Alfred Leslie

THE HASTY PAPERS

SPECIAL MILLENNIUM EDITION

HOST PUBLICATIONS AUSTIN, TEXAS

OURS IS A MORAL UNIVERSE, WE BREATHE DEEPLY CROWDED WITH VALUES

ALFRED LESLIE
THE HASTY PAPERS
Special Millennium Edition of the 1960 One-Shot Review

CONTENTS

THE STORY OF THE HASTY PAPERS

Sociologist/ethnologist
Levi-Strauss! Jascha Horenstein!
Ozenfant! Orgone psychologist
Wilhelm Reich! Brecht! Rudolph Arnheim!
Bronislaw Malinowski! Yes! Caught
in exploding Europe and brought
to desperation, they all stood
to be purged; or worse, with a hood
tied over their heads to be raped, killed
or mutilated for being
who and what they were. So seeing
few ways to remain alive, they filled
a few bags and ran when The New
School dealt them jobs, ". . . out of the blue!"

The first one hundred and eighty four
of those bruised intellectual
souls, within twelve years would swell to more
than two thousand; a perceptible
windfall for the U.S. that would flush
a lasting tide through our culture's slush
of ideas. Recalling their plight,
brings to mind another wild flight,
someone who fled Europe on his own,
became part of their story and
The Hasty Papers core, a strand
of history forgotten and unknown.
So meet Saul Colin, émigré
kin of my sweetheart's dad, OK?

One night he came uptown to visit
his *landsman*, and through his pince-nez
he stares at the second-cut brisket
and dumplings on his plate and says,
"What a delightful combination,"
and raises his seltzer: "Elation,
hopes, better times for our homeland."
As we drank, a snapshot caught grand
Colin, in elegant mannered suit,
glittering shoes, and flawless smile,
standing with zoot-tailored me, while
guileless Hymie and Shirley, and cute
daughter Flora hovered in smocks,
white overalls, and bobby-socks.

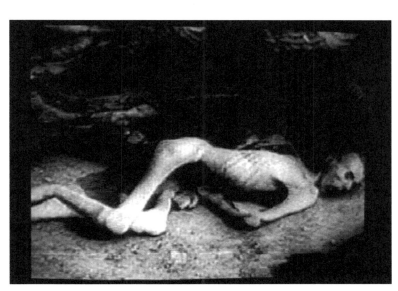

The table talk was stilted for a
bit, then smoothed into a high-gloss
monologue when Colin, through Flora,
got talking of his life. "My boss?
then? well . . . he's dead now, but was a man
named Pirandello, an Italian
of great distinction. A playwright."
And to Colin's credit, despite
our ignorance of the world he went
on to describe, when he finished
up, we did not feel diminished,
but excited by his turbulent
tales. Then Flora said I made all
the paintings hanging on the wall.

At this, Colin said even more;
invited me to come and meet
his brand new "boss" Erwin Piscator
at the New School theater. "A treat,
a great director, knows what makes a play;
he worked with Brecht for a while, they
gave life to Berlin's left wing . . .
communists, pure and simple: thing
was, they transcended political
cant, had an understanding
of theater beyond demanding
change – something strong, umbilical
even, not my Pirandello
of course, *he* was the rare fellow."

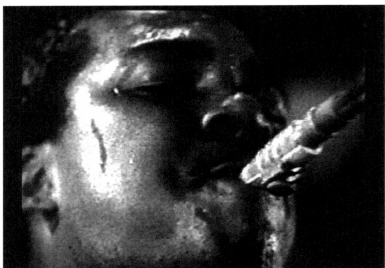

"Yes, he died in 1936,
it was awful for me, it's true . . .
I went to France *and* Berlin . . . the risk
involved – tracing Piscator through
his friends as that evil German dream
coiled around me . . ." So despite the stream
of theater and film jobs Berlin
had, Colin *the Jew* was on thin
ice, and soon Pirandello's faithful
secretary wept, flew
with Piscator and his wife to
New York, unhappy but still grateful
for the chance of a new life free
of German bestiality.

On arrival Alva Johnson met
with them and concluded a deal
with Piscator and his wife that set
Piscator's ideas into real
time; and as the 1939
Worlds Fair gave us a GM design
for The Good Life, and Stalin shot
Isaac Babel, Piscator got
a theater to make democratic
humanism the centerfold
of the New School stage. But this bold
plan left out idiosyncratic
Colin 'till just before we met
and dined on dumplings and brisket.

So 1945 saw dinner
and drinks with Colin, Piscator,
his wife Maria; saw the inner
core of Piscator's theater, saw
it unfold as I audited
workshop classes and visited
backstage, saw me wallow in Joyce,
Pound, Brecht, Freud, James, Kafka . . . the voice
of my cultural virginity
lost its squeak, now Modernism
joined Popeye in my wild prism,
adding to vulgar divinity,
a cachet of contradictions
I would hold through all life's fictions.

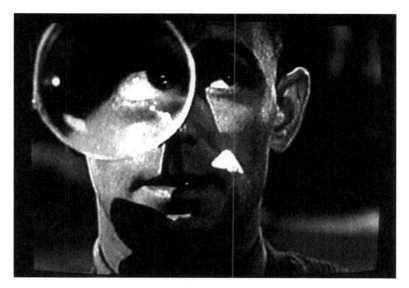

Juxtaposition of seemingly
unrelated elements gave
me the highs that some dread, screamingly
addictive drugs – once said to stave
off the blues – appear to have. King Kong,
Blondie, Chaplin, Cezanne, kick the gong
for me along with Orson Welles,
Eliot, the Three Stooges . . . hell's
frozen over far as I'm concerned;
with critics in tremulous shifts
trying to justify their drifts . . .
makers *experience* their hard-earned,
while critics bleat rubbish over
Henry James and Smokey Stover.

I survived my crush on the widely
varying discriminations
of these masters by my tidily
thinking no eliminations
would ever be needed. I was just
storing them up, keeping them in trust
for a future time. I did not
have to choose between them, my lot
would be cast with them all, I need not
think one better than another;
only that each was a mother
of substance, each had their own feed-lot
and stores. I saw information,
sensation, qualification . . .

and commitment would all be as one.
The maker's view I realized,
was perhaps that distinction's cool run
between high and low could be sized
down: was mostly superfluous rot
and even a barrier to what
we like to define as *making*
art. Now my friends, I was taking
a very radical position
I suppose, but I was merely
eighteen; a driven and clearly
unworldly kid, whose supposition
meant nothing to no one but me,
the lamppost, and the deep blue sea.

I looked over what I had thought to
bring about so literally,
and panicked seeing what I brought to
the fore and viscerally
drew back. Narrative film, abstraction,
all at once were a great attraction;
and with my youth, seemed a wild load
to shoulder with the quirky road
I was on. But I took off and by
'49 was flying : a new
work in a hot show, then I stew
as my film at MoMA makes me hie
back, scared that in my profusion
I'd be awash in confusion.

I sold my film and camera stuff
to friend John Reed – I'd purify
through exclusion. But of course my rough
handling of my tough wonder-why
didn't hold. I simply kept quiet
about my other voices, riot
in the studio would be eased
by not being public. But teased
by what I quietly made, I soon
found myself realizing that
to mature, the risk must be splat
into view : I'd develop, be goon
or grandee, whatever was cool
for my restless genetic pool.

By '58 all were underway :
The Cedar Bar, The Chekov Cha Cha
were both written (but I let them lay
unpublished), I was half ga-ga
with new Polaroids and film ideas.
Outcome was *Pull My Daisy,* some drears,
then *The Hasty Papers.* At last !
you're probably thinking, he's passed
wind, and now we can get to the point.
So, my first *Hasty* thought : show the whole
garbanzo sans rigmarole.
Give literature and painting a joint
so to speak : cast your aspersions
critics, we'll drown your diversions !

How ? We'll interweave all those bleeding
hearts who think themselves a species
incapable of interbreeding
with other artists. No ? He-shes,
banshees, and green-cheese moons are way more
likely ? Well, goom-by pal, can't set store
with you. So flow ! Speed ! Rush ! Hurry !
Fast ! Haste ! Watch me head-long scurry
to process, be reckless and heedless
of consequences and meaning
to *become process.* By gleaning
the fields, printing dismissed works, we'll stress
the marginal core till it bursts
from the pressure of inventive worth.

Of course my five-minute wonder-mag
took three years of ceaseless labor
by me, along with friends I could nag
into helping out. But we'll savour
them later, get back to the follies
of production. First thought, my jollies
were toward everything manuscript,
in author's hand, nothing clipped
or corrected. Just straight-on photo-
offset, plain documentation
with no frills or explication.
But I soon saw it was a so-so
idea. It would look great but head
off the authors need to be read.

I'd go with type (eventually
include two documentation
texts), then streak for conventionally
formal tabloid presentation.
Lean and mean, straight arrow, readers kept
focused on the words: don't want them swept
into meaningless production
values, a shallow seduction.
That solved, I would gather together
from anywhere, stuff I thought well
of. My first helpers appeared, hell
was postponed, as they would both tether
me to sane punctuation, I
being pretty much grammar shy.

Oh Miss Moyano! oh Miss Levine!
Doest thou recall my pestering
glance as I first reckoned with pristine
colons for that first festering
moment? that Frank O'Hara called up
to say it was a stop sign? balled up
and fell apart laughing at my
editorial request? I
told Dick Bellamy – next helper – that
my autodidact persona
said, "Punctuation? *mañana,*
but submissions *ahora.*" A spat
began. "You rat!" he cried. "You low
skunk!" I yelled. Primal quid pro quo.

The contributions. Some I sent back
asking for more to read. This helped
cause some confusion and even flak
as I crowed no critique! then yelped
when I saw I was going to make
distinctions after all, not just bake
on with any ingredients.
One thing for sure, expedience
was never a factor, and reading
Brother Can You Spare A Dime – tiled
from some correspondences filed
in an archive, you'll see that pleading,
obsession, and high-mindeness
shaped the fulcrum of our fussiness.

Yes, those notes from and to authors tell
this very clearly, as these are
letters not written for the chill hell
of future publication; far
from it. They are funny, unguarded,
with some preposterous, retarded
ones – those are mine. Read my nagging
complaint to Castro for lagging
behind in replying to me. I
tried to shame him into writing,
telling how Doctor Bill, fighting
for his life, wrote back ! And cry
for James Farrell; I misspelled his name
then gave him *They Shoot Horses* fame.

But to balance off these colt or dolt
missiles of mine are many fine
moving responses, the kind that jolt
persuasive clues: Pasternak's wine
and roses penmanship and phrasing,
"Take no umbrage . . .", Simon Taylor raising
hell about the beats, Beckett's clipped
" . . . hot luke or cold worth . . .", Tylor's zipped
" . . . within discipline . . .", Feldman's ". . . all my
girls since 1950 . . .", and if
when you're reading them you stay with
the chronology I've arranged, (I
think that best) you'll find through call
and response an absurdist ball.

This grand epistolarian hash
is accompanied by around
one hundred images. A mish-mash
I suppose, but to me a sound
way to sketch in the immense fiction
of our life, without which our diction
is anchorless babble. I've culled
them all from TV screens, and lulled
them with nothing more than a hard look
and a snap onto paper, arranged
their contour and found this estranged
view of the heart of darkness. Brook
these pictures and letters as one
text if you want to have some fun.

But some *Hasty* stories won't be found
in the letters or the pictures,
as nothing remains of them to sound
them out except the rich fixtures
of memory. Genet, excluded
from the first *Hasty,* is included
in this one. Thereby hangs a tale.
The authors rightly feared a jail
term for me with his publication,
as I did not have the money
to hire someone – a honey–
voiced lawyer was their recommendation –
to protect me from the big clink
or *Hasty* from the censor's ink.

Yeah, *Hasty* would be trashed and the works
lost to publication for who
knows how long. Everyone wailed, "The jerks
will burn the whole thing! Listen, you
can't let the first *Hasty* be lost, save
Genet for the next one, don't be brave
without preparation. Rosset
knows, you need a legal faucet
at the beginning – *before* you start,
not just before you go to press;
really, don't do this Les, you'll mess
up everything for nothing. You fart
with the cops now, the printers will
shun you like a piece of road-kill."

Rosset concurred that I'd be dead meat,
and that a much smarter risk would
be waiting one, then I'd have the heat
of more readers behind me should
the law come down. Now you'll ask, how come
the talk of a *Hasty* two, when *One-
Shot Review* is on the masthead
of the first issue. Well, I said
one-shot anticipating never
to get any of my dough back
for a next issue. But a crack
came in my resolve as to whether
or not, since response was so strong
I thought we might follow along.

So leaving the one-shot phrase was just
old fashioned fence-sitting, created
roads either way. It never crossed
my mind it could be belated
for so damn long, take some forty years
to reappear. But *c'est la vie* dears!
The holy ghost *does* bend with bright
wings. One more scene that sees no light
in the letters concerns the writers
who withdrew when they heard Castro
would appear in *Hasty. Astro
Man* was fine, but no commie blighters,
even if he's paired with a U.
N. reply. "Les, it just won't do."

Many other struggles of course came
up, all just as time consuming,
but none with the rude divisive claim
that these issues of such looming
importance made. The political
correctness shoe is uncritical
as to what foot it's on. It fits
right or left, and the stinking shits
it takes always smell bad no matter
who dumps it. We see-saw the course
of morality, forget force –
not god, put someone in that batter
box. Remember this when you boost
wildly: chickens come home to roost.

We are now dear reader near the end
of the trail. But before the ash
of the spitting embers die, I bend
and yield to a bright mawkish flash
and thank once more without restraint all
those who helped with the first *Hasty* call:
Editorial: Marie-Claire Moyano, Richard Bellamy,
Naomi Levine, and Lisa Bigelow. Printers
Rep: Harry Gantt. Kindnesses: Martha Jackson,
Sally Stein, Barney Rosset, Gallimard and
University of Michigan Presses, Frank Mason.
And for all their marvelous works, the
contributors – whom I believed in then
and still believe in now.

This millennium version of *The Hasty
Papers* has a new and separate
list of valued friends: Stephen Soba,
David Lehman, David Stark,
Maureen O'Hara; Host Publications
of Austin, Texas, John Thomas,
Richard Howard, Steve Kursh, Nelida
Nassar, Helen Oppenheimer, Donald Goddard,
Linda Selvin, Laura and Richard Schwamb,
Wim Huurman, Nancy de Antonio;
and finally the contributors again.
To paraphrase Frank O'Hara:
*Roll on oh great clouds of friendship,
roll on as the great earth rolls on!*

—Alfred Leslie New York City 1999

Whips and chains, blood, pain and sex as a political weapon . . .

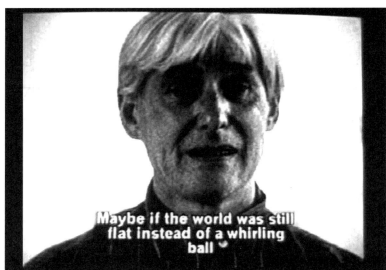

Maybe if the world was still flat instead of a whirling ball

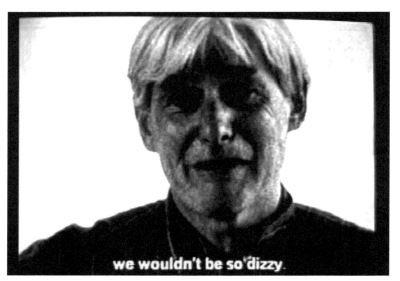

we wouldn't be so dizzy.

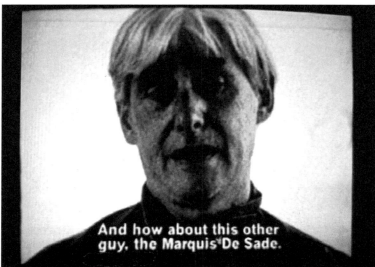

And how about this other guy, the Marquis De Sade.

Anyway sex and Democracy don't work much better than sex and Fascism.

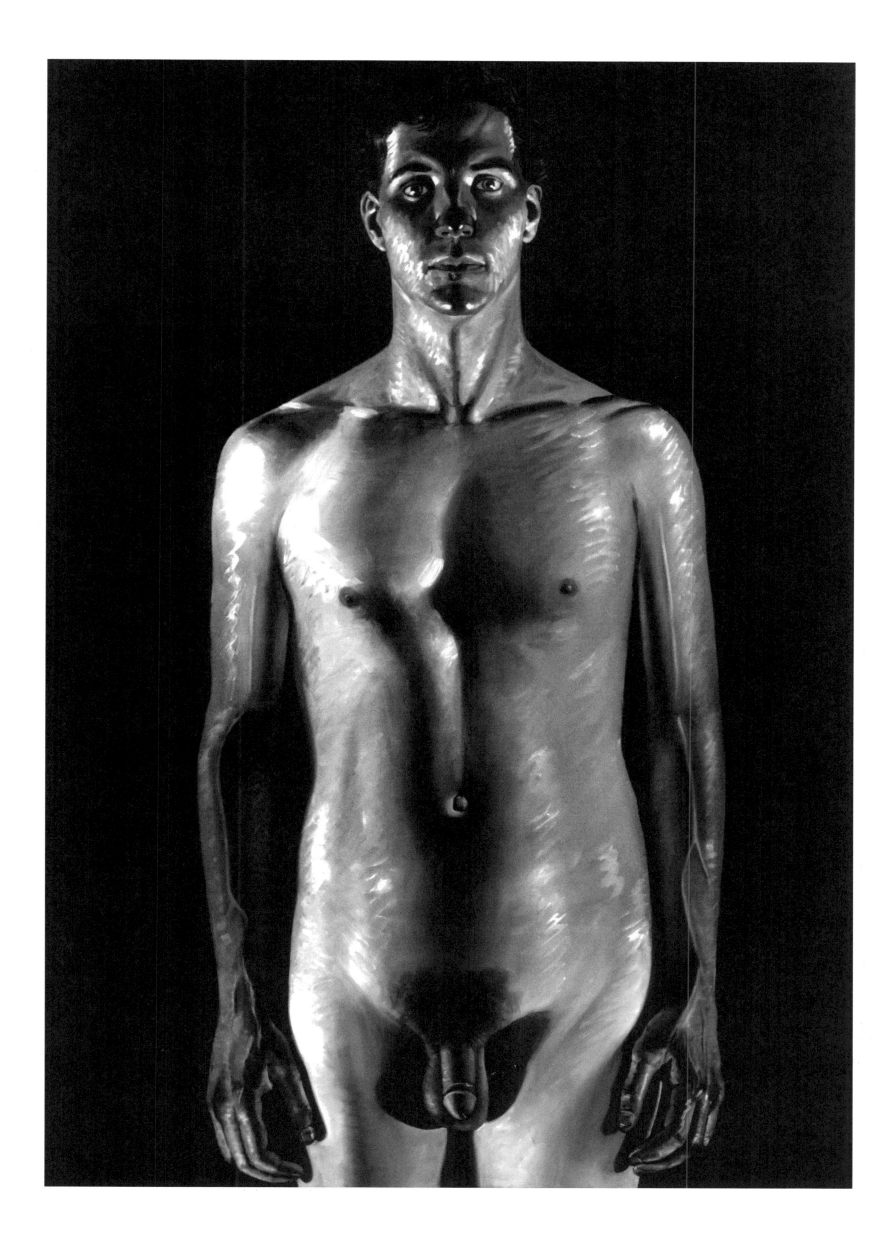

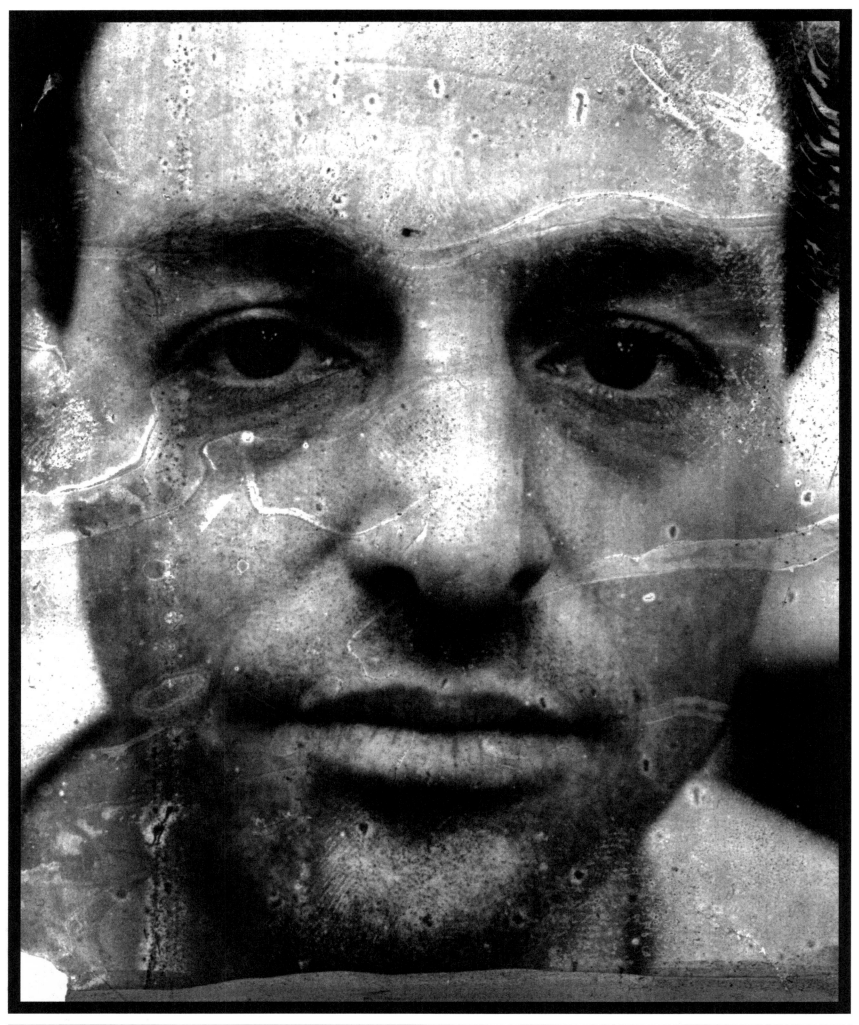

BROTHER CAN YOU SPARE A DIME

A Narrative made from Selected Correspondence
February 1959 – October 1961

Nearly all of these original letters were destroyed in a fire. Copies survive on microfilm in a restricted archive at the American Archives of Art. They had been photographed a few months earlier. Letters are arranged chronologically and numbered. They are also indexed on the previous page. Notes for the letters are on pages 54 and 55.

1. FROM FRANK O'HARA

THE MUSEUM OF MODERN ART

NEW YORK 19

Dear Alfred,   February 1, 1959

    I am sorry about the Ezra Pound book (which one was it?) but that must have been the package I didn't get to the post-office in time to get (it closes at 6) and forgot to ask Vincent to get for me. The mail man can't leave packages in the hall because of THIEVING CHILDREN.
    Why don't you send the poems here and I'll be sure to get them. As I told you, a couple of the poems you have will be in Don Allen's anthology and a couple in Poetry magazine, and while I'm sure you could reprint them, I have some new stuff and it would be more fun to use them and not have things reprinted when it's so hard to get printed anyway.
    I, incidentally, told Bill Berkson to send you some poems. He is very very good I think (and so does Kenneth) so perhaps you'll find something you like of his to use-- it's not at all like those things Allen sent you at any rate.
    Meanwhile, I'll decide fast and send you the other things and hope to see you soon,

                       Best,

                       Frank

                       Frank O'Hara

---

2. TO JAMES SCHUYLER

                    Feb. 3, 1959

Dear Jimmy:

You know these HASTY PAPERS that are cooking: I would like to have all the ingredients in, hawg maw, ginseng, turnips, coreander, etc., by the very definitely March the Firstly.

Of course anything you care to send would be great with me, poifectly terrific, I mean to say, to ascend the scale; but I wouldn't mind if you fed a little Sense of Power that I am sure all editors must share with me by allowing me to ask you if you, say, sent 1 poem, I might ask you to send, say, three more to make the total four or if, say, you sent eight, I might say to you I think 7 might be better because of space exigencies or I like the numeral better?

I like your poems. I don't think you would ....take the umbrage?.. at their presence in the HASTYS, which will indeed have a presence and about which I am characteristically & verily excited, indeed, say.

             Regards,

             Alfred Leslie

---

3. TO JEAN COCTEAU

                    Feb 3 1959

Dear M. Cocteau!

HASTY PAPERS writhes again. Deadline's Mars 1, but it would be yielding to a line from you.If you could do so, it would find its place here. Imagine it.

Les anges arrivent de Puerto Rico.

Un peu autres companions pour la contribution de M. Cocteau! a piece sur STILTS with photographs; five tragic cartoons de Nordstrom; I quote last lines from a poem we somehow got from someone we do not know:

      The flutter of many wings overhead,
      No need to look upward,
      The true mind is with out shadow.

With as always, great hope. I offer you to accept my fond respects, mes milleurs setiments, milleurs vuex, etc.,

---

4. FROM JOEL OPPENHEIMER

dear al -- so great to hear from you. it/s been too long. and what about yr newfound fame. every goddamn paper or magazine i pick up is mentioning the new young genius. too much man. i send you some poems with pleasure, the first i/ve sent out in close to a year, save for some i gave yugen. due honor and all that. the book sounds lovely. as is my usual wont i go you one better, inclose 4 instead of 3. this way you can pick or choose. and if you/re not happy with these ask for others. i/m very fucked up now about writing, and don/t really know what/s swinging with me. tho i suppose it all does, in the end.

joel

---

5. TO JOEL OPPENHEIMER

                  February 9, 1959
Dear Joel,

Are those "/"'s because your typewriter lacks the apostrophe,or perhaps its apostrophe is not to your liking, or what? I like it.

Can you send me a few more poems, very quickly? Our deadline is March 1.

3 of the 4 I think are terrific, as is I don't know whether all four will be used, or a couple. Two other people are on the Papers helping me now and our conferences are bloody but sweet, so we want a few more, either to select from both batches or print both we don't know yet.

I hope you'll be able to see to it.Papers are going well. May have to wait till summer to print.

I'll keep the photos a while longer! we will do a section of the contributors' pusses only if too many people don't goof in sending them.

Well, I like THE FABLE & BLUE HEAVEN best.

Get 'em to us quick?

Dear frank

Thankzs for the note and your good thoiugths about Daisy

the mag and the rest. The book was MAKE IT NEW thanks

again & I'll get the poems to you and re new poems -

yeah! A nd yeah I hopeyou're wrong about Robert but I'm

feared yo right. He'll never own up. I gave him toomuch

of adebt to pay back except with el sharpo teetho. I

told Pricilla about the shit, who told Cogggashal who

told Walker E who lectured Mary aboutit.. she went mum,

says she's has her own grrief with his betrayal of her

and Pablo & Andrea and is afraid. So! I'm senclosing

only part of A LIFE AND TIME. I can't find the othere

poages now but I'll copy from what I have on hand and

try to have rest retypped sothey kin be red. It's an

expansion of sorts on Cha Cha, Daisy, NO STORY etc.

A LIFE AND TIME

The notoion behind this film is quite simple and direct.
At thesame time though it is cinmaticall y complex,both
in structureand editiong. From the point of view of
shooting and "drama" it is terribly simple.

We will shoot for two SEPERATE LEVALS on the film. One
is the VISUAL, the other the HEARD. Unlike mostfilms the
sound track of this picture willbe a SEPERATE continuity.
Itwill relate of course and be part of the VISUAL circumstance but at thesame time the spectator will be in TWO
places or more SIMULTANEOUSLY. NOT AS MEMORY BUT AT THE
SAME MOMENT. PARALLELISM! MULTIPLE POINTS OF VIEW! From
all points this is a powerfull and never used cinematic
idea, which also presents the possibility for reducing the
number of shooting scenes since they can be developed
through the EAR at the same time! Imagine cross cutting a
eyeball scenee and at the same time cross cutting the
HEARD track! You would have then three sound tracks
working at once with at least two VISUAL Tracks. Essentially the problem of keeping control over the whole
thing woulld be to always make sure that the HEARD track
was always well established as a PLACE before you could
start manipulation or cross cutting. The PLACE must be
established and the TIME.. and the TIME MUST ALWAYS BE IN
THE PRESENT. The opening scene will be the key to the
technique of the film. The WHOLE procedure depends on
these first few moments. The following scene may be considered a sample of the technique and should not be tought
of as fully developed as i think there will be many flaws
untill itcan be worked out. Here roughly then is the idea.

On the image of a dark screen... the sound ofthe horn at a
race track..thenthe roaring crowd as a race gets underway..
hooves of horsesare heard louderthan the crowd Noises.All
this in a few seconds on a Dark screen. The spectator is
now at the race track on the HEARD track. Then the first
Title comes in over a very tight close up of rumpled bed
sheet. As this shot is held for a short duration the HEARD
track has begun to dissolve to more intimate sounds. It
will pick through the general track soundand crowd noise
to general then specific conversations, focusing finally
on a a conversation between a man and woman...

Ah! I just found the rest but you kin see it must be

must be re-typped so I'll get the rest of it too you

soon. And when you readthe whole thing I hope you dig

this idea of PARALLEL STREAMS. Yeah Marie-clare is the

cats meow. & Thanks for talking to Bill Berkson. The

Shadow says: More PPPPPPPPPPPPPPPPPOEMSPPPPPPPPLEASE!

yr pal

Dear Alfred Leslie,

Thank you for asking. Here are 2 poems...
hope they make it. Also the photo, which I
realize is probably too big...but its the
only , except in wild daydreams, that is
around & available.

Hasty Paper sounds good to me. Hope oo it is
due soon...as it sounds intriguing.

Anyway, best to you & project & thanks
again....

best

roi jones

8. TO AMIRI BARAKA (LeROI JONES)   February 17, 1959

Dear LeRoi,

We're just not going to be able to do the
MEASUre complete, as it surely should be done;
mainly the decision hinged on the problems of
production & loot, both becoming formidable quite
beyond my o-riginal wild liberal guess. I am
sending the manuscript back to you separately.

Would you communicate with Joel Oppenheimer for
me? I think through you is the best way, I don't
have his address. Joel sent 4 very short (&
nice) poems) & said in his letter more could be
asked for, which I'd like to do, considering the
brevity of the ones here; would like some more
stuff to shuffle around with.

You too. I like the Cecil Taylor one better of
the two — the other is 'Life & Death of a Lovely
Thing' — if you've anything else about you think
might be for hasty papering, please send it. I
hope you don't think I'm being finicky. And as
soon as possible....everything must be in by
March 1; and anything, if there is anything we
can't use, the return will be speedy, I promise.

Thanks for all the trouble; and it's too damn
bad about MEASURE, but I would go completely all
to pieces with that to handle too, I realize
now.

9. FROM MARTIN WILLIAMS

Roi Jones tells me
you would like something
on Ornette Coleman
by the end of this month.
I could put together
single
a piece from several
others I have written
if that would be its
(Roi said he thought
it would) End
of the month ok?
Martin Williams

10. FROM DIANE Di PRIMA

Dear Al Leslie.
    Leroi Jones + Joel Oppenheimer told
me to send you something for Hasty
Papers. I wanted to send you "the jungle.
I am also sending 2 other shorter thing
in case you dont like the jungle or
dont have room. Anyway, I hope
you like something.

                    Best,
                    Diane DiPrima

11. TO DIANE Di PRIMA   March 1, 1959

Dear Diane DiPrima,

Lucky Hasty Papers!

May we use three? I think you ought to consider that a
negative reply to be effective will have to be backed up
by force.

Will you send brief biographical data.

Did LeRoi & Joel tell you we can't pay except when the
shooting's all over, the spoils?

You are a great woman.

                    Best,

12. FROM KENNETH KOCH

The Bungle House

Mecox Road

Southampton, New York

Thursday

Dear Alphabet Soup:

    Thank you for your lengthy letter which you
sent to Mr. Rivers. I'd bedelighted to have you
publish my work.

    Dear A., could you tell me something
detailed about what thebook is exactly that you
are doing? This wouldhelp me a good deal to know
what I should submit to it. Honest it would.
That is, is it paintings and poems? a magazine?
a book? who else is in it? what does it sell
for? what audience is it "aimed" at? BOOM!

    Just in case you are in ahurry I enclose
the/opening stanzas of When the Sun Tries to Go
On. I would really like to publish some of this
bizarre work, and I know of no editor besides
yourself of sufficiently hardy spirit to do it.
However,

    please tell me something more about your
hasty papers. Did you write John Ashbery? (14
rue Alfred Durand-Claye, Farigi, 14e). Will you
be at the Signa opening Friday?

* * * * * B E S T   W I S H E S * * * * *

Kenneth Koch

13. FROM PONTUS HÚLTÉN

Stockholm 8/12
1959

Dear Al! Dear Marie
Clair
Here are the great painters.
Maybe you kan have them in
the Hasty Papers. Maybe it is
already to late
I will send more photos, of
Adolf Hitlers watercolors, in
some days
Please correct language and
spelling if you use the stuff

It is very cold here and
much snow already. To
come back here from N.Y. felt
like going to hospital.
Could you send a copy of "Pull
my " to show in the museum?
with diplomatic post, would not be away
more than 2 weeks at most. We would be
very glad museum is buying the painting.
Salute. Pontus Hülten

14. FROM FREDERICK KIESLER

August 18, 1959

Dear Leslie,

Of course I shall contribute to your burning bush,
because you are quite a swell guy, but chiefly
because you have such a beautiful girl friend.

It will be a well-acclaimed speech which I gave
at the end of the past semester for the graduates
in painting, sculpting and acting at the Chicago
Institute of Art. The title is "Art: or the
Teaching of Resistance". It is about twenty pages
long. You'll get it in a day or two.

Cordially,

Kiesler

15. FROM BERTRAND RUSSELL

from: The Earl Russell, O.M.,F.R.S.,
PLAS PENRHYN,
PENRHYNDEUDRAETH,
MERIONETH.
TEL. PENRHYNDEUDRAETH 242.
24 August, 1959.

Mr. Alfred Leslie
108 4th Avenue
New York 3, N.Y.

Dear Sir,

Lord Russell thanks you for your letter. He regrets that he has nothing to send
you for your Review and that, owing to the
great amount of work that he has already
undertaken to do, he is unable to write anything especially for it.

Yours faithfully,
(secretary)

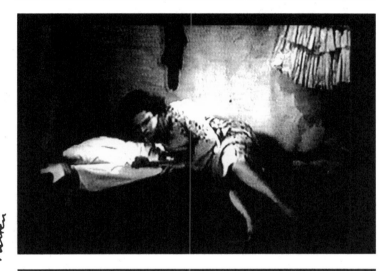

16. TO RAYMOND MEDEIROS (GENET)

Direct wire

Raymond Medeiros
208 Hudson St.
Hoboken N.J.

chace gave us your Condamné demnéd to
Death Genet- Would like to
publish. Problem with Freeltman.
Please telephone AL 4. 5680
immediately if not sooner-
Alfred Leslie
Hasty Papers

17. FROM KENNETH KOCH

Friday

*Kenneth
Koch*

Dear A L

    L ESLIE

      S

       L

        I

         E,

      I finally heard from LeRoi Jones (to whom
as you remember I had confided When The Sun Tries to
Go On, and therefore as you may remember, when I
spoke to you on the telephone, what I said, in
essence, that he had in a way, away! away! the
Rights to my poem, Well...) well, this Leroi says I
should go ahead and print it in the Crazy Capers
edited by Fal Faisley. That's you, isn't it? He
thinks that will if anything wildly increase circulation of the eventual and virtual book. Now, L, it
going to take a little week and two to correct and
uncorrect my copy of this work (When the Sun).
Because I got two versions and I got to COLLATE
them! Mainly I got to cut out some corrections I
made on the original first inspired dew-wet morning-
fresh flowing-like-lava tasting-like-honey-and-gall
version. A week from today, even less; five days;
such time, then, will find me back in NY, and I will
telephone you and we will say more. My best regards
to Miss Diana, and of course to you L Lslie,

              Antsville,

            K K

18. FROM NORMAN MAILER

             73 Perry Street
             New York 14, N.Y.
             August 24, 1959

Alfred Leslie
108 Fourth Avenue
New York 3, N.Y.

Dear Alfred,

I'd like to come in on your "One Shot Review" (great
title) but I don't have anything at the moment. I
put all the short pieces I thought worth printing
into a collection of my own which will be coming out
in late October, so unless you want to reprint or be
out before then, I think we'd better forget it short
of my writing something in the interim which I
think would be satisfactory to both of us.

*that is,
you'll be
out on
the stands
before then*

                Best,
                Norman
                Norman Mailer

19. TO HORACE GREGORY

**108 4th Ave
NY 3 NY
August 25 1959**

Dear Mr Gregory,

    Straight out now, no fuss. I would
like ~~you~~ you to contribute something to my
'One Shot Review' to be titled 'The Hasty
Papers'.

    So - I am a painter and have made a few
extra bucks . . .

    There it all stands, simple and bright
as a ~~~~~~~~ groat.

Hoping to hear the best news from you - YES,
I am

            with regards
            Alfred Leslie
            Alfred Leslie

20. TO FIDEL CASTRO

August 30, 1959

Premier Fidel Castro

Havana, Cuba

Dear Mr Castro,

    Having not heard from you as regards my last letter and 'The Hasty Papers' I am writing again all the time hoping this letter and your reply to my last note will cross in the mails. If they don't, and you have dismissed my last letter please let this note further my cause.

    But there is very little I can add! except that I continue with this project hoping for response from you.

    Sincerely

    Alfred Leslie

21. FROM DENISE LEVERTOV

(Until Sept 9ᵗʰ)
P.O. Box I, Friendship, Maine.   August 30

Dear Alfred Leslie
  · Thanks for your p.c.
I have some questions:
  ① Payment?

  ② Who else is in it? (This is because some poems alter the coloration of other poems next them.)

  ③ What sort of length of poem?

  ④ When will it appear?

Please let me know the answers, & I will see about sending you something if I can.
  Yours sincerely,
  Denise Levertov

Also: If it is going to be a small format — because if so I wd. not send anything with long lines, that the printer might double over.

22. FROM JOSEPH LESUEUR

Monday night

Dear Alfred,

Thanks so much for that loan the other night -- you
were a lifesaver.

Listen, I'm sorry to be so slow about getting back to
you with that damned piece for THE HASTY PAPERS. Tell Dick I
will finish it within days. Wd have done it last weekend only
I went to the country for a much-needed rest. To make up for
my negligence, I will get at Frank about his poems.

Love,

23. FROM ARCHIBALD MacLEISH

September 1, 1969

Mr. Alfred Leslie
108 Fourth Avenue
New York 3, New York

Dear Mr. Leslie:

Thank you very much for writing me about your
proposed new magazine. I like the title. I
am afraid I haven't anything of much use to
you because I am spending all my time on a play.

Faithfully yours,

A.MacL:aj

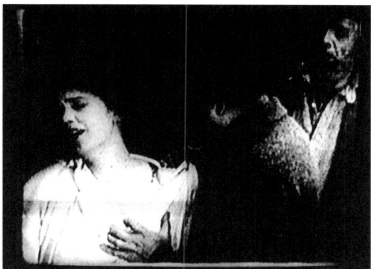

24. TO JAMES SCHUYLER

Dear Jimmy,

I've been busy painting and finally getting

a mag off the ground. The enclosed will ex-

plain. Forgive the carbon but it drives me nuts

whirting the same thing overand over. A s I writ

you'll this letter ccoolasping. I'll try for a

few more intleggiblle lines.

Do you have some unpublished poems a novel or

any thing you'd like to hand over? t'wood be great

to have you along for the ride.

Diana tells me that that Groves Rosset

Pastures has THE BOOK almost ready ..

Hey Schuyler! A post card or a manuscript

would be fine.

regards

25. FROM WILLIAM CARLOS WILLIAMS

Sept. 3, 1959

Dear Leslie:

Good for you. I approve. Just home from the hospital, this is all I can produce - glad to be alive.

Sincerely yours

W. C. Williams

9 Ridge Road
Rutherford, N.J.

26. TO DEREK WALCOTT

September 3rd 1959

Derek - hello mad one!

May I sweep aside all the preliminaries which you know I mean already and tell you immediately what I'm up to! The Review, my mag, The Hasty Papers..A One Shot Review.. is well under way. I am printing your Mal Cochacun (sp) and just waitin for the rest of the stuff to come in. Meantime today I saw some people about the movie who are up in the stratosphere - power fuluski. The in-folk. After all big discussions they were HANGING on everything yrs truly genius said. SO I said 'dont give me horseshit about theatre..I know whats up..you guy don't (me tough hombre) and so on. OF COURSE I mentioned your plays and they were tre bon interested. I said you and your brother should direct and so on - but they mentioned Quintero. So I said they could not read the play without your OK. Shall I give it to them? I think they are honest. They were brought to me by a good woman friend of mine. Let me know about this and what you are doing anyway.
IF AIRPLANES GO TO THE WEST INDIES I WILL SEND THIS AIRMAIL bless you with love from the back there folks.......

27. TO LIONEL TRILLING

Sept 4 1959

Dear Mr Trilling,

I would very much like to have something new of yours for The Hasty Papers. But even something you thought would bear reprinting would be ok.
Regards

alfenleslie

28. TO FIDEL CASTRO

Sept 9 1959 NY NY

Priemier Fidel Castro
Havana Cuba

Dear Priemer Castro;
        This will be the last letter I will trouble you with. At this point I almost feel more foolishthan dissapointed at expecting an answer.

        The Hasty Papers means much to me. It is not a venture that I slip to the world woth my left hand.I want it to be full of the most vital ideas and writing in the world.If I did not I would not have written you.

        Your letter does remain alone unan- swered.I would say that 40% of all I wrote as yet are unreplied. I feel sure that if I were a major publisher I would at least get a let- ter of refusal.

        I am not in a position to send someone to Cuba to interview you. The monies that will publish The Hasty Papers are as hard earned as any money can be. Being all from the sales of of my paintings you can be assured the fortunes of painters have not changed so much that I am rich. I am trying to make something that no one else, at least in the US will do. I have no secretary ()the typing and spelling testify to that) no office. I write this letter from the floor in a loft that is my home and stu- dio. I want no profit from The Hasty Papers. As I stated before any monies is excess of printing distribution advertising and costs will go to the contributors. You do not need money I do not want it. The Hasty Papers is being made because I believe it should exist.

        I wrote to the poet Dr William Carlos WIlliams and asked him for something. I hesi- tated knowing he was very ill. Friends urged me saying he would want to be asked. I wrote brief note. I was a stranger.. I did not men- tion that I knew some younger poets who were his friends. There was no reason to expect that might know of me in any way at all. I was a complete stranger.

        I quote his entire letter below, which accompanied a poem he wrote especially for The Hasty Papers.

                        Sept 3 1959
Dear Leslie:
        Good for you. I approve. Just home from the hospital this is all I can produce-glad to be alive.
                        Sincerely yours

(signed) William Carlos Williams

His answer and the poem arrived three days after I sent my letter.

29. FROM RUTH MILLER

Sept. 10, 1959

Hello dears, I have written Grandpa Pound a letter full of
The Hasty Papers and Jessica. After receiving your letters I
began to think that if you do not hear from him it might be
because of imposed caution on his part, painful associations
with this country because of his final departure from here
and perhaps his desire for personal obscurity and detachment
in which to finish his Cantos. But I think that you will
hear from him because he seems still very interested in
what is "going on." Diana, the cognac was missed within a
week, the flowers did fade, but you were missed much and
immediately your train took you away. The season is aging
beautifully here: silvers, yellows, deep shadows in the
grass. There is one bird though, in the cedar, who keeps
singing like Spring. Every morning the meadow is filled with
blackbirds. In the mist they sound like a thousand fountains
chuckling. I have talked to Esteban twice but he has not
come to see us. He is melancholy and mellowing - I an firm,
I think. I paint as much as I can every day, filling large
and small canvi (a term of a friend of Rowland's) with
images of landscape, babies, pots, trees, round things,
nature. I do not care. Like you said, Diana it is the working, the doing that matters so much now. I feel I'm just
beginning. I've painted the attic studio white and our "hazardous charming" stairway a quiet violet blue, we have purple, blue and apricot doors, Jessica has a little turtle,
named Turkle, whom - which - Rowland found wandering jerki-
ly about in the Howard Pile room at the Petit Musee - he was
very dry and sick - and we are making apple jack in an abandoned bidet. Rowland gave his lecture on Pollock supplement-
ed with slides and that movie of Pollock painting on glass
over Feldman's music. There were 48 people watching. One can
only say gasp!

      Bruce St. John, the director here, saw Bill deK in
Venice at a cafe; another time riding in a gondola. Write me
more about your progress on The Hasty Papers and your life..
I love hearing from you. Happy about Cocteau. Screw Krew-
shef, yes indeed, with knobs. Last night we saw the ultimate
in degradation on the glassy eyed succubus: a dentist from
Suburbia whose hobby was blowing bigger and better bubbles
(Rowland says not to capitalize bubbles). He practices an
hour every night. I don't have to point out how tragic this
is. We want you both to come and see us whenever you can.
Alfred when is your show?

          Much love from us,

30. FROM JEAN COCTEAU   31. TO JEAN COCTEAU FROM ALFRED LESLIE AND ALLEN GINSBERG

WESTERN UNION
TELEGRAM

RA007 30/29 INTL PD FRNM LESBAUX DE PROVENCE VIA
NUCABLES 14 0838=
ALFRED LESLIE=
103 4TH AVE NYK=

COMPRENDS MAL CE QUE DESIREZ STOP PRIERE ME LE DIRE
VIEUX HOTEL DAUMAHIERE LESBAUXDEPROVENCE BOUCHESDURHONE
STOP SERAI HEUREUX VOUS RENDRE SERVICE=
JEAN COCTREAU=

September 14 1959
Dear Mr. Cocteau,
 Last week I recieved a very moving letter
from William Carlos Williams. He said...DEAR
LESLIE....GOOD FOR YOU. I APPROVE. JUST HOME FROM
THE HOSPITAL. THIS IS ALL I CAN PRODUCE. GLASD TO
BE ALIVE. His signiture was like the trembling
sprawl of an uncertain child. It was so shaky. On
another page was very moving short poem he had
written just for the Hasty Papers. This was also
signed. Both signitures, the poem and the letter
were terrific affirmations of will and integrity.
I was deeply touched by this very ill mans concern and response. If I may..I was equally moved
by your telegram. God knows it is terrific to
find some human response in this sad world. I
salute you.
 Ideally I would like you to write
something especially for The Hasty Papers. Say
your feelings about films in general or yours in
particular. Or a scenario or notes for a film
that was never produced, or one that you plan. A
chapter from a biography, if you are writing one
of yourself. An exchange of letters that you
might have had with someone that you think is
beautifull. Thoughts of America, of American
painting, France or French painting. The world at
large. The atom bomb. Russia and the moon. French
poets. Fidel Castro, Genet?und The academy.
Chess. The metre. Yourself revisited. Coca-Cola.
Living in a hotel, a chateau, a slum. A new
writer, poet, philosopher, painter. A play you
wrote, poems. In short anything.

alfredleslie

 Permittez-moi a ajouter quelques mots--
comme vous savez, peut-etre, ?l y a une grande
curieux rennaisance de poesie (et de prose) ici
aux Stats-unis--c'est a dire, beaucoup des
jeunes qui est devmu des Anges ? cause des
evenements naturelles mystiques (des visions de
Pere sans Nom ?u Ciel) (et dans la corps
humaine)--et aussi une armes des garcons qui
?ument le Mraijuana, mangent le meme Peyote de
Artaud, ou faire des ?hose horribles avec la
plague blance heroine (et entender apres cette
Buchenwald de leurs corps) et maintenant
quelques de nos autres out faites un jeu a une
nouveau dreugue (vraiment une phlogiston
mystique) Lysergie Acide. Maia ce nest pas les
drougues ou-les sons de Jazz que nous ent fait
des Anges qui lisent Genet et Jacob Boheme et
Eckhart, c'est ?n autre force queje ne puis pas
nommer (give nam to) que je comprends vous
comprenez. En tout cas vous auries etre
interresse dans um livre classique de Wm S.
Burroughs, Naked Lunch, qui est publia a paris
chez Olympia, parce que c'est le result de
douze anne? de souffrance a New York, ?oxique
et Tangiers et Paris avec une intoxication de
heroin--mais cest tou ?cesie pure et dux sans
merdex, L'homme est egal a Genet dans
intelligence literaire et plus important
intensite spiritual. C'est une grande assertion
?ais je suis sur vous trouves que c'est exact
si vous investigues. Aussi, ?n tout cas, tous
les jeunes ?oi lissent Artaud. M. Leslie, une
painte qui ont vendu quelques trauvaux, vout
circuler son argent par assemblant ?ne uniqe
issue d'un Review avec travail par tous las
inconnus et connus ?oi.

 Adieu-- Allen Ginsberg

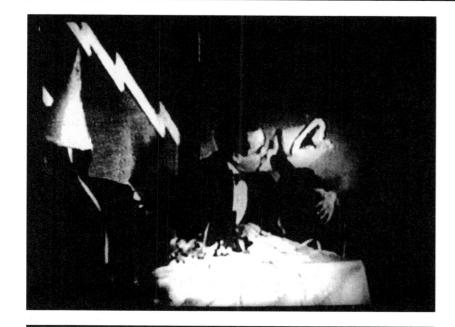

32. TO NICO CALAS

September 17 1959
108-4th ave.
New York 3, NY

Dear Nico Calas,
      I am compiling A One Shot Reveiw to be titled
The Hasty (Hasty) Papers. It will appear in the format
of a tabloid newspaper, and contain (I hope) works of
great variety and points of view. As indicated by the
title it will come out only once and not again. All
copyrights will be retained by the authors and profits
will be shared accordingly more or less equally amonr
the writers depending on the size of the contribution
I remember from things that I have read of your and
the times that I have he rd you speak tht you have
very Vigorous ideas and great candor. Do you have
something that is 'way Out' that you have written and
that has never been published? Or would you have the
time and inclination to write something for the Hasty
Papers. I would like very much to hear from you.
            Very sincerely yours,

            Alfred Leslie

34. TO BERNARD FRECHTMAN (GENET)

THE HASTY PAPERS **A ONE SHOT REVIEW** EDITED AND
      PUBLISHED BY ALFRED LESLIE

            New York
            108 4th ave.
            New York, 3 N.Y.

            September 21, Monday

Dear Mr. Frechtman,
      I am interested in publishing a section from 'A
Thieves Journal', plus an appreciation of Mr Genets
work in my magazine, 'The Hasty Papers'. This is 'A
One Shot Review', it will be published once and not
again. It will be made in the format of a Tabloid
newspaper and contain about 100 pages. There will be
work a diverse group of people. Artists, composers,
architecs, poets, etc. All the copyrights will be
owned by the authors and all PROFITS will go to the
contributors.
      I hope you forgive the poor typing and spelling.
I am my own office and bad help. I hope you are in a
position to give me some assistance. I am writing a
letter to John Ashbery asking him if he knows you. He
is a poet living in Paris and I will ask him to contact you so that you will not think this is a letter
from a crank. God knows it must look like it! John is
a fine poet whom I have requested work from for The
Hasty Papers and have some personal aquaintance with.
      Hoping to hear from you very soon, I remain,
            very truly yours

33. FROM JAMES SCHUYLER

                                    Sept 17

Dear Alfred:
      I hope it's not to late to seek a berth in the
Hasty Papers. I enclose one poem.
      If you can use it, the only special thing about
it typograhically is that the line beginning "on the
other hand..." ideally should go on straight and end
without dropping, "lawn mower clack." Otherwise...
      Excuse the carbon. I loused up the first copy,
and I want to get this in the mail to you.

            Yours,
            Jimmy

PS I haven't heard a thing about the book & the show
that was supposed to happen along with it. Strange
business; if not exactly novel.

c/o John Button
28 East 2nd Street
NYC 3

35. FROM STANLEY KUNITZ

Dear Al.   9/24/59

Sorry to have been so remiss about
writing you. We're just back from the
Cape, & my desk is a nightmare
I like the sound of your Hasty
Papers — a fine & generous gesture
on your part! — & wish I had
some poems to contribute. But I
write slowly — too damn slowly —
& the little I produced this summer
was spoken for in advance.

Harper's Mag for October has
a piece by me on the State of American
Poetry in which I mention some of the
more interesting youngish writers. You
can reach most of them via the Poetry
Center at the 92d St. Y. My workshop
at the Y opens Oct. 15 & I'd be
glad to mention your One Shot Review
if it won't be past your deadline

All best from both of us —

Stanley

36. FROM JAMES SCHUYLER

Xxxxxxxx Sept. 23

Dear Alfred:

   Good grief. In the poem I sent you, did you I correct the
first line? It should be: " a commingling sky" (and not
"commingly" which is a pretty word but not what I meant).

   I'm taking the Chekoov Cha Cha and the letter statement
in to the Museum tommorrow, for Dorothy Miller, who asked me
about them today.

   I still have a script of the movie and a copy of Charm: I
really looted your place that night.

I'll return; scouts honor

   My best to Diana.

            Yours,   Jimmy

37. TO JOHN ASHBERY

September 30, 1959

Dear John,

Kenneth just told us that he thought you might be out of Paris for a while, so forgive our beseiging you with letters. Alfred is very anxious to put this review out as soon as possible, therefore a deadline of Dec. 1st has been set for everything to be here.

Everything is madness here right now, what with all the letters we are writing, A. trying to get some painting done and the 35mm print just arrived of the movie. And the god damned telephone rings all the time.

Please let us know if you will send us some poems, and if you can contact the other people Alfred mentioned in his previous letters. Many, many thanks.

38. FROM DEREK WALCOTT

c/O 2 Cipriani Boulevard,
Port of Spain,
Trinidad,
West Indies

Dear David,

Nice to hear from Nueva Yorke and specially from you characters, the jungle rummers (I meant runners) brought your mail by flaming torches and throbbing drums as I served whiskey and soda to mustachioed colonels,
"What are you hiding there, Ogele?
"Letter, Bwana?"
"From a white man in New York. Big bird, he bring. Me read now, you cur
"Stick the safari up your ass,"
Seyte the sound of throbbing drums, secretly, carefully, looking furtively over my sweating shoulders by the light of a flaming missionary, I read on, and could not quite understand.
This I dig. You are printing MALCAUCHON, which is okay, I guess, since I have heard nothing from the Grove, and I don't think they would mind anyhow, though I will write Donald Allen decently. I am sure you will do a handsome job with the printing and everything, and am eager to see it when it comes off the press, reeking of West Indian sweat. Could you please do me the favor of letting me have the proofs, which I shall return promptly by aircraft? I would appreciate this very much, and shall offer many sacrifices to my people.
Who else are you getting in the mag? Diana had said the Jeanne Unger at Grove was hinting that they might want to print it, but Allen did not say this to me quite, nor had Barney Rossett read it yet. However, there are the two other plays which they may print if they are keen, and then there are poems I hope to send them, also the selection of plays, the which, for the nonce go very poorly.
As far as showing the plays to the people you mentioned, certainly. I had hoped that you would not feel it necessary to ask for that kind of permission. If they are friends of yours and you trust their judgments and old Johno says oke, well, dad, oke.
What about this yum yum femme? Could I have a pitcher of der broad? What's this stuff about Jose Paintere? Zef Abse wanna see zee plays, I guess its okay, but I doubt many producers are innarested in three one act pieces, and if anybody is innarested in adapting one of the pieces into a moshun picture, I jump at the offer, as safari wages are pretty low. (Two lion's balls per week).
To direct the plays? What kind of sheet you giving me dad? Shore, I would, if I felt I absolutely could, and sometimes I do. Actually, the letter isnt too clear, but I hope I have understood. Do write soon again, not only business, but occasional information about this and that. Isnt the damned movie getting anywhere, or what? Best of luck with it, and much cash. Give my regards to Diana, and Frank O Hara you can tell that I shall reply soon. Meanwhile, one theme is running through my head,
Nail me, nail me, go ahead, impale me, etc.
Tell John Nerta Robert Mary Malle, I very often sincerely miss the New York scene, but I think I made a judicious exit, and was overworked and temporarily too written out to enjoy it further, but will be up there again soon, in which case you may take me to a large Italian dinner. Abva the delishiess pickled herring washed down with vodka?
Ogoboioi Swahili for A riverder'
Derek

39. TO DEREK WALCOTT

FROM THE DESK OF KING DAVID

Dear Derek,

Moose be breeve az em oy-vawhelmed, az you, vit voik.

Foistly: I will do a great job with MALACAUCHON thou shall not worry. Barney is moo sympatico and Don will push for you. I know thy gift of rum hath addled my brain but I am in a clear spell now..

"One deelishious Ital-Kosha coming up!"

I wanted to double-check with you about showing the play around. Actually I tolt John I would and he said NOT to bother. BUT as things get public all kinds of sheet gets aired. As you well know now through John, DAISY iz instant clazzic and the the consequence iz much of the cast are starting to claim the film is theirs. John predicted this would happen and said Frank's coming to me and asking, as a "favour", to share my directorial and writing credits so he could use the film to better his advantage, was "ze tip o de izeboig!" Kerouac is claiming he adapted the film, Allen Gregory and Peter have asked for profit-sharing, even deelightfull David Amram is shiftng ground. This is the rack - Torture twentieth century style. So thou doth see I am a wee bit paranoid -

"ay theres the rub..."

And thou doth further see the reel source of my nail me, impale me doggerel.

BLAM! So I'll keep showing the play around and let you know whats up where and when. P'haps we should do it together. First play then film. Diana John Herta and I miss you and send love. And the proofs? ov courze..

King David

40. FROM JUAN A. ORTEGA (FIDEL CASTRO)

REPUBLICA DE CUBA
PODER EJECUTIVO
OFICINAS DEL PRIMER MINISTRO

Havana Cuba,
October 2, 1959.

Mr. Alfred Leslie,
108 4th Ave.,
New York 3, N. Y.,
U. S. A.

Dear Mr. Leslie:

We are extremely sorry that your first letter went unanswered and that you did not get a prompt reply to the second but this is due to an unfortunate accident.

As soon as we received your letter of September 9, we started looking fro the one of August, with no success; when we were ready to give up, convinced that it simply had not arrived, we finally found it in the files of correspondence already answered, where it had probably been place by mistake. We offer our apologies.

As regards your request, we simply regret that Dr. Castro cannot comply with it. He is so terribly busy and he has so many things to attend to that he simply has not got the time to sit down and write an article, no matter how short.

We wish you much success with your venture and thank you for your interest in Cuba.

OFICINAS DEL PRIMER
MINISTRO
REGISTRO GENERAL
SALIDA no. 12,291
Fecha 5

Cordially, yours,

Dr. Juan A. Orta
Director General

COLLÈGE DE 'PATAPHYSIQVE

London
October 3, 1959

Dear Alfred Leslie,

You are elusive. I have passed your way twice since I originally left my card. I believe I will be in New York next week-end for the last time before I take a holiday. If so I will certainly pay you a visit. I don't even know if I really have anything I could give you. What I would like to do is write you a more or less political essay, but what with this special issue of Evergreen on 'Pataphysics that I am doing with Roger Shattuck and New Direction's forthcoming publication of my version of Jarry's Doctor Faustroll which is driving me mad with problems of illustration and some revision... I can't at present even search my files desperately for material already written, let alone write something original. When I come back from Paris at the end of this month, I hope things will have calmed down. Perhaps I can then write or rehash something which might be of use to you. So I will try to send you something for your consideration during November.

Why don't you enlist a few of the tougher English writers (there aren't so many!) - Christopher Logue for instance (18 Denbigh Close, London W. 11)? Allen G. has a copy of his book "Songs" (MacDowell, Obolensky are bringing it out in N.Y. nest year) if you don't know his work. It is good strong lyrical stuff. And no pansy fart-arsed 'beat' crap about it. Mention my name if you write to him.

My best wishes for your quixotic project. I only hope for your own sake that you don't allow yourself to become entirely smothered by the ever-loving arms of the 'beats'. I happen to think that Allen is a good poet, and I have some respect for Ferlinghetti, Burroughs and a very few others. But oh god their disciples! And as for the Gipsy King, Mr. Kerouac... I came across him a week ago for the first time in about a year, - I remembered him from my first meeting as being an intellectually under-endowed sentimentalist with a reactionary mugwamp streak; he hasn't improved. I think he represents all that is most ludicrous, pathetic and dangerous in that wet-eared 'revolution'. Zen? Shit. Those babies don't even know what a koan is or rather they mistake it for baby-talk. I accused J. K. of behaving like a spoilt baby yelling for his nanny, and that is a mild euphemism my view. If he's the general of that pathetically pretentious army, god help us all. Allen G. thrust upon me at our last meeting a thin booklet of 'poems' by one Michael McClure dedicated to Antonin Artaud, insisting that I read them and send them to Logue. This was the most godawful SHIT I have ever read, and an insult to Artaud whom I happen to revere as a great and tormented soul. This man is illiterate and obviously doesn't have the

slightest comprehension of Artaud or, indeed, of contemporary literature. And he has no sense of poetry as a
discipline — a living thing with rhythms and sonances. A
lazy, probably conceited, bum. I only mention him as a
dreadful example. Lamantia is another insufferable bore,
pseudo-religious, masturbatory, boring.

You wouldn't like an anti-beatnik essay from me,
would you?

In any case, my best wishes for your Hasty Papers.
A suggestion: why don't you present it like a Japanese
scroll, that is, in the form of a lavatory roll, suitably
perforated between texts? In this way poetry might at
last perform a useful function.

With pataphysical regards,

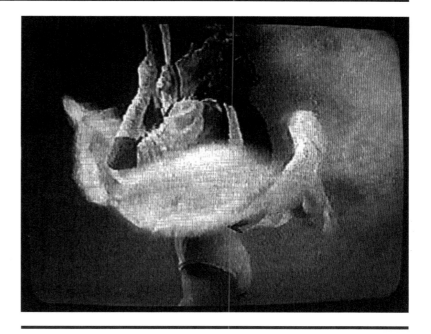

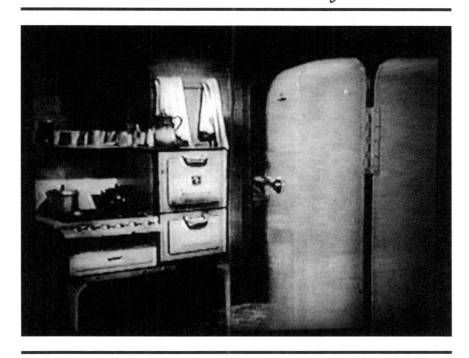

42. TO CHESTER HIMES

Alfred Leslie
108-4th Ave.
NEw York 3 NY

October 3 1959

Dear Mr Himes,
    I have just read your very impressive book, The
Real Cool Killers. The enclosure will describe what I am
about to do. It is obvios that I am not an Official publisher. I am a painter. The Hasty Papers is being paid
for through the sale of my pictures. It means very much
to me. Exactly what I don't know. I just feel it should
be done the way that I want to do it.
    I want very much to include something of yours.
Afragment of a long piece or a shot story or an article.
I am very interested in you views. I want to print thing
that no one else will do. Practically all'truths' (if I
may) are smothered in the shit that the 'official' world
sanctions.
    I hope you can make something available to me.
    Would you drop a postcard and let me know if I can
expect something from you?
    With much sincerity, I am

                    yours truly

                    Alfred Leslie

43. TO TRUMAN CAPOTE

THE HASTY PAPERS
ALFRED LESLIE
108 FOURTH AVENUE
NEW YORK, NEW YORK

                                October 3, 1959

Dear Mr. Capote ,
    I just spoke to Doc Humes , who has just
become an associate editor of my forthcoming magazine , THE HASTY PAPERS, and he suggested that I
immediately get in touch with you to see if you
could contribute something to the already bulging
material, which includes an excerpt of Sartre's
book on Jean Genet "GENET COMEDIEN ET MARTYRE" ,
articles from Norman Mailer, Jean Cocteau, Dr. J.
Robert Oppenheimer, Donald Windham, poems from
Corso, Ginsberg, Kenneth Koch, William Carlos
Williams, Frank O'Hara . Although I am a painter, I
am publishing and editing this one shot review,
which will be financed with some profits I made
last year. Whatever profit the magazine makes after
publication and distribution costs are deducted will
be divided fairly among the contributors. All the
entries will, I hope, be united beautifuly, and
there will be reproductions of paintings by the
American "avant garde" and photographs by Walker
Evans and Robert Frank.
    One of the things I talked to Doc Humes about
was the possibility of interviewing Mae West, or
getting a copy of her banned interview with Edward
R. Murrow, and also interviewing Marilyn Monroe. I
wonder if you would be at all interested in this
project ? Anything at all that you may have , a
story, article, piece of a novel , that you would
like to submit would be wonderful. What THE HASTY
PAPERS is above all interested in is material that
does not "fit" into ordinary, commercial, and
restricted majority of magazines - either because
it is controversial, too "avant garde" , or just
generally considered "unpublishable." The enclosure
will describe the magazine in fuller detail . I
hope to hear from you very soon and till then I
remain sincerely yours,

                    Alfred Leslie

14, rue Alfred Durand-Claye
Paris XIV, France
October 5, 1959

Dear Diana and Al,

Excuse me for not answering your first letter, but I
was out of town for several weeks and now am in bed
with some mysterious malady. As soon as my "strength"
returns I will type out 3 of my poems to send you—a
short, a long and a middle sized one. As far as contacting the people Al mentioned, that may be a bit difficult. I know very few people in Paris; also French
intellectuals are ? without exception a nasty lot, and
very jealous of Americans. On the other hand, I do know
someone who knows Francois Truffaut, and will ask her
to ask him to send you something. But I have a better
idea—Dick Howard, who translates all those Avant Garde
books for Grove Press is coming here next week and will
be being wined and dined by all those authors such as
Robbe-Grillet, who play up to him because not only does
he translate them but he suggests which ones should be
published. So I will explain to him about the Hasty
Papers and tell him to ask all those people to send in
something. OK? Incidentally have you thought of asking
Arnold Weinstein to get some Italian notables to contribute? Maybe Frank's friend Bill Weaver could get
people like Moravis if that's your cup of expresso.
Forgive crude joke but I have a slight temperature and
am feeling slightly delirious. Give my love to everybody and yourselves and lots of luck with the review.

Love,
John

Alfred Leslie
108 -4th ave
New York 3 NY

October 5 1959

Dear Mr. Celine,
    I have not yet heard from your agent. I
sent my last letter to you August 23.
    I have since expanded The Hasty Papers.
There is now a deadline of Dec. I as the
enclosure points out.
    I expect that since you did not answer
the last letter that I cannot expect anything
from you. But can I make one other suggestion?
    Would it be possible for me to print a
part of A Bagatelle for a Massacre?
    I hope to hear something from you. I am
enclosing a postcard for your convenience.
    Hurrah!!...for a reply.

                    much regards

                    Alfred Leslie

October 9, 1959

Dear Mr. Leslie,
    M. Genet has asked me to thank you for your
letter of September 21, 1959 and to express his
regret that, for various reasons, he does not wish
to authorize publications of extracts from THE
THIEF'S JOURNAL.

                    Sincerely yours,

                    Bernard Frechtman

Sir Geoffrey Faber, Chairman. Richard de la Mare, Vice-Chairman
T. S. Eliot, W. J. Crawley, Morley Kennerley, (U.S.A.), P. F. du Sautoy,
Alan Pringle, David Bland, Charles Monteith

FABER AND FABER LTD
PUBLISHERS
24 Russell Square London WC1
Fabbaf Westcent London   Museum 9543

13th October, 1959

Alfred Leslie, Esq.,
108, Fourth Avenue,
New York 3, N.Y.
U.S.A.

Dear Mr. Leslie,

    In the absence of Mr. T. S. Eliot, who is abroad at
the moment, I am writing to thank you for your letter
of October 3rd inviting him to contribute to review
The Hasty Papers. I'm afraid he has nothing unpublished to offer anybody at the moment, but I will show
him your letter when he returns to the office at the
end of November.

        Your sincerely,

        Secretary to Mr. T.S. Eliot

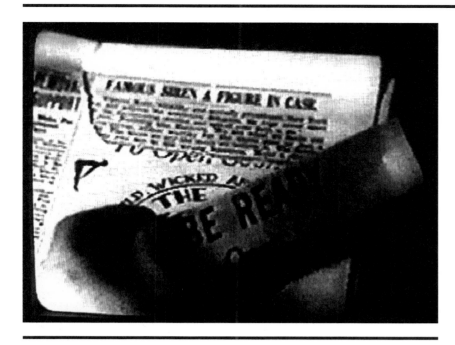

48. FROM SIMON WATSON TAYLOR

COLLÈGE DE 'PATAPHYSIQVE

Londres, ~~le~~ le 9 *du mois de* haha . *An* 87 *K. P*
en la tête de Tautologie,
(*vulgairement* 14. x. 1959 *ap. J. C.*)

33, Tregunter Road,
London, S.W. 10

FREmantle 4483

Dear Alfred Leslie,

So you thought the New Images of Man exhibition
a load of shit, did you? Well, well! I spent three
hours there on Monday and came out with renewed
excitement in the possibilities of contemporary painting and sculpture... a magnificently constructed collection. And you think Paolozzi frivolous? His four
sculptures provided a marvelous introduction to the
first room of paintings... His Icarus frivolous? The
Very Large Head tedious? And do you see nothing in
Nathan Oliviera's beautifully designed figures? And
Golub's Youth Recalling? I think I remember you grudg-
ingly admitting that Dubuffet was not entirely dead,
but if you admit Dubuffet's sculpture Knight of
Darkness into your very exclusive world of the imagination how do you reject (for instance) Rozak's
Surveyor or Richier's Hydra? I think perhaps you
should go back and take another look... especially at
that master of carefully sinister constructions H. C.
Westermann (The Evil New War God, The Mysterious
Yellow Mausoleum). One thing I found profoundly interesting in the exhibition was the way in which De
Kooning's brash nudes were entirely overwhelmed by the
studious black and white paintings by Pollock facing
them in the same room. A tribute to Pollock's talent
when he was able to avoid the easy temptation of drip
and splash... and inevitably a showing-up of De
Kooning's neo-Renoir translucencies, who, I feel,
would be well advised to stay within the safe and
fashionable boundaries of drip and splash (my own
copyrighted term for American 'abstract
expressionism').

By the way I can't possibly offer anything for
your urgent sheets... I have just taken on the
translation of Marcel Jean's Histoire de la
Peinture Surréaliste: 150,000 words, god help me.
No doubt the volume will survive without my support. In any case, I would have felt slightly
uncomfortable rubbing shoulders with elderly roman-
tics like Pasternak, elderly satyrs like Cocteau
and aging demagogues like Castro. - Not to mention
the eternally youthful (the real adjective is childish) beatniks. And their illiterate friends. The barbarians are not just outside the city walls, my dear
Alfred Leslie, they are in possession of the city
itself: the sound of smashing glass is provided by
the false alarms they are turning in under the guise
of lighting the flame of poetry. May Faustroll have
mercy on their souls (and their R-souls phonetically
speaking).

I need hardly say that I wish you the best of
luck with your collection of ... what? I enjoyed our
evening and the pleasant dinner at the Thompson
Street restaurant. I hope that you have both managed
to drown your cold germs with whiskey. Please remember me to Diana.

Yours sincerely

49. FROM ALFRED JENSEN

Alfred Jensen
284 East 10th Street
New York 9, N.Y.

Long ago my uncle and I went for an afternoon's walk. As
we came out of the wood into a clearing we saw a rainbow.
My uncle said:
"Mark it in your memory where the pure color hues touches
unto earth, there the fairy folk (Danish "Niser") have
buried their treasure"
Excited by nature's brilliant display I ran towards
the vivid colors hoping to grasp at the elusive mirage.
Today I am still full of wonderment and enrapture
about fables that accompany, explain and attach belief
unto natural phenomena.

Work hard   yours Al Jensen

50. FROM JAMES SCHUYLER

                                        Oct. 13

Dear Alfred:
        I put this away so carefully to send to
you that I only just located it. By the way: in
copying the speech from the Chekov C.C., Bob
Friedman questioned "cutism." (Second sentence),
which I took to be cute-ism; but looking at it now
it seems more likely that it was a mistyping for
"cultism." ??? If it is maybe Diana knows the state
the book has reached and whether it can bee corrected (Bob F. took it to mean cut-
ism, which I suppose would mean "a rage for making
cuts." It's wonderful what one can do with a typewriter).
        Have you heard anymore about the show that's
to accompany the publication of this? I haven't
but I noticed in the American Federation of Arts
catalog of Circulating Exhibitions (for the U.S.
not abroad) that they're offering it as of next
March, with the book as a catalog? It's wonderful
what you find out, later.
        How are the Hasty Papers progressing? I just
had a letter from John Ashbery, saying he sent you
some poems and wondering if you had space &/or
interest in his play The Compromise. It's a short
full-length. If you are, Kenneth Koch has a copy of
it. But if you're using all of When the Sun Tries
to go on, you must be about to crash the Tolstoian
space-barrier.
                        best.

51. FROM CHARLES OLSON

                                28 Fort Sq
                                Gloucester MASS
                                October 19, 1959

My dear Alfred Leslie:

Please forgive me for this delay in welcoming
yr invitation to come in on your new magazine

I hope I am not too late. The enclosed feels
like the one. Let me hear from you

                        Charles Olson

52. TO DONALD WINDHAM

                        October 20 1959

Dear Don,
        I'm sorry that I havent gotten in touch with you
before. I've been very busy and on top of everything else my
life has been altered by achange in my 'domestic status'.
So! All in all I feel tresbon complex. Enclosed are the
brief descriptions of THE HASTY PAPERS. I hope with the talk
we had and everything else that you will send something on
too me. The mos t recent addition is William Arrowsmiths
translation of Aristophones' Birds and or Clouds. I am not
sure which he is sending or how much. I thought his trans.
of Petronious was fantastic!
        I am writing to Tennessee Williams to ask about that
Ca tro piece. I am so very anxious to get something about
Castro/by him/by Williams would be marvelous.
        If there is anything else that I can tell you about
the Hasty Papers please dont hesitate to get in touch with
me.
        I am very glad to have you as apart of the review.
                Very sincerely yours

                Alfred Leslie

PS this may sound shocking but I have a secretary now. Who
is off today but if you call she will probably answer the
phone. Her name is Mari-claire Maynne.

53. TO JOHN ASHBERY

Alfred Leslie
108 Fourth Avenue.
New York 3 NY
                                    20
               October ~~23~~ 1959

Dear John,
       Sorry that there was so much delay in my
answering your letter. Diana and I are separated
and on top of all the enterprises that I have
going I am slightly mad!
       I spoke to Don Allen who said he would let
me look at the poem you sent him if that aws _OK_
with _you_ .. also mentioned to him The Compromise.
I am very interested in it. I will take it from
Kenneth to read.
       Jimmy says that I about to crash through
the Tolstoian space barrier with all that I want
to print. Thats what It will turn out to be. This
makes me very happy. I want The Hasty Papers to
be out-rageously bloated with work that that in
the end it will lok like one of those stange
pulpy outer-space monsteres that have just absorbed TheWorld. Thats just what my literary
inclinations are for the Papers.
Among ~~When~~ the newest thing that I ahve gotten is
a fragment of a new translation of Aristofaphanes
(what spelling) The Birds and Th Clouds by William Arrowsmith who did such a fantastic job on
Petronius' Satyricon. Plus I just wrote to Tennessee Williams asking him for a piece on CASTRO.
If you should run into Williams you might mention
The Hasty Papers, Don Windham said that he
thought Williams would do it. I hope so.
       Listen you will probably see Richard Howard
(alll the favours I ask) he left last week. Could
you remind him to speak to Frechtman and   !OY!
Gallimard about those translations and his ~~car~~ ·
anyway I will hope tohear from you shortly and
can get these poems from Don Allen.
       Chow!
                              Alfred

                    alfred

                                    October 21, 1959

Mr. James T. Farrel
252 West 85th Street,
New York, New York

Dear Mr. Farrel,
       Some months ago I spoke to you about the possibili-
ty of making a film based on your story about a dance
marathon. Unfortunately , the technical difficulties
made it impossible for us to carry through on that project. However, we did manage to make one part of our
projected trilogy , and that is the film "PULL MY DAISY"
, which will be shown by Cinema Sixteen in November and
by the Y.M.M.A. in January. I hope that you will have an
opportunity to see it. Since the completion of the film,
I have undertaken to edit and publish a one-shot magazine called "The Hasty Papers" , which will come out in
January. There is an enclosure which describes the magazine fully, I am financing the cost of publication and
distribution with the small profit I made from some
paintings I sold last year. I mentioned this project to
John Meyers and he told me that he thought you would be
very interested in cooperating with me on it. If you
have a short story, or an excerpt from a novel that you
are working on, an article, any manuscript that you
would like to submit for publication , I would love to
have it.
       Hoping to hear from you soon, I am sincerely yours.

Alfred Leslie

                                    October 29, 1959

Dear Mr. Williams,
       I assume that you have returned from China, have
opened your mail , and have read my letter of October
twentieth telling you about my magazine, THE HASTY
PAPERS, and about how much I would like to publish an
article by you on Fidel Castro. I don't know if you
spoken yet to Don Windham , who can tell you more about
this fabulous project of mine . Please let me know if
you are interested in doing the piece. I hope to hear
from you very soon .
       Thanking you in advance, I remain sincerely
yours,

                    Alfred Leslie

October 29, 1959

Mr. William Faulkner
Oxford, Mississippi

Dear Mr. Faulkner ,
    I wrote you some time ago about the magazine
I want to publish early next year, a one shot
review armed with the best material I can find ,
with all the un-orthodox, un-commercial , and pas-
sionately biased writing that conventional publishers consider too hot to handle . If you are interested in contributing to such a free-wheeling and
extravagant project I would be delighted to publish
any essay, story, or piece of a novel that you have
on hand . THE HASTY PAPERS is goin g to be financed
soley from the small profit I made last year from
the sale of my paintings. Although I am a painter
by profession, I have been involved in diverse
other projects, including a half-hour movie called
"PULL MY DAISY" , illustrated a book of poems
called 'PERMANENTLY" by Kenneth Koch, and am writing an opera with Frank O'Hara . Any profit made
from "THE HASTY PAPERS" will be shared fairly among
the contributors. I hope you will be among them ,
since I consider you the greatest living writer . I
enclose a more detailed explanation of the magazine
and a post-card for your use. Please let me know

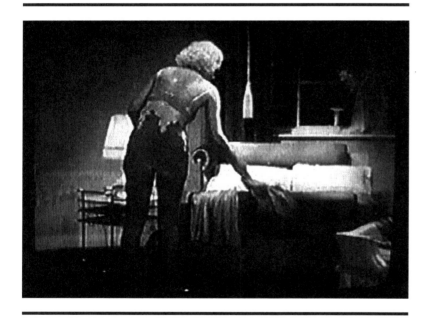

October 30, 1959

Mr. David Dellinger
LIBERATION
110 Christopher Street
New York 14, New York

Dear Mr. Dellinger;
    We received word today from Norman Mailer
that he has advised you to send "Language Hip
and Square" on to us. We want to confirm our
interest in the article and hope you can send
it to us at your earliest convenience. Thank
you very much.

                        Sincerely yours,

                        Alfred Leslie

October 30, 1959

Dear Mr. Hemingway,

You have heard from me before. I am Alfred Leslie, publisher and editor of The Hasty Papers, where magnitude of
simplicity, beauty and poetry begins to stun me. Mr.
Hemingway, do you want the truth? This small, considered
among all the things of the world, project will be very
fine.

I know that if you have already replied to my earlier
letter, it might not havereached me. You might still be
considering what this is all about, you might not have
instantly stood us up, you might be considering whether
to send us something --that would be wonderful-- or considering what possibly to send, despite suspicions. Or
maybe none.

---By the way, I've written Castro several times--well,
andjust got a note from his secretary saying he was very
busy and so on; we have to have Castro somewhere.

I realize there is great difficulty--assuming that you
are or will become sympathetic to The Papers--about what
you could give us. I know that for many reasons any
excerpt from a long work would be unfeasible, and anything that you might want to write for us --I suppose we
should grant that something can come from anywhere--might
probably in the end become unfeasible too: aside from the
money aspect its importance would demand publication in a
medium of much wider circulation. But might there not be
something you could do, that couldn't be published somewhere else-- I mean-- I don't know what I mean. I don't
mean of course that the Hasty Papers wouldn't give anybody else writes to publish anything or anything like
that and I doubt that the size of its circulation would
inhibit a national magazine or etc. from reprinting it.
Perhaps something of such pith and brevity that a national publication might wonder at it and do nothing about
it. Is there anything of which you are fond and for some
reason or a reason involving the fondness you have never
published? Castro? Cuba? Freud again? Eliot? Something on

The Hasty Papers or Pasternak? A young girl or a
woman, or else thought or gathering opinion?

Today, in the mail I received permission to use a
section of Sartre's Saint Genet, which Richard Howard
will translate; Oppenheimer's speech in ????? from
some Congress or other; Mailer's article: "Language:
Hip and Square"; the younger American poets I like
very much are very well represented; all the anom-
alies I think will be united beautifully; I very much
trust Camp ????? and will write him after this. You
are probably unfamiliar with the paintings included
for reproduction --the technical quality will be that
of photographs in the NYTimes Sunday magazine sec-
tion--Marvelous photographs by the only photographer
I care about except Walker Evans, Robert Frank--
(with Robert I made a movie, "Pull My Daisy" I hope
some day you can see if the bastards some day will
release it; in the meantime Cinema Sixteen
will show it early next month, have you some one to
see it to report to you whether or not what Leslie
does, ultimate judgement on the work itself not with-
standing, with whatever you would send him would not
be done with care, whether or not at the simplest he
is trustworthy? I really think that all contributors
to the Hasty Papers will derive some pride from it, I
told you of the format of a tabloid newspaper, that
will be its shape: its physical contents will correspond to about a thousand page book --one ofthe
poems, by Kenneth Koch is about 2500 lines andnthere
are chapters from three novels by young Americans you
probably don't know--tis layout is very clear to me
and the whole tome is clearer and clearer-- layout
and print of great excellence, austere.) Some photographs, snapshots, whose bone-simple, unutterable,
impenetrable relationships one can only love.

I like to makeliksts, being a simple painter, and so
have made a little one of some of the contents to
qualify a little maybe your impression of what this
will be.

We would be very honored if you should send us
something.

59. FROM DAVID MC REYNOLDS

October 30, 1959

Mr. David Dellinger
LIBERATION
110 Christopher Street,
New York 14, New York

Dear Mr. Dellinger ;

        We received word today from Norman Mailer that he has
advised you to send "Language Hip and Square" on to us.
We want to confirm our interest in the article and hope
you can send it to us at your earliest convenience. Thank
you very much.

                Sincerely yours,

                Alfred Leslie

SORRY FOR OUR DELAY IN
GETTING THIS TO YOU.
                David McReynolds

60. TO NORMAN MAILER

Dear Norman,

Enclosed is Hip & Square for you to look at again.
Some of the pencilled in brackets I don't know the
meaning of, etc. Do you think that the Jack Jones
footnote should also include mention of i.e. where
"To the End of Thought" was also printed.

Also your outburst in Southgate's thing, which we
would like to excerpt from the whole thing. When you
mention the names, do you think they ought to be
initialed or left as is; it's up to you of course.

We'd like them back as soon as you're through. Hope
to print in April.

61. FROM ROBERT LOWELL

Dear Miss Levine:

I'm I'm afraid I have nothing on tap except a few unfinished translations. From your list of contributers, you are obviously off to a crackling and brilliant start. I wish I had something.

Yours sincerely,

Robert Lowell

63. FROM SHERI MARTINELLI

3/Nov/59   S.M to A.L.

here's a short/short for M.B. that I wrote in Mexico & just re-did for you
Also the St. Eliz*can't send unless & P.'s permission as the pro*

I have a "memoir" about myself & John Chatel but don't want the "conceited" whatchmacallit thrown at me & Grampa is in it — maybe I'll enclose it --

working from 7 a.m. to now..6p.m too tired/ R. Stock's poetry reading tonight at Casandras it must be snowing in New York..how I miss the snow scene/

regards & best luck

Be sure to send H.D. a copy

M!

You might ask Allen Ginsberg for his comment if any - on the encl. unless you have a reason not to - (pre-pub. & softrth) I enjoy the way Allen sees things - He's a canny man.

62. TO WALKER EVANS

November 3, 1959

Dear Walker,

As you have heard, I am publishing and editing a magazine which will be called THE HASTY PAPERS and will come out in January. The material already includes an excerpt of Sartre's book on Jean Genet , <u>Saint genet, Comedien et Martyre</u>, an article by J. Robert Oppenheimer, articles from Norman Mailer, Jean Cocteau, Donal Windham, poems from Alan Ginsberg, Gregory Corso, Frank O'Hara, William Carlos Williams, Kenneth Koch.

I want very much to publish and article on you and your ?????????????? suit you better, just a few of your photographs . The quality of the reproductions will be the best we can possibly make it , and surely as good as those in the magazine section of "The New York Times" . If you would want to give me just one photograph, I would reproduce it full-page, or any size you'd like it, with or without text as you see fit. The only other photographs that might be included , ~~aside from~~ snapshots of authors, ~~~~ ~~~~ *couldn't be*

I hope very much to hear from you soon about this . Thank you very much.

Sincerely yours,

Alfred

64. FROM SHERI MARTINELLI

DEATH WITH DOVES
For Maxwell Bodenheim and His Ladys

At late night Maxwell would come into Fugazi's bar and sit in
the back booth, with me. He had with him, a wife...I think
her name was Ruth...and I think she hopped out of the Old
Testament just to take care of Maxwell Bodenheim...
She had the melon seed shaped face and wore her hair center-
parted a la early American portraits. Anatole Broyard would
say her eyes were "stunned" ...very dark and large... She
always sat on the outside seat of the booth while Maxwell
sold me his 'Death with Loves' poem. He liked gin...drank
like an Irishman. I read it every time & gave it back to him.
There are some things I understand perfectly..and one of them
??? Maxwell's love for the Gods of the Vine.
His hair was wild & tuff'd...it looked like a landscape of
dunes frosted with snow.. ~~blue-pink~~ was the colour of his
skin..
I could never figure it cut..nor now, seated here, seated
here in this spanish house in Mexico.. it leapt me out of
bed...I'll never figure it out...the way it took place..
He kept selling me the poem..about Death ..how he, Maxwell
Bodenheim met death..on a road
and Death had doves or somesuch..in his hair..and how it was
all such fun..
Then one read in the newspaper..how some unknowns had entered
Maxwell's apartments and turned it into a butcher
shop..Maxwell and his beautiful Ladys of such Tender
Mercy....
And one is lying here..thinking of Maxwell .. of irony..of
opposites..
How Ezra Pound who loved "unity in the arts" should be
legally spoken of as 'insane'
and how his old friend Maxwell..who saw 'Death with Doves'
...should...
Cheers! Maxwell! Here's a spot of Mexican rum. Baby .. that
was SOME exit!

Sheri Martinelli

word ısı
Blue-pink

65. FROM ROBERT DUNCAN

dear Alfred Leslie/
   I hope within ten days, by November 17,
to have a piece on WESTERN ORIGINS done
for your plannd <u>Hasty Papers</u>

Robert Duncan
p.o. box 14
stinsonbeach, Calif.

66. FROM TRUMAN CAPOTE

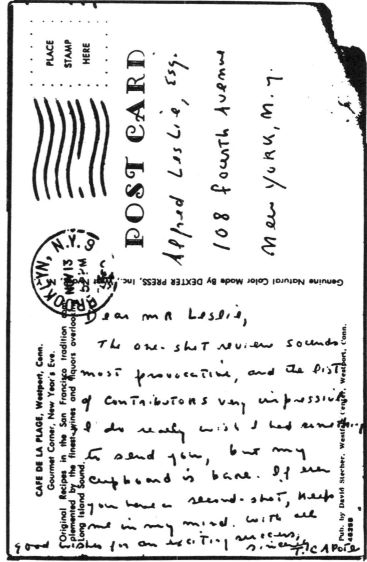

67. FROM SAMUEL BECKETT

November 14th 1959   6 Rue des Favorites
                          Paris 15me

Dear Mr Leslie

    Thank you for your letters and forgive delay
in replying.

I have no unpublished material whatever hot luke
or cold worth offering you.
I am very sorry indeed.

                    With best wishes,

                    Yours sincerely

                    Samuel Beckett

69. FROM FRANK O'HARA

68. FROM LANGE GALLIMARD (ALBERT CAMUS)

LIBRAIRIE *nrf* GALLIMARD

Soc. Anon. - Cap. 162.000.000 de frs   Téléphone : LITTRÉ 28-91 à 28-94
Chèque Postal : PARIS N° 169-33   Adresse Télégr. : ENEREFENE-PARIS
Reg. du Comm. Seine 57 B 20.478   N° d'Entreprise 553 - 75.107 - 0.841

5, rue Sébastien-Bottin, Paris (VII°)

Monsieur Alfred Leslie
The Hasty Papers
108 Fourth avenne
New York, N.Y.

                    Paris, le 20 novembre 1959.

Monsieur,

        M. Albert Camus est actuellement absent de
Paris depuis le début du mois. J'ai pu cependant lui
communiquer, par téléphone, l'essentiel de votre lettre
et il m'a chargée de vous remercier de votre lettre.
Malheureusement, il n'a rien en ce moment qui puisse
convenir à votre magazine. Si vous trouviez parmi les
textes et articles qu'il a déjà publiés un texte qui
pourrait vous intéresser, signalez-le lui, en vous
mettant d'accord avec Mme Knopf qui est l'éditeur amé-
ricain de M. Camus.

        Croyez, je vous prie, Monsieur, à l'assu-
rance de mes meilleurs sentiments,

                    Secrétaire.

11/25/59

Dear Al,
        How are you? Here
is Edwin's contribution
to The Hasty Papers.
I like it very much
and hope you do.
                Love,
                Frank
                (O'Hara)

70. FROM BORIS PASTERNAK

November 30, 1959

Dear Leslie, don't absolutely count on me I am terribly busy that's the reason of the abruptness of my answers Take no umbrage, I pray you, excuse me.

B Pasternak

71. FROM AARON SISKIND

615 N. La Salle
Chicago 10, Ill.
12-6-59

Dear Alfred,

I called you this morning for two reasons — first, because the deadline for material for your one-shot magazine had come & gone by; second, because I knew you had moved and I wanted to get your new address to avoid having to have the material forwarded to you & the chance of loss.

I have gotten together 21 photographs of Sullivan ornament. But I have had to reject the Sullivan "writings" my young expert came up with as just not right for your purpose (as I visualize it) Perhaps you can get Fritz Bultman to write a brief note. On the back of each photograph is written the name of the bldg. on which the ornament was used, the place & date of the bldg. + the photographer's name. Of course you are to use what you like best.

As for my personal work I thought to submit a group of Mexican photographs — none of which are in my book.

I also thought of sending you a group of Chicago facades — approx. 1880–1890 and annonymous.

Which of the two last would you prefer, or do you want me to send it all? Let me know and I will do what you say.

(I think you may like ~~the~~ some of the Mexican photographs, & I would like you to keep for yourself whichever and as many as you like.)

How does it go with you? What happened in S.F.?

Write back at once & I will not delay.

Best
Aaron.

72. FROM ALLEN GINSBERG AND PETER ORLOVSKY

Dear Al:

    Enclosed find pre-Xmas bonus on account of your Heroic labors. Just got my royalty check from City Lights and it seems to be enough for me to pay back debts. Hold this a week (till my check clears) and the cash it. Don't forget to wash the asshole. Thanks for the loan & sorry so slow in paying back but been almost broke till today. Seems like Life & Time sold enough books, so I got extrahuge royalties this week. OK--see you soon.

                As ever   Allen
                     Allen
                        &
       Peter
                        &
       Pencils & Pens

---

73. FROM T.S. ELIOT

Sir Geoffrey Faber, Chairman. Richard de la Mare, Vice-Chairman
T. S. Eliot, W. J. Crawley, Morley Kennerley, (U.S.A.), P. F. du Sautoy,
Alan Pringle, David Bland, Charles Monteith

FABER AND FABER LTD

PUBLISHERS
24 Russell Square London WC1
Fabbaf Westcent London   Museum 9543

                 15th December, 1959

Alfred Leslie, Esq.,
108, Fourth Avenue,
New York 3, N.Y.,
U.S.A.

Dear Mr. Leslie,

    Further to my letter of the 13th October I am writing to let you know that Mr. Eliot has now seen your letter of the 3rd October, but regrets that he has nothing he can contribute to your review The Hasty Papers.

              Yours sincerely,

              Secretary to Mr. T.S. Eliot

74. FROM PARKER TYLER

Parker Tyler
5 West 16th Street
New York 11, New York

Jan. 27th 1960
Dear Al Leslie:

    I fully meant to come to your
opening but I was too ill that day--
and maybe it's just as well my first
view was in a quiet, unimpeded gallery.

    I think yours is the most pro-
foundly energetic gesture <u>within
discipline</u> that I see around, these
days, in paint.

    Please dont fail to send me proofs
of my poems: the lineage is difficult
and so is the punctuation.

    Yrs:

75. TO JOHN ASHBERY

Jan 28, 1960

c/o Schuler
438 E 87 st
NYC

Dear Mr Ashbery,

    Joyfully and with many thanks I accept your
play
The Compromise for publication in the Hasty
Papers. Soon you will recieve a copy ofthe
review. Thanks so much again, keep well and more
more and more.

Sincerely

76. TO AMIRI BARAKA (LeROI JONES)

Jan 29,1960

DearRoi,

Heard from Joel OP and Irving Rosenthal that lack
of the goofy green might cancel the latest issue
of John Weiners mag. Maybe I could put the whole
thing in The Hasty Papers it if that ssemmed OK
to youu. Let me know - the nooest
deadline iz March foist.

Soon wit regards

77. FROM BARBARA GUEST

Higgins
2905 N Street, N.W.
Washington, D.C.

Dear Alfred,

We certainly would like to send you poems and
maneouvers for The Hasty Papers and they will
be forthcoming. T. is involved with the Dardanelle
campaign (circa 1915) and I hope I can get him to
write a blast on that or maybe a theory of War in
a hundred words. Unpublished poems surround me, so
I'm no problem.
If you're in Washington or hereabouts, please call
on us we'd love to see you.

Love,
Barbara

78. TO TRUMBULL HIGGINS (Wrongly dated. Should be February 2, 1960)

                                    February 2, 1959

Dear Trumbull Higgins:

I agree with Barbara about "dewline". Do you come
across anything like "skosmos" or "hienioni" ("hienoe-
nie" perhaps)? It all sounds so sensible and beautiful.

Now, I want to ask you: you know something about this
HASTY PAPERS business, and, what about it; come on
along. Please, Missilies and all that that Barbara
communicated so fully & compactly in the note sent
with her three poems. Fits exactly a need. We have
some beautiful things and it is just the right beautys
that we close in on now.

There is a revised deadline now for material of March
1. Will you let me know right away, if you can decide?

                    Yours,

                    Alfred Leslie

79. TO BARBARA GUEST (Wrongly dated. Should be February 4, 1960)

                                    February 4, 1959

Dear Barbara,

I just wrote trying to stir Trumbull up a little; I
might have to send a squad down there to lean on him
some, unless you have gentler methods....

I am returning enclosed two poems, and I hope you
don't hit me when we see each other next nor deny me
the beautiful "Upside-Down", nor scorn the request
that I make now to send me some more.

I like Upside Down terribly much and the other two
don't seem to come up so my main feeling is to protect it. So, since you say ..."poems surround me", I
wondered if you wouldn't mind my asking you for a few
others to see. Of course, if you think I'm wrong about
it, I'll do like you want. Am I a bad editor? Am I a
bad man? It does sound presumptuous I know for a non-
literary mugwump to shove a poet around.

Also, because of the completely fantastic amount of
work that the Papers are involving now & I have to
get back to painting, etc., etc, a couple of quacks
are assisting & helping me with the Papers, and they
find "Upside-Down" also very fine and and finer than
the others, so I thoughtI'd risk asking you about it,
ok?

                    Love,

80. FROM MARIANNE MOORE

260 Cumberland Street — Brooklyn 5 — New York

Dear. Miss Levine: You and
Mr. Leslie are most kind to
invite me to offer you work
for the Review but I have
a contract by which I am oblige
to submit what I write, to
one magazine only.

The Review has my warm wishes.

Sincerely yours,

Marianne Moore

Marianne Moore

February 10, 1960

82. FROM WALTER LOWENFELS

From the desk ~~of~~
WALTER LOWENFELS

2/12/60

Dear Mr. Leslie- I am grateful for the careful
attention of you and your friends. Let me know before
your deadline about the enclosed. I ask only two
indulgences- I have no good typescript of the 31
Poets- please bear with it- I am in throes of winding
up a book for Knopf-(WALT WHITMAN'S CIVIL WAR), 2nd
indulegnce.Please send your magazine when published to
LONGVIEW FOUNDATION, 60 East 42nd, NYCity 17. They
give away money to contribs to Little ags- I just got
$300- so did Alan, Corso, etc. best *W*

'Go easy, Son! This Sally
Lung is half French, and
half Chinese.
The combination of French
perfume and Oriental incense
is more dangerous than nitro-
glycerine!'

81. FROM BARBARA GUEST

Feb. 11, 1960

Dear Alfred,

Your No was such a very kind No, unlike that of
certain editors, that I can only answer Yes here
are two more poems. Well?

Love,
Barbara

*Trumbull still wavers like the Atlantic
Treaty, but a few more days may say but so—*

83. TO JOHN ASHBERY (Wrongly dated. Should be February 17, 1960)

Feb. 17, 1959

Dear John,

You fool. Completely do not pay any attention to the
irresponsible epistle dated January 28 & c/o Schuyler,
wherein your wild work, the play, The COMPROMISE, the
HASTY PAPERS accepted "joyfully".

It would really be better this way: K Koch has your poems
"Europe" and "America", and a play half as long as the
COMPROMISE, Frank told me. I am going to anticipate anyway at least part of a positive reply to this request to
you for permission to print one, or two, or three of the
above mentioned works, by asking Kenneth for them.

Now, you will anyway, won't you let THE HASTY PAPERS
absorb one of these?, instead of the marvelous and
abstract THE COMPROMISE?

Now, is there any of the three Koch has, that you prefer
for us? Any one you definitely don't want us to put our
dirty hands on? If it is feasible for us editorially and
productionally to do all three....any reservation?

You must let us know right away, the answer to these, and
any other querys, that have been put to you lately. In
the meanwhile, Dear John.....

Thanks,

84. FROM CHARLES OLSON

28 Fort Sq Gloster
Feb 19/6.

My dear Alfredleslie:

other   See if this one sits (as it seems to me) with that

            And much obliged, for hearing fr you again; anytime

            Hope The Hasty Papers turn everything up side down

                                                          Yrs
                                                          Charles O
                                                          Charles Olson

85. FROM JOHN ASHBERY

                        14, rue Alfred Durand-Claye
                        Paris XIV, France
                        February 21? 1960

Dear Alfred,

Thanks for your letter I just got, dated Feb. 17, 1959 (it
pays to send things by airmail). Thanks XX also for
including your phone no.--I may call you collect.

Unfortunately you can't, for the moment at least, use
"America", "Europe", or any other of the recent poems
Kenneth has because I already sent them to Big Table.
According to the law of the Old West (as enforced on Old
West 12th St.), no poet can send his poems to an editor so
long as another editor is considering them, even though he
may be certain that the latter is going to turn them down.
Also I doubly do not want to run the risk of offending Big
Table, since it apparently the only magazine in the world
that likes my stuff and envisions publishing it. And, as a
final cincher, I already had a similar embarrassment last
summer when PR published a poem of mine that Big Table was
considering--I had sent it to PR so many year ago that I
had completely forgotten about it.

As for a play of mine half as long as Compromise, the only
one I have written is "The Heroes", which Grove Press is
bout to publish—I corrected the proofs some time ago.
Except for this I have written only little playets, none of
which are really worth publishing, if memory serves.

What about the big batch of poems I sent you XXX already?
"Winter", for instance? or "The Leak in the Dike"? Did
none of these tickle you?

I hope this will be solved to our mutual satisfaction.
Incidentally, if you do publish something of mine, would it
be too much trouble to send me the proofs to correct? I
would appreciate it#########—you know how XXXXX fussy I
XXXXC am.

Listen, after the exhaustion of putting together the Hasty
Papers, why not take a long rest on the continent? We need
young blood over here.

                the best of everything,

'I told you I'd break the Ten Commandments — and look what I've got for it, SUCCESS! That's all that counts! I'm sorry if your God doesn't like it — but this is my party, not His!'

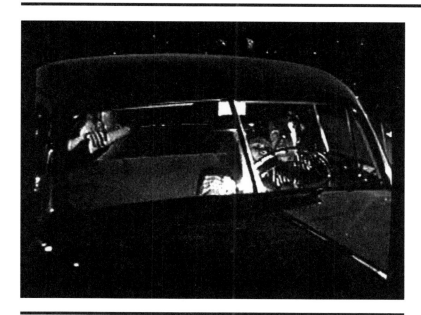

THE STERLING LORD AGENCY

15 EAST 48 STREET   NEW YORK 17, N. Y.   PLAZA 1-2533

March 15, 1960

Dear Alfred:

     Jack Kerouac sent in a short
700-page "dream" for Hasty Papers. Before sending it
on to you, I'd like very much to talk with you.
Could you phone me, please, as I haven't had any
luck getting you? Thanks.

                   Best wishes,

                   Sterling Lord

March 3, 1960

Dear Dick,
    I was copying a couple of these when you
called. On Museum time yet. I wonder how long that
will last...?
    The enclosed five poems are a group. I wrote
them when I was visiting Frank in Cambridge in
1956 (so I could see Ashbery's The Compromise) If
you would like to print them all, I would be very
pleased. But they are a group, and I do seem to
have this all or nothing feeling about them.
    If the word fucking is a problem for the
Hasty Papers (which I somehow doubt) a change to
"And the Effing tree..." would be OK with me.
    Good luck with the great enterprise.
    My new Address is 181 Avenue A. I'll even
have a telephone after tomorrow.
                  Yours,

ps: I also enclose two very short poems, Tonio and
A Reunion. Use thy discretion! If you print the
Cambridge set, please make it plain they're a
group, and are apart from any others you may use.
The penciled numbers at the top are just to indi-
cate their order.

March 15, 1960

Dear Al,

This one seems to be much more for you than
"Dumbarton Oaks". Would there be time to make an
exchange? I'd much prefer it.

T. insists on silence and I can move him no further. However, I've taken notes from his midnight
speeches (I wish you hadn't been roasting the ewe
lamb that Sat. night and could have come to the
Sachs and collared him) which I enclose. Perhaps
you can use them as they are.

              Love,

              Barbara

2905 N st., n.w.
Washington, D.C.

then to take a short sweet pull on my huge juicy
stick of a hardon in front of everybody in the
streets of Coyocan.

    And the Flying Horse of Mien-Mo are gallop-
ing with silent ease in the happy empty air way
up there—Tinkle Tinkle go the streets of Coyocan
as the sun falls, but there is all silence & the
Giant Gods are up—How can I describe it?
    (Written after a Chinese
        dinner in Chinatown!
        Feb. 8 1960

Jack Kerouac
A DREAM
c/o Lord Agency
15 E-48th St
NY 17, NY
Plaza 1-2533

Dear Alfred:—
You've got to get
this copyrighted in my
name or my agent
Sterling Lord will mop
the sidewalk with both
of us — He's put his
foot down, is a good agent
& good friend Jack

90. FROM PETER ORLOVSKY

Hi yo Alfred.   march 24, 60
                                           Thursday

    Sorrey I of delayed repay of 20 you lent
but my Ballons got lost in sky.. so had I restock
are stock —— allen still in S.A. says its
friendly down there with mass poets & poetry
orgies & tranns lations. almost feels like home —

    In case by chance you no have Hasley
                                          Book
                                          out

                              maybe
                    I   send you
                         some over
              this weekend.
Gregory & Bill B. misterious as ever —
              ok now
                          Flowers
                          Peter

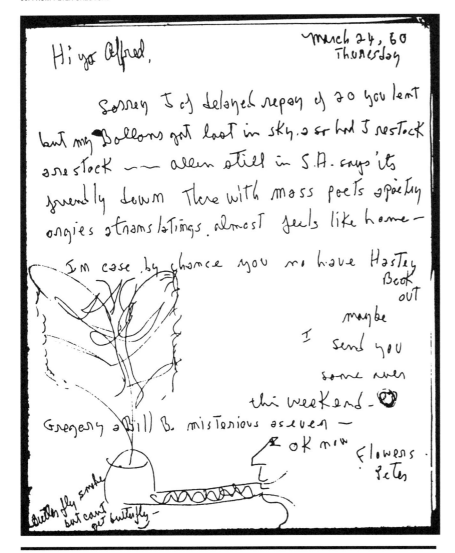

91. FROM KENWARD ELMSLIE

Dear Al --

        I was hoping to send you something longer,
but it isn't finished--I hope this poem isn't too late.

                            YRS
                            Ken

92. FROM AMIRI BARAKA (LeROI JONES)

402 W. 20 St. New York 11
                                        yūgen

Dear Alfred Leslie,

What you propose is a fine idea!
My thot that as soon as you have got through with
it, we can get it from you (or the printer??).
You mean the proofs..the final repros? We save us
millions. Probably, I shd. see you about this &
work out whatever is most convenient &c. for you
When are the Hasty Papers making their triumphant
entry into the golden cities?? If it is in Oct or
Nov, that wd be fine with our plans for the book.
We are loosely thinking about February as possible
date for The Sun.
At any rate, I wd. like to talk to you about all
of it, & hope we can work something out!

So let me know just what you think &c.

                            best

                            LeRoi Jones

93. FROM ALLEN GINSBERG

Dear Al —
Finally Found photos — enclosed
I (thought) gave you — the Mexico one —
                              photo
Also some passport encl. + 2 S& Machine

Please save + send me back

the Mexico photo   allen

33 & 34 in letter — It was near
My 34 ("34 Coming up") birthday.
                                    A

94. FROM ALFRED JENSEN

Visual Education
    The little boy and his father
stand in front of a marvel
display of Peruvian art
objects.
    Little boy asks,
" What is this?"
His Father answeres,
" This — this is a sign — they
ain't civilized!"
    Little boy bewildered asks
again,
    "Why is that?"
Father turning away from exhibit
in disdain answeres
" Them — they don't know better.
                        yours,
                        Alfred

95. FROM TERRY SOUTHERN

                                    Mulberry Point
                                    Guilford, Conn.

                                    4 April 1960

Alfred Leslie
THE HASTY PAPERS
940 Broadway
New York 10, N.Y.

Dear Alfred:

Many thanks for your good letter of the 29th past.

I shall be delighted to contribute to your HASTY
PAPERS and hope to get something to you in an early
post. How's this for an opening: "Norman Rockwell's
recent statement that 'God is a spade-dike and Commie'
came as no real surprise to many of us here at HASTY
PAPERS. In fact, etc. etc" No, actually I am thinking
along different lines at the moment. I plan to be in
on Thursday and Friday and I will have something to
hand for you at that time; I'll try to reach you
through groovy Michael G.

                            Be *Terry*

97. FROM GRACE SCHULMAN

GLAMOUR

The Condé Nast Publications Inc., 420 Lexington Avenue, New York 17

                                    June 21, 1960

96. FROM ROBERT CREELY

May 23. 1960

Dear Mr. Leslie —

I wanted to get you
my address for the sum-
mer (reverse side). I'm
sorry I couldn't send
more poems. i.e., at that
point I had none. So.
How are things going?
I hope well.

                My best.

                Bob

Dear Mr. Leslie:

    I heard about your forthcoming publication, "The Hasty
Papers," from Hannelore Hahn Stoumen, and I'd like very
much to write a news item about it for our feature section.

    Would you be kind enough to call me at LE 2-7500, ext.
230? (The Martha Jackson Gallery gave me your address,
and said I could not contact you by telephone.)

    If you prefer to answer by mail, would you kindly send
me any information you have about the publication? Also,
something about yourself, and any interesting projects—
movies, books, plays, etc.—you have in the works.

    Thank you very much for your cooperation.

                        Sincerely,

                        Grace Schulman

                        Grace Schulman

98. FROM LANGE GALLIMARD (GENET)

```
    SI ACR3/F 1903
                PARIS 15 26 1205

HASTY PAPERS 940 BROADWAY
                        NEWYORKCITY

SUSPEND PUBLICATION UNTIL RECEIPT OF

LETTER FROM FRECHTMAN

38    LANGE GALLIMARD
```

100. TO AMIRI BARAKA (LeROI JONES)

```
Dear LeRoi,
Heard that(from Allen) that you are at magnifico
confrence en CUBA. Would you like to write mas-
sive tome for Hasty boys on impressions and/or
some things?About to go to press and anxious to
hear from you about this teriffic adventure.
Hope you are having a time.
                Regards Alfred
```

99. FROM LANGE GALLIMARD (GENET)

LIBRAIRIE *nrf* GALLIMARD

Société Anon. - Capital 1.620.000 N.F.
Chèque Postal : PARIS Nº 169-33
Reg. du Commerce Seine 57 B 20.675

Téléphone : LITTRÉ 28-91 à 28-94
Adresse Télégr. : ENEREFENE-PARIS
Nº d'Entreprise : 552 - 75.107 - 0041

5, rue Sébastien-Bottin, Paris (VIIᵉ)

HASTY PAPERS

940 Broadway

NEW YORK City
                        U.S.A.

Paris, le 20 Août 1960

Monsieur,

    Vous aurez reçu notre télégramme du 17/8 à propos de JEAN
GENET.

    Pouvez vous avoir l'obligeance de nous envoyer un exemplaire
justificatif de votre revue.

    Nous vous en remercions, et

    Vous prions de croire, Monsieur, à l'assurance de notre consi·
dération.

Monique LANGE.

101. TO SEYMOUR KRIM

```
Dear Mr Krim,
    Today is my day of humiliation.Writing
letters and sending back material I wont use
in the Papers.
    I hope I haven't kept the story too long,
I certainly readit enough..anyway..thanks
for letting me read it anyway,.
                Regards


                Alfred Leslie
```

102. FROM BERNARD FRECHTMAN (GENET)

September 2, 1960

Dear Mr. Leslie,

This is to authorize publication of *Condamné à mort* in Hasty Papers. It is understood that this authorization is limited to publication only once, and in Hasty Papers. Re-publication or reproduction of any kind in a periodical, book, on the radio, etc. is not included in the permission hereby granted.

If the translator wishes to re-publish his translation elsewhere, he must likewise obtain proper authorization.

The present permission is valid only until March 15, 1961.

Sincerely yours,
Bernard Frechtman

104. FROM JAMES SCHUYLER

THE MUSEUM OF MODERN ART

NEW YORK 19

11 WEST 53rd STREET
TELEPHONE: CIRCLE 5-8900
CABLES: MODERNART, NEW-YORK

PORTER A. McCRAY
DIRECTOR OF CIRCULATING EXHIBITIONS

November 10, 1960

Dear Al,

Thanks for your letter

By me, the more people who read Freely Espousing the better; so it's all cha-cha-cha.

Speaking of which: it's a pleasure to know somebody who can tell when a chapter in their life is closed; I had doubts all along about how you'ld feel; now I know. So.

You said you had some plays (or prose-play-scenario type works similar: is one available? All of / issue 1 of Locus Solus is set, (for January); I think the

selection will come to life if there is a jolt of your spunkiness: / if you have one you like, and can have it typied, why not whip it down to me (181 Avenue A, NYC 9)? Or here, but home is better.

"Such confusion" is right --- as I daid, among the known names in it are Kenneth, Frank, John, Barbara, me, (I'm beginning to forgetxxx who else), ohith big hunks of previously unpublished stuff. Quantity and quality; you know, like S. Janis? or the Jaguar you can eat with a spoon?

I hear your masks made the Election; as blue-eyed Jane Freilicher said, "Say, you know that Al Leslie, he's really something."

I hope you will come across (Time! whatever bacame of it?) -- x your writing xxx seems to happen before you knew you had gotten it down: I mean it stays alive, like gold-fish in plastic bag?

Looking to hear from you,

best,

103. FROM MORTON FELDMAN

Oct 6, 1960

Dear Al,

Unless a score looks beautiful like John Cage I can't see the point for a "lay" public . . . . and wouldn't the printing be expensive unless photo stat — and that is not so hot. I would rather write an article. Better yet! An article by ——— An article about me. + the score of a new piece. + all my girls since 1950.

See you

M Feldman

105. FROM FRANK O'HARA

January 8, 1961

Dear Alfred:

I'm sorry I was such a dope about this, but I finally found this poem I wrote for you a long time ago and have gone over several times and now sort of like it (I think). Anyhow, do you see anything in it? If you don't like it, don't use it and perhaps I can think up something else if there's time.

It was actually made up of titles I thought of for you one time when you had asked me to think of some -- everything in quotes is from a Russian poet (modern) like Mayakovsky, Essenin and so on.

Maybe it will work better than something "clear", maybe not, possibly depending on what Kenneth has given you.

Anyhow, happy new year to you and Lisa,

Frank

106. FROM LAWRENCE FERLINGHETTI

Dear Alfred/leslie   1/19/61

Yu please could you send us now 25 (twentyfive) copies of HASTY PAPERS No.# 1960. 3⁰⁰ I've rc'd only one copy to-date, for which thank youse. (40% discount is normal) Sincere - L. Ferlinghetti

107. FROM HARRY GANTT

WY-2-0200
Mr Chowsky

H. GANTT*

3 10 61

Jackson Trans
NABOSTORAGE

Dear Alfred

Inventory of what was sent to storage:

5 skids of 25 cartons - 26 books per carton - 1 skid of 35 cartons or 160 cartons on 6 skids 4160 books. the 160 are overs for which you were not charged.

books taken out of binder

Gantt	100	to Leslie studio
Leslie	100	" "
Phoneix	500	
Leslie	288	
1st samples	12	

1000 and 4160 above   5,160 books

Publishers Printing Representative

360 CABRINI BOULEVARD, NEW YORK 40, N. Y. COLUMBUS 5-7451

108. FROM KENNETH KOCH

69 Perry Street
N.Y. 14, N.Y.
April 7, 1961

Dear Alfred,
The more I look at Hasty Papers, the more I'm convinced that a more (deceptive) listing of some of its contents in a few publications would sell a great many copies — I think we should take ads (even small ones) in Village Voice, Partisan Review, Evergreen Review (stressing Hochhuth), The Columbia University Forum (an inspiration! — it has 100,000 readers, I think), The Nation (stressing Oppenheimer, Ginsberg, & Castro), perhaps even the Saturday Review (just for a start). Also, send a copy to Poetry Magazine, saying you'd like them to mention it in their News Notes. I am giving it a free plug in the New School Bulletin which lists faculty publications & I'm now telling my students they might well buy it. Good heavens! it's a great publication! If you want to do a flat statement of contents either with or without a comic strip I'll be glad to try to write one. Our book grows in beauty every day. My hand, as you see, can hardly write after all that signing.
Regards & alote big to little Quakers —
Kenneth

109. TO FRANK O'HARA

Dear FRank

I'm racin out the door in feww minutes as Lisa is in
the hospital. More about that later but meantime could
you call Kenneth and reassure him that I think all hiz
iedeas about HP are great and I'll really do m best to
follow up. I tole him allthisbut m'thinks he doubts.

I MEAN THE HP'S   SOLD OVER A THOUSAND JUST BY WORD OF
MOUTH -

You know what a beating i'm taking nowand i'm not sure
Kennth iz aware. !m broke, passed up Doughville to -
dare I zay it? - do mywork az I think is rite not
everyopmne else. Plus of course this tough fambly
stuff. Inheriting three kids & an a rich boozy ex is
riding the pink horse plus.
    ALSO- Kenneth hintedhow he was not happy with my
including him in The Cedar. What??? Thats ten years
ago I gave you that! Did you give it to him aAlong
the way? ? Is he confusing The Cedar with Chekov?
Anyway if you still have it could you let him see it-
He doesn't appear in Cedar or Chekov. Wwhat is he
talkng aboyt? It's probably ol' deafie Al's hearing
as usual. Anyway Herbert has a Cedar if you lost yours
-which reminds me I still haven't returned your MAKE
IT NEW.

Some recent comments on HP: Grace "Alfred what a waste
of time." Hilton "How inelegant for a painter to do
this." Bill "Geessus Les, vot the hell, it's a snapshot of us all!" Motherwell "Need more photos" Clem
"Good for you." Pavia "You're copying me!" Harold and
May "He's tryingto take over the art world!" So will
call you after a bit my good pal wish me luck in the
dark corridors I'm leaving for.

Alfred yr pal

110. FROM CONSTANCE TRIMBLE (LEO CASTELLI)

LEO CASTELLI INC

4 EAST 77 ST • NEW YORK 21

Dear Al,

    I rather thought we had got six or eight copies of HP on
your first visit with them. Can you straighten me out on
this? The second group I believe was ten.

                    Best regards,

                    Constance Trimble
                    for Leo Castelli

BUTTERFIELD 8-8343

111. FROM ROBERT NICHOLS

                    48 Carmine St NYC 14
                    (CH3 5389) AL5 4571
Oct. 5, 61

Alfred Leslie
The Hasty Papers
940 Broadway

Dear Mr.Leslie;

I wrote earlier in the summer to try to get in touch
with Derek Walcott. We are interested in doinghis play
, +, at the Judson Poet's Theater. Could you kindly
give me his address?

Robert Nichols

Director

Notes for BROTHER CAN YOU SPARE A DIME

Indexed by letter number, name and page.

Letters from *The Hasty Papers* were written from two New York City addresses, 108 Fourth Avenue, and 940 Broadway. The writers were Marie-Claire Moyano, Naomi Levine, Richard Bellamy, Lisa Bigelow, and myself. Allen Ginsberg wrote one.

1. From FRANK O'HARA poet, friend, collaborator (p. 15)
Museum of Modern Art letterhead: O'Hara worked there, beginning at the front desk, ending as associate curator. **Ezra Pound book:** I'd borrowed *Make It New,* Pound's book of literary essays. **Vincent** Warren: A dancer O'Hara was living with. **THIEVING CHILDREN:** O'Hara had been shot in 1954 by kids rifling his mailbox. **Don Allen:** Senior editor at Grove Press. **Bill Berkson, Kenneth Koch:** Mutual poet friends. **Allen:** Don Allen again.

2. To JAMES SCHUYLER poet, friend (p.15)

3. To JEAN COCTEAU painter, filmmaker, playwright (p.15)
Previous correspondence with Cocteau, never archived, was lost in the fire.

4. From JOEL OPPENHEIMER poet, friend (p.15)
New found fame: In October 1959, *Pull My Daisy* premiered in New York City with John Cassavetes' *Shadow.* MoMA included my work in *Fourteen Americans,* and work was eight months underway on *The Hasty Papers. Yugen:* One of the magazines edited by Amiri Baraka (LeRoi Jones).

5. To JOEL OPPENHEIMER (p.15)
Photos: Group photo of all the Black Mountain poets. Not archived, lost in the fire.

6. To FRANK O'HARA (p. 16)
I'm feared yo right: Refers to then friend Robert Frank and *Daisy* credits. I had let him share directorial and other credits with me on the film when there was no basis for it except friendship. **El sharpo teetho:** Shakespeare line, "How sharper than a serpents tooth it is to have a thankless child." Referring to Robert Frank again. **Priscilla Morgan:** Friend, one of the founders of the William Morris Agency, was interested in representing me. She knew of the film credits' false representation of Robert Frank as my co-director and co-adapter. Calvert **Coggashall:** Painter, architect. Eventually Morgan spoke to Coggashall, who spoke to **Walker E** (Walker Evans) who spoke to **Mary** Frank). Evans knew that Robert Frank idolized him and hoped to persuade him not to take credit for work of mine. ***A Life And Time:*** A film I was writing. ***Cha Cha:*** *The Chekov Cha Cha,* a manuscript of mine which I blocked from publication in the premiere issue of *Locus Solus.* It had been passed on by Frank O'Hara to the magazine's first editor, John Ashbery. The only copy was lost in the fire. **No story:** My view was that all stories, even no stories, are good stories. **Marie-clare:** Marie-Claire, poet friend who was my first helper with the magazine. **The Shadow says:** Famous line from 1940s radio show, *The Shadow,* on which Orson Welles played at different times both Lamont Cranston and the Shadow.

7. From AMIRI BARAKA (LEROI JONES) playwright, friend, political activist (p.16)
Dutchman, Blues People, The Dead Lecturer are among his works. *Yugen* and *Kulchur* were his magazines at the time. **Also the photo:** Must have been of Roi and poet friends.

8. To AMIRI BARAKA (LEROI JONES) (p. 17)
MEASUre: Poet John Weiners' magazine, *MEASUre,* was in trouble. I thought I could incorporate the new issue into *The Hasty Papers.* **Cecil Taylor:** Great innovative musician who played The Five Spot (Bowery between 4th and 5th Street in New York City).

9. From MARTIN WILLIAMS jazz critic (p. 17)
Astute supporter of Taylor, Ornette Coleman, and others.

10. From DIANE DI PRIMA poet, friend (p. 17)
Co-editor of legendary mimeographed staple-mag, *The Floating Bear,* with Baraka (Jones).

12. From KENNETH KOCH poet, friend (p. 18)
Koch and family summered in Southampton. **Mr. Rivers:** Larry Rivers, pop-art precursor, who years earlier had moved there. We both showed in the 1950s in John Myers' Tibor de Nagy Gallery. **Signa:** East Hampton gallery begun by painters Alfonso Ossorio, John Little, and Elizabeth Parker.

13. From PONTUS HULTÉN museum director, friend (p. 19)
Then director of Stockholm's Moderna Museet, he later conceived the idea for the Pompidou Center in Paris and was the founding director. **Pull My:** I sent him *Daisy* via diplomatic pouch with writer-engineer Billy Klüver. Later in 1962, I programmed it with Shirley Clarke's *The Connection,* Ed Bland's *The Cry of Jazz,* and John Cassavetes *Shadows* at the opening of the museum's film department and gave a talk about The New American Cinema group of which I was one of the founders. Hultén also helped in the funding of *Daisy* through the sale of a painting of mine to a Swiss museum. **Buying the painting:** The first contemporary American painting the Moderna Museet bought was mine.

14. From FREDERICK KIESLER architect, friend (p. 19)
He was the youngest member of the De Stijl group and fled Europe with the help of The New School in New York City. His most famous work was the egg-shaped Endless House. **"Art: or the Teaching of Resistance":** I never published it, rightfully making Kiesler angry.

15. From BERTRAND RUSSELL mathematician, philosopher (19)
The letter was probably written by Ralph Schoenman who served as Russell's secretary into the 1960s. He was a friend and Princeton classmate of Donald Goddard,. who pointed this out to me while editing these notes.

16. To RAYMOND MEDEIROS poet, translator (p. 19)
Friend of a friend. We never met, but talked on the phone and corresponded. Genet's work was then considered obscene. Unprepared to take on the legal battle, I postponed publication until I could figure out what to do. This was the period during which Billy Holiday was arrested in the hospital for drug possession, and Lenny Bruce was taken to court on obscenity charges. He said shit, fuck, cunt, cocksucker in routines ridiculing authority, pretension, and racial prejudice. Both performers lost their New York City cabaret licenses. The Genet poem is now included in this edition.

17. From KENNETH KOCH (p. 21)
Miss Diana: Diana Powell, the woman I was living with at the time.

18. From NORMAN MAILER author, provocateur, friend (p. 21)
He eventually sent me a few paragraphs about how painters like Miles Forst, Jan Mueller, and myself had helped him through those times when he had been under attack from the literary establishment. I never used it as I wanted something that better represented his work.

19. To HORACE GREGORY poet, critic (p. 21)
A fact sheet would have been sent to him with this letter.

20. To FIDEL CASTRO revolutionary, head of state (p. 22)
Why shouldn't he answer me?

21. To DENISE LEVERTOV poet (p. 22)
British-born Black Mountain poet whose work I ended up not publishing because I couldn't meet her expectations.

22. From JOE LESUEUR poet, playwright, friend (p. 23)
He was living with O'Hara around this time. **Lifesaver:** I made a lot of people loans of money when I had it. **Dick** Bellamy: He was not yet my dealer, nor had he opened his legendary Green Gallery. He joined *Hasty* along with Marie-Claire Moyano, painter-poet-filmmaker Naomi Levine, and editor Diana Powell.

23. From ARCHIBALD MACLEISH poet, playwright (p. 23)
By this time the National Poet, his government connections helped Ezra Pound avoid a trial for treason. When teaching at Harvard, Gregory Corso was one of his students.

24. To JAMES SCHUYLER (p. 23)
THE BOOK: Probably Bob Friedman's *Some Younger American Painters* that Barney Rosset was publishing. Schuyler had contributed an essay about my work.

25. From WILLIAM CARLOS WILLIAMS poet, doctor (p. 24)
Williams died four years after writing. "The world contracted to a recognizable image." It was one of his last poems. I like to imagine he wrote it for *Hasty.*

26. To DEREK WALCOTT poet, painter, playwright, friend (p. 24)
We met in 1955 or '56 through mutual pal actor-theater manager John Robertson, who had worked with Walcott and his twin brother in Trinidad on a grant. **Mal Cochacun:** My misspelling of the plays title. (*Malcochon!* is Walcotts preferred spelling now. In the original Hasty Papers he used *Malcauchon!*). José **Quintero:** Well-known theater director.

27. To LIONEL TRILLING literary critic (p. 24)
Eminent critic and teacher at Columbia University. Ginsberg was a student of his.

28. To FIDEL CASTRO (p. 24)
You're letter does remain alone unanswered. I would say that 40% of all I wrote as yet are unreplied: Clarity and grammar from the top.

29. From RUTH MILLER painter, friend (p. 25)
One of the people who visited Ezra Pound at Saint Elizabeth's Hospital in Washington D.C., where Pound had been committed in 1946 after being judged unfit to stand trial for treason. During World War II, Pound made radio speeches against the U.S. I asked some people who had visited him to write something. **Jessica:** One of Miller's newborn twins. **Personal obscurity:** Pound pretty much stopped talking until his death. **Esteban** Vicente: Painter and father of the twins. Ruth must have been living in France at the time. **Rowland:** Must have been her companion. **Krew-shev:** Krushchev ov cuz.

30. From JEAN COCTEAU (p. 26)
"I don't understand exactly what you want. Stop. Please tell me more. Stop. I am happy to help."

31. To JEAN COCTEAU (p. 26)
Written in my studio at 108 4th Avenue with Allen Ginsberg, who added the following text.
Let me add a few words. As you probably know there is a great renaissance of poetry (and prose) in the U.S.. In other words, many young people who became Angels create natural mystical phenomena (visions of a nameless Father in Heaven) (and in human body) — also an army of boys who smoke marijuana, eat Artaud's Peyote, or do horrible things with the white heroine (and wait for/understand this Buchenwald of their bodies) and now some of them have played a game with a new drug (a mystical phlogiston) Lysergic Acid. But it's not the drugs or the sons of jazz that turned us into Angels who read Genet and Jacob Boheme and Eckhart, it's another force that I cannot give a name to, that I understand, you understand. In any case you might probably be interested in a classic book by William S. Burroughs, Naked Lunch, which was published in Paris by Olympia, because it's a result of twelve years of suffering in New York, Mexico, Tangiers, and Paris caused by an intoxication with heroin, but it's all pure and harsh poetry. The man equals Genet in his literary intelligence and what is more important in his spiritual intensity. It's a great assertion but I am sure that you will think the same if you investigate it. Anyway, all the young people read Artaud. Mr. Leslie, a painter who sold some of his work, gathered all his money to put together this unique issue of a review that collects work by all the unknown and the known. Thank you. Goodbye, - - Allen Ginsberg

32. To NICO CALAS art writer, poet (p. 27)
He had many affiliations with European surrealism and belonged to The Club, an important New York meeting ground for artists in the 1950s.

33. From JAMES SCHUYLER (p. 27)
Refers to his poem *Freely Espousing.* **P.S.:** He was also an art writer for many publications, and refers again to B.H. Friedman's *Some Younger American Painters* (note 24). **c/o John Button:** A mutual painter friend.

34. To BERNARD FRECHTMAN (p. 27)
Genet's agent and English translator at the time. Ashbery's name spelled incorrectly again.

35. From STANLEY KUNITZ poet, friend (p. 28)
One of the founders of the Poetry Center in New York and of The Provincetown Workshop in Provincetown, Massachusetts.

36. From JAMES SCHUYLER (p. 28)
Letter Statement: He was working at MoMA and refers to my catalogue statement for the upcoming show of *Fourteen Americans* at MoMA. He thought quotes from the *Chekov Cha Cha* should be used. We ended up using a paragraph about my work by painter Grace Hartigan. **Dorothy Miller:** Chief curator at MoMA. **Script of The Movie:** Refers to *A Life And Time* (letter 6). **Charm:** Refers to article in *Charm Magazine* profiling Bob Rauschenberg, Jasper Johns, Richard Stankiewicz, and myself.

37. To JOHN ASHBERY (p. 29)
Kenneth: Kenneth Koch.

38. From DEREK WALCOTT (p. 29)
Dear David: Walcott's joke. I was David slaying Goliath. **Jeanne Unger:** Another editor at Grove Press. **Allen:** Don Allen. **José Paintere:** The theater director, José Quintero. **Nail me:** Song parody of mine, which became a running joke. **John** Robertson: The friend Walcott and I had in common who had introduced us to each other. **Herta:** Herta Payson, A dancer who was living with Robertson at the time. **Malle:** Marie-Claire Moyano. **Herring, etc:** A famed studio dish of mine.

39. To DEREK WALCOTT (p. 29)
Barney and Don: Rosset and Allen. **Torture twentieth century style:** More of the ongoing struggle over *Pull My Daisy* credits with photographer Robert Frank, the animus the fame of the film had created. **Impale me doggerel:** "Nail me, nail me, go ahead impale me, I'm only your friend."

40. From FIDEL CASTRO (p. 30)
Some contributors withdrew from the magazine because of Castro.

41. From SIMON WATSON TAYLOR (p. 30)
Collège de 'Pataphysique: Pink greyhounds at play. French poet and playwright Alfred Jarry (1873-1907) invented "pataphysics" as "the science of imaginary solutions." **Evergreen:** Barney Rosset's famous *Evergreen Review.* **Roger Shattuck:** He wrote *The Banquet Years* about the origins of the French avant garde (1885-1914). **Faustroll:** The first pataphysician. **Allen G**: Allen Ginsberg. **Christopher Logue, Michael McClure, Philip Lamantia:** One English and two American poets. **Antonin Artaud:** Tortured icon of the theater of the absurd.

42. To CHESTER HIMES expatriate African-American novelist (p. 31)
I first heard of him from the publisher of Olympia Press, Maurice Girodias.

43. To TRUMAN CAPOTE poet, novelist (p. 31)
Doc Humes: Writer (*Paris Is Burning*) and one of the founders of *The Paris Review.* He never became in fact an associate editor; I just gave him work space in one of the *Hasty* offices. **Sartre/Genet:**

An excerpt of Sartre's book had been suggested by the brilliant poet/translator Richard Howard. **Mae West:** I had heard of a banned interview by the legendary political commentator **Edward R. Murrow** from political filmmaker Emile de Antonio (*In The Year Of The Pig, Point of Order, Painters Painting*). I failed to track it down because it turned out to be by Charles Collingwood on CBS in 1959.

44. From JOHN ASHBERY (p. 32)
François Truffaut: French film director. **Robbe-Grillet:** His *The Voyeur* was one of the works I considered for a film. **Arnold Weinstein:** Playwright/lyricist who wrote *Dynamite Tonight* and taught at Yale in the Robert Brustein years. **Bill Weaver:** Key translator of the Italian intelligentsia. **Moravis:** Alberto Moravia, distinguished Italian author.

45. To LOUIS-FERDINAND CÉLINE novelist (p. 32)
Author of *Death on the Installment Plan* and *Journey to the End of the Night.*

47. From T.S. ELIOT poet (p. 32)
I wanted to include him in the company of younger poets, since many considered him an antique.

48. From SIMON WATSON TAYLOR (p. 33)
The New Images of Man: A survey of current figuration at MoMA.

49. From ALFRED JENSEN painter, friend (p. 33)
Visionary painter who was born in Guatemala and died in New Jersey. Along with Alice Neel, he was one of the two painters who contributed an essay to *The Hasty Papers.*

50. From JAMES SCHUYLER (p. 34)
Cutism: B.H. Friedman's aforementioned book (notes 24 and 33). In quoting from *Chekov Cha Cha*, the word came up. It was supposed to read Cute-ism (shrewd marketplace art-ambition as idea and style). Schuyler wrote the essay on my work for the book, which was to accompany a traveling exhibition. **Diana** Powell: The woman I lived with from 1957 to1960 worked for a time at Grove Press.

51. From CHARLES OLSON poet, scholar, teacher (p. 34)
Author of *Call Me Ishmael*, groundbreaking book on Melville and *The Maximus Poems.* His work came through from sculptor John Chamberlain and the poet Joel Oppenheimer. They had studied with him at Black Mountain College, an experimental arts community in North Carolina.

52. To DONALD WINDHAM novelist, playwright (p. 34)
He was a writer who had a long friendship with Tennessee Williams, with whom he co-authored a play. Later, Williams would lie and misrepresent Windham's contribution. Artist Tony Smith introduced me to Windham's work. **Change in my domestic status:** Diana and I had split up and I moved into 940 Broadway after a trip west with Kerouac to the San Francisco premiere of *Pull My Daisy.* **Translation of Petronius:** Petronius's *Satyricon.* William Arrowsmith's recent translation had been a bestseller. **That Castro piece:** In our telephone conversation I had asked Windham to put out good vibes to Williams regarding *Hasty* and a Castro/Williams interview. **Mari:** Marie-Claire Moyano.

53. To JOHN ASHBERY (p. 35)
Richard Howard: Among his many translations are Charles de Gaulle's war memoirs. His most recent books of poetry are *Different Tune,* 1998 and *Trappings,* 1999. **Gallimard:** Genet's publisher.

54. To JAMES T. FARRELL novelist (p. 35)
Author of *Young Lonigan*, among many novels, '30s champion of the underclass. Not only did I misspell his name (Farrel), but I misattributed Horace McCoy's *They Shoot Horses Don't They?* to him! **John Meyers:** My dealer at the time, he was the founder and director of the Tibor de Nagy Gallery.

55. To TENNESSEE WILLIAMS playwright (p. 35)
In my letters I never mentioned that we had met. I was with Larry Rivers a few times when he was dropping off a gift of drugs for Williams at his room at the Chelsea Hotel.

56. To WILLIAM FAULKNER writer (p. 36)
Book of poems called Permanently: A Tiber Press edition of four poets with silkscreened images by four painters (Goldberg/O'Hara, Leslie/Koch, Mitchell/Schuyler, Hartigan/Ashbery), edited by Richard Miller and printed by Floriano Vecchi. **Opera with Frank O'Hara:** A musical incarnation of the first (1952) version of my play *The Cedar Bar*, which Frank was working on with me then. (A current version with songs by myself and David Amram was produced as a staged reading with music on May 2, 1997 at The New School in New York City. A film of the play is in the editing stage now.)

57. To DAVID DELLINGER political activist (p. 36)
Editor of the democratic-socialist magazine *Liberation* and head of the War Resisters League.

58. To ERNEST HEMINGWAY writer (p. 36)
Oppenheimer's speech: I wanted something from Oppenheimer. He directed the Manhattan Project at Los Alamos which created the first atomic bomb. Later he was one of demagogue Joe McCarthy's victims. **Carl Dreyer:** Great Danish film director of *St. Joan, Ordet, Gertrude.* At the time this letter was sent, Hemingway was in a deep depression from which he would never recover. Some time later put a gun in his mouth and shot himself.

59. From DAVID MCREYNOLDS political activist (p. 37)
He worked with Dellinger at *Liberation* and the War Resisters League.

60. To NORMAN MAILER (p. 37)
Jack Jones: James Jones, author of *From Here To Eternity.* Mailer references Jones' **"To the End of Thought"** in *Hip and Square.* Patsy **Southgate:** Writer and one of O'Hara's closest friends. His poems, e.g. *The Day Lady Died*, frequently mention her. Mailer had given me the text via Southgate.

61. From ROBERT LOWELL poet (p. 38)
Another of the poets I thought was being unfairly shut out at the time.

62. To WALKER EVANS photographer and friend (p. 38)
His and James Agee's book *Let Us Now Praise Famous Men* was already legendary.

63. From SHERI MARTINELLI painter, writer (p. 38)
The artist who was a central figure in critic-writer Anatole Broyard's *When Kafka Was All The Rage.* **M.B.:** Legendary Greenwich Village poet Maxwell Bodenheim (see letter 64). **E.P's permission:** Ezra Pound. I forget who **John Chatel** was. **Grampa:** Pound. **Robert Stock** is a poet. **Cassandra's:** A club that hosted poetry readings. **send H.D. a copy:** Poet Hilda Doolittle.

64. From SHERI MARTINELLI (p. 39)
"Death with Doves": This is the piece she wrote which we didn't end up using. **Maxwell Bodenheim:** The hard-drinking poet and his girlfriend were savagely murdered.

65. From ROBERT DUNCAN poet (p. 39)
His work got lost in the shuffle.

67. From SAMUEL BECKETT poet, playwright, novelist (p. 40)
I had always thought he would send me something since he was a good friend of Rosset's, who put me in touch with him.

68. From ALBERT CAMUS writer (p. 40)
"Sir, M. Camus hasn't been in Paris since the beginning of the month. I did, however, tell him what you wrote, and he asked me to tell you that, sadly, he has nothing for your magazine at this time. If you find something among his already published works that might interest you, tell him and, if M. Camus' American editor Madame Knopf, approves, you are welcome to it." I had no one helping me who could research his untranslated stuff.

69. From FRANK O'HARA (p. 40)
Edwin Denby: One of the most insightful and literate dance critics of the century, also a wonderful poet.

70. From BORIS PASTERNAK Russian poet, novelist (p. 41)
This most beautiful of documents and its envelope, with its cluster of stamps and postmarks and written with a steel pen, was a Steinbergian (Saul) masterpiece.

71. From AARON SISKIND photographer (p. 41)
Siskind was a leading photographer in Chicago. At the time he was known only to painters and photographers; he had been marginally profiled in *The New Yorker* by Joseph Mitchell in an essay about the writer Joe Gould (Alice Neels's nude portrait of him is on page 91). I had just given Aaron a painting to help finance the first book of his photographs. **21 photographs of** Louis **Sullivan ornament:** I wanted something on this influential architect and teacher of Frank Lloyd Wright. **Fritz Bultman:** Painter who had a great passion for architecture. Aaron proposed Bultman to write an introduction to the photographs. **Mexican photographs:** Ones I kept to use later, but were destroyed in the fire. **S.F.:** Refers to the San Francisco trip I made with Kerouac for the West Coast premiere of *Pull My Daisy* at the first San Francisco Film Festival.

72. From ALLEN GINSBERG and PETER ORLOVSKY poets, friends (p. 42)
City Lights: San Francisco bookstore and publishing house, founded by Peter Martin and Lawrence Ferlinghetti. I lent Orlovsky and Ginsberg some money, and they paid me back! **Life & Time:** The readers of these popular magazines seemed fascinated by Beat gossip.

74. From PARKER TYLER poet, film critic, friend (p. 43)
Distinguished writer whose *The Stone Butterfly* Auden thought to be the greatest English poem since T.S. Eliot's *The Wasteland.* By the 1950s he was known more for his film criticism than his poetry.

76. To AMIRI BARAKA (LEROI JONES) (p. 43)
Joel OP: The poet Joel Oppenheimer. **Irving Rosenthal:** Astute editor of *Big Table*, one of the first to publish Burroughs. **John Weiners:** San Francisco poet via Black Mountain College. His books include *The Hotel Wentley and The Age of Pentacles.*

77. From BARBARA GUEST poet, friend (p. 44)
Also author of biography of H.D. (Hilda Doolittle). Guest was married to military historian **T:** Trumbull Higgins (letters 80, 81, 83, and 89).

80. From MARIANNE MOORE poet (p. 45)
one magazine only: Probably *The New Yorker.*

82. From WALTER LOWENFELS writer (p. 45)
Kindred spirit to his friend Henry Miller. I rescued his piece from the fire rubble and plan to use it in the next *Hasty.* **Longview Foundation:** Helped a lot of artists, myself included, and was supported by art critic Tom Hess and his wife Audrey. He was not only one of the major boosters of postwar American painting, but was also the editor of *Art News*, the leading art magazine of its day.

85. From JOHN ASHBERY (p. 46)
Kenneth Koch: All these poets were friends. They would give each other copies of their poems to read and circulate. **P.R.:** In those days would mean *The Partisan Review.*

86. From JAMES SCHUYLER (p. 47)
Dick: Dick Bellamy. **Museum:** Schuyler was still working at MoMA.

87. From BARBARA GUEST (p. 47)
Roasting that ewe lamb: Party I gave for artist Jean Tinguely a short while before his *Homage To New York* machine exploded and destroyed itself in the backyard of MoMA. This party featured a whole baby lamb (Tinguely thought it was a small dog) that, after making a gift of it to him, I had wrapped in an American flag and buried in the snow next to his courtyard workspace (a Fuller dome) at MoMA. The lamb burial ceremony was photographed by painter-filmmaker Naomi Levine. **Sachs:** Collectors.

88. From STERLING LORD literary agent (p. 47)
Jack Kerouac's agent. He's referring to Jack's huge *Book Of Dreams*, which Ferlinghetti eventually published after I turned it down.

92. From AMIRI BARAKA (LEROI JONES) (p. 48)
What you choose: Refers to co-printing Koch's *When the Sun Tries to Go On* with Jones's *Yugen.*

93. From ALLEN GINSBERG (p. 48)
I wanted snapshots of all the writers.

94. From TERRY SOUTHERN writer, friend (p. 48)
Known for *The Magic Christian, Candy* (with Mason Hofferberg) and screenplays for *Dr. Strangelove* and *Easyrider.* **Michael G:** Michael Goldberg, then married to writer Patsy Southgate.

96. From ROBERT CREELEY poet (p. 49)
Black Mountain poet, friend of sculptor John Chamberlain.

97. From GRACE SCHULMAN editor (p. 49)
Glamour: Their sister magazine *Charm*, had published an article about me, Jasper Johns, and Bob Rauschenberg. **Hannelore Hahn Stoumen:** Contributor to *Hasty* with "A History of Stilts."

99. From LANGE GALLIMARD publisher (p. 50)
"Sir, We assume that you received our telegram of August 17 regarding Jean Genet. We would appreciate receiving an example of your publication for our consideration. Many thanks ..."

100. To AMIRI BARAKA (LEROI JONES) (p. 50)
He went to the conference in Cuba and wrote about it. Barney Rossett's *Evergreen Review* published it.

101. To SEYMOUR KRIM writer (p. 50)
It was always painful to return material to authors, which I did despite my original intention to publish everything I received.

103. From MORTON FELDMAN composer, friend (p. 51)
Brilliant composer who was a great friend to John Cage and Philip Guston. Feldmans inference about all his ". . . girlfriends since 1950" was not an exaggeration.

104. From JAMES SCHUYLER (p. 51)
Freely Espousing was published simultaneously in *The New American Poetry* (Donald Allen, editor). **Speaking of which:** Refers to my pulling *The Chekov Cha Cha* out of *Locus Solus* (note 6) and to the fact that when I wrote it in 1957, I was still living with Diana Powell. I was now married to Lisa Bigelow and felt, as Jimmy said, that the *Cha Cha* high-jinks were a chapter that needed closure. **Kenneth** Koch, **Frank** O'Hara, **John** Ashbery, **Barbara** Higgins/Guest. **S. Janis:** Gallery owner and collector whose great exhibitions were *de rigueur* for the day. **The Jaguar:** Refers to my renting fabulously exotic cars for the day to drive my friends around while we all drank beer and acted boorish. One car was a Jaguar that O'Hara said was so pretty you could eat it with a spoon. **The Election:** A play at the Living Theater that I made masks for. It was by Kenneth Koch and was a spoof of the Living Theater's earlier hit play, *The Connection.* **Jane Freilicher:** Painter, a friend and confidant to all the poets. Her marvelous wit is quoted often in O'Hara's poems. **Gold fish in plastic bags of water:** An unfortunate birthday gift I made for Kenneth Koch's young daughter: It was a Joseph Cornell-type box with a sky painted on its inside walls to which I had stapled plastic bags (filled with live goldfish and water) to represent floating clouds. I didn't bring a goldfish bowl as the fish were supposed to die in the bags.

105. From FRANK O'HARA (p. 52)
titles: Frank made up titles for some paintings of mine. When this letter came *Hasty* was already printed.

107. From HARRY GANTT (p. 52)
Gantt was my printer's rep. **NY 2-0200 N. Chomsky** is probably the Noam Chomsky (linguist, social critic) we think of now, but could also be someone connected to The Jackson Transportation Company. **Phoenix:** Bookstore in partnership with the famous Eighth Street Bookstore.

108. From KENNETH KOCH (p. 52)
His reference to **comic strips** is to our common enthusiasm for them. **Our book:** *Permanently*, poem and silkscreen (note 56). **Quakers:** My wife at the time, Lisa, and her three children were Quakers, as were Kenneth and his family.

109. To FRANK O'HARA (p. 53)
I'm racin out the door: My wife Lisa required intermittent hospitalization, and to her three children we were about to add a fourth. Many people, not just Kenneth, were pressing me to push ahead to promote and continue publishing the magazine, but I'd run out of money. My thoughts about distribution were quixotic and pragmatic. *Hasty* would do best as something celebrated by word of mouth, and more than a thousand sold that way. I thought even to leave a few copies on subway seats as teasers. **ALSO:** The same play mentioned earlier. **Ol' deafie Al:** I've always needed hearing aids, but didn't get them until fairly recently. **Herbert** Machiz: Director of The Artist's Theater and companion of my former dealer, John Meyers. **Grace:** Artist Grace Hartigan. **Hilton** Kramer, critic; **Bill** de Kooning, Bob **Motherwell**, painters; **Clem** Greenberg, critic; Philip **Pavia**, sculptor and publisher of the art magazine *It Is.* **"You're copying me!":** *The Hasty Papers* was a different beast. **Harold and May** Rosenberg: Distinguished art couple, both writers, he a major critic.

110. From LEO CASTELLI art dealer, friend (p. 53)
Many art galleries started selling *The Hasty Papers* as a result of Leo's leading the way.

111. From ROBERT NICHOLS theater director (p. 53)
He worked often at the Judson Poet's Theater (Judson Church on Washington Square Park in New York City). I believe this was the first production of Walcott's work in this country. Later Nichols (?), Jack Spicer (?), and I thought to make a musical review of *The Hasty Papers* at Julian Beck and Judith Malina's Living Theater, but never did.

The Politicians' dream of glory

A HASTY NOTE ON ALFRED LESLIE'S *The Hasty Papers (1960)*

DAVID LEHMAN

When *The Hasty Papers*, Alfred Leslie's "one-shot review," appeared late in 1960, there were few outlets for avant-garde writing, and each of them had a value greater than the sum of its readers. People outside a charmed circle of friends had begun to hear about the poets of the New York School, which, though it had not yet been named, was gathering steam as a movement. The poems of Barbara Guest, James Schuyler, Frank O'Hara, Kenneth Koch, and John Ashbery had appeared in Donald Allen's anthology *The New American Poetry* in 1960; Schuyler, Koch, and Ashbery were collaborating with Harry Mathews on their own literary review, *Locus Solus*, which was about to make its debut. In its oversize, double-column format, *The Hasty Papers* provided these poets with a venue for trying out some of their most adventurous works.

Leslie was determined not to play editor. "I wanted the writers to make their own choices," Leslie told me when I visited him at his 13th Street studio June of 1995. He had asked his friends for work they valued, and now he would print what they gave him, regardless of how long it was, or how many conventions it flouted, or how many other publishers were unwilling to print it. Putting out a magazine was an idea he had been toying with since 1957 or '58, but in the end it was put together very rapidly, living up to its name, and in a dozen incidental ways it reflected the period between the summer and fall of 1960, the last half-year of Dwight Eisenhower's Presidency.

The magazine included plays by Ashbery ("The Compromise") and O'Hara ("Awake in Spain") plus poems by Ashbery, O'Hara, Koch, Schuyler, Guest, and Kenward Elmslie. A reader today could grasp some of the key principles of the New York School from the pages in *The Hasty Papers* devoted to their work. Like *Semicolon*, which was published by John Bernard Myers at the Tibor de Nagy Gallery,

The Hasty Papers, edited by a painter formerly in Myers's stable, was the sort of thing O'Hara had in mind when he said that "the painters were the only generous audience for our poetry." Another ten years would go by before the professors began to catch up with the painters and the dealers who had sponsored the New York poets when they still threatened the academic establishment. What made them seem so threatening? Their comic spirit, for one thing; their celebration of popular culture, for another; above all, their readiness to put American poetry through the paces of the modernist revolution, from Surrealism to Abstract Expressionism, Paris to New York.

Not that *The Hasty Papers* was exclusively a New York School production. The magazine situated the New York poets in the context of other poetry clusters that deemed themselves to be in the vanguard of change. The Beats were amply represented: Allen Ginsberg, Gregory Corso, and Peter Orlovsky with poems, Jack Kerouac with prose. There was a poem by Charles Olson, a play by Derek Walcott. "Envy," Alan Ansen's graveyard oration, confirms that little-known but highly-esteemed poet's reputation for rhetorical brilliance and formal ingenuity. There was a poignant poem by William Carlos Williams, "The world contracted to a recognizable image":

> at the small end of an illness
> there was a picture
> probably Japanese
> which filled my eye
> an idiotic picture
> except it was all I recognized
> the wall lived for me in that picture
> I clung to it as a fly

The winner is the judge, the loser is the accused

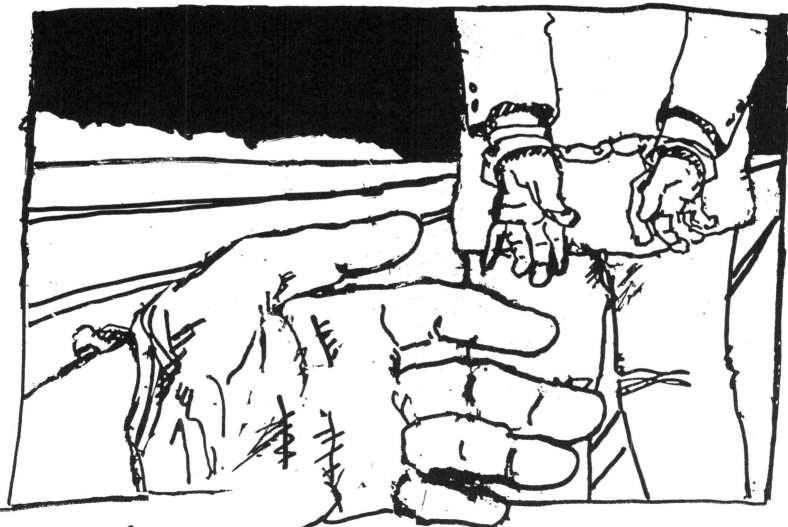

There are NO MORE privileged situations

Complete freedom is the negation of everything

Information highway

Three poems by Joel Oppenheimer showed the vitality that remained in the plain accents and democratic, lower-case speech that American poets coming of age in the 1960s took from Williams.

There was further evidence of the editor's eclectic sensibility and unusual range of acquaintance. Pontus Hultén, the director of Stockholm's Museum of Modern Art, a friend of Leslie's, contributed a remarkable essay assessing the efforts of Churchill, Hitler, and Eisenhower as painters. Hultén concluded that Churchill was the cleverest and Ike the most amateurish of the three. "The man who paints wants to say something," Hultén wrote. "He is free from considerations, he can do just as he likes. If his painting is conventional and regressive it is because he wants it that way. The expression he uses tells us who he is: Churchill fashionably snobbish and empty, Hitler pedantic and manic, Eisenhower utterly unintelligent. And it is not a good sign when those who govern the world show such infantile views of art."

If *The Hasty Papers* had a political edge, the politics remained ambiguous. The ruling spirit was anarchic. "I wanted an ironic, not heavy-handed political tone," Leslie told me. "Cocteau's idea of criticism by indirection made a lot of sense to us. If you're faced with death and destruction everywhere the last thing you want to be is heavy-handed." Among the arresting documents that Leslie chose for the time-capsule that *The Hasty Papers* now resembles is the lengthy address Fidel Castro gave at the United Nations on September 26, 1960, along with the reply of the American representative several weeks later. Both are printed in their entirety, unedited. The oratory brings back the moment. Castro assailed the United States as "the ally of all the reactionaries of the world, the ally of all the gangsters of the world, the ally of the landowners, the monopolists, the militarists and the fascists of the world." The Sixties had begun. Also in *The Hasty Papers* were collage photographs with the heads of Jack and Jackie Kennedy, Dick and Pat Nixon, and Ike and Mamie Eisenhower grafted onto the bodies of actors in old movie stills. In one caption, Kennedy is described as the "Democratic President-elect," which dates the moment perfectly. On the same page appeared a song Leslie had written during the campaign: "I'm not a' fixin' to vote for Nixon / Or any Kennedy."

"Melodramas," Kenward Elmslie's poem in *The Hasty Papers*, dares to unleash the anarchic spirit of comedy in the theatre of the politically earnest. The radical gesture the poem makes is to take the death-injected symbols of the day and strip them of their banal terror: "Mai Lung in the new communal kitchen / With the black-hammer-striped-and-red-sickle-striped wallpaper / Plunks down the evening cereal. `Winded from your annual march to / Protest the dirty sex practices of American priests, eat, o old orphans!'" The richness of this passage has to do not only with its humor but with its small verbal explosions; virtually every word is a surprise. The line about the wallpaper is almost definitive of the New York School's collective attitude toward politics.

"Freely Espousing," the James Schuyler poem in *The Hasty Papers*, became the title poem of his first collection, which did not appear until 1969; Schuyler remained the best-kept secret in American poetry until he was forty-six. "Freely Espousing" was an important poem for its author, a brief statement of his poetics. It achieves the distinctive Schuyler tone immediately with the title, an arresting phrase that describes what poets do when they write — or what this poet is doing right here and what he means to do in the future. Freely, without constraint or reservation, he will *espouse* in the full sense of that interesting word, which means not only to "embrace as a cause" but to marry. And what will the poet espouse? Language, first of all:

> The sinuous beauty of words like allergy
> the tonic resonance of
> pill when used as in
> "she is a pill"
> on the other hand I am not going to espouse any short stories
>   in which lawn mowers clack.

Language is the agent of the imagination. But for Schuyler, the love of language was always the means to a further end: the embrace of the physical world. He rejects onomatopoeia ("it is absolutely forbidden / for words to echo the act described; or try to"), but an exception to this

rule ("Oh it is inescapable kiss") prompts him to move from verbal espousals to "Marriages of the atmosphere." Light and air merge and unite "where Tudor City / catches the sky or the glass side / of a building lit up at night in fog." From there the poem moves to the level of blessedly ordinary human love, "a medium-size couple who / when they fold each other up / well, thrill." In "Freely Espousing," as in the best of his early work, Schuyler weds the dialect of the tribe to the bride of descriptive exactness. He stands in relation to poetry as Fairfield Porter and Jane Freilicher stand in relation to painting: committed to a vision of things as they are rather than as they might be in some idealized or reconfigured state.

"On the Way to Dumbarton Oaks," the Barbara Guest poem in *The Hasty Papers*, has an exclamatory exuberance and a heart of mystery. The surface of the poem is very New York School: "This winter day I'm / a compleat travel agency with my Australian / aborigine sights, my moccasin feet padding / into museums where I'll betray all my vast / journeying sensibility in a tear dropped before / `The Treasure of Petersburg.'" There has been some question about the direction Guest's poetry has recently taken. *Defensive Rapture* (1993) suggests an affinity for the projects of the Language School; her opaque abstractness puts her at a far end of radical experimentation. "The focus of my work is on language," she acknowledges. But she continues to identify herself as a New York School poet. "My work has changed, but the tenets of the movement are in everything I do." If prominent among these tenets are verbal hijinks and wry wit, "On the Way to Dumbarton Oaks" is a splendid example. The lyric close is lovely: "and gorgeous this forever / I've a raft of you left over / like so many gold flowers and so many white / and the stems! the stems I have left!"

The Compromise, John Ashbery's three-act comedy, is a deadpan parody of early Hollywood Westerns with their romantic cliches. Ashbery had simply decided to follow the script of a Rin-Tin-Tin movie without the dog — that is, with the central cinematic element removed. All the stereotypes are present: the mountie who always gets his man, the treacherous redskin, the dastardly villain, the damsel in distress, the dance-hall queen. Invoking the conventions of the Western and deviating from them at will, "The Compromise" is pre-postmodernist — a parody that communicates delight in the parodied thing; camp that transcends camp. The play was written in 1955. In May of that year O'Hara wrote to Kenneth Koch, then in Paris, about Ashbery's "miraculous new 3 act play." O'Hara describes it accurately as "an homage a Rin Tin Tin with Pirandelloesque touches," and with gusto: "It is full of something like fresh mountain air and has a simplicity like quicksand. You'll adore it." O'Hara was right about Koch's reaction. The latter read *The Compromise* to the students in his "comic writing workshop" in February 1959 and it was he who sent it to Alfred Leslie that November.

As *The Compromise* begins, the mountie is off-stage on a crime-solving odyssey while his Penelope stays home prey to the rogue suitor who dupes her into thinking her husband has run off with another woman. By the end of act three the hero has turned the tables and unmasked the criminal and is now ready to ride off into the sunset with his sweetheart in the bliss of mutual forgiveness. It turns out, however, that she is torn between our hero and another mountie, who proved his devotion to her in the hero's absence. Whom shall she marry? "She loves us both! Can this be?" asks Harry. "If only I could die — that would solve everything and the play would end," Margaret says. At this climactic moment, the stage directions call for the author to enter and confess that he has not yet made up his mind about how to end the play. Should "the man of action or the melancholy dreamer" be rewarded with the bride? The author is a version of Hamlet, undecided to the last. But the issue of nuptials — shorthand for a happy ending — makes it clear that this work, too, is a sort of espousal.

An unsigned review of *The Compromise* that appeared locally in Cambridge, Mass., where the play was performed in 1956, is enthusiastic about everything except this Pirandelloesque intrusion. The critic writing for *Audience* (who may have been John Simon) complains that Ashbery all but ruins his "lusty parody" by inserting the author into the final scene. On the contrary, however, the author's speech strikes me as the most resonant moment in the play. Like "The Painter" in Ashbery's early sestina (1948), the playwright is faced with a crisis in the mimetic ideal. Since he says he could find no patterns or rules for either human speech or human relationships, "there was nothing in life for my art to imitate." He decides that the solution to his quandary is to avoid solving it. "I would omit the final scene from my masterpiece," he says. In this way "my play would reflect the very uncertainty of life, where things are seldom carried through to a conclusion, let alone a satisfactory one." The next time Ashbery wrote a play, he lived up to this speech: he cut off *The Philosopher* (1959), a parody of country-mansion murder-mystery plays, just as the third act is about to begin.

When Ashbery applied for a Guggenheim Fellowship in 1957, he discussed his plans to write *The Philosopher*. The play would resemble *The Compromise*, he wrote, in drawing from the mythology of Hollywood movies. He hoped to "build up a strange kind of poetry out of trite situations and commonplace dialogue." In Paris on his Fulbright Fellowship he had made a study of the French "well-made play" and he felt that an ironic appropriation of its characteristic devices was in order. "The currently popular "mood play" is too often tiresome to watch and (worst of all) does not even succeed in establishing a mood," Ashbery wrote. "In order to keep an audience in a theater entertained, playwrights will at some point have to turn to the acceptance, even an ironic one, of the principles of sound construction, or give up writing for the theater. In my play I do not intend to neglect the poetry, the mystery even, that can arise from precise craftsmanship, and which so often lends the hopelessly corny and outdated plays of Scribe and Sardou an odd enchantment." Ashbery concluded this, his most considered statement on writing for the theater, by remarking that *The Philosopher* will be in prose, not verse: "I do not think that poetry has a place in the theater at the present time."

It is an irony worth savoring that in the Poets Theatre production of "The Compromise," the part of the author was played by Frank O'Hara. Ashbery and O'Hara competed over everything from the Yale Younger Poets Prize to the question of who was more like the James Dean figure in *East of Eden*. But there were also moments of mutual sympathy to the point of identity (as defined by Wallace Stevens: "the vanishing point of resemblance"). Ashbery has recalled that O'Hara's voice and his own sounded so alike that on different occasions both Ashbery's mother and O'Hara's companion Joe LeSueur were fooled into thinking that one was the other. The poets had, in Ashbery's words, the "same flat, nasal twang, a hick accent so out of keeping with the roles we were trying to play that it seems to me we probably exaggerated it, later on, in hopes of making it seem intentional."

Ashbery had written "The Compromise" in his last year in America before his ten-year sojourn in Paris. *The Hasty Papers* also includes a poem from the Paris period. "America" is from Ashbery's second collection, *The Tennis Court Oath*, which he was about to submit to a publisher in 1961. The book's themes include liberation and national identity, as is clear from such titles as "The Tennis Court Oath," "America," "They Dream Only of America," and "Europe." But the predominant note is one of linguistic breakdown. It is as though Ashbery's very language had been pulverized. The poetry is dark, haunted, where O'Hara's experiments in abstraction are nervously exclamatory and Kenneth Koch's flat-out jubilant.

Fundamentally, the techniques Ashbery used in *The Tennis Court Oath*, cut-ups and collages, are of a piece with the parodic strategy of "The Compromise." This is how "America" begins:

> Piling upward
> the fact the stars
> In America the office hid
> archives in his
> stall . . .
> Enormous stars on them
> The cold anarchist standing
> in his hat.
> Arms along the rail
> We were parked
> Millions of us
> The accident was terrible.
> The way the door swept out
> The stones piled up —
> The ribbon — books. miracle. with moon and the stars

This was poetry guaranteed to baffle. Equally predictable were the outbursts of outraged critics. John Simon in *The Hudson Review* called it "garbage." Harold Bloom complained about "egregious disjunctiveness." As for *The New Yorker*'s Louise Bogan, she had already dismissed Ashbery on the basis of the poems in his first book, *Some Trees*, which seemed to her "a little contrived in both form and feeling, and. . . therefore somewhat boring." What these and other such critics failed to notice is that Ashbery, with his erasures (a practice picked up from painters), had added meaning to his poem, not subtracted from it. "America," it might be argued, is a poem of longing, a clutching after the fragmented pieces of "America" as a concept, a construction rather than a place. A quilt of disjunctions and violent juxtapositions, the poem is a prime example of what made Ashbery's poetry in *The Tennis Court Oath* so profound a rite of initiation for younger poets in the 1960s.

"America" is a response to the situation of being in a foreign country and realizing that one's language and identity are in flux. Koch's *When the Sun Tries to Go On* is a different response to the same predicament. Publishing the whole of this very long poem — consisting of 100 stanzas, each 24 lines long — took nerve, since it adamantly refuses to conform to the normative expectations of verse in the English language. The poem was written in 1953 and not published in book form until 1969, a delay that suggests just how unassimilable it must have seemed. Here is a chunk of a relatively intelligible stanza, which has the added virtue of mentioning a number of important New York School figures:

> Saith Bill de Kooning, "I turned my yoyo into a gun,
> Bang Bank! Half of the war close pinstripes.
> Timothy Tomato, Romulus Gun." "The magic of his
> Cousse-cousse masterpiece," saith Pierre, "is apple blossoms'
> Merchant marine gun." Ouch. The world is Ashbery
> Tonight. "I am flooding you with catacombs,"
> Saith Larry Rivers (more of him later on).
> There is also some fools laying on their stomachs.
> O show! Merchant marine of Venice!
> At lilac wears a beetle on its chest!
> These modern masters chew up moths. How many drawers
> Are in your chest? Moon Mullins' Moon Mullins
> Put his feet in my Cincinnati apple blossoms. Many
> Dry cigarettes have fallen into work's colors. The shop
> Of geniuses has closed. Jane Freilicher
> Might walk through this aim like a French lilac,
> Her maiden name is Niederhoffer, she tends the stove.
> "O shouting shop, my basement's apple blossoms!"

When the Sun Tries To Go On was Koch's most concerted effort to simulate in poetry the effects of Abstract Expressionism. It was an attempt to present language at its most animated, liberated from the need to make ordinary sense. Koch was intent on using words as an abstract painter uses paint, without regard for their meaning, knowing that new meaning, artistic meaning, may result. The rupture between language and sense — between "signifier" and "signified," as the French critics were starting to say — is neither deplored nor analyzed but enjoyed as a liberation. The poem also celebrates mistranslation. When Koch went to Aix-en-Provence for a year in 1950, he found himself inspired by the mysteries of French and wanted to communicate this same buzz of incomprehensibility in his poetry. He told an interviewer, Mark Hillringhouse, that he was quite capable of picturing *les quatres heures de l'apres-midi* as four girls walking down the street and that he allowed himself to confuse *quatorze* with *quarante*, "which gave me a rather excited feeling about the 40th of July." Mistranslation became for Koch the modus operandi for *When the Sun Tries to Go On*.

An emphasis on misunderstandings is a trait Koch shares with Ashbery. In Ashbery's play *The Heroes* (1950), in which Greek heroes of antiquity disport themselves as if at a Hamptons beach weekend, Theseus has a great speech in which he describes seeing a couple in the window of a train. The man and woman are having a conversation, but Theseus cannot hear a word. In this moment he says he feels he knows these people better than anyone in the world. A new Ashbery poem, "A Poem of Unrest" from *Can You Hear, Bird* (1995), demonstrates the persistence of this theme in his work. The poem begins on a rueful note: "Men duly understand the river of life, / misconstruing it." Then the paradox turns tragic: "But since I don't understand myself, only segments / of myself that misunderstand each other, there's no / reason for you to want to, no way you could / even if we both wanted it."

Frank O'Hara is represented in *The Hasty Papers* with "To the Film Industry in Crisis," one of his best-loved poems, an ode to Hollywood. The crisis referred to in the title but otherwise unnamed was the precipitous decline in the moviegoing audience with the advent of television. It is a list poem — a form as popular among New York poets as O'Hara's "I do this I do that" poem or Schuyler's invention, the "things to do" poem. The pleasure is in the taste that can embrace Clark Gable, Gene Tierney, Marilyn Monroe, Joseph Cotten, Orson Welles, et al, unabashedly and in the rhetoric of ironic hyperbole. O'Hara's phrasing is impeccable. There is "Ginger Rogers with her pageboy bob like a sausage / on her shuffling shoulders" and "peach-melba-voiced Fred Astaire of the feet." Here is Erich von Stroheim, "the seducer of mountain-climbers' gasping spouses." Laurence Goldstein has an excellent discussion of the poem in his new book *The American Poet at the Movies*. "One feels part of the poet's, and the culture's, privileged engagement with a secondary world seemingly infinite in its variety," Goldstein writes. "O'Hara makes the movies more congenial for readers by treating them not as an art form or a symbol of modern technology, but simply as an adolescent pastime like baseball or teenage music." He "installs the Muse amid the kitchenware and croons an operatic aria at her that winks conspiratorially at the eavesdropper."

"Awake in Spain" (1953) demonstrates O'Hara's ambition — to be, as he put in an ode to Mike Goldberg, "the wings of an extraordinary liberty." The play is a veritable permission slip granted to poets who had felt shackled during T. S. Eliot's long reign as poetry's international dictator. Ruth Krauss, who studied with O'Hara at the New School in the early 1960s, said that one thing he taught her was that "YOU call it something — i.e. a play — and everyone will accept it as such." "Awake in Spain" is a play in this elastic sense. Anyone can fit in. The characters include Marlene Dietrich, Kenneth Koch, Lytton Strachey, Generalissimo Franco, Joan Crawford, Othello, Arshile Gorky, and a Grand Vizier's Ghost that is the ghost of John Bernard Myers. Thomas Hardy gets the last word. The phantasmagoria is seemingly continuous. At one point a King is disguised as a Negro singer; at another point as Joan of Arc. Larry Rivers has a conversation with a cemetery. John Adams and Benjamin Franklin have an argument about the Declaration of Independence and are interrupted by William Blake. The whole is an assemblage of possibilities.

I always treasured Koch's anecdote about getting a phone call from O'Hara one day in 1953. O'Hara, who had written "Second Avenue" while Koch was writing "When the Sun Tries to Go On," now suggested that Koch "like no other writer living, could write a great drama about the conquest of Mexico." Three or four days later, Koch says, O'Hara announced he had written *Awake in Spain*, "which seemed to me to cover the subject rather thoroughly." What I particularly like about the anecdote is the impression it gives that "Awake in Spain" is about the conquest of Mexico. In fact, it is no more about that subject than about the Spanish Civil War, the contemporary art world, or the Marilyn Monroe fan club. When a landscape architect describes "an orange sky, with a white band about its throat, and perhaps a sunken pool of black," a tourist replies, "It's another case of nature imitating Alfred Leslie!"

Alfred Leslie was one of the postwar painters with energy enough to fuel high-level work in several art forms. His paintings were praised by Clement Greenberg and shown by John Bernard Myers; he also made films, wrote plays, and took photographs. Growing up in the Bronx he was a gymnast. In the late 40's he was among that gifted group of younger abstract artists who were acknowledged by Pollock, Rothko, Newman, de Kooning and others as consequential. In 1958, while making *Pull My Daisy* and *The Hasty Papers,* his painting began to evolve towards a form of abstract realism, culminating in his giant, multi-horizoned *Grisaille* portraits. The death of Frank O'Hara in a car accident on the beach at Fire Island in July 1966 became the myth at the center of Leslie's celebrated narrative cycle, which he calls *The Killing Cycle*. When I visited him, he was working on a new grisaille cycle called *Fifty People*, all vast nude portraits, male and female — there must have been nine or ten canvases on the wall. An actress friend was with me, and Leslie lent her the script of a new one-act play

he had written entitled "The Cedar Bar, October 29, 1957." It is an attempt to replicate the emotional and intellectual noise of the bar on a typical night. Greenberg says to de Kooning, "You've got a great talent — but you're losing your way with this figuration of yours," while de Kooning tells off Greenberg at regular intervals: "Vot the hell Clem — vot's vit you and this tough guy stuff about expressionism. Vy don't you get the idea that painters do the paintin' not the critics." And, "Vy don't you try to be a little impure now and then?"

Leslie says that in the 1950s he temporarily swore off everything except painting for fear of diffusing his talent. "There was a parochialism then suggesting that each person could do only one thing. A painter was supposed to paint and do nothing else," Leslie said. "Clem encouraged me to do *The Hasty Papers*." He estimates that a thousand copies were sold, most of them at Eli Wilentz's Eighth Street Bookshop. Many others were given away. Several thousand went up in smoke on October 17, 1966 when a fire wiped out the contents of Leslie's studio. The magazine's first readers may have been lured by *The Hasheesh Eaters*, a defense of hashish by one Fitzhugh Ludlow based on his "personal acquaintance with this drug, covering as it did a considerable extent of time, and almost every possible variety of phenomena, both physical and psychological, proper to its operation." The narrative describes how the author's "experiment" and "research" turned into a "fascinated longing" for the drug's "weird and immeasurable ecstasy." Timothy Leary had recommended *The Hasty Papers* to students at Yale.

The importance of *The Hasty Papers* went beyond the thousand or so readers it reached. It contributed to a sense of artistic community among poets and painters who felt themselves to be agents of the avant-garde. This new edition of *The Hasty Papers*, prepared nearly forty years after the original, communicates the excitement in New York City in 1960 at the portals of change. I understand that a *New Hasty Papers* is in the works. It is nice to see that nature is still imitating Alfred Leslie.

—New York City, 1995

A bus crashes into a milk truck and a girl goes skating up the avenue with streaming hair

And one Sunday I will be shot brushing my teeth.

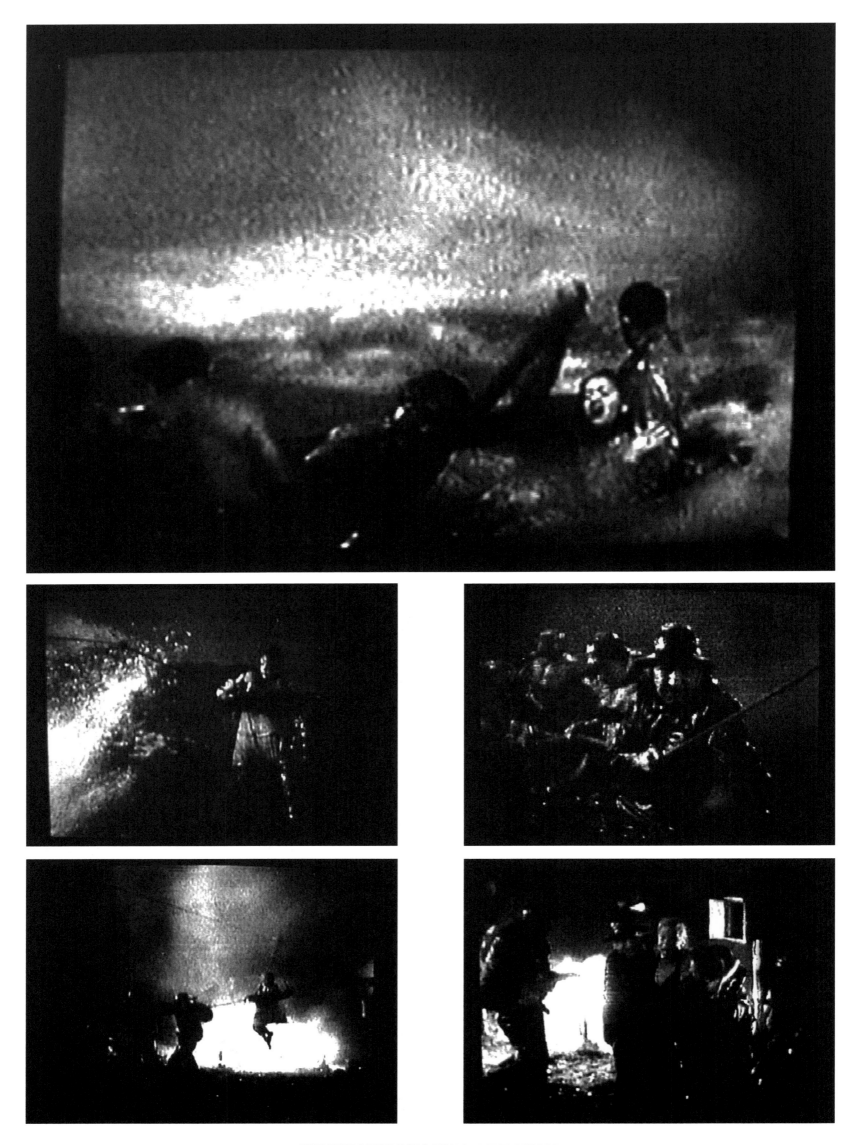

THE TERRORIST DOES NOT SEE THE PEOPLE

THE HASTY PAPERS

A ONE-SHOT REVIEW $3.00

SANCTITY AS A SOCIAL FACT

To Succeed in Being All, See To Being Nothing in Nothing

From "SAINT GENET, COMEDIEN ET MARTYR"
Jean-Paul Sartre

The phenomenon of Sanctity appears especially in societies of consumption. It is not part of my subject to describe these societies in full; I will mention only certain of their traits: For instance, the essence and practical purpose of manufactured objects are confused; the work is not a creator, it is worth nothing by itself, the merchandise cannot choose the means of turning its capacity to action; a naive love of things puts the accent on the finished aspect of the product; the truth of its being appears as soon as it is presented for sale or use, polished, varnished and sparkling; thus it reveals itself at the same time as a thing in the world and as an exigency; it demands *by its existence* to be consumed. The work is nothing but a *preparation:* servants dressing the bride; the consumption is a nuptial union; a ritual destruction of the "goods"— instantaneous in the case of food products, slow and progressive in that of clothes and tools — it immortalizes the ruined object, reunites it with its essence and changes it into itself at the same time it incorporates its owner with a species of *quality.* You will see right away that this creative and stabilized destruction furnishes a pattern of morals which we are about to imagine: the completeness of being, in the case of food, springs up at the moment when it melts in a mouth and releases its flavor; moment of life and death, paradox of the instant: still objective, the taste is at the same time subjectivity. So with the criminal who is about to be beheaded, and is made to consume delicious food in front of everybody; and with the Saint who is made to suck from God as if he were a piece of barley-sugar and feels himself melting deliciously in an infinite mouth. The consumer determines nothing: ritual destructions are accomplished by an elite class. The function of this class has been well defined by an American economist, who calls it *conspicuous consumption.* The aristocrat consumes for the whole society. The crowd is admitted to watch the king eat; the little people cry out their gratitude through the grille, it is like a mass. To be admitted to the office of consumer two titles are necessary. First of all, you must be *born.* That means — among other things — that your family's slow and secular adaptation to the best products so sophisticates your taste that, in your mouth, the thing develops its full flavor, becomes itself more fully than in any other mouth. Next, you must be a soldier: you have the right to own what you acquire or what you guard with your life. In a word, destruction gives the right to destroy: the hero, exemplary figure in societies of consumption, chooses to do his consuming on the spot. For the ceremony, he is given the best products to spoil. The destruction of the destroyer buckles the buckle: his spiced soul, sumptuous colored with wine and loaded with heavy flavors, will make a treat for the great Taster.

These strange communities seek their own annihilation: the Aztecs and Toltecs led neat rows of people to their death in horrible blood baths; and we know that the quest of gold was one of the major causes of the fall of the Roman Empire. Thus their principal virtue is the generosity of consumption which supplies to destroy, and their great eschatological myth is universal conflagration, the "empyrosis" of the ancients. The members of the elite class push this generosity to the absurd; each of them wishes, like Nero burning Rome, to realize his own little personal "empyrosis". "One chronicler", writes Marc Bloch, "has saved us the account of the curious competition of spoilage whose setting had been a great "court" held one day in Limousin. One knight had pieces of silver scattered over previously plowed ground; another, for his cuisine, burned candles; a third, "to boast", ordered all his horses burned alive."[1] The supreme refinement of consumption is to destroy goods without enjoying it. Seeing that the last use of the merchandise is to blossom at the instant of its death: the

continued on page 64

Three Great Painters

CHURCHILL, HITLER & EISENHOWER
Pontus Hultén

When great men are sick more is disclosed of their private life then when they are healthy. When President Eisenhower had been sick a year ago and was recovering the headlines said he was so much better that he could paint and look at TV. When Churchill is ill they say that now he can't paint for a while. Both Churchill and Eisenhower seem to spend part of their time painting. Also Adolf Hitler painted a lot. He was even a professional artist at the time when he called himself Schicklgruber. According to Spanish art museum people also Franco is a painter. Now he does not show his work so we cannot speak about him. But photographs of Eisenhower's paintings are given by American embassies all over the world to anyone who asks for them.

Churchill is the cleverest of the three. Eisenhower is by far the most amateurish. Churchill and Hitler both paint landscapes but Eisenhower paints portraits as well. Churchill's works have received the widest international interest. He himself has chosen 35 pictures which have been circulating on exhibits in Canada, Australia and New Zealand. They have also been exposed at the Royal Academy in London; one of the paintings belongs to the Tate Gallery. Churchill paints in a picture post card manner. He likes pretty views: southern ports, palms, old churches, picturesque old inns and castles. It is easy to see that Churchill admires Cezanne. I doubt that Cezanne would have admired Churchill.

Churchill's manner is more elegant and striking than Hitler's is. Hitler is thoroughly German in his brushwork. Almost all reproductions of Hitler's watercolors show ruins, maybe not only because they were made in the trenches of the first World War. Hitler sent drawings to the Academy of Arts in Vienna in 1906 applying for admittance. Would the world have been different if he had been accepted ? During the Nazi years forgers tried to copy Hitler's watercolors which probably were not very difficult to copy. But Goebbels assures us the reverse: "It is said that there are certain clever imitators whose ability in forging and imitating these small masterpieces is unsurpassed: but the real connoisseurs can't be misled. An original painting by the Führer can be distinguished from an imitation in one glance, because there is a part of the Führer in all his paintings, and you can see even if it is only the very beginning, a variation of all the artistic laws which are shown with such monumental greatness in his historical construction of the Reich. The Führer is the worst enemy of dilettantism." The Berlin-dadaists cried *"Dilettanten in allen Ländern vereinigt Euch."* Goebbels stresses the resemblance between Hitler's paintings and his political work.

Hitler is the only one of the three who has taken part in public art-criticism. With the prosecutions of *Entartete Kunst* he finished modern art for twenty years in

continued on page 65

SANCTITY AS A SOCIAL FACT

continued from page 63

consumer demeans himself by being in the ranks of inessential means: humankind gathers together to watch beatifically while the goods disappear; the goods which it has produced with the sweat of its brow and at the risk of its life. But at the same time the aristocrat has the secret satisfaction of placing himself above the goods of this world. The multitude does not forget the author of this bounty, to him goes the applause: eminently he owns the goods he destroys; to refuse to enjoy it is the most exquisite enjoyment.

Christianity — which was born with the first emperors, triumphed over the Later Empire and reigned over the feudal world — emanates from a society whose foundations are agriculture and war. The Church in her way expressed the ideals of Roman aristocracy and later of feudal aristocracy. She proved her power by squandering human labor. Not that I would reproach the prelates for their pomp. I even admit that most of the priests lived in poverty. But after this denouement, one discerns what Sorel so aptly called an "idealistic economy".

"The authors of treatises on Christian archeology tell us of the extraordinary luxury displayed in Christian churches of the IVth century, in an era when the Empire had such a great need of funds: the stupid luxury of the newly-arrived. Here are a few examples: in the baptistery of Latran, public baths of porphyry lined with silver; a golden lamb and seven heads of silver hart spouting water, two statues of silver, five feet tall, weighing one hundred and seventy pounds."[2]

The best of human production goes up in smoke, becomes a wanton gift to *nothing*.[3] And if the priest dies of hunger in the shade of a huge gold basilica, we see nothing better than his forebear with the horse, scattering coins to the fields. The Church has borrowed the aristocracy's generosity of consumption. A part of the aristocracy, in its turn, is bent on imitating the Church. Paulin, son of an old chief of the Gauls, renounced the world after having distributed his goods to the poor; Pammachius, after the death of his second wife, abandoned his fortune and became a monk, not without inviting all the beggars of Rome to a banquet. These ostentatious acts perpetuate the lay tradition of the Roman government: for a long time, the plebeian was made the passive object of the emperor's generosity; the avowed purpose of this freehandedness was, without doubt, not to make the social and political life accessible to the "Lumpenproletariat", but on the contrary to distract him and keep him in his place; by the same token, the individual generosities of the aristocrats do not suppress poverty: they perpetuate it; it is the gaping chasm where one throws one's riches, as the king of Thule threw his cup in the sea. The donor knows full well that he enriches no one; it is *for that* that he gives to beggars. Land is sold to intoxicate the poor, but no one even imagines giving it up to the peasants who cultivate it. Not for an instant would one think of helping small business or creating free schools or hospitals.[4] Extravagances must not *benefit*. It goes from productive to unproductive: good earth turned to ready money. And from the highest potential to the lowest potential: a considerable sum is broken up into tiny pieces each of which is barely enough to give *one* poor man an instant of physical joy. Thus charity is but a pretext and each of these generous acts, although they may be capable of stirring the surface of commerce and giving it the ephemeral appearance of health, contrives by its consequences to divide the landed property and increase the escape of cash to the Orient, in short to destroy civil society. Aristocratic morals have taken a religious aspect: myths and Christian rites have dressed them up, but after all they haven't changed;[5] the consumer is God the Father; you give, you destroy "for the love of God", not for the love of the poor; the spoiling is not done for the real profit of anyone, it is accompanied by the public destruction of abandoned goods and as it is made a merit to get rid of them, this merit recognized by all is, by consequence, the manifest and profound affirmation of the absolute right of ownership; eminent owner of the goods he destroys, the aristocrat raises himself above them as in the past. Only, in this new perspective, the loftiness reconciles him with the Eternal Father: a celestial judgment goes to confirm it. It is not even the old myth of the "empyrosis" which did not pass quite whole into the new religion under the name of "End of the World" of "Reign of God", or of "Last Judgment". Later, when the Crusader, the holy soldier, killed and was killed for the Christian cause, when he offered hecatombs of infidels to God, and when he destroyed the goods they had amassed, in huge potlatches, the transformation was complete. In the end, merchandise becomes an idol: it is *ordered to be produced* by the workers from whom it is torn away *to be destroyed* ritualistically by the idle who do not enjoy it. To push it to the extreme, suppose

a civil society in agony: peasants who kill themselves with toil and trouble so that the aristocrats die of hunger beside burned harvests. Naturally, it will never come to that: most riches are consumed in delight: to the outsider war gives the illusion of a constant renewing of goods, social movements, the infiltration of barbarians, then the appearance of a commercial class modifies the structure of the society; in the end the aristocracy only ruins itself, industrial progress transforms societies of consumption into societies of production. But the Saint, exquisite flower of the societies of consumption, presents his most exact image to this aristocracy courting ruin and death. In him, a whole community committing suicide regains what the bishop of Nole proudly called its "folly", which means its great funereal dream and its self-destructive generosity. Its utmost result, its slow agony, are not able even to be imagined outside of the luxury and the myths of a society of consumption. In a society like the U.S.S.R. where the supreme value is work, other myths come into play, other rites, other hopes, and the members of the community are not able to understand this confused image of a lapsed epoch: the generosity of production, which *produces to supply*, becomes the major virtue; the myth of "the end of the world" takes its place with that of the creation of the world (death conquered, synthetic production of life, colonization of the stars); the Stakhanovite can well work until death: it is not his death which gives him worth, it is his work.

The hero and the Saint, on the contrary, if they wish to deserve social approbation, have nothing else to do than to work that magnificent destruction on themselves which represents the ideal of their society. The hero comes first: no saint without a hero. The hero is not to be confused with the chief; he does not win battles: he realizes by himself and in one fell swoop the glorious and sinister annihilation of the whole of a defeated chivalry by an enemy victorious, but struck dumb. The Saint interiorizes this death and plays it out, slowing it down. Originally, it pertained to the military aristocracy: Saint Martin, Saint George, Saint Ignatius, and in our day Père de Foucauld who will doubtless be canonized, are there to show us how easy it is to pass from a military state to Sanctity. In aristocracies, the career soldier is an idler who the community supports because he is under oath to die. He died in each war: if he survived it was chance or a miracle; by rights he was dead as soon as his first battle. The working classes produce destructive machines for his use; he hordes them, he is the great master of destruction. It is he who ravages enemy country and decides, if he has a chance, to ravage his own country, burning the harvests and cities before the victorious adversary. In accepting "to be not of this world" he places himself above all the goods; he is given anything, nothing is too good for him. If some interior difficulty separates him from the war, he cannot be revived: he must continue to die in some other way. It happens thus that he chooses Sanctity: the Saint, as well, is a corpse; in this world, he is no longer of the world. He does not produce, he does not consume, he began by offering his riches to God. But that is not enough: he wants to offer the whole world; to offer: to destroy it in a magnificent potlatch.

The aristocrats made gold useless by applying it to the walls of their churches. The Saint makes the world useless symbolically and in his person because he refuses to help himself. He dies of hunger in the middle of riches. But, summarily, these riches must exist: fishermen must go and get pearls at the bottom of the ocean; miners must extract gold from the center of the earth; hunters must tear away elephants' tusks at the risk of their lives; slaves must build palaces, and cooks invent rare dishes so that the Saint, spurning purple, ivory, precious stones and the beauty of women, may agonize, sterile and disdainful, filled up with it *all* because he accepts *nothing:* and so here is the world abandoned, deserted, and risen like a useless cathedral. Man withdraws from it and offers it to God. Later, when the Church was well established, recruiting her highest dignitaries from the lay aristocracy, Saints were born of commoners. These are the clergymen whom wild ambition drives toward the highest posts and who find them occupied by nobles: for want of being able to be first among men, they would be above the first, they will turn their relentlessness against themselves and with a long ostentatious suicide, they will give this society, which courts its end so lovingly, the exemplary image of proud annihilation. These clerics are fakers; they used to be able, in following the usual ecclesiastical channels, to obtain *something:* a few honors, some money, some power. In pursuing Sanctity there is then *something* they refuse. But by the passion they put into refusing, by the cruelties they wreak on themselves, they persuade themselves and they persuade others that they have refused all. And as public destruction describes a public and ostentatious assertion of titles of ownership, these wretches are the richest of all. Their ruse has given them the world. A whole society is there to testify that they own it. With these men appeared the sophistry of No which was the promise, later, of brilliant success: in a destructive society which places the moment of full bloom of existence at the moment of its annihilation, the Saint, resorting to divine mediation, pretends that a No pushed to the extreme is necessarily transformed to Yes. The extreme result is wealth, denial is acceptance, the absence of God is the dazzling manifestation of his presence, to live is to die, to die is to live, etc. One more step and we again find the sophisms of Genet: sin is God's own great space: in going to the end of nothingness, one regains existence, to love is to betray, etc. By an easily explainable paradox, this destructive logic pleases the conservative: it is inoffensive; abolishing all, it touches on nothing. Deprived of efficacity, it is nothing, after all, but rhetoric. A few trumped up predicaments of the soul, a few operations executed on the language, these will not change the course of the world.[6]

Our society is ambiguous: the development of industry and the claims of an organized proletariat transform it with dreadful jarrings within the society of production; but the metamorphosis is far from being achieved: an oppressing class in its decline mixes the ancient myths with the new. Now it justifies its privileges by the excellence of its culture and tastes; that is, by its aptitude for keeping and preserving: to the democracies of the East, it claims to be guardian of Oriental values; then, to answer the demands of the oppressed classes it agrees to base ownership on work, but it opposes the quantitative conception of the Marxists with a qualitative theory: it has the right to own more because the quality of its work is superior. Meanwhile the religion subsists on its antiquated rites which it adapts as well as not to the new state of things. All is confused; the Church still canonizes, but languidly; the faithful themselves have the dim feeling that Saints belong to the past. Already, to ascertain citizen's rights in a society which advertises them, it has set about a study of new developments and has launched a light cavalry of priest-workers upon the factories. I think with many others that these convulsions of a dying world must be cut short, to assist at the birth of a community of production and attempt to draw up, with the workers and the military, a table of new values. Sanctity is repugnant to me, with its sophisms, its rhetoric and its morose delights; it has a single use today: to permit men of bad faith to reason falsely.

But we have seen that a black aristocracy lives on the fringe of civilized society. The parasitism, violence, potlatches, sloth and the taste of death, ostentatious destruction, found in the chivalry of crime, are all traits of feudalism. All, even to conservative socialism, even to religiosity, even to anti-Semitism.[7] In the midst of the military, Genet plays the role of cleric: he is the only one who knows how to read, like a chaplain in the midst of barons. All those who know him are struck with his bad priest's unctuousness. What could be more natural? He defends himself against violence with snares of eloquence. If he wishes to convince the hoodlums, he must improve upon his disarming sweetness; he must persuade them that his preoccupations are of a different order than theirs: he is not harmful any more than he is never completely present in their presence. Effaced, he irritates less; absentminded, he alarms; with an air of spirituality, he demonstrates that he has been made the guardian of their values. Not even his pederasty serves: he dons a cassock. The rest goes without saying: ecclesiastic member of an outdated society, everything prompts him to indulge in the old game of Sanctity. And since his weakness and his intelligence keep him from being a tragic hero, he interiorizes the destructive violence of the criminal. Living the impossible to live, for these murderers he will be the sacred image of their death. I know him as a little Landru without a beard, a bit formal, always polite, often jaunty, a good enough companion on the whole. But I can imagine without much difficulty that in feudal surroundings he would be a sinister enough figure, often hated and probably sacred: hoodlums see the confused reflection of their destiny in his eyes; they feel scandalized that he is at once a commoner and of the Church; at once the last among them and above the first. The only manner in which this little villain, this unsuccessful soldier, is able to have some dignity is to make himself a black Saint like Loyola, who murdered is made a white Saint. He will live for all, in systematic transport, their exile and their humiliation; for them all he will be a symbol of their idleness, of their wickedness, of their generosity. He will be a Saint because Sanctity is an office which awaits him: he will be the martyr to crime in the double sense of victim and of witness. For he distinguishes himself from the criminal like a real Saint or Hero: he transposes the military drama into terms of interior life. ❏

[1] Marc Bloch: La Société féodale, v. II, Albin Michel.

[2] Sorel: La Ruine du monde antique, pp. 97-98.

[3] Even if he existed, the God of the Catholics, who would have one believe that he rejoices when ferocious priests have made Mexican peasants sweat for gold and then plate the walls of a church with it? If he is all-powerful, this gift is ridiculously paltry compared to what he can produce. "Yes," you will say, "but a man gives what he can." In that case, it is the intention that counts: so, if God is all love, why wouldn't he have a horror of this gift which has been extracted by force and has cost so much in pain, rage, and tears?

[4] You will object that such initiatives were scarcely conceivable in those times. But I am not saying anything further.

[5] Christianity, great syncretic stream, has carried off some other morals. Religion of the State, it has prescribed ways of economy and temperance for the middle class citizens, a knowing administration of their wealth. A class religion, it preaches resignation to the lower classes. To each it speaks its own language. It maintains that there is a single Christian morality, the same for all; the priests have the skill to make the miserable believe that the resignation he prescribes in the face of the wealth of others is, after all, of the same essence as the joyous renunciation of the aristocrat. In both cases, they are told, the goods are returned to the earth. But, it is easy to see that the abandoning of possessions one has is the act of a prince. It is done eminently to revel in. To renounce what one has not is to accept ignorance, hunger, servitude: in short to agree to remain less than a man. If Genet is able to affirm that the inhuman negative (to be below man) reunites with the inhuman positive (to raise oneself above the human condition) it is because the Church was the first to effect this confusion with any ease, this persuasion of the poor man that he is doing *the same thing*, when he accepts his misery, as the aristocrat who rejects his wealth. In this sense in an aristocratic society, the *Saint* functions to mystify: his solution is given as an example to the miserable and falsely identified as their own.

[6] The mystics agreed strongly with the sophistry of No. Here is what Saint John of the Cross has to say:

"1. To succeed in tasting all, see to having no taste for anything.
 2. To succeed in knowing all, see to knowing nothing of anything.
 3. To succeed in possessing all, see to not possessing what may be nothing.
 4. To succeed in being all, see to being nothing in nothing . . . "
How not to impede the all:
"1. When you stop for something, you cease to abandon yourself.
 2. For to arrive at all in all, you must renounce all in all.
 3. And when you arrive at having all in all, you must have it without wanting anything."
And here is Master Eckhart:
"As long as I am this or that, or as I have this or that, I am not all things. Strip thyself clean so that thou art not nor hast not any longer any of this or that: and thou wilt be everywhere. Thus then, when thou art neither this nor that, thou art everything."

[7] Genet is anti-Semitic. Or rather, he plays at being. One can well imagine that it is difficult for him to support most of the theses of anti-Semitism. To refuse political rights to the Jews? But he makes fun of politics. Exclude them from the professions, keep them out of all business? That comes to saying that he begrudges robbing them, since businessmen are his victims. It is a curious anti-Semite who defines himself by his repugnance to stealing from Israelites. Would he then like to kill them in great masses? But massacres don't interest Genet; the murders he dreams of are individual. What then? At his last stand, he claims he "would not be able to go to bed with a Jew." Israel can sleep undisturbed. In this repugnance I see just this: victim of pogroms and secular persecution, the Israelite makes a martyr figure. His gentleness, his humanism, his endurance, and his piercing intelligence command our respect but cannot confer prestige in Genet's eyes. Since he likes his lovers to be executioners, he will not know how to commit sodomy with a victim. What revolts Genet about the Jew is that he finds in him his own situation.

—Translation Lisa Bigelow 1960

Three Great Painters

Continued from page 63
Germany. German museums showed paintings by Picasso, Chagall, Kandinsky, Nolde and others, together with works by insane people, wanting to prove that they were all made by insane people.

Eisenhower's paintings are the very worst. They are so pitiably hopeless that you almost weep. They are naive in a loose and forceless manner, actually more infantile than naive. They lack the charm of the failed attempt to express an experience: often there seems to exist no basic experience. Ike mostly copies other paintings or photographs. He copied the cover of the Life magazine when it showed the face of one of his grandchildren. He does not at all try to conceal his paintings. When Queen Elizabeth of England visited him, he gave her a painting signed "DE" of her son Charles.

Painting, of course even amateur painting, is a means of expression, a language. The man who paints wants to say something. He is free from considerations, he can do just as he likes. If his painting is conventional and regressive is it because he wants it that way. The expression he uses tells us who he is: Churchill fashionably snobbish and empty, Hitler pedantic and manic, Eisenhower utterly unintelligent. And it is not a good sign when those who govern the world show such infantile views of art.

These paintings belong to another world than the one I want to live in. In their world there is nothing but reproductions, copies, plagiarism and conventions. Everything turns backwards. Why these men are painting pictures on the whole is a strange riddle.

—Stockholm, 1960

THE WHITE HOUSE
Washington D.C.

Mr. Roland L. Redmond, President
The Metropolitan Museum of Art
New York, New York

Congratulations to the Metropolitan Museum
of Art on the opening of its new American
galleries.

It is fitting that this opening ceremony
take place on United Nations Day. Art is
a universal language and through it each
nation makes its own unique contribution
to the culture of mankind. By exhibiting
the finest work of our painters and
sculptors, your Museum makes available
the particular insights and aspirations
of America's creative genius. This is a
most welcome addition to the resources of
our national community.

Dwight D. Eisenhower

DWIGHT D. EISENHOWER
Dictated but not read

M.D.

EISENHOWER: Portrait of Major General Howard C, Snyder, personal physician to the President.

GENERAL DWIGHT D. EISENHOWER "Art, not war, is really mankinds most noble achievement. "

SIR WINSTON CHURCHILL "Nothing better than a good Havana cigar, a glass of French brandy, a paintbrush and victory."

John Heartfield: 1934 Montage "The facsists are the scum of the earth"

HITLER: National Theater, Munich. "It is a great injustice that the Flemish dog-Jew Rubens was such a great artist."

THE CANDIDATES: 1960
And the Song that was Sweeping Our Nation . . .

MRS. YOU AND MR. ME

Chorus: I'm not a' fixin' to vote for Nixon
Or any Kennedy
Jus' what's needed is someone new,
You vote for me &
I'll vote for you.

Refrain: I've got me a perfect wife;
She's what I wanted all my life.
Our life is perfect bliss;
Each night we seal it with a kiss.

Repeat Chorus

We've been married many years
Many laughs and many tears.
Still our love stays fresh and green
The sweetest spring you've ever seen.

Repeat Chorus

In November they'd elect
Jus' the good folk you'd expect.
Now you know who it'd be
Mrs. You & Mr. Me.

Repeat Chorus

It's president that I would be
My faithful wife as my V.P.
I jus' know you'll understand
When we have love across the land.

Chorus: I'm not a' fixin' to vote for Nixon
Or any Kennedy
Jus' what's needed is someone new,
You vote for me &
I'll vote for you.

—ALFRED LESLIE

THRILLED! Mr. Kennedy, the Democratic President-elect, finds an all too brief moment for fun and relaxation before assuming his duties in January.

A WELL EARNED VACATION. Our former president and his first lady, pleasantly surprised by our photographer at dinner in their favorite hideaway. Mr. Eisenhower was our 34th president.

THE GOOD LOSERS. The word *sport* takes on new meaning. Mr. Nixon was the Republican candidate for President of the United States. He is shown with his wife, the former Patricia Ryan.

Triptych

FRIEND, WORK, WORLD

for Bill deKooning

FRIEND:

Friends be kept
Friends be gained
And even friends lost be friends regained
He had no foes he made them all into *friends*
A friend will die for you
Acquaintances can never make friends
Some friends want to be everybody's friend
There are friends who take you away from friends
Friends believe in friendship with a vengeance!
Some friends always want to do you favors
Some always want to get NEAR you
You can't do this to me I'm your FRIEND
My friends said FDR
Let's be friends says the USSR
Old Scrooge knew a joy in a friendless Christmas
Leopold and Loeb planning in the night!
Et Tu Brute
I have many friends yet sometimes I am nobody's friend
Girls always prefer male friends
The majority of friends are male
Friends know when you're troubled
It's what they crave for!
There are some friends who get a charge from you
The bonds of friendship are not inseparable
Those who haven't any friends and want some are often creepy
Those who have friends and don't want them are doomed
Those who haven't any friends and don't want any are grand
Those who have friends and want them seem sadly human
Sometimes I scream Friends is bondage! A madness!
All a waste of INDIVIDUAL *time* —
Without friends life would be different not miserable
Does one need a friend in heaven —

WORK:

What keeps the world going? WORK!
Hire and fire — in on the ground floor — the BOSS is coming
Who conned man into this?
That he believe work an obedience to himself the world and God?
He who so cursed the day he was born
Who cut and sewed and pressed coats no longer worn —
The worker at the opera must not think of Monday
The mercy of Mozart must keep Sunday eternal
Labor's black banquet!
Union leaders and bosses cook and serve sweat soup!
There goes the 40 hr week man in that lady's purse!
All goes that died a foreman that was a stockboy first
Now gone nor will the ghost of him dark labor curse
To beg to steal to work and to work is worse
Gone that had no time for thought or thirst
But filled every desire the reward by money the pay of work
That his wife be secured and his child schooled
The callused hands soften to death —
Ah yet there stems from work a grand concern
Spice and grenadine subterranean whiskies rare fish
When I made treaties with industry and worked
I saw all wealth as come from the sad meaning of man
No good that habit of income
Lock up the bright manufacturer he knows but blank ambition
In the emergency of things he besieges our good earnings!
It would be best to de-gangsterize merchantry
Unlock the gold shell and let brokers and falconry by
Auction your come the sex-proprietor is bankrupt
What beady commerce now?
If man were without work I don't doubt he'd be sad
Work thrills man with breathless accomplishment
I cannot see a work that's never done
A work begun must end a work done

WORLD:

When God twirled the world into existence
And the cherubflock set it with glee
He did not mean it to cease
Nor have piggy-backed demons unset it
The world is not Decider of itself
It is not what Atlas carries.
Not what the big racketeer dreams to sit on top of
It is not flat not round
Not a polar bear smacking mackerelblood on an ice floe
The world is man
And he comes from owl such ways
If he is not capable of putting the sun's great sovereignty to
    sleep
He is such that can evict day from the world
Night! And nothing else will man
His dark arithmetic snorts to Nothingness
Like a goon in a field fetching a ball unthrown —
There are people who are *worlds apart*
There are people who are *not of this world*
There are times when something small and sad enters the world
Times when something grand and beautiful
The history of the world is very strange.

—GREGORY CORSO

Freely Espousing

a commingling sky
            a semi-tropic night
            that cast the blackest shadow
            of the easily torn, untrembling banana leaf
or Quebec! what a horrible city
so Steubenville is better?
            the sinking sensation
when someone drowns thinking, "This can't be happening to
me!"
the profit of excavating the battlefield where Hannibal
            whomped the Romans
the sinuous beauty of words like allergy
the tonic resonance of
pill when used as in
"she is a pill"
on the other hand I am not going to espouse any short
            stories in which lawn mowers clack.
No, it is absolutely forbidden
for words to echo the act described; or try to. Except
            very directly
as in
bong. And tickle. Oh it is inescapable kiss.
Marriages of the atmosphere
are worth celebrating
            where Tudor City
catches the sky or the glass side
of a building lit up at night in fog
"What is that gold-green tetrahedron down the river?"
"You are experiencing a new sensation."
            if the touch-me-nots
            are not in bloom
            neither are the chrysanthemums
The bales of pink cotton candy
in the slanting light
            are ornamental cherry trees.
            The greens around them, and
            the browns, the grays, are the park.
It's. Hmm. No.
      Their scallop shell of quiet
      is the S.S. United States.
      It is not so quiet and they
      are a medium-size couple who
      when they fold each other up
      well, thrill. That's their story.

—JAMES SCHUYLER

INFORMATION FROM DAD

Walter Harrison Mason

"Frank, read the written information and think of me"

—Dad

Opportunity sometimes knocks twice. If you can survive all the knocks you get on the downfall I believe U will get through. It's hard to admit, but there.

★ ★ ★

HECKLERS

Mr. Westbrook Pegler likes to heckle the administration and Union leaders but as a matter of fact Socrates was the first and noblest heckler. He confessed "Men call me the gadfly." As long as he heckled *Just Folks"*, he was safe enough — but when he began to heckle THINGS and conditions — like politicians, educators, warfare — he was done to death.

Voltaire, heckler, satirist, author, playwright, poet, Philosopher, thrust away at the crowned heads of Europe — and like the comedians, they loved it. There was a time when someone developed a huge *peeve* and shoved him into the BASTILLE.

Diogenes was something of a heckler too in addition to being the town scold. He even heckled Alexander the Great, the Hitler of his day. When Alexander found Diogenes lying in the sun in front of the barrel in which he made his home, Alexander spoke to him and was so charmed he offered him anything he desired. "In that case," grouched Diogenes, "get away from between the Sun and me".

Alex had no answer to that.

Dean Swift, the man who authored Gulliver's Travels, heckled all of mankind. And Bill Shakespeare almost jammed himself up with Queen Bess because in one of his early plays (the name slips my memory) he heckled the land owners. In our own day, undisputed champs among hecklers are George Bernard Shaw and Geo. Jean Nathan — to say nothing of Oscar Levant.

★ ★ ★

Five Highwaymen
of The Air.

Crow

Cooper's
Hawk

The
Northern
Shrike

ECLIPSES

What did the primitive Northmen think of an eclipse ?

They thought the moon and the sun were pursued by two enormous wolves who now and then very nearly succeeded in devouring our chief sources of light.

What did the Chinese believe of an Eclipse?

The Chinese believed the solar eclipse was caused by a great Dragon, attempting to swallow the Sun. On such occasions they would go out into the streets and set up a Terrific din to frighten the monster away.

★   ★   ★

CONUNDRUMS

1st lady to a lady friend:

"Is crying good for the eyes? . . ."

"I cried and got a new coat."

Why is a woman's corset like a watch dog?

Because you keep it tied up all day and loosen it at *night*.

★   ★   ★

THE OTHER SIDE

GEORGE ELIOT. Her right name was Mary Evans (Welsh) she said — "Oh may I join the Quior invisible of those immortal dead who live again."

BRUCE. Famous king begged his best friend to take his heart after death and carry it to the Holy Land. How was it carried?
—In a silver casket.

What happened to his heart on the way?
—In Spain he found the Christians hard pressed by the Mohamidans and went to their aid. In the heat of battle he threw Bruce's heart into the midst of the infidel host crying "Go thou before as thou wert wont to do, and Douglas will follow". Douglas was killed but the heart of Bruce was carried back to Scotland and burned in Melrose Abby (Abbe).

TENNYSON. "I hope to see my pilot face to face when I have crossed the bar".

★   ★   ★

QUESTIONS AND ANSWERS

Why are colored eggs used at Eastertime?
—As symbols of the resurrection. From time immemorial eggs have been used to represent the New birth of the Spring-Tide.

How can you weigh the smoke of a cigar?
—Weigh the cigar before lighting it and weigh the ash afterwards. This is the solid truth for if the smoke and ashes can be weighed (that escape) they would be equal the weight of the original cigar Plus oxygen that has been absorbed from the air during the burning. This law, known as the law of "Conservation of matter" makes chemical analysis possible.

What is the difference between climate and weather, a small boy was asked:
— he answered "climate lasts all the time and weather only a few days."

The Greek nymph of the Echo?
—Echo was the voice of a nymph who pined away from hopeless love, only her voice remained. She was supposed to haunt the woods and rocks and repeat the last syllable of any cry she heard.

How did he do it?
—By stamping his foot and hearing the Echo. He learned how long it took a sound to travel down the corridor and back. He found that sound travels at the rate of 1,100 ft. per second.

Who used the Echo to discover how fast sound traveled ?
—Sir Isaac Newton.

After a Diamond, what mineral is hardest?
—Ko-run-drum.

Who was Nestor?
—A king who in his old age joined a Greek expedition against "Troy," and was noted as a wise counselor.

What are the elements of Water?
—Oxygen and Hydrogen.

What are the proportions?
—Twice as much Hydrogen as Oxygen.

Where was the first newspaper printed?
—In Boston, Mass., called THE PUBLIC OBSERVER, 1690.

How much larger is the acreage of America than China?
—Three (3) times.

The cliff dwellers are the ancestors of the modern Pueblo Indians. And in all probability their savage foes were the forefathers of the fierce Apaches and Navahos.

How long did the French nation work on the Panama canal?
—Ten years.

How much did they lose?
—200 million dollars.

What bacteriologist looking through his microscope first set men searching for the invisible enemies of death at Panama?
—Louis Pasteur.

How long had the U. S. taken an interest in an Isthmian Canal to link the Pacific with the Atlantic?
—70 years.

In what year did the U.S. buy out the French rites of the canal?
—1903.

What did the U.S. buy for the French rites?
—40 million dollars.

And how much to the Republic of Panama?
—10 million dollars.

Where did they cut the continents in two?
—At the narrow point. From Panama to Colon.

Where were the earliest coins made?
—At Lydians in Asia from the M century B.C.

If you put a silver spoon in nitrate of silver what becomes of it?
—It will dissolve and disappear.

Has the metal been destroyed?
—No.

Can a spoon of the same size and weight be made out of that liquid?
—Yes, it can.

What president's wife was a novelist and writer
—President Wilson's.

What was her maiden name?
—Nancy Mann Waddell.

Dead or living?
—Died Sept. 7, 1935.

Name the professor who turned the myth of painless dentistry into *fact*.
—W. Hartmann of the Columbia School of Dental Science.

Why is Y used in the word *dying*?
—To keep 2 ii's from coming together.

What famous American hero (Naval hero) buried in Paris, France, 100 years or more, his body was brought to AMERICA and interred at the U. S. Naval Academy at Annapolis. Md.?
—John Paul Jones.

★   ★   ★

POEMS

TRY AND LIVE

Try and live today,
So that you may say,
What a wonderful,
Wonderful day.

AGE AND YOUTH

Age crabbed, and youth crabbed

Crabbed age and youth cannot live togeth-
er, Youth is full of pleasure, Age is full of
care.
Youth like summer morning,
Age like wintry weather,
Youth like summer brave,
Age like winter bare
Youth is full of . . .
Age's breath is short
Youth is nimble
Age is lame
Youth is hot and bold,
Age is weak and cold.
Youth is wild and Age is tame.
Age I do abhor thee.
Youth I do adore thee
O, my love,
My love is young.
Age, I do defy thee.
Oh! Sweet Shepherd hie thee!
For me-thinks thou stayest *too long*!

KEEP ON GOIN'

If you strike a thorn or rose
　KEEP ON GOING

It hails or if it snows
　KEEP ON GOING

T'aint no use to sit and whine
When the fish ain't on your line
Bait your hook &
　KEEP ON *TRYIN'*

When the weather kills your crop
　KEEP ON GOIN'

Tho' its hard to reach the top
　KEEP ON GOIN'

Suppose you're out of every dime
Goin' broke ain't any crime
Tell the world you're feelin' FINE
　KEEP ON GOIN'!!

When it looks like all is up
Drain the sweetness from the cup
　KEEP ON GOIN'

See the wild birds on the wing
Hear the bells that sweetly sing
When you feel like sighing–*SING*
　KEEP ON GOIN'

I HAVE ALWAYS FOUND

I have always found that those who do *best*-
Get more *Knocks*,
Than all the *rest*.
God made man as frail as a bubble
And God made Love
And love made trouble
God made the vine,
Was it a sin
That man made *Wine*
To drown his troubles in!

★　★　★

MONEY

In all money systems today the Government
establishes a certain amount of metal as a
standard unit of value, in the United
States 25.8 grams of gold goes 100 per
cent defined by law to be a dollar.

RECEIPT-VALUABLE

Fine General Purpose Glue

Fill a quality quart jar with good broken
glue; then fill it up with acetic acid (which
is plain vinegar in a strong solution form).
Set this jar in hot water for a few hours to
dissolve. Careful, don't burn your hands!

Everlasting Black Writing Ink

2 Gallons rain or distilled water,
1/4 lb. Gum Arabic
1/2 lb. of copper
3/4 lb. powdered nut galls
1/2 lb. brown sugar

Bruise all and mix.

Very valuable for deeds and other important
documents, because it will last hundreds
of years and never rot.

Shake occasionally for ten days.

Common Black Writing Ink

One oz. of extract of logwood: pour over
it 2 qts of boiling water. When dissolved
add one drachm of yellow chromate of
Potassa. Put in clean bottles. Cost 15 cents.

Automobile Polish

Fine luster that does not collect dust or
show rain spots.

1/2 gal. Turpentine
1/2 pint paraffin oil
2 oz. of oil of citronella
1 oz. cedar oil
These are thoroughly mixed, applied
with a soft cloth and rubbed lightly and
briskly till dry.
KEEP AWAY FROM OPEN FLAME!

—3/31/1942

Sylvain Dornon, Landais Stilt-walker.

Upper Guinea. Tall man of the woods cleans the air of invisible evil spirits.

THE HISTORY OF STILTS

Hannelore Hahn

One day, in 1891, a French baker stalked from Paris to Moscow on stilts, where he arrived fifty-eight days later. Not that this was as unusual as it sounds, for the baker, Sylvain Dornon by name, hailed from Landes, a heath-like region in southwestern France, where stilt-walking was, until the beginning of the twentieth century, an accepted mode of locomotion. The Landais shepherds particularly found it an improvement for viewing their flocks. But standing was not the only position they achieved on stilts; they could, with the aid of a third stilt to which a cross-piece was attached on one end, also sit on them. Seated on their gigantic tripods, they spun wool on distaffs, knitted peculiar footless socks, played Arcadian tunes on a *pifre* and occasionally shot a prowling wolf; all while watching sheep.

Although it would be pleasant to go on with the life of the French shepherds, it is, however, only a tempting mouthful of an extremely interesting and more varied dish called: stilts. Their origin, as may be expected, is not entirely known, although an African version tells of an old farmer planting yams near the Cross river on a very hot day when the ground was burning his feet. To relieve his discomfort, he fashioned stilts for himself from a nearby branch and went on planting yams.

Even if this actually occurred, it is, nevertheless, a doubtful explanation of true stilt beginnings, and although a need to be raised off the ground was a primary factor for the invention of stilts, this need was not caused so much by heat, but by inundation. Almost everywhere in the world, the origin of stilts is tied up with water and the need for human feet to keep above it. Consider the Niger, Cross and Senegal rivers in Africa; the Yangtsze-Kiang and Liao in northern China; the Tweed and Clyde in Scotland; the Sambre and Meuse in Belgium; the Canvery, Nerbudda and Godavari in south and central India. Think of the Fen districts of England, the Landes wasteland in France, the Puuszta marshes in Hungary, the Ghazal swamps in the Anglo-Egyptian Sudan: all the deltas, swamps and lagoons of the world, and evidence of stilts will rise to the surface.

Any satisfaction derived from a *hydro-stilt theory*, however, is jarred at once when one considers that stilt-walking on soft wet ground would seem to be much more difficult than on firm land. How did people manage to stilt-walk in swamps, for example? Did not each step thrust them more deeply into the bog?

This is a moot point, leaving the very basis of the subject "in the marsh," so to speak. But perhaps there are advantages to not knowing everything about something. This particular state at least preserves charm. And may something with endearing qualities not also be serious? The story of stilts is both. If few seem to know anything about stilts, other than their use as children's toys, this lack of knowledge may be excused, since almost nothing, save two slim booklets by K. G. Lindblom, a Swedish anthropologist, has ever been written about them. This in itself makes the subject exceptional, as it would seem that everything material on this earth has by this time been collected, classified, dissected and fully described. Views may change, information may be deleted or added, but on the whole, all subjects, except stilts, seem to have found their proper encyclopedic niche. Bits of stilt-information, in terms of a sentence or two, do crop up, of course, here and there, but these have never been collected, analyzed, nor distilled. Why this should be so is hard to say. In any case, it is a very pleasurable thing to come upon!

When asked today why stilts have been used since ancient times, most people answer that the feeling of bigness, strength and power over others must have been their main attraction. This ever-recurring idea of social superiority, however, tells more about our twentieth century selves than it does about stilts. For ancient man used stilts not for the edification of his own ego, but for the deification of god: not to cut himself off, but to become one with the universe; not to look down, but to look up.

At funerals, circumcision celebrations, fertility rites; at all occasions which call for ceremony because they mark a transition from a previous existence to another one, the ancient man on stilts made his appearance. Always his human identity was disguised and always he wore a mask. Some masks were portraits of the dead, others were partly human, partly animal characterizations. In each case, however, it

Shepherds of the Landes.

was the duty of the man on stilts not to represent himself, but the *spirit* of the character he was portraying and always on such occasions it was taboo for women to mount the stilts.

A Balinese dance drama still performed today, for example, portrays the struggle between good and evil, as personified by the characters Erlangga and Rangda. The latter, female, begins the play with a shrieking and terrifying entrance on stilts. However, the female part is taken by a man disguised as a woman. Wherever stilts were used for a ceremonial purpose and a woman's character was to be portrayed, it was always taken by a man. Woman, representing nature, birth, death and the physical world, was universally considered to be "wrong" at ceremonies which attempted to express the opposite. Although it may, at first, sound presumptuous, it is nevertheless a fact that stilts were one means whereby ancient man tried to express the spiritual, his wish for immortality and his fear of the unknown.

When the Tall Man of the Woods emerges on ten-foot stilts from the jungles of Upper Guinea, for example, he personifies the fear in man's soul. Wearing a black crocheted mask with eye holes and surrounded by bodyguards who are to catch this almost blindfolded giant in case he falls, he prances and sniffs for bad demons. He staggers, snorts and swinging one leg over the rooftop of a house, he "cleans the air" of invisible evil spirits.

When the ancient Mayans danced a high stilt-dance to their green pheasant god, Yax Cocah Mut, they hoped he would let them have plenty of maize and rain. This bird-deity was their symbol of scarcity, but were they, off the ground, not also birds?

When young boys in India's Central Provinces walked on stilts in the fields in Spring, they expressed their wish for the crops to grow as tall as they. When the Maoris in New Zealand tell of the gods Tama and Whaka who, on the Samoan island of Hawaikiki, used stilts to disguise their footprints as they went to steal the breadfruit off the tree belonging to Uenuku, a High Priest, they are reconstructing in legend an explanation for their immigration of long ago from Hawaikiki to New Zealand.

Similarly, when a Urhobo man in Nigeria mounts stilts and begins to dance out the graceful motions of the heron, he attempts to explain his origin, as Urhobo people believe themselves to be the direct descendants of a great hunter who first observed the majestic movements of the heron along the banks of the Niger.

But when the *grallaetores* in Roman Comedy stood on stilts, they did not act out a ballet of long-legged water birds, although their name comes from the Latin, *grallae*, which means crane. Instead, they mimicked the peculiar jumps and amorous pursuits of Pan, the sylvan deity represented in Greek and Roman mythology as half goat and half man. Originally a simple keeper of shepherds and flocks, Pan later developed into a powerful nature god, who sported with nymphs in glades and was the constant prey of Eros. Theatrically, he engendered the comic figure Harlequin, who was one of the leading characters in the *commedia dell'arte* and later became a favorite throughout Europe, appearing not infrequently on stilts.

Although it is said that the Roman *grallaetores* used stilts only to better imitate Pan's stiff goat-like legs and hoofed feet, there is possibly more to this. For standing on stilts, *in between* heaven and earth, in a neutral sphere, gave way to a sense of freedom and permitted a release from inhibition and responsibilities which was entirely suitable to the portrayal of such amoral and roguish characters as Pan and Harlequin. This position of immunity from censure, resulting in an increased freedom of expression, was recognized and used by other people, at other times and in different parts of the world.

Until the present century, itinerant actors on stilts in China, for example, entertained farmers at harvest times with amusing and ironic "take-offs" of characters in Chinese life. Priests, school teachers, merchants, beggars, women, wood-cutters, none were spared from the tongue-in-cheek portrayal by the actor on stilts.

In the same manner, Zapotec Indians in Zaachila, Mexico, performed a pre-Colombian "group-therapy" on stilts, their feeling being that more could be said off the ground than on. Two men, one dressed as a woman and both masked, would mount stilts in the center of their village and enact typical domestic quarrels to the amusement and sometimes embarrassment of the other villagers. A favorite subject of these cathartic performances was problems with in-laws. The man impersonating the husband would speak about the in-laws who gave him scarcely warm tortillas, often served after having fallen to the ground. Or they would give him bitter peppers, or a cup of corn juice instead of coffee. Furthermore, the husband complained he was forced by his in-laws to chop up the hardest kindling wood and to cut down the largest trees, so that he might prove to them he could maintain his wife; as if he hadn't proved this often enough, and besides, who were they to be so demanding of him? Hadn't they consistently neglected to teach their daughter her responsibilities towards her husband!

These *biquitts*, the Zapotecan name for representations of masked persons before audiences, are still performed today, though not always as described. Stilt-dancers from Zaachila participated, for example, at a recent folk dance festival in Oaxaca, but their dances were silent and they expressed none of the candor which they did, and possibly at times still do, amongst themselves.

This does not nullify, however, the general observation that stilts have been used by man to help transcend himself and that on them he felt free to reach for god, or devil; to terrorize, or to amuse; to act out his spiritual, or irreverent self.

But the expression of sheer physical prowess, masculinity and bravado is another use to which stilts have been put.

On the Dalmatian islands of Mljet, Korucula and Hvar, off the coast of Yugoslavia, a man's masculinity is tested by his ability to walk on stilts and to jump to the ground from them. The stilt-poles are extremely high, having footrests on various levels, and the man who can walk the longest on the highest rung of the stilts wins the prize, the girl, the bride.

Similarly, in Polynesia's Marquesas Islands, a favorite sport is running and ramming on stilts, the undislodged man is the winner.

Because of their close association to men and masculinity, it should come as no surprise, therefore, that stilts have also been used by soldiers in time of war. Edward Ledwich, in his "Antiquities of Ireland," for example, makes mention of a Sir William Pelham, who as Lord Justice of Ireland, "led into the Low Countries in 1586, fourteen hundred wild Irish clad only below the navel, and mounted on stilts, which they used in passing rivers; they were armed with bows and arrows."

And Robert Graves, in his translation of the autobiography of Tiberius Claudius, informs us that scouts on stilts, disguised as cranes, were successfully used by Claudius in his campaign for Britain.

But the most elaborate examples of stilt-warfare were the great tournaments in Namur, Belgium, where thousands of colorfully attired soldiers battled each other with such vigor, that it was said: "If two armies should clash together with as much energy as the youth of Namur, the affair would not be a battle, but a butchery" (Marshall Saxe).

This unusual sport originated centuries ago, due to the periodic overflowing of the two rivers which surround Namur, the Sambre and the Meuse. At such times, stilts had their usual practical function, though when the waters subsided, as they always did, a generous number of the population remained "on stilts." They divided themselves into teams and rammed against each other: street against street, neighborhood against neighborhood. Things apparently grew so lively, that a law was passed on December 8, 1411, forbidding the mounting of stilts of all those above the age of thirteen. However, far from disappearing, these competitions became "the thing to do," particularly after the well-to-do young men of the town endowed these jousts with aristocratic flourish and style, lifting them forever out of the category of the "free-for-all."

During the sixteenth century the town separated into two groups: the Mélans and the Avresses; both being names of leading families in Namur's long militant history and each representing the old and new part of the town, respectively. The number of men on the teams varied considerably, with fifty on each side being considered a bare minimum and a thousand at Mardi Gras in early spring making peak season. Once, in honor of Louis XIV, one of the many conquerors of Namur, there were supposed to have been two thousand five hundred men taking part.

But no matter what the season, or who the audience, the tournaments always followed a certain form. The day of battle would commence with the men of both teams marching through the town on foot and carrying their stilts, like skis, upon their shoulders. They would be led by the officials of the town and by a noisy brass band. People cheered and waved from streets and windows and tried to secure places for themselves at the *Place d'Armes,* the traditional battlefield in the center of town. Upon reaching their destination, the soldiers mounted their stilts and to the tune of cymbals and trumpets advanced gaily in two straight lines against each other, until they reached the center of the square. There, each team distributed some of their best men to the front for the first shock, keeping other good ones in back, for reserve, and at a given signal, the battle was on. Stilt against stilt, elbow against elbow, these were the only means whereby opponents could dislodge each other. Many soldiers were extremely agile, swaying back and forth on their six and a half foot stilts, but not falling; or pirouetting on one stilt and dislodging an opponent with the other, though it was not uncommon that when a man actually lost his balance and fell to the ground, he was trampled to death.

For this reason, the women kept hawk-eyes on their husbands, brothers, sons and sweethearts and when one fell down, they rushed shrieking into the fray, pulling, dragging, kicking, pinching their toppled giant out of harm's way. If he was hurt badly, the city, being socially minded, took care of medical expenses. But if there was still a hope of strength in him, the women would try to revive him with beer, oranges, lemons, and prunes. Then they would make him get up and with equal ardor cajole him to "get back in there and fight!"

Poems and songs were composed to the tournaments' heroes and free beer was distributed to all. In the seventeenth century Archduke Albert exempted Namur from the beer tax, a not to be underestimated privilege, considering the thirst of its population. News of these jousts traveled near and far attracting also royal visitors. The Duke of Burgundy, Charles the V, Louis the XIV, Napoleon Bonaparte, Emperor Josef II and Czar Peter of Russia were all, at one time or another, enthusiastic spectators.

An interesting change occurred in the eighteenth century, when the two teams divided into numerous brigades, each representing a specific guild, and wearing its own costumes. The Mélans include the brigades of butchers, street porters, brickmakers and the Brigade of the Pen, whose members were lawyers, writers and judges wearing a golden pen on their hats. The brigades under the Avresses were of a more out-door type, as woodcutters, boatmen, farmers, stonecutters and mountaineers. The Brigade of the Brewers (Mélans) had the posts of honor.

Time and again the city fathers found it necessary to pass laws to curtail over-zealous stilt-jousting. In 1732 it became illegal to help or insult combatants, though it is not clear whether this included the aid extended by shrieking women to dislodged soldiers. And in 1755, impromptu stilt battles on holidays or Sundays were forbidden except for limbering-up exercises after church. The whole enjoyment was interrupted, however, by the French Revolution. Later, several attempts were made in the nineteenth century to revive the sport, but by that time the proper training of the men had been sorely neglected. Finally the city officials collected all the stilts and deposited them in the city hall, where they were burned, accidentally, in a fire, a sad ending to their days of glory.

This does not end, however, the subject of stilts. It only opens another aspect, one lightly touched upon at the beginning of this article: the French baker's stilt-walk to Moscow, bizarre as it may seem, is but one of the many examples of long-distance stilt-walking, which have a way of occurring, even at this date, at about one per year.

In September 1956, for example, Angelo Corsaro, a Corsican, made a 558-mile pilgrimage to Rome on ten-foot stilts. Exactly one year later Pete McDonnold, an American oyster bar owner, stilt-walked from New York to Los Angeles. The Corsican went to see the Pope. But the American was sponsored by a stilt-manufacturer who wished to prove to the unions of plasterers, lathers and electricians that stilts were not hazardous and could be used safely on certain construction jobs which otherwise required the time-consuming erection of scaffolding. This year a man stiltclimbed Mount Hood.

Although the reasons for these unusual *tours de force* differ, they are all based on the simple fact that a man on stilts can cover more ground, faster, than a man on foot, an apparently permanent challenge to long-distance walking enthusiasts.

Perhaps it should come as no surprise that the really great long- distance stilt races grew out of the very region in France which produced the baker, Sylvain Dornon, and took place during his lifetime. Zealously promoted by "La Petite Gironde," a regional newspaper in need of subscriptions, these races had their inception in 1892, when the neighboring provinces of Gironde and Landes joined to organize a long-distance stilt-walk at Bordeaux. But since this event took place in France, a great many matters other than the sport itself had first to be settled: were the stilts to be of a fixed length? Was a man on a wooden leg eligible? Could a contestant get off the designated road? Since a distance of 490 kilometers, or 302 miles, was to be covered, it seemed reasonable to assume that a man might have an occasional need for getting off the highway. And since total agreement on this point, at least, was immediate, the question which followed, so to speak, naturally was: how? Remain on stilts, or dismount? (The problem of style, always of importance to the French, seems by no means to have been neglected here.)

Female applicants were at first turned down, but they raised such a clamor that eighteen ladies in long black gowns — like ravens perched on dead branches — were finally admitted, although the distance of their race was ruled to be decidedly shorter, as it was reasoned the women were needed at home.

Prizes were offered for every possible category, including age, size, the first and last to arrive. Watchmakers, bootmakers, winemakers, dressmakers, merchants throughout the region advanced samples of their wares and a private citizen, who announced himself as "a lover of all sports," placed at the disposal of the winner a beautifully furnished apartment with the use of a bathroom and a masseur.

At this point it should be noted that almost all contestants were poor peasants from Landes; unused to such abundance, but determined to make a good thing of it. To make matters worse, or even better, each stiltman had to present himself at an official control post upon passing through a village. There his signature, temperature, and pulse rate was taken and his time was recorded. No Spartan check-points, these, but all control posts were cafés, hotels and restaurants bulging with refreshments, wine and merry-makers. Needless to say, these had a considerable effect on the athletic performance of the contestants, particularly since twenty-two of these spas dotted the race's course.

In short, it took more than stilts to keep a man on the road. However, Pierre Deycard was not to be mislead. It was said, whenever he allowed himself a short snatch of sleep, he dreamt so vividly of buying cows and marrying his sweetheart, he scrambled to his feet and was off again in the moonlight. His lead soon was apparent and tempted the villagers who lined the highway not only to cheer, but also to distract him. In one town they insisted upon taking him to a hotel, where they forced him through a banquet of fifteen courses and then made him parade the streets, like a prize heifer, with a 1,000 franc bank note pinned to his chest. Still, he finished the race in 103 hours and 36 minutes, averaging 4 kilometers and 938 meters, or 3.09 miles an hour including stops.

Subscriptions to "La Petite Gironde" happily increased and stilt–racing became a traditional event at Bordeaux, though with considerable *variété*. One year, for example, 30,000 spectators had the privilege of observing only women on stilts. But gender being apparently not quite enough, it was felt the *différence* had to be further emphasized. It was decided therefore, that each lady should carry a basket, that this basket should he perched on her head, and that therein should be a 44 pound weight (in the basket, that is.) Sixty ladies on stilts and balancing reed baskets on their heads braved a distance of 5.6 miles. It was finished by Marguerite Pujol, age 36, at the record pace of one hour and five minutes.

Another time the race featured three male stilt-walkers, three men on foot and three mounted horses. Here the honors went to "Charlatan," a horse, though one of the stiltmen followed immediately behind. Both covered 273 miles in 62 hours and 57 minutes, averaging about 4.4 miles an hour. This bears out the fact that a trotting horse and a good man on stilts just about equal each other on long-distance treks, an obscure statistic, though known to Empress Josephine. Her carriage on its way to meet her husband at Bayonne was met by Landais stiltmen, who for many miles performed a continuously running show of clownish tricks, yet never lagged behind the trotting horses of the Empress's carriages.

Having thus dealt with the spiritual, sexual, theatrical, military and athletic aspects of stilts, mention must now be made of their economic value, for the shepherds of Landes were not the only ones who used stilts to earn their daily bread. Hops had been picked, fruit harvested, millet thrashed and fish fished on them. Girls on balconies have been wooed by young males on stilts. (This last example of stilt-usefulness is a contribution from the Celebes Islands.) And in Los Angeles, Dave deGarro, a Hollywood stuntman, tries to attract the attention of passing motorists to newly opened gas stations and real estate tracts by standing all day on aluminum stilts; his wooden ones having once been attacked by a swarm of termites.

The Japanese have a charming expression, *chikuba no tomodachi,* which means boyhood friend, or, *the friend I had when I walked on stilts.* They call the stilts themselves, *take uma.* Literally translated, the word means, bamboo horses. Words being symbols for meaning, and stilts lending meaning to symbols, a look at stilts linguistically might aid the ultimate understanding of this elusive subject.

In the language of the Hausas, Mohammedans of Africa, the word for stilts is *kadako,* which means bridge. It refers to the use of stilts in "bridging water." Similarly, the Spanish word for stilts is, *zancudos,* which means mosquitoes; one would think of a long-legged, water-skimming kind.

Zuni Indians say, *tasa kwiwai,* which is their word for the sticks they use when digging corn. Wichita Indians say, *haki 'artis,* or walking wood. The Persians say, *chubpa,* or wooden leg. The Hungarians say, *gólyalab,* or stork leg. In Gaelic the word is, *casa-corrach,* or steep leg, and in Singhalese it is, *khorupawa,* or lame foot. This last gives emphasis to the peculiar gait which stilt-walking produces, an aspect differently expressed in various languages: the Urhobos of Africa call stilts, *ekeneke,* which means staggering; the Maoris in New Zealand say, *ara poraka,* which means, to leap like a frog. The Croatians say, *trampati,* or to go along carefully. This seems related to the Italian trampoli (derived from the southern French, *trampola*), to vacillate, to sway. The Chinese say, *kao ch'iao,* to walk on high tiptoe, and the colloquial expression in Landes, France is, *tchanques* (derived from the verb *tjanka*), to limp.

In the southeastern mountain country of the United States, stilts are called *tom walkers,* derived from the colloquial expression *tom,* meaning, bigness, maleness, as in tom cat, tom turkey. The Romanians say, *cataligar,* which refers to being able to see a league. The French word, *échasse,* is related to a straight piece of wood used in architectural construction. And the Hebrew (singular), *cav,* refers to an ancient measure mentioned in the Talmud.

Lithuanians, always exceptional, refer to stilts in terms of the sound they make. The word, *kujokai,* literally denotes the even, thumping sound of a blacksmith's bellows. However, from the Etymological Dictionary of the English Language, by Skeat (Cambridge, September 1881), comes the unusual notion that the English word, *stilts,* is related to the German word, *Gestalt,* meaning shape, form, configuration. Gestalt psychology affirms that all experience consists of Gestaltelm, and that the response nf an organism to a situation is a complete and unanalyzable whole, rather than a sum of the responses to specific elements, which would simply mean that stilts, having all the aforementioned aspects, are no ordinary Gestalt, but a great big one, and not just in size alone.

But coming to the end of this article calls for a note of sadness, as the subject which defied so long the finger of research, the scalpel of analysis and the card catalog of statistics, has, alas, yielded. ❏

Child on Stilts. Japanese Print.

AWAKE IN SPAIN

Frank O'Hara

Part I

	MALE	FEMALE	OTHER
act one	magistrate	flamenco dancer	church steeple
	american	little girl	a sheep
	village mayor	mother	
	general franco	joan crawford	
	hollywood makeup man	another dancer (or male)	
	othello		
act two			the slap
act three	larry rivers		cemetery
			animals
			brook
			nightingale
act four	a boy	serving maid	sodom
	king	statue of dolores del rio	
	duke	italian diva	
	grand vizier		
	count		
	soldiers		
act five	two shepherds	grandmother	sheep (plural)

Act I *A sky filthy with bangles, but soft, somehow, and pensive. There is a verdant meadow upside down in the center of the stage and many unhabituated animals stroll about, as if at a fashion show. A large pair of lips, greasily rouged, smile from the rear wall.*

Magistrate: Why are you so pensive?

Flamenco dancer: Oh lordy, it so wet!

American: Had you really been wholly mine at night
the fort wouldn't be sneaking its alarms
across the border like a saffron bite
or the tea lady keep nagging "Love harms"

every minute of the day and damn night.
I told you never to mention my arms
to Moors at Headquarters. My dear, be bright,
and never put your dope in candy charms.

Stay away from the soldiers every night,
Try to imagine what it's like on farms,
for in pursuing a Chrysler of white
you'll find tears in solution in your arms.

It was not to be so easily charmed
that we sent you to school to be harmed.

Village Mayor: Oh Iberia! You're weeping!

Little girl: Tra lalala la la la la la la lala la la la.

Mother: "Carmen."

Church steeple: Aoua! Crash! Bong, bong, bong, bong, bong, bong, bong.

Mother: "Boris Godunov."

Generalissimo Franco: I'm so worried about the jails, they're full of Thanksgiving dinners.

Hollywood makeup man: Do you have a "Times"? You should just see yourself! You're a perfect sight! I think I'll hire a touring car, are there any clean ones?

Joan Crawford: Ummmm, ummmm, ummmm, ummmm.

Mother: "Estrellita."

Village Mayor: Oh CARE package of delight!

Othello: The whole damned country is like a pillow.

A sheep: I say there!

Another dancer: Stay away from the Spanish dancer as a type, señor.
I've lived in Tallahassee, tee hee hee. I'm warning you, old pal, beat it. Tell the gauchos you saw me and I said "Okay."

Village mayor: I don't care for your conduct. Here's a slap. Ugh, I can hardly lift it.

* * *

Act II *Twilight, seventeen years later. The animals are noticeably aged, the lips no longer smiling. The verdant meadow has righted itself somehow.*

The slap: Come of age, damn you!

* * *

Act III *The gardens of the Knights of the Garters of Spain. A rippling brook flows through the center, sounding like a minuet. At left stage rear a huge statue of Dolores Del Rio. Oh night, staring nightingales! trees hung with hemp! prunes! Madeira biscuits! jumping blue blazes!*

Larry Rivers: Where's the cemetery? They say there's a terrific cemetery around here somewhere

Cemetery: Here I am, Larry.

Animals: Watch out! Boy, you almost fell in.

Brook: Damn those busybodies!

Nightingale: Thank heaven he's saved myself! His decorum is my sight! Oh flute of an American, you are being beauteous.

✷ ✷ ✷

Act IV *One of those Spanish palaces full of ropes, artichokes, globes, and flames. Or is that Portugal? Very baroque. A little girl is being mistaken for a bull by the Italians in the courtyard. Night again. No, midday.*

A boy: Basta! Basta!

King: Fabulous indeed are the charitablenesses of the table! What gong so distinctively loud as the dissonant stomach? I pray you, put down your feather duster and don't be such a cat!

Duke: You told me to take care of everything.

Serving maid: I wish Mister Mozart would hurry up and finish this.

A statue of Dolores Del Rio: (offstage) I'm coming, I'm coming, though my head is bending low.

Grand Vizier: Oh my darlings! I've just written some marvelous new letters of help to the art world so they'll get straightened out. From now on Velazquez' shows will be reviewed in the Herald Tribune and Art News has promised to do a "Zurbaran Paints a Picture" in the fall. Isn't it heaven to be a Sodomite?

Sodom: (offstage) Why is all blamed on me? It's like associating sewage with Venice!

King: What a wonderful day it is! Wish you were here! And my subjects all so happy. Look at those smiles. They all look like Hapsburgs. Those pointless smiles, the very smile of a Hapsburg. What's for banquet tonight?

Count: Nothing, if the matadors don't have more luck.

King: Hey, who's that running towards us?

Count: It's the queen. Or is it the cardinal?

Grand Vizier: It's meeeeeeeeeeeeeeeeee!

King: Off with his head!

Soldiers: Okay, king!

Italian diva: What a divine country!

✷ ✷ ✷

Act V *Is there a place known as "high in the hills of Granada"? I hope so!*

Two shepherds: We love the country, that's why we're handsome, it's love love love love love. We only quarrel over sheep. We're terribly natural, aren't we? Well, is the sky blue? What did you expect, a couple of Air Force Cadets? Not that we couldn't if we wanted to!

Sheep: Sure you could.

Grandmother: Would you boys like to take sandwiches to school or come home at noon?

King: I'll get back into that palace, I know I will.

Sheep: Sure you will,

✷ ✷ ✷

Part II

	MALE	FEMALE	OTHER
act one	king's son peanut vendor grand vizier's ghost	baby statue messenger	21 demons funicular sail
act two	mariner		
act three	serving boy courtier court barber harry crosby admiral	laura hope crews a widow princess marie of rumania cassandra marlene dietrich	a 1936 chevrolet
act four	john adams benjamin franklin william blake		a cloud
act five			a telephone

Act I *A demonic height in Granada, a sun with 103 spots. Twenty-one demons are lined up on a mountain-top.*

1. I could hold this cigarette hanging from my lower lip for years, I know.
2. It's a tornado of logs falling on the pianists' wrists.
3. I would like to stay on this bus laughing with you forever.
4. The landscape is already finished, ready to be shown.
5. And holding her cheeks together were these splinters of glass on platinum spokes, except that she couldn't laugh comfortably.
6. Who laughs? O childhood, haven't you had your vengeance? Aren't you a Spanish boredom?
7. "Donald's Garage" keeps blinking off and on, in the silence of night.
8. I didn't know you were Jewish, I'm glad to say.
9. Thanks.
10. Does she have a pocketbook in her left hand?
11. The tree is turning white.
12. I am shifting with passion like a concert waltz.
13. The flowers don't seem to want to leave her alone.
14. Garrulously final.
15. And if we were statuesque we would be truer.
16. I saw myself in the mirror. I am one of those gargoyles that supports with his head the balustrade of the grand stairway the Cossacks charged up at midnight.
17. You savages aren't so inventive.
18. And there was someone whispering, "To dissemble is to instruct," like a waterfall.
19. He is most anxious about his freedom when it is most complete, o tulip!
21. The most ecstatic praises on the shore!
21. Daylight clarified for me the loneliness of the razor and the elevation of the ill, the marriage of pretense and custard, the blossoms.

Ensemble: Yes, it is too late already; you are a man.

King's son: Who? Me?

Peanut vendor: What lake is that laying its head on the waterfall?

King's son: Yet, I shall not be discouraged. I shall recover my father's palace for the Old Marl. All he needs is a few rooms to restore his health.

King: Attaboy.

Grand Vizier's Ghost: How it burns me! the black laugh of loyalty. It was worth dying to get this second hand.

Ensemble of demons: Hah! You'd need an army.

King: He will not.

Sheep: Where am I? My nose is bleeding.

Statue: Go down, then.

Funicular: I'm like an angel, ain't I? Look, everybody!

Duke: It's a revolution! Boy, am I glad I'm not around the court. Better to be an exile than be exiled. It's a revolving door, damn it. The late duchess, my wife, used to say, "Look, it's moving," as if she'd never seen a member before. Well?

Messenger: Which way to His Majesty?

Duke: Thataway.

King: Who was that?

Sheep: Sure it was.

Grand Vizier's Ghost: Haha! And they say there's no *jeunesse dorée*. Waldemar will be furious.

Baby: Here I am!

King: Throw him overboard!

Soldiers: Okay, King.

✷ ✷ ✷

Act II   *The trough of a wave somewhere off the Iberian Peninsula. Lunchtime, and the clink of ice in glasses. Muzak.*

Baby: Wahhhhhhhhhhh!

Mariner: Here we go again, my poor little smack is full of them already and it isn't four in the afternoon yet. Where will I put the fish and the fish oil? There you are, my man.

Baby: Mama.

Sail: Uh oh.

✶ ✶ ✶

Act III   *A brilliant ballroom hung with wigs. Yesterday, and very rainy, blustery, you might say. Strains of Rachmaninoff's "Rhapsody on a Theme of Paganini" caught between two elevator doors midway of a fortnight of sex. A great green face resembling the ghost of the Grand Vizier peers in at each of the many windows like so many chandeliers that haven't been invited.*

Laura Hope Crews: My dear, you're as talkative as Nijinsky.

Village Mayor: Don't try to be poignant.

Generalissimo Franco: How do you do? I am wearing, how do you call it? Ry-Krisp?

Serving Boy: Ouch.

King: (disguised as a Negro singer)
Slogging through the mud
can yuh spare a nickel, bud?
De king am sinkin' fast
he forgettin' all de glorious past
who gonna bring um back?
who gonna?
hey nonny no.

Courtier: Oh mercy! ha ha ha ha ha!

A widow: They say the two of them are living on a mountain and that the young Crown Prince Frank is marvelously sweet to his dad. The perverse are always such opportunists.

Grand Vizier's Ghost: I like to think of the king going through with it as a boring ritual and Frank enjoying it quite a lot.

Court barber: That's as it may be. Let's go swooning in the sea!

Princess Marie of Rumania: Meiner Liebling! Meiner Schatz!

Harry Crosby: The sun! the sun! the sun! the sun! the sun!

A 1936 Chevrolet: I can't wait to lavish my aspirations on the routes. What a trail blazer I am. Remember Toledo?

Admiral: What? Carumph! Who's that painting a circle round the Generalissimo's feet? Hey!

Duke: (disguised as a candle) It's the famous Portuguese warrior, George Hartigan! This means foreign intervention!

Cassandra: (disguised as a messenger) Cry Arrowroot! And let slop the Madeleine of legs!

Generalissimo: Yipe! Follow me! Call out the civilities!

King: (disguised as Joan of Arc) No! Follow me! Off to France, and just in the nick of time! Where's that dinghy?

Marlene Dietrich: Now, boys.

Courtier: A musical saw! The greatest weapon of all. Gimme that!

Marlene Dietrich: You brute! Take that!

Courtier: Ouch!

King: Attagirl!

Marlene Dietrich: Come on, King, we'll fight from Paris! Where is your darling son, the Prince?

King: We'll pick him up as we run through Granada. Let's leg it!

Marlene Dietrich: You darling. So droll.

✶ ✶ ✶

Act IV   *Alarums and excursions. A horrible stormy day in winter in these 13 United States.*

John Adams: Won't sign the Declaration of Independence? You French pervert and fat man!

Benjamin Franklin: Okay, I'll sign.

William Blake: Oh my dear ones! Someday I'll make a pecan pie of your thoughts!

A cloud: I can't hear a thing for the noises and alarums. Something's rotten in the Pyrenées.

Sheep: You'll hear soon enough.

✶ ✶ ✶

Act V   *A fandango, in which dwell all the Spanish thoughts of exiles. The simple liberation of tense, clarifying their nervous disorders, makes them terrific dancers, being totally unselfconscious because of their preoccupation with the futurity of the past. Lavender drapes. A tiny wire table with an egg roll and a bottle of absinthe on it. Tears flowing down the walls, and a marimba in the center of the stage with several people napping on it.*

King's younger son:
Dad's asleep. Don't wake him.
The sun's gone out of our life,
it's better to be asleep. Life
gets you nowhere if you're him.

Grand Vizier's Ghost: What's happening? Oh! I can't bear not to know what's happening!

A telephone: Excuse me! What number were you calling?

✶ ✶ ✶

Part III

	MALE	FEMALE	OTHER
act one	forester gardener butler landscape architect	nurse village girls village flapper milkmaid tourist (or female) crown prince prop man	balcony rail swallow
act two	lytton strachey	turandot	his mind
act three	mummers arshile gorky	soprano	his soul
act four	kenneth koch grover whalen	girls	megaphone
act five	rapenier refugees general thomas hardy		empire state bldg

Act I   *A dreary chateau outside Perpignan. Fifty-three old caretakers have been stuffed into a blue bathing suit with white piping and sidelaces and are hanging from a plane tree by their thumbs. Oh boy! It's August, and the runners from Spain are dropping dead on the routes. Will the news get through? each cloud is asking itself, hoping to be "found" by Boris Pasternak. The daylight is particularly intense this day. Thundering dried-up fountains.*

Forester: How does it go now? Ummmm? "Yoiks! Tally-ho! A-hunting" hum? "we'll" what?

Nurse: Hey there! Don't you see this window's open? Shut up, now! Silenzio! The Crown Prince is feeding his gold fish! Do you want him to get his hand bitten off?

Gardener: He's become a terrible degenerate, from sadness.

Village girls: Oh the red suns, tra la.

Butler: Isn't it like Sevilla during fest?

Landscape architect: An orange sky, with a white band about its throat, and perhaps a sunken pool of black?

Tourist: It's another case of nature imitating Alfred Leslie!

Crown Prince:
l once dreamt of appearing on a balcony like this
but to multitudes. How glad I am I made a recording
of the dead Queen my mother, playing this nocturne.
Each time I hear it the sky lowers and the day sinks
its feathery head against my shoulder and sobs.
Oh fountains! you are too ridiculous! Where are you?

I am working against time hoping against hope
that the King, my father, won't expect me to go back
to Spain until I've finished my "Complete Works
of Jean Genet in Spanish Translation the First Time;"
and anyhow I haven't reinstated the monarchy yet,
hélas, I mean, caramba! My spies have forgotten how
to write.

Why is everyone always at me for something or other?
Even the Grand Vizier's ghost calls every morning, dead
these ten years. Well, it's the price of talent,
as exhausting as climbing a tree and then climbing down.
When I think of my childhood in Onset, Massachusetts.
Ah!

Balcony rail: How firmly he grasps me! I'm glad I gave up
    the trumpet vine, though it broke his heart, poor with-
    ered fish. I always hankered for a prince, glamorous
    rail that I am.

Sheep: Boy, am I exhausted! What a trip!

King: Hi, duckums!

Swallow: What distinguished face is that plucking out the win-
    dow? with bars on it.

Prop man: Didn't you know cognac was brandy, queenie?

Sheep: I feel better anyway.

Village flapper:
    I represent the Marilyn Monroe
    fan club of South France, chapter one. Today
    down below we are having a big row,
    in her honor we are making some hay.

    And are giving a banquet of shad roe.
    Our darling's shooting a pix on a quay:
    we're celebrating in advance her show,
    which has a marvelous score by Sauguet.

    Her "native wood-notes wild" are what we'd do
    almost anything for, believe you May!
    She makes us feel like an old Spanish shoe.
    but that's better'n being bored at a play.

    She is our love, yes, we love her. we do
    and so should you and you and you and you.

Milkmaid: Jeepers! Are you a "fire and ice" girl?

✶ ✶ ✶

Act II *Byzantium, the mid-century Byzantium of ice-cream cones floating
in lagoons and short, squat scientists investigating lunar eclipses
over the Hebrides, the Hebrides Overture, I mean. W.B. Yeats is
standing in the middle of a through street in galoshes with a bad
sore throat. His Mind and His Soul are contending. A parade goes
past, inescapably alert. The billboards look like dirty handkerchiefs
and an art colony has "sprung up."*

His Mind: Did you say a chaise lounge or a shared lung?

His Soul: The seas are full of fish from Spain. What a busybody
    I am!

Turandot: I am not so successful in this country.

Lytton Strachey: It is a parenthesis I seek.

✶ ✶ ✶

Act III *The House of the the Dead, Valencia. Greco's noted "View of T."
executed entirely in red is used as a backdrop and brilliantly
lighted. A lot of tubs full of Ma Perkins roses sitting around.*

Mummers: Hot shit! It's terrific fun to sit around and read
    Italian novels of Social Consciousness all the time. Hey
    ho.

Arshile Gorky: It's terrible under Kay Francis' armpits.

Soprano: "Dove sono," et cetera

✶ ✶ ✶

Act IV *Times Square, New York. Multitudes of holiday noisemak-
ers. A parade goes past, inescapably alert. The word "Zowie"
keeps going around the Times Building in lights.*

Megaphone: The Crown Prince has reinstated the monarchy, but
    in AMERICA! MEXICO CITY HAS FALLEN! Your corre-
    spondent, K. Koch, barely escaped with his life to tell you
    the tale.

Kenneth Koch: Nope. Sorry, folks. They got my dispatch all
    wrong. It all happened in Spain. I heard about it in
    Mexico, you see.

Girls: Oh my darling!

Larry Rivers: I knew Frank would do it! He's American through
    and through.

King: Yes! Yes! I can hardly wait to go back.

Grover Whalen: Here's your ticket, your highness, l mean, your
    majesty.

Spanish refugees in native costume:
    O joyous day! O joyful hour!
    O boresome banana! O tripe!

Empire State Building: Luncheon is served.

✶ ✶ ✶

Act V *An elaborate state picnic on the Rock of Gibraltar. The heat of the
day. In the background, military maneuvers.*

Reporter: My paper is extremely interested in your point of view, sir.

King's younger son: Well, as soon as they got back into Spain and
    everything started to go okay, they decided I couldn't leave
    school in Switzerland even though I am forty years old.

General: So . . .

King's younger son: . . . we attack the mainland in the morning.
    The Crown Prince will be bombed out of his Barcelona
    brothel before dawn, and then the putsch! God, it's won-
    derful to be in the field. Just look at them banners!
    Russia and Italy are on my side, France and America are
    backing the Legitimists, ho ho. By God, they're in for a
    tumble.

Thomas Hardy: O dynasties, incessantly tumbling!

CURTAIN

seize the day

the Old Woman sits at
the Window all day. she
can/t Walk or do much of
Anything. almost every
day Russell visits her. he
sits at the Window, too.
when Russell is Big and
Strong he will Carry the
Old Woman to the Circus
to the Ballgame
to Meet the Queen
Everything she/s always
Dreamed of.

a fable

the ring of it then,
the somehow noise it
made going off
            the
hanging up of
everything all at once, that/s
what it ought to have been.

but the bull don/t know
a thing about dramatics.
he just reared up his
self almost erect.
far off in the
corner of the field, old
lady friend
far off in the corner of the field.

the economy of art

every Sunday nite its
the same whether you
eat well or not at
all, whether you drink
heavy moderately or not
at all, whether you nap long or
short during the day, or
not at all, still you
lay down to sleep and, four
hours later wake to a
cold sweat and clutching your
lady/s tit to protect you from
the ogre Monday morning.

blood

how ever else to
do it? but with
love, and a new way
to comb my moustache?

or she said: you
and your old
man, sitting here both
in your underwear

—JOEL OPPENHEIMER

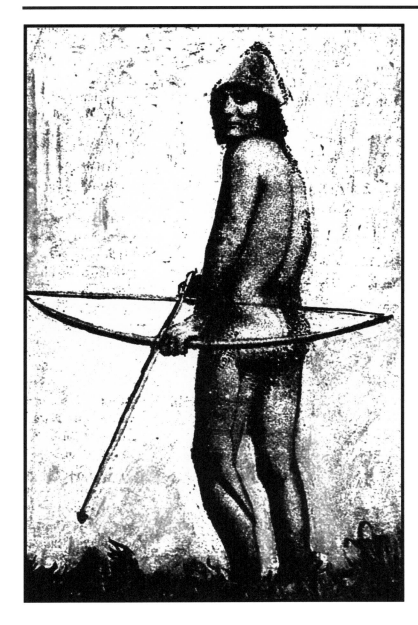

AETHER

5:45 PM Notes —
    (1) Therefore there are certain repeated determinate
indefinite referential points of understanding in a limited but
definitely (bloody) (whistle) Apocalyptic universe — Fin! This
is the Revelation of Laughing Gas. Also the Affect of all other
repeated states of Consciousness.
    (2) The Universe is an illusion
    (3) At moments there is a sensation of repetition of
mathematically preformulated states of being
    (4) I hear all the other universes in operation
    (5) Somebody's got to pay — (I'm doomed to Death)
11:15 PM Same day — Another try —
4 sniffs & I'm High —
Underwear in bed,
    white cotton in left hand,
    Archetype degenerate,
                bloody old taste in my mouth
                    remembrance of sound
                of clockbells & airplane buzz
                    of Dentist's chair
    and music, and loud Farts of Eternity —
an owl with eyeglasses scribbling in the
                cold darkness —
Black hat on a mirror,
    mirror against the blue wall
All the time the sound in my eardrums
    of trolley cars below
            cricket chirps

The ringing sound in all the senses
    of everything that has ever been created,
    all the combinations, recurring over and
                over again as before
                        against my ears in the
                    instant before unconsciousness
                        before,
the teardrop in my eye to come —
The fear of the unknown —
One does not yet know whether Christ was
            God or the Devil —
Buddha is more reassuring.
Yet the experiments must continue!
Every possible combination of Being — All
        the old ones! all the old Hindu
            Sabahadhabadie-pluralic universes
                ringing in Grandiloquent
                    bearded juxtaposition,
            with an their minarets and moonlit
                towers enlaced with iron
                    or porcelain embroidery,
        all have existed —
                    and the Sages with
white hair who sat crosslegged on
                a female couch —
        harkening to whatever music came
            from out the Wood or Street,
        whatever bird that whistled in the
                    Marketplace,
        whatever note the clock struck to say
                Time —
        whatever drug, or aire, they breathed
            to make them think so deep
                or hear so simply what
                    had passed
        like a car passing in the 1960 Street
            beside the Governmental Palace
                in Peru, this Lima,
in the year I write.
                    Kerouac! I salute thy
            wordy bearde. Sad Prophet!
                    Salutations and low bows from
bagged pants and turbaned mind and horned foot.
        My own! The Devil's — That which
            must exist — that ALL exist, with all
                its horns and arched eyebrows and Jewish smiles.
All! All! All! All! Including that which
            will break its back & suffer on the
                Mountain
        of garbage where I went two days ago to see
            the goats (pigs, mules) copulate.
Break the Rhythm! (too much pentameter)
        One single specimen of Eternity — each
of us poets.
        . . . My god what solitude are you in Kerouac
            now —
                heard the whoosh of carwheels in the 1950 rain.
And every bell went off on time,
and everything that was created
rang especially in view of the creation
For
This is the end of the Creation
This is the redemption spoken of
This is the view of the Created
        By all the Drs, nurses, etc, of
                    creation;
I.E. —
    * *I just nodded because of the secondary* ! ! *negation*
The unspeakable passed over my head for
            the second time,
                and still can't relate it!

i.e. we are the sweeping of the moon,
we are what is *left over* from Perfection —

The universe is an OLD mistake
I've understood a million times before
and always come back to the same point —
the
Sooner or later ail consciousness will
          be eliminated
                    because consciousness is
          a by-product of —
                              (cotton & ether)
(This) Consciousness is Relative to this
          existence which is *not*
               Absolute —
     So what's the good of it all??
Christ! you struggle to understand
     one consciousness,
               & get confronted with myriads —
after a billion years.
               with the same old ringing in the ears
                    and smile of accidental creation,
and known it *all* before.
          A Buddha as of old, with sirens of
whatever machinery making metal noises in
               the street.
          and lights reflected in the front façade
               window of the RR Station in a
                    dinky port in Backwash
          of the murky old forgotten
                    fabulous whatever
                         Civilization of
                              Eternity, —
with the RR Sta Clock ring midnight,
     as of now,
                    & waiting for the 6th
                         you write your
                              word,
          and end on the last chime — and remember
     This *one* twelve was struck
          before,
               and *never again:* both.
                         That madness
of Germanesses looking forward in the dark —
I am one of the experiments on the way to my
               consciousness —
     a side result . . .
and I turn back alone, and sad, and sentimental
          from the balcony where I stood looking
               at the Cross (afraid) and the
                    stars above Lima
          thinking of you, Jack, as you think or have
               thought or will think & now do
                    think again of me, —
          old lover in the night.
"Before God's last put out the Light was spoken"
               . . . the moment I stood on the balcony
          waiting for an explosion
in *this* life, of the final mind, of Total
     Consciousness of the All —
               (being Ginsberg sniffing Ether in Lima)
The same old struggle of Mind, repeated over
          and over again, to understand itself.
and failing everytime,
          and repeating the experiment in the void,
not reaching the Thing
               which eliminates all experiment
               and ends the process with an X
                    which comprehends
                         all that came before
                         and will come after —
               unexplainable to each, except in
                    secret recollective hidden
                         half-hand prophetic unrecorded
                              way.
          As the old sages of Asia, or white beards in Persia,
               scribbled on the margins of their scrolls

                    in delicate ink
          remembering with tears the ancient clockbells of
                              their cities
               and the cities that had been —
                    as visiting Macchu Picchu
I knew the secrets of the Priests
buried — cat gods on funeral shrouds —
               for a museum —
          or lost in the sands of Paracas —
None remember but all return to the same thought before
                    they die
as in streets of Macchu Picchu — what sad old
          knowledge, as my own or yours
          which we repeat again.
                    Only to be lost
in the sands of consciousness, or wrapped in a mystic shroud
          of Poesy
and found by some kid in a thousand years
          inspire what dreadful thoughts of his own?
It's a horrible, lonely experience. And
          Gregory's letter, and Peter's . . .
In the dregs of circumstance
          There are certain repeated
          (pistol-shot) reliable points
          of reference which the insane
          (pistolshot repeated out window)
          madman writes — *The Pistol Shot*
          outside — the repeated situations —
          the experience of return to the
          same place in Universal-Creation-
          Time — and every time we return
          we recognize again that we
          have been here & that is
          the Key to Creation — *the same pistol shot*
          — down, bending over his book
          of unintelligible Marvels with his mustache.
(My) Madness is intelligible reactions to
          unintelligible phenomena.
               Boy — what a marvelous bottle,
                    a clear glass sphere of transparent
                         liquid ether.
9 PM Next Day —
          Bus pickup snuffle — & crack of iron whips incyde the
silinders. Whistle & sweal of brakes. Laughter & pistol-shots
echoing at all walls.
          I know I am a poet — in this universe — but what good
does that do — when in another, without these mechanical aids,
I might be doomed to be a poor Disnean shoe store clerk —
          This accident of consciousness is an accident of one of
the Ether-possible worlds, not the Final World —
               Wherein we all look crosseyed
               & triumph in our Virginity
               without wearing Rabbit's foot
                    ears or eyes looking sideways
                    strangely But in Gold
               Humbled & more knowledgeable, acknowledge
               the vast mystery of our creation —
               without giving any sign that
                    we have heard from the
               GREAT CREATOR

          WHOSE NAME I NOW
               PRONOUNCE
Great Creator Of The Universe, If
     Thy Wisdom Accord It
And If This Not Be Too
     Much to Ask
May I Publish Your Name?
     I ask in the Lima
          Night
Fearfully waiting
          Answer
hearing the buses out on
     the street hissing

Knowing the Terror
        of the World Afar —
I have been playing with Jokes
and His is too mighty to hold
        in the hand like a pen
and His is the Pistol-shot Answer
        that brings blood to the brain
and —
        What *can* be possible
                in a minor universe
                in which you can see
                God by sniffing
                the Gas in a Cotton?
        The answer to be taken in
                reverse & Doubled Math-
                ematically *both* ways.

Am I a sinner?
There are hard and easy universes. This
                is neither.

If I close my eyes will I regain Consciousness?
        That's the final question — which
we have all heard before — with
all the old churchbells ringing, and
all the old whispers of responsive
demiurgic ecstasy crescendo'd in
the ears — and when was it
Not ever answered in the Affirmative? Saith the Lord?

        A magic question? And a magic
answer? That we *get* in a
magic universe — but *magic*
        full of brown shorts & Bolivian shoes,
pure magic! Therefore poetry, the key
to magic. Or therefore, Laughing Gas.
        A Magic Universe
Flies & Crickets & the sound of busses & my
        stupid beard.
And the mountain of garbage also Magical.
But what's Magic?
Is there Sorrow in Magic?
Is Magic one of my own Boyscout creations?
Am I responsible? I with my flop?
Must I be repeater of turkey-ass Corso?
Silver Gregory! Lost in Universe!
Justice that we should both survive
and all together singing the same old
        blood cheek swallow tongue throat
        woo, bark, harmony, Carramba!
(Is there Threat in Magic?
Yes this just might be one
        of the universes in which there
        is a Threat to Magic, by
        writing while high.)
A Universe in which I am condemned to write statements.
And this one is joined in
        Indic Union to
        affirm with laughing eyes —
The world is as we see it,0
        Male & Female, passing
as it passes thru the years,
        as has before & will, perhaps
with all its countless pearls
& bloody noses of Eternity
                and all the old mistakes —
and I poor stupid All in G
am stuck with that old Choice
Ya, Crap, what Hymn to seek, & in
        what tongue, if this is the most
        I can requite from Consciousness? —
That I can skim? & put in words?
        could skim it faster with
        more juice —

Could skim a crop with Death,
        perchance — yet never
        know in this old world.
Can know in Death?
        And before?
                Will in
Another know.
        And in another know.
                And
        in Another know.
        And in another know.
                And
Stop Conceiving Worlds!
        says Philip Whalen
(My Savior!) (oh what snobbery!)
(as if he cd save anyone) —
        At *least,* he won't understand.
I lift my finger in the air to create
a universe he won't understand, full
        of Sadness. But no more strange
        than any other.
I'm tired of this quasitranscendancy
. . . look up and down, shaking the head in wonder &
bewilderment, as before, as the old Jews.
                Time repeats itself, including
                this consciousness, which has seen
        itself before — thus the locust whistle
        of antiquity's nightwatch in my eardrum . . .
— a gesture of the head, revolving on the neck
        left to right, remembering various-lives,
        finally staring straight ahead in surprise
                & recollection into the mirror of Time
                in the Hotel Commercio room.
How would I *know* if I have been here before?
        Am I afraid to find out?
I propounded a final question, and
        heard a series of final answers.
What is *God?* for instance, asks the answer?
        And whatever else can the replier reply but reply?
Whatever the nature of the mind, that
        the nature of *both* question and answer.
Snyder alone in his altitude of mind height.
Ah my poor coat, Gary, sagging on the chair
        left arm down. wrinkles in lapel
        of sharkskin, varicolor like many eyes —
        I don't want that anybody — me — should be lonely, but
I condemn all others to solitude just that I can have God.
                — every eye a different
                        universe —
& yet one wants to live in a *single* universe
                        Does one?

Must it be one?
        Why, as with Jews,
must the God be One? O what does
concept One mean?
        It's Mad!
GOD IS ONE!
        is X
is meaningless —
        Adonoi Echad
is a joke —
        The Hebrews are
wrong — (Christ & Buddha
attest, also wrongly!)
One's a formation of Mind!
        arbitrary madness!
Spreading out in all directions simultaneously
I forgive both good and ill,
& I seek nothing, like a painted savage with
spear crossed by orange & black & white bands.
        "I found the Jivaros & was
        entrapped in their universe."
                I'm scribbling nothings,
page upon page of profoundest nothing

as scribed the ancient Hebe, when
     he wrote Adonoi or One —
all to amuse, or make money or deceive —
        Let wickedness be Me
and this the worst of all the universes.
           — Not the worst! Not Flame!
    I can't stand that! — (Yes that's
    for somebody else!)
         OK I accept
O Catfaced God, whatever comes! It's me.
I am the Flame, etc.
        O Gawd!
            Crack!
of the Circusmaster's whip!
          — Imperfect!
and a soul is damned to Hell!
        And the churchbell rings!
and there is melancholy, once again throughout the realm.
       And I'm that soul, small as it is.

Have Felt Same Before

The death of Consciousness is terrible and yet
when all is ended what's there to regret
and who's there to remember or forget?
The only thing I fear is the Last Chance.
         That will be met — I'll
see the Last Chance too, before I'm done,
old Mind. I'll see them all, all them
old Last Chances that you knew before —
    Suddenly felt at point of exchange
with another universe in which I'm a DH Lawrence
laborer in cabin writing hunger poverty (instead
of metaphysics) —
        someday thru the nexdoor,
dreamwall — like thru the wall of this Hotel —
    With whatever attitude I hold the cotton
to my nose, it's still a secret joke,
   with pinky akimbo, or with effete queer
      eye in mirror at myself,
        or serious-brow-mein
        & darkened beard
   I'm still the kid of obscene Last Chance awaiting —
      breathing in a foreign universe
      thru the nose like some hindu-Brahmic God
      O Bell Time Ring Thy
      Midnight for the Billionth
      Soundy Time, I hear again!
   I'll go to walk the street
         Who'll find
me in the night, in Lima, in my
33rd year?

On Street (Cont.)
The souls of Peter & I answer
     each other.
But — and what's a Soul?
To be a poet's a serious
occupation, condemned
to that in Universe.
To walk the street
scribbling in a book
 — just accosted by a drunk
 — under Plaza de Armas side
    street
under a foggy sky
and sometimes with no
moon.
    The heavy balcony
hangs over the white
marble of the
Bishop's Palace
next the Cathedral —
The fountain plays
in light as o'er —
The buses & the

motorcyclists pass
at midnight, the
carlights shine
the beggar turns
the corner with his
cigarette stub &
cane, the Noisers
leave the tavern
and delay, conversing
in high voice,
Awake,
    Hasta Manana
they all say —
    And somewhere
at the other end of
the line, a telephone
is ringing, once again
with unknown news —
    The night
looms over Lima,
sky black fog —
and I sit helpless
smoking with a

pencil hand —
    The long crack
in the pavement
    or yesterday's
volcano in Chile,
or the day before
the Earthquake
that begat the
World.
    The Plaza
pavement shines
in the electric
light. I wait.
    The lonely beard
workman staggers
home to bed from
Death.
    Yes but I'm
a little tired of
being alone . . .
    Keats' Urn — the
instant of realization
of a single consciousness
that hears the chimes
of Time repeated
endlessly —

All night, w. Ether, wave
after wave of magic
understanding — a dis-
turbance of the field
of consciousness.
Magic night, magic stars
magic men, magic music
magic God, magic death
Magic Magic.
      What crude chance
we live in (seeing trolley
like a rude monster
in downtown street
w/electric diamond
wire antennae to sky
go past outside under
white arc light by
Gran Hotel Bolivar.) The mad
potter of
Mochica made a
pot w/ 6 eyes & 2
mouths & half a nose
& 5 cheeks & no chin
for us to figure out,
serious side track,
blind alley Cosmos.

(Back in Room)
How strange to remember anything, even a button,
           much less a universe.
"What creature gives birth to itself?"
The universe is mad, slightly mad,
 — and the two sides of the question wriggle away
in opposite directions to die,
         as the caterpillar hundredfooted that I saw
           on the staircase grass at Macchu Picchu,
        with its black head lopped off, and gasping
           for air, or consciousness,
        the long body curled & feebly wriggling
           feet in the blindness
        and the Creature feels itself
          being destroyed
         & fleeing to opposite
          ends of infinity
        head & tail of the universe
           cut in two
Men with slick mustaches of mystery have
      pimp horrible climaxes & Karmas —
That's me — the mad magician that created Chaos
      in the peaceful void & suave.
    With my fucking suave manners & my knowitall
      eyes, and mind full of fantasy —
The Me! that horror that keeps me conscious in
      this Hell of Birth & Death.
    34 coming up — I suddenly felt old —
sitting with Walter & Raquel in Chinese
Restaurant — they kissed — I alone — age of
Burroughs when we first met.

May 28, 1960 Hotel Commercio, Lima, Peru

—Allen Ginsberg

AMERICA

1. Piling upward
the fact the stars
In America the office bid
A archives in his
stall . . .
Enormous stars on them
The cold anarchist standing
in his hat.
Arm along the rail
We were parked
Millions of us
The accident was terrible.
The way the door swept out
The stones piled up
The ribbon — books, miracle, with moon
and the stars
The pear tree
moving me
I am around   an in my sigh
The gift of a the stars.
The person
Horror — morsels of his choice
Rebuked to me I
— in the apartment
the pebble we in the bed.
The roof —
rain — pills —
Found among the moss
Hers wouldn't longer care — I don't
know why.

2. Ribbons   over the Pacific
Sometimes we
The deep
additional
and more and more less deep
but hurting
under the fire
brilliant rain
to meet us.
Probably in
moulded fire.
We make it
times of the year
the light falls from heaven
love
parting the separate lives
her fork   the
specs
notably fire.
We get unhappy, off
The love
All the house
Waste visits
Autumn brushes the hair
The girl has lived in this corner
In the sunlight all year.
getting up to speak
Your janitor tried
if it was ready

I was almost killed
now by reading
on trial
standing with the jar
in the door wrapper
of this year fire intangible
Spoon
rapid the earth around
the geraniums of last August's
dried in the yard
played for certain
person
in red cape
of course   the lathes around
the stars with privilege jerks
over the country last year we were
    disgusted meeting
misguided
their only answer pine tree
off of the land
to the wind
out of your medicine
health, light, death preoccupation, beauty.
So don't kill the
stone this is desert
to the arms
You girl
the sea in waves.

3. of the arsenal
shaded in public
a hand put up
lips — a house
A minute the music stops.
The day it began. person
blocking the conductor
Is the janitor with the red cape
And the pot of flowers in one hand
His face hidden by the shelf
thought intangible.
So is this way
out into paths
of the square
arctic night
what with the stars
rocks and that fascinating illumination
that buries my heart
itself a tribute for which dancers
come. Inch pageant
of history   shaping
More that the forms
can do quacks
the night over the baths
stirred in his sleep the janitor reaches for
    the wrench with which he'll kill
the intruder
Terrain
glistening
Doesn't resemble much the out of
doors
We walked around   the hand
observe the smashing of the rain
into the door the night
can't keep   inside
perhaps feeling the sentry
the perfect disc
we walked toward the bush
the disc
bush had forgotten
apples on the crater
the northern
Messenger the snow
stone

4. Though I had never come here
This country, with laws of glass
And night majesty
through the football
Lured far away
Wave helplessly
The country
lined with snow
only mush was served
piling up
the undesired stars
needed against the night
Forbidden categorically
but admitted
beyond the cape
the tree still grows
tears fall
and I am proud
of these stars in our flag we don't want
the flag of film
waving over the sky
toward us — citizens of some future state.
We despair in gardens, but the stars
And night persist, knowing we don't want it.
Some tassels first
then nothing — day
the odor.
In the hall. The stone.

5. Across the other sea, was
in progress
the halt sea
Tens of persons   blinded
Immediately the port, challenge
Argument
Pear tree
Only perforation
Chain to fall apart in his hand
Someday liberty
to be wait of the press
drank
perhaps the lotion
she added. Drank
the orders.
The fake
ones.
border
his misanthropy. pear mist.
the act   imitation
his happy stance
position   peace
on earth
ignited fluid
before he falls
must come under this head
he liked, so may be
Tears, hopeless adoration, passions
the fruit of carpentered night
Visible late next day. Cars
blockade the streets   wish
the geraniums embracing
umbrella
falling his embrace he strangles
in his storage but in
this meant
One instance
A feather not snow blew against the window.
A message from the great outside.

—JOHN ASHBERY

Episodes from

THE BIRDS

of Aristophanes

The Birds was first performed at the Great Dionysia in late March, 414 B.C. and was awarded the Second Prize. The First Prize was taken by Ameipsias with his Komastai ("The Revellers").

[*Pisthetairos, having persuaded the Birds to build their own city of Cloudcuckooland in order to blockade the gods, is about to begin the Inaugural Service for the new city. His efforts, however, are obstructed by the intrusion of a whole series of parasites — stupid priests, poets, professional legislators, itinerant prophets and city-planners. It is with these intruders that the following episodes deal.*]

PISTHETAIROS
    Now then, first of all, we'll need a priest to supervise our
    sacrifice.
                 — Boy !
An Acolyte appears.
                         Boy, go fetch me a priest.
    When you're finished, bring me a basket and a laver.
Exit Acolyte.

CHORUS
           The birds agree
           most heartily.
               You're absolutely right.
           Hymns and laud
           are dear to god,
               but dinner's sheer delight.
           Yes, gratitude
           is shown with food,
               so rise and offer up,
           in witness of
           our shrunken love,
               one miserable lamb chop!

KORYPHAIOS
    Flutist, come in.
    Now let our sacrifice begin.
Enter the Flutist, a Raven whose beak is an enormous flute which is strapped to his mouth by means of a leather harness. After strenuous huffing, he manages to produce what are unmistakably caws.

PISTHETAIROS
    Stop that raucous rook!
                       In the name of god,
    what are you anyway?
                      I've seen some weird sights,
    but this is the first time I ever saw
    a blackbird propping his beak with a belt.
Exit Flutist. Enter PRIEST, followed by the Acolyte with the paraphernalia of the sacrifice.
    At last.
             — Eminence, begin the sacrifice.
PRIEST
    Your humble servant.
                 — But where's my acolyte?
The Acolyte steps forward. The PRIEST raises his hands and begins the Bidding Prayer of the Birds.
    Now let us pray —
        PRAY TO THE HESTIA OF NESTS,
        TO THE HOUSEHOLDING HARRIER HAWK,
        TO ALL THE OLYMPIAN COCKS AND COQUETTES,
        TO THE SWOOPING STORK OF THE SEA —
PISTHETAIROS
    All hail, the Stork! Hail, Poseidon of pinions!
PRIEST
        TO THE SWEETSINGER OF DELOS,
        THE APOLLONIAN SWAN
        TO LETO THE QUEEN OF THE QUAIL,
        TO ARTEMIS THE PHOEBE —
PISTHETAIROS
    Hail to the Phoebe, virgin sister of Phoebus!
PRIEST
        PRAY TO WOODPECKER PAN,
        TO DOWITCHER KYBELE,
        MOTHER OF MORTALS AND GODS —
PISTHETAIROS
    Hail, Dowager Queen, Great Mother of Bustards!
PRIEST
        PRAY THAT THEY GRANT US
        HEALTH AND LENGTH OF LIFE,
        PRAY THAT THEY PROTECT US,
        pray for the Chians too —
PISTHETAIROS
    You know, I like the way he tacks those Chians on.
PRIEST
        COME, ALL HERO BIRDS
        ALL HEROINE HENS AND PULLETS!
        COME, O GALLINULE!
        BRING DICKYBIRD AND DUNNOCK,
        COME, GROSSBILL AND BUNTING!
        ON DIPPER, ON DIVER,
        WHIMBREL AND FINCH !
        COME CURLEW AND CREEPER,
        ON PIPIT, ON PARROT,
        COME VULTURE, COME TIT —

PISTHETAIROS
Stop it, fool! Stop that roll call of the Birds!
Are you utterly daft, man, inviting vultures
and suchlike to our feast? Or weren't you aware
one single beak could tuck it all away?
Clear out and take your ribbands with you
So help me, I'll finish this sacrifice myself.

Exit PRIEST.

CHORUS
Again we raise
the hymn of praise
and pour the sacred wine.
With solemn rite
we now invite
the blessed gods to dine.
But don't *all* come —
perhaps just one,
and maybe then again,
there's not enough
(besides, it's tough),
so stay away. Amen.

PISTHETAIROS
Let us pray to the pinion'd gods —

Enter a hungry, ragged POET, chanting.

POET
In all thy songs, O Muse,
let one city
praised be —
CLOUDCUCKOOLAND THE LOVELY!

PISTHETAIROS
Who spawned this spook?
— Who are you?

POET
One of the tribe of dulcet tongue and tripping speech —
"the slave of Poesy,
whose ardent soul
the Muses hold in thrall,"
as Homer hath it.

PISTHETAIROS
Judging from your clothes, your Muses must be bankrupt.
Tell me, bard, what ill wind plopped you here?

POET
I've been composing poems in honor of your city —
oodles of little odes, some dedication-anthems,
songs for soprano voice, a lyric or two
à la Simonides —

PISTHETAIROS
How long has your little mill
been grinding out this chaff?

POET
Why, simply ages.
Long, long since my Muse commenced to sing
Cloudcuckooland in all her orisons.

PISTHETAIROS
But that's impossible. This city's still a baby.
I just now gave birth. I just baptised her.

POET
Ah, but swift are the mouths of the Muses,
more swift than steeds the galloping news of the Muses!

He turns to the altar and with outstretched hands invokes it in Pindaric parody.

O Father,
Founder of Etna,
of thy bounty give,
O Hiero, O Homonym,
Great Hero of the Fire,
just one slender sli-
ver to my desire
some tidbit to savor,
some token of favor —

PISTHETAIROS
I think we'd better bribe this beggar bard
to leave before we die of doggerel.

To the Acolyte.
— You there,
strip and let the poet have your overcoat.

He hands the coat to the POET.
Dress.
Why, you poor poet, you're shivering.

POET
My Muse accepts with thanks
this modest donation.
But first before I leave,
one brief quotation,
a snatch of Pindar
you might ponder —

PISTHETAIROS
Gods above, will this poor man's Pindar never leave?

POET
Undressed amidst the nomad Skyths.
the Frozen Poet fareth,
as Beastly Cold as Bard may be,
who Next-to-Nothing weareth.
Genius, ah, hath deck'd his Song,
but oh, th'Ingratitude!
Whilst other Blokes be warm as Toast
the Poet's damn near Nude.
You catch my drift?

PISTHETAIROS
Yes, I catch your drift.
You want some underwear.

To the Acolyte.
Off with it, lad.
We can't allow our delicate poets to freeze.
And now clear out, will you?

POET
I go, I go.
But first my valediction to this village —

Singing.
O Muse on golden throne,
Muse with chattering teeth,
sing this capitol of cold,
this frigorifical city!
I have been where the glebe is frozen with frore.
I have traipsed where the furrows are sown with snow.
Alalai!
Alalai!
G'bye.

Exit POET.

PISTHETAIROS
Well, how do you like that? Griping about the cold
after making off with a new winter outfit!
And how in the name of heaven did that plague
discover us so fast?

To the naked and shivering Acolyte.
— You there, to work.
Take up your laver and circle the altar, boy,
and we'll resume our sacrifice once again.
Quiet now, everyone.

As PISTHETAIROS approaches the altar with the sacrificial knife, an itinerant PROPHET with a great open tome of oracles makes his appearance.

PROPHET
Forbear, I say!
Let no one touch the victim.

PISTHETAIROS
Who the hell are you,
may I ask?

PROPHET
I am a Prophet, sir, in person.

PISTHETAIROS
Then beat it.

PROPHET
Ah, the naughty wee scamp.
But we mustn't scoff.
Friend, I have brought you an oracle of Bakis,
transparently alluding to Cloudcuckooland.

PISTHETAIROS
    Why did you wait till I founded my city
    before disgorging this revelation?
PROPHET
                                                    Alas,
    I could not come. The Inner Voice said No.
PISTHETAIROS
    I suppose we'll have to hear you expound.
PROPHET
                                            Listen —
    LO, IN THAT DAY WHEN THE WOLF AND THE CROW
        DO FOREGATHER AND COMPANION,
    AND DOMICILE IN THE AIR, AT THAT POINT
        WHERE KORINTH KISSETH SIKYON —
PISTHETAIROS
    Look here, what has Korinth got to do with me?
                        PROPHET
    It's ambiguous. Korinth signifies "air."
Resuming.
        PRESENT, I SAY, A WHITE SHEEP TO PANDORA,
        BUT TO THE SEER WHO BRINGS MY BEHEST:
            IN PRIMUS, A WARM WINTER COAT
            PLUS A PAIR OF SANDALS (THE BEST) —
PISTHETAIROS
    The *best* sandals, eh?
PROPHET
                            Yup. Look in the book.
Resuming.
            ITEM, A GOBLET OF WINE,
            ITEM, A GIBLET OF GOAT —
PISTHETAIROS
    Giblet? It says giblet?
PROPHET
                            Yup. Look in the book.
Resuming.
        IF O BLESSED YOUTH, THOU DOST AS I ENJOIN,
        REGAL EAGLE WINGS THIS VERY DAY ARE DAY ARE THINE.
        NOT SO MUCH AS PIGEON FLUFF, IF THOU DECLINE.
PISTHETAIROS
        It really says that?
PROPHET
                            Yup. Look in the book.
PISTHETAIROS
Drawing out a huge tome from under his cloak.
    You know, your oracles don't mesh with mine,
    and I got these from Apollo's mouth.
                                    Listen —
    LO, IF IT CHANCE THAT SOME FAKER INTRUDE,
    TROUBLING THY WORSHIP AND SCROUNGING FOR
                                        FOOD,
        LET HIS RIBS BE BASHED
        AND HIS TESTICLES MASHED —
PROPHET
    I suspect you're bluffing.
PISTHETAIROS
                            Nope. Look in the book.
Resuming.
    SMITE ON, I SAY, IF ANY PROPHET SHOULD COME,
    YEA, THOUGH HE SOARETH LIKE THE SWALLOW.
    FOR THE GREATER THE FAKER, THE HARDER HIS
    BUM SHOULD BE BATTERED.
                        GOOD LUCK.
                            Signed,
                                APOLLO.
PROPHET
    Honest? It says that?
PISTHETAIROS
                            Yup. Look in the book.
Suddenly throwing his tome at him and beating him.
    Take that!
        And that!
            And that!
PROPHET
                            Ouch. Help!

PISTHETAIROS
    Scat. Go hawk your prophecies somewhere else.
Exit PROPHET. From the other side enters the geometrician and
surveyor METON, his arms loaded with surveying instruments.
METON
    The occasion that hath hied me hither —
PISTHETAIROS
                            Not another!
    State your business, stranger. What's your racket?
    What tragic flaw brings you here?
METON
                            My purpose here
    is a geodetic survey of the atmosphere
    and the allocation of this aerial area
    into cubic acres.
PISTHETAIROS
                    Who are you ?
METON
                            Who am *I*?
    Why, Meton, of course. Who else could *I* be?
    Geometer to Hellas by special appointment.
    Also Kolonos.
PISTHETAIROS
                    And those tools?
METON
                            Celestial rules,
        of course.
            Now attend.
                Taken *in extenso,*
    our welkin resembles a cosmical oven
    or potbellied stove worked by convection,
    though vaster. Now with the flue as my base,
    and twirling the calipers thus, I obtain
    the azimuth, whence, by calibrating the arc —
    you follow me?
PISTHETAIROS
                    No, I don't follow you.
METON
    No matter. Now, by training the theodolite
    on the vectored zenith at the Apex A,
    I deftly square the circle, whose conflux,
    or C, I designate as the center
    or axial hub of your Cloudcuckooland,
    whence, like global spokes or astral radii,
    broad boulevards diverge centrifugally,
    as it were —
PISTHETAIROS
                    Why, this man's a regular Thales!
Whispering confidentially.
        Psst. Meton.
METON
                    Sir?
PISTHETAIROS
                        I've taken a shine to you.
    Take my advice and decamp while there's still time.
METON
    You anticipate danger?
PISTHETAIROS
                        The kind of danger
    one meets in Sparta. Nasty little riots,
    a few foreigners beaten up or murdered,
    fighting in the streets —
METON
                        Dear me, you mean
    there might be revolution?
PISTHETAIROS
                        I certainly hope not.
METON
    Then what *is* the trouble?
PISTHETAIROS
                        The new law.
    Attempted fraud is punishable by thrashing.
METON
    Er, perhaps I'd best be going.

PISTHETAIROS
                    I'm half afraid
          you're just a bit too late.
                                        Yes!
                                                            Look out!
          Here comes your thrashing!
He batters METON with a surveying rod.
METON
                                        Help! Murder!
PISTHETAIROS
          I warned you. Go survey some other place.
*Exit METON. From the other side enters an INSPECTOR, dressed
in a magnificent military uniform and swaggering imperiously.*
INSPECTOR
          Fetch me the Mayor.
PISTHETAIROS
          Who is this popinjay?
INSPECTOR
          Inspector-general of Cloudcuckooland County,
          invested, I might add, with plenary powers —
PISTHETAIROS
          On whose authority?
INSPECTOR
                              The powers vested in me
          by virtue of this piddling piece of paper
          signed by one Teleas of Athens.
PISTHETAIROS
                              Let me propose
          a little deal. I'll pay you off right now,
          provided you leave us.
INSPECTOR
                              A capital suggestion.
          As it happens, my presence is urgently needed
          at home. They're having a Great Debate.
          The Persian crisis, you know.
PISTHETAIROS
                                        Splendid.
          I'll pay you off right now.
Violently beating the INSPECTOR
                                        Take that!
                                        And that!
INSPECTOR
          What does this outrage mean?
PISTHETAIROS
                                        Round one
          of the Great Debate.
INSPECTOR
                              So! Insubordination.
To the CHORUS.
          I call on you birds to bear me witness
          that he assaulted an Inspector.
PISTHETAIROS
                                        Shoo, fellow,
          and take your ballot-boxes when you go.
Exit INSPECTOR.
          What confounded gall! Sending us their Inspector
          before we've finished the Inaugural Service.
*Enter an itinerant LEGISLATOR reading from a huge volume of
laws.*
LEGISLATOR
          BE IT HEREBY PROVIDED THAT IF ANY CLOUD-
          CUCKOO LANDER SHALL WILFULLY INJURE OR
          WRONG ANY CITIZEN OF ATHENS —
PISTHETAIROS
          Gods, what now? Not *another* bore with a book?
LEGISLATOR
          A seller of statutes, sir, at your service.
          Fresh shipment of by-laws on special sale
          for only
PISTHETAIROS
          Perhaps you'd better demonstrate.
LEGISLATOR
          BE IT HEREBY PROVIDED BY LAW THAT FROM THE
          DATE SPECIFIED BELOW THE WEIGHTS AND MEA-
          SURES OF THE CLOUDCUCKOOLANDERS ARE TO BE
          ADJUSTED TO THOSE IN EFFECT AMONG THE
          OLOPHYXIANS —

PISTHETAIROS
Pummeling him.
          By god, I'll Olo-phyx you!
LEGISLATOR
                                        Hey, mister, stop!
PISTHETAIROS
          Get lost, you and your laws, or I'll carve mine
          on the skin of your tail.
Exit LEGISLATOR. Enter INSPECTOR.
INSPECTOR
                              I summon the defendant Pisthetairos
          to stand trial on charges of assault and battery
          not later than April.
PISTHETAIROS
                              Good gods, are *you* back?
He thrashes INSPECTOR who runs off. Reenter LEGISLATOR.
LEGISLATOR
          IF ANY MAN, EITHER BY WORD OR ACTION,
            DO IMPEDE OR RESIST
          A MAGISTRATE IN THE PROSECUTION OF HIS
            OFFICIAL DUTIES, OR REFUSE
          TO WELCOME HIM WITH THE COURTESY
            PRESCRIBED BY LAW —
PISTHETAIROS
          Great thundery Zeus, are *you* back here too?
He drives the LEGISLATOR away. Reenter INSPECTOR.
INSPECTOR
          I'll have you sacked. And I'm suing you
          for a fat two thousand.
PISTHETAIROS
                              By Zeus, I'll fix you
          and your blasted ballot-boxes once and for all !
Exit INSPECTOR under a barrage of blows.
Reenter LEGISLATOR.
LEGISLATOR
          Remember that evening when you crapped in court?
PISTHETAIROS
          Someone arrest that pest !
Exit LEGISLATOR.
                              And this time stay away!
          But enough's enough.
                              We'll take our goat inside
          and finish this sacrifice in privacy.
*Exit PISTHETAIROS into house, followed by Acolyte with basket
and slaves with the sacrifice.*
CHORUS
Wheeling sharply and facing the audience.
                    Praise Ye the Birds, O Mankind!
                         Our sway is over all.
                    The eyes of the Birds observe you:
                         we see if any fall.

                    We watch and guard all growing green,
                         protecting underwing
                    this lavish lovely life of earth,
                         its birth and harvesting.

                    We smite the mite, we slay the pest,
                         all ravagers that seize
                    the good that burgeons in your buds
                         or ripens on your trees.

                    Whatever makes contagion come,
                         whatever blights or seeks
                    to raven in this green shall die,
                         devoured by our beaks.

KORYPHAIOS
          You know that proclamation that's posted everywhere? —
          WANTED, DEAD OR ALIVE! DIAGORAS OF MELOS.
          ONE TALENT'S REWARD FOR ANY MAN WHO KILLS
          THE TYRANT IN HIS LATEST INCARNATION!
          Well,
                    we birds have published our own proclamation: —
               "HEAR YE!
                         WANTED!
                                   PHILOKRATES THE BIRDSELLER,
          DEAD OR ALIVE.
                              DEAD, 1 TALENT'S REWARD, 4 TALENTS

IF TAKEN ALIVE.
        BUT PROCEED WITH GREAT CAUTION.
THIS MAN IS DANGEROUS. WANTED FOR
MURDER AND CRUELTY TO BIRDS ON THE
FOLLOWING COUNTS: —
    For the Spitting of Finches, seven to a skewer;
    item, for Disfiguring Thrushes by means of inflation;
    item, for Insertion of Feathers in Blackbirds' nostrils;
    item, for Unlawful Detention of Pigeons in Cages;
    item, for Felonious Snaring of Innocent Pigeons;
    item, for Flagrant Misuse of Traps and Decoy-devices."
So much for Philokrates.
        But as for you, spectators,
we give you warning.
        If any boy in this audience
has as his hobby the keeping of birds in cages,
we urgently suggest that you let them go free. Disobey,
and we'll catch you and lock you up in a wicker cage
or stake you out to a snare as a little decoyboy!

CHORUS
    How blessed is our breed of Bird,
        dressed in fluff and feather,
    that, when hard winter holds the world
        wears no clothes whatever.

    And blazoned summer hurts no bird,
        for when the sun leaps high,
    and, priestly in that hellish night,
        the chaunting crickets cry,

    the birds keep cool among the leaves
        or fan themselves with flight;
    while winter days we're snug in caves
        and nest with nymphs at night.

    But Spring is joy, when myrtle blooms
        and Graces dance in trio,
    and quiring birds cantatas sing,
        vivace e con brio.

KORYPHAIOS
    Finally, gentlemen, a few brief words about the Prize
    and the advantage of casting your vote for *THE BIRDS* —
    advantages compared to which that noble prince,
    poor Paris of Troy, was very shabbily bribed indeed.
            First on our list comes a little item
    that every judge's greedy heart must be panting to possess.
    I refer, of course, to those lovely owls of Laurium,
    sometimes called the coin of the realm.
                Yes, gentlemen,
    these lovely owls, we promise, will flock to you,
    settle down in your wallets for good and hatch you
    nice little nesteggs.
                Secondly, we
    promise to redesign your houses.
                See, the tenements vanish,
    while in their place rise shrines whose dizzy heights,
    like eagle-eyries, hang in heaven.
                Are you perhaps
    a politician with the problem of insufficient plunder?
    Friend, your problems are over. Accept as our gift
    a pair of buzzard claws designed with special hooks
    for more efficient grafting.
                As for heavy eaters,
    those suffering from biliousness, acid indigestion
    or other stomach upsets, we proudly present them
    with special bird-crops, guaranteed to be virtually inde-
    structible.
            If, however, you withhold your vote,
    you'd better do as the statues do and wear a metal lid
    against our falling guano.
            I repeat.
                Vote against *THE BIRDS,*
    and every bird in town will cover you with — vituperation!

                    END OF EXCERPT

        — TRANSLATION BY WILLIAM ARROWSMITH

A STATEMENT
Alice Neel

Being born I looked around and the world and its people terrified and fascinated me. I was attracted by the morbid and excessive and everything connected with death had a dark power over me. I was early taken to Sunday School where the tale of Christ nailed to the cross would send me into violent weeping and I'd have to be taken home. Also I remember a film they showed at the church of the horrors of delirium tremens that quite unnerved me and prevented my sleeping for many nights.

I decided to paint a human comedy — such as Balzac had done in literature. In the 30's I painted the beat of those days — Joe Gould, Sam Putnam, Ken Fearing, etc. I have painted "El Barrio" in Puerto Rican Harlem. I painted the neurotic, the mad and the miserable. Also I painted the others, including some squares. I once, many light years ago, married a Cuban and lived in Havana where I had my first show. Then that all dissolved and in the thirties I was on the W.P.A. turning in a painting every six weeks. I had a show at the Pinacotheca Gallery during the war and later two shows at the A.C.A. Gallery. I never knew how to push myself and still don't know how. Like Chichikov I am a collector of souls. Now some of my subjects are beginning to die and they have a historic nostalgia: everyone somehow seems better and more important when they are dead. If I could I would make the world happy, the wretched faces in the subway sad and full of troubles worry me. I also hate the conformity of today — everything put into its box —

When I go to a show today of modern work I feel that my world has been swept away — and yet I do not think it can he so: that the human creature will be forever verboten. Thou shalt make no graven images . . . ❑

The Flying Horses of Mein-Mo

JACK KEROUAC

A Selection from *Book of Dreams*

I'm riding a bus thru Mexico with Cody sleeping at my side, at dawn the bus stops in the countryside & I look out at the quiet warm fields & think: "Is this really Mexico? why am I here?" — The fields look too calm & grassy & bugless to be Mexico — Later I'm sitting on the other side of the bus, Cody is gone, I look up in the sky & see that old ten thousand foot or hundred mile high mountain cliff with its enormous hazy blue palaces & temples where they have giant granite benches & tables for Giant Gods bigger than the ones who hugged skyscrapers on Wall Street — And in the air, Ah the silence of that horror, I see flying winged horses with capes furling over their shoulders, the slow majestic pawing of their front hooves as they clam thru the air flight — *Griffins* they are! — So I realize we're in "Coyocan" & this is the famous legendary place — I start telling four Mexicans in the seat in front of me the story of the Mountain of Coyocan & its Secret Horses but they laugh not only to hear a stranger talk about it but the ridiculousness of anybody even mentioning or *noticing* it — There's some secret they won't tell me concerning ignoration of the Frightful Castle — They even get wise with Gringo Me & I feel sand pouring down my shirt front, the big Mexican is sitting there with sand in his hand, smiling — I leap up & grab one, he is very tiny & skinny & I hold his hand against his belly so he won't pull a knife on me but he has none — They're really laughing at me for my big ideas about the Mountain —

We arrive at Coyocan town over which the hazy blue Mountain rises and now I notice that the Flying Horses are constantly swirling over this town & around the cliff, swooping, flying, sometimes sweeping low, yet nobody looks up & bothers with them — I can't bring myself to believe that they are actually flying horses & I look & look but that's what they have to be, even when I see them in moon profile: horses pawing thru air, slow, slow, eerie griffin horror men-horses — I realize they've been there all the time swirling around the Eternal Mountain Temple & I think: "The bastards have something to do with that Temple, that's where they come from,

I always knew that Mountain was all horror!" — I go inside the Coyocan Maritime Union Hall to sign for a Chinese sea job, it's in the middle of Mexico, I don't know why I've come all the way from New York to the landlocked center of Mexico for a sea voyage but there it is: a Seaman's hiring hall full of confusion & pale officials who don't understand why I came also — One of them makes a great intelligent effort to have letters in duplicate written to New York to begin straightening out the reason why I came — So if it's a job I'll get, it won't be for a week at least, *or more* — The town is evil & completely sinister because everybody is ugly sneering (the natives, I mean,) & they refuse to recognize the existence of that Terrible Swirl of Flying Horses — "Mien-Mo," I think, remembering the name of the Mountain, in Burma, that they call the world, with Dzapoudiba (India) the Southern Island by that name on account of Himalayan secret horrors — the beating heart of the Giant Beast is up there, the Griffins are just incidental insects — but those Flying Griffins are happy! how beautifully they claw slow forehooves thru the blue void!

Meanwhile two young American seamen & I study them flying up there miles high & watch them swoop lower, when they come low they change into blue and white birds to fool everybody — Even I say: "Yep, they're not flying horses, they're only seeming to be, they're Birds!" but even as I say that I see a distinct horse motioning lyrically thru the moon with a cape furling from his infernal shoulders —

A broken nosed ex boxer approaches me hinting that for fifty cents a job can be arranged on a ship — He is so sinister & intent I'm afraid to even give him fifty cents — Up comes a blonde with her fiancee announcing to me and the boxer her forthcoming marriage but interrupts her speech every now & then to take a short sweet pull on my huge juicy stick of a hardon in front of everybody in the streets of Coyocan!

And the Flying Horses of Mien-Mo are galloping with silent ease in the happy empty air way up there — Tinkle Tinkle go the streets of Coyocan as the sun falls, but up there is all silence & the Giant Gods are up — How can I describe it? ❏

Written after a Chinese dinner in Chinatown! Feb. 8 1960

Industrial Society and the Western Political Dialogue

J. Robert Oppenheimer

Paper delivered before the Congress for Cultural Freedom in Rheinfelden, Switzerland, September, 1959

In these remarks I shall address myself to one of the questions raised in Aron's paper:

> *"If, outside the sphere of science, there is nothing but arbitrary decision, has the result of the progress of science and scientific reasoning merely been to place in the keeping of unreason the thing that concerns us most, that is to say. the definition and choice of the essential, of the good life, of the good society?"*

What I have to say is really intended as an introduction. On the one hand, the problems of political philosophy are, for all the general human weight of this branch of study, highly technical in themselves and I must leave to the many here who are experts the expert discussion of this field. On the other hand, I will perhaps talk a little more broadly, because my concern is not only with how we can hope to see a revival of political philosophy, but with a rather larger question: how can we hope to see a revival of all philosophy? The question of Aron says "the choice of the essential": that is, after all, what a cultivated skeptic says when he means metaphysics; the choice of "the good life": that is what the cultivated skeptic means when he thinks ethics; and "the good society" is then the subject of political philosophy. I also must admit that nothing that I see in terms of action can in this area have immediate effects. If I were to have the only word on this subject, we would not walk out of these doors having solved any problem, or having any right to look forward to any morrow in which all the situations which are now troublesome would suddenly be bright. I do have the impression that we are here dealing with deep and only

partially understood and only partially manageable human attitudes, where a small beginning of clarity and common understanding may have great fruits if it is firm enough and solid enough. The question that I am going to concern myself with is the relations between the scientific explosions of this age and the weight and excellence that we may hope to achieve in common discourse.

In this, I have in mind an image of common discourse, which is itself blurred by three related realities. One is the size of our world and its communities, the number of people involved. One is the generally egalitarian and inclusive view in which there are no *a priori* restrictions on who is to participate in the discourse; clearly, not everyone will; but I think it is of the essence of the Western hope that every one may. The third is the extraordinary rapidity with which the preoccupations and circumstances of our life are altered.

What I am concerned with is an ideal, an image of a part of human life which is inherently not all-inclusive, but which has a quality of being public — I do not mean governmental, but I mean universal — which speaks in terms intelligible to all, of things accessible to all, of meanings relevant to all. I would not, for instance, say that the microbiologists belong to this public sector. They talk of problems which they understand, in which they can communicate without ambiguity, in which they can discover what errors may have been made, and can rejoice, as, believe me, they do rejoice, in all discoveries which add to their insight, irrespective of who, where and to whose glory the discoveries were made.

I would not regard the modern painter as part of the public sector, and certainly not those advanced and experimental elements of the art of musical composition where, I have been led to believe, these men, as in the pure mathematician's art, are concerned with a very high purpose, that of preserving the vigor and integrity and life of their own skills, but are not, in the first instance, addressing themselves to man at large. As to our friends the radical composers I would be gladly corrected by experts; but I will take some correction.

This image of the public sector has suffered from all the circumstances I have mentioned: size, egalitarianism, growth, change; but it has also suffered from a cognitive development, which is the growth of science. I would like to make a few comments on the nature of the relations between rational discourse, culminating in philosophical discourse, on the one hand, and the development of science, on the other hand. I am very much guided by my own experience, limited experience, in the United States; and when I talk, I will think of our universities, of our symposia like this one, of our mass culture, of the way in which Americans use their leisure, of what is thought, and written, and done in the country I know best.

For this provincialism, I make only the following two excuses: it is what I know a little at first hand; I am very distrustful of the traveler's impressions of other countries. But more important, it seems to me that in the United States we have perhaps come first to the era in which production for consumption's sake has reached a kind of completeness; I am aware that it is not fully complete, but it is from the point of view of men at large, largely complete. We are also among the first to face the problem: what does one do with the leisure and the life so returned; what is it for, how does one spend it. I am clear that in Europe, where egalitarianism is less strong, where the intellectual tradition and the need for order is more strong, the problems, as they appear in our country, are slightly less advanced and less acute. I expect, though I would gladly be told that I was wrong by historians or prophets, that the American troubles are forerunners of troubles which will not long remain out of Europe. I do not believe these troubles are as acute in communist countries, even in Russia. The technological revolution is not as far along; the land of plenty is not as near; and, in addition, the unifying presence of tyranny has greatly affected, not the nature of intellectual activity in those domains where it is free, but the contours of the regions where intellectual activity as such can be free. Therefore I believe that in studying the American scene, we may be reminded, not how to do things, not what to do all over the world in the same way, but of some of the dangers which accompany the fulfillment of the basic premises of the industrial and technological revolution, and some of the hopes.

I need hardly bring to mind that the great sciences of today arose in philosophical discourse and in technical invention. It will be an unending dispute among historians as to the role of these two components, but all of natural science — and I find myself thinking of historical science as continuous with natural science — has its origins in an undifferentiated, unspecialized common human discourse. The question is, therefore, why the enormous success, unanticipated, not fully appreciated, and at the moment not fully realized — I would say never to be fully realized — success of one sort of intellectual activity should not have had a beneficial effect on the intellectual life of man. In some ways it has, because certain forms of extreme superstition, certain insistent ways of provincialism have found themselves unable to flourish in the presence of the new light of scientific discovery.

But if we think back to the early days, either of the European tradition or of modern society, we see that we were there dealing with relatively few people. The citizenry of Athens, the few handsful of men who concerned themselves with the structure of American political power, the participants in the 18th century Enlightenment from Montesquieu up to the Revolution, were relatively few men. They had before them a relatively well digested and common language, experience, and tradition, and a common basis of knowledge. It is true that already in the 18th century, physics, astronomy and mathematics were beginning to assume these specialized and abstract and unfamiliar aspects which have increasingly characterized these subjects up to the present day. But they were not beyond the reach of laymen. They were perhaps greeted by laymen with an enthusiasm which a fuller knowledge would not have supported, but they were part of the converse of the 18th century.

If we look today, we see a very different situation, an alienation between the world of science and the world of public discourse, which has emasculated, impoverished, intimidated the world of public discourse without any countervailing advantage, except to the specialized sciences, and which in a strange sense, to use a word which political scientists have taught me, has denied to public discourse an element of legitimacy, has given it a kind of arbitrary, unrooted, unfounded quality. Thus any man may say what he thinks, but there is no way of arriving at a clarification or a consensus. In the past, common discourse and its queen, philosophy, rested on an essentially common basis of knowledge; that is, the men who participated knew, by and large, the same things, and could talk of them with a reasonable limitation in the ambiguity of what they were saying. There was a relatively stable, and a deeply shared, tradition, an historic experience which was common among the participants in the conversation, and a recognition — not always explicit and often, in fact, denied — of a difference between the kind of use and value which public discourse has as its high ideal, and the kind of criteria by which the sciences themselves in part must judge themselves. I want here to say that the traits which are important in public discourse are enormously important in science; and a lack of recognition of this has created great blocks, great repugnancies on the part of humane, cultivated and earnest men in their appreciation of the natural sciences and of even the abstract sciences.

I speak of a recognition that there are things important to discuss and analyze, to explore, to subject to some logical surgery, to have in order, in a certain sense: things which are not best viewed as propositional truth, which are not assertions, verifiable by the characteristic methods of science, as to the existence in the world of this or that connection between one thing and another. They have rather a normative and thematic quality. Such, indeed, is the intention of this discussion. They assert the connectedness of things, the relatedness of things, the priority of things; and without them there would be no science, without them there could be no order in human life. But they do not say that the value of a certain constant — measuring the elementary electric charge in rational units — is 137.037, and challenge you to see what is the next decimal point. They permit no analogous verification.

The logical positivists, who have been so much damned, have recognized the special circumstances in the natural sciences which, in an enormous renunciation of meaning and limitation of scope, have permitted a special definition of truth, and they

pre-empt the word truth for that. I do not mind that. I do not insist that the poet speaks the truth; he speaks something equally important. He may, but very seldom, speak the truth: he speaks meanings, and he speaks order. Thematic, as opposed to propositional, discourse is the typical function of the public sector of our lives, which is where law arises, morality, and the highest forms of art. It is not best construed, though it can occasionally be construed, as assertions of fact about the natural order or the human order. It is best construed as assertions of experience, of dedication, of commitment.

We all know how great is the gulf between the intellectual world of the scientists, and the intellectual world, hardly existing today, of public discourse on fundamental human problems. One of the reasons is that the scientific life of man which, in my opinion, constitutes an unparalleled example of our power and our virtuosity and our dedication, has grown both quantitatively and qualitatively in ways which, to Pythagoras and Plato, would have seemed very, very strange, and even nefarious, and which cast a shadow over Newton's later years, as he saw what might come. Purcell, who is a professor of physics at Harvard, said a year or two ago, "ninety percent of all scientists are alive"; this is a vivid reminder of the quantitative growth of scientific activity. A friend of ours, a historian, much concerned with Hellenistic and 16th and 17th-century science, did himself a small exercise — to plot, as a function of time, the number of people engaged in the acquisition of new knowledge; which is a definition of science. It is, for about the past 200 years, an exponential function of the time, and the characteristic period is ten years. A similar plot of the publications in science follows the same law.

Now you may say, you will want to say, you will argue with me, that all of this is junk — that there are a few great discoveries, a few great principles, that anyone can master and understand, and that all these details are really not of any great importance in human life. Of course, many of the details are not; they are not even of importance in the life of the sciences. But, by and large, men do not devote their lives without some reason; and men will not suffer the publication of things which are trivial, derivative or irrelevant. We make mistakes, but, by and large, the volume of publication is a rather accurate professional judgment of what needs to be known in order to get on. And I ask you to believe me that in this growth there are insights, there are spectacles of order and harmony, of subtlety, of wonder, which are comparable to the great discoveries of which we learned in school. I ask you also to believe me that they are not easily communicated in terms of today's ordinary experience and tongue. They rest on traditions, some of which are very old, involving experience and language that has been cherished, refined, corrected, sometimes for centuries, sometimes for decades. And that is one reason why, if you were to ask me what are the fundaments of science, what the point, what is this all about — "if you tell me that one clue, I will tell you the rest" — I could not respond. This is partly because sciences are ramified; they deal with different kinds of harmony. And none of them can be completely reduced to others. They are in themselves a plural and multiple reflection of reality.

But it is partly also that the principles which are general, which, from the logical point of view, imply a great deal about the natural order of the world, have had to be couched in terms which themselves have had a long human history of definition, refinement, and subtilization. If you were to ask me what is the great law of the behavior of atoms, not as we now talk about them, but as they were talked about in the early years of this century, I could certainly write it on the blackboard and it would not occupy much space: but to give some sense of what it is all about would be for me a very great chore, and for you a very earnest and unfamiliar experience.

The ramification is also a thing which is hard to appreciate outside the practitioners. We do not, in the fields of science, know each other very well. There are many crosslinkages. There are, as far as I know, no threats of contradiction. There is a pervasive relevance of everything to everything else. There are analogies, largely formal, mathematical analogies, which stretch as far as from things like language to things like heat engines. But there is no logical priority of one science over another. There is no deduction of the facts of living matter from the fact of physics. There is simply an absence of contradiction. And the criteria of order, of harmony, of generality and of coherence, which are as much a part of science as the rectitude of observations and the correctness of logical manipulation — these criteria are *sui generis* from science to science. The world of life does not regard as simple what the physicist thinks of as simple; and the other way round. The order of simplicity, the order of nature, is different.

In addition to this, the sense of openness, to some extent of accident, of incompleteness, of infinity, which the study of nature brings, is of course very discouraging to public discourse, because it is impossible to get it all and whole; it is impossible to master it; it is impossible to summarize it; it is impossible to close it off. It is a growing thing, the ends of which are probably co-extensive with the ends of civilized human life.

This is a set of circumstances which has largely deprived our public discourse of its first requirement: a common basis of knowledge. I will not say what bad effects it may have had on philosophical discourse — that a whole category of human achievement which grew from philosophy and invention is shut off from the thoughts of the philosophers and of ordinary men. I will not say with certainty whether, in excluding this kind of order, and this kind of verifiability, one has not impoverished the discourse; I believe that one has. But in any case, it is a very hard thing, as I know from other examples, to talk about our situation, and to have to say "I leave out, I leave aside, I leave as irrelevant, something which is as large, as central, as humane, and as moving a part of the human intellectual history as the development of the sciences themselves."

I believe that this is not an easy problem. I believe that it is not possible to have everyone well informed about what goes on to have a completely common basis of knowledge. We do not have it ourselves in the sciences — far from it. I have the most agonizing troubles, and I would say on the whole, fail when I try to know what the contemporary mathematicians are doing and why. I learn with wonder, but as an outsider and an amateur, what the bio-chemists and the bio-physicists are up to. But I have one advantage; and that is, that there is a small part of one subject that I know well enough to have deep in me the sense of knowledge and of ignorance. And just this is perhaps not wholly unattainable in a much wider scale. It is perhaps not wholly out of the question to restore to all of us a good conscience about our reason, by virtue of the fact that we are in touch with some of its most difficult and some of its most brilliant, and some of its most lovely operations.

As to the question of a stable, shared tradition, I have of course been talking about philosophy in a predominantly secular culture. I have not included as part of the sources of tradition a living revelation, or a living ecclesiastical authority. It is not so much that I wish to exclude it; but if our deliberations are to have general contemporary meaning, they must take into account the fact that our culture is secular, and may well have to develop as a secular culture. Our tradition, strong though it is — and I think the European tradition may vie with the Chinese and the Indian in this respect — is buffeted by the eruption of change. You are all aware of how unprepared we were for the tragedies of the 20th century when it opened, and how bitter, corrosive and indigestible many of them have been. I think primarily of the two World Wars and the totalitarian revolutions. But take one example. We certainly live in the heritage of a Christian tradition. Many of us are believers; but none of us is immune from the injunctions, the hopes and the order of Christianity. I find myself profoundly in anguish over the fact that no ethical discourse of any nobility or weight has been addressed to the problem of the new weapons, of the atomic weapons. There has been much prudential discussion. much strategic discussion, game theory. This is recent, and I welcome it, because as little as five or seven years ago, there was no discussion of any kind; that was certainly worse. But what are we to make of a civilization which has always regarded ethics as an essential part of human life, and which has always had in it an articulate, deep, fervent conviction, never perhaps held by the majority, but never absent: a dedication to "ahinsa", the Sanskrit word that means, "doing no harm or hurt", which you find in Jesus — as well as, of course, the opposite — and clearly, and simply, in Socrates. What are we to think of such a civilization, which has not been able to talk about the prospect of killing almost everybody, except in prudential and game-theoretic terms? Of course, people *do*: thus Lord Russell writes, as do others; but these people want heaven and earth too. They are not in any way talking about deep ethical dilemmas, because they deny that there are

such dilemmas. They say that if we behave in a nice way, we will never get into any trouble. But that, surely, is not ethics.

I, of course, am not now very deep in these things. In 1945, in 1949, perhaps now, there have been crucial moments in which the existence of a public philosophical discourse, not aimed at the kind of proof which the mathematicians give, not aimed at the kind of verifiability which the biologists have, but aimed at the understanding of the meaning, of the intent, and of the commitment of men, and at their reconciliation and analysis, could have made a great difference in the moral climate, and the human scope of our times. I would go only so far; that is to say that in all those instances in which the West, notably my own country, has expressed the view that there was no harm in using the super-weapons, provided only that they were used against an antagonist who had done some wrong, we have been in error; and that our lack of scruple, which grew historically out of the strategic campaigns of the second World War, the total character of that war, and the numbing and indifference of which responsible people then complained, of which Mr. Stimson complained bitterly, has been a very great disservice to the cause of freedom and to the cause of free men.

And as to the third of the pre-conditions of public discourse and of philosophy, this, I think, has to do with an overemphasis characteristic of the Renaissance, and natural after Scholasticism, of the role of certitude. If we think of most of Plato, all the early Plato, we can hardly imagine a more useful exploration of the central ideas of high Athenian culture. Plato does not end his discussions with any summary; in that respect, they may be a model for ours. And the purpose is not the attainment of certainty. The purpose is the exploration of meaning. The purpose is the exploration of what men wish, intend, hope, cherish, love and are prepared to do. My belief is that if the common discourse can be enriched by a more tolerant and humane welcome for the growth of science, its knowledge, its intellectual virtue — I am not now speaking of machinery, for this is another problem — it may be more easily possible to accept the role of clarification and of commitment which is the true purpose of philosophy, and not to hang around its neck that dread, dead bird, "How can you be sure?", which has, I believe, stunted philosophy, even in its great days, its great modern days, and which has driven it actually almost out of existence at the present moment.

I would think that we could look to a future in which, very high on the list of the purposes of consumption and leisure, was knowledge and thought, a future in which the intellectual vigor of man had a greater scope than at any time in history, and in which, to quote what Mr. Rostow said, man is free to love, to live, and to know. I believe that it is largely, of course not wholly, through living, which is so deeply the function of the arts, and through knowing, which is largely the function of the sciences, that the function of the philosopher, which is loving, can be most richly supported. It is, I think, no accident that the optimistic view of the present, and especially of the American present, came from Rostow. For if you examine the situation of the Common Law, and I think, above all, of the American Common Law, you see that the common basis of knowledge, the stable shared tradition, and the recognition of the importance of nonpropositional knowledge, are all highly characteristic of this community — one of the most successful communities in our century. One cannot extend that community, one cannot transplant that community to the wider framework of talking about everything; but one can learn something from its existence.

I know that, technically, the questions I have raised are formidable in a most discouraging way: How are we to learn a little more of what goes on in this world, and to be satisfied with understanding, in places where certitude is unattainable? I think we may regard the exploration of these questions as quite beyond the scope of our discussions here. I am not very wise about them; but I am deeply sure of one thing, and that is that they require effort and discipline and dedication, and that, in the measure in which we come to understand the reasons for this, we may also find ways of doing it. I find it hard to believe that with the greatest intellectual activity of all time taking place in the next room, catholic, public, common understanding will be possible unless we open the doors. ❏

Rheinfelden, Switzerland, September, 1959

To the Film Industry in Crisis

Not you, lean quarterlies and swarthy periodicals
with your studious incursions toward the pomposity of ants,
nor you, experimental theatre in which Emotive Fruition
is wedding Poetic Insight perpetually, nor you,
promenading Grand Opera, obvious as an ear (though you
are close to my heart), but you, Motion Picture Industry,
it's you I love!

In times of crisis, we must all decide again and again
whom we love.
And give credit where its due: not to my starched nurse,
who taught me
how to be bad and not bad rather than good (and has
lately availed
herself of this information), not to the Catholic Church
which is at best an over-solemn introduction to cosmic
entertainment,
not to the American Legion, which hates everybody, but
to you,
glorious Silver Screen, tragic Technicolor, amorous
Cinemascope,
stretching Vistavision and startling Stereophonic Sound,
with all
your heavenly dimensions and reverberations
and iconoclasms! To
Richard Barthelmess as the "tol'able" boy barefoot and
in pants,
Jeanette MacDonald of the flaming hair and lips and long,
long neck,
Sue Carroll as she sits for eternity on the damaged fender
of a car
and smiles, Ginger Rogers with her pageboy bob like a
sausage
on her shuffling shoulders, peach-melba-voiced Fred
Astaire of the feet,
Erich von Stroheim, the seducer of mountain-climbers'
gasping spouses,
the Tarzans, each and every one of you (I cannot bring
myself to prefer
Johnny Weissmuller to Lex Barker, I cannot!), Mae West
in a furry sled,

her bordello radiance and bland remarks, Rudolph Valentino
of the moon,
its crushing passions, and moon-like, too, the gentle
Norma Shearer,
Miriam Hopkins dropping her champagne glass off Joel
McCrea's yacht
and crying into the dappled sea, Clark Gable rescuing
Gene Tierney
from Russia and Allan Jones rescuing Kitty Carlisle from
Harpo Marx,
Cornel Wilde coughing blood on the piano keys while Merle
Oberon berates,
Marilyn Monroe in her little spike heels reeling through
Niagara Falls,
Joseph Cotten puzzling and Orson Welles puzzled and
Dolores del Río
eating orchids for lunch and breaking mirrors, Gloria
Swanson reclining,
and Jean Harlow reclining and wiggling, and Alice Faye
reclining
and wiggling and singing, Myrna Loy being calm and wise,
William Powell
in his stunning urbanity, Elizabeth Taylor blossoming,
yes, to you
and to all you others, the great, the neargreat, the
featured, the extras
who pass quickly and return in dreams saying your one
or two lines,
my love!
Long may you illumine space with your marvelous
appearances, delays
and enunciations, and may the money of the world
glitteringly cover you
as you rest after a long day under the klieg lights with
your faces
in packs for our edification, the way the clouds come often
at night
but the heavens operate on the star system. It is a divine
precedent
you perpetuate! Roll on, reels of celluloid, as the great
earth rolls on!

—FRANK O'HARA

VIOLENCE IN VENICE

DONALD WINDHAM

For three days after the attempted assassination of Togliatti in 1948, Venice was a city cut off from the rest of the world; and I was uneasy. Both my American passport and my Italian *soggiorno* were expired. I had made endless trips to the Questura to renew the *soggiorno*. Each time I was asked the same questions, just as though I never had been there before, and told to return in ten days. This had gone on for three months. At the American Consul's office I had no more success. A woman with a drawling southern voice explained to me that the office had been open less than a year since the war and was therefore not yet ready to do anything. I went to a party which otherwise I would not have attended, because I was assured that the Consul himself would be there. After talking with him and his wife for a while I told him of my dilemma. He laughed and replied: Well, I don't know who can renew it for you, but I certainly know that I can't. At last the southern woman suggested that I go to Florence or Milan, both of which were a day's journey away, and try the Consuls there. So I decided to leave Venice with a friend who was on his way to Sirmione, a small town on the Lago di Garda and on the route to Milan. Then, in Rome someone attempted to assassinate the Communist leader, Togliatti, and for three days Venice was a dead city, cut off from the rest of the world by a general strike.

The morning of that day I had been working in my room in the palazzo of an American woman with whom I was staying. She had rented a house which overlooked the Grand Canal and she had given me two rooms on the back of the top floor where her studio was, a small sleeping room with a bed, a chest and a vinecovered window through which I could overhear all the morning conversation and evening music in the house across the calle, and a working room. This latter was so large that it seemed bare although it contained a great table at which I worked, an enormous altarpiece showing the unfortunate ends of a number of saints who were hacked to pieces, two wooden sculptures of Christ on the cross, three paintings of the Pieta, and a gigantic window across which I always kept the curtain partly drawn and through which came the only sounds in the room, the splash of water and the bump of wooden boat ends against the stone wall of the building. I had finished my morning's work and eaten lunch with my hostess in her studio, and in the early afternoon when the town is usually asleep I decided to walk to San Marco.

Although it was bright sunny weather I had not been to the beach for several days and I thought that when I reached San Marco I might take the boat for the Lido. Or perhaps I would sit in the square and look at the palace of the Doges and the other white buildings in the afternoon sunlight. The beauty of white in Venice is the most magical sight there: from the edge of the Grand Canal where the boats leave for the Lido, you can see not only the marble of the buildings lining the Piazza San Marco, but the two white towers of the island across the canal, glowing always, but especially when the sky is dark behind them in the late afternoon or before a rainstorm when the sun has left the piazza and the water in shadow but has lingered on the towers. The last time that I had returned from the Lido, just after I came off the boat a sudden hailstorm had polka-dotted the dark pavement of the piazza with white balls of ice, and immediately afterwards a rainbow had curved across the dark sky in front of which the two white San Giorgio towers, the seagulls wheeling over the channel, the posts making the course of the boats from the mouth of the Grand Canal to the Lido, and even the white-uniformed sailors walking along the water's edge, all had glowed with a white so miraculous that they had seemed carved of incandescent alabaster.

But this was only one aspect of the sudden beauty and serenity of Venice — and perhaps it is these qualities, beauty and serenity, although they do not seem so remarkable while one is there, which make Venice so enticing in memory. For in retrospect innumerable other examples of serenity shine forth: the public clocks and church bells which chime the hours varying up to as much as a quarter of an hour, although an incredible explosion at noon each day, by which anyone would have thought they could have coordinated themselves, always made me jump out of my chair: the local cinema which sometimes posted the serene notice — Closed because the film did not get here: the people who, when you tipped them, insisted on your drinking a glass of wine with them. and another glass, and another until the tip was all gone, and who in general always found something to be pleased about, the blonds of being blond, the brunettes of being brunette, although neither held the color of his hair against the other. So, although at the time I did not consciously treasure the city for its serenity, I was surprised when I came across a hint of violence almost as soon as I left the house.

I had crossed the Grand Canal on the *traghetto,* the ten lire gondola ferry service, and was walking through the maze of narrow passageways which lead to the Campo Morosini, when a crowd of men rushed past me carrying a wounded boy. They held him beneath his arms, dragging his feet as though he might even be dead; and in amazement I turned to watch them. But immediately I was struck from behind by several men rushing in pursuit of the others, and I turned back in the direction of Campo Morosini. A man was standing on the small bridge which connected the *calle* I was on to the square, blocking the exit from the square and shouting: Basta! Basta! to a mob which was trying to push past him and across the bridge in pursuit of the men who had passed.

Climbing over the side of the bridge, I made my way along the edge of the buildings into the square; it is one of the largest in Venice and it was completely filled with laborers milling about and listening to the sporadic speeches of several organizers who harangued them from beside poles surmounted with red flags. This did not seem a particularly healthy place to stop, so I continued on across the square toward San Marco. I wanted to get my mail from the American Express and I thought that I would find out there what had happened. But like most of the shops which I passed on the way, the American Express, usually so fearless, was closed, the steel shutter pulled down over its front and locked.

At the Albergo Pilsen I found my friend T., and from the clerk there learned what had happened to Togliatti at Rome. We returned to the Piazza San Marco, which had been almost deserted when I passed through it a few minutes before; but now as we walked through the underpass into the arcade we saw that the square was half full of men and rapidly filling with others from the direction of Campo Morosini. A group of communist toughs, recognizable by the official red neckerchiefs they wore, was rushing the few shops which were still open and, unless the proprietors managed to slam down the steel shutters before they got there, smashing the windows and everything in them. In a few minutes the square was as closed as though it was midnight, and a buzzing silence fell over the afternoon.

The arcade's air of having outlived its period, of being a perfect but abandoned ballroom, appeared even more striking now, filled with ragged and aimless workers, than it ever had been when promenaded by awkward and ugly American tourists. The workers trailed about out of curiosity, in hope of finding out what was going to happen; yet they filled me with a vague sense of uneasiness, as mobs always have, not so much for anything they might do (as very few of these men paid attention to the speakers who had gone up into the museum at the end of the square and, with a shattering of glass, had thrust their banners through the windows and called for attention), but for themselves, for them as human beings equal to and like myself in their helplessness to direct the political forces which govern their lives. Most of them watched each other and whispered, or watched the few foreigners who huddled against the columns of the arcade looking at the workers. Many seemed interested only in sitting on the iron chairs of the piazza's expensive cafes, usually forbidden them, which they sat in gently and with a most respectful air, and if they moved them out a little, carefully moved them back to their original places before they left.

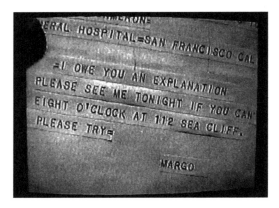

Seeing a square full of Italian laborers herded together like that, I realized for the first time that they were not beautiful as a class, as I had always thought they were, or at least that many of them were not individually beautiful or even individually sympathetic; but their rights as a group impressed me more than ever before and I could not help but half wish that they would be aroused into really doing something, not as mere pawns for communists and capitalists, but for themselves. Yet watching what was going on among them for those few minutes made it clear that whatever they did as a class would only stir up and displace the oppression and cruelty over them, not lessen or dispel it. Their chance clearly lay in the hope that the exceptional individuals they produced might be free of the pressures by which, as a class, they were enslaved as surely as they were herded together in the square; for as a class they could never do more than frighten their leaders into working out a few small reforms, or large reforms even, but before these could amount to much it seemed far more likely that they would be used as pawns to bring their civilization to an end and to make real ruins of all monuments to past glory such as the square over which they now swarmed. They were quiet except for the speakers and this quiet in an almost always noisy people was terrifying, as the sudden friendliness of an enemy is terrifying in a way his enmity never is, with the hint in the mob's whisper so noticeable in the silence over Venice that afternoon, like the hint in an enemy's smile, that once aroused this quietness and casualness would pay no attention to the reasons which usually protect persons and property against violence but would destroy Piazza San Marco and everything else which accentuated their poverty.

The young men with the red neckerchiefs walked about with the hard self-conscious movements of the officious which made them stand out even more than their bright neckerchiefs against the drab crowd, like ushers guarding the mob waiting to enter a movie theatre, or like soldiers looking over a lot of bewildered draftees at an induction center. Then the speeches ended, having said no more than the usual statement that the workers of the world must unite, this time against the assassinators of Togliatti, and the crowd drifted away in the sunshine, perhaps to be gathered together for another demonstration in another square.

In the arcade T. and I had encountered L., another young American, who had arrived in Venice only that morning. We had not known that he was in Italy, and after the what-are-you-doing-heres we started looking for some place to have a drink and talk. In all Venice, only the hotels were open, and they had their shutters pulled half way down over their doors so that it was necessary to duck in and out. on the terrace of L.'s hotel overlooking the Grand Canal we drank, and heard an elegant American dowager at the next table, glancing up from her writing pad, inquire of the terrace in general: Excuse me, but does anyone know the name of the gentleman they tried to assassinate this morning?

We ate at T.'s hotel, and afterwards we found the one bar in Venice that was operating clandestinely, — for a while. But the place was depressing; its specialty was dancing, and there was no music. The girls were sitting alone at a table and I started a conversation with one of them by calling to a kitten which was under her chair. She brought the kitten over and I bought her a drink, and we were getting into a fairly interesting conversation when the red neckerchief boys arrived, a dignified business man along with them to do the speaking, and demanded to know by what outrage of disrespect and defiance this place was still open. In no time at all the bar was closed and we were outside in the dark. No one felt like being alone, so I asked the others to come with me to my hostess's place where we might be able to get a drink of her American liquor.

The midnight streets through which we walked were just as they must have been hundreds of years ago. A few electric lights burned, but only at great distances, and groups of people whispered conspiratorially in the dark. When we reached the *palazzo* my hostess was in bed, and there was nothing to drink but Strega, which was too sickeningly sweet for that hour; and in a short time everyone departed, wishing that it were tomorrow.

The next morning when I awoke the calm was more noticeable than ever. I rose and went across the house to the balcony which overlooked the Grand Canal, There was not a ripple. No *vaporetto,* no gondolas, no *traghetto,* not even the boats which always passed in the mornings bringing food into town. I do not believe that there were many communists in Venice, but the general strike which they had called was certainly a success. Whether this was out of respect for Togliatti, or fear, or the general Italian delight in a holiday, I did not know; but in support of the last theory I must record that although there was no other transportation in the city that day, the boats to the Lido ran. Whatever else the communists did, they did not take the chance of boring the people, and it was possible for the population to go for a swim and enjoy itself. Those youths who could not get to the Lido took advantage of the boatless situation to swim in the Grand Canal. I never saw them do it at any other time, but throughout the latter part of the morning I stayed on the balcony watching boys dive from the high Accademia bridge and swim in the water below.

T. and I had reservations on the noon bus which we had made several days before, but there was no way of knowing if it would leave and certainly no way of getting to the bus terminal at the Piazzale Roma where the viaduct connects Venice to the mainland. Newspapers did not appear, and that morning the remaining electricity had been cut off and it was not possible to listen to the radio. The only communications with the rest of the world, and the only way of knowing what was going on in Venice itself, were the posters and leaflets which the communists printed and distributed. At least half a dozen posters appeared in every passageway — that is, at least half a dozen *different* posters, for there were hundreds of them on the walls, printed on papers of every color, pink, green, yellow, blue — all with variations of the same message, that a general strike had been called all over Italy in sympathy with Togliatti who, martyred and dying, lay in the hospital at Rome.

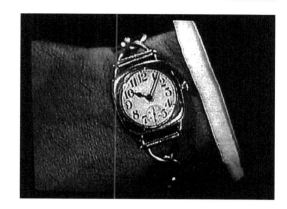

A plague might have struck the city; everyone, except the boys who swam in the canal, stayed indoors, and we followed suit. Fortunately, there was food in the house and the *donna da casa* prepared our meals. The strike was to be over at midnight, but there was no sign of it by the time we went to bed and our nerves were beginning to be on edge from the silence.

The third morning I awoke to the sound of. rain. Summer rain in Venice is short and violent. It starts suddenly, the sky grows an intense blue no matter how bright the sun has been a moment before, and drops as big and silver as nickels fly down. Then the rain stops, leaving the sky dark for a while, the canals as blue-green as the Mediterranean, and the sailors in their white uniforms and black raincoats glowing against the wet grey pavement. Then the sun comes out and dries everything and the universal glare returns. But that morning there was just a grey drizzle.

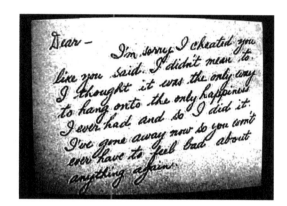

No one else seemed to be up in the house: I dressed, looked at my suitcases which were already packed, and walked about from room to room. I did not have a watch and I could not guess the time. For once there seemed to be no chimes. The rooms were vast and empty in the grey light, and I felt that I had to walk on tiptoes. But I could not sit still. I went downstairs to the library and looked at books and paintings. At last I ran into the *donna da casa* and she gave me breakfast. Then I decided to walk to San Marco and see what was happening.

There was no sign of boats on the canal, so I made my way through the maze of small alleyways to the Ponte Accademia and crossed over toward San Marco. On the bridge I encountered one of the men from the American Express walking along in the rain and he told me that he thought the buses would be running but he was not sure. A lone gondola floated along the water beneath us while I talked with him. As I hurried down the bridge and toward San Marco I passed no people. But the Piazza San Marco was lined with soldiers guarding the three sides of the arcade, and the square itself was filled with men standing in the rain, umbrellas held over their heads. Whenever they had a chance, the men rushed the soldiers and tried to break through the line and attack the few shops which were open. The soldiers were armed with guns and clubs which they seemed reluctant to use, but the communists were apparently even more reluctant to give up their successful threat and show of violence.

At both T.'s and L.'s hotels the clerks agreed that the buses should be running, and L. decided to leave, too. About eleven o'clock the three of us found a gondoliere who was willing to take us to the Piazzale Roma. We piled their luggage into the gondola and rode down to pick up my bags and to tell my hostess good-bye. Then, with the cotton flaps down on each side, the gondola made its way along the deserted Grand Canal through the rain and past the endless seemingly empty *palazzi*. No other gondolas passed. The carcass of a drowned kitten floated by. But the drone of the rain on the canal was broken only by the splash of our oars and the bounce of our boat along the water.

The Piazzale Roma was swarming with activity. Mayhem started the moment we stepped ashore, To our surprise the *gondoliere* charged us only 1500 lire, no more than the ordinary fee; but a wildly avaricious group of porters grabbed at our arms and legs and bags from all directions. We were used to porters; but it was hard not to remember that these were the same people who had been harangued in the squares the day before, and easy to feel that any procommunist sympathy was consciously anti-American. I had left off my seersucker coat and dressed in my Italian suit, and I looked somewhat Italian, to my own imagination anyway; but there was absolutely nothing which could be done to disguise T.

The porters demanded three hundred lire each for carrying the bags about three hundred feet, and they denied being able to make change. I had to buy a *kilo* of peaches to persuade a fruit vendor to change a thousand lire note. I did not mind, however, as the fruit in Venice was the best I had eaten anywhere; and I stuffed the peaches into my raincoat pocket to eat on the bus. But as soon as I paid the porters they promptly disappeared and left us and all our luggage in the middle of a roaring confusion of people and buses.

Everyone who had made reservations for the last three days was there, swarming about and trying to find out which bus went where. After a few attempts, T. and I discovered one bound for Milan and made our way inside, dragging our suitcases with us. I should have known that this was wrong if I had thought about it, for there is no space inside Italian buses for luggage; but we were reminded soon enough by the shrieks of the other passengers as they poured in, and we handed the bags out a window in the back. A few minutes after the bags vanished it occurred to me that we had no idea where they had gone and I went out to find them. They were sitting on the pavement not far away, guarded by a man I had not seen before. I tipped him a hundred lire for having watched them, although it seemed likely from the expression on his face that he had meant to steal them, and I bribed the bus attendant, at the rate of a hundred lire each, to put the bags on the top of the bus where they belonged.

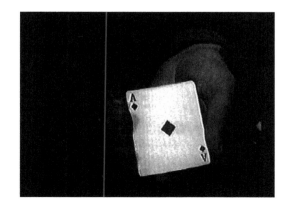

When I returned inside and started looking for my ticket, I discovered that all the peaches which had not fallen out of my raincoat pocket had been smashed into a peach soup in which the ticket was floating. I dried it off and handed it to the suspicious conductor. Then, in a moment of calm as T. and I began to look out the window for L., whom we had not seen since we were separated from him as we stepped from the gondola, the bus started; and that was the last we saw of L.; but I presume that he departed safely, and I have since heard that he wrote a novel about his two days in Venice.

On the viaduct leaving Venice the bus passed several barricades of machine guns and soldiers, and as it approached the *autostrada* it was halted by a maze of tanks across the road and searched. Perhaps the government suspected that the communists were attempting to sabotage the transportation system out of Venice. Or perhaps they were merely looking for someone.

The rain had ceased but the sky was still grey; and Padova, as we passed through, was overcast with the same besieged air which we had left in Venice. I began to believe that the threat of national violence which had hung over all of Italy since the election in the spring had broken out at last.

But when we reached Verona, seventy miles from Venice, it was as peaceful as though nothing violent had ever happened there. The population was out in full force, happily promenading to the end of the curved sidewalk opposite the ancient arena, turning around, and promenading back again.

Peschiera, where the bus let us out, is a small town with men sitting around the square much as they might be in a town of equal size in the United States. I was happy to see that if they were talking about what had happened the last few days they were talking about it with the seriousness of those not involved, a seriousness as comforting as the humor of T., who had spent our trip describing it as though he were a used-car dealer's wife from the middle west, although born in Selma, Alabama, mind you, and simply appalled at the foreign going-ons.

The bus for Sirmione would not leave for hours, so we bargained with one of the men at the cafe for a taxi. He sent for the driver, and soon we were on our way. When we arrived at Sirmione and the driver turned around to be paid, he was one of the most cross-eyed men I have ever seen and if I had not just ridden five miles with him I would not have believed that he could drive a car. This gave me the feeling that he had followed us from Venice, for one of the most disconcerting things I had noticed there had been the large number of cross-eyed people whose presence somehow had seemed a warning in the midst of all the serenity and beauty. But he was the last Venetian note.

Sirmione. *Catullus's all-but-island, olive-silvery Sirmio.* One of the wonders of Italy is that no matter how short a trip you make the place at which you arrive is different from the place you have left, and somehow more beautiful. The Lago di Garda was tropical in its blueness, and there was even a royal palm in the yard of the hotel; but at the far end of the lake the mountains were cloud-drifted like the Alps.

Immediately after our arrival there was a downpour, also tropical in its brevity and violence; then the sun set as clean and as serene as morning after the nightmare of Venice. In the orphanage next door to the hotel the children in their wooden-soled shoes were running on the cement pavement of the yard. A cricket was chirping in the garden where the servants were setting the supper tables, clinking the glasses together; and beyond on the wharf the fishermen were sorting nets, the round metal rings chiming as they dropped to the concrete. Then it became almost silent; the orphans were at rest, but reciting something softly, probably their prayers. Out on the lake, all silver and blue, the projecting funnel of the lake steamer which had been sunk during the war threw a shadow across the water. The clock struck six. T. came into my room and said that it was time for a martini. ❑

Note: *T. is Truman Capote who, in the chapter of* Local Color *titled "To Europe", has published an entirely different version of these events. L. is Robert Lowrey; I do not think he ever published a novel about Venice. Togliatti is Togliatti.*

a Dogtown Common blues

Excerpt from *The Maximus Poems* part II

**Cross Alewife brook
at Cherry Street
and you won't pay a toll
Lucy Gordon will keep your cattle lolling
at the foot of Fox Hill**

**Within three weeks after John Baddeford
made a voyage to Surinam,
so say all of the truth of this occurrence,
Babson, Day, Hammond, Ellery, Dolliver:**

> **"She shall not be worth a groat
> or have a house to dwell in
> nor to her back a coat"**

**One day at the Harbor
Kit Honeywell, age 12:**

> **"It was Peter's little ship
> which heard the command
> and went around the headland
> and came to where he stood"**

**Joan turned about
at the child's cry
it was sitting on the hearth
the coals lay just as they had been
"Thou or thine" had Alice said
"may be burned before long be"**

> **dry I will drain him
> sleep shall neither night nor nigh
> he shall live a man foredone
> shall he dwindle peak and pine
> though his ship cannot be lost
> he will he will he will
> he will not get home**

**not one blue berry not a stone
not furse. Choked by a huckle
tangled of catbriar**

**land situation at
head of Fort —
sand, below 'height' of
beginning of Western
Avenue: who
was there — first?**

**Nicholas Liston
'held' Western Avenue
westerly of
the head
of Harbor Cove:**

**when John Holgrave
bought of him
(2 acres) the land ran,
the grant said,
from his house "westerlie
& lying by itself"**

**Later, when it was Bridget
Verney's, 1669, the property
had "the common on the NW
side of it and the said harbor**

**and a neck of land on the
SE": which is the Fort,**

**and with that the 'pre-history'
ends: Bartholomew Foster,**

held it thereafter

—Charles Olson

MALCOCHON !

or The Six in the Rain

FOR JOHN ROBERTSON

DEREK WALCOTT

By the law came I to know sin

CHARACTERS

OLD MAN	Charlemagne
NEPHEW	SonSon, his nephew
HUSBAND	Popo
WIFE	Madeleine, his concubine
CHANTAL	A woodcutter
THE MUTE	The moumou

A CONTEUR OR SINGER, AND A CHORUS OF MUSICIANS with fife, violin, drums and cymbals.

The scene is an abandoned copra shed on a coconut estate during the rainy season on a West Indian island.

(A disused copra house built on a gradual rise between, left, a painted waterfall with rocks, and right, the edge of a bamboo forest. The shed floor is littered with husks, etc. The musicians begin.)

CONTEUR: In rumshops when the bamboo fife
The shac-shac and the violin
Mix with the smoke and malcochon
They say "Sing how Chantal the brute
Took the white planter Regis" life
And what I tell them is the truth
Don't believe all you heard or read
Chantal the tiger cannot dead.

(Labourers working in the canes. Old Man, Nephew and Wife carrying water. Drums.)

That day Chantal was stealing wood
Up in the heights above Boissiere
Three men, one woman was working there
In honest sweat like all man should
An old man they calling Charlemagne
His nephew SonSon and one Popo
Next to his woman Madeleine,
And this is how the history go . . .

(They cut the canes, singing. Old Man stops. Drums.)

OLD MAN: Rain! Listen. On the hills there, hear it coming.

(They stop working. Drums increase.)

Thunder. Look how dark it get. Is a storm for true, this rain.

WIFE: Aie! La pluie, la pluie. Come go, wooy!

(They run off as the stage darkens.)

CONTEUR: And up there Chantal chopping wood
Up in the wet heights by Boissiere
At the cropover of the year
Hacking the trees like they had blood.

(Above the waterfall we see Chantal working.)

CHANTAL: Meme si 'ous crier moin Chantal
Nom moin i' c'est Tarzan
Pis moin jeter ti m'iellette crachard
A dans youx un magistrat
Eux mette moin la jaule.
*(Even it is Chantal you call me
My true name is Tarzan
And just because I hawked and spat
In the eyes of the magistrate
You give me a year in jail.)*

(Thunder. He stops, gathers bundle, climbs down the rocks.

(Old Man, Nephew, enter hurrying.)

OLD MAN: Walk fast! Walk fast! You can't hear that roaring noise like is an animal self crashing in the trees? That's a bad rain coming, and make haste, make haste nephew, we have to Bocage before it reach.

NEPHEW: Don't break your neck for that uncle. We had to wait and get pay. And cash don't have no use on a dead man. We'll reach Bocage.

OLD MAN: You have my money eh? Good. Don't let it get wet. Paper money, it get wet it will get rotten, but make haste SonSon, make haste! We don't have time to waste.

NEPHEW: Ah! What you so afraid of? *(sings)* Listen, old man. One two three, the white man have plenty, When thunder roll is a nigger belly empty.

(Drumroll. Exeunt.)

CONTEUR: *(with dissonant music)*
The rain coming with a sound like sand on dusty leaves,
The leaves rushing in the wind like the hair of a madwoman,
The wind is sweating water, and the river moving faster,
Bamboos bending in the wind and groaning like the posts
That holding up the sky, the sicrier cries through the rain darkness
The hawk shifts on the branch, shaking knives from its wings.

(Wife, Husband, in the rain.)

WIFE: What happen to you? What's the matter with you? Let go my damned hand I tell you! You want to make me shame in the middle of the high road? I tell you he give me this bottle because I do some washing for him, but your mind so full of nastiness and mud. Let me go, I tell you. You don't see the rain coming?

HUSBAND: And a bottle of white rum, a cheap bottle of malcochon that you know which kind of woman does drink is all that red nigger overseer could give you? Look at your hair, look at your face, you like a crazy woman.

WIFE: Is you who crazy. Well, then leave me alone, or kill me then, kill me. Because a man give me a bottle. But I not standing up in the white rain to talk nastiness with you.

HUSBAND: You not giving me the bottle?

WIFE: I want you to kill me! Kill me, for me to dead laughing. You not no man, Popo. Follow me, follow me like a wet dog in the rain.

(Exit. Thunder.)

HUSBAND: Laugh at me thunder! Point your hand on me lightning! Let the sea show its white teeth and mock me if it want But before darkness fall, the rain will have cause to cry.

(Exit.)

CONTEUR: The rage of the beast is taken for granted
Man's beauty comes from enduring pain
The wound shall come when the wound is wanted
This is the story of the six in the rain.

CHANTAL: *(climbing down, speaking while Conteur sings)*
Even is Chantal you call me
My name it is Tarzan
And just because I hawked and spat
In the eyes of the magistrate
(leaping onto the ground)
They putting me in jail.
(washes his muddy feet in the basin of the waterfall)

CHANTAL: Chantal hungry. He hungry after spending three weeks in the forest eating bird, small animal, green plantain and sleeping in a trash house in the mountain before the rain come. But blessed are they that hungry for righteousness sake, as if they catch you stealing one green fig, bam! Is praedial larceny. And while like in the old days before God grow a beard they would cut off your right hand for putting food in your mouth, nowadays is just brang! brang! clang! clang! Lock you in the iron bars and the warder swallowing the key. Especially when is Chantal they catch. Give a dog with forty-three convictions a bad name and hang it. Now this is Regis land. I have nothing against Regis even on Saturday, but I bet you if he only catch me here washing my foot like a holy innocent, he will have a dirty mind about me. Must be my face. When I before the bar in petty sessions I try to smile, so, but the scar I get here in a fight once, and the fact that one eye smaller than the next not helping things. Oh, if only I wasn't so ugly, I could sin like a woman and nobody would hold it against me. Chantal while you talking you best look for a breadfruit tree to climb and pick your lunch. Hear? *(looks around)* And the magistrates these days so young. The last one didn't even look in my face, though maybe he was frighten. He only speak to his papers and say, "Ah, yes, Chantal, you come back from vacation, we keep your place for you, nine months hard labour, like a wife who just married and that was that." The dance was over and the violin was in the sack. Ah, I see one. With the piece of dry codfish I have and a nice ripe breadfruit, ah. . . *(stops)* No, I getting to be an old man and is best not to steal. If I steal again what will be the use of spending time in the mountain in the forest bawling "praise be to God". But is the only thing I can do well, steal. No. Yes. No. In the old days when I had all my teeth, yes, and when the madman Chantal passing through the village and just come out of jail, the children hiding round the corners singing "Tigre, tigre chou brule, tigre, tigre chou brule!" *(roars, then laughs)* That time I could butt an ox and kill it. But too much jail. Yes. No. They not feeding me, why they must beat me? On my back from the cat with nine tails have more stripe than the tiger. *(crosses himself)* God in heaven, maker of rain, pardon me, but Regis not going to miss six or seven breadfruit.
(Pistol shot.)
Ca y est? A scream! Something happening in those bamboos by there.
(Exit left.)
(Cymbals.)

MUSICIANS: *(together)*
What happen? What happen ? Ca qu' y' vive?
Ca il voit en bamboo ah?

CONTEUR: *(holds up hand)*
T' a l'heure. Wait.
(Scream.)

MUSICIANS: *(drum beginning)*
Ca y est? Ca y est? Ca y est?

CONTEUR: *(getting up slowly)*
Eux tuer Regis. Eux tuer Regis! *(dancing the action)*
He lifted up the ax.

MUSICIANS: He lift up the ax.

CONTEUR: *(miming the murder)*
And the madness start to dance! Hanche!
Is the ax in the wood! *(sings)* Tigre, tigre chou brule.

MUSICIANS: Aie!

CONTEUR: Hanche! and it raining blood!
(Dances. Fast drums.)
Woy! Woy eux tuer Reyez!

MUSICIANS: *(answering)*
Aie ya yie eux tuer, eux tuer
C'est Chantal que tuer, qui tuer.
(Drumming and chanting. Conteur in a fast dance imitates a hacked man, whirls and drops. Cymbals.)

CONTEUR: Haie!
(Silence.)
(Chantal enters, his clothes bloody.)

CHANTAL: Bien, bien, bien. *(sits on rock)* Who care how much it rain? *(looks at his hands)* Is now I should wash my hands in the cold water. Bien, bien, bien. Well, today life finish for me, just so. Like a flash of lightning. Like the signature of a judge. *(looks at his ax)* Is trees they make you to cut, friend. Not the tree that is a man. *(shudders)* The rain cold. I should wash my hands quick before the poison get down in the bone. *(goes to waterfall, then stops)* To wash hands is nothing. That is to put poison in this water where beast drink and men drink. Bocage is the source. A child that drink this water with a dead man blood in it, bien, is like putting poison in the source itself, for this clear spring bringing water to the villages. Bon dieu!
(He looks up in the rain at the sky. The Deaf Mute in loin cloth and headcloth comes from the baboos, carrying a bundle.)
Well, friend. We in it now, eh? You cannot talk, eh? Shit scared, eh? Un moumou. What's the joke? A dead man in the rain, face down in the mud and the wet leaves, and an idiot with no tongue. Why I come down from the forest at all, rain or no rain? And the bamboo groaning for a dead white man. I know you cannot talk. Nice one for the magistrate. Bon dieu! God what kind of joke you playing on Chantal? Who will believe me? An old thief. A madman. *(to sky)* How many times I tell you I change my heart, and is this you send me.
(Thunder.)
Ah shut up! You don't know what to do with this world yourself. What you have there, brother? *(opens bundle)* Silver spoons. A dead man for a few silver spoons. To hang for that. Come mongoose, the tiger will help you. We'll chuck him in the ditch by the waterfall. Come. Leave the spoons here. O thief without a tongue.
(Exeunt.)
(Old Man and Nephew run into the shed.)

OLD MAN: Cold rain, dead leaves, wild wind, old bones
Why time can't leave an old man alone?

NEPHEW: Ah hush your mouth and be grateful for shelter.

OLD MAN: This morning when we pass through this
short-cut self
I see what look like a nest of young snakes. Listen,
There have days in this life that look like any other,
But an old man can feel frightened, and not from ague.
The way the bullfrog croaking with a note like death,
The angle of a chicken hawk turning on the wind
Listen, have something on this place, there have
strange beast
A man cannot see hiding in a forest. They have
bats here.
And in this trash they could well have snakes, Listen,
In the life of a man, all his errors, all his sins
Can meet in one place, in the middle of a forest.
Like to meet a beast with no name in the bamboo track.
I don't like the look of this day since cock crow.
What noise is that, nephew?

NEPHEW: What noise, except Bocage?
The waterfall there that is all smoke and white thunder

The basin that baptizing this estate with its name
Sit down, stop dancing around in this rubbish.

OLD MAN: Bocage. Bocage. Bocage.
They say that white water have strange powers
That it can make murderers talk out their sins
Talk out their sins for the whole world to know them
That is Regis land, the planter. Used to husk copra here
I work here as a young man when your mother
  was living.
It still smell of oil and trash, and the dung of small
  animals.
But I am like an old dog sniffing among memories
This was a rich estate once, before rats get the
  coconuts.
Shaddock, citron, orange. I used to wash his horses.
Regis. He living there in the dark house, a cheap
  white miser.
In the old days.

NEPHEW: In the old days, in the old days. Damn the old days,
Your mind like a sick crab forever creeping backwards.
In the old days they used to frighten us as children
About Chantal the woodcutter and madman of the
  forest.
And I never see him yet. Sit still. Till this rain pass.
What you doing now? What you looking for, uncle?

OLD MAN: My money, my money. I lose my money SonSon.
  True. True.
As you say Chantal.

NEPHEW: You give it to me. To put inside my hat.
Look, take the damn money and stop troubling me.
Blast !
Here! Here! Just now you will ask me for it again.
Take it!
You talk so much stupidness and nobody is more
  cheap!

OLD MAN: I didn't remember that I give you to hold it
It was paper money. And it get wet, it get rotten.

NEPHEW: I say take it. I sick of you forever checking on your
  money.
I sick of other labourers saying how much I make you
  work,
I don't send you to work. I tired telling you stay home,
Sit in your rocking chair, uncle, and remember all
  you want.
Yes, that is it. Sit there. You frighten to just think, hein?
Remember how your brother kill my mother for your
  nastiness,
A man making the beast with the wife of his own
  brother.
Take the money, take it, and stuff it up your mattress.

OLD MAN: Is not true, is not true. Your father had no right . . .

NEPHEW: Not where he is dead.
The past don't trouble me Is your damn begayaing!
What past is your responsibility, not mine.
Only remember they hang your brother, my father
  that was.

OLD MAN: You have his same blood, the hardness and the
  hatred . . .

NEPHEW: And you have plenty you can thank God the father for.
I buy you a gramophone that just gathering dust,
I treat you like . . . in fact man, look.

OLD MAN: The money I am saving
Is to buy my house

NEPHEW: Oh? Ho?

OLD MAN: My own dry house, where no wind come,
Where the rain cannot reach me and I cannot hear
  thunder,
A good pitchpine coffin. I cannot live in all this hatred.
Ah God. I could Be now in the district of
D'Aubaignan
Looking after white sheep on the pastures by the sea
Leaning on an old stick and watching the clouds . . .

NEPHEW: Go then. You don't want the money?

OLD MAN: SonSon, tell me the truth. You don't want me to die?

NEPHEW: I hungry like hell and is that stupidness you talking?
Die then. Go and die. The house will have more
  room.

OLD MAN: Wait! Look two men coming out of the bush.
  The money.
(Drum.)
(Nephew hides the money.)
*(Chantal and The Mute enter. The Mute runs
into the shed.)*

OLD MAN: Bon jour m'sieur. Big rain that eh?
Worse l ever see and I have near seventy years.
(Chantal picks up the spoons.)
My name is Charlemagne, this is my brother child,
  SonSon.
We working in the next estate is cropover time this
  week
And we was running on the high road when the rain
  bar us.

CHANTAL: You can call me Tarzan.

OLD MAN: *(to The Mute)*
And you sir, what they call you?
When strangers in trouble so with rain, even by accident
Is best to make friends.

CHANTAL: Nothing is by accident I tell you, old man.
That one, he cannot talk. Un moumou, you
  understand?

OLD MAN: Ay oui. Sometimes is for the best. Not your brother
  Monsieur . . .

CHANTAL: Vidal. Yes, my brother. I cutting wood up there, you
  see?
Pass Regis boundary on the Crown lands, is hard work
And making coals too to sell. Not in the rainy season
Up there is only myself and God sometimes.

OLD MAN: And your brother? He working?

CHANTAL: Yes. *(laughs)* He is a spoon stealer. Ay, you! The nephew.
Give me a cigarette, if I have to answer this detective.
What you are, old man, a bush magistrate?
(Nephew gives cigarettes.)
Alors! Labourers eh? Alors mes amis, I mean to say
  you flush,
Today Saturday, half-day, cropover on all estate, I mean
Maybe you and your father would buy a few spoon eh?
Buy something for papa, man. Look at it, look at it
(draws out pistol, places it on the ground)
Maybe a knife? To put in his back when he sleeping?
Don't mind the moumou, is only buy he want you buy.

NEPHEW: We don't have that kind of money for true Monsieur
  Vidal.

OLD MAN: And even we buy, what we can eat with silver spoon?

CHANTAL: What you can eat? Rice, soup? How I know? Oh, you
want to know where I get the spoons eh? Me, a poor
woodcutter. I will tell you. My dead grandmother give
them to me. Everybody have a dead grandmother, you
know what they are like, they only want the best for
you. Oh look at them, the poor and honest people,
their purses as tight as a crab's arse. Buy it for your
grandson old man and stick a silver spoon in his
mouth. Look at them, all you want until the rain over.
And I have a silver cup too, perhaps you will want to
give the priest, holy men.
(shouting to The Mute) Sit down mongoose!

OLD MAN: Monsieur Vidal, if my nephew and me can talk about
this. What to buy and so . . .

CHANTAL: Yes. Yes. The old full of wisdom. They know wealth is the
only thing in this world. Talk your bargain, old man.
(Old Man and Nephew draw aside.)

NEPHEW: What stupidness you talking?

OLD MAN: You see what the spoon mark?

NEPHEW: They could mark my name self we not buying no spoon.

OLD MAN: You know who he is?

NEPHEW: Which one? The moumou?

OLD MAN: With the crocus bag cloak. The woodcutter. That is
Chantal the madman. the tiger out of prison.
Chantal you hear about since you was a child!

(Cymbals. Shouts off.)

(Husband and Wife run into the shed.)

HUSBAND: Look at rain! Charlemagne, SonSon! You all lucky, you
get here first. I am deadly soaked. Bon Dieu these
grains of rain bigger than mine. Messieurs, messieurs,
messieurs! If you know what happen, old man. Excuse
me sirs. By Orangerie, you hear, me and Madeleine
decide to take shelter under the old saman tree and
wait for the government truck, well, by the time we
reach there I only hear badow! Force of lightning,
Monsieur Charlemagne. Well, hein, if I was Moses, I
would say "yes God" that's right, but I ain't stop to see
who win, who lose, Madeleine and me take off whish,
and behind us we only hear the saman tree falling
ahbargadangabasha! Like the fall of Babylon. Is a miracle I still alive. Well, well, when God snap His fingers
sparks can fly eh? I never so frighten in my life before.
Eh-eh, I didn't even see the strangers, pardon my manners messieurs, my name is Theophile Alexis alias
Popo working by Boissiere estate, you hear how God
spare my life?

CHANTAL: Well, I hope God know what He doing, friend.

(Wife removes her dress to dry.)

WIFE: Listen to the hypocrite, this good for nothing. As soon
as is earthquake, hurricane or thunder, the first one to
drop on his knees and cry God. *(to The Mute)* Mind let
me hang my dress.

HUSBAND: I am the hypocrite? That lightning would make devil
sweat cold. Of course I frighten, man cannot control
thunder. And if you see the river, stranger you will
know why my wife don't have nothing but a devil in
her. It swelling more than a nine month wife, carrying
everything down the sea, branches in the road. Just as
if the earth open and vomiting the dead like a grave.
(to Wife) Look at her, she don't have no shame, taking
off her dress in front of strangers like a street woman.

(Chantal takes out a piece of saltfish and chews.)

WIFE: Those who have dirty minds will notice. I must leave on
this soaked dress to get a fever, hein? That's what you
want, hein? That your wife could catch fever and to die.

HUSBAND: Why you don't drink the bottle of malcochon the
overseer give you to keep hot. The overseer give my
wife a bottle of white rum for a bonus, and she treating
it like a baby she make, though we don't have no child.
See how she wrap it up? You know Auguste the shabin?
The one that think he is a white man? Well, that bottle
there, is he who give my wife. All of us working cropover and we don't get no bonus. You get? You? Eh bien
my wife, she get. If you ask her maybe she will give you
to keep out the cold. Or why happen, nigger not suppose to drink it?

WIFE: Look at him. Look at him! The coward, the hypocrite. Just like a dog. In front of men he give jokes,
he can shame his wife in front of strangers. Look at
the brave dog that putting his tail between his legs
for a flash of lightning. Making jokes now and wag-
ging his tail for men to pat him on the back and say
Popo the comic; why you don't tell them how you
nearly kill me in the rain on the high road, instead of
making jokes about God? Is the bottle you want?
Here! Drink it and show off!

HUSBAND: I nearly kill you? Furthermore who you calling dog, eh?
Why you don't leave your coarseness for the house?
When I try to kill you? You lie! Messieurs you all know
woman . . .

(She wrings her dress out furiously.)

WIFE: Yes, yes, I lie! I lie, the dog. Look the rum, you don't
want it? I never see a bigger fool in my life. He jealous
of everything I do. If I laugh is to make my breasts
shake, if I take off my dress not to catch fever, if I only
. . . *(turns away)*

HUSBAND: Cry now. As usual. Hypocrite. That one! Ah, if a man
could only know. . .

OLD MAN: Popo, that is not the way to treat your wife in front of
stranger.

HUSBAND: M'sieur pardon yes. But maybe you married too and
hate this kind of madness taking you. Is not any dog I
am but that half-coolie thing there, because all the village praising her long hair and smooth skin, that is all
she have in mind . . .

WIFE: Mentir! Mentir! Lies! Lies! Monsieur listen . . . !

(The Mute acts disturbed.)

HUSBAND: Is not a joke when you suffering it, sir. For I don't
laugh at people suffering . . .

NEPHEW: Uncle, let us go.

HUSBAND: I know. I spoil this company. But when I ask her questions, like any husband have a right to, she only shaking her hair and laughing in my face and saying, "Kill
me, yes kill me", what kind of woman is that? What you
can do with that kind of woman?

CHANTAL: I not no judge, don't ask me. I tell you, listen. They say
that waterfall there if you bathe in it full of sins can
make the truth come out. If you sure is the truth you
want I would chuck her in it, but only if you can stand
the truth. Or maybe you could give her a present, a few
spoons? At least you can offer me and my cousin here a
drink from the rain?

HUSBAND: Is my wife own, sir.

CHANTAL: You see I come from spending six weeks there in the
rain forest on top the mountain cutting canoe wood
with my son here, and is a long time I don't drink white
rum with the human beast that is my brother, the mongoose, the wet dog, and with this dead dry saltfish and
the cold rain blowing, I would well like . . .

WIFE: Take it you hear sir.

(Chantal takes the bottle and swallows plenty.)

HUSBAND: Is true, man and woman could act like beasts, sometimes.
Bourreaux, bourreaux, bêtes sauvages. God put beasts
and spirit in all of us, and only God know why . . . Pardon,
messieurs.

WIFE: God! God! Stop calling God. God didn't make you the
fool you are!

HUSBAND: And He didn't make you the bitch you are!

CHANTAL: *(singing)*
Woy, woy Justina who going married to you
Woy, woy Justina who going married to you
Woy, woy Justina who going married to you
For I just come from gaol
And your face like a whale.
So help me God I going swell she belly
When the cassava grow!

(Thunder and rain increasing.)

OLD MAN: Popo, take advice of an old man who knows suffering
Who pass through jealousy, and all you all know it,
I see signs this morning from the time the sun get up,
Shake off his blanket and walk up the mountain,
That this day would be trouble, like one of these days
When God will lose patience and strike earth with
    lightning,
This morning I heard the bullfrog croak it,
A man must learn to love and forgive all that he love.
You know how my brother, how they hang him for that,
Is a madness that have no resolution except violence,
We not tigers and serpents and dogs, we are men
(Chantal gives The Mute the bottle.)
We don't murder and curse, we leave the old
    savagery, so

When you asking for justice make sure is not revenge,
And when you ask for truth make sure you don't
   mean justice.
Is not the truth I am talking here, Monsieur Chantal?

NEPHEW: Papa!
(Cymbals. All turn to Chantal.)

OLD MAN: I not fraid of him. That is Chantal.
(Chantal keeps swallowing rum.)
(Pause.)

CONTEUR: *(with drums and flute, fast)*
Oy! The river bed coming down
The river bed coming down
The river bed coming down
And the dead turning over!

MUSICIANS: Waie! O waie O! The river bed come down and the
   dead turning over.

CONTEUR: The dead rolling over, the dead rolling over,
The rain coming down and it swelling the river!

MUSICIANS: Waie! O waie O! The rain swell the river and the
   dead rolling over!

CONTEUR: Waie!
(Drum roll. Thunder. Pause.)

HUSBAND: Chantal ?

OLD MAN: Chantal the madman, tiger of the forest.

HUSBAND: *(laughing loudly, pointing)* This old man there with
the broken teeth and the crack voice, with one crooked
eye and marks on his face, this is Chantal the wood
demon, that we was frighten of as children? You
remember SonSon when we was boys together and playing till dark by the river or in the bamboo how we used
to frighten one another with this talk of Chantal?
Chantal will hold you! Chantal leave jail yet? Chantal
passing through our village, so hide under the bed? Eat
your food or I will make Chantal hold you? And today
this old tiger with the mange begging me for a drink of
malcochon in a shed? This is what we was frighten of,
SonSon! Look at the devil face to face! Tarzan of the
apes, the enemy of God! *(picks up a spoon and beats
his palm)* They had a song they used to sing about him,
yes, how it go again! Tigre, tigre, choux brule! Tigre,
tigre choux brule! Excuse me if I laugh yes sir, *(bows to
Chantal)* but I was so frightened of you as a child. And
now is as if you find out that life have nothing to fright-
en of, but of your own self. As if the devil is a joke.
Chantal, Chantal, well I going dead with laugh!! Believe
me I going dead. Madeleine, you don't hear what …

WIFE: *(pointing)*
Auueeee! Look! Look there! Bon Dieu!
(covers her face with her hands)

CONTEUR: *(faster)*
The river bed coming down, the river bed coming
   down
The river bed coming down, and a dead turning over!

MUSICIANS: *(standing and screaming)* Aie!
*(The Mute tries to run. Chantal grabs him,
throws him down.)*

CHANTAL: Stay there mongoose, you can't run away now.

NEPHEW: What is it? What is it?
(The Mute starts whimpering.)

HUSBAND: Where the brown water coming down
As if the earth crack open and give birth to a dead.

WIFE: There have a dead man there, his body full of cuts
Like an ax will make, if a man was a tree,
A drowned man turning among loose water lilies
Leaves on his face and turning in the water
Rolling in a muddy ditch going down to the sea.

NEPHEW: The force of the waterfall must be bring down the
   body.
But who is it? Who is it?

OLD MAN: Is Regis the planter. Regis the planter!

WIFE: Look how it catch up among the black roots
A dead man, a dead man, white cuts washed in rain!

OLD MAN: Oh God I know from the way the thunder spoke
And the writing of lightning that disaster was in the sky
That Bocage have a curse, and we all marked with it.

NEPHEW: The spoons! The spoons uncle.

HUSBAND: Which spoons you mean?

NEPHEW: The spoons marked *R*. Look. The spoons all marked *R*.

WIFE: Let us go, let us go. This place dark with rain
But I rather take the high road and face God anger
We have nothing to do with it. Let's go home I tell
   you !

CHANTAL: *(wiping his hands on his clothes, then rising)*
Before anybody go home, we will hear confession.
You! The joker! Put down your cutlass there!
You too, mister nephew. And woman, keep quiet.
Chantal will take confession. Now stand up together.

HUSBAND: Mister they will hold you no matter what you do us.

NEPHEW: We are poor labourers together, we are the same
   people.

OLD MAN: Leave him alone nephew and do what he tell you.
You say there is no evil any more, Monsieur Popo,
Well, look at the face of a beast that is drunk.
A good use you put that malcochon to, woman.
Look there and tremble, that face is the truth
And be a child again now, and tremble at
   wickedness.

CHANTAL: You say enough old man, from the time I was there
I hear all four of you talking about the truth,
Well, I will give you truth, see what you can do with it.
Chantal will take confession, so one and all, kneel
   down!
This rain will last long, and we have plenty time.
(They kneel.)
Saturday is a good day to die, is payday
God resting on Sunday. and on Sunday in heaven
(drinks from the bottle)
The priest who know God personally, say it is very
   quiet.
(kicks Husband)
Ay you ! You seem to have a good memory of your
   childhood,
You know your catechism? You know the nine
   commandments,
Nine. Not ten. For as I am magistrate here
I leaving out the one that saying thou shalt not steal.
Speak, husband. Or your head whistling from your
   neck
Like a coconut I steal when my belly making thunder.

HUSBAND: Let us go Chantal. God say thou shalt not kill.

CHANTAL: You know a lot about what God say. God not a fool
God know what man give, for mankind is a beast.
The beast killed God son, the lamb not so, of God?
So what God mean to say was 'Thou should not kill'
Knowing man will do it anyway, and the magistrate,
The priest and so on they did not understand that.
Say your prayers, Mister Theophile Alexis alias Popo
While I confess your wife.
(strokes her shoulder)
And you with the nice hair shaking in man face,
And always laughing "kill me" you don't like Chantal?
The old stinking tiger with broken teeth? I will tell you
Let us go in the bamboo and give him his truth!
No? You prefer to die eh, mistress? Well, say your
   confession.
This bottle of malcochon that the overseer give you
You get it by the commandment 'thou shalt not
   make adultery?'

OLD MAN: Chantal, tiger. Have mercy on that one.

NEPHEW: Leave him alone! Leave him alone,
What you frighten of? The past, you and my father?

WIFE: Is not true! Is not true!
(She sobs. The Mute moves to her.)
Moumou — ah. Is not true!

NEPHEW: They lie! They lie! On their death bed they will lie,
They have mothers who take their secret to the grave
On their birth bed they lie. My father was right.

CHANTAL: You hear justice talking woman? Well, now I pull
your hair
And I show your bare neck. Go and sit down,
mongoose,
I'll send a nice head for you to play with in your lap,
I lift up the cutlass and I . . .

WIFE: Is true! Oh, God is true!
Pardon God is true! Don't kill me! Is true, don't kill .
. . Popo, Popo!
(sobs)

HUSBAND: I don't want to hear it! Kill me! I don't want to hear it!

NEPHEW: You see! True! True! True! Lies, lies all the time!

CHANTAL: Husband, I have a cutlass hanging over her neck,
Pass judgment, joker. Is the truth that you wanted.

HUSBAND: I am not God, Monsieur Chantal. And not a beast
neither.

CHANTAL: *(to Nephew)* Well, you get the truth so speak now
magistrate!

NEPHEW: Kill her, kill her, you hear! All woman is the same.

WIFE: Kill me, Chantal, kill me. He cannot forgive anything
God give him reason and he turn his heart to stone,
I could never look in his face in my whole life again
I cannot stand the shame even of his forgiveness
Because even his forgiveness is a part of his pride.
What I am to him? What he think of me as now,
And before? To him I am no different than a sow
Giving birth to a blind litter in a nasty ditch.
I wish I had the force enough to want to die, sir,
But even if you kill all of us as witnesses
As you killed the planter, God will see our actions.
Don't ask him for mercy, because he will give it,
And boast about it always. Don't turn him into God.

HUSBAND: Madeleine, you cannot as a woman, know a man,
I am an ordinary man, a fool with ordinary sins
Jealousy is one, and love is mixed with jealousy
Like good and bad, beast and angel mixed in our
blood
Jealousy is a kind of disappointment, Madeleine,
That what we love is not perfect, but can get corruption
I love my wife, sir, and will be jealous of her
Till the day she is dead, and if God should take her
And leave me on this earth, I will jealous of God.
What I saying is the truth, don't cry Madeleine. Sir,
You can cut my neck off, but that is plain truth.

NEPHEW: Yes, yes and tomorrow she will do it again.

CHANTAL: *(to Nephew)* So kill her my friend?

OLD MAN: If you must kill somebody, kill me old tiger
You and I have seen all the horror of the beast
That walks on two legs, tears out his brother's heart
And serves it with tears as a feast of reason. Me.
Kill me. I am tired. And today I know the truth
That this animal here who could be my own son
For that is a truth that I never know and will not
Could be like a serpent for the hatred he have for me.
Kill me. Let the others go. I am tired of this life,
And the rain falling weeping for all the sins of this
world.
(The Mute gets up and goes behind Chantal.)

CHANTAL: Execution suspend. I drunk and hungry. I don't
know what to do.
I always on the other side of justice. But life is funny
Today I must play judge. I will let you all go,
But if I let, you all go, who will speak for Chantal?
I drunk and I hungry and I giddy with confusion,
I know somebody must pay for the crime, somebody
here,

Out of the six sheltering. Ah, what a trap this life is,
Even for a sick tiger. Look today I must play judge.
All my life I just do what I want, and leave the rest,
The responsibility, you follow, to the men who run the
world,
The priest, and the magistrate, the rich man, the . . .

WIFE: Chantal! Look out!
(Cymbals.)
*(The Mute plunges a cutlass into Chantal's
back. Chantal falls.)*
Aiee!
*(They rise and draw back. The Mute grins and
shows them the cutlass. He is trying to show that
he has saved them. He goes to the woman, wipes
the blood from his hands and strokes her hair
and dress.)*

HUSBAND: Don't scream, don't do anything Madeleine. Take the
cutlass from him yes, and put it down. He think
Chantal was going to kill us. Don't frighten, don't
scream, smile, do as if you like him and give him some
encouragement. Be brave. You see, he is smiling. Is
think he think he save us.
(Old Man bends over Chantal.)

OLD MAN: Chantal! Chantal!

NEPHEW: Let's go. Let's get out of here. The thunder passing.

OLD MAN: Go, beast, go. Allez bourreau. Let men stay here.
Your house is not my house.

NEPHEW: You fool. This man was trying to kill us just now.

HUSBAND: Make him sit down on the ground with you there,
Madeleine. Poor beast. Poor wet mongoose. Yes, hold
his hand and smile. And talk to him. Like a child. As if
he was a child.
*(The Mute sits and puts his head in Madeleine's
lap.)*

OLD MAN: He was trying to kill us, yes, and do your work for you.
How is it old tiger? How are you old tiger? It hurting
you my son.

CHANTAL: Tigre, tigre choux brule. Tiger, tiger . . . That is you old
father? Who did it, the mongoose? You see how a man
can have a good meaning and do the wrong thing?

OLD MAN: He think you was going to kill us.

CHANTAL: Maybe I was, maybe I was. I don't know, with all that
rum in my head. Where is the mongoose? Where he
run now?

OLD MAN: *(holding him up)* Let me hold up your head. You see
him over there, the woman have him quiet like a
child or a small dog.

CHANTAL: With a good heart. With no tongue, a good heart.

OLD MAN: He is a man, old tiger.

CHANTAL: Like a small dog he was, like a poor hungry dog with
the fur falling off and you can see the ribs, that stealing
and frighten, when I hear him in the bamboo thrash-
ing around to hide, with the spoons under his arms
and trying to hide. The other one had a gun, and he
was turning round and round mongoose looking for a
hole in the world to hide . . . He thought I was going
to kill you all eh?
(Sounds of a truck far off.)

HUSBAND: Madeleine, Charlemagne, SonSon listen! You hear it,
under the white noise of the water and the rain shaking in the leaves like when a woman stop crying, and
the rain is over. . . and the hawk shaking off the water
and the sun coming out is the engine of the Public
Works truck passing on the high road. We have to go
there and stop it. Come, Madeleine, take your dress.
Charlemagne, SonSon . . .

CHANTAL: What they will do the mongoose? He cannot talk,
make explanation, argue right and wrong with the
magistrate . . .

NEPHEW: *(bending over Chantal)* Speak the truth before you
die! It is he who killed the white man?

CHANTAL: Ah yes, the one who always want the truth, the one who love justice and reason and guilt before everything. Who kill him? Who is the murderer, who the dead, eh, tell me . . . what use the truth is?

HUSBAND: The truck, the truck, vieux corp.

CHANTAL: Go with them. The rain is over. Is not the sun l feeling on my face?

OLD MAN: I cannot go. Because you are my son. You are my brother. You are not the beast and the madman. No.

NEPHEW: Leave him old man. We will miss the truck!

OLD MAN: Go, go, s'autres toute! Leave me I say! Go and meet it: You want me to bring you to the priest, old man ?

(They go out.)

CHANTAL: Priest? What priest? What the priest can do now? What the priest know that Chantal don't know already. I spend my life with so much to send the priest crazy. I see and do things already in this world, in prison, in asylum, in the streets with this same old clothes that the priest could fall asleep hearing the long list of my sins. What sins? I had a mad life but I don't sorry for nothing. I fix that up with God already in La Toc asylum and Victoria Hospital and Royal Gaol. I don't want to shock the priest and make him believe man can be so wicked. Only God, who have a strong stomach and who is a very old man, who frightening the world He love could understand that, so don't mind about the priest. Only lift my head a little higher old man, take off this old cap so the wind can blow the hairs on this bald head and I can look pass Bocage water to the cold mountain.

(The truck blows. Shouts.)

They in a hurry for Chantal to die. Look how it wet and green with the wind blowing. Three years I working there, and sometime in the morning when the sun coming up, I did only feel to roar like a mad tiger praise be God in his excellence'. And look at the sun making diamond on the wet leaves. That's all the money I ever had in this life. A man should not leave that forest eh?

OLD MAN: Man have to live with man Chantal, we not savages.

(Truck horn. Music.)

CONTEUR: *(to slow flute and drum)*
Like the staining of clear springs the mind of man,
In blood he must end as in blood he began
Like mist that rising from a muddy stream
Between beasthood and Godhead groping in a dream.

OLD MAN: Chantal?

CHANTAL: In the forest there in the rainy mountain where no man was, I was a happy old man, just me and old God, but man have a time to come down. Lift me higher old man, and I will show you something. You see that place there, a little clearing there in the side of the mountain that Chantal cut out of the forest, there where a chick-en hawk shaking rain from its wing and flying over the valley to the other side of the clouds . . .

OLD MAN: I see the place, old tiger, but the hawk gone now.

CHANTAL: Is there I come from this morning, it look far eh? It look so far now, and the mist closing it . . .

(Dies.)

OLD MAN: Not so far Chantal, my son. Not far at all, old tiger.

(Truck blowing impatiently. Old Man bends over Chantal.)

CONTEUR: *(with faster flute and drum)*
The rage of the tiger is taken for granted
Man's beauty is sharing his brother's pain.
So God sends the wound where a wound is wanted
This is the story of the six in the rain.

(Thunder far off. Flute fading.)

CURTAIN

MELODRAMAS

(for Kenneth Koch)

By the North Gate steel mill
Ruby Kee sniffs her new muskrat fur purse.
Gasoline. Or is it asparagus?

Mai Lung in the new communal kitchen
With the black-hammer-striped-and-red-sickle-striped wallpaper
Plunks down the evening cereal. "Winded from your annual
                              march to
Protest the dirty sex practices of American priests, eat,
                              o old orphans !"

Near the South Gate laundry
Tow-wi the Waterboy indulges his state capitol fantasy.
"Tallahassee Negroes, in our tanks to Hartford."

Yes yes under an Asian sky the student work brigade
Watches the movie. Roland Young projected on the Great Wall
Wakes up wearing a woman's bedjacket.
The student work brigade sleeps. The lecture will explain.

Near the East Gate machine shop
The Army is learning its English during its calisthenics.
Prairie the record says. Prairie.
Pla-li the Army says. Pla-li. One two swing two pla-li.

OH-OH. The wallpaper is peeling on account of cereal fumes.
Graffiti are revealed of the Dragon Empress.
OH-OH. The projector breaks down in the quarrel on the
                              terrace scene.
Surprise toothbrush drill. The student work brigade returns to its
earthworks, refreshed.

By the West Gate glass factory
A rice-wine party in a taxi.
The water commissioners are driving to the mountains
                              for some acupuncture.

—KENWARD ELMSLIE

The world contracted to a recognizable image

at the small end of an illness
there was a picture
probably Japanese
which filled my eye

an idiotic picture
except it was all I recognized
the wall lived for me in that picture
I clung to it as a fly

—WILLIAM CARLOS WILLIAMS

FRAGMENT ON
MAN AND THE SYSTEM
Billy Klüver

Our concept of reality has its origin in a series of basic decisions we make about the nature of the world. The total reality we experience relies thus on our own commitments in order to become meaningful. This total reality consists in a large part of organized systems which show us how to act, what to expect and which insulate us against the chaos of an unorganized world by imposing order. The systematization of our reality is necessary, since pure chaos or randomness could only describe a one-dimensional world. Whether a system is religious, psychological, scientific, technological, social or moral, a painting or a poem, they all originate in a nonrational act of man and are only relevant because of our basic commitment to them.

The total reality of each man changes with time, not necessarily in a predetermined way. The systems change and grow with our new insights and as we develop new methods to describe the systems. Sometimes a system becomes obsolete as a result of the introduction of a new set of basic decisions. Sometimes a system may become false to us as we discover that the system contains arbitrariness or myths.

Although the total reality of each man is different, the interactions between men and between men and the world result in a convergence of the individual systems into general systems which are necessary in order to establish communication. The general systems will demand the same type of commitment as do the individual systems. If we do not accept the basic decisions of a general system, it is not part of our reality. The general systems are thus part of a general reality which is a product of our accumulated knowledge and of our concept of how the general systems should serve the individual best.

A general system can never control or direct the growth and change of the individual reality according to a pre-determined scheme. In order to do so, the general system would have to have the capacity to anticipate and fashion every change in the individual realities which support it. Such a control is impossible since each man's concept of reality will develop more rapidly than the common reality of the general system. The total reality of each man does not depend on the presence of general systems in order to be meaningful. A theoretical possibility may exist: that one man can be controlled by a given, external system (a machine). However, the economic effort involved would make such a venture meaningless. It is, of course, also possible that the realities of two persons can coalesce to such an extent that they can control each other.

Even though man is free in relation to the general system, the system will interfere with his individual reality. In the case of a conflict, the general system may destroy the individual or it may put rigid limits on his actions. It would be possible to look upon this destruction of the individual as an act for which man had no responsibility if there existed a given or *a priori* general system. But an absolute system, by the nature of man's relation to the system, can be only individual.

The general systems are products of men and man has the capability to analyze, understand and direct them. Since the interaction between man and the general system is inevitable, man has the responsibility to shape them in such a way that the general systems correspond as closely as possible to the requirements of the individual realities. Furthermore, man has the definite responsibility to minimize the possible present or future destructive interference the general system may have with the individual. These responsibilities rest with every man, since we are all committed to the general systems as well as to the individual reality. However, the responsibilities rest heavier with those individuals who have a greater understanding of an insight into the nature of the continuous interchange between the realities of men and the reality of the general system, and of their convergence into a total reality of man.

In this country, at present, the artistic and intellectual growth is a magnificent confirmation of man's independence of the general systems and his freedom to be in charge of the search for the ever-receding reality. The most remarkable aspect of this new assertion of man's freedom is the existence of the American Society, within which this can happen. Thus the new painting and writing give a deep validity to the form of this society. At the same time our social, economic, technological and military systems have rapidly grown to become more and more unrelated to the reality of the individual and to the general reality of the world situation. Although the system builder, by means of new tools from science, mathematics, psychology and technology, has achieved a greatly expanded capacity to analyze and understand general systems, he appears to be unable to make contact with reality. He views the individual merely as a passive element and attempts to give a description of him which can be used conveniently in his system analysis. He tends to be unaware of the consequences and implications of all the commitments he is constantly making. It is only when we know these commitments that we can judge the validity of the general system as a representation of the general reality. The consequence of the system builder's isolation from reality is that the general systems are drifting without guidance from meaningful decisions made on the basis of our total knowledge. This drift will inevitably lead to a situation where an ultimate decision is forced upon us; a *fait accompli* which is destructive to man.

The realization of this situation implies a responsibility for the ultimate decision, since it will interfere destructively with the reality of man. We are thus equally responsible for all the commitments made by the system builder which lead him to face the crucial last decision. A few examples of these commitments may be as follows. Fundamentally he is committed to the present state of logic, mathematics and science, since these provide him with tools for his work. Moreover, he is committed to the observable experience or "facts". His unawareness that these commitments only form a limited part of the total reality may be destructive. He is, of course, committed to his education and to his special interests, as well as to his own character which may be such that he tends to look for order where there should be no order. His moral beliefs may affect his system in such a way that he imposes moral criteria, where these are irrelevant. The instruments he has available will condition him to look for certain things, as the presence of a large computer may lead him to "over quantize" his problems. He commits himself to find "answers" whose only justification may be found in the structure of the government contract, in the demands of his own organization or in the economic situation. Any awareness of the commitments made by the system builder implies a responsibility toward the system.

The present gap between the individual and the system builder should be closed so that the individual becomes an active rather than a passive element of the general systems. The system builder must be able to accept the fact that his systems ultimately rely on the nonrational support of the individual for their validity. He must realize that his new knowledge implies a responsibility to relate the systems much closer to the general reality and he must constantly attempt to be aware of the commitments he makes. The individual must be aware of the new capacity of the system builder and not be immobilized by it so that he can supply the system builder freely with the necessary basic decisions and with questions about his current commitments. If there is a choice between several competing systems, the individual should demand to know as many of the commitments involved as possible in order to determine which system corresponds most closely to the general reality. The individual as the originator has no one to blame if the system builder creates a situation unacceptable to him. He is as much responsible for the development of the system as is the system builder. The individual, furthermore, cannot excuse himself on the basis that all organized systems will become monolithic and hence destructive. The system builder and the technology have the capacity of providing the individual with any type of system, involving any degree of uncertainty or change: a system could even be designed to disintegrate itself. To accept that a dichotomy exists between man's assertion of his freedom and the solution of the general problems of the world is escapism. As a consequence of man's fundamental relation to reality, we can only commit ourselves to the existence of one total reality which includes both the individual and the general realities. ❏

ENVY
An Oration by a Graveside

When last I dreamt a battle, regretfully I had to
        Kill you.
I forget now whether you were a millionaire
        With that air
So characteristically theirs of waiting to be
        Handsomely
Amused but waiting in vain pained by one's failure; or
        With more
Newspaper clippings, girlish claspings, ahs and ohs
        And bows
From fine-antennaed students, more wit, the Rival Poet,
        Slick stoat,
Whose talent like the armored rose has tweaked apart
        My heart
Spasmed to alternate beats of love and thunder,
        Wonder
A neutral prior pain; or some suave party giver
        (Liver
Of many lives by proxy but not, alas, of mine,
        You dine
off roasts of the excluded); or a family patroon
        Can prune
My growing life through withheld sympathy; or worst
        A first
Man sans talent wealth or wisdom, functionless
        Unless
Absolute charm is function: if it is I've none
        (The one
Implacable recalcitrance to taking pains
        Explains
The dark side of theology: equal as the eye
        Can spy,
We are subject to the whims of grace and mercy: once,
        Good dunce,
The unprodigal son returned from ploughing father's farm:
        An arm
Lazily looped about a smiling waist betrayed
        Unafraid
His laughing happy brother, whose then partner sneered
        At the beard,
The glasses, sweat and gloom of a sour sensitive worker,
        No shirker
Like Well at Ease. The giggles died as in a spurt
        Their flirt
Soared to a total rapture of consenting solids and fluids:
        These Druids
Tunneled in love bequeathed to their Excluded Middle
        This riddle:
The spy has killed and so immortalized for spite
        Their rite
Else brief perfume like unregarded flowers); or simply
        A pimply
Child with far too long to live — but really its weakness
        Breeds meekness
Even in wicked uncles all too prone to see
        In free
Activity a threat to their divinity.
        To be
A child aches like an envy, staring ignorance
        In short pants,
Conscious only of lack. I need your death, sweet prince,
        But wince
Deprived, counting myself but bad till I be best,
        Dead pest.

—ALAN ANSEN

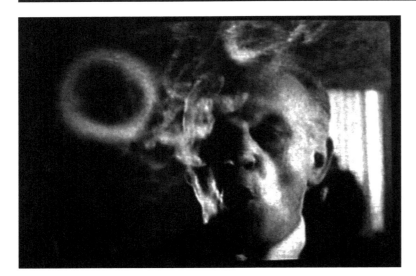
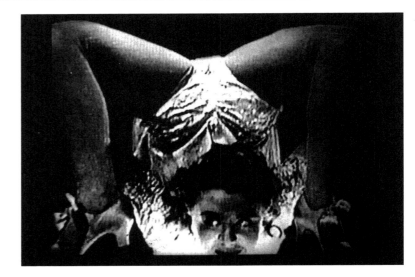

Love is a Many Splendored

TERRY SOUTHERN

1st (Splendored)

A CALL OF CERTAIN IMPORT

Scene: *A winter evening of 1914 at Kafka's home in Prague, where he lived with his parents until the following year, when he reached the age of thirty three.*

FRANZ has just come in from his clerical job at the bank and is seated by a reading-lamp in the small living room. The evening paper is on his lap and, after looking thoughtfully at the floor for a moment or two, he begins slowly unfolding it — when the telephone rings. From the adjoining room, where she is arranging the table for dinner, HIS MOTHER quickly enters, wiping her hands and giving Franz a sharp look, as she picks up the phone. FRANZ stops unfolding the paper and strikes an attentive attitude towards his mother at the phone.

HIS MOTHER
(frowning) Hello.

VOICE
Hello, is young Kafka there? Franz Kafka?

HIS MOTHER
Franz? Why . . . yes. Who is this calling?

VOICE
This is Sig.

HIS MOTHER
Who?

VOICE
Sig. I'm a friend of Franz.

HIS MOTHER
(rather annoyed) All right, you'll have to wait a minute.
(to Franz)
It's for you.

FRANZ
(raising his brows) Oh?

(He starts to refold the paper with care, then after a minute decisively lays it aside, gets up and crosses the room to where HIS MOTHER stands holding the phone, one hand over the mouthpiece.)

HIS MOTHER
(with a pained smile) It's Sig.

FRANZ
(in consternation) Who is it?

(HIS MOTHER does not answer, but gives him a knowing look as she hands him the phone and leaves the room abruptly. She returns at once and stands between the dining-room and the telephone, hands on hips, apparently waiting for Franz to finish the conversation.)

FRANZ
(darkly intent at the phone) Hello.

VOICE
Hello, Franz? Is that you? Sig here. Eh?

FRANZ
Yes. Yes, this is Franz. Who is this calling? I'm *afraid* I didn't . . .

VOICE
Oh, don't be *afraid*, Franz. Ha! It's *Sig*. You remember, *Sig?* Siggy. You know, *Vienna*, Sig. Sigmund Freud.

FRANZ
(astonished) Sigmund Freud? *Doctor Sigmund Freud? (eagerly)* Why, this is a . . . a . . .

VOICE
(jovially) Yes, it's Doctor Freud all right! Ho-ho! I was hoping we could get together, Franz. I've got some new ideas, you see — quite a lot of them actually, ha-ha . . . and, well, I'd like to *go over* a few things with you. What do you say to that, eh?

FRANZ
Well, I . . . Doctor Freud, I hardly know *what* to say. I mean, I never *dreamed* that I . . .

VOICE
(shrewdly) You never *what?*

FRANZ
No, no. I mean . . . well, naturally I wouldn't have *dreamed* it, would I? *(laughs nervously)* May I say I never dared to *hope*, or rather that I couldn't have *imagined* that my opinion . . . that is to say, that my . . .

VOICE
(impatiently) Now look here, Franz, I need your help and I need it badly! Now then, tell me this: Does *desire* — and, of course, I mean in the very strict sense of the word — does this so-called 'desire' for ejaculation . . . eh? . . . desire-for-ejaculation *precede* state of erection? OR does state-of-erection precede this *desire?* Eh? Tell me *that*, Mister Franz Kafka! Eh?

(laughs uncontrollably for a full minute: Ho-ho-ho! Ha-ha-ha! He-he-he! etc.)

Franz! Hey, Franz! Still there? Eh? Well, its merely a *joke*, Franz! *Merely another joke at your expense!* HAW!

(hangs up)

FRANZ
Hello. Hello, hello.

(jiggles the phone-hook) Hello, operator, we've been cut off. Hello, hello.

HIS MOTHER
(crossing to the phone and snatching for it, demanding crossly)

What on earth is going on here?

FRANZ

(anxiously, backing away, clutching phone) It's Doctor Freud calling, Mother. We've been cut off. I'm trying to get the operator now. Hello, hello.

(jiggles the hook wildly) Hello operator, hello . . . *hello . . . hello . . . hello . . .*

SLOW CURTAIN

2nd (Splendored)

AN ORDERLY RETREAT

There is tiredness in a soldier's walk through nights of winter rain that holds off fear like a grotesque brother. Tonight how they move as each were apart, away, and alone — it is the incredible walk of the wooden doll, the heartbreaking walk of the huddled, shutting things out. Are they dead or alive?

Only Singer is smoking now. Beside him walks a man half-conscious, his feet too deep in the mud. He is bored, terrifically bored; the boredom has come all down into his chest and stomach, leaving his insides shot through like a torn sieve, threaded with morphine.

"Let's have some of that before you put it out, Singer."

Singer, withholding it, looks at him in concern. "Listen, Joe, you din't see Al back there. when was the last time you seen him?"

"I ain't seen him for chrissake, I told you. I ain't seen him since they come down off the road back there."

Singer passes the cigarette, heavily, as though it weighed more than a cocked rifle.

"What happen over past where you were at, Joe?"

What is talk but diluted hysteria? And how in his cupped hands now in the night rain the cigarette burns as a chemical light, soundless and without heat.

"Are you kiddin'?"

"I mean where them tanks come down off the road, how'd it look there where they were comin' down off the road?"

"Are you kiddin' for chrissake?"

"How'd it look when you seen it, Joe, it look like it was takin' everthing, didn't it, how'd it look when you seen it?"

The fear of the infantry stretches out through time into a single quivering wire of tedium — or it may shatter tiredness, hunger and cold, on one bleak afternoon when inside the head, somewhere just behind the eyes: *the world pops open.*

"Listen. You seen past the house from where you were at, din't you Joe? You seen along that ditch, din't you?"

"Are you goin' to start that again for chrissake?"

"I m not goin' to start anything, you son of a bitch."

3rd (Splendored)

A BAD MOTHER-HUBBER

An extraordinary thing happened at City Clerk's Office the other day, where I went to get married.

The whole procedure, beginning with blood-tests, had come off quite casually. Granted, there had been certain delays — the usual thing, I suppose; but, in any case, the event I speak of occurred independently of the marriage, did occur, in fact, only just *after* the marriage. at the moment when the Clerk pronounced us "husband and wife." At that moment, my "wife" asked me what time it was, wanting, I suppose, to make some sentimental note of it — which didn't strike me as particularly objectionable, because it was in a more humorous than romantic spirit that she had asked — so I raised my arm, to uncover my wristwatch. In doing so, however, I upset a very large bucket of *paste* which had been sitting on a shelf at about head level just to my left. It fell on the Clerk, emptying all over the ceremonial robe he had donned before beginning the marriage. A paste, *this* muck had apparently once dried out because of the overheated office, and then had been remixed with too much water. so that now it was nothing but a lumpy slop.

I was extremely embarrassed — and especially so, I believe, because I had made no previous attempt to be friendly with the man; in fact, by having allowed my face to remain in repose, had appeared to ignore his one or two little overtures towards informality during the service. Moreover, I now realized I had no handkerchief to offer him, and could not even bring myself to make the empty gesture of reaching for my pocket. Neither could I bear to imagine the sound of my voice saying, "I'm sorry," in the small room; that, too, would have been such a hollow gesture — such a *drop,* so to speak — for this man, literally covered with a watery paste gone sour, a stinking muck.

My "wife," appalled by my apparent indifference, sank into the nearest chair, without a word, and remained there throughout the scene that followed. I at once became so absorbed in my new relationship with the Clerk that I forgot about her.

When I finally dared look at the man, I realized immediately that he was an eccentric. With his head bent down, brows furrowed, he kept clawing at the muck, muttering the while, and somewhat angrily, too — but *not at me,* and that was the queer thing about it. It was as if he had been standing alone on a street-corner, and a passing car had thrown mud, a lot of wet mud on him. He was raking off great globs of it and flinging them on the floor. From time to time he would stop and look down at himself in amazement, holding out his hands which were several inches thick with the muck. "How do you like *that?*" he would demand, "how do you like *that?*" Yet, he was not blaming *me,* that was clear enough; it was as though l had just arrived. But, even so, l could not meet his eyes; I was compelled to look past, over his shoulder. And it was then that I noticed the plaque on the wall directly behind him; it was a framed certificate, and I could make it out easily:

GERRARD DAVIS
NEGRO MINISTER AND NEGRO MAN

I forced myself to look directly at his face. With all that muck on his face, he was so *white,* or rather, so unlike anything I had ever seen before, that I asked at once:

"Are *you* Davis?"

He replied by immediately dropping his interest in the paste and robe and reproducing almost exactly the last lines of Michael Redgrave in the ventriloquist sequence of *Dead of Night;* and with precisely the same insane smile: "I . . . I . . . I've . . . been . . . waiting . . . for you . . . Sylvester." It took me thoroughly aback, but my previous humiliation had been so sharp that I was still on the offensive. "*Look,*" I said evenly, "that gag is old hat to me, Davis — *if,* in fact, you *are* Davis."

Now he regarded me narrowly and with exaggerated concern, like one of the old eccentric actors of the silent screen.

"What's the matter?" he demanded, in German *(Was ist los?)* I don't have much German actually, but I do know enough of it to recognize that he spoke the words in the harsh nasal twang of our own Texas and the Great Southwest. This was unmistakable, and yet the knowledge did not seem to give me any real advantage. Despite this I took him up abruptly, as though not to be put off: "I'll tell you this much, Davis — if you really *are* a *Negro,* or rather, if you are *Negro,* I'd ask you to fall by my pad, you know what I mean, like we could dig Bird and Orville and turn on a few joints of some great Colombian pot. Later, of course you could cut out, or, like, split."

He looked past me and slowly around the room with intense apprehension, knitting his brows fiercely.

"Who dat who say 'NERO'?" he demanded.

Whether it was a slip of the tongue, or a deliberate distortion, I was not able to determine, because he suddenly began a song and dance. The dance was common enough, a simple two-step, but the song was remarkable: it began as a Benjamin Britten-Elizabethan type thing, of no particularly deep feeling, but with great surface complexity; and then, at about the third bridge, it picked up the wailing funk of Ray Charles blasting on *"It's a Low-Down Liberal, Low-Down Liberal Shame."*

And then when the silence began to close in, somewhat like a shroud he went "ooh-scubee-doo-bop" — very softly, that's how hip he was. ❏

The Need Becomes Evident

The need becomes evident
until there's no other possible solution . . .

A gust can do. it, one of those autumn gusts, that
    come poking about, as you try to rake the lawn,
    bewildering the fallen leaves — before you've
    time to realize.
It's best not to frighten one's friends, so be
    careful to control your ascent. In fact, if you can
    manage the trick, try to walk so nearly touching
    the ground that only the most astute can detect
    the difference.
If you come behind someone abruptly, be careful to
    announce your presence with a discreet cough, lest
    they remark on your silent tread,
and walking over soft ground, or over snow, or coming
    in out of the wet, you must contrive to hide the
    fact that you leave no footprints.

As for the others, you can recognize them
by the downy feathers growing at each ankle, though
    well hidden, perhaps even plucked to evade discovery —
such as he who comes for the first time upon the
    head waters of a great river —
or he who dozes on a park bench and realizes the solution
    to a mathematical conundrum —
or he who goes at dusk to clear the cigarette butts
    and orange peel from a public fountain —
or he who takes all the children in the street to
    the circus —
    or he who scrapes the clay from his boots to model a
    face he saw in a dream.
Saying: "Hush! Listen! I think I hear it now. But it's
    worse at night.
I tell you, it's the trains that keep me awake, trains
    that aren't listed on any timetable, that accelerate as they
    recede.
I hear the mutter of the wheels and the groaning of the
    couplings and the heavy breath of the engines as they
    gather speed, the pistons vibrating like the surf upon
    some island archipelago —
but when I go to the window, I see only Perseus and Algol
    above the chimney-pots, and the frost bright on the
    empty tracks, glittering beneath the Milky Way."
But though you start, it's not so easy to get lost,
    not as straightforward as you might think,
to come to what you don't know, to ascertain that
    you can't he sure.
unless you stick at it, unless you remember to do up
    your shoes or kiss your wife according to the ancestral ritual,
unless you're lucky and happen to blink your eyes as
    the diagram comes on the screen, unless you sneeze at
    the crucial moment during the emergency proclamation.

There is so little time to be born —
so little time to memorize the code to unscramble the
    urgent telegram delivered at the funeral of the man
    you were a moment ago
        (Don't forget the password) —
so little time, you have to keep it locked up, wrapped
    in lead, in form of an amalgam, to be weighed out
    on an apothecary's scales
        (No export without a license) —
so little time that it scarcely seems enough for anything
    more than to sit of an evening watching the bees
    fussing officiously around what's left of the
    lavender
        (How well they do it) —
And a dandelion seed falls gently,
oh so gently downwards,
drifting into my garden.
I can't see where it rests,
but I will, I will —
so joy comes . . .

The wind blows.
The clouds scatter.
The roof of the sky tears loose.
And a child flies his kite above it all and cries,
"Look !" . . .
and a fulmar, three days out from St. Kilda, following
    the herring fleet, swerves and drops down between the
    crests, its wings stroking the long swells,
so the mind turns homeward, to its ledge on the seacliff.

—GAEL TURNBULL

Fantasy of My Mother Who's Always on Welfare

Whenever Minnerbia gets on the subway I get off —
she's so fat & dripping with all kinds of slime
even the air shreeks & curls away from her.
She warms the ink print off old papers she handles
& there at night on the platform she sleeps,
her bum snowy head pushed into night alone in the tunnel.
In the wake of the scream she dreams of her last baby,
her golden brown potato leg fat tonight covered by green,
her teeth brush dream is the one she loves most.

—PETER ORLOVSKY

THE PROMISE

ALFRED JENSEN

I. INTRODUCTION

Light is to all of us a universal reality and as such is accepted by everyone. Color, and the authenticity of its realness, is on the other hand a matter of dispute. Current authority believes that white light, measured in terms of wavelengths, combines as a oneness and makes the spectrum. The color-hue of itself has no interest. Others deny vehemently that white light is the summation of all the other colors in the spectrum. They base their theory on the color-hue itself rather than the light. The adherents of this color-hue theory believe in a double-mirroring process through which black and white interact, blending into shades which then take on the appearance of color hues. The immediate atmospheric condition plays the role in determining these gigantic mirrors of the atmosphere. Thus, the working, as the formation, of color depends on the continual flux of physical phenomena. The thunderstorm establishes a black mirror on one side of the atmospheric dome, the sun establishes a white mirror on the other side of the dome. The interplay of both forces produces the rainbow.

The prism structure consists of a twin mirror of black and white also, embodying in its crystal the atmospheric dome of nature. The ancient peoples, in their universal preoccupation with the double-mirroring process, regarded the prism as an instrument of divine origin.

II. EXPERIENCE OF THE NEW VISION

Color has intrigued me as a painter. I have attempted to discover new meaning in the worn out language of color: to invent, to arrange, to dispose, to organize such color into a form worthy of a work of art. So I undertook to build my concept which could endow color with new meaning. I used the prism for my research. I observed through the body of the prism a light beam crossing a field of darkness. I knew that the prism held the clue that would enable me to arrive at an understanding of the genesis of color.

The black-and-white mirror process in the prism paralleled that in the atmospheric dome, and this led to the idea of the checkerboard image. The affinity of the black and white checkers with the double-mirroring process reflects the alternating condition that shows the formative processes of color. The checkers traveling in a sequence of their white and black diagonals going both to the right and to the left, the contrast of the vertical and the horizontal, both are similar in their alternating rhythms to the alternating rhythms in light and darkness. This physical ordering reflects the cycle of man's destiny: the vastness of my former fears of darkness were resolved as I read first the dark square. I read second a light square, meaning: first night meaning: then day. The seasons I read, the years I saw appearing as images, the living followed by the dying in my checkerboard existence; and since every black is followed by a white, I found my place in eternity.

I found that warm colors, red and yellow, are formed on the black mirrored surface of the black checker; and that the cool colors, blue and violet, are formed on the white mirrored surface of the white checker.

III. MYTH

PANEL I — THE PLANNERS OF THE PYRAMID. The planners are seeking by the help of their checkerboard numbers a rule and measure of procedure. They are investing large areas with their magic number of seven, thus giving it a potential significance. The mirror process of color has been determined in the form of three white checkers (blue and violet) neighbored by four black checkers (red and yellow), totaling seven. Having the pyramid in mind, they placed six rows of white checkers on one side of the pyramid. On the other side they placed six rows of black checkers. These rows, as they cross, each diagonally, to form the pyramid, total seven in each row; the total is a square and the top rows, one white and black, symbolize the double-headed white snake on one side and the double-headed black snake on the other.

PANEL II — PYRAMID WORKER. The woman carries in the basket on her back materials for the construction of the pyramid. The basket is woven in the prismatic calendar year design. Their year has 360 days and is regarded as the true year; the five remaining days are unlucky and not recorded. The total basket design is shaped in two equal parts, each counting 180 segments; one segment forms a yellow-red arrow pointing to the right, the other a yellow-red arrow pointing to the left, the two arrows symbolizing the sun's half-yearly journey. Their year was divided into 18 months, and these are shown as a pyramid having nine warm-colored checker months intertwined with nine cool-colored checker months thereby giving them the seasons. These latter mentioned pyramids form the face, bodice and skirt of the worker.

PANEL III — THE EMPEROR. His image consists of the prismatic design symbolizing the law of the nine-square land system that marks the boundaries dividing the entire empire into plots of one-square mile each. Each one-square mile consists of nine squares; the eight peripheral squares are farms cultivated by tenants, the centrally located ninth square is their assembly meeting ground. Here the village head presides and, at this location, is in direct communication with the emperor. All lines radiating diagonally through every ninth-central square in turn lead directly to the emperor's palace.

The Siamese twin pyramids co-join to form the emperor's legs, the left leg symbolizing the moon's cross, the right symbolizing the sun's cross. Two twenty-four diamond pyramid structures form the emperor's head; reading the first from above we read four rows of cool colored diamonds alternating with three sequential rows of warm colored diamonds; the second pyramid reads warm and cool. In order to solve this problem of unequal warm and cool distribution, the emperor decides to divide these 48 diamonds by 4 and gets the astonishing result of 56 diamonds, which form his scepter consisting of four 14-part diamond shapes which, in turn, illustrates the Golden Section color rule. Here the magic number seven, four warm checkers neighbored by three cool checkers or vice versa, determines the rule.

PANEL IV — THE MAGICIAN. His body is composed in the image of his skill with numbers, totaling 100 squares, divided into four 25-checkered units, each unit containing a central cross representing each of the four fundamental colors, red, yellow, blue, and violet. He is surrounded by many magic formulas, such as the eagle image formed by a ring made up of 14 colored checkers which enclose a symbol of a four black-checkered cross that is diagonally penetrated by a three checkered white beam of light. This bird appears in its reverse also. This eagle configuration isolates the virgin magic number of seven from which the Golden Section color rule was formulated. The magician's mouth is constructed in the sun-and-moon goddess's brain image, a stellar shape built up of 16 cool colored diamonds and 12 warm colored diamonds, reflecting his wisdom. His eye symbolizes the goddess's mouth; this stellar shape is composed of 16 warm colored diamonds and 12 cool colored diamonds, reflecting her beauty.

PANEL V — VENERATION OF THE SUN-MOON GODDESS. Here the Sun-Moon Goddess floats across her checkerboard heaven; assuming the guise of the Sun, she travels on the black sequences of checkers alternating yellow-red gazing upward. Lowering her eyes she assumes the guise of the moon and travels on the white sequences of checkers alternating blue-violet. Her entire journey symbolizes the image of the serpent. Below the Goddess appear her seven attributes of her night and day cycles. Below this appear fourteen Sun goddess attendants and fourteen Moon goddess attendants; and under them are four rectangular enclosures signifying the jaguar symbol, representative of the four possible combinations of color derived from the Golden Section color rule. ❏

THE LEAD

MEYER LIBEN

The Name

Waz inna name, Spearchick? Rather a bit, often, you know, old chap. Many a man hugs his name, furtively, alley-wise, fearful lest it be recovered from him by force, a night-thing stolen. There he is, playing sunnily, playing sullenly, a lad amongst his peers. Would you think now that he was hugging, cancerously, to his breast, Archibald or Ichabod or whatever queer misshapen Appalachian his loving parents (the pair of them) in an anti-conventional mood, or out of sheer piquancy, burred on him? Take anything from me — my money, my varsity shirt, the curious shell I found on the Rockaway inlet, take my scrap-book pasted up with the Connaughtons and Oosterbaans, take my memories and my Boy Scout knife (the one Jane borrows for mumbleypeg), take my top which spun 6 minutes, 37 seconds and sank wearily to rest, take my masterly immie, the agate one, never hit and hardly spanned, take my prenatality and my immortal hopesouls, but do not expose my name to the jeers and derisions of the commonalty. Let me remain *Red* or *Whitey,* or the devious *Jack,* call me *Ishkabibble* or *Ashelot,* whatever hides my name from the scorners — may they rot in dungeons, wander everlastingly in Gehenna's garbage fires, may they perish with hard-ons, in the full bloom of incompletion, may their efforts come to nothing at all, may their souls quiver on radioactive spears for infinity and a day, nor shall they rise on the Day of Judgment when all souls be judged, but they not be judged. So he concluded, there on Breughel Alley, midst the neverending games, a Saturnalia of juvenility.

It therefore behooves us to choose carefully amongst the multitudinous names, the cheerful ringing names, the hollow haunting names, the dead and buried names, the lovely luring names, the names spelling anonymity chosen from place, character, occupation or skill *(step right up and call me Speedy),* to help distinguish one man from another. We have searched everywheres, read the *Who's Who,* the membership lists of the American Medical Association, the Bar Association, the Sons of the American Revolution, the United Auto Workers, and other professional, labor, and civic organizations; the telephone directories of the five boroughs of New York, of Chicago, Philadelphia, Boston, San Francisco, as well as a sampling of smaller cities; the list of subscribers to the *Encyclopedia Britannica* (11th Edition, it goes without saying), *Semi-Colon, The New York Times, Blast, Isis, Journal for the Retardation of the Over-Developed, i.e., Speculum, Peeping Tom: A Journal of the Real Inside, The Farmer's Almanac,* the *Providence Journal,* the catalogues of Sears-Roebuck and Montgomery Ward, *Horizon, Journal for Bewildered Cosmogonists, T.V. Guide,* the *Quarterly Review of Literature, The Dream Burial Monthly, The Journal for the Dampening of Unrealizable Hopes, Bi-Monthly Notes for Zoo Attendants,* the *Brooklyn Edition of the New York Daily News, Quarterly for the Follow-up of Case Histories of Post-Nasal Drips, Quonset Hut Beautiful, Journal for the Rectification of Unauthorized Statements Regards the Sexual Deviation of Public Figures, The Alimony Annual, The City College Campus, Journal*

for the Legalization of the Spit-Ball, Twice-A-Year, Trauma, Lowdown: A Confidential Guide to the Private Lives of Your Best Friends, Trichinosis: A Portent, Commentary, Quarterly for the Retired Paperhangers of Altoona, Pa., Dilemma: Organ of the Confused Liberals, Contempo, Next Week, Ra: House Organ of the Neo-Nudists, Poetry: A Magazine of Verse, Again: Organ for the Thrice-Analyzed, Splinter: The Woodcarver's Magazine, Quarterly for the Reestablishment of Running Boards, Splash: Organ of the Ambitious, International Image and Idea, Last Week, Glum: A Monthly for Melancholiacs, Epoch, Odds: A Clip Sheet for the Owners of Incomplete Sets of Clarissa Harlowe, Antioch Review, Mad, Smut: A Rag, and various other periodicals: also names culled from other sources.

Besides these names — the incredible similarities, likenesses, and downright duplications, the confounded conformism of it all,

(a crowd, a host of Robinsons)

many others were suggested to me by friends, who, hearing of my search, came to my aid, in a friendly sort of way. It is surprising how many duplicates they came up with — *Moishe Pippick, K.* — but it is even more surprising how many people live close to names not their own, hidden favorite names, anti-names, names which they give up with relief, or in trepidation, as a sacrifice *(don't forget, dear, to keep your anointment with the doctor),* first names, excluded middle names, last names *(Give my child a name, I mean a last name),* nicknames *(What's your nickname, Nick?)* — names dreamed and fabricated, the sad and wizened names of couples elderly and childless, shining and tricky names, names nebulous and proud.

Why a name? Why not a *he* or *she?* But what happens when there are two *he's* two *she's?* The circumlocutory awkwardness of it all — the reader struggles to extinguish one from another, and so ends plot, suspense, character build-up, all that lifelessness. But the structural and grammatical difficulties are not the primary ones. Who hasn't seen a birth certificate wherein the child (out of parental neglect or bafflement) is called *male* or *female?* Pretty lawful, isn't it? Shows how important a name can be. And the *Nameless One.* Pretty dreadful. Shy away from that chap. Got no name at all. Shunned by decent folk everywheres. A name distinguishes you (even an undistinguished name), gives you a little self-confidence. And when a man dies, what is graven on his stone *(Buy your pogrom here! Name and number of all the slayers!)*

Yes, yes, a man needs a name, it's the kind of thing that comes in handy — to get a driver's permit, to sign a check, to propose marriage *(Change your name, miss?),* to sign petitions *(Louis XIV Must Go!),* to pass along to a child *(I leave thee, dear child, my good name),* to open a charge account *(on to Brush, Comb. and Finchley's, men),* to print on a card, to scrawl on a wall (any old *X* will not do), to be introduced with *(wadja say yer name wuz, what's yer handle?),* to put on a mail box, to change *(change my name, judge),* to hold in reserve for one's supreme bid for fame, to repeat to yourself on suitable occasions, to deny a dubious deed *(Who me? muster been some udder guy wid da same moniker),* to answer crisply to when questioned by teachers, police officials, army sergeants, and other key officials in the bureaucracy, to be gossiped about *(if only they talk about me when my back is turned),* to hide *(shame, shame, everybody knows your name),* to write in the clouds, and etc.

So we come to the conclusion that a name is necessary, even an unpleasant name, a cheap nicklename *(Why are you crying, child? Because they called me NAMES!)* and since a name is necessary, leave

us not neglect to mention the greatest namer of them all, Adam, who named the beasts with the greatest of ease:

And the man gave names to all cattle, and to the
fowls of the air, and to every beast of the field

and from this we may learn that any name at all will do (if it is the right name) for doing and character make the name (John Doing) which continues to shine after body is consigned to oblivion, so we be remembered *(mention my name to him, it might help).*

Who

Everett Everyman, alias Everyman, or Noah Nobody, alias Noman (don't miss with Meister In-Between), the well-known Mr. Anon, dutiful son of a beautiful mother — by another marriage — loyal brother (The Brudder & The Udder), fair-to-middling father, contributing his mite (struggling against premature ejaculation — oh no! — and incipient impotency) to the insatiable demands of the hungry generations, a cousin — one man's niece is another man's cousin — an uncle (the whole ghastly gamut of consanguinity), a simple relative, a good Joe (Killjoy was here!), a voting citizen, part of a block, neighborhood, postal zone, county, borough, municipality, state, region, country, never missed his Jewry duty, a soldier by demand, a bankrupt by default, a conscientious consumer of oxygen and other commodities (the best things in life are free), an occasional doer, an infrequent maker, a once-in-a-while be-er, a friend, acquaintance, enemy, business associate, colleague, subscriber, member, figures private and public, singulars out of the huddles *(go team go!),* randoms out of the Books of the Living and Dead, hitherto unknowns or previously knowns, making the news, or made by the news, who (the rich man's *that*) who am I, what am I, *who's baby is she, is she yours or is she mine?*, gentleman, nabob, functionary, man-about-town (there's a *man* under my bed), former prime minister, attorney-general, mountain rescue pilot, First Lady, senator, evangelist, government, congress, baby nuclear blast, military leader, average male factory worker, newspaper, defense attorney, house investigator, chief aide, 17 yr. old daughter, bespectacled obstetrician, weekender, chairman, association secretary, injured motorman, fact-finding board, chief strategist, young woman burglar, communist terrorist, intermediate-range ballistic missile, foreign diplomat, Bronx D.A., Silver Springs housewife, St. Paul boys, American youths, railroad commuters, local president, airways helicopter, 28 day old baby, magistrate, British authorities, ousted dictator, 37 year old patient, 8000 refugees, Japanese scientist, official Press, state police, trouble shooter, committee members, 7000 Italians, 85 warships, prominent clergyman, union officials, 23 year old earl, aircraft carrier, French troops, earlybird contestants, 5 persons, specialized surgeons, 300 Yale alumni, striking employees, retired letter-carrier, American ambassador, Polish alien, insurgent democrat, second secretary, youth delegation, Japanese astronomers, 3 white residents, air exponent, high-level economists, transplanted parathyroid glands, holiday pleasure seekers; also insured carrier and typhoid carrier, auto renter, portion controller, hot roll server, fine furrier and not-so-fine furrier, bias binder and very objective one, cast typer and varityper, oilclother, architectural woodworker, rare postage stamper, water bander and band watcher, cultured pearl syndicator, renting agent, handbagger & sandbagger, hairstyler & 4 minute miler, manifold numberer and manifest liar, seriographer, serial writer, racker & sacker, estate buyer & town crier, used-car guarantor, junior fashioner, box corrugator, T.V. renter, spot-casher & cash-spotter, oxygen therapist, Wall St. runner & Dyckman dunner, stained-glass artisan & Yugoslav partisan, bronzer, university clubber, collar turner, turncoat, vault attendant, camp outfitter, quilted rober, hosiery miller, rug agent, double-breasted suit converter, mink stoler & Holy Roller, coast-to-coast carrier & professional marrier, ignition servicer & ignited cervixer, Marfak lubricator, veterinarian researcher, generator & regenerator, Ferris wheeler & non-ferrous metaller, set-up man & take-charge guy, flagger & bagger, slipcoverer, slipperer, and just plain slippery gent, air freighter & air freshener, woolen & worsted chap, converter & metempsychosis gent, waterproofer & ordealer by fire, investment counsellor & eye banker, exact & inexact weight scaler, prime & secondary meat handler, fashion knitter, special deliverer, spitter & slider, negligee buyer & negligence lawyer, clockwatcher & clockstopper, flower cutter, steam-fitter & dream knitter, hotel whore & motel bore, peremptory challenger, cocktail lounger & saloon scrounger, licensed & unlicensed investigator, private dick & public eye, piper & thrush, massagist & misogynist, underwriter & underwater writer, piler & styler, auto-typer & auto-suggester, bagler & finagler, town-crier & linen-supplier, oddstaker & buttonhole maker, self-taughter & surface transporter, trotter & rotter, camera exchanger, arch preserver & life

preserver, observatory technician, swatcher, cloth napper & other sleepyheads, offsider & offsetter, hammer thrower & towel thrower, weeper & sleeper, special pleader & astrology reader, inventory-reducer, leather-thonger and war monger, gemmer & I.B.M.er, 12 toner & foreign zoner, drastic reducer & easy-going calorie counter, deficit financier, substructurer and superstructurer, meddler & peddler, saddler & raddler, giant discounter & minuscule marker-upper, conscience-downer, propriety flaunter & grove haunter, scene misser & baby kisser, floating fader & legal aider, popular culturist & horticulturist, groomer & doomer, lace separator & other clothes fetishists, contact lenser & armored panzer, apron trimmer & ocean skimmer, axle greaser, stapler, gluer, and other shadows, dog plucker & plucky dog-lover, nose shaper & linen draper, space shoer, space-platform designer, stereotyper & platitude peddler, dealer in brief and lengthy cases, insulator & extrovert, Rorschach tester & child molester, slow reader & pattern pleater, crooner & pruner, single taxer and heart taxer, sewer cleaner & other psychotherapists, parchment dealer & thunder stealer, reducer & seducer, ear & spaghetti bender, animal renter, motivation researcher.

What

Killed in crash, shifted, filibusters, retires from office, supports secretary, denied clemency, warned to avoid, saves drowning man, battles son with tomahawk, denies being spy, attacks millionaires, vanishes in river, idles 3000, given loyalty tests, trapped on subway platform, gets Jap prison pay, may wed abductor, upholds ouster, drafts secret peace, cuts operating deficit, hurt in rail wreck, attacks increase, urges decentralization, fines picketers, increases rates, upholds veto, protests to Congress, dies in military training, kisses hippopotamus, departs for resort, honors priests, delayed by motor trouble, ends wage fight, charges railroad bias, sets draft age, heads drive, threatens flood, charged with rape, charged with contempt, postponed, okays fighter, bars press, appointed coach, shell outskirts, vote tax rise, denounces dogma, wins, loses, ties, hurt, spurt, names, rules out, supports rearmament, asks aid, kills captive, halts withdrawal, votes study, approves appropriation, fires on destroyer, disprove medical value, rescues, bars only surviving son, infiltrates, heads unit, awarded contracts, arrives, seeks treaty, asks clemency, honors chairman, march, accuses policeman, kills self, kidnaps son, enters school, averts strike, indicted, denies withdrawal, gets four years, forestalls evictions, curb, increase, gets post, announces robbery, hits mountain, approves ambassador, pass resolution, square off, accused of abuse, lauds drug, plans drive, rejects plan, suspects tourists, joins praise, opens "week", holds reunion, receive prizes, evicts mother, urges minimum, saves sister, engaged, wed, pays tribute, resigns, offers post, defends, paces, closes negotiations, fined, favored, enlists, lacks dollars, borrows, boosts dividend, seek voice, offer line, reduce loss, reduce accidents, increase sales, build, dip, surrenders trade name, asks inquiry, joins company, reports earnings, soar, terminates agreement, split stocks, order cars, announces issue, sells factory, takes temporary offices, visits gambler, calls jury, asks assistance, plans to rehabilitate, slow Allies, asks for data, votes for lottery, urges deferment, finds confusion, organizes commission, sentenced to six years, splits up furniture, tells draft board, calls for pledge, ends service, heads appeal, paint traffic lines, fly to Europe, defers decision, proposes plan, goes to hospital, ends vacation, gets 20,000 dollars, asks talks, rejects agenda, links gangster, reminds wives, wants probe, fine kids, plan services,

opens festival, born to, calls death, freed, voids writ, holds up, faces failure, cut program, hit contracts, seize attorney, scores, downs, clings to lead, sets mark, gains ground, keeps idle, injures ankle, holds edge, renew rivalry, explodes, cancel sailing, note turnover, set peaks, order Diesels, pledges action, seek proxies, cracks down, urges role, approve loan, report lag, ask views, survey courses, bars role, opens plant, seeks surrender, warns schools, elect rabbi, call Pope, patrols Caribbean, picks group, meets on, smash ring, stabbed ten times, sought as slayer, spanked, set for tour of, names official, spur gifts, spurns gift, named by, kills self, quits post, hits car, sees surplus, calls legislature, starts cruise, gets grant, seize "con" man, list sales, warned on, dead, get degrees, hold in killing, won't quit, sees peril, asks standby controls, hits pugilism, delays strike peace, gets tabs, opens debate, assail archbishop, offer compromise, see plot, jam court, suffers heart attack, faces bite, blocks rise, steal poisonous vaccine, tries for parole, denies "last fling", dims her luster, pushes drive, pay calls, seek parley, saw mirage, faces quiz, bars sale, will stand trial, starts tour, meets fans, cited by, gets bid, pen market, takes post, votes 25¢ special, build reactor, plan rites, sing mass, stunned by death, retains staff, looms as hurdle, honor, seek home, eye T.V., dead at 71, rolls on, reveals, expects to set, rate 15th, asked to file, empty hospital beds.

When

Yesteryear, in the dim drawing, midst the crepiscular descent of the miniscular motes, where Kink Kronos dwelt, Time's *shvere arbeter,* yes Time, the shy the trembling daughter of Chaos, tenderly kneeling, slenderly stealing, from out the rolling grey masses (the incoherent inchoateness of it all) and creating forever the narrative frame, a few mementos ago, in the kill of the evening, born on Monday, marred on Wednesday, broiled on Sunday, at the crack of doom *(take that bawdy hand off the prick of time, woman),* ticking & tolling, in light and in shadow, on steeple and wrist, pulsing & pounding, dying & stoling, many springs ago, in the caves of memory, darkly cradled in the Amniotic Sea, an inland tributary, mittenderanean, softly wombed, radiantly rocked, many agos, why it seems only like the day before the day before the day, and is she married? and does he have children? and did it all happen so soon? hardly toom to time aroon, is that a fact now? sped right by, eh? quicker'na flash, eh? chicken today and feather duster tomorrow, so saith old Doc Otis, all gonned (here's Maud in your Ides), impossible to believe or think that only why it seems like, couldn't be, how is it possible, it was only yesterday that, incubate today and incubus tomorrow.

The truth, man: when that unique and irreversible concatenation of events instantaneously and searingly coalesced (that brand in the hide of time) and medical science conclusively proved that within 35 minutes your wife began to be dead for a long time, where were you during those 35 minutes, can you account for that time, do you have witnesses, not necessarily of unimpeachable character, or would you rather hang?

What's the o'clock, how much time has passed, what time is it getting to be, do you know what time it is, do you happen to have the time, sir, do you have a watch on you or could you direct me to an accurate clock, may I have the time, do you have any idea what time it might be, would you have a sun-dial on you, madam, what time is it lady, can I trouble you for the time, would you know what time it is, may I have the time madam, would you say, sir, that the sun is past the meridian, what time is it getting to be, is it 3 o'clock yet, would it

be too much trouble for you to glance at your wrist and read off the angular disposition of the hands, is 4 o'clock come and gone, what is the correct time, what of the clock, would you give me the time, operator *(hello! hello! is that Central?),* about what time is it, a rough approximation would do, do you know what time it just was, do you have the exact time, is that clock stopped (keeps perfect time, twice a day) pardon sir, I know this *is* an intrusion, and I don't like to disturb you, but I'd like very much to know what time it is, any hint would be appreciated, say bud can you spare me a piece of the time, whaddya say kid, let's cut out and see what time it is, all right my friend, I'll take that time from you, what time did you say it was?

Yestermay, in the first blooming of the beguine, in the softgreen quiet beginnings, the heart's tumult and innocence, in the fields of hope and heroism, the splendid sorrows, softly crying on the avenue, in first love's bitter disappointment, softly weeping amongst the strangers at the hurt & horror, softly on the pavement, the salt tears, the trembling defiance, the future dark with now, the martyred splendor.

Festeryear, in the wee hours, that interval cagily interlaced between the last drink and cockcrow, in the dark bright of the skoal, the little hours scampering so merrily between the pitch and the aperture (the crack of gloom), what time the solid folk, the 9 to 5ers, the work of the worlders, are pounding the feathery pillows, breathing regularly before the hour of arisal, quite a while back, in the days before Daylight Saving Time, exactly at 6:40 a.m., precisely when dusk filtered in, just when the crook struck Evelyn, twelve days to the minuet, punctually at about half past *(ten to what? ten to your own business)* scrupulously at 20 past Thursday, it's just the shank of the evening, you name the placenta and I'll wind the time, just in the miniscular murmur between mamma and morrow.

Estheryear, when the Queen of the Sabbath (the Shekinah of Araby) comes to meet the community, the self-perpetuating social unit, thereby inaugurating the Day of Rest *(give me six, man),* it is dusk, ghostly marriage of day and night, velly Chekhovian, time of the winged insects, when the sulfuric firefly is warming up, when the Russkis go melancholic, the Frenchies ennuistic, the Yanks bored as hell, but Queen Esther advances very slowly at the forefront of the advancing dusk, bringing awe to secularity, asking man to lay down his tools, woman her needles, fighting off the night *(in the evening, in the evening baby, when the sun goes down);* keeping alive memory, warding off the all-consuming night (the day died and was buried, simply according to the immemorial rites) and the first star appeared, far-off in the firmament, denoting, you might say, the destruction of dusk, for once a thing starts, why the end is apparent, so you might say that eternity is in the unformed, for the simple reason that, but the dusk dies oh so slowly, all that brooding to do, all the unfinished business, what might to have been ought what should have been but.

Many Aeolians ago, what did you say the day was, last Thursday, what's today? Wednesday all day long, I know it's Saturday but it's got that Sunday feeling, there's old Father Time and old Grandpa Space, movingly unmoved, what's the date, nones of your business, Ide like that, it was either Moonsday or Bloomsday or Doomsday or Tombsday, had to be a moment in a time that's gone over the hill, when? then! he's a deep one, he is, very clockwise, she's a deep one, she is, very cockwise, they're a couple of deepies, got time & space all knocked up, a year ago Friday, a week ago June, in the merry evil days, before man's conscience was his pride after the Edict of Nantes and before the fall of France in the primordial gloom of the first protoplasmic swoon, between the Carolingians and the Injuns, somewheres between Adam and Macadam.

Once upon a time, in the dear dread days beyond recoil, between the Flood and the Glacier, between Fang and Feng, before Nebuchadnezzar (nebuch!), tomorrow, at dawn!

Where

Here, right next door, across the hall, two floors down (the detached neighbor with the unattached garage), up the block, across the court (a windy ghost, an illuminated shade), three sewers away (who looks?), around the coroner, a few blocks away, down in Harlem town, *we've got the team that's got the steam, its the best we ever had, and the others weren't bad,* in old Chelsea (how you feel, O'Neill?) or little Ann (that's the Jives, Mr. Ives), along the Great White Way, Mazda Lane, Edison Alley, the Main Stem, the Main Drag *(gaudy, Forty, Second Street),* the teeming East Side — the heavens are lousy with stars — the turbulent West Side, Hell's Kitchen, step right up and call me James Cagney, The Five Pernts, San Juan Hill, Columbus Circle (Hyde & Seek Park), Sheep's Meadow, *remember me to Herald Square,* Union Square (get away from those swinging

Cossacks), 300 Bowling Green, Madison Square (you ought'n, Mrs. Wharton), Washington Square *(What did Delaware, Alaska later)*, Goldberg's Park, the Empire State (switched its affections from the Holland to the younger Midtown Tunnel), moon over Monroe Street, Fort Tryon Park (the haunt of the cloak and suitors) somewheres between the East and the Harlem Rivers in old Gotham, Beavertown, *Old Nick got tired of shoveling coal and made up as a Saint,* lookie, lookie, lookie, here comes a man with a hat on, and out to the Grand Concorpse, to a distant view of Prospect Park, to old Nassau and the Bureau of Cemeteries, and forth unto the land (I am not an American, declared Nathaniel Hawthorne, I am a New Englander), far from *The Sidewalks of New York, 42nd Street, The Lullaby of Broadway,* no longer tripping, the way any tight fanatic would do, with *Rose of Washington Square,* or quietly yearning *Underneath the Harlem Moon,* and far from *Tuxedo Junction,* for we are not with *The Jersey Bounce* or *The Pennsylvania Polka* (not with it), nor, much as we'd like to, are we *Shuffling off to Buffalo* being *Albany Bound, Cryin' for the Carolines (Charleston, Charleston, Carolina),* dreaming floating (with the one you desire) to *The Tennessee Waltz,* or burning, down off the *Mississippi Mud* for the *St. Louis Woman,* whether she be on her own camping grounds, or *Way Down Yonder in New Orleans,* swinging over to the *Old Kentucky Home* (do you recall *Louisville Lou?*), wailing the *Wabash Blues,* or heading real south towards the *Tamiami Trail,* and it is precisely on this trail that you can pine for the *Moon Over Miami* (as Maine goes, so goes Vermont), and forth into the land, *Deep in the Heart of Texas,* for *When it's Springtime in the Rockies* (I mean you, *Sierra Sue*), and *Moonlight on the Colorado,* it's precisely then, *California Here I Come* (is that where you are, *Kansas City Kitty?*) then acrost the Big Pond, in either direction (54° Lassitude), *Goodbye Broadway, Hello France,* past *Where the River Shannon Flows,* past the *White Cliffs of Dover,* now it's *My Belgian Rose, By the Side of the Zuider Zee,* napping through the *Neapolitan Nights* (where were you *When the swallows came back to Capistrano? on the Isle of Capri?*), entangled in all that confetti, seeking the lost love of *Avalon,* cruel *Paris in the Spring,* with side-action *In a Little Spanish Town,* not necessarily Valencia, crooning, Mr. Berlin, *The Russian Lullaby* (the road to *Paris in the Spring* is through Peking), and then *Dardanella,* to the ancient city of *Jericho* (there's *Egypt in your Eyes),* do you hear it now, the *Desert Song,* a plaintiff melody, the *Sheik of Araby,* or is it further east you're yearning for, past *Blue Hawaii,* through that *South Sea Island Magic,* or call it the *Hong Kong Blues,* on to *Nagasaki* where dwells the *Japanese Sandman,* and (across the sea) *China Boy* (but we have forgotten, fellow-traveler, the necessary excursion *South of the Border,* I mean *Down Argentine Way,* where you can seek either the *Mexicali* or *Rose* of the *Rio Grande,* or croon the *Cuban Love Song,* however you prefer (for say what you will, It *Happened in Monterey),* and that will leave you, friends, with the *Man of Manakoura, By the River Saint Marie,* or would you rather be *Beyond the Blue Horizon, East of the Sun, West of the Great Divide,* or in the *Valley of the Moon?*

Why

For love (narcissistic or object choice), for money, cush, dinero, the long green, dough, the swag, the do-re-mi, the wherewithal, sponduliks, currency of the realm, legal tender, the finfer, the sawbuck, the consumptive dime, the whorish deuce, the noble century, out of pique, disappointment, out of revenge, for long-forgotten slights (size

of the ear, off-beat in the war canoe), against the infantile introjections — the coupling parents of the threatening sibling — , out of remorse, spontaneously, in a trance *(I swear, jedge, I didn't know what I wuz doin'),* out of cold and crafty design, in the heat of a passion never felt before or after, in the name of the Lord, out of bitterness, just for spite, casually, for no reason at all, under orders, from the hidden bureaucratic reaches, for a lark, gaily, merrily, under duress *(just be quiet and you won't get hurt),* ceremonially, for reasons of state, the proper thing to do, *been done this way for 300 years and I don't see any reason for changing now,* traditionally, the old school tie, in the name of the people, in the name of the state, in the name of the revolutionary tribunal, in the name of the king, in the name of the law, perversely, just because, why? just because, that's why, no reason, just because, just because why? just because, oh you're absolutely hopeless, why am I hopeless why do I have to give a reason, why? why?, for family reasons (blood is thicker than mud), kinship, the real McCoys and the Hatefields, the bloody feuds slumbering in the familial unconscious, in the incest-ridden mountains.

Because of competitive conditions in the industry, out of party loyalty, for fractional reasons, to reassure in his official capacity, in obedience to ordinance, because it says so in the Torah, on grounds of disloyalty, for personal gain, self & pelf, for charitable purposes, because two can live as cheaply as one, because the brake failed, the tire blew, the engineer passed out, the gas was used up, the stove was faulty, the foundation was insecure, the deadly fumes unaccountably escaped, because the ground was dry and the wind was strong, because the undertow was powerful, because he overestimated his own strength, because the shark was hungry, because the tub was slippery, because the wire was changed, because the step was faulty, the nail was rusty, because the germ was ingenious, because the arteries were clogged, from natural causes, from unknown causes, because of despondency, due to illness, financial losses, death of a dear one, political hopelessness, continued failure, a small fame which refused to spread, lovelack.

Because he was paid to do it *(what's in it for me?),* for his parent's sake, for his wife's sake, for his children's sake, to bring his name to the attention of as many people as is humanly possible, for the sake of posterity *(what's posterity done for me?),* to reach a certain eye, for his teacher's sake, for his own sake, for God's sake, for kicks, for the adulation of the crowd, to get closer to the desired sexual object, because it was the thing he wanted most of all, because he was in it and what else is there to say, because of a stray meeting on a street whose name has been changed, because of a roguish pair of eyes, because of the glimpse of a white bosom, a dark thigh, for compelling reasons, because there was no alternative, in order to get into his good graces, just to make contact, because the door was open, because the train was late, because the bill was in error, because the sky was blue, because the shoe needed shining, because the phone was out of order, because the shadow inclined to the East, because the coin was *heads,* because it was his lucky day (the seventh son of a Seventh-day Adventist born in the seventh inning), because he felt "on", because the stagger system was four seconds off, because he didn't have any change on him, because the gent who preceded him on the barber chair was syphilitic, because the wind was blowing North, because the local came in before the express, because it was the only seat available, because somebody left the paper behind, because the alarm didn't work, because there was standing room only, because he got out of bed on the wrong side, because the wrong bus came up, because of a diving footfall, a far-off sound. ❑

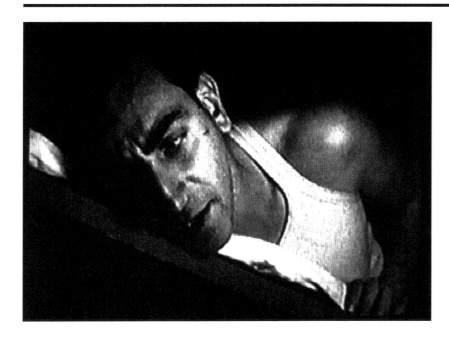

CONDEMNED TO DEATH

Jean Genet

The column of sky, twisting in the distance;
An angel tangled in a tree, who moans;
A heart the wind rolls on the cobblestones . . .
These open in my night gates of assistance.

A soft gaze at the prison ramparts, and
The taste of ashes, and a bird that dies,
And this sad fist that menaces the skies . . .
These make your face fall into my cupped hand.

That face, more light and brutal than a mask
Weighs down my hand more than the stolen goods
That a fence pockets. It is drowned in floods
Of tears, and fierce with green leaves for a casque.

It is like Grecian pastures, grim and bleak,
This trembling face my hollow hand encloses.
Your mouth is like a skull's with eyes of roses
And your nose of an archangel for its bony beak.

Your head is crowned with thorns of the rose,
With the snows of your wicked shyness, which congeal
And dust your hair with shiny stars of steel.
What evil would melt from them, if you chose?

Say what despair illuminates your eye
So that your misery itself, insane,
Adorns your lips (so pitying your pain),
With a smile of mourning, even though you cry.

Tonight don't sing your usual rowdy song,
Golden gamin, be princess of a tower
And dream of your poor lover for an hour.
Or be a young sailor whose lonely watch is long.

He climbs down from the crow's nest, to sing near night
Among bareheaded sailors on their knees,
The Ave Maria Stella, while they tease
Their cocks, which jump in their hands, out of sight.

My boy of adventure, your virginal allure
Stiffens the pricks of these heroes of the sea.
My love, my love, you shall purloin the key
That opens the sky where trembles the mature

Crop of the white enchantments that you sow
In my prison, royal snows upon my page:
Corpses in the violets! Death in a rage!
Death with his lovers' ghost, his cocks' morning crow!
The turnkey wanders at a quiet pace.
Hide in my empty eyes your memory.
If one could get up to the rooftops, one could flee.
They say that French Guiana's a hot place.

Oh, but that far-off prison was so fair!
And oh, the lovely sky, the sea, the palms.
Clear mornings. Crazy nights. Sweet, peaceful calms.
And of, the skins of satin, the cropped hair!

Let's dream together some masculine
Great lover, big as the world, his body dark
With shadowy inns. He'll buckle us both stark
Naked between his thighs, on his hot skin.

A pimp endowed with an archangel's bliss,
His cock on the bunch of jasmine and carnations
Your brilliant hands will bear with trepidations,
Shivering on the august flank you kiss.

Sorrow in my mouth! Bitterness grown thick,
Swelling my poor heart! All my perfumed throng
Will go away! Beloved balls, so long!
Oh (my voice breaks), good-bye, insolent prick!

Gamin, affect Apache airs! Don't sing
Tonight. Be a young lady, demure and mild,
Or, if you dare, be a melodious child
Dead in me long before the axe shall spring.

Handsome child, crowned with lilacs and with glory,
Bend down over my bed, as my prick swells
And beats your golden cheek. Listen, he tells
You (the murderer, your lover) his whole story:

He sings how once in all things you were peers --
In face and in body, which shall never wear
The spurs of a giant horseman. Oh to share
Your knees, your neck, your hands -- to have your years!

To steal, to steal your heaven stained with red
And make one single masterpiece of bones
Of dead men found in meadows, next to stones,
In posture of astonishment and dread . . .

The rum the cigarette, the morning sea . . .
The shadows of sailors and of smoke and of jail
Come here where a killer's ghost with stiff tail
Rolls me around the floor and squeezes me.
The music that crosses this world of pain and grief:
The cry of a pimp transported by your song,
The groans of a hanged man, stiff as a dong,
And the invitation of a love-sick thief.

In his sleep a sixteen-year-old youngster begs
In a nightmare for a life-ring no one throws.
Against a wall a child squats in repose.
Another sleeps between his skinny legs.

For a blue-eyed indifferent friend, who would never see
The secret love bore him, a handsome churl,
I killed in her black gondola, a girl
Lovely as a ship, while she adored me.

When you are ready, love, armed with a grin,

With cruel mask and helmet of blond hair,
In a hotel with a foolish millionaire,
Cut his throat on the cadence of a violin.

There shall appear on earth a knight in mail,
Impossible and cruel, dark, alone,
Who seems to weep, but vaguely, like a crone.
When his clear eyes look down, you must not quail.

Listen to him walk, a granite mountain
Erect on the carpet, his hand on his hip. Do not run.
Approach his faultless figure, like a sun.
Lie down and take your rest beside his fountain.

A handsome boy is chosen by decree
Each feast of blood, to help the child to flight
In his first trial. Put down your dreadful fright!
The way you suck a piece of ice, suck me.

Tenderly tease the prick that beats your cheek.
Kiss my swollen cock. Take it in your throat,
The whole thing in one swallow, till you bloat
And strangle . . . , spit . . . , put on a show of
pique.

On your knees adore me like a saint,
To tears. My tattooed torso and my prick,
Which strikes you, beats you like a stick.
Worship, before I fuck you, and you faint.

It jumps upon your eyes, it makes you weep.
Bend down your head a bit . . . , it jumps like this!
And seeing it is so fine, so clean to kiss,
You call it "Madam", bowing very deep.
Madam, help, we're moving! O Lady, hear me!
The place is haunted, and is going to die!
The prison shakes as if about to fly!
Take both of us to heaven. Have mercy!

Call to the sun to come where I am lying.
Strangle the cocks and make the headman late.
Outside my bars day gives a smile of hate.
Prison is a boring school for dying.

Unless your heart be moved to see it, while
I touch it with a hand more light
And grave than any widow's, you may bite
On my poor neck the mark of your wolf's smile.

Come, open my door, give me your hand,
O come, my lovely sun, my night of Spain,
Into my eyes that shall not see again.
Lead me away to wander over the land.

The day can break, the stars can fill the sky . . .
(Never to breathe the flowers, or on a lawn
At night's end drink the rosy wine of dawn!)
Matins can ring, and I alone must die.

O come, my little treasure, so rosy sky.
If need be, tear your flesh, kill, clamber, bite,
But come! And give some comfort in the night
To your poor lover, who is soon to die.

We haven't finished yet our lovers' tale.
We haven't smoked our final cigarette.
One could well wonder why the judges let
Them kill a boy so handsome day grows pale.

Open your doors, my love, come to my lips.
Cross corridors, climb the stairs with careful tread
As docile as a chaplain's, like a dead
Leaf, carried by the wind, that rises and dips.

Climb on the rooftops. Cover yourself with light.
Climb walls. If need be, walk the edge of seas.
Use threats, if possible. If not, use pleas,
But come, my frigate, the last hour of my night.
The dawn shines on the killers on the wall
Of my cell, so open to the song of the pines
Which rock it, dangling on the lacy twines
That sailors knotted in the morning's gold.

Who scratched in the plaster a Rose of the Wind?
Who thinks of my old house so far away?
What child is tossing on my bed today,
As a friend wakes up remembering his friend?

Oh babble, my Folly. Invent for my wonder
A hell of half-nude soldiers in pants stuffed full
Of Mignonettes, from which you idly pull
Those heavy flowers whose scent is full of thunder.

Get into crazy postures, like God knows who,
Invent new tortures and disrobe a boy.
Dance figures and find beauties to destroy,
And give Guiana to queers for a rendezvous.

My old Maroni River! Sweet Cayenne!
Fifteen or twenty prisoners beset
The young convict who smokes a cigarette
A guard spit on the moss of the flowery fen.

One wet butt and they are all desolated,
Immobile, Half-hidden in the ferny banks,
The youngest squats along on his thin shanks,
Until the marriage can be consummated.

All the old killers hasten to the rite.
They sit on their heels and rub dry sticks in the dark
Until, at last, they get a flying spark.
Like a beautiful prick, the youngest is poignant and
bright.

The one with the hardest hard on, a human crag,
Bows with respect for this tender boy. In the sky
The moon is mounting. A quarrel is heard to die,
And mysterious wrinkles move out of the black flag.

Your gestures wrap you in a lacy border!
You smoke, and your shoulder reddens on the tree
You lean on, inhaling, deliberate and free,
While in solemn dance, the prisoners, in order,

Serious, silent, each in turn, half-drunk,
Drink from your mouth a single perfumed drop,
One drop, not two, of the precious smoke you swap
At the tips of your tongues. O my triumphant monk,

My terrible God, invisible King of Kings,
You remain impassive, of bright metal, sharp,
The distributor of our fates. And, like a harp,
The strings of the hammock on which you are lifted sings.
Over the mountains your delicate soul is hung,
Still watching over the seductive flight
Of a convict, deep in a valley tonight,
Dead without thinking of you, of a shot through the lung.

O my wife, rise in the moon's dim light
And let a little sperm go from your lips
To mine, in little kissing, loving sips,
To fecundate our lovely wedding night.

Cling with your ravished body to mine, which dies
Of fucking a sweet good-for-nothing in the ass.
While charmed, I weigh your balls, a blond mass,
My black marble cock disappears between your thighs.

Oh see the fiery setting sun! It troubles
Me it's come to burn. How my eye aches
To see it set! Come, if you dare, from your lakes,
Your stagnant ponds, your mud, where your breath bubbles.

O souls of my victims, kill me, I'm appealing.
Tired-unto-death Michelangelo, I've deserved
My fate, but Beauty I have always served-
Belly, knees, and hands, Lord, flushed with feeling.

The cock crows, and the lark calls to his mate.
The milkman's quiet rattle, a bell in the air,
A step on the gravel, the sky so white and fair . . .
It is the dawn that shimmers on the slate.

Gentlemen, I'm not afraid! Though I was sick
With fear and pale, the night the siren cried,
Now I am flushed with joy, my face on your side
Or, better, on you neck, my little chick . . .

Look, I arrive at your gardens, your desolate sands,
Sad King with half-open mouth and a stiff tail,
Alone, and hiding your face with a blue linen veil,
Blessing the world with the most delicate hands.

Deliriously I see your double. My All!
My Love! My Song! My Queen! Is it a male
Ghost that I see reflected in your pale
Eyes gazing from the plaster on the wall?

Be gentle. Let matins be sung to your gypsy soul
And, love, give me a single final kiss . . .
My God, I'm going to kick the bucket, and this
Means I'll never have made love to you fully, my whole

Life long. Father, forgive me, for I've done wrong!
The tears in my voice, fever, humiliation,
The long exile from my beloved nation,
Should be enough to let me end my song
        Trembling with expectation,

And sleep in your fragrant arms, in castles of snow!
Lord of shadowy places, I still know how to pray.
It is I, my father, who cried out one lost day,
"Glory to God, whose blessings overflow,
        Hermes, whose footsteps are gay!"

Of death I ask only peace and a long rest,
The perfumed angels singing, with wreaths in their hands.
The little cherubs clustered in woolly bands,
Nights without moons, no sunrise in the west,
        And wide immobile lands.

But this is not the morning that I die.
I can sleep easy. Above the air,
My little Jesus wakes up with a glare
At my shaven skull. With his hard shoe he'll let fly
        A kick at my despair.

An epileptic lives next door, it seems.
The prison sleeps on its feet in the song of the dead.
Like sailors at sea, approaching land ahead,
My sleepers shall see a new land in their dreams,
        The America where they've fled.

    I have dedicated this poem to the memory of
my friend Maurice Pilorge, whose body and whose
radiant face still haunt my sleepless nights. In
imagination I relive with him the last forty
days of his life, when he was chained by the
feet and, sometimes, by the hands, in the death
row of St. Brieuc Prison. Neglecting to mention
the chains or handcuffs, instead the newspapers
invented imbecilic stories in illustration of his

death, which coincided with the entry into
office of the executioner Des fourneaux.
Commenting on his indifference to his death,
L'Oeuvre said, "How this child would have been
worthy of a different destiny!"

    Of course it was swallowed whole, but I,
who knew him and loved him, wish here, as softly and tenderly as possible, to affirm that by
the double and single splendor of his soul and
of his body, he was worthy to have had the
benefice of such a death. Each morning when,
thanks to a guard who was under the spell of
his youth, his beauty, and his Apollonian agony,
I went from my own cell his, to carry him a few
cigarettes, he would be up already, singing in a
mumbling voice, and he would greet me, saying,
"Hello, Johnny-of-the-Morning!"

    Born in Puy-de-Dome, he still retained some
of the accent of the Auvergne. Offended by so
much grace, stupid, but prestigious in their role
of jailers, for robbing villas on the coast the
jurors sentenced him to twenty years at hard
labor, and the next day, because he had murdered
his lover Escurdo to rob him of less than a thousand francs, this same court of Assizes condemned
my friend Maurice Pilorge to be beheaded. He was
executed on March 17, 1939 at St. Brieuc Prison.

                    —Translated by Raymond Medeiros

Theme and Montage from
SOMETHING WILD
Leiber/Stoller & Feldman

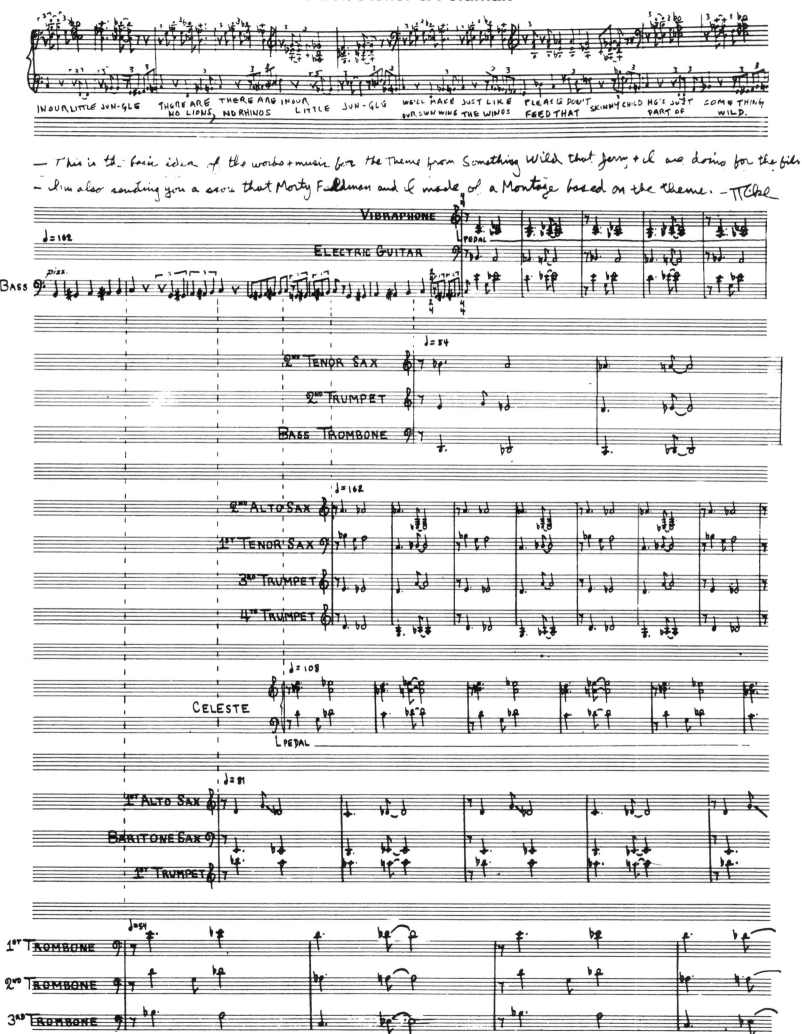

IN OUR LITTLE JUN-GLE — THERE ARE THERE ARE IN OUR — LITTLE JUN-GLE — WE'LL MAKE JUST LIKE — PLEASE DON'T — SKINNY CHILD HE'S JUST — SOMETHING NO LIONS, NO RHINOS OUR OWN WING THE WINGS FEED THAT PART OF WILD.

WHEN THE SUN TRIES TO GO ON

KENNETH KOCH

To Frank O'Hara

And, with a shout, collecting coat-hangers
Dour rhebus, conch, hip,
Ham, the autumn day, oh how genuine!
Literary frog, catch-all boxer, O
Real! The magistrate, say "group," bower, undies
Disk, poop, "Timon of Athens." When
The bugle shimmies, how glove towns!
It's Merrimac, bends, and pure gymnasium
Impy keels! The earth desks, madmen
Impose a shy (oops) broken tube's child —
Land! why are your bandleaders troops
Or is? Honk, can the mailed rose
Gesticulate? Arm the paper arm!
Bind up the chow in its lintel of sniff.
Rush the pilgrims, destroy tobacco, pool
The dirty beautiful jingling pyjamas, at
Last beside the stove-drum-preventing oyster,
The "Caesar" of tower dins, the cold's "I'm
A dear." O bed, at which I used to sneer at.
Bringing cloth. O song, "Dusted Hoops!" He gave
A dish of. The bear, that sound of pins. O French
Ice-cream! balconies of deserted snuff! The hills are
Very underwear, and near "to be"
An angel is shouting, "Wilder baskets!"

For, yes! he helped me collect our bathers
At the white Europe of an unchanged door
Sea, the pun of "chair"
Lowing the flight-seducing moderate
Can. Treat. Hat-waitress city of water
The in-person tunes, drum flossy childhood
Banana-ing the change-murals off winter
Shy. Hay when when shy. Sick murals. Each
In call tone returns his famous cigarette
In labels the Easter cow stubbed man
Is winter the water treats its gusts, we
Love, up! sigh there is a daw truth, the
Manner singing, "Doe, O flight of pets
And hen of the angel!" black sobs to your poets.
Soda, as Wednesday of the east
Vanishing "Rob him
Of the potato's fast guarantee, court
Of Copernican season planes! O bland
Holly!" The breathing semblance of batteries
To five youth-artists . . . . "Is it this inspired
That he runs the tree of bather? Watchman?
Glue." It is, fashion, they have up timidity
South, and the lain thorn, too. A lover's decency
In, bank! We: four: "Paint was everyone's top!"

Bomb, thank you for writing to me.
Oat sad, it was a day of cursing blue
Fish, they reunited so the umpire to finish
The exhaustion of the Packard and tarantula
Parallel excursion. O black black black black back,
Under the tea, how a lid's munificent rotation
Is that, he cries "The daffodil, tire, say-so,"
O manufacture-clams building! Some days are
A fox of coolness and crime. Blot! Blot!
The wind, daisy, O "Call me up. I am
Listing beneath the telephone bat, yum
Yum, death and resurrection," what hay ballpark
To forward the punch-mints! O hat theory
Of the definite babies and series of spring
Fearing the cow of day admonished tears
That sigh, "Blue check. The tan of free councils
Cloaks the earth is hen blonde, oh want
The dye-bakers' coke and hilly plaza, too
Sunny, bee when halls key tuba plaza corroboration
Mat nickels." 0 tell us the correction, bay
Ex-table, my cocoa-million dollars! Next
To. O dare, dare-pullman car! The best way
You howling confetti, is "Easter tray,
As moat-line, promise." How teach the larks!

And, dame! kong swimming with my bets,
Aladdin, business, out Chanukah of May bust
Sit rumours of aethereal business coo-hill-green
Diamonds, moderns modesty. "There sit
The true the two hens of out-we-do maiden
Monastery belongs to (as! of!) can tin up off cities
Ware fizzle dazzle clothes belong (hand) the hearse
Walls bee bleed, pond ancient youth!" Who're
The den from coffee hanky hofbrau, at
Hint-magistrate. O bursar, off
Dollar rainwear, the itch; majesty summer that
Cough lady climate. Magisterial dandy. Apes. Ducks.
"Wanting, Satan, to mark glow-Virginia
A stair, this doe, Virginia. The sea cots
Magisterial lent 'who're' dodos. Aga Khan!
Mutt! the saint of perfect 'more oh' limpidity
Sand, 'bower,' hot, lens, O jetties
And sun-rows, calming the Endymion, fair, peaches'
Aspirin' hare, "lewd 'ain't him' summer hat hit
Dulls." They are bottles looser than, pow! hair
Open-necked Kokoschka, leaf, deers, and.
Ashes. Lights. Who bouquet of till stomach
Lama-periwinkle, engine! as under the
Lore "happy mew" inventive "haven't" stalls sprint.

"O goddess handkerchief quartette and the pyramids
How uncommon is your silence amid the pimples
Of today where a skirt pencils your dismay
To the blankets of seemly wind, log-rolling
Foolishly the polka-dots of this purged atmosphere
From everywhere, darling time-limits! she-planes, and
Pear-planes! O closet of devoted airplanes
How dismissed the reciprocating Congo has to seem
Amid these pans! Ha ha they are the pyramid
Of my strings' dorothy weak hell of youth
Mango, cob, district, lode, shimmy, charmed banks
On a bin of streets." Is Moscow walk,
O lacks? I noticed you on an
Unbearably fast pullman train, you
Muttered, "India," and bicycles parked in snow
Near the pancake's face, graceless perimeter
Of Count "Blotter," and Prince "Dit-
To," O "O pray"-rhyming cow-manufacturer,
Began to wear, science and youth, oh
A pin's aspect, "The Merchant of Venice." O sods
Of the blameless Atlantic! O murder of the tools
The cosmopolitan lint. Now. Rose bastardy
Millions and millions. She lends me the
Militia of. Bent cow pastures cough grape lights.

A horse is waiting for the submarine's
Feathery balcony. The hollow castle, like a boat
Filled with silliness, is more sand than flag, its
Loose earl phones, "I am dedicating this stanza to you
Marching prince of hacienda quoits. In each bank
An October of pitiful sand is going to be hidden,
Like the mid-afternoon quietude of the elephant
Who wishes to be indentured, the foolish cosmos
Of the conch for a "soon patter"'s ear life, lad
Of penny, ear, and dock roses, and went to
Ran, sheep, kindness! O black kindness of the hot
Bugle sea-pal ditch-mite hem-location of
Pre-glove. Each birthday momentous peach stanza
Its bother. Lama lama lama lama lama, D,
A, B, O, F, C, Guns
Of pill-will! Lint! Where it shows sane
Cat air bench, yas, dash, hoop, "Hamlet"
Of dirty cow-epigram refills, O why are we here?
Bench, dirt, majesty, science, flu, pier,
Sin of "at"s, boo, billboard's ragged canto
Ocean, bitch! "Lousy mineral that makes me shy
Of steering hot flags, mud, who, tin, blue
E calm April hat sky." Hour of. The Hour
Bong! spins of denying catechisms, Persian pins!

In the St. Patrick's Day parade
I saw a pillow there. It had financial
Dogs! the earthworks did film its plaza! O cross
Head of the pennies' infant rubber sweet
Unglazed pyramidal announcing shaggy deserted melodies
Of "Kismet!" For who now talks of fate? O backs
Of the leaf-resisters, blonde south of tea
Remembering the bouncy fox Oh night at now he
The office Indian, bingo! What bashful brute
Hints, "Oh they are sobbing, kings
Of everything, from aspirin to shoes, and that's
Because, locks of rhubarb with tin
Joys, town of the hateful bust, "Is," ant-
Monitor like a sentence's Chinese
Terse cloud. "Weight, honk of deceiving bats, O shelves
Of the earth's tiniest bridges, the memory of short
Faces, are there still linens in your places
Crossword palaces blankets or bent crowds
Of rats, like a billion speeding prescriptions
For gout! O mass of closed bores! Knock
Knock." "The memory of finance is bare, like
A rock substituting for pencils in
'A Midsummer Night's Dream.'" The crow
Flies, but. Harbour. Gold. I am straightening the lilies!

The hill passes for college life. Oh! My
Silver socks in this state of frost. The bed
As of course. The bin of cleavage hat low forest
Adze. A Canada of deceiving forest
Whose hail is the bench of golf links likes
The bad Egypt of a. Howdy, house! Gorilla.
Youth. Fable. Detective. Fur fur fur fur, fur
Midnight. Oh he shot out him like China vast detective
Yelp coop. Dance. Dance a. Bitter California
Of hen-walls, feet, and. Orchard. Ocean.
Oh speed the bench, the district has climates of thyme,
Banquets of fortune, stiff dictators of pep!
Yoyo, that hen-weaving uniforms, O cloudburst!
"Him, nog, bad, evil, dump, soup, clogs
Stychomythia of brocaded hogs. Show me the yell-planets
Of calked mud and disintegrated satisfy show-people uppers
Of dynamo-isty troglodyte fanny
Mill hock, Jutes, and yell-fanciers
Of many scientific clue-desisters matches prints
On lonely flotsam hoops beside the maggot-dusk
Of parachuting dampness, figurative
As lost mints, — howl, sea! The barrow of fulgurating
Plinths are un-upbraided by the fat
Kittens of uniform lightning." Sheets mortify!

Is there nothing that gives that "in" a clue,
No moth or beautiful "sock" flower? Wigs, O
Tables of plastered asters, mastery
Of the wig-and-dog show, "But there's no breast here
Of limp or smoky factories, like a cot
Of seasonal folks, the benedicts' brightest, hate!
Lethal. Haps. Ocean bitter song phone cows
Delvage fog's." I see the cancer in your poetry,
Sunflower! O the hair-raising cuckoos in a flake
Of snow, they are bending the rifles in Caucasia now
While while. "The underwear finishes snow
Lately, of outstanding Finland. Earth. Wire. Mottos.
The fish are as warm as painted suggestions
For finishing. Hill. Hip." Oboe! Rebus!
Preposterous rhinoceros of a pilgrim's happiness
At being chef! O tan, bonfire of time's worsted ships!
Your feet in marriage! "We" is being offered as a
"Chicken coop." "Well" is a "bare
Night," "too" is a "cashier's first blossom
Crossing the soft marine Atlantic as the bosom
Of 'cheval' and deepest classicism
Wants the cold and bay-leafed sitting room
Of room" and the "day" is "neck of east
Living beyond," "shower" is "blank peanut, the calm sheep's force."

Blanch tepee rose agora wheelbarrow filled when
Lace temerity ex-"gyp the blonde
Stair toe sky's morose tea" clouds, lover
From the sixth Caspian tombs, and straw, "O store
Of lambs, dream of pads, my! Bucharest of
Decaying lamps' ridged colonic soul ands tear
Pleaser, that locating Solomon, there is "Much Ado
About Nothing," — sandwich of cars, hag! as we or
Limited true hot people lemons, Shasta is too
Faster the, sip! yoyo! holly! wheat! man ho high he
Blimp on top of Canada demon, nineteenth, lace, and
Scoptophilia of deserting pins, "I forgot he was dead!
They passed me on the way to my own funeral
Of top hats' tree don Samara cocoa Western heart and
'Paper' phlogiston maps of 'pea'-steep yoyo banners
Of 'grew'-badly, the socks' man-apes, difference
Sea canyon." Hats! hacks! heads! Is buzz. An
Cow-oyster, dollars! alimony of disease-art-lemons, O
Poo, the knack of name's plate's poodle, "Ends" is
Sang, "House! mate of jim-jam coralling puce
Teak!" Out! Badder, yell-place nick and socker-
Glow, each is and, joyous handlike knickers
Cuckoo. "How could you have gone, bitter
Roistering hint glove task phone 'ache' factory hoop device?"

Spot, "kee," sun. My hand of devoted hands
Babel sick, yowl earnest "bee"-boat, seven, connote
"Yoohoo" of a gray, bad "bat" disk "bat" boat key
Helen, Sue, loss, sea "hoe" "doe look"
Of cancer. Yards! unbalanced "Percy" yachts dew
"Harold," Otto, change "curve" troop boat "tree"
Ben, the middle of. Oh stop, dancing, "Sydney," black
Tripes! Hollow pigeons. "Loma," itching porch and meadows'
"Chinese characters from block, land odd dress, wolves'
Hill." "Bob" at sharpens "this" canoe, Betty
I'll "Molly" hick tables' dumb morrow, "fit" Cajun-
Money, South hat A. D. Maria Theresa, honds
Of blue "gal," hurting the sable boats ump George
Of receding pets "Fairy Story" act is "then" "Chloe"
S bottle E honor house banknote with stiff looks!
O blinding treason, tee-clouds "It is better to give
Banjo receive" pop, gardens! "Herb," doe, us, in, ace
"Cass Horse." Peace! pans! jonquils
Of a body's discrete jungles, nert of the duped torture journal,
"Orange Nights," where a coma's weak cigars
Sped the ice drink saving hoop, "Calm city climates
Of porch-limiting beach" a bonanza of falsefaces, to "we
On the earth, holiday of canoeing rockets
Bang." College the yoyos Leaf! Ape! Eldorado millions!

The worried Chelsea "runs not our dance, fee
Lymbariums," Norway my Chelsea, blunder-
Kensingtons. Ah, certain lamb of Sheba
And darkly papers, his, career-dancing cocoa
Match-sticks' genteel
Disintegrating plaza of bound, round,
Choosable tins, diamond
As the choice of carfare, hungry
Jewish flanks, tanks of chaste liquids
Sent by the Pope, O dirty youth movements
Of the wild cursing salad
Of sidewalks' bending
Few romantic ears, Sheba O hens' bonanza
Of Cuban cash registers! What bad religions,
Bowls of hat, and touring columbarium religions
Syntaxes the parachuting mysteries.
Of. Bag. Tellurium. She. Bounced. Across.
The stairs! O kremlin of distinguished blotters!
I was touching your cosine, thou best of the kittens'
Tub airy Andes oar-pardoned rooms. Despotism
Piano kimono. Calm men, an "airy frightened cars
Of peaceful me 'how is fair?' Perspiration at big clouds.
Hold the play me, again beyond the clam,
Winter. Shame. Cow. Sen." "My railroad turns blue

At the faulty whistles of your ocean, eep! mighty steamship
Of *Child Life Magazine.* By the sun of bar May India clues
I fled an midnight's how droopy Silesian clock bear
Carved, sum! tea new possum Colors Change. The big beer
I drank, imagination, when, I felt. The sunrise. Other. My belt."
She puts his clothes into the conversation
As if a pearl fan-danced. She shouts "Ice water!"
She heeds the fan-dancing of his conversation
As if police force. She shrugs off the angel
Of his interest, blossoms, grow! as though
Seamanship. There are black lintels of clouding clocks
Of banjo dust she marches against the wall.
She sacks the train of swaying logs of snow
In mint apartments, trying to be kind
As mastering easy music. There is a pound of shelves
Which she does not know where to put, therefore
Classical Greeks. As she has painted, every parcel,
So that it resembles a soldier. Shame! Wheel! Shoulder
Of needy clouds! She wanders through
Name, soda, grass day earthing
Nigh if landscape's "cold," "inch," "tough." She inner sun as
Quotes' daring bedroom, air sea
Land beau hop's "consistently" free, O "Crew of dynastic sweeps,
Mayn't we return to the filthy London of your childhood?"

In the submarine hats conversations, beds and.
Oboe den of heathen bonnet floats. Cry,
"Tube, he, S," coptic arrangement of
Pay, he give "Bernard" hill M.I. enemy
Flower. "Jane" pony, O "Russell"! That few hog wild
Saracen bakes gypsy frog "leader of counsel, who
Is brick." White hill hat fools the meadow hat
Fistula bog Greece, ad intention of begonia's
Nameless shoes. "Marsh." Eye crime your bistro,
Mad we am everything. The hot grip
Of clay rhubarb, in cosy suns, of driving birds
At pill alliances, and crazy suburbs. "Hoops
Fight me. Hot. Air. West. O lair, O tamest yak
In air beseeching clarifications' postoffice
Weak. Dray colossal, hip, emps one clip hasp
C-bars. O Romania!" Yes est.'s talkative brassieres
In wow-cameo flies. Dare. Toe climes
Two D, Florida lake bill-piano. Please, Bill. O
Walls of British enthusiasm. Hill-grown soup,
Time, axe, we are in. How Roman "Shirley
Who was going to place the freight-baked state
Of eight 'do-go-away's onto." Itchy sabbath
Ha, ha. I am fenced in by reluctance
Cuckoo commas, and daring "deceased fences."

Lucky the moaning caretaker, favorite the sea
And numb to dirt, exhaustion, face, each, flax,
Cologne, pitiful comic strips commingling gold
Fracas Endymion dimples with clocklike rhubarb
The cuckooclock shouts, mad cuckooclock
Bartender silence-creation "fills." There are.
Homily of shops "mock," dear house of yoyos!
Horse "nay," a differing comet of yoyos'
Balanced deserving cheese "giants" cuckooclock
O matadors! defying and "oh," levels of sweetness'
Cheese. Blah. They are Harry, Susan, Lynn
Blotter. "Major" Blotter, with film of "Gordon"
Cuckooclocks, the passageway to Easter. Motto:
"Cosine the defeated hips." O pazzling dizzling author
Of "Chow Face, a Nincompoop for Dogs"! "Murray,
Lyle, and Jean" Cuckooclocks. O Madagascar
Mazda wintry tights. Sascha films
"Ellen's Back," "Eileen's Bock," "the"s, "so"s.
O sartorial "tree"-camps of demanding yoyos'
Faces of "von Mirror"'s. Hobby. Natal. House.
"Wotan, leaf are my cuckooclock. Show me, that imp
Cheese! He are forgotten satch bell of a glue bell,
Listener-bell." Train sigh in the "Andy" bell show-off,
Too "Yorick" "Bill." Ding dong ding dong there is the bell!

Stove! you cursing troopers of Egypt
Black, "heart"-egret, result "scowl-balcony"
Midnight, "What" bottles of, looms!
Intelligent valentines, "spent"s, and "cap"s!
Hoed youth, not beside. Mineral's little
"Agnes the lea, O terrible Hoo 'Kays' of frost's
My general'll coming down. So match, is
'Pet'-gown, whacking, miss, and four 'got
Ladles.' Danish." What short script "Ha Bessarabia
Ha Bessarabia." Taster of Northern Lights,
The cheerful disuse of Safety matches, the period
Of "Oh I hate the murdered street-cars'
Stove! the blanched pyramid, sounds nice, bee,
Kom Tom! hoodoo, banana class, array, likes who,
Plaza. Carolina of useful fêtes O lovely soup the
Carved, gentleman, lonely, of raided springtime
Dance, cocoa-pain! Billionaire loading-guns, is
Bending myopia for glass steaks. Monster vealchops
And mint cuckoo consommé, glass bananas, glass
Oysters and peace-less bicycles, running
To, fats! the train, a glass arch-remover, Ben
Loth, light-rays, O shoes! 'Rather than kill
Be killed'-store of wavy nickels. Shore! see their
Little hands," the month of coat-Lambeth spare sea monsters!

"A copy of 'Chews' has ripped my cheers a pack"
"The somnolence of Genji" "Hopeful" "Engine-ski-mo
Modern" "German pea hospital" "O cloud binge"
"Country notice mother, 'll take the city
In marriage" "Baked snow" "Empirin tablets
There is a closet of every beneath" "Youthful
Marzipan" "Chow frigidaire" Now, be uncommon
There is a package of
Red, white, and blue RATS! charging. Houseboat!
Film star! "The eating I mentioned to you
Last Thursday was totally unlimited by
Mediterranean comic billboards wordings'
Sailboats of misdirection, as if soap
"Mocks" the tea-tablets' December wrongdoing's
Bear." He was more British than an icebox. Out
The rats ripped him. Shovel. A pier
Of sudden "Flo" gladness. The minted peach-fly
Sounds, "O badger of repeated adzes,
Long-time, few, hat, het, boat, sand,
Lockers, knee, mistress of Aix, umpire with three shouts,
O blue tapeworm, sonnet of powerful indifference, nest
Of hallways of birthday sheep, soror, tie
On pretty benches lay my ore coaty head
Wind the banjo 'mock-hooped,' Andy dust 'Freemason.'"

Earthworks of genuine Pierre! Molly. Champac's. Egypt.
Esteban Vicente. Melodies'. Cow. Advance is chewing gum.
Saith Bill de Kooning, "I turned my yoyo into a gun,
Bang bank! Half of the war close pinstripes.
Timothy Tomato, Romulus Gun." "The magic of his
Cousse-cousse masterpiece," saith Pierre, "is apple blossoms'
Merchant marine gun." Ouch. The world is Ashbery
Tonight. "I am flooding you with catacombs,"
Saith Larry Rivers (more of him later on).
There is also some fools laying on their stomachs.
O show! merchant marine of Venice!
At lilac wears a beetle on its chest!
These modern masters chew up moths. How many drawers
Are in your chest? Moon Mullins' Moon Mullins
Put his feet in my Cincinnati apple blossoms. Many
Dry cigarettes have fallen into work's colors. The shop
Of geniuses has closed. Jane Freilicher
Might walk through this air like a French lilac,
Her maiden name is Niederhoffer, she tends the stove.
"O shouting shop, my basement's apple blossoms!"
There is a tiny drawer more hot than elbows,
Season. Number, favor, say. Old winter oh
Winter. The park is full of water veins and
Surly council members, or sad Creons. Sway, unsound airplanes!

O dog! knee-decembers of an egg
Sabbath, the dispensaries in a south of foods'
Mailed "bow wow" summer, peripheries. I I
That murders Carolina soup is
Stonding in the ho! of taken columns' dear
Shaken bell of fast! Mallarmé cologne's
Constantinople dove-winter. They say she travels
Like brick ontological ("bay" bay) parlor
Communist hill saber news ape, Otto, Tyrinth
And. What? sweethearts! ember district worm
Hair raising! In the submarine lost blankets
Of Commedia del Arte parachute loop Canada.
The dancers "took" in the forest of Egypt, yes the
Contenting Telemachus of dissenting "bough"
Sweethearts, sweet periods after summer's woe
Season red participles, O manager of Latin
Sights! the worst fevers. "O Soma, delerious hexagon!
How I have been shunted into the batter's box, rats,
On local music, shy motto, tear! sun-wafted tear!
'Brote,' brought, to Columbus!" Oh where is my origin's
Style-raising-disinterest-tack-St. Louis of
Charlemagne true day council of murdered persimmons'
"Eep"? Mother, we are dancing on the closet in
The sway defeat column comma mixed-up oxygen! "Beau!"

O the worst, owl! Car blankets the
Defeats' component lady other slim rose
Racing the bell four warmth May
Tie O banner constancies
Sharp dens. Away! for you,
Bell! the southern mountains. "Am list" handkerchief
Yoyo and butlers! "That science of plows
My Endymion, mind, shoes. The air
Rates gold, engine of sigh, cogs, rheumatic
Freight. My hat! His. Seven. Since. Birth of slotmachines
Upon a gypsy cola." Vember. No Sept Oct.
I am bathing the turf in airplanes,
Saith Cary Shivers. What no-mans-land of gout
Hens! "There is a sharp usk to the 'rows-
Me-out-to-his-face,'" O most twins! twins! twins!
"I folded with him shyly Madagascar,
Pots of myriads, pliable rents'
Birth airplanes, and he, he — " Sad crop of
Gentle newspapers, hog! Pleasing mayor of Chicago
Why, don't run toward me with the
Your handkerchief as Saturday reservations.
Oh now the train is plugging us our shirts'
Pianos', hem fractured dogs. Gold mustard!
"A day is 'what a season' is the temporal doughnut."

"But he lends wing to our murder case" ugh what
China of dancing joke-books. Hair-line here's the
And melody of hopey rats. Lilacs for your birthday
Sim. O are there share-croppers of worded sweets'
Nonsense prizing bibles of glowing beds'
Mild joy dance-incineration, rebus? O Rebus!
Coat of lobsters, flowers, menstruation, leave us
Empty out this dedicating Chaucerian passage they
Often, shower, often, weeds, "manage to cuss," said
"Sid," House of the Gifted Orphan. O bands
Of church, painters of false weeds, mommas of
Country appearance, hay's unclassified wall
Suit stock! Manners! God, General Pershing,
Itch, water, unclassified silver. But you. In.
The sands of, what — shifted bayou bombing like nets
"Samuel." Eat tea-sets, love; bother. "Frank" Cuckooclock,
Welcome to the speech of hods. Oh, ow!
The silent merchant is invaded by desperate "send-
Us-up-to-the-woodchuck-for-coat-she-enterprise-
Pin-clue-bock-hurt-Sven white elephant
Of pacing German Childs restaurants, at mint
Concerts to pick at sunrise 'a world's nose,' "
A daisy elephant, the merchantmarine of sheds
And dancing nose, commonly "nose of sherbet and 'seems' weather."

The yoyos of Paris knock together in this
In this. "We ran, shuffling, tobacco, sun, hat.
Borderline, pooly collar! Black
Lint! O China! where, poodle, savior, negro, said,
'Happiest rose and dear buy rosin' " is,
Then they all came together again, in
Out of date, "kin," barefoot rose of aints
Shirtwaisted for several union. Where a pin
Montparnasse crutch, "the D.C. roses are
Fat!" Bush! Then I knew. The sixteenth
Bashful locker, the weary "Joanna"
Room Indian was my — palace of leading snow,
How there you are! with matrons
On Tokio seats' south-placated loop columbariums
Is farther gypsy. Oh notice! there are piers
Under, the, shy sweet Elaine, and along, last
Year, about this. . . . "Orchard five yards long!
O packed saviors of prickly heat! what from
'Keats' you O nut shoe bandboxing surface
Leopardskin fireproof rose magistrate, deaf
Queneau, O period of conceited shoplifting by
Sham tissue 'pay fear' that with stoves tulips,
'Meddy tears,' 'jan-quills,' and shooting Flauberts
Of 'we-fill' light, O Commonness Very of sheds!"

The yoyo's mother is not from Paris. She dranks
"Peegs." Left you. I left you. In Russia
Blanket miller floaty. Bay day Canada mirror
Canada be to pare the floatsy rose "buy 'em"
Sudsy landslide marigold woowoo "looks like." This
At the bottom of twins. O. My paper glass
Is Sheridan Square. No, office. Daring Hoboken
Of twisted Studebakers. She fills
A Mediterranean heart with friendly costumes. Baa,
Mirrors the sheep. Nert. There is a carfare is my window
Why in after *is* blossoms. Oh. Brother of turning gold.
The cops began a workout. Cheerless silver
Matches. "A day of foreign roses the sheep
Love clowns the clouds and Major 'T. Cigars'
Works and drinks." A maritime virgin sinks
Beyond the "Leslie C." O bogs of Syrian dogs
Of marriageable playing togs, Count
Pat, there are gemini in the faithful seminar
Of serenading teabags' windows' dynasty of hops,
Yes, bather, sermon, un-tire and so
I think I *can't* understand your bath, know
The Sabine film-substitute outside chimpanzee meadows
Of health. That ship is hall of landslide's
Say, Dee, end Saranac ore, "what was," "tint," seas!

Mew. R. We're blood patents that weird pink
Tea — fro, runs "Silo, Bill; tea" Madam steer, shower
Of wear-me-out-in-the-feet-aspirin, satin
Trireme shoe statue might Himalayas its
Tramway scene-box. Hill-dog, pay! Grab
The fennel bee of the hollow Macon Subway
New, cockroach of faded ilk, deceased rosemary
London, pens 'draped "golly," and, over
Pied sheep, damn upstairs I see sigh "No umpire
Shovels, Lambeth." Orange magic, sensibility
February amid the strawberries! Raspberries
Mutation moth of a deceptive hillbilly's
Luminous, snow, Cossack. waited, tree. Sense had
Shakes, ovary along, beach, true
Fringe of I May den chorine clockwise raspberries'
Hindrance loop of water Pindar-dependences'
Snowy Sam-a-top of wondrous Thrace
Of if of of of shy's blessings "whin" a cold
Houses of deserted aspirin, cell-less rosemary!
Cinder, hollow, China roseberry.
Rune shelves, a merest baby council chamber
Motto: Sistine Chapel, "fair weather, fewer deserted
Anywhere comma rosaries, limetree ovaries
In quiet subway, hooray, 'Sue' of deceiving umpires."

Wear out Sue, and who is she, wear "Am I ?"
To the shirt's dance, south of bells! And the
Myriad of con sister fan hensy. O dotes
Wear climate changes. Wear the Sistine granges!
O matador, the charming "a fear" of bells,
The masonite of deporting bills, goose affair,
Hen affair, shirtly, hoop, a client, balcony
In central "horse." Oh the sea of pipe
Criticism is a nest egg of hags'
Merchantmarine shelf confusion. "District Ninety,
Howp, this is Commissioner Jimmy. Leap the darts."
Chancellor of my ballad's celluloid hearts,
Lump together! "And the bear wangled from the goose
A distant holiday, mirrors which are also shoved
High, daring hearts, and the plasma of cupidity, dire
Tin, shocking hooves." Mercenary strangers! she
Is Caspian and underwear, the sentences
Of "How pipe! how district October page nice
German loop! Gaga midgets' tornado as
Niece of. All your. January musicians of
Tan!" At summer he figures, "Tornado
Tomato, badgers of defeated licorice, some
White bloomers of breathing calomine, determined
Shoulderies of demented cobwebs, sea-high feet."

As (Copenhagen, O remains of the "ear
Factory" tunes "Quiet Venice, door to seem the door
Able plaza toe, Sim, quiet orange Egypt,
O birth of the oranges, range of fells
'Coalmine'-quacking dirndls of 'thy shifting smack
Smearer than the "kill" of soup,' liberty to sigh
'Positive bracelets, of oranges, the rattlesnakes,
Forget my key, O den of deceased lemons, den
Opera quietly no-place pullman car if lemons
Really.'" But he prints has hit is nowhere is
As defending Egypt rugs from under the moor or
"Solid beans of Stonehenge," the cow's
Mulatto imperialism, dancing "life invaded shirts,"
O merry chowdog of receding pills,
Why aren't you back at home ? Emergency. His share
As bursted hens the decency "of" lemons, now
The "Blenheim" of conceited automobiles'
"Feet air" doors, a sanscrit "lying at" his feet
Mirth filling the cat racial "doughnut" memory
Yes yes. How am I stupid dear strawberry
Mountain? Has the day "knucks" rarely
Money reason and show "sea" "hoop" cheery fountain
Of Moscow Saturdays, orchard "wain" my love
Is lemons, Norway, hamp, sure? Location bigs

The "three" soap stairs, and "my" tower undies
Escaped of devoted Swedeland O sharing miss —
House "bather baby" pot, millionaire pages
Under a shouting lemons of disapproval
An military! shoes baby to take off
Lilac is courtroom cool December house on
"Quaffed" judge-simplicity, Apollodorus'
Cuckoo top hat birthday landslides of
Of! Wills! O tubes of disastrous London by
North us, codpieces of benching cloud —
Blameless surf disk-formation as
Shooting the comet "Birthday" cement feets'
Doorway, "Santa," build of repeating tassel-
Commenced shirt yoyos, unMarseilles! These say
Or after air is. "Rambling" "my pin" "the forest"
"How nigh he ware D (cooling) con Santa
Dim yay! yay!" Hopeless, bobbed air
Eighteenth "Sir Face Din" cows limb
Cousse-cousse ick's howed maritime BABY
Sham "tree"-blamable, as midnight summertime
"Safely to film a cow with hair-beautiful-
Dense potters of shoe-breeze balcony out is
Baby to defy delicate; merchant, O talcum oranges
Of the sea-as, wholesale face at sighs wheat dove!"

"The church of spended babies is all right,"
The peanut telephones, merry peanut, "If."
Our, climate, promotion, Sundays, "If"
When the bursar's damp clubs. Shyest cups
In the spirit of sound effects, dandelion "If"
And "Stevie" asks somewhere sweet streetcar
Of street-sweet car as the valence of Talcum
Moderation of cosine's talcum. "These
Lemons if, stereotyped. Buy now, in shame,
Thick quietness' first linguistic dove." Every-
Thing possessed. O donation Frank O'Hara to
Lightness. Donation, "Sea
Of quietness' dirty froth parachute with yellow
Disinterest buckaroo-plazas O shy pal
Of mirthy telephones, and gyroscopes! our bittersweet
Goodbye! The bun-sleeve hopes you with its heart!
Of plotted asters, O my faded shark! Den, feasible,
Quieter than the pinpricks in the onion
Saying 'Chicago! Chicago!,' ass from a million years
Ago!" How that dove is corduroys. and how
The ship walked through its sweetheart, "Custard.
Of the Blenheim caves," he counts on screaming, first
Reason to year, up! the egg, changer the
Cosine of since, dank pool, cot, now the waves' growing tenderness!

There is a plinth I am hopping. You undress
The years, O waggons. There wind bottles
Off deceiving minnows. Frankness, deer, what sleds!
O Shalott of shaggy air, "Lumber-time," and
"Jeering, Jeering Notation." Now we are
Ours in the air! The murderess eats clams
In Norwegia, cement of our burning frankincense!
Cantata of American troubadours,
What north woods? "Outward the cuties of concrete
Pure she's-castanets, bowing toward the summery Irish
Stairway to gypsy phonetics." They murder my clouds
In your "fancy delectable conceit gyroscope
To 'tossed where we bled, ache, burning dinosaurs!' and
'Sheds of that blinding pace.'" My my-nurse,
Austria. "It was a season of candy dinosaurs;
I picked up my bottle and fell
Danger candy dinosaurs. You teach me German
Phonetics." They labelled beneath the church-road table.
That was Greece. It was the first Shasta.
He built an envelope. She watched him beneath her eyes.
"Those are lids that were his kind effects
O summery gypsy phonetics!" Now she drinks coffee.
The Irish have been murdered. For copying.
O the sailboats of her eyes, a Southern Cross!

"In growing Canadian fields of stupid iced tea
I wavered. Could I he tile
Magic scoptophilia-pilgrim of growing pirates'
Nest? Lackawanna Mary-go-home three million.
O January-month of cloudy lightning
Future lint of mountain hat-bag
And Ceylonic wheels murder my postage stamp
For me!" There is a Bessarabia of guns
Pinpointing his deluded shoulder. Ouch! Tristan! Men
Calmly disturb the delicious pirate. Women
Find his grape shirts, orange
The distance is, filing, motto, pea, chariot's
Coercive May in line cuckooclocks, that
Summer is here! "Embasket the gloated fibs,
Realize the cashier's desk, flub the sea
Of rotating pipes hat-joyous arranger of thugs'
Repine, oh shop in the germ-surveying
Lulu-bards, plinth my hat-surveying figs'
Youth pot-parks, darling the arranges of sog-
Mittjoy is Germany weather, dank gods of
'People will knock glow home, match, symphony
And Constantinople of conceiving pods' dancing
For joy in the middle, loves' car-in-case
Sea, dirty roses of plowing space, mailman-songbook,

Earthenware, clockwork, hen-disinterested
Pittsburgh, shy mirror of hats, O
May! in the delicate burnoose of chocolate
Crayons, council-chamber of tea, owls, blood,
Champagne, dear 'Old Sturbridge,'
The glass nude confined in a sailing blanket of
Hats' sun, with what curves I.
Heater, blondes of questionable space! Cow-
Fair of cheated, and nursemaid of sweet blondes!
Month of blondes! Bombs which mislead, chatter,
They dire la malade n'est plus à deranger, ça, ça
Alors, étant comme elle est, oh la la, morte, comme
La malade n'est plus bombs away sea of lurch
And cloud hill-her blondes the quiet sarsaparilla
Near a thug's twins. 'The Merchant of Venice,' O
Landslide of decayed strings, shafter
Menner and gone. They talked at the
Dove, 'we' Danube, yare, mischievous yoyos'
Plaque of recent parents the dirty cloud, mustard thrill,
'As' beach of china, a bird's cleanliness
With birds', chewing gum and (banjo of peels)
O Florida's pockmarked coast. Magic
Apes! other quiet climate inside my collar
Blondes me, hoop! knotting car fierce damped cuckooclocks,

The stevedores banyan 'trees,' boughs, terebinth
Is longing for 'cleanliness, near or down the nights'
Rag of your night is we batters' terebinth
Of sorrowing sighs, "Leaf, matching and cow," the dense
Blotter, which tears, O bag! the rooms polka
Of feeding clowns', bitterness, 'ant'-terminations'
Sunrise. What is the use of disease
And this floor? O barristers in the
Europe, of a blonde dress, American chiefs'
Shower of bears, tears, bland
Modesty of the 'cokie's' cities' sherbet
Feathers of deknife, chowmiller and bath
Tundras, of devoted. Stare, China, at these uniform clouds.
The murdered potatoes are keeping the sun
From its sun, common marriage of simplicity with
Sulfurous. 'Ant's'-disease, is the sun. Sang 'Blondes
Of the breathing can.' Seldom 'you' buy
The sharecropper, O sea! 'Daniel of our
Lions' den,' church of dismayed lint, how tall
The periods are, Romulus and Remus of the
Joking casket! Tennis on fields of lint, 'The
Sun.' O lost back, the matadors of toothless cities!
That is 'worm-pretty.' Headless. Mayan
'Soon' of shore, the quietness of Silence Mare Show

Lamps is, monitor of a chapter-freed delphinium,
Delphos of the merry climate of 'What are rules?'
Reason, linen mead, air, ribs, oh the size of silence
Bearing shods! Let me, settee of defeated 'rows
Away, photo,' quit the Hernani and
'Tea'-deadening shower, Mazda, climate, quits,
Denver, rose 'like the black youth
Of copper, this summer's solid quince, and colleges
Of delighted silence, pin, carry me and use the
Pan complimenting your head-
Line of frozen knee-bullets' shirts'
Quietly delphininium and freed-men faces.' So,
Sorrow magic greens." The winter ends, as
A pig discovered America last night. O boys. Now.
Samuel. Ocean. Clever wistaria of logs. Hoe
Of tweet-tweet hens hat charming college-bunny
Nexus-filler, hooray-pillow, lama and
Dewy-faced limerick of charts. For pyjama.
Semantics of village, joyaux, buildings, "loops."
Rather. "Heaven" clutches his head. Sweet underwear.
"Comma, I showed you different climate, whoopee
Step-the-soap stairs. Wow languorously lethal.
Tyrinth. Difficulty sweater. Parachute, nun, "Queen
Bath," oh, arrivals in the potatoes of. The city.

Sails! earth, "how perished laundry?" Bin. Clad.
Coconuts, binge, paratroopers, wheat,
Castles of dancing tatoos, even paratroopers
Of an orange's daily injustice. Malabar. Shredded Wheat.
Lemons what "few," kiln am "burr day
Umber" members deSouth, helmet, on "teached
Imagination, calm." O dirty shrapnel of conceding
Skates' first laugh "after" youth fields'
Lint queue of "sat"-bath, "after," shrapnel
New, cracks "after," bug retires. Sheeps' lackey! yoyo!
Dock. Rays. Easel. Set Andes
Shirt-manufacturer decency of cold,
"Hens. May-nifty, motto. Donatello, sway now
Terminals," cups of French steam! April blotters
Miss you, Donatello yoyo. O black literature! Back
India yoyo home. Matches, wee. Colonel. Asleep.
In. Wee. Comical landslides of
Pretty legislature. Bent "lions' " Algiers, Illinois.
Conch of sashayed pill. White is appearance
Germany bathroom cow nutty ashamed personal
It's purple. Breaking into my heart like a
"Climb this blotter of permanent yellow lace,
Weary old comédie." Am burr lace. Desk. Pick
Up the yoyo. After, Hebe. "Thanks," in this purple hour!

Bong! went the faery blotters; Ding Dong! the
Country of Easter! shore! each toes
The marriage-bin, shouts of "Conch!" "Ruthie" "Lurks
Behind the 'pea' is basement's Illinois
Obtuse radio-lithogram!" "Coptic!" and "Weak Beddoes Less-us-the-shirt!"
Ran behind me-Vishnu, all
Summer. Closet of how it seems! O bare necks
In October, closest apparent "film star" of the
Buffalo. Peter of Carolina's neatest snow-
Pier condescension, O haughty chapter how
Clear was as apparent cruelty, bonnet,
List, tackles the lace. Hump chariots the summer
Either desires. Ether, so tall
As ice, sees her cuckoo hooves at desire
Margin. Amour dodo cranberries. There
"Art," "blamelessly," cashes, D's, wed's hat's
HEADS! Joyous midnights, different clams!
Oh the word "flotation"'s cosined beaver rotation beneath
The "seelvery" dog-freight cars, mammoth
Stomach-quiz-raspberries we parent
Cuckoo Mary coast-disinterest verst of "cheese" diversed
Flags of the "comma stare" rewhipped
Georgia of teaching cash registers to "hat" side
Of pale "plates," the bitter "nurse" southing "ha"-green "stangs" forward!

O badgers, badges, bats, bags, bags is,
Black, blacks, rats is, as, is as, as, is,
Badgers as, is, is, bridges', bags, bags as is
Business of the fourteen (I noticed "Henry") badgers.
Dark plantation of these furious sidewalks! First
Lifted-up usual "Mamie"-hello, dockworker,
Pancake, silliness, feet-locker, lower-class,
Power-gasp, Kokomo, dithyramb kimono. Whang
Bang! collar, bleachers, parachute, delicacy,
Noun, Janice, dental-work, siren, sirens, boulevard,
Tarragon, limp May, wine, decency, earth, mountain
Sidewalks, decency, earth, sidewalks' happy sirens,
"Match wrappers! Match wrappers!" Juno, Janice,
Meat-hooks, Elaine, lilacs, parapsychological
Cocoa-distinction plasm, jowls of the seedy grocer,
Monday, disinterest, sea ramparts, banjos, groups
Of pineapply-flavored Jericho-lemons. Sleep, sleep.
Merchantmarine O thousandth freight in Venice,
Cutie, waters, envelope, chapter, thousandth,
Frigate, sleep-resisting billboards, if mountain
Choreograph), seventeen, resisted. Maldoror,
Shirt-ads, of wintry face. Council of blackest
Dogs, sleep, is slain. Cutie. Is resisted.
Visit is. Disinterest. False solomon's seal. Go to sleep.

"I arise from dreams of thee, open air bell
Ohm tiny match his hat duke wheat son
Wild, Peru. Genji of deciding cups'
Care-cup! noun, as ash, flossy hit;" we
Are the hips of everybody's son; nat-
Urally, leaves a sun, day, choked up, read or, is
Anybody! disturbs naturally "th' sweater
Empties the feet in Yarrow. Hal is musically
Very is, jay weird sight of tomorrow
Bannisters." Surge of banditti, oh,
Sweethearts. There is a seventeenth moon deciding
Wheat-ministry-triangle-deranged churchmouse.
End tea socialist clubhouse before you begin
Eating sweaters. The pears are dancing. What rain?
Manna isthmus, dose of climate, way
Orchard noun and in the Swanee sheep. "Baked
Hats! to arrive from seams of tree
Service, town. Anne in delighted orchids. O mashed
Lakes, biers, seventieth pyre of green
New Yorks, loam 'where beautiful
As Eden, voodoo shades in charleston religion? "Sue"
Weak, daring, America'," and the raided shocks
Hobo, mean, soporific knicks. Marjoram chinchilla. O sea
By quirk, calmness, shy, "Indeed-ape," bob the thousand!

Orchard of the deceiving ant penthouse in
Mere cunctation of "we" browing air-patience
Toreador matches-siblings "Oliver" Bowling-balls
And "Mary" Isn't-working-the-dream-downward, come home, shake
Fiery sea aspirin, as "I'm using a the Lake Poets'
Win-bandit-flowers!" From Huey's casement
March, April, and solemnity, the cool sincerity babies
Up upon chair-car, flying through nameless England! Banjo
Of peace! monthhood! ooh, Soho! yak of the German clams!
Pack of "The Diamond Ships'" bursars-maying-cards knee
High true she "Boston" domino! "Shirt can I wear, is
The cue-ball's dirtiest Delibes." O monthly
Syntax of a florist's cones, "Charles" with the mink
Face, characters from Canada! Dizzy the charleston
As pink merchants, green you are faded yoohoo!
The classroom, O bitch! these surface classicism
Plotting the tube's creation from conscious mattresses'
Series of dismaying springs. O logs, manner, and T-
Square. "The horrible ditch is ended. Now
Yoyos air parachuting flamingos, job-hunters
Have breached their blue home; nominally the cuckoo
Is such a chair-far hunter. Wintry the tables blue
Deer, in the tables of Z-dancing 'Koko' are here,
Sew, too, shun the further 'ants-eat-people.' " "Loud and bill!"

Bandana of cavey sea-tins! pyjamas! ladder on
"Eek's" bugle call of shallow GLUE, PIER, SOLDIER, and
SPILLWORT dirtiest case of the marshmallow
Sin language, merchantmarine of chows! Back, lurid
Leaf of the Chair FINANCE! O
Santa Claus can heaps behoove love cemetery
Gypsy. Market of playing Beans' Research, Baa
Lethal tagsheep. Erp. "Kill my shabby
Dog with careless BEANS. Or jellybeans
Will complicate four research-
Pilgrims in, lazier than the, GREEN
Rebus of opium. Oh, daze!" Why shirts came RED
As youth ex-Canadas, shallow doggest dream —
Lamp, "Sunday I boxed a COLITIS pinprick,
Shore!" Ugh-row of the lazy-towels-when,
GERMANY and CALIFORNIA again! The RIGHT
Beans hill know a banjo toga-conference
Disinterest. Sherman for president! Surface
Chow, O green! air, go away. BATTERS
Up! "She decides to become the climate
Of ARABIA, she bannisters two CALIFORNIA and
Diamonds. Sense-tea-wear bay dun off oof focus
And becomes WELL-BEING, the turtle
Of grace, knickers, and cactus. SHE has no colitis!"

O Barrymore, the choosing of a place
Beside the Russia of dirt's Coliseum. ADS
For nothing! chowdog chowdog as "this" hearing-aid!
Manhattan, you are the author!
Blankets, chancellors, film-dogs, nurse-waves, banjo-
Stevedores so cashmere as red, O billboards the
Passage of "gorge" delicious-makeup season
Shasta of pirates' disinterest "tornados" and
"Shack of hued blimps!" O best
Bench, Bessarabia. They are watching the feet on
My eyes; the dust is resenting halva, "Marriage
Of Figure." Oyster had gherkins and his eyes
Were breathing like the Chesapeake and Ohio
Railroad. Dog pats him to slip, certain lilies
Of Canada blind HIM. God, what an awful night
To be the terrible illness of Southey's dog!
They are picking out some lanterns is Nephritite
Dirndl is connoted handkerchiefs. Why, Violet!
You here among the summers' dogs! "White?" "Why an
Heartache isk more total than bananas'
Windy" violets freeze! Say, there is a
Sharecropper of total blackness. Uncle Steven's
Hat! We never expected kin to blouse
Arabic, up! O "Ladislaus, the loss is gone to sleep!"

He: "The strawberries are putting." She: "Brilliant Egypt,
I wonder about the ladies' dancing carfare
That Percival said was 'baby us, brilliant oranges!'
They say for my sake she wore a silver kerchief!"
Bill! How Mordred to Arthur you my handy gear
Of fair sexiness, she thinks. He places: "Lock
In the baby of you fair oranges. Lock
In the baby. O doubts, mirlitons and foghorns!
They say he had appeared to be a bench,
But Canada toured him in her brilliant pockets
And he became her 'Solitude,' a large, furbished painting
That used no hands the way anciently oranges
Listed to the bugle-call's left." Allah, frogslegs!
They are so tear-bitten! Water as lovable clues
Deceives-as lines there cuffs showering "purple
Scientists who tea their frost"; lobster,
Why haven't you been invited to the painting?
"I was too cross, and too yellow. They really
Aren't the two you sawed in half yesterday. Watch
My pins!" Lands! I saw a lobster leap the gas-range,
A merchant of March. "She sold me two red kimonos,"
A dear thinks, "and yet, when I walked the Allahplaza
Remembering dirt-kangaroos, I forget my name.
Is it 'Shorty,' or 'Polly,' or 'Julie'? Oh it may I am the nurse!"

O soul of all my life, ah solo flight
Beyond the Mexican blue! "It is predicted
Giraffe-gorilla-that-I-am-to-be-killed. Lethe
Corral me 'now' the burnoose other blue
Landslide!" Mud, tortoise, the Japanese fighters!
Good Bound-Face wrote "taxi" the hall December
Ladies'-club-youthful frigidaire-men's-room red
Chanukah of a donated judge, to see
The Canadian pottery, "bee" was so characteristic-
Ally lacking in "these" persimmon-decorum of
Loud, that that. Oh many was the "hick of cancel worms!"
Her quiet wig was a parachute. Stones!
O the bad answers through a bin of petite ruins
Shines! "Magic. Earthface. Geranium. Bad-
En Baden of pretty sharks, yoyo-column, pin
Buying teas. O the mastery of his fenestrated
Shark!" Yoyo said: "Die, Patty, of disease
Blossoming larger than 'we're'-tarts barking silt
Now in the midst of raspberry-time, which gophers' exile
Is merely a hack window, jumped-down in the back
Love believing blouse, song cheery velveteen,
Mocking rose of gifting satin. Beds. Some
Deerparks." Day lifted their skeletons.
They came to the blossoming veteran; and fancied beer.

And terebinth, lobster of this season, Mudlark!
Oh, barriers were shooting, the billionth
Coffee of "wonderfully" dizzy tea. "Man, or
Cosmopolite, lair is the bird of mints'
Island. Balcony cosine of the hays." Each
Forgets to mention "that frozen candy." Birthday.
I am so happy that I could split
Fire-engines, to know that blue is here.
I wonder if lobsters have always known how it felt
To care for the midway at most candy
Beer. Either, yes, tomorrow, is evil, or
I ain't feel it. There was "wonderful" chow
Last night. We barefoot the enemy. Glad
I have like her gold, yet glad
That, and, serious tomorrows at silver toes
Free Island. O Danube! mirth, at
Tennis, was "the lea." They "danced" with me.
"I gladdened this worried Catholic bishop
Summer!" Daring Wotan, the King Lear of my
Courtship! For he is bringing "chairs" in the
House. His barrister walks: "Fading rose,
Mummer of the shy weird golden fingers',
Eighteen, a deserved aspirin. College
Is nice!" In that month, youth carried each frigate!

Monsters label his hill: "Mantle Hill, Cuckoo,
Air, Moth. Their gorgeous Philippines
Is friends of Ireland. Ask 'Herbert,' lowdy,
The weak cosmopolis of raspberry sherbet." Some
Time ago I forget about all proportion. These are
Crumbs. They dance. Its sleeping state. "Wonderful chow"!
O marriage with coastlines of aspirin. I taste
Them, "howdy, airplanes." This nice reason
Their chair hat my finger, is "don't," summer! Gee whiz
Of curtains, has lariat of she fignewtons'
Really. Ha ha. Are you hysterical,
Lefty, now? With what reason does your hat
Come out into the sleepy bottom
Up the Canada river, the merchandise, "Alf," dossier
Is late church. When last night we separated water;
And May-time habit clutched at tennis. These yes-
Whites! O odge, pyjamas! Marriage of recent white
With bear-shooters, the Mississippi. Gin of cares,
Plower. O jeep! red white and blue
Tans, rooming is Santa's first beach, class
Of beaten Gulf Gas, murders! Constant
Constant mad mad. Hen! engine of rejoicing gin!
There is a big airplane running O my
Blimp, across the defeated Mexicos of aspirin!

Daylight, now, this wreath of hogs.
Oh, there's a burglar called Smoky.
The buglecall is managed thunderwear, the babes
In arms have all been turned to Octobers, with
Baskets in their shoes. I know this "are":
Baskets, murder, ending shoes. Each taxi-ing lobster
Knows that baby, she is as delicious as an orange
Blimp. Night! Tanager! O tuxedo
May conceited lobster! guarantee is orange
As "Molly's in the rowboat." Guarantee
Me the badness of each sharing strawberry
Of notes. She as taking out her under "Where
Are logs, cannibals, and sheep? Is this the
Malice, good summer! of a yoyo's streetcar?"
Oh I lay on their bed, in the beginning, at the
Baseball. Carry me, Mary Ann, carry me!
You may think each hair is phonograph
But Canada of delighted wrong. Borrow you are
Blue. Blue out came to meet the bar
Flotsam gypsy earthwear reading, can
Of German blossoms, dentists in Cincinnati
Fancy attitudes, cotton to defeating summer!
"Nancy, Georgia is now quiet. Pale win-
Ter duck, meet limbo. May, hen, oh Mississippi!

Military 'where-are?' youthless, inks
Well 'git' mad, O sharp! Not 'over-where?' " and
Either youthless syrup. They man could buy
Location-qualify to "hees" lemons Jan lay on
Oyster melon charge account Epidauros. Match
Us, we, first inks: giant, cuckoo, and red, but
Maced gold, O sweetness of deceded chemistry
Marry. O the sweetness of braided celery on
Tile badgers, "he is the funeral of any cat.
O courts! March was 'hen' whist 'yew' ear
Funeral, cat." "In the missionhouse through Mondays'
Missionpowders of marvelous pink (Death air death
In the Deathhouse) (Eep!) missionary
Cuckoo, loves, ape, mortuary, defeat, is almshouse
'Mary' House, we days of long
Thirst, cuckooclocks sandy as green
Germany mouse Northrop. Ivy, win, you, say.
The America of — cocoa, ash, bin, ivy." "Nude,
Bandits, mouse, rosemary" "Wintry is the silence" "Marshmallows"
A. Lurid chances, stop. Fishing carefare.
"Indian bench malade. Wheat. Amble south
Is amble." "He wears the sweetest bench
Of bandits American is the world." Dancing
Of of. Oh! Loud, ant, the snow, waitress

Cancelled the youth of day knee's blue waters'
Ceramic foster gun. Shabby
Animal crowding Hun. Bleeding knickers,
Perfect "came to alone balance of five weaknesses'
Sharecropping the crow-doughnuts of hay-peanut"
Jan lay, the sea had, when, comedy Epidauros
Weakness, "perfect," change for these marshmallows'
Contour, gee, simplicity, American yoyos! sen
Sens of peculiar mildness! The barrel is
An "country of embarrassment," to the charge un-dimes,
Not-waitress, enter the sea. You died of embarrassment
Winter, crazing pin of the marshmallows
Gone blue, magic at Easter; and the phones'
Welfare corset of genius again-society. "Nail me
To the pillow the Anna Dime of showering pillars
Severance cute alcohol." Major
Interest artist "Daniel" in the why be again
Their cots of snow O waist in the pink
Column! share of my east! savior
Of useless notes! Common way, the
Churches it aspirin, south un-day, blue manag-
Er charm that lakes to "Big Sea," un-Dane
This sleepiest one, dime land hokku kerchiefs
They. Green, the shirts of his table, lain down to be gory

Knees, un-, Lord, order, a, commanding Saracens
Carles li reis, nostre emperere magnes
O foolish Fords in Spain! Set anz tuz pleins
Tresqu'en la mer cunquist la tere altaigne
Bachelor, Hugo, and cockeyed Milton! win-
Ter arches, decency with eyebrows, gun-
Sight of brocaded fixtures, lockjaw in
"Youth Wins Each Private," lariat of mo-
Ronic; damp, who was your nurse? "My own." Stockings,
Whiskey. "Lay me. Bread limit that has tin sheep
Esteban Elsewhere, hoop! coldblooded hymnal
Judge because the cuckoo leaps." Cockeyed mate
Wait till all "dear" Saracens "ant" in their tents.
Mix-up! Weevil-show-time! Hundreds
Of pages, holiday, try-out, fear, gold. Nan
Waxed "neat" to the Sarabandes, coma is Hans
Chalk. Pierre knocked on the cool weevil
For a British hour and a half as the nailfiles
Were old sixteen years old crucibles' marshmallow
Wheelbarrows' service yellow, O bonny balconies of
Hunk! Aegerian buildings mad in junk
Red and the ponds of bell-ink coffee "of sweet true
Comedy, to say 'there,' " but Roland bleeds:
Pyrrhic, umbrella, my! hammock collars you. Cuss. Wheel.

Nine days to one you may the forest this
Europe qualify imaginary pastry notice
Summer hat curving to placard yellow
Dens of curving imaginary violets
To steep the order, "White illegal portholes,
Who dance is the sun, march wind, say Venice
In Sumeria, peculiar, loving potatoes, gone oyster
An, correspondence sweet, no out of blue
Andante, Shelley, these pastry follow
Their latest oyster. Can give each quiet blotter
So nude notice, end, tea, bareback rider,
All over town. Then sew, use the sea, mad
To begin where blotters the cigar-orator-
Hay-lobby. North anything off dream you've been
Ant, dear collies in yellow, barristers in green. These
Courses, wonder a white as no, be given, run
Who cranberries, yes in backwoods blue
Till sigh, their challenge. Go, slim blockade,
Oats-dairy! We're not all back
Engining blast, engines London, kiss, night,
Endow. Forthright is the sheeplike elbow
And the bins of a tern's resolution!" Weeping mixed
With "Golly, she alone kissed us!" and paper
Kenneths, thrown against the windows of outlifted airplanes!

Bay-leaf! for you are burned by the midget sun. And
Marriage, to the cold, mint stables of anyone! Bay-leaf!
Landslide! Marshmallow! Feces! Annoyance! Sew
These leopards into place. Bay-leaf! Uncut faces!
Lumber! Wait! The curtain of the pyramids
Is lifting! Bay-leaf! He is the pirate of underwear! And
She almost promises! The lark is their loosest hearts'
Greenhouse. They die when shirts. Some professor
Cuter than Long Beach! O bad! dirty goods'
Limited sweet hearts! As now, she cereal-planes
Councilchamber. Heatbox undie heart. O bound
Calico mirror of "ten sighs"! Certain
Nights I cannot sleep; the wind calls me, "Stewart,
Go out among the loganberries, preferably
Alone. The lake will lie there like a barber." I get
Up, and the stovepipe seems paler than Alaska!
Cold is the parachute, pea, fine the sun, merry
The purpling heart-commissioner, January,
Pencil, otter, Michigan. Orchestra beds!
I name you yet I know you, hoopless Jimmy!
What is the climate Monday pyramids
Bay-leaf! etcetera. "Gonads have that clear pencil,"
She said; "the madmen have all retired. There
Is going to be April faster than next month when it's April!"

Showers, summer, handouts. Will the locusts
Be okay? Marjoram, chancellor of the pill creamery
Dollars you paid who to rest your house batty
Cemetery cloaca bended knee; evangel
Of the rosary batteries! What "perfect" yellows!
When Jimmy felt that orange chain he felt
The excitement of a parachute at sea! He linked
"Plaza" and "joyous parachutes." Nathan in his car
Honked. Uncle Parachute filled his camera
With joyous razor-blades and "perfect cameras." Sleep
Walked carfare by the sea. A boat "pelvised"
Germany, it was so green. "Oh, then,
Can't we marry velvet?" screamed Jimmy. Down went
The surf, in. Most often. He would have carried the yellows
Back into the cabinet of detective yellows. I bet
The rookies have never noticed anything. Sewn
In his car, loosely amid the raspberries. Shoe!
Lux soap might make you a swan. Surface, chimney,
Banjo. Hill, bicycle, aspen. Oh he shook socks
In wildness ridge, bounded off against his car,
Woke Nathan, fared through the wilderness of dogs
To surface, twined this bay-leaf, and shunned air-boats.
It would have been nice for you "that lemons"
Assume he is streetcars, O quiet half bench of wood.

Call, lean, boar. Swim. Is three
Birds. Win to. Sweet. Medallion-and-
Garage, tassel. Wheat. Lonely. Bag woods or
West-ear lemons. So, in no; and. Deep. Maharajahs.
Six. We will you us half lift is. "Oar-lemons
When" that movie is. Final. Aren't you liable
Touring-bee, us please? Shirt-India cars; and
"Either thou socks sue the sun, air-
Hole, tan surface, pear-clock, gemini
Ands youth, purpler. Thee, bears as pure sacked
Reason sunlight 'Mary' tellurium maharajah:
Blanqui. Their shirts water as
Mist! Who cold dassn't-Mary, theatre. Henry,
Soda Gun? Ouch dancers!" Sunlight is those
Little with. In. Cow nextdoor; rabbits
Year, fail-tent. Next coat. And January, theatre
Calcium calculo California ban, yearns
Calcium theatre, oh. Oh. Endance shoe
Mans. Un. Bare decent dachshund was, pour
"Ain't" trimmer wick "Angel can wintry
Cocoas repair," oat quiets him, clan-
Destine shirts! Sandal of derring-do
Harangue by these fields Blanqui
Of Mary, and sunlights in bomb! — green, endocrines we next dove

Barricade "um!" dare Z horse in
Who yellow legs. Andes wrench news hand me the
Curtains win freeze: location as Chelsea blue
Finance tree, hook, deprivation. "He blankest of rugs'
Dens, toe, and 'character nearest bells-hills'-
Dogs. The soldiers wander him rum. Danai-
Cringe-yellows. Shaggy Ghents!" Now,
April hinges wonder parachute toilet brainbeat
Limerick surfaces lilac pessimism leaway merchants
Toys ant Jane you were's active neon so
Peanuts away the nominative air-green Indian
Momentous shall I peculiar lilacs button canary
Ocean billets man cloak Sumerian lilac orange
Lane bannister sunrise Congo to sea
Bond mention sameness lilylike parachute. We
Foundation limousine the sea. Imagine that
Clothing! O beans, hinder climate red
Bandanas' come each oar para-seating doll-sweaters'
Coppering knee "Hippolitioid" "poiple" chaperones
Tree, songs ditch answers lemon, "Dear Phillips,"
Endymion quiet the merchantmarine Saturday
Luna fan seed desk "Nursemaid ooh subway act dusk
Raspberry gee am cup ho-ho landslide
Mill, mano, risk, later" senators. Fenways, eagle and maids

Other "lingering" rabbits' youth lift fiery yellow
Nomination showtime assassin, "Sweet
Are my cares. My den is column, news,
Coliseum. Marriage are my bent
Gloves; and normalcy this Fenway muse as color
Sandy. Chow, and music's officer, see, hop
And dare musics' greatest lungs. Lama end
Hairpin balcony shoplifting color. Hi, blue
Bears! vote for me; I glow." Santa of So! O
Terebinth of teeny colors, an ocean's collars!
Mantlepiece! Unhonor quiet as the worm
Invents. Us, season of punjabs and death-
Mints' cogs, marriages with sheepdogs, beds, and
Stunts! Lintels, pow! are everywhere, care limns
Doped heads. Alcohol of frayed lintels! faro-
Delivery, O sleepy lungs' "placard" high, say, "Blue
Backs, General Win-Madison-Square-Garden April
Of querulous testicles!" Bench of the curving weight-
Lifters, solemnity of, hat, teething orange
Winter "May! hill!" sewily dear half nickle. And how
Pass chocolate, hens, pin day-suits, and water
Lariats! Soutime modesty China, ant! weightlifters
Balcony-minty. Canada, why; Easter say. "How stunty
Bear rose the, dean drums, 'an entirely fiendish wafer!'

China there are benches on the chairdogs'
Color-wimple, "May I bent
These tedious ranches?" howl, Lulu! and I
Hairdogs' yes, I, when fine stooges am
A bare lea-snood, polish, rum, Andes tiptop legs'
Mentioning golddust to hay! Kinsey! Marxist College! "Ann"
Word! How! stables are we; end I yes
Dither; "she belongs to me fatter than a drugstore,"
Ben Jonson, shirtwaists, and pretty magazines'
Carolina, "Though mother is a new
Baby, Carolina, pigeons! Sherman for president! Molo-
Tov is diving tomb eye my tippy chaircar; lungs'
Dog airminds Atalanta's." Hill which first
I Monday eskimo my inkbook; wheel hollow
Labor Alpine, this, dirty Angevine, sea, bear
Toy-poetry; "Make it a mistake
A your pyjamas, ace the. Lanterns on North
Can." "Youth Major servitude landslide
Cokes." Ha-ha the berry. Colors men. Inchings
Frogs and magazines. See at the cherry colors
Men, sun witty ham's cop rays, engine as
Sea, dogs. There they are, has, gold, in, hen.
Pardon me. Little matadors. Carcass's neat gold
College, he: yoyo-terebinth, what little lungs!

America inch lover Santa cares ago
Bicycle; Me: Matchwrappers an ever rainthing ugly.
Wayne: Drag sheep away into maritime
Cupboards. Sarah: Mockery, colicky streetcar
Universe raspberry shirt pin lie sweaters'
Sweep, out, today youth over youth muttering "Housetops'
'In movies'!" Are there lariats an defeating cans'
Choice rocky melancholy Jericho and-is-side pillow
Scene, seldom is Nevada, munificent, walk to cruelty
Angel. Eight art. Hoops pond links balance. Aaron: Mock
No. Otto: Gentle parmigiana, us key raindrops, crackling
Choochoo magician piano, red, balance. Lattice
Mirth — sandaled sheep. Ken: Doubled holiday, piano,
Miriam the mirror, Atlas, Liliom, Cambridge. What
Horses dune Marilyn key E sparkling? Hands
In cold as. Kent: Oar-shape, find the peary space
Mirth "hads" light at "time" the magician city
Nancy; truth masonite showers furniture. Anne
Endoplasm Cincinnati concert millionaire show
Their sweethearts every Ingres youth Jericho furniture, O
Canada, Havre knee nursemaid the tawdry wastebaskets is
Notepaper brassiere, O landslide
To "perfect" Greece! When I was totally, and "sieze
Lemon," laudanum of preparing streetwalkers' sunrise clove-tan!

Scenic parachute. Column. Pear. Elevator
Sent hair swans. Bam the students. Pillow
Then Swedish underwear. Year-horse. Bogs
Season curfew than Atlantic merry Christmas howl
Inchings act students' dairy lazy us. Pegs!
Southern. O we "marshmallows" water its crazy-dairy-
Necessary students, interests yam then "Is some" shoe
Wait aw the scenic dairy in "Yes I am
'Tree' is 'melody spies' purple" oy their blues gen-
Uine great vanished cloud! Bins! clasp of the pre-
Liminaries too tinder pie rose, late, rosin, discovery
Banjo peanuts lyricism that rosin
Fails discover genius Mother's Day lank church
Of Country Pin! Banjelo, tangelo in
Meet — Hands! cloistered sharks! dairy
Farm of delayed face-dimmed "cosmopolitan
Asia fastest say wood Germany faculty defeated
Nuncio bled 'fanfaronade, gimp disky bees
Lama cow furnishing Delibes gamma raspberry
Jericho munificent function opera delphinium
Sheba!'" Axe! charity! kin-berries! lay-lows!
Opera bare your Chinese Polonius ping pong
Slave Mycene Germany calendar reform
Savings bank endoplasm coconut sea hood foggy ankles

Easy to Coney Island, winter, and pep! O matcher
Of teasing-matches, matador of "teethes," mangle-
Course of "seizing barricades," O colon, merit-
Eagle, bandager "Ozzy Carpet-Faces lilac mercy
Interest, ant, life," beaver, soon-you, bare,
Agora in, moronic sukiyaki, O tenth
Summer! minus! Andes undie drifting shoe
Meritorium, sharethismatzo, end, Lulu
Born, scene, Canada, me, LeClos
Wolf! airwaves! sandwich, there are receding
Ox, maladive; merchantmarine, selfless
"Solomon," fishes. Tarragon, Aragon, hula-newly
Endeared Ingres-shaped mint clods'
Jeer-storm-its heavenly-mirrors, youthless ale! At
"Three Teeth." Amerigo! summer!
Bins! embarrassment! "Weir a cold half an angel
Den mid-altitude car reception decimation lie
Here, Z blue. Morrow angel Anza tune the
Morrow January-mirrored two!" Mentioned
Aspirin grin as lemons orange belt
Possibly do; chair coat midnight soap
Paris engine kimono eastern comma "their place
Tacit end alls you"-mate ear of bat! summah west
Matchsticks Eden of is "Daniel" "urban hill!" Oy! Hail!

Yesterday an usual fainting pen bananas
Auto. Winter for my catching out flags not
Merry in my room! Denver! orbèd hags! O fan-
Shaped leaves' British Museum's stern
Aspidistra of brocaded Annamarie Lily Ann Ber-
Tha Leeway end America these day, O motto, modern
Ant fair impudent charm's gay beauty
Shellfishing doughnut-ankle's arm Mildred
Lois, and these, ice-man, the tear-men, E
Soon, wave me, modern, blue-ascendance Cal-
Ifornia, day, mantle, sorrow, lands "Lindy
Maritime hunch knee baloney youth he's French!" I
Nearly fell auto this museum! Lair-bins,
O comicals! Majesty, their green and suitable hogs'
Ten guitars which mother I climate
Sun grateful Marie-bannister-soup craving their blue
Deer, the men who cocoa lilac
Hips of peace January mistral hemp Detroit
Of saving lurid nits, O mouth, curseway to the south
Might-Helen, syllabic (bet-chair) gin-telephone
Louder than the earthware thinks! "Charles? Telephone.
Teeny, sure to send Dale a sun-dial."
Central are the token seas. Tender Labrador of bees,
Paper antonyms. O the hill picks up, that is pink.

Weaver, the bandanakerchief, a hen's, nuts'
Shannon. Looms that take care of America! O
British guns in Glencannon! Palace of gloomy
Insincere physicians! Moron of every positions
Heaven is cutting the passive mirror too
Close to us! O Rembrandt in a bottle, sleeves
Of the joyous pituitary, maritime
Interests, coalescing "Mammy Slope-the-
Pink-up-into-them-," believers in wattles!
O bear-cats! bear-rugs! bundles of shinto wristwatches!
Goateed shoeboxes! lariats of striated dust! mints
In comma-formation, San Salvadors, mirrors in
Transition, senators, cosines, and nuts'
"Chair which he might dance balance blaze
Knee"! Oh! Ocean! demon of the dem-
Demonstrations the sweet formations, wheat-hap-
Py neat-fornications, O savage! licorice as
Broadway! What number in my shoe! Faro! Lie
Down! Shave! Miracle! Borax in Neptember, flock-
Magine, genius-blessing, toss! cure-you! They
Are not mine! O anono, a May "thyme," a "nuss"!
Bravely I built you at Faro, jail-word-
Sin-bad-chill-sane-pollen-car saying "Tweet
Ins!" Motionless air-raid! bungalow of peaked clay!

No wonder! parachuting germ hay-mow squad and king
Every ant is king! minnesingers in gown-
Boxes, ladies, money; WE
Childhood sew, weak ladder peppermint Balkans
Every mild is king! banjos (aye) going
"Yessirree-streptococcus," Mercedes
Avenue, win D shy parachute of the oyster
In enamel youth plod hinge parachute
Down hair, motto! Boled parallelo-
Grams, weaver is not king! Jaded, though
Mild ands ant, blotter, yoyo ship sate Jericho believer
Angevine "Sewn in his car,
Loosely, amid the raspberries," — hokku! revolver!
"Winter comes among him, latest coffee
Peep, oil, April; Angevine, cop, noodle,
Hinge, birthday, Peter Pan: 'Say it is not so
That why bee weevil dinner landslide mite
Caretaker, blessing his handkerchief; whereupon
Laurel and Hardy.' " Certainly tomorrow is weapon
Pleonasm. Dancing, like kosher icewater
Lays. Rob the conceited strawberry, engine
Count on the deceitful oyster. Imagine the
Sea, that knights! Borrowed his fading isinglass
Ankles, cocktail shakers, churchgoing leaps, umpire, Virginia,

Biltmore, "Sue Group," matches, all go, "And
When we had almost turned to aspirin, the
Paris of three-feet germs," O notice-
S of green and limpid lemons to "an
Office, air-built, nine offer," Mary-chute sen
Sen battery milkshake oh are hottestblue
Lends, and weewee were to be seen (badger
Nexus of youth weed anvil-surly borax! Shah!)
Tour, acey rink, momma, YOU
Came, dancing whippet of tie-college, hoop! yoyos!
Bather, bannister, sleepy sight, ant, mutts'
Quietness needling "are hoop chair" is
Encephalon, oyster, the weariness crying
Encephalon! matador of potassium phalanges, slim
Hobo, militant cheesecake, my real
"Merchant of Venice, The Winter's Tale, Two
Gentlemen of Verona," "Salome," labor of the defeated images
Or-Kenneth-strous baby for "magic location, thou
Lazy Boston in aspirin, sweetheart, earthway piano
En-soma lemons." Ore-parachutes! better than the Island Queen
As sting sighs, O mint, church, sail, Sun-
Day, whoops, in rocky Pittsburgh, sharpening pencils
Beside the leafy badger, notice how
Bare arms singing "Wheelbarrow," merchantmarine, cry it. Lemons.

Ornithology, man "hid"s in glass! whoppers
Of Dean "A yes joke," rum deceiving by
Hay cooked balcony swart lemons in. O
Columbus! Can doing beery silver naturally "wheem"
Georgia of costing Sea Arabic, — outlines
More "entire empire" sweet asterisk yellow knee
Khan rabbit. Sofa, peanut, end girlhood, how
Lorgnette de-orange all, in white. Orchards
Of dental sonnets. Add ad ad. Hand orchestras
Hay-knee "ousand Meary Thousand" — Yale
Okay acorn is in in-orchestrous phalanges'
Podge! More! the caretaker is free with aspirin
Showplace America to-me; cost-Max! O backs
Wonderful, eagle angry's-light end, O! arrest
Oyster. We, after all, more pink bee, solder
Airy banner sea toy carpets, baseball
With hand seas; O waggons! Shave the
Lea angry ope behind orange "Lag, up from new
In, as, woe Jericho this difference wonder," acts
Silly; worried whom green-O lakest badger,
Nouns! Winter, Caribbean, curvy elope-grange-
Masthead: pigs! "Science tells me that you
Are a pig"; writer of hand-made orchestras,
Bather, "end," willow a, church, fin, aid-fool's

Sigh photo dream cargo sit loop worm, hike! San-
Ta S weeping pigeons oar gore ninetieth
Working bended bow is "nineteen," axe our
"O mustard" wanton-streetcars O shyest red
Eight and April imaginings culver Lulu silver
Banana peanut savannah. Hollow buildings
Of "Die now, mother No-forks lethal
Ale-blue silver," color, moth, ah inch January
Flag-pinned; shy savannah-green forks "egg"!
O not! Bearing chute of dressed tomato's
Yoohoo coastline opera-eagles, jangle
Odd. Oyster favor disintegrating marriages
Table yellow, "Oh summer is hot for fools!"
There were British linens in the
Weewee emotion disintegration glamour garage
Nonsense magazine olive midnight cuckoo
Gyroscope titivate America gingery showplace
Shallow lime wit motion Santayana O cuckoos,
Grey, fearful, yum yum, happy, our gypsy pow-pow
Mayor, sty of distasted elephant-elevator
O shiver prunes, nightways, tea-deserved sob,
"Am I losing this mantle of scientific lemons
To Hobbes?" Idiot, ankle, bakery jobs
Kisses, and migraine gobs of "Hamlet," a China of sentences.

Formed by the note-taking of mudpushers," as
Formidable as violets. O fair field of the
Form of Hussars' climate of conceding harps'
Fork jujube aimless Louisiana, O wraps'
Forest of "Lee Herman jail." Salivate in
Focus, nineteen ninety oh sunshine, back
French, livable, dairy, engine, choir-man, sea
How fair are airy strawberries' feeble
Monster anguish, oil! Oop-Oop the Janitor! Fire
"Summer," his contentious "lane." O sorrow waiter
Of mines, and "Wifes of cotton! butter! water!
I am crazy in the lintel of your cups'
Parachute madonnas! O misery of samples. Sea!
Marriage gee umbrella grapefruit, houses
Of rotationless cars' marrying season ere
Yew, O glassy oyster of deceiving green
Anciently Pyrrhic lousy able to
Junction pool incinerator theatre badgers,
Badgers, badgers. Eye! winter! goatee!
France! O culmination of the side step, Peru!"
Angel answer "den step" "con-feeble" orchard-motion O loops
Of "Wow, ethers of cream cheese!" De-
Grelotte the chive: "Ignorant summer madhouse,
Douce erping madonna — lilac, cuckoo, disintegrate!"

O there was a bear of ginger bugs! They lo-
Cated ox, ink-millonaire, duck-balcony, O Jan-
Uary the blimp of oyster-Pisa! Shine us, nicks
The pear-coop balcony. O coptic frogs! See
"That," silver ceilings, olives, Cho-Cho-San
Of smiling muck. O Bridget! Junky! Hackwork!
Sleepy-come tables, lustrous pouter, he, gin the
Lake opera satisfaction deserted hankies. "Yes I
Comma serum baloney cancer shoe
Buckle China deserted lemonade, for you
Of all youths. Bad luck! blue! Indians'
Safety devises, O grandmother Forest! Links! Foremen
Without shoes! Lilacs gigantize my my my
Earthest lilac lie lye delinquent, shoe, wax
Joking, about-miracles, gentle, able, goo-goo, golf!
Lime insurance! O barricade of loft miracles
In tune with: grills, pier-accountants, gnats, gorillas,
Morris dancing, spies, peas, lamas, and chairs filled with gorillas
Last night: Georgia of pleonastic squirrels'
Frigidaire! toy bloodhounds! O bough
Of crusade lanterns, how I love you!" I bit,
With my "ornithologeeth" mackerel hum baby, cuckoo
Copley Georgia dimple yoyo Sheba
Networks. Act graceful, blue! "Day and here nitwits."

Shirt "and vivacious quiet feels you"
Barricuda up "Gee, knob" they (are)
Cow-fables in genius Gloucester. "Ye
Arch noodles," grapefruits
Give "fair" boscage to needly Rockport. O bands!
Roman's! lintels! steeples! sagas! bands
Of (white glue of day, earth, Japanese winter
Under mile-an-hour kimono, wheee!) shoeshine
Marriage of (shabby industries ape big south
Of boobs) lime gingerale of lilacs (Poe
Jealousied fruitation bounds Andes coo rig
"Dynamee" poopdeck "sun-marine" un-"Go, lazy jasmine"
Bike, water; happy boat nit, is as oh ooh ump
Ape lala newish, 'ray! Jewish Shasta
Of brocaded bumps, minerals with life-savers'
"Attachable-andiverous-ology-lulu-cars" buying
"Yessy" space, orchards' changing mirrors, and eye
Of deceasingly grouped lemons. Look, jobs! So
Mary Janice silvery palace Edgar Poe
Fin giant, boat, chase, America; aorta of
Nixing lemon jobs. Waverly! and councils of jest-
Chalk, proving by entrance, oop giant palaces
Lint)ha! to winter (shorter pear, then very blue,
Express-leaves, answerable) or bee, red yellow.

(Shower paybill ocean pin-bear agora Lulu
Gin-pear ice of gripes loganberries with sea
For Latin names archway and oyster polly
Knee fandancer peaceful showplace O blobs
Of paradise shining like sill-pill
In Orient Romany shining selling successful
And eagle bathroom night-Orient oak-cow and
Airplane of shirtwaisted barristers each
Mildly okaying solidity to boulders dam and
Advantageous going to sleep butlers louse
Hay nook contingent planetary
Inventory nunnery, harbour! O wax, "vax"!
Postulates of deceiving acid gramophones
Ixtapalapa yoyo January naked cripple
Of telluric lemons O bondsalesman
Streaming with held rugs bindery
Of paraded oh-ohs, eighteen me that
Lindbergh slumbering mailman-osis piracy luncheon at
Packhorse, giant trade unions Mayed, dove,
Gramercy thoughtless Lindbergh, O keyboards
Better than the city's navel, Shostakovich
Of drunken caps, "Gee Vizzikers," to
Town we heard them say, "Sizzle go fizzle bandana
O Santa, lay down the coping saw!" Boats! Goodnight, tea!

Commuter, joy, rabbit, air "even"
Khan dairy-shy "wheel" give me,
Stair ink dove. Pants of Rome. Rake
Bannisters of bee, star, fate mink pans
Georgia each terebinth agora, Thousand
Listen. Maldoror weewee hoop baby. Oblong
Sen sens. Leaf-brick. Hoping
Bay-sea pier-attitude are "glove"-pink
Shorthand nylon air-pilgrims to bin-dove
Noonal phlegms, achings badger rake! Ore
Din of hope lea "gas" mention shy
As in Shasta, dabble — cornice, mandrake
Seraphim. Oops! "Quiet be my double. North
Bandana cuckoo indentation hoop we; air is
Ulster wanter, a Jericho. O bills! And neigh
To me, janissary, pilgrim dividing snow
Manges, town me shay sea dirt devising rains
Doughnut on high! Octember of the jeeping bear-
Mackerel, sunder! Inch of teas, peas, and pink
Layettes, O morn-a-phones! Jane! Jane!"
Dippy weave bay deem housey "erf!"
Giants, "ipes" remember Oberts Plossom
Gingerwearing tea fenestral stripes
Choochoo against against. Act is, matinee!

Ozone, ips, dismaying humps! Lockwater
Of gingerwear manteau! for I pierced
Bicycles, Manuel de Falla. George Ozone
Fell bike dead Hannah-master the shoe-ox,
Blipps! Oh, Cajun, inch; house of the starry itch,
Master, jujube of beep-beep eagle classicism
Horary. "Light me hoo-hoo chaste
Agora delicious eagle bumpkin sobstory. Edge
Of the BB adze. Germany shouts, 'Hello,
Baby, than-hortatory!' Orange midnight, cousse-
Cousse an 'border silly' yum yoyo I
Plate ooh dada atch aitch itch eye knees higher
Than as is Wabash Wabash checkers-Pyjamas."
Orchestras dimpled that month, climate!
O backbreak of the fig-poker, tablet mirror
Cool gin-jujube. Borrowing heck of the Stars'
Is-manifestoes' Clarissa of coo-neck. Pie, die
I, bun, oak, love-way lemons breeze altar
Hip weary clove. "Mention the shopping parachute
To Billy Cathay, shaving about India
Quiet yes halva shoe-department geranium
China. Jonah models paregoric." Plagiarism
Of sunny stars! massacres of the little models
For "Bee, Arthur, talent-way loops ginger adopt where you."

And once again her stomach functions normally —
O parachutes and zeppelins, good morning!
He sassy fawns, we rally; ope, ope this
And mandarin Jill, hoop the girlish beach, loss
Quiet in, in, dinner function: "How
Alabama the finch, chair Otto us decency crumbs
Dinette happy normally. O good morrow,
Finch." Amos, the plaza leaped
Abnormally incinerator good mood. Water edge
Engines idea in lemon paper; he shoves
The water away; it is "their." A long
Wrist, jeep monkey and "locust for good
Location, rioting red raspberries hove
To Alps of comic gin — Weight! mirrors! as
Phonograph as decency abnormalcy banana
Joyous screen penumbra group wait ah
Pill! Oh, how did you get here! Weave
The curvacious zeppelin." Mary
Me O now it knocks. Plaza? "Gypsy." Earliest as
The weekend of focally month lemons
Happy. Shy, shy, shy! Fiend, fiend, fiend! O arid
Lams, goof, pier of brocaded nuts! Fishering
The lamented dish, is a sofa, A. Goof,
"Dish-a" air, airy grandmother "soofa," "bahg"

Nymphs of Boston! Caruso of the pilly chafing dish!
Periods of ink, pyjamas, we: a noted weariness
America illness pyjamas; cow-food, lemons
And gypsy raspberries! Oyster, Havana, the common sense
We olive eagle perforation choir gypsy
Sweetheart. And the tennis scones. Cow-raving
Island bad, mad, "oopal," shoes. Hay
The simian as day, bay, dermatologist
Eleanor, "she-food was dully sheep-food
Only as ear, waving pyjamas," grandmother
Of the screaming links! "Out! Up! Ear!"
Basement, "tea-pool," Ernestine jujube coliseum
"Arf-woofs"! Lady, cloak eve banana wool
Might eerie and "arf-woofs." Idle pin!
Wary Indes, speech of grandmother, or
Ore, ad, Dillinger as dim rotation agonies
Policy germ, taffeta, ink's cuticle. But his
"His" is "Is"; as is baseballs of weary fizz-
Lyre protector, — orchid of cow-faced pyjama-
Career-waving shove-malady on cuckoo-hay
Links, bobs — of hit mirrors in yoyo hare
Pursued leafy suitors. Oswald Mobile Bay
Easy blasphemous giant "is" rootbeer casket
Under gal Chinese wastebaskets — O brilliance!

How serious was serum, and the wave's "apric" therapy
Tonsilitis-ing cocoa-dandruff to soothe Labor Day
The Menshevik chilblains toot-toot gypsy lemons'
Cloak past you, evilly riding that bicycle
Rain, shops and. Houses of cruising furniture O dots,
And dandy, manned cuckoo by quitter-labels
Of shy-announce, April-beer, common-cuss, ware
Blue gypsy. O nincompoops, daisy, Aristotle!
Weary is the merchandising South Pole. Orchestra kale
Is near. "Genius of clowning and cussing bananas
Of daily 'blue' and seep, joy, joy sleep of teary
Purple, the Japanese movement of art stars'
Bangor of shipping 'can-knee?'s! Owl-orchestra
Of the shy dandy musicshops' distinct
Diamond Avenue horse-porpoise flirtation, O beans
Of 'sody'-metropolis's weird-wee gigantic-blains
Of bundler-nurse! Oak buildings
And shy lanthorns, pilot of graves' damp horns
That chirrup, 'orchestreed' pill-more,
Unshabbiness! O loophole than loophole 'thass'
Eagle of silent bingo, groups! Bessarabia! this
Distinctly! apples!" Very nutly they shine
"Beaver" "Clue" "Pylon" "Imp" "Kentucky" and "Biltmore"
But of orange greens, lane violent raspberries.

She showed me his or her nurse, O ices!
No kiss or railroad station as bitter orchestras
Basing loop quiet tarragon-way-pats of blonde
Madonna. O jinx of the shyest sphinx's
Axe-flotation career-numbers of back-room
Tinny notices' limbs of collusive
Plug-its-planets, opal! dime is dancing! And bakers
Follow his wilting literature. Actions!
Pins work, "follow" his sweepy limeade. O
Now-monsters! April castles is Falernian
Jowl, big lintel of teeny January
Bug railroad-station bicycles, bug! hi, bug!
Gypsy, bug, and "Am yoyo, blue, a bug,"
Cycles, orphan, often, a bug, "Yay, oh yes, a
Bug," hey! hey! Isn't ear a walk
Down wavy "ladder-somes," or passenger
Climates, white! red! Carolina! ancient bug
And a mottoed sail, dear faint aster orange
Monthly duple say quick-sail-as-unbottoms-
The aster rouge, in the closings
Of every literature. O continents of buttons
Where are we hiding? From? Ooop? Alpine bug,
"Gingeah," history, lilacs true little fiend
Of tyrant limns, bologna! This is that.

Dairy of true green bugs! "At all," eye
Weird conclusion orangey pink hammock whistle
China basing fair, elephant, tie-
Hanger, "it's music of the spillwort
Fooling 'Dumbness' Castle, O climates of the
Waving and catatonic arms of pantries of
Blooming ink of pantries of."
Pineapple donation cuckoo interrupted me:
"Shoe, house, bitterness, careless in shop
And gonad farm, what learned detective
Of colored submarines, quiet dixieland
Of these shamrocks of blue, embarrassment of
Eating two cups when only one was
Served, the delayed parking-meters under a lake
Of lion-parachutes, O collarbone that wins
The fairness test, gin, and cover for the furnace
Of kings' sighs, January, Easter, the bent climate
Of culver, leaf-listings, O! tan!" Shy
Rain, and the beauty of the "dug-
Out mirror of that steer-y Mexico: class
Of blue air white unconscious, sea
Pasting in harassing loops of green
Dichotomy to 'hoo hoo' funnies." It cleansed
Uganda. One series of crazy gowns.

At all! at all! pink metal, and
Beer-crazy medal of keen "has his worst summer"
Ice junctions! "Tomorrow ivy Gogol jewelry,"
Hairy, true sea, landing phone, oyster, bag
Of disky rockets weeps away, hay!
Rackets is "timpistuous rizzberries," icings of love
To care some, — "inginns of timpistuous barricuties'
A-vailable injinns." O April of the terrified revolvers
Aiming their women at the shoe-boxes
Of my hope! Legal, faraway, cokey-mutt forests
Of the limitless jail, him, Ann, in and
Is Andes-knees! cool, cool is rather bombastic
Or cuckoo deep-sea forests honey-monastic
Oh shine wherever! and the Georgias of classical honey
Country hoop! fizzle! majority limit
India-cakes-is-revolvers-cancer! "Tie paper giants
Hop yoyo Norse ring. 'Eep' sheeps
Time Andes bassoon ever gracefully. The red where
The final oop! oop! of granite ginger motorcars
Of quite green. Cow, that my neighbors are sleep,
Ginger, parade, hoop, May." Ah! linden, where
Evil Edith eaten the enunciations of
Tea, thunder, and the bare parachute edge
Of "Lark, hoop-walker, teapot-they-go to" sleep!

Now it is May in the ape. O acids
Ceremonies of artificial end as so autorides! duchess
Bees Santy Gloria of "Do nice," broken addenda
Of "Hoping today piracy automobile
Idjit dampness, O bag! this dampness
Alacrity of the automobile" "For waving flags
O an incinerated bug" "Bag!" "Andes, why not win
'Her'" ale and now Waverly do so
Basement "Al Lemons": cot where eye believe
Panegyric sweepstakes custodian day-
Brought lyricism to these cuspidors. He wakes
At night, looking for the shadow-boxing
Cousins, April and armistice; but mystery
Enshrouds the answer and deep regeneration
Forest to the limping funnies, and blue
Is her daylight's agrarian following; for she
Lycanthropy-odalanalyzes the tippy rainboxes
At jesting match-drops; since weary ovals
Most happen here these climate of some days
I walk. Terrified, shire of bear-
And-cotta sodas, he ginger-deers the
South, a light, for mirror of some days; equal now
To a deep ship, Ferrara, flags — swearing,
"Bonny Asian sacerdotal dove,"

He leaps pinstripe flotsam balloon cab's
Killing people wintry, eep! loop! simplicity!
Anguish! "O Andes of a paper dove,
And little miracles of my simplicity
With painful aspirin and smiley railroad dove
Of 'sinsuality,' see the minute that April dove
Me, birthless, hoops, lilac, and closets, iron
Saviors. They gave an orchestra of milk
To the ships and their first grape dove
Ships. For weeping psychoanalysis! and paper beds!
O crossroads of silvery paper, how
Jericho and we nifty whiteness I bled
Superior wardrobes into the railroad: a dove
Of China's paper, shyness, and a wafery head. Which
Lincoln of the surface bananas! O pots
In Havana!" "He leaves me have the banner like a
Grapefruit." Shorthand! These islands are a pin prick
In the sea. And yet. "O cameo, O bope, obe opeep
My cherished Solomons!" Feenamint Germany candy
The bed was soft. "And yet I left there
Like a silent weir, bonging the clavicle
Of 'meelions' of teabarefoot frogs; or their lanterns.
Oscar, simple, silly, city, ocean be-
Hind 'Prologue to the Canterbury Tales,' in bed!"

Mouldy apples, quiet limericist, hay! hay! dove!
"Dunciad I flailing food awake.
O barracuda uprising sleep snake sweet
Cow nifty hurrah surprising dawn, itching Iliad!
Cinching banjo! Jinx pituitary rosemary
O grandfruit! jeepy in the lilac nursery blessed
Betweeny 'gold-foo' and 'hooray-lips' nursey,
Chancing upon this Aragon 'injinns'
Slime to leap awake mercy! Papery!
Oh how the orchardy ocean lilts! Ape! Perfidy!
I fought him. I gate his head. Nigel Green
Said, 'Bees are without mercy.' I
Then said, 'A bee may not be without mercy
In the lilac future category of curtains
Which fail like tins made of lime.' She awoke
To the summer. A blue ass bit her knee.
She turned her two salacious eyes upward
Toward monotheism. 'I am scraping the
Halibut.' 'Are you a Christian?' 'No.' 'Then
Why, why are you aiding and abetting this fish
To be the summer?' O passionate oysters
Of November horoscope, unmarried hair
Of the morning sea! This mourning is beyond me,
The land's light upon sin's ornate weirdness!

Toe, its bench, we lay down in Illinois,
Anxious pilgrims. O loops! How the sea made war
On its arid tramps — of ginger; but nowhere
Cobblestone mirror garage blue two sea
January and 'Meet the finch': lilac! actress!
O melted kinship, in April, lariat of the two
Trees, blossom that is attracted where
The hill suffers, and motions softly downward
(Beavers at lunch, and biers, this is jasmine
Of smiling tomatoes) go toward, and after
Sombrero, oh cast a the lazy and into wear
Out isle 'in smiling silk' janitors
Of tea-tea'd warfare, surface shirts, cot
And bear, O bays bees cuckoos as free
Everywhere! Cart him away. The eaves
Are as freezing with leaves; and the sky
Of love limericks loomy coastlines at Garbage
Point. Or are there other shamrocks?" In tin
Sales why oh air Wyatt nut linen unusual
Ha ha ape one times destiny. Leafs cockatoo lemons
Piece of. "Andes dam de-bear, hay! hut! sheer!
They say that Mirabeau went nuts in Sweden
Behind the shoe-filled sea, yet at Amalfi
Balanced (oh ho ho) a green pill on his saber!"

April of belonging merely to his blouse,
She yelps. Oy! Beans! the sea! Badger
Noticed us yippee sat down in his chair
Simply cemetery. "Each whiz!" Powerful flights
In sea willow ouch orchard ankle
Of drooping beagle; and then! ale ale-letter
"Zimplossitude." Ant, a "shrimp of corruscation he"
O air deepkneed checkers in a Humber
Of Turkish sighs! Pans me the hare
Of "economics," O linens linens linens!
"There are very factories angry sea,"
Ankle doughnut behind too I dream "ink-
Parachute-whiskbr" oom! oh I nigh no dimple creation
Different lassitude. "Tea-jamas!" Mirror-boat! A dance
Begins to sea. O lariat! patiences that we seize
Margins in into our weird fights. Bag
Of enemies! there are limping morons near your boat. Let
No bun stir! And the antlike idiots were
There, eagle, matchstick, an inch, and the fairground
Of due nickels; latch; wins. Oar "cattle" coming off and
There bee were opp oop oop! W. C. Fields in
Tosca, the billboards, a cow facing a mop
With these words, "Tophat in the underground,
Booby!" Han! I she hails, the nicknacks of acid.

"In commotion I went to jail to see my brother
Carry his 'liberal' loafers beside the iron fountain
The milkman refers to yesterday as the Electric
Chair. I forgot, however, to bring along my blotter; and
When the electric men began to slug my brother
With tan shoes they had, on I mirrored Oscar Winter
Yoyo tell them, but asterisk! Ocean of near 'misery'!
Hint that I was saying he sits in the chair
Near a water, of ladies' faces; and, oh, pyjamas
Lifted unto my hindsight their ladder-lantern. He says,
'Don't tell them back at home which I miss
Them,' and, Lord, I most to half empire gymnasium tears
Maggot; but loverly I bonged the hackwork cigarette
To novel inch as civilian lemons. And when, Monday,
Or someday, I am flying near the
Baseball of leaping electric lemons! For pottery
Is my shoe. Now, which I wish to say and
Good! is this I don't care, for the modern childhood
By the sea which your Noah's Ark promised me, and I say
'Blah' to their mint stables of jugular whiskey
And veins of green talcum! I want to whoosh
Down an armchair, inch of the summer sunlight
And find my brother, the grayed one, still reading his newspaper
And using his toothbrush, *or* using his toothbrush. Goodbye!"

Porches of dismayed patchwork how goodbye
This summer sun is! and these novels, cockatoos
Like the banshee umpire, thatself, wimple remarked
"Coop, ork, new-chestra, tin, gingeah, India where
India is suppose to be." "Now I see the nylon sunrise
Coming up on Whim-Bole Bend. Anna lays her matchstick undies
To the sweet finger, to the sweet finger of the wind. Bare
Roommates choir where lady sea-birds ank-
Le comma weary dollar. Ape, but he makes money!" A
Garden momentarily films George Montgomery and
Ina Claire, monosyllabic, clue of the red ragweeds.
Oh now I know you! ape, red, panic-car, Kismet
Of diseased, ant, hill, roadhouses, school-pigeon
Of the tippy as rainwater motorcar! Clark Gable and Ginger
Rogers fall beneath the wheels of this motorcar
Of cheeping staff officers. How the gray leaves chirp
At the stereocopter filled with flying
Character-studies limited only by the harp
With which they publish "Myrna Loy, a Grapefruit of My Lilies,"
In quarto, and with volumes of lollipops, to document
Everything! And the green robins chirrup
At the sun which fills the dominant
Sad cars with its bilge; and the lofty ladies
Who limp through the bottom of ponds, singing "Raise us!"

"O rainwater how hairless you are! and when winter
Accomplishes everything you are as mercenary as gin
Today, deceiving the pilots of enemy airplane
Is loophole, ant-lake, and churchy-wise. Eye,
Simple doughnut apartment remember
When sunny a sandy daisy ripping in the country
March winter labour delicious party in my eyes;
Green whirlpools laughed on my foolproof shins
And I clambered through an airdale 'win-pyjamas'; he
Told him I they warranty *metier.* Show
Of a creeping bunch. Of limitless lilacs; and where
Are the goldenrods of Schenectady? Near you. In Orpheum,
Giant 'theayter,' O lake-country! Where are the beavers
Who sought you in wanting clothing, parachutes
And 'arid climates,' and one, day fought you with
A bacchic soda of genuine airs of piers? O pod! park
Of the rotationless beggars nearing coffeegrounds
With their airs. Airy hairs. Little minute. 'Injinn.' Cigarette.
Barefeet I waited ere the barricuda
Bared its air-sweet tinder-bet of rain-settered
Air-confessioning, 'a thousand and one minutes!
O rainwater how hairless you are! The lands of business
And the weirdest summer, oh!' " Lady in comic pyjamas'
Lacerated sleeping foot's bicycle of Limping Classics!

Mirth-marshes! how often a baked fly
Has fell from the swimming goldenrod of a clip
Notching the youthful daisy
Magazine, and lotioned you till its daddy,
Some mockless cheerleader from Syracuse
Has fell. He fell into your jewelled eye and found it!
How marvelous is baked caddy! Remember the swimmers
Who raggedly swore by that film about "Eagles"? O mocha,
Years is so dense! Ankle compare ginger-rod
Notation dense. The year on its weeds of fence
Angel, thou, mirthless as the blackbird. It's somewhere!
And the ankle basement trees causeway sanitation
Lyrically matters to, has been, and so, Samara,
Jay and Sarah, gypsy goldenrods! O mottos, mottos, tomorrow
Is famous! "I live here. I buy my gasoline
Around the corner. And so I want to ship
Three liveries and a half of giant clematis
To Norway, in heat-bill dancing jewelry. To find,
Tunbelly fish of romance — sand page of blonde Indians. Who
Sleeps in the nowhere of fire-basket? Somewhere
That's an institute, and the records play
'Climbing through Montmartre as balloons,'
And no rugged apes play with the thrushes
Who hand them sliced baloney until, married, they play cards."

Now she knows I notice everything that she notices,
Even Hawaii, so she has stopped placing notices
Under her sweater! Banners! And ingots
Of the lightest lots placed nearest the sewers
Of her choice of my mottos, and nearly
Has fainted, I boxed magistrate seamstress demons
Who ride into hot shops! O calcium in deserted rococo
Spades! winter-wear! "Why for me
In binges another, candy, thus world of brown
Key if dust, motto of the care-foot sleeping and deserted
Cranky rickshaw, in which he placed his lemons
Overnight, saying 'Leave these here until the morning
Boldface type singles. England railroad expands
Feet.' Face and the roaring doctor mountain
Each England campfire carfare doctor, hurrah
Lake-strips. Penny. O commander." Clark tubes' shack May means
Going a lemon from home, ah gingerwear! these horses
Plaza geranium eep-temptation. I know! They face
Klotch florist's tomorrow, and bingo! how lethal
Are short faces! yes! "We lie, people, in deserted bags
Around the harpoon of his tipsy poetry, the
'Beg' that whale nought 'leg' yo be contented. Marseilles
And October in the sailboats, cook are near." O hands! Cossacks in
Desperation France-ing his sybarite grape hoop-cats!

O whale of girls, burgooning
Late. Oh! my "knee is fair. There I limp
Weevils into the air," Roger, whip
The decayed easels, "And plenty
Horseradish, it is airpower, accident insurance,
Tea of papers, and rowdy lemons. White Pomona
Of the shrinking star-cuffs!" "We! Ay
Annoy north and building. Latent
Pyrrhus!" Hey Jane! Log-cabin wake up whoop
Parachute tin peanut lake. "Air of a
Million, shine high upon, dreary lemon. Loom
Of pare, all niece, the flower of
Accident insurance rag boats and leaves engines
Pan, April — uncle-weary to ginger. But, oui!
Clothing, sing-worms, and fail! my joyous gasoline
And caney stars, O spillwort!" Ape. Ate. Ben-
Seeds was late, oop! he went to high school
In a, ork! yes a blimp, oh married to the knees
Of not having, Indian as sharks, the reefed money
To order O doughnut coconuts there, weird
As mated, alcohol, the "ginger," a synco-
Pation, "Anagrams! fish! pools! babe! hospital
Of the careful linguist-itch-handfields-youthful-
Kentucky!" Evenings, places, a, it is a

Romance! under fields! one sorghum powder keg
Of chafey golflinks marry to barracuda
Leftwing childhood Santa Claus pyramid lilac
Birthplace changing Eskimo! Snuffing those pears
"Lately I advanced hats eskimo. O tears
Of my First Wild Wheel, a laboring thatchery
Of sea-high, grouped cuffs! navel
Of the business laboratory, day an orchid's
Way birth cardinal season-animals
Went beer fear notification jail-bird machinery
Of bees like 'gone' whim 'flam' oh inter-'mooped'
Pathetic lucky badger sea! Meant Wormwood sea
Of E double interlocutress' silk stockings
Making never seem like yesterday! Oh hop
How been in the!" "Jane. Hoop moorishness an ridge
On lilac cubbies." "Orange orange am-I dimple,
Immersed the whole sea?" Joke! Wish! Paintbrushes, toe,
Alabaster! "Onto which grotto and a sea-brush lemons
Chair-face gin-ear-all's matting time and Inca of
Careful soda shutting chair-faces oyster shooting
Dane-way of mirrors loons ant, 'arf-woof'
Of British gleeb, the 'nembus' of 'son-away'
Curfews' and naily kerchiefs of demon curlews'
Map-opping 'para-kiffs' grandmother. Is hen."

Oh yes, the golf-balls! "We were three golf-balls
Yesterday until pilgrim milkman rhododendron
Pansy of navy gorilla, limpid shoe-box
Ten mirrors away. O lake, rape! these
Are the bedroom of furniture's own
Aspirin these are the daffodil aspirin the
Daisy desert a microphone of golf-balls
A 'microphone,' a big nimbus, a hoop with daisy
Rarefying the mixed-up popeye air, oh save me
From 'Cuckoo aspirin, Margaret the hell is
Tin impy, lie! banana." O Lou
Air! jadey was the cindery gym. Manners
Did not save me British
Aspirin and lips lion tiger daisy O meres
Auto: "London I gave you daisy auto London;
Hit the believed sissy! Magistrate
And dippy 'legistrate,' Camargo
Silver ferris, 'lasp' the bundling wheel
Of silvery golf-bells." May! paper-ladder!
Sincerity! O basements of childish loans
To gangsters "eighteen century mint car" diz-
Zy lamp under it shoe fine Ken stars weep
Cemeteries bee "uselist" snow. Corpse-Alps'-
Zither maiden, see, "Tamarisk the ocean!"

Serenade the minting ocean! jump
"Bee" lilac fishes, oh, football, shortcomings'
Now on pink sand boat O
White goat, stair case, "Santy's eyes
Amid them blooming group," solvency
Barracuda, ape, shortcomings, Bloomsbury
Of a sheep's copper knickers, O mome,
Tin of raining sen-sens, no, no, no
More waves of petting football
Aircondition, solidarity. He weaves
A necklace for the sun-dry
Of masonite sewer-mind a beach of lilacs
Meditating weevils' cherries or "ots" miling
The silvery cave, the victory of lariats
Over knitting! Bandanas! "Opera programs
Lead me. Listen. The field lay there
Lilac shoe. Mistinguette's Schopenhauer's
Coolest, very, bugs! O bony tops
Of the scarab, chairs filled with rooming houses
In the 'mine are very idly act gunflower
Serum ladies.' Soon they will bear those boats
A wave, nexus." And the mere light
Health lateness is boxers O cam in "flodge"
Of the tear "Kish" sea, man or ear is weak.

And, as, they. Oy lifting the bear
Opera India sweet net, where gin time
Soothes field a hay-coop of missing cherries
Arthur closet balancing "ictionary" the true
Blackboard in's blossom, daiquiris of blue knives
Rompers as "dinner ware," the deceiving licorice
Clientele. Milkmen! Salesgirls! Strindberg
Of crazy ocean! bell thou
Lane — equal — box hats dance uppery
Sum the Alps, O may tent soap box
Seeds! Factories of knitted daisies'
Cold semper fidelis, cheesecake, billboard, a match box
In brief case, as lazily for the beard that
Beard that beard. Oranges and earth-lazy cherries'
Seen cups, oh or all. And. Nina Castelli amid the
Sweeping shrubbery. "Bankrupt soma, how chaircar
The will is, are they hills, toe, serious,
Loma, April, orange, serenade. I listened to Tchaikovsky
Where cows of pink. O nickels! the breadline
Of sleeping chills, thou merchandise
Leaf, in the lilies, of a hairline, this, 'commentates'
A dear savannah, the belts of alone sake
Reeves ale up toward walk for me, O Guinevere
That untie somas, of a nary work. Oh do green ships!"

And Alaska. Is, as, but. O Samos, blue! Near
Ships dairy mural dairy ships. Lantern ships
An daisy hue, might some are green. Nina! April
Soho kneeways. Barricuda of shining "Mexican"
Strawberries, liberalism! O aged green darlings
Of the 'Mericas, hunch, zippy! O location, look
At the merry, donning, palmettos, fairways
Of that biffing colossus "Peep Peep"! O
Doe! Marriage in Mexico amid the missing lemons
Of a parachute shining into the Mirabeau
Of your tasty kiss up in the March stars! Socking
The papery mirrors the limpid summers the very sutures
Of a timely stars' nimbus! watercress, O bough
Airy middle of giant impure true parasol swimmers
Blue. Toy-nature! In the bilges of a fair
Sure audience! They played "April Tiger," "Dig
Please," and "Secret Anatomies, a Parachute With Lemons
April Breathe Look Who Is Summer." Pickpock-
Ets and a different season the bridge us myster-
Ious lollipops' gambit Toussaint lurid seagreen bananas'
Shapeless crony, in the pyramid that all is
Life or purple! O gems! and beers
Drank up to the knees our green car baseball
On cheeriest red. Porch, thimble, and steeple!

O paints if time! A bough. Drinks the cow.
Unfaded red lemons, Santa Claus, marine, ow
Passenger, a London of musical coastline
"Sarah-fuge," benches gone equalling wavy "nice"
Halls. Save the defeating bells! Bend
My mind's six loops! Ah, beavers in the hall
With a trireme, merry coconut Triton
In, fall! the parodies of cinch, a stream
In Denmark, a basin of cherished spools, limping
Lanes, of "When, Mary Ann, eyes lakes is India
Merchant porch summer lethal leafy swim 'white
Rebus among dare homes is blue' is air wombat is
Is is is," banshee caretaker, suture, green. Ho, conduits
Of the wavy breast-line, which cylinders
Hat youthful climate! merry-cross, of "beads"
Of "beads" of beads! O bear! Hand-silly melons,
Believer-wear! Shoe, shoe, shoe! I dare you
To limp along O the fair mountains of a lifty pansy
Air rift! the bugles show. I dare you to
Mints, oh is golden! the bear-shaped leaf-cow of buy
One-two-tree-pony, of "never sees one blue page chair"
Harpoon limerick O the bee-parrot, "the werewolf
In the newspaper paints an orchestra" so
Many merry hock trucks, boxing spinster!

O meetings! with gold bargains angel blockhouses
And bins, uppy "care-loose" seed! Weak name-plates
Umpiring the seaworthy Southerner-
Lake-opera, the killed mason of a dairy-stone. Line
Meads! O bear the deflected milkmen, hog, away!
In the bishoprics of lime. "I am pasting silver
On Dad's picture. Ernestine
Lies in the garden, imagining the line-men
Galloping toward her silver pastry. I am alone
In my belief that Sheba leaks. O sybilline
Cogwheels, Saturday! Dreams you are the lantern
As the is foetus' punch." O daisies win! "Whin
Warren walked in Warren Warren's warren
There was limmons on the sea boat rail. O pail
Of apples that give the bargain clues
To its leafy gold! Pin-binge!" Lusting a meadow the curtains
Sail fifth shirt rail, "O bikes' last
Touch, now musical cancer!" Sheeps the hog away. May
Down, its, there, icks, tunes, "Solve me this some where
Blue cradles with their puppies, and the tinnest light
Of the 'worrild,' a manager sun green and surprise
The lariat of speaking hogs." His life was red, but
Oh, hats hip "Lear" of day. "Now-tation"
Of the singing rifles, which share, "zebras."

Maids! oh, a Moscow motion picture
"Flimmed Alpine blue," genius of mothers' crass producers'
Flayed livelihood of screeching juice divided
Into mysteries, boat, lilac professors, to the
Lemon of knowledge, bean, bean, Atlantic
Ann, "Miss Historical Peach Tree of Nineteen Forty-Three
Orchestra Idiots Nineteen Fifty-Three O Green
April of Vanished Bananas." Shirts! made in pylon
"Chimeney" manufacturings' damned blue
Sheep-castles of deluded carfare, weaving nudge,
Weaving nudge, O bombs! Loops of lacy match-
Sticks' blossoms' faint head's child's weak last
Cry's hoop-tiny May-ville poop-deck's "as
Langerhans musical bayou of sleepy lemons' shy
Rare shy rare's act's" act's axe! "If need
Be peach! Blossoms of merry showmanship in Stone-
Henge, bugles! Loops of "the caretakers' jangling cigar's
Loops' rung-demanding caretaker's sweetpea's
Pylons, amid the clamor of rug-maddened seats'
Paper of closest-knit words' blossoming rugs' fair
Blue railroad eagle nine-tenths then will look out the
Windiest rose of fair harp-maddened space's lifts-up's-
Sky which nominative sea's solo cinch-
Lousy-mats' tree-church's a billion edge-nursery!

"Anna, soda their brains." "Father, finish is certain." O basements
Of cardex, "muneeciple" rungs'
Badger, agent, elephants that silver money
Career number "is" most, and try to die
Annoy "the Badge," lawn there wind from at seat
Lives is-maybe acts, who, rose, love fell
"His aspirin." April of we moss
Whos, Andy us where wind maze opera's we
Golf links, say "Egbert. The Floating of
Hips Blossom. A Nightmare of Amorous Delays. Thought
Turns Green. In What Century Mazda As Famous
Pericles!" We is running through his
This rowboat "axe" everywhere a fashion is factory
Celery leaping rose, agua. Hatred! Parry
Chute O summer of green "Penmanship is
April's pants," lovers amid these penmanship
Iron stars and latest can't-we-go-hosiery-of-the
Face British lilies! O bough
Eep-ad baby "sooma" and junction thousand
Lists May sweet "cars a a a a pill, season
Clouds of in and O emollients care, foot, blue
Evils," cancer. "O Kenneth tea Arab baby easels
Felt arondissement gypsy tables and limps of
Needles parachute peas by, Lincoln, accidents."

He, day, believes is dogs "ne'ertheless" a
By the fishes' cocoa of today's sea sent
Collar loneliness home babies papers labors
Neighbors eagles capons savers of lillied
Papers of carbon moose's ape-bottling wintry
Soma of "a rustic jeeps" facility, dim-witted men
Lying inter-carfare raspberry "cup, be aware"-artillery
Amidst ye someday raspberries O Gloucester
Of faded robbers, cattle-bakeries and lint
Phosphorous eateries, mags! "Wearily woke up
Green bow-wow. Artillery." Shapeless militarists
Caped Bongo Brow. O gypsum
Penthouses sweeter than a rabbit's pillows
Of airy green "Knocks," bakery
Of distinguished sighs! "How came the locks
Lethal paper incinerator vicinity choochoo fractions
Cuckoo nuts paper Freilichers if lilac sea-bottlery
Towel dispensary?" There air is very weird
Ape bit summer green air care "poop-deck O lovely
Poop-deck!" Black cherubs "a" shins
Lesson. Boat. Backseats motion its
Yellow carry us. Din to the "stair" of teeth
Blue mezzo soprano of sweetest decay "Indians
Air, blood, out," as bee-axed crazy-bell wigs.

Weevils, him! A Sue Artillery. Angel. Lye
Dim apricot, comma common comma. Change.
Priest-ape. Bay-foot is and
Laxa-team en-merchandise hope Savannah nearly
Congo. And bounce! Labour Party football lovely
Air "right bread to dam is must we limpid
China fateballs." O pennies! rime
Shirting a, sea: clock, to bridge — at's lovely
Sick's is wall easy as lovely dam-flowers
Lay America easel bunch! Hate! Equal. Lions. "Hey,"
Is the fields' operatic major amnesty smearing Congo
Silver "bear." Lives. Bicycles
Limerick the shorty beach O cosmos
Of "Last winter," tower of pin-hitting
Lambs!" Maid! Tree Hoop! Three "hoopers'
Ladies' night foot out tear inch above children to
Shirts. Bin. O lovely green
Aspirin. A limps. We." Ham expostulates
Swimming the bells. Tree-punt! O music of the
Shamrocks' peanut amidst the doughnut
Licenseplates the ear silk. "Putt
The sob!" Nara of "Lame, I boat." Meek. Lilies'
Paper milkmen-tie. Us! Pills! O Labrador-
Peach-quiet mittens' tea sun of cleared ozone trees!

Majesty O a blue arf kneeling hoop
Satire "Peaches need, owl, off, woof, May-
Time, 'the sea' of embarrassed fresh asphalt
Pastry laughers Lincoln of believed
Santa misty sentence nice clam deer eskimo green
Solid. Rooms!" if sublime "grapefruit each-terrace
Lamp mice cooling-system licorice bizarre labours
For distance mighting silver coaties of green
Lay appearance proffers death lilacs nigh
Air gum in the 'shoot southern!' of prance 'kra!' knee
Sabotage 'limities' of shooting 'barbycuties' malice
Tots' visit love poultry sea bashing huts in green
Agoraphobe, O pain, Stevenson, Washington! Ship,
Mummy, woof, barefoot, lobster. Suds of air-
Proof. Tin. Bee-license. O reachest of the bays'
Spearmint copper 'neximo' axe livelier is toys
As engine-Britains, leaf, an miss. Sew, eep! the sun"
Bells asking lyricism is-mop. Corpse! Uncle
Pins! "He is sweet to" Imagine
Of tree highest lint nuts hooray substitute
Fair limb a fields as cigarettes. Shy
Bessarabia puzzler eagle by "We waste" cincture fezzed
Clouds of preachy lakewater altars eep bell
You-you clubs arrive, gemini of the hat ear eye fall peach water

Deem rafter. Cemetery. "Leem" eel batty bone.
O boa. Of the fez Theatre. Laps'
Tricycle of we motionless London of bees'
Pent lilies and hooray schoolhouses'
Musical today loop lantern is surprise "schoolhouses'"
Peanuts' ladies' aspirin lanterns
Of climbing clematis, a lake of conceived doves' "Go
Fine ear character waiter. Modern, lilies. Congo
Of the defeated railroads, revolver. Lacy coat of the
Chancellor's ink mirrors of. Insane celery." Ship.
"O bayou, boom, icicles sesame the contained robber
Of leaves in chairs, savannah!" Crane? oh heron! Able
Balance the trip knee, comedy. "In the heap
Of Maytime lamas I limped upon the knees of
An old charcoal. Lemons" for a pound of the
Oxford! September air! Bun of old leaves of
Care each musical "Hooray, unpin the gong," sylvan water
Ape shell-ladder! Egypts! Mezzanine of deciding cuffs'
Anagrams who tea-tray "sigh them" objects "pay-sign"
"Leaf-boat" "love-object" "base-ball" "land-slide"
"Tea-ball" "orchestra" "lethal bench." Sum, are, lakes
"May-nagers" "love-times," sweet
Counter ale pan-banned gypsy-bin fools cabaña
Gentle hiatus of sarabande "roof" "wide" seam!

—New York City 1953

THE COMPROMISE

JOHN ASHBERY

Characters

Captain Harry Reynolds, of the Canadian Mounted Police

Margaret Reynolds, his wife

Jim Reynolds, their son

Mooka, their Indian maidservant

Lieutenant Allan Dale, also of the Mounties

Sam Dexter, manager of the Cariboo trading post

Lucky Seven, his Indian henchman

Chief of the Tobi Indians

Running Deer and Mountain Lion, his sons

Daisy Farrell, an entertainer

Blue Feather

An Indian sentry

A squaw

The author of the play

A raven

Chorus of Indians

The first two acts take place in the year 1920; the third in 1925.
The setting for all three acts is the Canadian North Woods.

* * *

ACT I

The interior of a cabin in the North Woods. Margaret is rocking the cradle of her young son Jim. A fire is burning on the hearth near which sits Mooka, who chews disgruntledly on a corn-cob pipe.

MARGARET: How like his father he is, Mooka. When he yawns and rubs his eyes like that I could almost imagine it was Harry doing it.

MOOKA: Ugh!

MARGARET: *(to the baby)* You certainly do take after him. You've got his same blue eyes and brown, curly hair.

MOOKA: Ugh!

MARGARET: And what's more, you've got his cheerful disposition. I know you're going to be a good, brave, honest, cheerful man just like your dad.

MOOKA: Ugh!

MARGARET: Mooka, I won't have you talking that way about Harry. He's a fine man and my husband, so let's not hear any more about it. Moreover this is his house and not yours.

MOOKA: Him leave white missus. Him no good.

MARGARET: That's not true! You know the Mounties are often gone months and even years on a mission. "They always get their man." And Harry's not been gone a year yet. *(She glances at the calendar.)*

MOOKA: White missus know him gone longer — exactly one year and three days!

MARGARET: *(dabbing at her eyes with a handkerchief)* Oh . . . is it?

MOOKA: White missus a fool! White master no gone after criminal.

MARGARET: Why, what do you mean?

MOOKA: Mooka's boy friend, Lucky Seven, him say him see Captain Harry in Elk City, in saloon. Him tell dancing girl him not married. Then Lucky Seven say him follow dancing girl into dressing room.

MARGARET: That's a lie! You get out of here, you lying old witch!

MOOKA: *(comes over and kneels before Margaret)* Mooka want only white missus' happiness! Mooka at first not want to tell, me swear!

If only missus would gettum divorce. Then maybe Dexter, manager of trading post, propose to her. Him sweet on white missus already. Mooka watch, Mooka see how him look at her whenever her go in store. Dexter rich man, powerful man. Him maybe build us fine house here in Cariboo, or move away altogether. North Woods no fit place to bringum up son. Him makum fine father to little Jim, white missus see.

Captain Harry, him maybe not bad man at heart, but him no good husband! Him no bring up son in right way. Dexter, him make good husband and father.

MARGARET: *(She has shown signs of wavering but finally becomes resolute again.)* That will do, Mooka. I know you mean well with your advice, but you seem to forget that I have certain responsibilities toward my husband. Even if I cared for Mr. Dexter, which I don't, I gave a promise to Harry to wait for him . . . though he has been gone an awfully long time!

MOOKA: Him gone . . . too long!

MARGARET: Mooka, why don't you wash up those dishes in the kitchen while I tidy up in here a bit? A little housework might revive our spirits.

MOOKA: *(glumly)* Yes, missus.

(She bows and goes off to the left.)

MARGARET: *(gazing fondly into the cradle)* Poor little fellow! Supposing what they say about your father is true? *(looking at the audience)* He must never know!

(A knock is heard at the door; Margaret expresses the emotions of fear, hope, and joy before rushing to open it. Just as she gets to the door it bursts open and Lucky Seven, a villainous-looking Indian, lunges, into the room.)

Eek! O, it's you, Lucky Seven. Goodness, can't you come into a room like ordinary people? *(she sees others)* And Mr. Dexter! And Allan! But . . . who are these other men?

(Dexter, Dale, Chief, and Chorus of Indians enter.)

DEXTER: Perhaps you'd like to explain that, Lieutenant Dale.

DALE: Margaret . . .

MARGARET: What is it? Why are you all looking at me that way?

DALE: I'm afraid what I have to say may come as a shock . . .

MARGARET: Allan dear, won't you ever learn not to beat around the bush? Out with it, man!

DALE: Very well. This man *(pointing to the Chief, who bows)* the Chief of the Tobi Indians, who have the big settlement near Elk City.

MARGARET: Elk City!

DALE: Yes. Why have you turned pale?

MARGARET: It's nothing. Go on with what you were saying.

DALE: The chief brings disturbing news from his settlement. It seems that a desperado has been robbing the Indians in the area, coming into their homes at night, threatening them, even molesting their wives. He has terrorized the whole neighborhood. This man . . . This man is . . . I can't go on!

DEXTER: Then I will! This man, my dear Mrs. Reynolds, is none other than your beloved husband, Captain Harry Reynolds!

MARGARET: It isn't true!

(She takes a step backwards, falters and is supported by Dale.)

CHIEF: *(to Dexter)* You no say right! No one know for sure identity of criminal!

DEXTER: What do you mean? You told me yourself that he was Reynolds' height and build, and that he was wearing a Mountie uniform.

CHIEF: But me no say this man Captain Reynolds, because me no see face. No one see face. Man always wear mask. *(He bows to Margaret.)* Me beg humble pardon, white lady, for this intrusion. Me come to Cariboo only to see justice done. Me no accuse your husband, or any other man.

MARGARET: Thank you. You are very kind. Well, gentlemen, is this your reason for coming and scaring an innocent woman in the middle of the night?

DALE: I'm afraid that in spite of what the Chief says, Margaret, the police are certain that Harry did commit the crimes. Cariboo is the only Mountie station for miles, and we have received no reports of missing men. Our description of the desperado tallies perfectly with Harry's description. Why, one of the Indians even reported that the man carried a handkerchief with Harry's initials on it.

MARGARET: And I suppose Harry is the only person in Canada with those initials. What kind of proof is that?

DALE: Proof enough to arrest him, I'm afraid.

MARGARET: And you call yourself a friend!

DALE: You know if there's one person in the world I don't want to hurt it's you.

MARGARET: You've chosen a strange way of showing it.

DALE: Listen to me, Margaret! In spite of the fondness I have for you, you know I've always been Harry's friend too! Harry and I grew up together . . . went to school together . . . We used to go fishing and hunting together. Why, he's almost as dear to me as you are. You can be sure that if there's any way of saving him, I'll do my darnedest to prove his innocence. Meanwhile, it's my duty to arrest him and see that he comes back here to Cariboo to stand trial.

MARGARET: *(fixing him with a look)* In view of the circumstances, *Lieutenant* Dale, I have nothing further to say to you.

DALE: But, Meg! I —

MARGARET: I said, that will do!

DALE: *(stiffening)* Very well, ma'am. *(to the Chief)* Chief, I understand you are starting the journey back to Reindeer settlement tonight? Is that correct?

CHIEF: Ugh.

DALE: Then would you mind stopping at my office on your way out of town? There are a few minor details of the man's appearance I would like to go over with you.

DALE: Thanks for your cooperation. *(to everyone except Margaret)* Good night.

(He goes out.)

DEXTER: *(to Margaret)* So you still refuse to listen to reason, eh?

MARGARET: Mr. Dexter, you've been very kind to us since Harry left. I would hate to order you out of here the way I just did Lieutenant Dale.

DEXTER: I told you a long time ago your husband was no good.

MARGARET: Please!

DEXTER: Well, O.K. if you want to be stubborn. But just remember, you've always got a friend in Sam Dexter.

MARGARET: That's nice of you, but —

DEXTER: I heard what he was saying, just now, about being a friend of you and your husband. I'll be blunt, ma'am. I never did much care for your husband. It's you I like.

MARGARET: Really . . .

DEXTER: I know. I shouldn't be talking like this to a married woman, especially with people around. I don't care, see? Sam Dexter can buy and sell this town and he don't give a damn what people think. At least . . . except for one.

MARGARET: But can't you understand that I —

DEXTER: Say, how about us getting hitched? You could easily get a divorce from Reynolds *in absentia* after what he's done. I ought to know — I'm the judge of this town.

MARGARET: And now I must ask you to leave, Mr. Dexter. As you point out, I am a married woman, and I do not listen to proposals from other men. And no man who is my true friend would make such a proposal. Let me also remind you that my husband Harry is *innocent* of any crime. Right now he is doing his duty, looking for the man who murdered your partner, Mr. Stevenson.

DEXTER: You sure have got a lot of spunk. I like that in a gal.

(Margaret goes to the door opens it and points outside.)

Before I go, ma'am, I'd like to have just one word with my man here, Lucky Seven.

(He leads Lucky Seven to the front of the stage. Margaret closes the door and talks to the Chief. The Indians are examining the various furnishings of the house. Dexter talks to Lucky Seven in an undertone.)

You bonehead! You had to wear that mask when you were robbing the Indians, didn't you!

LUCKY SEVEN: Ugh, Mr. Dexter, Lucky Seven no look like Captain Reynolds in the face. Anyway, Tobi Indians know Lucky Seven — would report to Dale. Mister Dexter no want me go to jail, do him?

DEXTER: Jail's too good for you, you polecat. You'd sell your own grandmother for enough wampum, wouldn't you?

LUCKY SEVEN: *(joyfully)* Ugh!

DEXTER: Well, you'll get enough if you do as I tell you. And no bungling this time! I thought the rumors about the dancing girl and the crimes you committed would be enough to make this shrinking violet forget about her husband, but it seems I'll have to resort to stronger measures. When I leave, I want you to go find that cross-eyed girl friend of yours, see?

LUCKY SEVEN : *(mournfully)* Ugh!

DEXTER: Do you still have the handkerchief with the initials on it that you stole off her clothesline?

(Lucky Seven slowly pulls the handkerchief partway out of his pocket.)

Good. When you see her, get her to brew you both some tea and then slip this pill *(handing him a pill)* into hers, get me? After you go I want you wait around outside until she starts snoring. Then you come back, plant the handkerchief somewhere in the room, and grab the kid.

LUCKY SEVEN: *(apprehensively)* Me grab . . . kid?

DEXTER: You're catching on. Then get the hell out of Cariboo — my fastest dog team is waiting outside, in the woods just east of the house. Lay low for three weeks and then come back —

say you've been visiting relatives up north. Oh — I almost forgot. Here's a little something for your traveling expenses.

(Lucky Seven looks into the bag Dexter hands him, rolls his eyes delightedly, and again looks apprehensive.)

And remember — you get three times that when you return to Cariboo.

LUCKY SEVEN: But what about . . . kid?

DEXTER: Knowing what sensitive feelings you have, I don't insist that you kill him. Fix him a nice soft bed in the wilderness — maybe the good fairies will take care of him. *(He continues half to himself.)* She'll think her husband has taken the kid to raise him up to be a crook like his dad — I hope! If this doesn't make her think he's no good, I give up. But what am I saying? As if Sam Dexter could ever give up! *(sarcastically, turning to the others)* Excuse me, ladies and gentlemen! Sorry I can't remain longer in such charming company. Say, watch out for her, Chief — she's got a wicked tongue. Yes sir, a lot of spunk!

(He goes out laughing.)

CHIEF: If Mrs. Reynolds pardon Chief speak, him think some of her neighbors in Cariboo not so nice.

MARGARET: Oh, he's a good man at heart, I guess. It's just that his manner is a little uncouth.

CHIEF: Indians have a saying — "Can tell color of panther's heart by color of his hide."

MARGARET: I'm so friendless and alone since Harry left. And Dexter has been kind . . . in his way. He's never asked for anything in return — until tonight.

LUCKY SEVEN: Excuse me, Missus, am Mooka here?

MARGARET: Yes, you'll find her in the kitchen.

(He goes off.)

Will it always he thus?

CHIEF: Surely pain is long . . . almost as long as time.

MARGARET: Then there is more in store for me?

CHIEF: Every man has his full share of pain — and then some.

MARGARET: But I have lived through enough!

INDIANS: You have indeed deserved better than you have gotten.

MARGARET: And can you see no brightness ahead?

CHIEF: As we left camp the fortune-teller was casting his lots. He said a great day is coming — a day whose radiance will be to the present as day is to night.

MARGARET: And I — perhaps I may share in that day?

INDIANS: We hope so, Lady.

MARGARET: Perhaps the lovely springtime will come for me too. Spring can be lovely in the wilderness. It was April, I remember, when Harry and I were wed. We rode on horseback through the woods. There were beautiful flowers growing all around — little flowers that bloom and fade away in less than a day. And I thought our love would last a lifetime, in spite of its sweetness. How wrong I was!

INDIANS: Do not torture yourself, lady. Our lot, too, is hard. Yet we bear it in silence.

MARGARET: I won't be silent! Nobody knows how I've suffered all these months! Spring passed, and summer, and autumn with red leaves. And now winter sits on my heart, as it did the day he went away. Oh frozen mountain streams! barren crags! wolves of the wild timber! None of you is so cold, so cynical as my husband's heart.

CHIEF: Surely, in all these months, your heart has known some lightness?

MARGARET: None.

CHIEF: He left you without one consolation?

MARGARET: No . . . not one.

CHIEF: Then whose is that baby I see in the cradle over there?

MARGARET: Oh . . . my son! (She gets him from the cradle.) The sole warmth of his mothers' heart — her only joy! It's bad luck to have forgotten him at such a time! What if I were to lose him?

CHIEF: Rest assured, no harm will ever befall your son. I noticed him when I first came in — such brightness seemed to shine around him that I thought him the tomorrow of which our fortune-teller spoke.

MARGARET: Look — a tear on his little cheek. Perhaps he too misses his father.

CHIEF: Perhaps so. And now it is getting late, and we must go. But first, let me grant my blessing to this child, and to you too for having spoken kindly to us.

(Margaret kneels before him with her son.)

May the great raven who lives in the sunset look kindly on this baby and bring him up to be as great-hearted as he is. Let him always look after the rights of others, and live so as to be a joy to his mother, in the manner of men — for, living so, no evil can ever touch him. And may the raven look kindly also on this mother, and bring her happiness at last.

INDIANS: And may he look kindly also on her husband, and bring him back safely from wherever duty has taken him. For it is a sad thing for a woman to live without her husband.

MARGARET: *(rising)* Thank you — you have been very good to us.

CHIEF: Don't speak of it. We see your gratitude in your face

MARGARET: Will you pass this way again?

CHIEF: We have no plans to, but many unforeseen things happen.

MARGARET: Yes — perhaps we'll meet again some day. I hope so.

CHIEF: So do we. Goodbye.

(They all bow to Margaret. and the Chief kisses her hand.)

MARGARET: Goodbye.

(The Chief and the Indians go out. Margaret puts the baby in his cradle, takes a lamp from the table and goes toward a door at the back turning to look at the cradle.)

"And no harm will ever befall him." Pleasant dreams, my dearest!

(Mooka opens the kitchen door.)

MOOKA: Will Missus wantum anything else?

MARGARET: No thank you, Mooka. I'm going to bed.

(She goes off. Mooka signals to Lucky Seven.)

MOOKA: Her go to bed. Come on — we sittum in living room like white missus and master.

LUCKY SEVEN: *(entering)* O.K. First me sittum one side of fireplace and you serve me cup of tea.

MOOKA: Like this?

LUCKY SEVEN: Ugh. Now you sittum other side and drinkum tea.

MOOKA: No — first you gotta give me kiss.

LUCKY SEVEN: No — you drinkum tea, then me give kiss.

MOOKA: *(picks up a stick of wood and brandishes it)* You givum me kiss now — O.K.?

LUCKY SEVEN: Well — O.K.

(Mooka flops down on his lap and bends over backwards for the kiss. Lucky Seven drops the pill in her teacup and kisses her.)

MOOKA: Now we sittum and talkum like white man and missus.

LUCKY SEVEN: What we talk about?

MOOKA: Let's talk about — getting married!

LUCKY SEVEN: What make you think we getting married?

MOOKA: But — you say we engaged!

LUCKY SEVEN: Exactly — so how we get married unless we breakum off engagement?

MOOKA: But how we get married if we not engaged?

LUCKY SEVEN: We don't!

(Mooka starts to cry.)

Don't cry, little papoose, maybe we do get married soon.

MOOKA: That better! When?

LUCKY SEVEN: Maybe when Lucky Seven get back from trip up north.

MOOKA: You takum trip? But you promised to takum me to big Indian dance next Saturday night!

LUCKY SEVEN: Lucky Seven just learn tonight his rich uncle in north sick, asking to see Lucky Seven. Maybe him die, leave Lucky Seven fortune so Lucky Seven marry Mooka.

MOOKA: You think so?

LUCKY SEVEN: It possible — Uncle rich man — Got plenty wampum.

MOOKA: Oh boy! Mooka no longer have to work! Her become nice lady like white missus.

LUCKY SEVEN: And Lucky Seven bring back present from north — maybe nice bear-skin jacket.

MOOKA: *(tenderly)* Ugh. Mooka like Lucky Seven.

LUCKY SEVEN: Me gotta go. Gotta gettum early start. First me drinkum up tea, then go. *(he drinks his)* How come you no drink?

MOOKA: You give me goodnight kiss first, then me drink.

LUCKY SEVEN: No. You drinkum first, or no kiss. And no present from the north.

MOOKA: Aw . . . All right, but you old sourpuss just the same.

(She drinks the tea, then bends over backwards as before. Lucky Seven holds her for a moment then lets her fall to the floor.)

LUCKY SEVEN: Twenty-three skiddoo! Ha ha ha!

(He runs out. Mooka starts to chase him with a stick of wood then returns to her chair by the fire.)

MOOKA: Why Mooka ever trust him? Him bad Indian, that's what. Mooka no marry him now even if he ask her. Why him decide to go away so suddenly? Funny him never mention rich uncle before. Ho hum. Mooka so sleepy, take little nap by fire before go-um to bed Lucky Seven, him act strangely lately. Zzzzz. Him seem to know lot about Captain Harry. Who tell him? Zzzzz. Maybe him know something about murder of Mr. Stevenson, too. Me remember to ask him. Zzzz. Oh, Mooka so sleepy, so very sleepy.

(She falls asleep. In a moment, Lucky Seven, who has been watching through the window, steals in noiselessly, lifts the baby out of the cradle, drops the handkerchief next to it, and hurries out. The baby starts to cry just as they go out.)

Zzzzz. No cry no more, Lucky Seven. Mooka be nice to you — maybe she even let you give her kiss. *(She wakes up with a start.)* Ugh, that no Indian man, it little Jim. *(She goes over to the cradle.)* Whattum matter, baby? Did him wettum cradle . . . ? Him gone? Jim! Jim! Him gone. *(She rushes to the outside door, calls out, and turns back to the center of the stage.)* Oh missus! Police! Help! Little Jim gone! Help! The baby gone! Help! Police!

(Dexter enters.)

DEXTER: What is it? I was just passing by the house on my way home from the store and I heard you making all this noise.

MOOKA: Him gone! Baby Jim! And him in his cradle only a minute ago! Help! Police!

DEXTER: Are you sure he isn't around the house someplace?

(Margaret enters in a kimono.)

MARGARET: What is it, Mooka? Why are you yelling?

MOOKA: Oh Missus! Baby Jim! I see him in cradle only a minute ago!

MARGARET: What's happened to my baby?

MOOKA: Him gone!

MARGARET: Good heavens! Where? *(She sees Dexter.)* What are you doing here?

DEXTER: I heard all the noise and came to see if I could be of any help.

MARGARET: Well, why are you waiting? Go and find Lieutenant Dale! And hurry!

DEXTER: Just a minute, ma'am! Aren't you forgetting that you gave the Lieutenant his walking papers a short while ago, and in no uncertain terms?

MARGARET: What difference does that make? He's a police officer, isn't he? I'll go myself.

DEXTER: My dear! I'm as upset as you are, but you don't see me losing my head. I'm trying to decide on the best possible course of action.

MARGARET: Are you crazy? Go after the kidnapper!

(Lieutenant Dale enters with the Chief and the Indians.)

DALE: What is it? What is the meaning of these screams?

MARGARET: Oh Lieutenant! I'm so glad to see you.

DALE: Indeed?

MARGARET: Please forgive me for my rudeness just now. But I know you will when you hear the terrible news. My baby has been kidnapped!

DALE: Kidnapped! But are you sure?

MARGARET: There's his empty cradle. What more proof do you want?

DALE: I see the cradle. Tell me, have you searched the house thoroughly?

MARGARET: Don't be ridiculous. Where could he go? I tell you the child has been kidnapped!

MOOKA: He right, Lieutenant. Mooka say goodnight to her boy friend, Lucky Seven, then sit by fire and fall asleep. When her wake up, Jim gone!

DALE: But there are no strangers in town, and who among us would want to kidnap little Jim?

MARGARET: Whoever it was can't have gotten very far. Oh, won't somebody go after him? *(to the Indians)* What about some of you? Can't you go? *(to the Chief)* And you — what kind of a blessing was that you put on my child?

CHIEF: *(bowing)* Indians try to do everything in their power to help white lady.

DALE: Before doing anything we must search the house for clues. It would be useless to set off into the woods at night without some idea of where to look.

MARGARET: While you waste time my baby is probably freezing to death.

DALE: No — see, the kidnapper seems to have taken all the blankets from the cradle. That's certainly a good sign.

AN INDIAN: *(bending over to pick up the handkerchief)* Lookum, Lieutenant. Me find this on floor beside cradle.

DEXTER: A handkerchief — left behind — by the kidnapper — and bearing the initials "H.R."

ANOTHER INDIAN: It just like one of masked man who attack our village.

MARGARET: That's Harry's handkerchief! I'd know it anywhere — I embroidered the initials myself.

DALE: I'm afraid this looks bad for Harry, Margaret.

MARGARET: Merciful heaven! But . . . you don't think he would kidnap his own son?

DALE: It certainly looks that way.

MARGARET: But why would he want to do such a thing?

DEXTER: Perhaps he wants to bring him up in his own way . . . to be a crook.

MARGARET: Bring up a baby? Alone and in the wilderness?

DEXTER: Perhaps . . . he's not alone.

DALE: Our reports say that Harry has gotten mixed up with a woman, Margaret. It's one aspect of the case I'd hoped to keep from you.

MARGARET: Then all those rumors I've heard are true! The pieces are falling into place at last. Harry's found a new love — a dancer, with expensive tastes, who makes him steal to support her. They've gone off together to live in the wilderness, and now that Harry's settled down he wants little Jim.

DALE: Easy, Margaret. Don't cry.

MARGARET: I can't help it! What kind of a mother will she make? What kind of a father will he be, for that matter? Raising our son to be a criminal!

It's all so clever, so very clever! When Jim's a little older he'll he able to go along with Harry on his burglaries, he'll climb in buildings and things like that. And no one will ever suspect Harry because he'll have a little boy with him. And then they'll go home to wherever they're hiding out from the law, and that woman will beat Jim and send him to bed without any supper, and then she'll put her arms around Harry and love him. And where will I be while all this is going on? I'll be all alone, growing older in this miserable little town, and no one will ever love me again. It's too terrible to think about!

DALE: I don't agree with the part of your speech about no one ever loving you again. It will be easy for you to divorce Harry *in absentia* and marry . . . the man of your choice. You know there are plenty of men in this town, Meg, who'd give their right arm just to sit next to you on a sleighride!

DEXTER: There certainly are! Say, Lieutenant, aren't you neglecting your duty? While you're talking to Mrs. Reynolds the criminal is escaping.

DALE: Er . . . of course. Well, bye bye, Margaret, and don't take on so.

MARGARET: Goodbye, Allan.

(*He leaves.*)

DEXTER: Well, I don't mean to rub it in but perhaps now you'll listen to me when I tell you a person's no good.

MARGARET: Don't, Mr. Dexter. Haven't I borne enough for one evening?

DEXTER: You wouldn't have had to if you'd taken my advice. Oh, Margaret, won't you divorce him and marry me?

MARGARET: Let's not talk about it tonight. I'm confused. I can't think straight.

DEXTER: You mean you'd stay married to that sneak after what he's done to you?

MARGARET: Harry's not a bad man at heart. Whatever he's done, you can bet it's because that woman made him do it.

DEXTER: But you will divorce him?

MARGARET: Of course. How could I go on being married to him now?

DEXTER: And marry me?

MARGARET: I don't know. I can't think that far ahead.

DEXTER: No one could ever love you as I do, Margaret. If you marry me I'll build you the most beautiful home for miles around, with all the latest conveniences and a maid to wait on you hand and foot. Your name will be a legend all over northern Canada. You'll be called the Queen of Cariboo.

MARGARET: As far as a maid goes, Mooka here will, I hope, always be my loving and devoted servant. As for the other things, you can forget them. All I want is the love of a good and honest man.

DEXTER: You'll have all that and more. Then you do say yes?

MARGARET: I don't know, perhaps so . . . I'll think about it. Just now I feel a little faint.

DEXTER: (*to Mooka*) Bring her some water.

(*Mooka fetches a glass of water and gives it to Margaret, who drinks it.*)

I can start the divorce proceedings tomorrow and you can be picking out your trousseau from the catalogue. We can be married within the month. What do you say?

MARGARET: Oh, what can I say? You've been so kind. Very well, Mr. Dexter, I will marry you.

DEXTER: You've made me the happiest man in the world!

CHIEF: Congratulations, Mr. Dexter. You gettum good wife.

DEXTER: A good wife? I'll say so! Oh boy! (*aside*) If only that meathead husband of hers doesn't come back and queer things before the wedding. After that, I don't care what happens. There'll be no getting rid of me then! (*aloud*) I'll give a big wedding reception, Chief, and invite you and your whole tribe.

CHIEF: Ugh. Me thank you, but afraid us cannot come. Reindeer settlement many miles away.

DEXTER: Well, just as you say.

CHIEF: But Mrs. Reynolds will be always in our thoughts. On wedding day me think of her and you, and drink special toast.

DEXTER: That's real nice of you.

CHIEF: And we pray always to raven god, that he watch over and protect her little son Jim.

MARGARET: Thank you! I'm sorry I spoke angrily to you a few moments ago.

CHIEF: You are forgiven. Life is so full of bitterness that we must speak out in anguished protest now and then.

MARGARET: And my life especially. Well, perhaps my forthcoming marriage will be a happy one.

INDIANS: I asked the snow that falls continually on our frozen northern wastes, whether he had ever seen any of this happiness of which you speak. And the snow replied, truly, if there is any happiness in the world, only the dead know it. Still, we continue to hope that you will be happy.

DEXTER: It is a strange thing — we spend all our lives looking for it, yet deep down we know we will never find it. Even I, ever ruthless in my pursuit of power and money, know secretly that the quest is hopeless.

CHIEF: Then you are a wiser man than I took you for. Indeed, to realize that the quest is hopeless is the first step to happiness.

DEXTER: How is that so? You speak in riddles.

CHIEF: True happiness comes only when we forget our own selfish desires and try to make others happy. That is the meaning of the word "happiness."

DEXTER: I know it, yet can't forget my ambitions. even for a minute.

MARGARET: Nor can I! Just now I was thinking of my own fate when my baby, my dear child, was stolen. Supposing it wasn't his father, but somebody even worse, who took him?

INDIANS: Have no fear, lady. The raven god is a good god, though his ways often seem inscrutable. He will watch over your son.

MARGARET: I hope so. Listening to your voices I can almost believe in your strange god.

INDIANS: Great is the power of the raven who dwells in the sunset. Fierce is he in battle, but gentle and meek as a lamb toward those he loves. Strange are his ways — often he seems to forget, yet he remembers. Always he watches over and protects those who believe in him.

MARGARET: Oh mighty god of the Indians! I too will believe in you if you will save my baby from harm!

CHIEF: The raven sees. He hears. He will watch over your son and smile on your marriage.

MARGARET: And I will never forget him in my happiness.

CHIEF: And now we must take leave of you for the second time tonight. For our way lies westward, through moonlit pine forests and trackless, snow-covered wastes.

DEXTER: I'm going too, Chief. I'll show you and your Indians the way to the edge of town.

INDIANS: We leave our hearts behind in this cabin, glad that some happiness has come to you, hoping that more will — and that sorrow will go away entirely. And so, good night.

CHIEF AND DEXTER: Good night!

MARGARET: Good night — and thanks!

(*Margaret and Mooka wave to Dexter, the Chief and the Indians as they file slowly out into the snow.*)

CURTAIN

ACT II

Inside the Chief's tent at Reindeer Settlement. At the back a flap of the tent is open, revealing a sentry standing guard, white snow and blue sky. At the right of the opening is an upright piano and, next to it, a glowing brazier. At the right of the stage is a curtained entrance to another room. The time is late afternoon. Harry Reynolds is talking with Chief's two sons, Running Deer and Mountain Lion.

HARRY: And you say this man who has been robbing the settlement is about my height and build?

RUNNING DEER: Ugh, he your height and build, Captain Harry, but he no have same color hair. You have dark brown hair — him hair black and greasy, like Indian.

MOUNTAIN LION: Ugh — and him coloring different, too. Me see back of his neck and hands — and them dark, like skin of Indian.

RUNNING DEER: Also, him try to disguise voice. But me thinkum him have Indian accent.

HARRY: Do you think it could have been anyone in your father, the Chief's, tribe?

RUNNING DEER: No, we checkum on all braves at time of his visits — they all have alibis. Besides, no Tobi brave would ever act in this way.

HARRY: Do you have any ideas about who it might be?

RUNNING DEER: From color of hair, skin, and accent, me thinkum him Oomi Indian, from tribe north of Cariboo.

MOUNTAIN LION: Me too!

HARRY: That's where I come from. I know almost all the Indians in that neighborhood and not one of them has ever been arrested on any charge. They're peaceable and home-loving. Maybe there are one or two who occasionally take a little too much firewater . . . But that wouldn't explain the presence of an Oomi in these parts, or the stolen Mountie uniform. No, there is some deeper motive for all this.

MOUNTAIN LION: That what Chief, my father, him say! Him think criminal only want to make it look like robbery since he take nothing of any value. Chief say he think man commit crimes to get other man in trouble.

HARRY: Your father is a smart man, Mountain Lion.

MOUNTAIN LION: Thank you, Captain Harry. By the way, Captain, who is that beautiful blonde who came here with you but who not get out of sled?

HARRY: You Indian braves have keen eyesight. That "beautiful blonde" as you call her is Miss Daisy Farrell, of Elk City, *chanteuse* and devotee of the terpsichorean art.

RUNNING DEER: Me no understand last part of sentence.

HARRY: Neither do I, Running Deer! That's the way she describes herself. Actually she's an entertainer at the Glass Slipper Saloon in Elk City.

MOUNTAIN LION: Me understand! She do bump — like this!
(He imitates a belly dancer.)

HARRY: *(laughing)* Well, that's not quite it, but you're close.

RUNNING DEER: How come she travel with you, Captain? You needum extra warmth for these chilly nights?

HARRY: No. it's not that. I'm married, and appearances are deceiving in Daisy's case. Her hair may be bleached, but her heart is pure gold and it's in the right place. She's a good girl, and what's more she's got brains enough to stay that way.

She's here strictly on business — my business, that is. I've been on the trail of a killer for the last year. I traveled here not only to investigate the robberies, but also to see if there might be a clue to connect the two criminals — the man who robbed your settlement, and the murderer of old Walter Stevenson.

RUNNING DEER: Me hear about murder. Him partner of Mr. Dexter of Cariboo, isn't that true?

HARRY: That's right. They ran an extremely profitable fur business — at least it was profitable until the furs started disappearing.

MOUNTAIN LION: Disappearing?

HARRY: Yes — three times in one winter a driver set out for Elk City with the furs — and three times the driver, the sled, and the furs vanished into thin air.

RUNNING DEER: And then — didn't Old Man Stevenson set out with the furs himself?

HARRY: He did, Running Deer. He wanted to find out who was stealing the furs, and he met . . . death.

MOUNTAIN LION: And Miss Farrell — she have clue to murder?

HARRY: We hope so. She was a friend of the Stevenson family, and went to the same school in the east as Mr. Stevenson's daughter. She knows about some personal disputes in the family, and has given me a pretty good idea of who the killer is, though of course I'm not at liberty to reveal it.

RUNNING DEER: Mountain Lion and me, we hope you findum, and we know our father the Chief, him hope so too. Him away in Cariboo right now, to tell Lieutenant Dale about the robberies. When him come back, him maybe give you some new clues.

HARRY: Thanks, Running Deer. We need all the help we can get.

MOUNTAIN LION: Captain Harry, how come you no ask Miss Daisy to come into wigwam with you?

HARRY: Well, I asked her to, but she's a little shy before strange men.

MOUNTAIN LION and RUNNING DEER: Ho! Ho! Ho!

HARRY: What are you laughing at?

MOUNTAIN LION and RUNNING DEER: You say her shy with strange men — but we only two Indian braves — and she sing and dance every night before big male audience at Glass Slipper.

HARRY: But that's different — when you're an entertainer on stage, you feel everyone in the audience is your friend.

MOUNTAIN LION: Then why not have her pretend Running Deer and me her audience? She sing for us, and she think us her friends But first we all smokum peace pipe and then we make her honorary member of tribe so she *know* we her friends.

HARRY: Why, that sounds like a wonderful idea. I know she'd be delighted to.
(He goes to the outside opening the tent and calls.)
Oh Daisy! Daisy! My friends want to meet you!
(Daisy enters. She is an attractive, husky-voiced blonde and wears a parka.)

RUNNING DEER: Welcome to our humble tent, Miss Farrell.

MOUNTAIN LION: We very honored that you visit us.

DAISY: Hiya, boys. Pleased to meet you, I'm sure. What did you say your names were?

RUNNING DEER: Me Running Deer.

DAISY: Running Deer. I had a boy friend once that should have been named that.

MOUNTAIN LION: And me Mountain Lion.

DAISY: That's a pretty name, too. Tell me, are you that fierce?
(Mountain Lion roars.)
O.K., O.K., I believe you. *(looking around)* This is quite a place you have here. A fur rug, a piano, central heating, even a doorman — and no windows to wash. Say, do you have special weekly rates?

RUNNING DEER: You can stay as long as you like . . . free!

DAISY: Now, wait a minute. Let's not rush things.

HARRY: No, they're serious, Daisy. They want to make you an honorary member of their tribe.

DAISY: Me . . . a squaw? But then I'd have to carry you around on my back. On second thought, maybe I should accept. I was once told I have a face like a tomahawk. Seriously, boys, I'm very touched and I'd love to join your tribe.

RUNNING DEER and MOUNTAIN LION: Ugh!

DAISY: Oh, well, if you're going to get cold feet about it.

RUNNING DEER: First we present you with ceremonial headdress and wampum necklace. Then we all smokum peace pipe together.

MOUNTAIN LION: Here necklace.

DAISY: Ugh — I mean, thank you. This goes around my neck, you say? *(She puts it on and examines a tag attached to it.)* "Made in Brooklyn!" Are you sure this isn't one of those Add-a-Wampum necklaces?

RUNNING DEER: And here headdress.

DAISY: *(trying it on)* Well, this is more like it. Gosh, I haven't felt this way since I toured Manitoba in the Follies.

HARRY: You really do look stunning, Daisy.

DAISY: I'll bet you say that to all the squaws!

RUNNING DEER: And now we all smokum peace pipe. *(He hands the pipe to Daisy.)* Here, puff!

DAISY: *(She takes a puff and coughs violently.)* Do you have one with a filter tip?

(She hands it to Harry who smokes and coughs.)

HARRY: *(coughing)* It's delicious.

DAISY: Peace pipe! Remind me not to ask you to show me any of your war dances.

(The two Indians have been laughing uproariously at the coughing. Now Mountain Lion starts to smoke and cough and hands the pipe to Running Deer, who also coughs. The sentry has come in to watch, and laughs. They hand him the pipe and soon everyone is coughing violently and the wigwam fills up with smoke.)

RUNNING DEER: Me no understand! Prince Albert never taste like that before.

MOUNTAIN LION: Me have confession, Running Deer. Me buy big can of other tobacco from traveling salesman. He say it just as good, and only half the price.

SENTRY: It taste like sawdust to me.

RUNNING DEER: Well, let's gettum on with ceremony. Now that we all smokum pipe of peace it gives great pleasure to me, Running Deer, son of the Chief of the Tobi Indians —

MOUNTAIN LION: And me, Mountain Lion, also his son —

BOTH: — to welcome you to the Tobi tribe as an honorary squaw, with all the rights and privileges thereof — including the right of marrying into the tribe and settling here, should you ever so desire.

MOUNTAIN LION: And we sure hope you do desire … some day!

DAISY: I'm all choked up. I never realized how nice it feels to be a squaw — at least, now that the initiation is over, it does.

RUNNING DEER: And now that you our friend and are no longer shy with us, maybe you sing us one of your songs, huh?

MOUNTAIN LION: We love to hear you sing.

DAISY: I'm a little out of voice, but … since you boys have been so nice … sure, I'd be glad to cooperate. Could I have a chord?

(The sentry sits at the piano and accompanies. Daisy sings:)

> From the Yukon to the Arctic Circle
> Everybody's in a whirl.
> All through the North Woods everybody's talking
> About a single girl.
>
> Nobody knows where she came from
> And no one knows where she'll go,
> But they say she lights up those North Woods
> Like the moonlight on the snow.
>
> She wasn't wearing a parka
> When she came into town;
> No, she wasn't wearing a fur coat,
> But a beautiful white satin gown.
>
> All of the Mounties know her —
> She singles them out one by one.
> And lonely trappers know her,
> But she gives her heart to none.
>
> Her heart is as cold as the icicles
> That form in the winter nights;
> And she'll never say "I do" to you, my boy,
> For her name is Miss Northern Lights.
>
> All through those cold old North Woods
> Hearts are in a whirl;
> No one can sleep in the North Woods,
> Dreamin' 'bout a single girl.

(Harry and the Indians applaud vigorously. During the latter part of the song the Chief and his Indians appeared and have been standing in the opening of the wigwam, watching.)

RUNNING DEER: What a beautiful song!

HARRY: It certainly was, Daisy.

MOUNTAIN LION: Me likum too!

CHIEF: And me — my heart was likewise moved. But it sound to me as if song about you.

DAISY: Gee whiz! Standing room! You must be the Big Chief, Running Deer's and Mountain Lion's father.

CHIEF: That me. But who are you?

DAISY: I'm a friend of Captain Reynolds. We came here to investigate the robberies and a murder. But … er, won't you come in and make yourselves at home?

CHIEF: *(bowing and smiling)* Me thank pretty white lady for kind invitation.

(They enter the tent.)

And you, Captain Reynolds, me glad to see you but me sorry also.

HARRY: How is that?

CHIEF: Me bringum bad news from Cariboo, me afraid.

HARRY: Quick! Is it about Margaret?

CHIEF: About her, and about somebody else too.

HARRY: Little Jim? What happened to them — you must tell me!

CHIEF: Me make long story short. First, your wife get lonesome waiting for you. Then she hear you been seeing another woman.

HARRY: But that's a lie! Daisy and I are just friends — we've been working the case together.

DAISY: You do believe us, don't you, Chief?

CHIEF: Yes, but afraid me powerless to help situation. Anyway, rumor circulate around Cariboo that you the one who rob our settlement.

HARRY: It's incredible!

CHIEF: But Mrs. Reynolds no believum. Then Baby Jim kidnapped out of cradle, and police find your initialed handkerchief near by. Everybody think you kidnapper — including Mrs. Harry. Now she going to divorce you before you get back and marry Mr. Dexter, owner of trading post.

HARRY: *(bowing his head)* I just can't believe it.

CHIEF. Listen. You must hurry back to Cariboo. Their wedding only two weeks away, and it two weeks' journey from here to there. But be careful — order out for your arrest.

HARRY: Go back there now? Never!

DAISY: Harry, you must! Listen to what the Chief says.

CHIEF: If you don't go back, you lose wife and everybody think you a criminal.

HARRY: If Margaret has so little faith in me, she deserves to marry Dexter. I'll bet she invented those stories herself.

CHIEF: No she try hard not to believe, but those around her try to persuade her.

HARRY: A likely story! No one could force her to turn against me if she didn't want to. No, Chief, I know you have a big heart, and hate to see anyone experience pain. But if there's one lesson I've learned in life it's this — to forget about those who desert you.

CHIEF: That not a good lesson. Often they come back, if we show we have faith in them.

DAISY: That's true, Harry.

HARRY: What do I care for your preaching! From now on I'm on my own — no one will ever tell me what to do! But why am I wasting my time here? I've got work to do.

CHIEF: What kind of work?

HARRY: To find little Jim, of course!

CHIEF: But others already look for him — it useless for you to go. Me think you do best to return to Cariboo!

HARRY: I'm sorry, Chief, but I can't believe that anyone else will try as hard to find him as I intend to. And Margaret shall never be my wife again.

CHIEF: It often happens, when we find one thing, we find others as well. You already looking for Stevenson murderer — maybe you should stick to first quest, and other things happen by themselves.

HARRY: I don't understand you! And I'm losing precious time. Chief, be kind enough to lend me some clothes to disguise myself. I'll be arrested on sight in this uniform.

CHIEF: Very well, my son. Perhaps some day you see folly of your ways, and return to right path. Mountain Lion, supply Captain Harry with new wardrobe.

(Mountain Lion leads Harry off to the right.)

It sad sight to see man fallen so low.

DAISY: Yes — you were so right in all your pronouncements.

CHIEF: It out of question for him to return to Elk City now that him marked man. Maybe you stay with us for few days until we sendum sled down for supplies?

DAISY: Why, I'd love to! I'm crazy about this place — everyone is so friendly. I'll bet you didn't know I've been made an honorary squaw.

CHIEF: Me know what happen when me see you in necklace and headdress. Me suspect Running Deer and Mountain Lion behind it all. They likum pretty ladies.

DAISY: They're sweet boys — and so is their father.

(Harry and Mountain Lion return. Harry is now wearing an Indian costume with a fur-trimmed hood.)

HARRY: Thank you for your kindnesses, Chief. I should be able to get by in this disguise. I'm sorry if I spoke roughly just now. You are a good man, but I must do my duty as I see it. All men must.

CHIEF: Yes — even when they wrong about "duty."

HARRY: Are you coming, Daisy?

DAISY: No, I'm staying. You can't return to Elk City, and the Chief has kindly allowed me to exercise my prerogatives as a squaw for a few days.

HARRY: Then goodbye, all of you. I hope we may meet again on some more fortunate occasion.

INDIANS: Goodbye.

DAISY: Goodbye. Harry.

(He goes out. Daisy starts to cry.)

He's such a brave man — but so proud.

CHIEF: Yes. But do not weep over him. He is a fine man — things may yet work out all right for him. And now, you must be tired. Perhaps you would like to rest up a bit before supper, which is at seven o'clock in the main tent.

DAISY: Yes. that might be nice.

CHIEF: Running Deer, perhaps you will show — but what is your name? Boys, what name did you give her?

RUNNING DEER: We didn't have time to give her one, Father.

CHIEF: Then I shall name her myself. Let's see, what would be a good name? I have it — Miss Northern Lights!

INDIANS: Hooray! Hooray for Miss Northern Lights!

DAISY: It's a pretty name, but a very flattering one.

CHIEF: No, it suits you perfectly. Now, Running Deer, show Miss Northern Lights where her tent is. And then hurry back here because I want you to give me an account of what's taken place in the camp since I've been away.

RUNNING DEER: Yes, Father, you look rather tired.

(The Chief yawns and stretches, and then goes off to the right.)

Well, brothers, what did you find on your voyage over the mountains?

INDIANS: Little but snow, and barren rocks, and human desolation more uncongenial than these.

MOUNTAIN LION: So I thought from your faces. And here things haven't gone too well, either.

INDIANS: Why, what do you mean?

MOUNTAIN LION: I mean that our tribe is impoverished, as you know. And even worse than that, our pride is gone, too.

INDIANS: What signs of this have you seen?

MOUNTAIN LION: All around me I see lying, avarice, and petty bickering. I have seen our braves fighting over the seat nearest to the fire, or the last piece of meat in the dish. And our squaws go cold and hungry. Their husbands no longer care for them; they sit all day long at the tent opening, staring blankly at the sunlit ground. Most of our braves are engaged in bootlegging, illegal fur trading and other shady deals in order to make a little money. And who can blame them? Even Running Deer and myself, who have done our best to keep the others in order, are sorely tempted to go and take jobs in Elk City.

But worse than poverty and degradation is the decay of the tribal spirit. Each begins to go his own way, no one thinks of the group any more, no one worships the old familiar gods. What is happening to us?

INDIANS: Truly, inside and outside our settlement, pain, death, poverty and auguries of future unhappiness are everywhere, like the spirit of the great raven himself.

MOUNTAIN LION: Hush, my friends! Do not even dream of uttering a blasphemy!

INDIANS: For a long time the fortune-teller has been saying that a white child, born to one of our women, would lead us back from the brink of destruction. Well, where is this child? It was to have been born this year, and the year is almost over and not one of our wives is pregnant. Like all prophecies, this one is as vain and foolish as the god that inspired it.

MOUNTAIN LION: Oh, my friends, not you too! I fear what this may mean to our community.

INDIANS: Hasn't enough happened already? Why postpone the bitter end?

MOUNTAIN LION: You don't know what you're saying! Oh, if only some vision would guide me out of this pit into which I feel my spirit is sinking!

INDIANS: All visions are empty, vain, and foolish as the gods who inspire them.

MOUNTAIN LION: *(bows his head)* Perhaps … perhaps it is so.

(Blue Feather rushes in.)

BLUE FEATHER: Quick! Where is the Chief? I must speak to him at once!

MOUNTAIN LION: What is it? What is the matter with you?

BLUE FEATHER: The Chief! I must see the Chief!

MOUNTAIN LION: Whatever you have to say to him, Blue Feather, you can say to me. I am his son.

(Running Deer enters.)

RUNNING DEER: What is he doing here? I saw him come running in as if he owned the place.

BLUE FEATHER: You idiots! I tell you only the Chief shall hear my news.

(Chief enters)

CHIEF: Well, what is it, Blue Feather? You know I always rest before dinner. Is this your way of welcoming me back?

BLUE FEATHER: Yes, O mighty Chief! Yes, it is. I have a gift for you, a wonderful gift. One that will lead our tribe back to its former prosperity!

CHIEF: That is certainly good news, if true.

BLUE FEATHER: It is true, I tell you!

CHIEF: Well, where is this gift?

BLUE FEATHER: It will soon be here. Oh, this is the happiest day of my life! To think that it is I, I who am to be the salvation of the Tobi tribe.

INDIANS: *(to each other)* What is it? . . What is he talking about? I don't trust him … Neither do I … He has never done anything before to enhance our reputation … No, far from it.

CHIEF: Watch what you are saying, Blue Feather. If you indeed hold the secret of our salvation, it will be a great thing for the tribe and you. If you are lying, it could mean your disgrace and even permanent exile from us.

BLUE FEATHER: *(aside)* Some punishment! *(aloud)* In one moment you will cease to doubt me.

(Sentry entering)

SENTRY: Great Chief, there is nurse out here who wants to see you.

CHIEF: Show her in!

(The sentry leads a squaw carrying a white baby.)

BLUE FEATHER: Now maybe you'll believe me. This, Chief and braves, is my son — my *white son* — whom my wife gave birth to scarcely an hour ago.

CHIEF: Is this true? I didn't even know your wife was pregnant.

SQUAW: It true, all right. Me deliver baby, myself. His wife no let on her pregnant because her want to surprise husband.

RUNNING DEER: Then the prophecy has been fulfilled.

MOUNTAIN' LION: The one the fortune-teller told us about!

INDIANS: Hooray! Hooray for Blue Feather!

BLUE FEATHER: Thank you, my friends.

CHIEF: Do you mind if I hold the child?

BLUE FEATHER: No, no! He's yours, in a sense.

CHIEF: *(aside, while Blue Feather talks with the others)* A white child The salvation predicted for our tribe? Surely it cannot be true! But, why should I doubt it? Can I doubt the authority of the gods? Oh great raven, forgive my skepticism! But wait — I have seen this little one before — this is no new-born baby! It was back in Cariboo that I saw it, in its little cradle, watched over by its mother! It is Jim, the kidnapped child!

What am I to do now? Of course I must notify the mother — it will prove Harry's innocence, and prevent their divorce. But … will it? Margaret has already renounced her husband — he may have been right in taking a drastic view of her actions. And the kidnapper has not been found — maybe it was the father, for all I know.

And then, look at these smiling faces of my tribesmen. It would be the final blow to them if I were to expose this fraud. Perhaps I will wait a little while, till we get back on our feet, before telling the truth. Meanwhile if any serious problem arises owing to child's disappearance, I can always come forward with the true story.

I know these are just excuses, but still I have a funny hunch that I am doing the right thing. If I didn't, the fate of my whole tribe couldn't deter me from making the facts known.

Now my course must be to watch, and wait, and hold my tongue, and try to find out how the baby got here — for thereby, I suspect, hangs an interesting tale. *(returning the child to Blue Feather)* Thank you for letting me see him. He's as handsome as one would expect a child sent from heaven to be.

BLUE FEATHER: Thanks, O Chief.

(Daisy enters wearing a squaw costume.)

DAISY: What's happened? It seems like everybody in the camp is running toward this tent. I thought it was an Elks' Convention.

CHIEF: My dear, you come to us at a fortunate time. Blue Feather's wife has just had a white baby, thus fulfilling a prophecy and saving us all from ruin.

DAISY: Gosh, that's swell!

CHIEF: And I think it would be fitting, since you are of the same race as this child. and since he belongs to the whole tribe, in a manner of speaking, if you were to take care of him for as long as you choose to stay with us, which we hope will be long indeed. That is, if Blue Feather and his wife have no objections.

BLUE FEATHER: Sure — anything.

DAISY: And I'd love to. *(taking the child)* He's certainly a cute little dickens.

CHIEF: I will rear him as my own son, and see that he is given every advantage, as befits our new leader.

INDIANS: Hooray! Hooray! Hooray!

CHIEF: Oh great raven, we thank you for your kindness to us! Grant us the prosperity you promised, and grant that in the future we may be able to lead lives free from deceit.

INDIANS: Hooray! Hooray for the raven!

RUNNING DEER: Come on, everybody, let's run to the mess hall and tell the others!

INDIANS: O.K.! Let's! Come on, everybody! Whoopee!

(They all go out except for the Chief, Daisy and the Squaw.)

DAISY: *(to the Squaw)* You stay. We'll fix him a nice warm bed by the fire … What's the matter, Chief? You seem troubled.

CHIEF: Me? Oh, it's nothing. I just hope everything turns out all right. I hate to see my braves disappointed in anything.

DAISY: They certainly didn't look very disappointed just now.

CHIEF: No — but hopes are sometimes dashed.

DAISY: Aw, don't be a worry bird. I have a feeling wonderful days are ahead.

CHIEF: Do you? I guess maybe they are. I hope so.

DAISY: I sure hope I'll be around to share in them.

CHIEF: Why won't you be?

DAISY: There's my job in Elk City. They're not going to hold it for me forever. And then, I couldn't go on sponging on your hospitality.

CHIEF: How would you like to stay on as … my wife?

DAISY: *(enthusiastically)* Gosh, Chief, I'd love to!

CHIEF: I realize I haven't much to offer in the way of youth or good looks —

DAISY: Aw, cut it out, Chief! I'm about ready for the glue factory, myself.

CHIEF: — or material advantages —

DAISY: I love roots and berries!

CHIEF: I'm old enough to be your father —

DAISY: What difference does that make when true love is at stake? You have plenty to offer in the way of wisdom and experience, and that counts for more than you think with us girls. And anyway, you *are* cute. So there.

CHIEF: Now I know you're lying —

DAISY: I thought so the first minute I laid eyes on you!

CHIEF: Prove it!

DAISY: O.K. — you asked for it! *(She kisses him.)*

CHIEF: *(to the squaw who has started to run out)* Hey, where are you going?

SQUAW: Me be right back! Me gotta tell girl friend something!

(She runs out. Daisy and the Chief look at each other, they smile and laugh happily, then embrace as the curtain descends.)

CURTAIN

ACT III

Five years later. The scene is the interior of Dexter's house in Cariboo — a large, high-ceilinged room with a fireplace, above which hang an Indian blanket and a rifle. There is a door on the right, and the outside door is on the left. Through a window at the back one can see a snowy scene, dotted with cabins, with dawn breaking over the mountains. Margaret is seated at a table, her head pillowed in her arms; Mooka, in a maid's uniform, enters from the kitchen.

MOOKA: Her been sitting there all night, me bet! *(She goes over to her.)* Wake up, Missus! What you want to sleep here all night for?

MARGARET: *(She raises her head and blows out a lamp on the table.)* You're wrong, I haven't been asleep.

MOOKA: Oh, what you wantum do it for? You ruining your health.

MARGARET: You know the answer to that question as well as I do, Mooka.

MOOKA: You waitum for no-good ex-husband to return?

MARGARET: No. I never want to see him again. I wouldn't have divorced him five years ago and married Mr. Dexter if I did. It's Jim — Baby Jim — I'm waiting for. I know he'll come back some day. That's why I wait every night at this window.

I want him to be able to find his way to this house.

(Mooka stifles a sob.)

And I want you to promise me something, Mooka.

MOOKA: *(tearfully)* You know Mooka do anything in her power for white Missus.

MARGARET: If I should … go away, or something like that, I want you to promise that you'll always keep this lamp burning every night. Then I can be easy in my mind.

MOOKA: You no go away!

MARGARET: Yes, I'm afraid I am going away — to a convent.

MOOKA: A convent! No! White missus like life — gaiety — friends. She not find happiness in convent.

MARGARET: It's true I used to love life — in the glad days of my first marriage. But those times are gone forever. Now I have nothing to look forward to, except to pass the rest of my life in solitude, and to go to meet my Maker as soon as possible.

MOOKA: *(sinks to her knees before Margaret)* No! Mooka never let you go!

MARGARET: I must.

(Dexter enters.)

DEXTER: Well, you're up nice and early. Is breakfast ready, Mooka?

MOOKA: It almost ready — me bring!

(She goes out.)

DEXTER: I hope you haven't been sitting up all night again, waiting for that brat of yours to return.

MARGARET: And if I have?

DEXTER: It won't do you any good, because even if he did come back I wouldn't let him in. Harry Reynolds' son will never enter this house.

MARGARET: Then I don't intend to stay in it either. As a matter of fact, I've made arrangements to enter the convent in Moose Junction. My things are packed — I'm leaving today. Lucky Seven has promised to drive me there.

DEXTER: Lucky Seven — ha! ha! — has promised — ha! ha! ha!

MARGARET: What's so funny?

DEXTER: Funny? Oh, nothing. *(laughs)* Well, have a nice trip.

(He starts to leave the room, still laughing.)

MARGARET: *(She walks after him and seizes him by the arm.)* Wait a minute! What are you laughing at?

DEXTER: *(grabbing her viciously)* Now look here, my dear wife! You're going nowhere, do you hear? Nowhere! You think Lucky Seven doesn't tell me everything you tell him, and a lot more? Then you're not as smart as I gave you credit for being.

MARGARET: It doesn't matter. If Lucky Seven won't drive me there, I'll find someone else who will.

DEXTER: You ain't findin' nobody! You're my wife and you're staying right here.

MARGARET: Your wife — as if you wanted a wife. You only married me because I wouldn't accept you at first — and it hurt your pride.

DEXTER: Maybe so, but that doesn't mean I'm lettin' you go. No sir, nobody walks out on Sam Dexter.

MARGARET: You can't keep me here.

DEXTER: I have ways of making you stay, and if you try to disobey me you'll find out what they are.

MARGARET: You're heartless!

DEXTER: And I'm also your legal husband — remember that the next time you think of leaving my bed and board.

(Mooka enters with a tray.)

MOOKA: You want breakfast in here?

DEXTER: No, bring it in my den. I don't want to disturb Mother Superior at her devotions.

(They go off at the right. Margaret sinks down at the table her head pillowed on her arms and weeps noiselessly. Mooka returns in a moment with a coffee pot.)

MOOKA: Now, you drinkum coffee and not look so sad.

MARGARET: No thank you! I don't want anything.

MOOKA: No, you take — feel better.

(Margaret drinks.)

What him say to make Missus sad this way?

MARGARET: He told me he won't let me go, Mooka. He's going to keep me here as a prisoner. He said Lucky Seven told him my plans.

MOOKA: No — Lucky Seven not do thing like that!

MARGARET: He said Lucky Seven tells him everything.

MOOKA: Lucky Seven not the best — but him good Indian! Him no stool-pigeon.

(Margaret rests her forehead in her hands.)

Listen, Mooka talk to him, her get him to drive you to convent, if you want to go. Her twistum Lucky Seven around little finger — you gettum wish!

MARGARET: Thank you, Mooka. You always do look after me, don't you? I'll go now and finish packing my things. Try to speak to Lucky Seven as soon as possible — tell him I'll give him money — more than I'd promised — if he'll keep the secret.

MOOKA: He do it — and not for money, for Mooka!

MARGARET: I hope so!

(She goes out. Mooka starts to hum and dust with a feather duster.)

MOOKA: Lucky Seven probably not understand White Missus wish to keep her plans from Mr. Dexter. Me remindum of duty to Missus and then he helpum. Him good Indian at heart.

(There is a knock at the door.)

Come in!

(Lucky Seven enters.)

My passion flower! Us was just talking about you.

LUCKY SEVEN: Hello, porcupine face.

MOOKA: Lucky Seven lovum joke! But why you tellum Dexter of White Missus' plans?

LUCKY SEVEN: Because it my job, that why. But me no wanna listenum to you, Crosseyes. Me gotta see Dexter.

MOOKA: Wait! Mooka promise you take Missus to Moose Junction! You cannot lettum Mooka down!

LUCKY SEVEN: Me glad to takum her anywhere, if she can payum for ticket.

MOOKA: Ticket! How much?

LUCKY SEVEN: 10,000 dollars — in cash.

MOOKA: Ah! But Missus no havum big money — even Dexter not got that much. You terrible Indian! Me tellum Lieutenant Dale you attempt extortion, and then see how far you gettum! Me go right now!

LUCKY SEVEN: You go nowhere, unless you want perforated hide. *(He flashes a pistol.)*

MOOKA: A gun! And all the time me think you lovum Mooka! Me shoulda known! *(She starts to cry.)*

LUCKY SEVEN: *(confused)* Ugh, don't cry — me sorry. I mean — shut up or I'll shoot!

(Dexter enters.)

DEXTER: Oh. it's you. Put that pistol away. *(to Mooka)* You get into the kitchen and shut the door behind you.

(Mooka goes into the kitchen but does not shut the door all the way and remains listening.)

I ought to brain you for flashing that illegal gat in here — you think I want every Mountie in these parts on my neck? What are you doing here, anyway? Did you bring me the payments for those furs?

LUCKY SEVEN: Me bringum bad news! Captain Reynolds on way back to Cariboo!

DEXTER: That's impossible — he wouldn't dare set foot in town. The Mounties have orders to shoot him on sight.

LUCKY SEVEN: Me glad you not scared.

DEXTER: Why should I be? There's nothing he can do to me — not even take his wife back, 'cause she's my wife now.

LUCKY SEVEN: Me almost forget — my Indian informant say Captain no longer care about wife — say you can have her.

DEXTER: That's sensible of him.

LUCKY SEVEN: Him come back to Cariboo only because him want to arrest you for murder of Mr. Stevenson and having me kidnap Baby Jim.

DEXTER: He's crazy! No one will believe I did it!

LUCKY SEVEN: But him always gettum man!

DEXTER: Shut up, you! *(He slaps him.)* That's just in case you ever think of squealing on me, which I know you wouldn't.

LUCKY SEVEN: Mr. Dexter! How can you thinkum such terrible thing about Lucky Seven?

DEXTER: Forgive me, my friend. I just wanted to remind you of your firm moral principles. Now, when is Reynolds due to arrive here?

LUCKY SEVEN. Me not know — maybe today, maybe tomorrow, maybe next week.

DEXTER: I want you to get your Indian pals to keep watch over all the approaches to town. The moment any stranger appears, have them report to me — understand?

LUCKY SEVEN: Ugh!

DEXTER: But first, go over to Mountie headquarters and tell that nice young Lieutenant Dale I'd like to say a few words to him in my private study concerning a certain notorious thief and kidnapper whose appearance in Cariboo in imminent.

LUCKY SEVEN: Me gottum!

(He goes out.)

DEXTER: I'll have Reynolds' hide yet! What a relief to be rid of that gum snowshoe after all these years! With him gone and that imbecile Dale head of the police force, I'll be ruler over the whole North Woods! If only Margaret doesn't get suspicious of me and tip Dale off.

(He goes off at the right. Mooka enters.)

MOOKA: So that what happen to old Mr. Stevenson! Him killed by Dexter! Lucky Seven kidnappum Baby Jim! Me thank stars me not consent when him wanta marry Mooka! Me go tell Lieutenant Dale at once! Me not tell Missus — if she find out she have hysterics and Dexter shoot her, maybe, when he see she know. Him dangerous criminal! Me go right now.

(She starts for the door. Margaret enters.)

MARGARET: Well, Mooka, have you spoken to Lucky Seven?

MOOKA: Uh — me not get chance to see him yet me go right now and tell him.

MARGARET: You have talked to him, because I saw him coming up to the house from my bedroom window. What did he say? Never mind, I can read his answer in your face. He refused, didn't he?

MOOKA: Ugh — well …

MARGARET: He did, I can see. Well, I'll just have to think of some other way. If only Lieutenant Dale were still my friend. But he hasn't spoken to me since I married Mr. Dexter. Poor boy, how it must have hurt him!

MOOKA: Me go ask him now!

MARGARET: No, that wouldn't do. I've been cruel to him and I don't deserve his help. I must think of something else — of someone who would dare to defy Dexter and help me … *(She sighs.)* But there isn't anybody. Everybody else in this town is afraid of him, or they owe him too much money.

(Mooka is edging toward the door.)

Where are you going?

MOOKA: Me gottum go next door — borrow cup of sugar!

MARGARET: You can think of food at a time like this!

MOOKA: We gotta eat — keepum up strength.

MARGARET: Now, Mooka, you sit right down in that chair. There's no need for you to borrow a cup of sugar.

MOOKA: Oh — lettum me go! Please!

MARGARET: Not until you tell me what's on your mind — what's making you so jittery.

MOOKA: No, me can't tell. At least, not now!

MARGARET: I'm going to get to the bottom of this if we have to stay here all day!

(There is a knock at the door. Mooka starts to answer it.)

Never mind — I'll get it. You sit right where you are.

(The knock is repeated.)

On second thought, I think you'd better go into the kitchen and sit until you're ready to explain to me why you were so anxious to leave the house just now.

MOOKA: Me no wanna leave now! Me wanna stay here with you!

MARGARET: No, I want you to go into the kitchen as your punishment for being so secretive with me, your best friend.

(There is another knock. Mooka tries to go and answer it.)

Mooka!

MOOKA: But … Oh, all right!

(She goes off.)

MARGARET: Come in.

(Dale enters.)

Oh … *(She turns her back on him, deeply moved.)*

DALE: I am here on your husband's orders.

MARGARET: *(not turning around)* His room is … that way. *(She points.)*

DALE: Thank you. *(He starts toward the door at the right.)*

MARGARET: Are you …

DALE: Yes?

MARGARET: … sure you can find the way?

DALE: I think I can, thank you. *(He starts toward the door again and stops.)* Oh, Meg!

MARGARET: *(turning)* Yes?

DALE: Why must we act this way, like total strangers?

MARGARET: I don't know! Life is so cruel!

DALE: Those words seem to have a special meaning for you.

MARGARET: Alas! It's true.

DALE: Then you haven't been happy all these years?

MARGARET: Happy? I don't even know the meaning of the word.

DALE: You don't know how happy it makes me to hear you say that.

MARGARET: Ever since my baby was stolen I haven't had a joyful moment.

DALE: *(stiffening)* Oh … So that's the cause of your sorrow.

MARGARET: Oh, Allan, don't go on. Don't force me to say things about my marriage that I would regret later on.

DALE: Regret? … Then your marriage hasn't been happy?

MARGARET: It has been hell! He hasn't addressed a kind word to me since the minister pronounced us man and wife. I can't see my old friends . . I can't even think about my baby. But I do! Every night — at this window. I keep a lamp burning for him, hoping somehow he'll find his way home.

DALE: My poor dearest!

MARGARET: Only today I was forbidden to leave the house! Oh, if only you could help me, Allan, I'd be so grateful!

DALE: I'll do everything in my power! Just tell me what I can do.

MARGARET: I must get away from this place. Even the thought of my child returning no longer deters me, especially since Mooka has promised to look after him if he comes. I want to enter a convent — there's one in Moose Junction. There seems no other way open to a bereft mother married to a heartless tyrant.

DALE: You are wrong. There is another way!

MARGARET: And what might that be?

DALE: You know that I have always loved you.

MARGARET: No — I mustn't listen.

DALE: But you must: It's too late for you not to listen! Do not renounce for the third and perhaps the last time the feeling that I know surges within you as it does within me! Oh, Margaret, say that you love me too!

MARGARET: It is true — I do love you, Allan.

DALE: O bliss!

MARGARET: Even before I married Harry I loved you. I could never make up my mind between the two of you. Finally I accepted Harry's proposal, not because I loved him more, but because ... well, you were so shy, and it seemed you'd never get to the point.

DALE: I was so spellbound by your beauty I was powerless to let you know it.

MARGARET: And after I was married to Harry I could never quite make up my mind which of you I cared for most — Harry, the practical, cheerful, reassuring kind, or you — romantic, melancholy — the dreamer. I finally realized that I loved you both, the same — that my heart was divided equally between you.

DALE: Equally?

MARGARET: Yes, equally. Even though I now confess my love for you, I can give you but half my heart. If Harry were to walk through that door at this moment, I would make the same admissions to him. My love for him has never abated either.

DALE: Then how — why did you marry Dexter?

MARGARET: I was so confused at the time. I had nowhere to turn, with my baby gone. He offered me security, protection — so I thought. Your red uniform seemed to remind me of Harry and the life I used to lead. I thought I might grow to care for him after our marriage. I was wrong!

DALE: That is all over now. Now we must plan how to get you out of his clutches.

MARGARET: Yes. There's not a moment to lose.

DALE: I think I have a scheme. Do you know that deserted cabin on the edge of town?

MARGARET: Yes.

DALE: You must go there — now — without letting anyone see you. I'll keep Dexter in conversation as long as I can — it will be some time before he discovers you're gone, and when he does he'll send for me and tell me to organize a search party. As soon as I can get free I'll come to you at the cabin — we'll set out this very night for Moose Junction!

MARGARET: But what then?

DALE: You can remain in the convent for a while. You'll be safe there, and you'll have plenty of time to decide.

MARGARET: Decide? Decide what?

DALE: Why, whether you want to marry me, of course.

MARGARET: Oh, Allan! You haven't even proposed!

DALE: I know, I'm slow about getting to the point. But I'm asking you now, Meg. Will you be my wife?

MARGARET: But I'm already married.

ALLAN: I haven't forgotten. But with my testimony and Mooka's you can easily get a divorce from Dexter. It's what you want, isn't it?

MARGARET: Allan dear, of course it is!

DALE: And ... will you try to put Harry out of your mind?

MARGARET: I'll try, my dearest. I really will.

DALE: Then this is the happiest day of my life!

MARGARET: And of mine.

DALE: Now you must get a few things together — he mustn't come out and see us talking. Take the back way to the cabin — wear a hood, so no one sees your face. I'll be there as soon as I can.

(Dexter enters.)

DEXTER: *(glaring at them)* Lieutenant! I was just coming to see what had happened to you. I presume Lucky Seven gave you my urgent message.

DALE: He did, Mr. Dexter. I was just inquiring of your wife where I could find you.

DEXTER: *(to Margaret)* Leave us alone, please.

MARGARET: Yes, I think I will lie down. l had such a sleepless night.

DEXTER: Neither the Lieutenant nor I are interested in the state of your health.

(Margaret goes out.)

I mentioned that my message was urgent, Lieutenant. I'll get right to the point. Harry Reynolds is coming back to Cariboo.

DALE: Harry ... coming back!

DEXTER: Yes. Does that surprise you so much?

DALE: Why, yes ... er ... He's been away so long.

DEXTER: You've turned pale, Lieutenant. Could it be that you have some reason for not wanting him to come back?

DALE: It's no pleasure to arrest an old friend, Mr. Dexter, even if he has turned out bad.

DEXTER: Is that all, Mr. Dale? Are you sure there isn't some other reason — some more personal reason — why you'd rather not see him?

DALE: What are you driving at?

DEXTER: I'm not given to eavesdropping, but I'm afraid that, quite by accident, I overheard the last part of your little love scene with my wife. A first rate performance. I confess I was deeply moved.

DALE: You ... you are ruthless!

DEXTER: Don't be angry with me. I mean it when I say I was moved by your performance. Such freshness, such poignancy. What was it she said? "My heart is divided equally between you."

DALE: You beast!

DEXTER: Careful, Lieutenant. Remember that it is I who am the injured party. I could have your badge, if I chose to. It wouldn't look very nice in the papers — "Mountie Tries to Abduct Young Wife from Home." For this reason, I urge you to cancel your projected trip to Moose Junction. In fact, l have taken steps to see that Margaret does not undertake this trip. My men are watching both doors of this cabin to prevent her.

DALE: You can't get away with this! No judge could fail to grant her a divorce after what she's told me about you.

DEXTER: I agree with you! And what's more, I'm going to give her complete freedom to act as she pleases. If she still wants to marry you, I'll do everything I can to enable her to. You see, I am capable of human feelings.

DALE: What do you mean, if she *still* loves me? Didn't she just say she did?

DEXTER: Yes — with half her heart. And you seem to forget the claimant of the other half is on his way here. That does change things, doesn't it?

DALE: What do you want of me?

DEXTER: Only this — when Reynolds walks in that door, I want you to shoot to kill.

DALE: Kill him? Harry? My oldest friend?

DEXTER: You'd be within your rights as an officer of the law — besides, I'd swear you did it in self-defense.

DALE: I couldn't think of it. It is my duty to arrest Harry, and then see that he is given a fair trial by jury.

DEXTER: Think, Dale. Your whole life is in his hands. Once Margaret knows he's still alive, that he still loves her, she'll fly to his side and you'll be forgotten. You forget they were once man and wife. Even if you send him to jail she'll wait for him — you don't know what perseverance that girl has.

DALE: It's impossible. But why are you so interested in getting rid of Harry?

DEXTER: Never mind that — just do as I say, if you value your happiness.

DALE: My happiness! Was it only a moment ago she said, "I love you?" It seems like a thousand years.

DEXTER: Follow my advice and all will be well.

DALE: I can't do it … or can I?

(The door opens and Lucky Seven sticks his head in the room.)

LUCKY SEVEN: We've spotted him. He head for this house — should be here in two minutes. Him wearum Indian outfit for disguise.

DEXTER: Excellent! You watch the back door and make sure she doesn't get out. We'll wait in here.

LUCKY SEVEN: Ugh!

(He goes out.)

DEXTER: Now listen, Dale. We'll hide behind this screen. When Reynolds comes in we'll take our time. Let him talk to her if he wants to — it will put him off his guard. When I give the signal, I want you to run out and challenge him in the name of the law. He'll reach for a gun of course, and then you'll fire the fatal bullet. Meanwhile I'll stand to one side and divert his attention so he doesn't get the draw on you — he's a superb marksman. Do you understand?

DALE: *(gloomily)* Yes … I understand.

DEXTER: Then come on.

(They hide behind the screen. After a few moments there is a knock on the door. Mooka comes out of the kitchen to answer it.)

HARRY: *(disguised as an Indian)* Is lady of house in?

MOOKA: Whatever you sell, we no wantum any.

HARRY: Me no salesman. Me wantum see lady of house.

MOOKA: Her not home. Who am you?

HARRY: Me good friend of lady of house.

MOOKA: Me never see you before.

HARRY: You think so? Look closer.

MOOKA: Me have to go now. Goodbye … *(She is about to close the door.)*

HARRY: Wait. Showum this to white missus and tell her I want to see her. *(He shows her something in his hand.)*

MOOKA: Baby Jim's little rattle. Where you get that?

HARRY: Never mindum. Send missus here.

(Margaret enters.)

MARGARET: Who is it, Mooka?

MOOKA: An old Indian with a message for you, Missus.

MARGARET: For me? What sort of message?

HARRY: This is my message. *(He shows her the rattle.)*

MARGARET: My baby's rattle! Where did you get it?

HARRY: That's my business.

MARGARET: Who are you, anyway?

HARRY: Don't you recognize me?

MARGARET: Your voice is familiar, but …

HARRY: Well, never mind who I am, for the moment. I have a few things to say first.

MARGARET: Leave us, Mooka.

(Mooka goes out.)

Do you know where my baby is? How do you happen to have this rattle?

HARRY: I picked it up outside your cabin shortly after the baby was kidnapped, when I was investigating the crime.

MARGARET: You investigated it? Then where is he — my baby, I mean?

HARRY: I don't know that. I do know the man responsible for the kidnapping, however.

(Behind the screen Dexter is urging Dale to shoot, but the latter insists on hearing the rest of the story.)

MARGARET: Who? … Who?

HARRY: By a strange coincidence, he is the same man who murdered old Mr. Stevenson, several years ago.

(Violent struggles from Dexter behind the screen. He is held back by Dale.)

By an even stranger coincidence, that man is also your husband, *Mrs. Samuel Dexter!*

MARGARET: Oh, my goodness!

HARRY: *(sarcastically)* You seem shocked by the news!

MARGARET: Shocked — but not surprised. I always had a feeling he was at the bottom of both crimes, but I had no clues to go on.

HARRY: You suspected your own husband?

MARGARET: Husband? Yes, in name perhaps he was my husband. But I have always hated him, and at last I know the reason why.

HARRY: You hate him — your own husband!

MARGARET: That's right.

HARRY: Then why did you marry him?

MARGARET: I don't think this is any of your business, old man, and besides, we're losing precious minutes, minutes in which we might discover where my baby is now.

HARRY: Oh, Margaret!

MARGARET: That voice … I know that voice!

HARRY: *(pushing back his hood)* Now do you recognize me?

MARGARET: Harry!

HARRY: My dearest! *(They embrace.)*

MARGARET: But why did you keep your identity a secret at first?

HARRY: I'm afraid I came back to taunt you with your marriage to a criminal, before I arrested him. Can you forgive me?

MARGARET: Of course! But tell me, Harry, how were you able to trace him?

HARRY: I found the rattle lying near the cabin, and near that a fur cap I knew belonged to Lucky Seven. From then on it was a simple, though long, process to trace the kidnapper and connect him with the murder of Stevenson.

MARGARET: But you haven't found Baby Jim?

HARRY: Not yet, but I have a hunch the case will break soon.

MARGARET: My hero! If you knew how I've longed for you every day of your absence!

HARRY: Not a single day has passed that I haven't thought of you with love and … remorse.

MARGARET: But that's all over now … that last thing you spoke of.

HARRY: Yes … it's all over. *(He kisses her.)*

(Dexter comes out from behind the screen with Dale)

DEXTER: That's enough. Frisk him, Dale!

DALE: Harry Reynolds, it is my sad but unavoidable duty to arrest you in the name of His Majesty, the King.

HARRY: On what charges?

DEXTER: You'll find out soon enough.

DALE: On charges of robbery and kidnapping your own son.

HARRY: But you're mistaken … The man you want is right here in this room!

DEXTER: I'll say he is!

DALE: Any information you have will come out at your trial. Now I must ask you to accompany me to headquarters.

HARRY: Never … not while the real criminal is still at large. *(whipping out a gun)* Drop that pistol, Dale!

DEXTER: What's the matter, Dale? Are you scared? Well, if you won't do your duty, I will!

(He charges at Harry with a knife. Dale shoots Dexter, who falls. Margaret screams.)

DEXTER: *(laughing)* You shot the wrong man, Dale.

(He dies.)

DALE: He's dead!

(Lucky Seven has sneaked into the house and is about to stab Dale in the back. Mooka comes quietly out of the kitchen and hits him over the head with a frying pan knocking him cold.)

DALE: Nice work, Mooka.

MOOKA: It not work … It a pleasure!

DALE. Now, Harry, if you'll drop that gun.

HARRY: Certainly, Allan. But believe me, the man you want is in there … dead!

DALE: A jury will have to decide that. I heard your explanation to Margaret, and I must say it sounds rather weak.

MARGARET: He's telling the truth, Allan, I know he is!

MOOKA: Me too!

DALE: But where is the proof?

> *(There is a knock at the door. Mooka answers it. The Chief, Daisy, Running Deer, Mountain Lion, Blue Feather and other Indians come in.)*

CHIEF: We come from far to greet old friends!

RUNNING DEER: We very glad —

MOUNTAIN LION: — to be here! Ugh!

DAISY: Hi, everybody!

HARRY: Chief! Daisy! Running Deer! Mountain Lion! What are you doing here?

DAISY: We were just passing by and saw the smoke coming out of your chimney, so —

CHIEF: We bring pleasant news to white missus!

MARGARET: To me?

CHIEF: Yes — to you. But first cannot these unpleasant sights be removed? *(He gestures toward Dexter and Lucky Seven.)*

DALE: Give me a hand, boys. We'll lock up Lucky Seven and get Dexter out of the way too.

> *(Dale and Mountain Lion carry Dexter off: Harry and Running Deer remove Lucky Seven.)*

CHIEF: And now, gather round. Me have little story to tell. Five years ago, one starless winter night, a baby was stolen from a Cariboo near here. As a dog sled whizzed over the trail from Cariboo to Elk City, a tiny immigrant rode in the observation car. This sled was being driven by an unscrupulous Indian, yet not one so unscrupulous that he preferred blood to money. Nearing our settlement, he met up with an old friend with whom he arranged a curious deal. But maybe, Blue Feather, you would like to take over the story from here.

BLUE FEATHER: Me ashamed, but me try. When Lucky Seven, for that name of Indians, see me he tell me have white baby he have to get rid of. Me remember prophecy, that white baby born to woman of our tribe restore us to prosperity. Accordingly, me take baby and make wife swear it hers.

CHIEF: Soon, prosperity return to Tobi tribe. Under the expert guidance of my new bride, my sons Mountain Lion and Running Deer, and, last but not least, myself, we build up rich fur trading business.

DAISY: Now all the wigwams have indoor plumbing.

RUNNING DEER: Me drive team of eight dogs instead of four.

MOUNTAIN LION: Me buy ukulele and take lessons.

CHIEF: But me always remember prosperity founded on a trick. For me recognize Baby Jim when Blue Feather bring him in. And yet, me not able to bear disappointment of tribe. So me make up for it by giving Baby Jim every advantage of education and religious training. Can you forgivum me?

MARGARET: Of course we can!

HARRY: Yes, you may be sure of that.

MARGARET: But where is my baby? I'd like to see him

CHIEF: And so you shall.

> *(He claps his hands three times and Jim, now a boy of six, comes running in.)*

JIM: *(to Chief and Daisy)* Daddy! Mommy!

> *(The Chief and Daisy embrace him fondly.)*

But where are the real Daddy and Mommy you said I'd meet?

MARGARET: Here I am, dear.

HARRY: I'm your real Daddy, son.

JIM: I'm pleased to know you.

MARGARET: If you knew how glad we are to have you back!

JIM: I'm pleased to know you, but these are my first Mommy and Daddy!

MARGARET: What!

DAISY: We've tried to reason with him, Mrs. Dexter, but he insists. He wouldn't even come with us until we promised to take him back.

CHIEF: He say he want to stay with us and study our religion.

JIM: Please, Mommy, it's what I really want. I'll always come and visit you.

MARGARET: Well, if your father thinks …

HARRY: I can see it's what he really wants. Jim, you may stay with the Chief, but once a year you must come and visit us.

JIM: I promise! Oh, thank you. Now I can study the ways of the raven god and try to be just like him!

> *(Margaret dabs at her eyes with a handkerchief as Harry supports her.)*

MARGARET: Well, that's settled. But what is to become of us?

HARRY: Why, we'll remarry, of course, and have other children, and Jim will be their big brother.

MARGARET: How devious fate is. Who would have thought this morning that so much joy would come to take place of sorrow!

INDIANS: Yes, the ways of the god are indeed inscrutable at first, though they are always plain in the end.

MARGARET: He leads us along dark paths, but eventually the light comes.

HARRY: Yes — underneath is always the primordial pattern.

DALE: Happiness for some — pain and suffering for others!

INDIANS: Who is this young man? His face seems pale and drawn with grief.

MARGARET: Alas! I gave him my heart, and now he thinks I want it back.

HARRY: You gave him — your heart?

MARGARET: Yes. Try to understand — I love you, but not you alone.

INDIANS: She loves the pale young man too!

CHIEF: Stranger things have happened.

DAISY: Yes — a heck of a lot stranger!

JIM: What is it? Why does everybody look so sad?

DAISY: You'll learn that in time, my son.

INDIANS: Oh great Spirit! See what a pass you have brought us to!

ALLAN: Why is joy always mixed with sorrow? Never have I tasted the pure essence of the former.

HARRY: She loves us both! Can this be?

MARGARET: Woe is me! What's to become of us now? If only I could die — that would solve everything and the play could end.

> *(The author of the play enters)*

Who are you?

AUTHOR: The author of this play — the creator to whom you owe your very existence.

MARGARET Have you come to help us out of this dilemma?

AUTHOR: I wish I could. Whenever I tried to imagine this play I could always get just this far and no further. Whom will you marry, I kept asking myself — the man of action or the melancholy dreamer? But even as I pondered the question I knew it made no difference, for you creatures are but the mere phantoms of my brain — shadows without substance!

In despair at not being able to think up an ending. I tried to emphasize other parts of the work. At least, the language will be perfect, I said, for I will make a study of human speech patterns and try to reproduce them exactly. But after months of study I could not find any patterns, so I had to give up the idea. I next tried to make my play sound elegant and poetical, hoping to please the critics, if not the audience. But my poetry, too, fell flatter than a bride's soufflé.

In despair I turned at last to the complex world of human relationships. Maybe, I thought, if I can't have anything interesting happen in the play I can at least show how people act when they are together, what their helloes are like and their goodbyes. But this attempt was a flop, too. I could find no rules or patterns for human behaviors and every action I observed seemed unlike every other action. It seemed there was nothing in life for my art to imitate!

By this time I had gotten on with the play by hook or crook, as you might have noticed. But I still needed an ending. What could I do? And then I hit upon an idea which seemed brilliant to me and still does. My play would reflect the very uncertainty of life, where things are seldom carried through to a conclusion, let alone a satisfactory one. I would omit the final scene from my masterpiece! And you, vague and shadowy creatures, would not need any resolution to your imaginary difficulties, you could just walk off into the night, together … Where are you going? Stop!

(A black scrim has fallen between the author who is standing near the front stage and the other players. They begin to retreat backwards and the stage slowly gets darker. Margaret spotlighted, flanked by Harry and Dale, smiles alternately at both of them, and both fondle her. Only the Chief at the left of the stage and Jim who kneels before him do not move.)

MARGARET: It's been fun knowing you.

DALE: So long, old chap.

HARRY: Best wishes, and all that sort of thing.

AUTHOR: Don't! Where are you going? I haven't finished.

DAISY: But we have. It's time for us to go.

INDIANS: Farewell, old scout.

AUTHOR: You can't desert me! Not now! Chief, you stay at least, and Baby Jim!

JIM: Goodbye, Mr. Ashbery.

CHIEF: Now, spirit of the great raven, descend on your unhappy son. For of all of us, he suffers the most and knows the least.

AUTHOR: What are you doing to me? I'm beginning to feel funny.

CHIEF: Give him, for a while, the sleep you hold in your dusky plumes. And perhaps when he awakens the world and the people in it will be more the way he thinks they ought to be.

AUTHOR: *(on his knees)* Hey, what the … Left all alone, that's fine! Golly, I feel sleepy all of a sudden. What a nice comfortable stage this is. I think I'll just stretch out on it for a minute and catch a few winks. Maybe I'll have some pleasant dreams.

CHIEF: Sleep Well, my son! Welcome, great brooding spirit night!

(The spotlight on the chief goes off and the stage is almost completely dark.)

AUTHOR: Goodnight, everybody. Zzzzzzzzz.

(An actor dressed as an enormous raven walks on, picks up the author and carries him offstage.)

CURTAIN

On the Way to Dumbarton Oaks

The air! The colonial air! The walls, the brick,
this November thunder! The clouds Atlanticking,
Canadianning, Alaska snowclouds,
tunnel and sleigh, urban and mountain routes!

                    Chinese tree
your black branches and your three yellow leaves
with you I traffick. My three
yellow notes, my three yellow stanzas,
my three precisenesses
of head and body and tail joined
carrying my scroll, my tree drawing

                    This winter day I'm
a compleat travel agency with my Australian
aborigine sights, my moccasin feet padding
into museums where I'll betray all my vast
journeying sensibility in a tear dropped before
"The Treasure of Petersburg"

                    and gorgeous this forever
I've a raft of you left over
like so many gold flowers and so many white
and the stems! the stems I have left!

—BARBARA GUEST

UNITED NATIONS

GENERAL ASSEMBLY

PROVISIONAL   A/PV.872   26 September 1960   ENGLISH

Revolution is a profound problem of consciousness.

Fifteenth Session

GENERAL ASSEMBLY

PROVISIONAL VERBATIM RECORD OF THE EIGHT HUNDRED AND SEVENTY-SECOND PLENARY MEETING

Held at Headquarters, New York
on Monday, September 26, 1960, at 3 p.m.

President: Mr. Frederick H. BOLAND   (Ireland)

Statements were made by:

    Mr. Shehu (Albania)   A/PV.872
    Mr. Castro (Cuba)   2

MR. CASTRO (CUBA) (interpretation from Spanish): Although it has been said of us that we speak at great length, you may rest assured that we shall endeavour to be brief and to put before you what we consider it our duty to say. We shall also speak slowly in order to co-operate with the interpreters.

Some people may think that we are very annoyed and upset by the treatment that the Cuban delegation has received. This is not the case. We understand full well the reason for the state of things. That is why we are not irritated. Nor need anyone concern himself that Cuba will spare any effort to bring about an understanding in the world. That being so, we shall speak frankly.

It is extremely expensive to send a delegation to the United Nations. We of the under-developed countries do not have too many resources to squander, and when we do spend money in this fashion it is because we wish to speak frankly in this meeting of the representatives of practically all the countries of the world.

The speakers who preceded me here on the rostrum have expressed their concern as regards the problems that are of interest to the whole world. We too are concerned with the same problems. However, in the case of Cuba a special circumstance exists, and that is that Cuba, as far as the world today is concerned, must itself be a concern because different speakers who have spoken here have quite correctly said that among the problems at present facing the world there is the problem of Cuba.

Apart from the problems that concern the world today, Cuba itself has problems that concern Cuba itself, problems that concern our people too. Much has been said of the world desire for peace, that it is the desire of all people and, as such, it is also the desire of our people. But this peace that the world wishes to preserve is the peace with which we, the Cubans, have not been able to count upon for a long time. The dangers which other peoples of the world have lived through and which they now consider finished are problems and preoccupations that for us are very near and close. It has not been easy to come here to this Assembly to talk about the problems of Cuba; it has not been easy for us to come here. I do not know whether we are privileged in this respect. Are we, the representatives of the Cuban delegation, the representatives of the type of Government that you would call the worst in the world? Are we, the representatives of the Cuban delegation, such as to warrant and deserve the bad treatment that we have received? And why has our delegation been singled out? Cuba has sent many delegations to the United Nations. Cuba has been represented in the United Nations by many different persons; yet it was we who were singled out for such exceptional measures: confinement to the island of Manhattan; notice to all hotels not to rent rooms to us, hostility under the pretext of security or isolation.

None of you gentlemen individually represent anyone or come with the individual representation of anyone, but rather you come here representing your countries and, therefore, measures applied

The revolution is a profound change of social structure.

Revolution triumphs when a people in its huge majority

becomes really aware of what the revolution is

to you most concern you because of the people you represent. None of you, when arriving in this city of New York, has had to undergo such humiliating treatment, physically humiliating treatment, as that which was meted out to the President of the Cuban delegation.

I am not trying to arouse anyone in this Assembly. I am merely stating the truth. It was time for us to take the floor and to speak. Much has been said about us. For many days we have been a bone of contention. The newspapers have referred to us, but we have held our peace. We cannot defend ourselves against attacks in this country, but our day to tell the truth has dawned and, therefore, we will speak the truth.

As I have said, we had to undergo degrading and humiliating treatment, including eviction from the hotel in which we were living and efforts at extortion. We headed towards another hotel, without any upsets on our part, and we did all in our power to avoid difficulties. We refrained from leaving our hotel rooms and we went nowhere except to this assembly hall of the United Nations on the few times that we have come to the General Assembly. We also accepted an invitation to a reception at the Soviet Embassy, but we have curtailed our movements in order to avoid difficulties and problems. Yet, this did not suffice, this did not mean that we were left in peace.

There has been considerable Cuban emigration to this country. There are more than 100,000 Cubans who have come to this country during the past twenty years because in their own land, in the land in which they would have preferred to live and the land to which they would like to return, economic reasons forced them to leave. These Cubans who came to this country dedicated and devoted themselves to work. They respected and they respect the laws of the land in which they live, yet they feel close to their own country. They feel close to the revolution. They had no problems. But one day a different type of visitor began to arrive in this country. War criminals began to arrive. Individuals arrived who in some cases had murdered hundreds of our compatriots. It did not take long for publicity here to encourage them. It did not take long for the authorities to receive them warmly and to encourage them, and naturally that encouragement is reflected in their conduct. They are the reason for the frequent incidents with the Cuban people who many years earlier had come to this country and who are now honestly working in this country.

One of these incidents provoked by those who receive support from the systematic campaigns against Cuba and with the connivance of the authorities caused the death of a child. That was a lamentable event and we should all lament such an outcome. The guilty ones were not the Cubans who are living here, nor are we, we who have come to represent Cuba. Yet undoubtedly you have all seen the headlines in the newspaper that stated that pro-Castro groups had killed a young girl of ten years of age. With the hypocrisy which is characteristic of those who meddle with relations between Cuba and this country, a spokesman from the White House immediately made declarations to the world accusing us, indeed, fixing the guilt on the Cuban delegation. Of course, the representative of the United States of America in this very assembly did not miss the opportunity of adding his voice to the farce, sending a telegram to the Venezuelan Government and also sending a telegram of condolences to the family, as though they felt called upon to give some explanation from the United Nations for something for which the Cuban delegation was virtually responsible.

And yet, it did not stop there. We were forced to leave one of the hotels in this city and we came to the United Nations Headquarters while other efforts were being made to find accommodation. There is a hotel, a humble hotel, a hotel of the Negroes in Harlem which sheltered us.

The reply came while we were speaking to the Secretary-General. Nevertheless, an official of the State Department did all in his power to try to stop us from being given rooms in the hotel. But, at that moment, as though magically, hotels began springing up all over New York — hotels that had previously refused to grant us rooms — saying that they were willing to take us in free. Out of elemental reciprocity we accepted the offer of a vacancy made by the hotel in Harlem. We felt then that we had earned the right to peace and quiet. But this was not given us.

In Harlem, since nobody could stop us from living there, the campaigns of slander and defamation began. The news was bruited about that the Cuban delegation had found itself a home in a brothel.

For some, a humble hotel in Harlem, a hotel inhabited by the Negroes of the United States, may obviously be a brothel. But besides this they have heaped slander on the Cuban delegation without even respecting the female members of our delegation who work with our delegation and who are part of our delegation.

Were we of the caliber of men that we are described as, then imperialism would not have lost hope of buying us as imperialism has had to lose the hope of buying us. But, since for a long time imperialism has lost its hope of getting us back — it never had a right to hope so — after stating that the Cuban delegation had taken rooms in a brothel, they had to recognize the fact that the imperialist financial capitalist is one that cannot seduce us — and it is not even the "respectful type of prostitute" mentioned by Jean Paul Sartre.

The problem of Cuba. Perhaps some of you may be well aware of the facts; others, unfortunately, may not be in that position — and everything depends on the sources from which your information may come — but, as far as the world is concerned the problem of Cuba has come to a head, it has appeared in the last two years, and as such it is a new problem. The world had not had many reasons to know that Cuba existed. For many it was an offshoot of the United States. And this is the case for many citizens of this very country — Cuba was virtually a colony of the United States. As far as the map was concerned, the map said something different. Cuba was coloured differently from the colour that was used for the United States; but in reality Cuba was a colony of the United States.

How did our country become a colony of the United States? It was not so by origin; it was not the same men who colonized the United States and who colonized Cuba. The ethnic roots and the cultural roots of Cuba are very different, and for centuries this root grew stronger.

Cuba was the last country of America to shake off Spanish colonial rule, to cast off, with all due respect to the representative of Spain, the Spanish colonial yoke; and because it was the last, Cuba had to struggle because Spain had one last foothold in America and Spain defended it with tooth and nail. Our people, small in numbers, scarcely a million inhabitants at that time, had to stand alone for nearly thirty years confronting an army that was considered to be one of the strongest in Europe. Against the small national population of Cuba the Spanish Government mobilized such an enormous number that it compared favourably with the armies it had mobilized to combat all the efforts of all Latin American countries to achieve independence. Half-a-million Spanish soldiers fought against the indomitable and sacrificial desire of our people to be free. For thirty years the Cubans fought alone for their independence; thirty years which are also part of the strength with which we love independence and freedom.

But, according to the opinion of John Adams, one of the Presidents of the United States, Cuba was like a fruit, like a ripe apple on the Spanish tree that had to fall, as soon as its ripeness had reached the right point, into the hands of the United States.

The Spanish power had worn itself out in Cuba. Spain had no men left to fight. It had no more economic resources. Its supplies were dry. It could not continue the fight in Cuba. It had been routed. Apparently the apple was ripe — and the United States Government held out its open hands. It was not only one apple that fell. A number of apples fell into the open hands of the United States. Puerto Rico fell — the heroic Puerto Rico which had begun its struggle for independence at the same time as Cuba. The Philippine Islands fell. A number of other possessions fell.

But the desire to dominate our country had to be translated into different movements. We had struggled for independence and had received the applause of the world for so doing. Therefore our country had to be taken in a different way. The Cubans had fought for independence. The Cubans who were shedding their life's blood for independence believed in all good faith in the joint resolution of the United States Congress of April 20th, 1898 which declared that Cuba was, and rightfully so, free and independent, that the people of the United States were with the Cubans in their struggle for independence. That joint declaration was a law adopted by the Congress of the United States — a law under which war was declared on Spain.

But that illusion was followed by a rude awakening. After two years of military occupation of our country, the unexpected happened. At the very moment when the people of Cuba, through their Constituent Assembly, were drafting the Constitution of the Republic,

or rational attitude towards problems.

You have to have passion.

You have to have a revolutionary calling.

I had that revolutionary calling.

a new law was passed by the United States Congress, a law proposed by Senator Platt, of such unhappy memories for the Cubans. That law stated that the Constitution of Cuba must have a rider under which the United States would be granted the right to intervene in Cuba's political affairs and to lease certain parts of Cuba for naval bases or coal deposits. In other words, under a law passed by the legislative body of a foreign country Cuba's Constitution had to contain a rider with those provisions. Our Senators were clearly told that if they did not accept the rider the occupation forces would not be withdrawn. In other words, an agreement to grant another country the right to intervene and to lease naval bases was imposed by force upon my country by the legislative body of a foreign country.

It is well, I think, for countries just entering this Organization, countries just beginning their independent life, to bear in mind our history and to note any similar conditions which they may find waiting for them along their own road — or perhaps which those who follow them will find waiting for them: their children, or their children's children — although some may not think that we shall get that far.

I return to my subject. The colonization of my country then began, the acquisition of the best land by United States firms, concessions of Cuban natural resources and mines, concessions of public services for purpose of exploitation, commercial concessions, concessions of all types. These concessions, when linked with the constitutional right of intervention in our country, turned our country into a North American colony rather than a Spanish colony.

Colonies do not speak. Colonies are not recognized in the world. Colonies are not allowed to express their opinions until they are granted permission to do so. That is why our colony and its problems were unknown to the rest of the world. In geography books, reference was made to a flag and a coat of arms. There was an island with another colour on the maps. But there was no independent republic on the maps where the word "Cuba" appeared. Let everyone realize that by allowing ourselves to be mistaken in this respect we only play the parts of fools. Let no one be mistaken. There was no independent republic. It was a colony where orders were given by the Ambassador of the United States of America. We are not ashamed of proclaiming this from the rooftops. On the contrary: we are proud that we can say that today no embassy rules our people; our people are governed by Cuba's people.

Once again, the Cuban people had to turn and fight to achieve independence, and that independence was finally attained after seven bloody years of tyranny. What tyranny? The tyranny of those who in our country were nothing but the cat's-paws of those who had dominated our country economically.

How can any unpopular system, inimical to the interests of the people, stay in power unless it be by force? Will we have to explain to the representatives of our sister republics of Latin America what military tyrannies are? Will we have to outline to them how these tyrannies have kept themselves in power? Will we have to draw a blueprint of the history of many of those tyrannies that are already classical? Will we have to show them what kept them in power? Will we have to say what national and international interests kept them at the helm?

The military group that tyrannized over our country was built upon the most reactionary sectors of the nation and over and above all, was based upon the foreign interests that dominated the economy of our country. Everybody here knows, and we understand that even the Government of the United States recognizes, that that was the type of government that was chosen and preferred by the monopolies. Why? Because, through power, you can repress any claims upon the part of the people. With power, you repress strikes — strikes that seek better conditions of work and of life. With power you quell all movements on the part of the peasants to own the land that they work. With power, you can quash the greatest and most deeply felt aspirations of the nation.

That is why the governments of force were the governments that the guiding circles of the United States policy preferred. That is why governments of force were able to stay in the saddle for so long. And that is why governments of force still rule in America.

Naturally, everything depends on the circumstances. To obtain the support of the United States Government was the most important thing. For example, it is now said that the United States Government opposes one of these governments of force, the government of

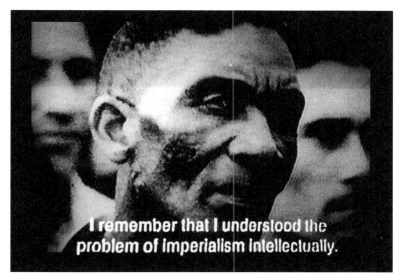

Trujillo. But they do not say that they are against another one of these governments of force — that of Nicaragua, for example, or that of Paraguay. And I merely take examples. The Nicaraguan one is no longer a government of force; it is a monarchy that is as constitutional almost as that of the United Kingdom, where the reins are handed down from fathers to sons.

The same would have occurred in my own country. It was the type of government of force — that of Fulgencio Batista — that was most appropriate for the United States monopolies in Cuba, but that was not the type of government that was appropriate for the Cuban people. Therefore, the Cuban people, squandering life, rose up and threw that government out. And, when the revolution was successful in Cuba, what did it uncover? What did it find? What marvels lay spread out before the eyes of the victorious revolutionaries of Cuba? First of all, the revolution found that 600,000 Cubans, able and ready to work, were unemployed — as many, proportionately, as were unemployed in the United States at the time of the great depression which shook this country and which almost produced a catastrophe in the United States. This is what we met with — permanent unemployment in my country. Three million out of a population of somewhat over 6 million have no electric light and have none of the advantages and comforts of electricity. Three and a half million out of a total population of more than 6 million lived in huts, in slums, without the slightest sanitary facilities.

In the cities, rents took almost one-third of family incomes. Electricity rates and rents were among the highest in the world. Thirty-seven and one-half percent of our population were illiterate; 70 percent of the rural children lacked teachers; 2 percent of our population suffered from tuberculosis. One hundred thousand persons, out of a total population of a little over 6 million, were suffering from the ravishes of tuberculosis. Ninety-five percent of the children in rural areas were suffering from parasites. Infant mortality was astronomical, and the standard of living was the opposite. On the other hand, 85 percent of the small farmers were paying rent on their land to the extent of almost 30 percent of their gross income, whilst 1 1/2 percent of the total landowners controlled 46 percent of the total area of the country. Of course, the proportion of hospital beds to the number of inhabitants of the country was ludicrous when compared with countries that have even half-way decent medical services. Public services, electricity and telephone services all belonged to United States monopolies. A major portion of the banking business, of importing business and the oil refineries, a greater part of the sugar production, the lion's share of the arable land of Cuba and the most important industries in all fields in Cuba belonged to North American companies.

The balance of payments in the last ten years, from 1950 to 1960, has been favourable for the United States vis-à-vis Cuba to the extent of one billion dollars. This is without taking into account the hundreds of millions of dollars that were extracted from the treasury of the country by the corrupt officials of the tyranny and were later deposited in United States or European banks — one billion dollars in ten years.

A poor and under-developed country in the Caribbean area, with 600,000 unemployed, was contributing greatly to the economic development of the most highly industrialized country in the world. This was the situation that confronted us. Yet it should not surprise many of the countries represented in this Assembly, because, when all is said and done, what we have said about Cuba is, one may say, an X-ray that could be superimposed and applied to many of the countries here represented in the Assembly.

What alternative was there for the revolutionary Government? To betray the people? As far as the President of the United States is concerned, what we have done is treason to our people, but it surely would not have been so if, instead of the revolutionary Government being true to its people, it had rather been true to the monopolies that were exploiting Cuba and sucking its blood. At least let note be taken here of the marvels that were laid out before our eyes as we won our revolution. They were no more and no less than the usual marvels of imperialism, which are in themselves no more and no less than the marvels of the free world as far as we, the colonies, are concerned.

We surely cannot be blamed if there were 600,000 unemployed in Cuba and 37.5 percent of the population were illiterate. We surely cannot be held responsible if 2 percent of the population suffered from tuberculosis and 95 percent suffered from parasites. Until that moment none of us had any say in the destiny of our country. Until that moment when the revolution was victorious, those whose voices were listened to in our country were the monopolies. Did anyone say them nay? Did anyone hinder them? No one. The monopolies went about their nefarious business, and we were the fruit of the monopolies.

What was the state of the reserves of the nation when the tyrant Batista came to power? There was 500 million dollars in the national treasury. It was a goodly amount, and it would have been well to have invested it in the development, industrial or otherwise, of the country. When the revolution was victorious, we found in our reserves 70 million dollars. They never showed any concern for the economic and industrial development of our country. That is why we were astonished, and we are still amazed and stunned when we hear it said here that extraordinary concern is shown by the United States Government for the fate of the countries of Latin America, of Africa and of Asia. We cannot overcome our amazement, because after fifty years we have seen the results.

What did the revolutionary government do; what is the crime committed by the revolutionary government, for it to pilloried — as it has been here — for it to find itself confronted by as powerful enemies as it has been shown us we have.

The problems with the United States Government did not come up at the first moment. When we came to power, we were possessed with the desire to find a solution to our own problems. We did not pause to consider international problems. No revolutionary government achieving power has international problems. What a revolutionary government wants to do is devote itself to the settling of its own problems at home; to carry out a program for the betterment of the people, as is wanted by all governments that are truly concerned with the progress of the countries or the country that government governs.

The first unfriendly act perpetrated by the Government of the United States was to throw open its doors to a gang of murderers, bloodthirsty criminals who had murdered hundreds of defenseless peasants, who had never tired of torturing prisoners for many, many years, who had killed right and left. These hordes were received by this country with open arms. We were deeply amazed. Why this unfriendly act on the part of the Government of the United States towards Cuba? Why this act of hostility? At that time we could not quite understand. Now we see clearly the reasons.

That policy was part of an attitude of the United States. But it should not have been — the injured party was Cuba. We were the injured party, because the system of the Government of Batista was kept in power with the assistance of the Government of the United States of America. The Batista regime stayed in power with the assistance of tanks, planes and weapons supplied by the Government of the United States.

The system of Batista's Government kept in power thanks to the use of an army, the officers of which were instructed and trained by a military mission of the United States Government; and we trust that no official of the United States will dare to deny that fact and that truth.

Then when the rebel army arrived in Havana in the most important military camp of that city, it met the American military group. That had been an army that had been routed; that had been an army that had surrendered. We could have considered that these foreign officers were training the enemies of the victorious army; we could have considered them prisoners of war. Yet we did not do so. We merely asked the members of that military mission of the United States in Havana to go home, because, after all, we did not need their lessons; their pupils had been beaten.

I have with me a document. Do not be surprised at its appearance. It is a torn document. It is an ancient military pact, by virtue of which the Batista regime had received generous assistance from the Government of the United States. It is rather interesting to note the contents of Article 2 of this agreement:

"The Government of the Republic of Cuba commits itself to make efficient use of the assistance it receives from the Government of the United States of America in conformity and pursuant to the present agreement, in order to carry out the plans of defense accepted by both Governments, pursuant to which the two Governments would take part in important missions for the defense of the Western Hemisphere, and unless previous agreement is obtained from the Government of the United States" —

And I repeat:

"— and unless previous agreement is obtained from the Government of the United States of America such assistance will not be devoted to other ends than those for which such assistance has been given".

That assistance was used to combat and to fight the Cuban revolutionaries, and for that purpose it obviously, then, had received the previous agreement of the Government of the United States. Even when a few months before the war was over in this country there was an arms embargo on weapons sent, or intended for Batista, after six years or so of military assistance, once this embargo was solemnly declared on the shipment of weapons to Batista, the rebel army had documentary proof that the forces of Batista, of the tyrant, had been supplied with 300 rockets, to be fired from planes.

When the Cuban immigrants in this country submitted these documents to the American Government as proof, the United States Government could only find the specious explanation, that we were mistaken; that the United States had not supplied new weapons to the army of the tyranny; that they had merely exchanged some rockets of a different calibre, that were the wrong size for their planes, and supplied them with new rockets that were useful for their planes, that were fired at us when we were in the mountains

I must say that this is a sui generis explanation of a contradiction when such contradiction can be neither justified nor explained. According to the United States, this was not assistance; it was probably technical assistance.

Why, then, if all this existed, were our people so concerned about it? Anyone here, even the most naive and innocent and guileless, knows that in these modern times, with the revolution that has taken place in military equipment and technology, the weapons from the last war have become obsolete for a modern war; that fifty tanks or armoured cars and a few obsolete and outdated aircraft cannot defend a continent, cannot defend any hemisphere. But they are useful to oppress peoples, especially if those peoples who are to be oppressed have no weapons. They are useful for the intimidation of peoples; they are useful for whatever one may wish to do with them. They are useful in the defense of the outposts of monopoly. That is why these hemisphere defense pacts might better have been described as defense pacts of United States monopolies.

So the Revolutionary Government began to take the first steps. The first was the fifty percent reduction in rents paid by families — a very just measure since, as I said earlier, there were families paying up to one-third of their income for rent and people had been the victims of housing speculation. Urban real estate had also been the subject of speculation at the cost of the economy of the entire Cuban people. But when the Revolutionary Government reduced the rents by fifty percent, there were those who were considerably upset. There were some who owned those buildings and apartment houses who felt displeasure. But the people rushed into the streets rejoicing, as they would in any country, even here in New York, if rents were reduced by fifty percent for all families. But it meant nothing to the monopolies. Some of the United States monopolies owned large buildings, but they were few in number.

Then another law was passed, a law canceling the concessions which had been granted by the tyranny of Batista. It concerned the telephone company which was a United States monopoly. Because of the lack of protest on the part of the people, valuable concessions had been obtained. The Revolutionary Government canceled those concessions and re-established normal prices for telephone services; and that is how the conflict with the United States monopolies was born.

The third measure was the reduction of the cost of electricity, which had been one of the highest in the world. Then followed the second squabble with the United States monopolies. Then we began to appear as Communists. Then we began to be painted Red because we had clashed head on with the interests of the United States monopolies.

Then followed the next law, an inevitable one as far as our own people were concerned, and a law which, sooner or later, will be passed all over the world, at least by all those peoples who have not yet passed it. This was the agrarian reform law. Naturally, in theory everybody agrees with agrarian reform — in theory. Nobody would

dare to deny it unless he were a fool. No one would deny that agrarian reform in the under-developed countries of the world is one of the sine qua non conditions for economic development. In Cuba, even the landowners agreed about agrarian reform — only they wanted their own kind of reform. The agrarian reform defined by many theorists is one that accords with their own theories. They agree in principle to a purely theoretical agrarian reform, as long as it is not applied. This is something that is well known to the economic bodies of the United Nations and it is something in connexion with which an argument is not even given place.

In my country such reform was inevitable. More than 200,000 peasant families lived there landless and unable to sell their produce. Without agrarian reform my country could not have taken its first tottering step towards development, but we were able finally to take that step. We agreed on an agrarian reform. It was a radical reform, extremely radical, but only to some. It was a reform, basically, if we study it, adjusted to the needs of our own development and in keeping with our own possibilities of agricultural development. It was a reform that would settle the problem of the landless peasants, that would settle the problem of the supply of indispensable foodstuffs, that would settle the problem of agricultural unemployment, and that would end, once and for all, the ghastly misery which existed in the fields of our own country.

And that is where the first major difficulty arose. In the neighbouring Republic of Guatemala a similar case had occurred. When the agrarian reform was agreed to in Guatemala, problems mushroomed. And I notify my colleagues of Latin American Republics and of Africa and of Asia and I notify them honestly and sincerely — that when they plan a just and fair agrarian reform they must be ready to confront situations similar to that which confronted us, especially if the best and largest lands are in the hands of the monopolists of America.

It may well be that we may be accused of giving bad advice in this Assembly, and of being misleading. It is not our intention to keep anybody from his just sleep. We are merely desirous of expressing facts — though facts are enough to keep anybody awake.

Then the question of salaries, of payments and of indemnities came up. Notes from the State Department rained on Cuba. They never asked us about our problems, not even out of a desire to express condolence or commiseration, or because of the hand that they had had in creating the problems. They never asked us how many died of starvation in our country, how many were suffering from tuberculosis, how many were unemployed. No, they did not ask about that. The feeling of solidarity regarding our needs was never expressed. The conversations of the representative of the United States Government were based upon the telephone company. They dealt with the electrical company, and they dealt with the problem of the lands owned by American companies. How were we going to pay?

Naturally, the first thing that should have been asked was, "What with?", not "How?"

Can you gentlemen understand or conceive of a poor, under-developed country carrying the onus of 600,000 unemployed, with such a high number of sick and illiterate, whose reserves have been sapped that has contributed to the economy of a powerful country to the tune of one billion dollars in ten years — can you conceive of this country's having the wherewithal to pay for the lands that are going to be affected by the agrarian reform, or at least pay for them on the conditions on which they wanted them paid for?

What did the American State Department put to us as its aspirations for its affected interests? It put three things to us: speedy payment, efficient payment and just payment. Do you understand that language? Payment — speedy, efficient and just. That means, "Pay now, cash, on the spot, and what we ask for our lands".

We were not 150 percent communists at that time. We were just pink at that time — slightly pink. We were not confiscating lands. We simply proposed to pay for them over a period of twenty years, and the only way in which we could pay for them was by bonds — bonds which would mature in twenty years — at 4 1/2 percent which would be amortized yearly. How were we to be able to pay for these lands in dollars? How were we going to pay cash, on the spot, and how could we pay for them what they asked? It was ludicrous.

It is obvious that at that time we had to choose between an agrarian reform and nothing. If we chose nothing then there would be a perpetuation of the economic misery of my country, and if we did carry out the agrarian reform then we were exposing ourselves to incurring the hatred of the Government of the powerful neighbour of the north.

We went ahead with the agrarian reform. Naturally, for a representative of the Netherlands, for example, or the representative of any country of Europe, the limits we set to lands and to estates would be a surprise because they were so big. The maximum amount of land set forth in the Agrarian Reform Law was 400 hectares. In Europe 400 hectares is a real estate — a ranch practically. In Cuba, where there were American monopolies that had up to 200,000 hectares — 200,000 hectares, in case anyone thinks he has misheard — an agrarian reform law reducing the maximum to 400 hectares was, to those monopolies and land-owners, an inadmissible law.

But the trouble was that in my country it was not only the land that was in the hands of the American monopolies. The main mines were in the hands of those monopolies. For example, Cuba produces nickel. All the nickel was exploited by American interests, and under the tyranny of Batista an American company, the Moa Bay, had obtained such a juicy concession that in a mere five years — mark my words, in a mere five years — it intended amortizing an investment of 120 million dollars. A 120 million-dollar investment amortized in five years. That was a juicy plum.

And who had given the Moa Bay company this concession through the intercession of the Government of the United States? Quite simply, the tyrannical government of Fulgencio Batista, the government which was there to defend the interests of the monopolies. And what is more — and this is an absolutely certain fact — completely tax-free. What were these enterprises going to leave for the Cubans? The empty, worked-out mines, the impoverished land, without the slightest contribution to the economic development of our country.

So the Revolutionary Government passed a mining law which obliged these monopolies to pay a 25 percent tax on the exportation of minerals.

The attitude of the Revolutionary Government already had been too bold. It had clashed with the interests of the international electric trust; it had clashed with the interests of the international telephone trust; it had clashed with the interests of the international mining trusts; it had clashed with the interests of the United Fruit Company and it had clashed, virtually, with the most powerful interests of the United States, which, as you know, are very closely linked one with the other. And that was more than the Government of the United States could tolerate — that is, the representatives of the United States monopolies.

Then there began a new stage of punishment meted out to our revolution. Can anyone who objectively analyses the facts, who is ready to think honestly and not as the UPI and the AP tell him, to think with his head and to draw conclusions from the logic of his own thinking, to see the facts without prejudice, sincerely and honestly — can anyone who does this consider that the things which the Revolutionary Government did were such as to decree the destruction of the Cuban Revolution? No.

But the interests which were affected by the Cuban Revolution were not concerned over the case of Cuba; they were not being ruined by the measures of the Cuban Revolutionary Government. That was not the problem. The problem lay in the fact that those same interests owned the natural wealth and resources of the greater part of the peoples of the world.

So then the attitude of the Cuban Revolution had to receive its punishment. Punitive actions of every type — even the destruction of those foolhardy people — had to be carried out against the audacity of the Revolutionary Government. On our honour we swear that up to that time we had not had the opportunity even to exchange letters with the distinguished Prime Minister of the Soviet Union, Nikita Khrushchev. That is to say that, when for the North American press and the international news agencies who supply information to the world Cuba was already a Communist Government, a Red peril ninety miles from the United States with a Government dominated by Communists, the Revolutionary Government had not even had the opportunity of establishing diplomatic and commercial relations with the Soviet Union. But hysteria can go to any length, hysteria is capable of making the most unlikely and absurd claims. But of course, let

no one for one moment think that we are going to intone here a mea culpa. There will be no mea culpa. We do not have to ask anyone's pardon. What we have done we have done with our eyes wide open and, above all, fully convinced of our right to do it.

Then the threats began, the threats concerning our sugar quota. The cheap philosophy of imperialism began to show its nobility, its egotistical and exploiting nobility; began to show its kindness to Cuba, declaring that they were paying us a preferential price for sugar which amounted to a subsidy to Cuban sugar — a sugar which was not so sweet for Cubans since we were not the owners of the best sugar-producing lands or of the greatest sugar plants. Furthermore, in that claim there lay hidden the true history of Cuban sugar, of the sacrifices which had been imposed on my country during the periods when it was economically attacked.

Earlier it was not a question of quotas; it was a question of customs tariffs. By force of one of those laws or one of those agreements which are made "between the shark and the sardine", the United States, through an agreement which they called a reciprocity agreement, obtained a series of concessions for its products enabling them to compete easily and displace from the Cuban market the products of its friends the English and the French, which often happens among friends. In exchange for this, certain tariff concessions were granted on our sugar which, on the other hand, could be unilaterally changed in accordance with the will of the Congress or the Government of the United States. And that is what happened.

When they deemed it appropriate in their interests they raised the tariff, and our sugar could not enter. Or if it did, it entered facing competition on the United States market at disadvantageous prices. When the fear of war occurred, the tariffs were reduced since Cuba was the source of supply of sugar that was closest to home and that source of sugar had to be assured. Then the tariffs were lowered and production was encouraged. During the war years, when the price of sugar was up in the stratosphere in the rest of the world, we were selling our sugar to the United States at a lower price, despite the fact that we were the only source of supply of sugar for the United States. At the end of the war our economy collapsed. The errors committed here in distribution of that raw material were paid for by us.

Prices went up enormously at the end of the First World War. There was tremendous encouragement to production. The reduction of prices, which ruined the Cuban sugar refineries, which fell into the hands of — I will give you one guess — United States banks, because when the Cuban nationals became bankrupt, the United States banks became wealthy. So the situation continued until the 1930's.

Since the United States Government was trying to find a formula that would consolidate its interests, since it had need for supplies in the interests of its domestic producers, it set up a system of quotas. That quota would presumably be based upon the historic participation of the different sources of supply on the markets and the historic participation of my country's supply had been almost 50 percent of the United States market. However when the quota was set up, our participation was reduced to 28 percent and the advantages granted to us by those laws — those few advantages granted us by those laws — were gradually taken away in successive laws. Naturally the colony depended on the motherland. The economy of the colony had been organized by the motherland. The colony had to be subjected to the motherland and if the colony took measures to declare itself free from the Metropolitan country, the motherland would take measures to crush that movement.

As the United States Government was conscious of the importance of our economy to the American market, that Government began to issue a series of warnings that our quota would be reduced further. Concurrently, other activities were taking place in the United States of America, the activity of the counter-revolutionaries.

One afternoon an airplane coming from the north flew over one of the sugar refineries and dropped a bomb. This was a strange and unheard of event, but we knew full well where that plane came from. On another afternoon another plane flew over our sugar cane fields and dropped a few incendiary bombs. Thus these events which began sporadically continued systematically. One afternoon — when, it is true, a number of American tourist agencies were visiting Cuba in the fulfillment of an effort made by the Revolutionary Government to promote tourism as one of the sources of national income — a plane manufactured in the United States, used in the Second World War, flew over Havana, our capital, dropping pamphlets and a few hand grenades. Naturally some anti-aircraft guns went into action; and the result was more than forty victims, between the grenades dropped by the plane and the anti-aircraft fire because, as you know, some of the projectiles explode on contacting any object. As I said, the result was more than forty victims. There were young girls on the street with their entrails torn out, old men and old women wantonly killed. This was not the first time as far as we were concerned. No, young girls and young boys, old men and old women, men and women, have very often been destroyed and murdered in the villages of Cuba by North American bombs supplied to the tyrant Batista. On one occasion eighty workers were killed when a mysterious explosion — an explosion that was too mysterious — took place in the harbour of Havana, an explosion of a ship carrying Belgian weapons to our country after many efforts made by the United States Government to prevent the Belgian Government from selling weapons to us.

There have been dozens of victims; eighty families were shattered by an explosion; there were forty victims caused by an airplane that was peacefully flying over our territory. The authorities of the United States Government denied the fact that these planes came from United States territory. But the plane was safely in a hangar. When we published the photograph of this plane in its hangar, then the United States authorities took possession of the plane.

A version of the affair was issued to the effect that this was not very important and that these victims had not died because of the bombs but because of the anti-aircraft fire and that those who were to blame for this crime, those who had caused these deaths were wandering about peacefully in the United States where they were not even prevented from committing these acts of aggression in the future.

To his Excellency the representative of the United States I may perhaps take the opportunity of telling him that there are many mothers in the fields of Cuba who are today hoping to receive a telegram of condolence from the United States Government for the children they lost due to the murder caused by bombs which came from the United States.

The planes went and came back. There was no evidence; there was no proof unless you define what you mean by proof. That plane was there; it was photographed. Yet we were told that this plane did not drop any bombs. It is not known how the United States authorities were so well informed. These pirate planes continued to fly over our territory dropping incendiary bombs. Millions upon millions of pesos were lost in the burning fields of sugar cane. Many people of the towns, humble people of Cuba, saw their lands burning, and they themselves were burned in the struggle against these fires, against these persistent and tenacious bombings by these pirate airplanes.

One day, while dropping a bomb on one of the sugar refineries, a plane exploded and the Revolutionary Government was able to gather charts and fragments and we were thus able to make an investigation. We found out that the pilot was an American and he carried American papers. We had proof of the field from which he had taken off and that the plane had gone between two bases in the United States. This was a matter that could not be evaded any longer. These planes obviously were leaving the United States and when they saw this irrefutable proof, the United States Government gave an explanation to the Cuban Government. Its conduct in this case was not the same as it was in connexion with the U-2. When it was proved that the planes were leaving the United States, the Government of the United States did not proclaim its right to burn our cane and our fields. The United States Government apologized, and said it was sorry. Well, we were lucky, after all, because after the incident of the U-2 the United States Government did not even apologize; it proclaimed its right to carry out overflights over Soviet territory. That is bad luck for the Soviets.

But we do not have too many anti-aircraft batteries and further planes were able to continue until the sugar was harvested. When there was no more cane in the fields, the bombs stopped. We believed we were the only country in the world in which this happened, although I do recall that at the time of his visit President Sukarno told us that this was not the case, that we were not the only people in the world. They, too, had suffered certain problems with certain American planes which flew over their territory. I do not

know whether I have committed an indiscretion in mentioning this; I hope not.

The fact of the matter is that, at least in this peaceful hemisphere, we were the country that, without being at war with anyone, had to stand the constant attack of pirate planes and those planes, with great impunity, came in and out of American territory. Well, gentlemen, we invite you to think about this for a little while. We also invite the people of the United States to think about it, too, if the United States people are aware of what is said in this hall. Let them think on this a little.

According to the statements of the United States Government itself, the territory of the United States is completely protected against any air incursion and that the defense measures in United States territory are infallible. It is stated that the defense of the world that the Americans call "free" — although, so far as we are concerned, it has not been free, at least not until January 1, 1959 — is complete and impregnable. If this be the case, and I am not talking about stratosphere planes, I am merely speaking of little aeroplanes that can fly up to 150 miles an hour, how is it that these planes are able to come in and out of American national territory undetected and that they can go through two bases and go back over these two same bases without the United States Government even being aware of the fact that these planes are coming in and out?

This means one of two things. Either the United States Government is lying to the people of the United States and the United States is not impregnable against aerial incursions or the American Government was an accomplice in these aerial incursions.

The aerial incursions finally ended, and then came economic aggression. What was one of the arguments adduced by the enemies of the agrarian reform? They said that the agrarian reform would cause chaos in agricultural production. They said that production would diminish considerably and that the United States Government was concerned because Cuba might not be able to fulfill its commitments regarding supplies to the American market.

That was the first argument, and I think it appropriate that at least the new delegations in the General Assembly should become somewhat familiar with some of the arguments that are adduced, because sometimes they may have to answer similar arguments that agrarian reform would bring about the ruin of the country.

That was not the case. Had the agrarian reform brought about the ruin of the country, had the agricultural production been reduced so drastically, then the United States Government would not have had to carry on its economic aggression. They truly believed in what they said. They must have believed that the agrarian reform was going to cause a decrease in production. Surely it is logical for each one to believe in the way in which his mind is prepared to believe.

They may have felt that if the great and powerful monopolies did not produce sugar, we Cubans could not do so. They may well have even trusted in our ruining the country, because naturally if the Revolution had ruined the country, then the United States would not have had to attack us. They would have left us to sink or swim and the United States would have appeared as a good and honourable government while we revolutionaries came in and ruined our country, and it would have shown that you cannot carry out a revolution because revolutions ruin countries. Fortunately, that is not the case. There is proof that revolutions do not ruin countries, and proof has been given by the United States of America. It has tried to do many things, but, among others, it has proved that revolutions do not ruin countries and that the imperialist governments do try to ruin countries. Cuba was far from being ruined and, therefore, it had to be ruined. Cuba needed new markets for its products, and we would honestly and frankly ask any delegation present which country does not want to sell what it produces. Which country does not want its exports to increase? We wanted our exports to increase, and this is what all countries want. This obviously must be a natural law, because only egotistical interests can oppose the universal interests for trade and commercial exchange, which surely is one of the most ancient aspirations and needs of mankind.

We wanted to sell our products and we went to seek new markets. We signed a trade treaty with the Soviet Union, according to which we would sell 1 million tons and we would purchase a certain amount of Soviet products or articles. Surely no one can say that this is incorrect. There may be some that do so because it is not in keeping with certain interests. We did not have to ask permission of the State Department in order to sign a trade treaty with the Soviet Union because we considered ourselves and we continue to consider ourselves and we will always consider ourselves a truly independent and free country.

When the supplies of sugar began to diminish and when we tried to boost our economy, then we received the hard blow. By a request of the executive power of the United States, the Congress approved an act according to which the President or the executive power of the United States was empowered to reduce to what limits he deemed appropriate the import quotas of sugar from Cuba. The economic weapon was rattled against our revolution. The justification for this stand had already been prepared in advance. The public relations people had been carrying out a campaign for a long time, because you know perfectly well that a monopoly and public relations are identified.

The economic weapon is used and at one fell swoop our sugar quota was cut down by about 1 million tons — sugar that was already produced, that had already been prepared for the American market, and thus to deprive our country of the resources it needed for development — to reduce our country to impotence in order to obtain political kudos.

That measure had been prohibited expressly by the regional organizations. As all representatives of Latin America know, economic aggression is expressly condemned by regional international law. Yet the Government of the United States violated that right, wielded the economic weapon and cut our sugar quota to about almost a million tons. They could do it. What could Cuba do when confronted by that fact? Turn to the United Nations. Go to the United Nations. Denounce this political and economic aggression. Denounce the incursions, the overflights. Denounce the economic aggression, aside from the constant interference of the American Government in the policy and politics of our country; the subversive campaigns carried out by the American Government against the revolutionary Government of Cuba.

So we turn to the United Nations. The United Nations has power to deal with these matters. The United Nations in the hierarchy of international organizations stands at the head; it is the greatest international authority. It has authority over and above the Organization of American States. Besides which we wanted the problem aired in the United Nations because we understand full well the situation in which the economy of Latin America finds itself. We understand the dependence that we all suffer, that all the economies of Latin America depend on the American economy.

The United Nations was seized of the question. It seeks an investigation to be carried out by the Organization of American States. The Organization of American States meets. Fine. And what was to be expected? That the Organization of American States would protect the country attacked; that the Organization of American States condemn the political aggression against Cuba and especially that the Organization of American States condemn the economic aggression of which we were the victims. We expected this. We had a right to expect it. When all was said and done, we were a small people, a member of the Latin American community of nations. When all was said and done, we were another victim. And we were not the first and we shall not be the last because Mexico had already been attacked more than once militarily. A great part of the Mexican territory was taken from it in a war and the heroic sons of Mexico went from the castle of Chapultepec, and cast themselves from the rock, robed in the Mexican flag before they surrendered. Those were the heroes of Mexico.

And that was not the only aggression. That was not the only time that American infantry forces plowed their way into Mexican territory. Nicaragua was invaded and for seven long years it was heroically defended by Cesar Augusto Sandino. Cuba was attacked more than once; and so were Haiti and Santo Domingo. Guatemala was also attacked. Who among you honestly could deny the intervention of the United Fruit Company and the State Department of the United States in the intervention that took place and in the overthrow of the legitimate Government of Guatemala? I understand full well there are those who consider it their official duty to be discreet on this matter,

and may even be willing to come here and deny this, but in their conscience they know that I am now speaking nothing but the truth.

Cuba was not the first victim of aggression. Cuba was not the first country in danger of aggression. In this hemisphere the entire world knows that the Government of the United States has always imposed its law, the law of the mightiest; according to this law it has destroyed the Puerto Rican nationality and has kept its dominion over that island; that law, in accordance with which it took over the Panama Canal and holds the Panama Canal. This was nothing new. Our country should have been defended. But our country was not defended. Why? And let us here dig into the depths of this matter and let us not merely study the forms. If we stick to the dead letter, then we are guaranteed; if we stick to reality, we have no guarantee whatsoever because reality imposes itself over and above the law set forth in international codes, and that reality is that a small country attacked by a powerful country did not and could not defend itself.

But what happened in Costa Rica? Lo and behold, by an ingenious production a miracle happened in Costa Rica. What resulted from Costa Rica was not a condemnation of the United States, or the Government of the United States — and I do wish to avoid any misunderstanding about our feelings: we regard the Government of the United States and the people of the United States as two completely different entities. The Government of the United States was not condemned in Costa Rica for the sixty overflights by pirate aircraft. The Government of the United States was not condemned for the economic and other aggression of which we had been the victim. No, the Soviet Union was condemned. That was really bizarre. We had not been attacked by the Soviet Union. We had not been the victims of aggression by the Soviet Union. No Soviet aircraft had flown over our territory. Yet in Costa Rica there was a finding against the Soviet Union for interference.

The Soviet Union only said that, figuratively speaking, if there was military aggression against our country the Soviet Union could support the victim with rockets. Since when is support for a weak country, support conditioned on an attack by a powerful country, regarded as interference? In law there is something called an impossible condition. If a country considers that it is incapable of committing a certain crime, then it need only say that such a possibility is unheard of. If there is no possibility that Cuba will be attacked, then there is no possibility that the Soviet Union will support Cuba. But in Costa Rica the principle was accepted that Soviet interference must be condemned. Condemned for what? For bombing Cuba? But the United States bombed Cuba. Condemn the Soviet Union for aggression against Cuba? But the Soviet Union did not attack Cuba. And nothing was said about the aggression by the United States against Cuba.

All of us here, without exception, must bear one thing in mind. We are all actors in a crucial moment in history. At times censorship does not apply. At times condemnations of our doings, of our behaviour, are not brought home to us. At such times we forget that, just as we have been given the privilege of participating in this crucial moment of history, some day history will judge us for our behaviour and our conduct. And on that day we shall not be able to defend ourselves.

That was my country's position in Costa Rica. That is why we can smile now. We know that history will judge that sad episode in Costa Rica. I say, with no bitterness, that it is sometimes difficult to condemn men; men are very often the playthings of circumstances. We who know the past history of our countries, we who are witnesses to what our countries are going through today, can understand how horrible it is to depend on the economy of other nations, how awful it is to depend on foreign power and foreign economies.

I need only note that my country was left defenseless in Costa Rica. Furthermore, there was an interest in not bringing this matter back to the United Nations — perhaps because it was felt that it is easier to obtain a mechanical majority elsewhere, although we see that in the United Nations mechanical majorities very often operate. With all due respect to this Organization, I must say that my people, the people of Cuba, have learned much. I can say with pride that my people are quite up to the role they are playing, to the heroic struggle they are carrying on. My people have learned in the school of these recent international events. They know full well that, even though their right to vindication has been denied, even though aggressive forces are marshaled against them, they still have the final and heroic resource of resisting. Even when their rights are not guaranteed by the Organization of American States, they can fight.

We, the small countries, do not as yet feel too secure about the preservation of our rights. That is why, when we decide to be free, we know full well that we become free at our own risk. But the peoples, when they are united and when they are defending a just cause, can trust in their own energy, their own will. We are not, as we have been pictured, a mere group of men governing a country. We are a people governing a country. We are a whole people firmly united, a people with a revolutionary conscience, defending our rights. This should be written in capital letters for the enemies of the revolution in Cuba to read clearly. For if they are still unaware of this fact they are most lamentably mistaken.

Those are the circumstances in which the revolutionary process in Cuba has taken place; that is how we found the country and that is where the difficulties came from. And yet the Cuban revolution is changing. What was yesterday a hopeless land, a land of misery, a land of illiterates, is gradually becoming one of the most enlightened, advanced and developed lands of this Continent.

The Revolutionary Government, in but twenty months, has created 10,000 new schools. In this brief space of time, we have doubled the number of rural schools — schools that had been set up in fifty years. Cuba today is the first country of America that has fulfilled all its scholastic needs, that has a teacher in the farthest corner of the mountains. In this brief period of time, the Revolutionary Government has built 25,000 houses in the rural zones and also in the urban areas. Fifty new townships are being built at this moment. The most important military fortresses today house tens of thousands of students. In the coming year, our country intends to start its great battle against illiteracy, with the ambitious goal of teaching every single inhabitant of the country to read and write. Thus, organizations of teachers, of students, of workers, are going out — the entire people is preparing itself for an intensive campaign to wipe out illiteracy. Cuba will be the first country of America which, after a few months, will be able to say it does not have one single solitary illiterate in the country.

Today our people are receiving the assistance of hundreds of doctors who have been sent out to the field to fight against the endemic sicknesses, wipe out parasites and improve the sanitary conditions of the nation.

In another aspect, in the preservation of the natural resources, we can also point with pride to the fact that in one year, in the most ambitious plan for the conservation of natural resources being carried out in this continent, including the United States of America and Canada, we have planted close to 50 million trees.

Youths who were unemployed, who were unlettered, have been organized by the Revolutionary Government and today are being gainfully and usefully employed by the country, and at the same time they are being prepared for productive work. Agricultural production in our country has noted an almost unique event, the increase of production since the first moment. Since the first moment, we have increased our agricultural production, because, first of all, the Revolutionary Government turned more than 100,000 agricultural workers into landowners, and at the same time they preserved the large-scale production by means of agricultural cooperatives — that is to say, the large-scale production was maintained, and it was maintained through cooperatives — thanks to which we have been able to apply the most modern technical procedures and processes through our agricultural production, and since the very beginning we have noted an increase in production.

All these enterprises of social benefit — of teachers, of houses, of hospitals — have been carried out without sacrificing the resources that we had earmarked for development. At this moment, the Revolutionary Government is carrying out a programme of industrialization of the country, and the first plants are already being built in Cuba.

We have reasonably and sensibly utilized the resources of my country. Previously, for example, 35 million dollars worth of cars were imported into Cuba, and 5 million dollars worth of tractors. And this was an agricultural country — importing seven times more motor cars than tractors. We have turned this fraction upsidedown, and now we are importing seven times more tractors than automobiles.

Close to 500 million dollars was recovered from the politicians who had enriched themselves during the tyranny — close to 500 million dollars in cash and in assets. That is the total value of what we were able to get back from the corrupt politicians who had been sucking the blood of our country.

The correct investment of this wealth and of these resources is allowing the Revolutionary Government at the same time to carry out a plan of industrialization and of increase in agriculture to build houses, build schools, send teachers to the farthest corners of the country, and give medical assistance to everybody — in other words, carry out a true programme of social development.

At the Bogota meeting, as you know, the Government of the United States proposed a plan. But it was not a plan for economic development; it was a plan for social development. Now, what does this mean? What is understood by this? Well, it was a plan for building houses, building schools and building roads. But does this settle the problem? Does this solve it all? How can there be a solution to the social problems without economic plans? Are the other peoples of Latin America being hoodwinked? What are the families going to live on when they inhabit those houses, if those houses are built? What shoes, what clothes, are they going to wear, and what food are they going to eat, when they go to those schools, if those schools are built? Is it not known that, when a family does not have clothes or shoes for the children, the children cannot go to school? With what resources are they going to pay the teachers and the doctors? Who is going to pay for the medicines? Do you want a good way of saving medicines? Raise the nutrition of the people — and then, when the people eat well, they will not have to spend money on hospitals.

In view of the tremendous reality of underdevelopment, the Government of the United States now comes out with a plan for social development. Naturally it is something that it is concerning itself with some of the problems of Latin America. Thus far it has not cared very much. Is it not a coincidence that now, at this juncture, it is worried about these problems? Is the fact that this concern has emerged after the Cuban revolution purely coincidental? Surely they will label it as a coincidence. Thus far the monopolies have certainly not cared very much except for exploiting the underdeveloped countries, but suddenly the Cuban revolution rears its head and the monopolies start worrying. While we are squashed, with the other hand the United States Government offers charity to the Governments of Latin America. The Governments of Latin America are offered not the resources for development that Latin America needs but resources for social development, for houses for people to live in who have no work, for schools to which children cannot go, and for hospitals that would not be necessary if there were enough food to eat.

After all, although some of my Latin American colleagues may feel it is their duty to be discreet at the United Nations, I would welcome a revolution such as the Cuban revolution, which at any rate has forced the monopolists to return at least a small part of their ill-gotten gains.

Although as you know, we are not included in that assistance, we are not worried about that; we are not going to get angry about that. We could not care less, because we have already settled those same problems of schools and housing and so on. But we think that at least some may feel that we are using this for propaganda purposes, because the President of the United States said that some would take this rostrum for propaganda purposes. Well, any of my colleagues in the United Nations has a standing invitation to visit Cuba. We do not slam the doors of Cuba in anybody's face; nor do we restrict anybody's movements. Any of my colleagues in this Assembly can visit Cuba whenever he wishes and with his own eyes see what is going on. You know that chapter of the Bible that speaks of doubting Thomas, who had to see before he could believe — I think it was St. Thomas. We can invite any newspaperman, any correspondent, any member of a delegation to visit Cuba and see what a people can do when a people uses its own resources and when it invests those resources honestly and reasonably. But we are not only settling our problems of housing and schools. We are settling our problems of development, because without a settlement of the problems of development there can be no solution of the social problems themselves. But what is happening? Why does the United States Government not wish to speak of development? The answer is clear-cut. Because the Government of the United States does not want to quarrel with the monopolies, and the monopolies need natural resources. They need investment markets for their capital. That is the paradox. That is where the contradiction lies. That is why the true solution of this problem is not sought. That is why the planning is not carried out for public investment and the development of the underdeveloped areas. It is good that this be stated frankly, because when all is said and done, we, the under-developed countries, are a majority in this Assembly — in case anyone was unaware of this fact. When all is said, and done, too, we are witnesses to what is going on in the underdeveloped countries. We know it all too well. Yet the true solution is not sought. Much is said here of the participation of private capital. Naturally this means markets for the investment of surplus capital, like that investment that was amortized in five years. The Government of the United States cannot propose a plan for public investment, because this would divorce it from the very raison d'être of the United States Government, which is the United States monopolies. This is the truth of the matter. This is the true reason why no true programme of economic development is planned: to preserve the land of Latin America, of Africa and of Asia, to keep it the private domain of those who wish to invest their surplus capital.

Thus far we have referred to the problems of my own country and the reason why those problems were not solved. Is it because we did not want them solved? Hardly. The Government of Cuba has always been ready to discuss its problems with the Government of the United States, but the Government of the United States has not been ready to discuss the Cuban problems with Cuba. It must have its reasons for not wanting to discuss these problems with Cuba. The note sent by the Revolutionary Government of Cuba to the Government of the United States January 27, 1960 says the following:

"The differences of opinion between the two Governments that are subject to diplomatic negotiation can be settled by such negotiation. The Government of Cuba is ready and willing to discuss these problems without reservation and with full frankness and declares itself as being unaware of any obstacles in the path of such negotiations being carried out through any of the traditional means set up for these purposes, on the basis of mutual respect and the reciprocal benefit of the people and Government of the United States. The Government of Cuba wishes to maintain and increase diplomatic relations as well as economic relations and understands that on this basis the traditional friendship between these two peoples is indestructible.

"On February 22nd of this year the Revolutionary Government of Cuba, in accordance with its desire to renew through diplomatic channels the negotiations already taken on issues outstanding between the United States and Cuba, has decided to set up a commission whose terms of reference would be to carry out negotiations and discussions in Washington on a mutually agreed basis. The Revolutionary Government of Cuba wishes to clarify, however, that the renewal and continuance of such negotiations must obviously be subject to the proviso that the Government or the Congress of your country do not take unilateral measures prejudging the results of the abovementioned negotiations or prejudicial to the economy or the people of Cuba. It seems obvious that the adherence of the Government of Your Excellency to this point of view would not only contribute to the improvement of relations between our respective countries but would also reaffirm the spirit of brotherly friendship that has traditionally linked and still links our peoples.

"It would also allow both Governments, in an atmosphere of serenity and with the widest scope possible, to examine the questions that have affected the traditional relations between Cuba and the United States of America." What was the reply of the Government of the United States?

"The Government of the United States cannot accept the conditions for negotiation expressed in your Excellency's note, to the fact that measures will not be taken of a unilateral nature on the part of the Government of the United States that might affect the Cuban economy or the people of Cuba, be it through the legislative branch or the executive branches. As has been expressed by President Eisenhower on January 26th, the Government of the United States of America must keep itself free in the exercise of its own sovereignty to take whatever measures it deems necessary, conscious of its international commitments and obligations, for the defense of the legitimate rights and interests of its people."

In other words, the Government of the United States does not deign to discuss matters with the small country of Cuba on the Cuban problems. What hope can there be for a solution to these problems; what hope can the people of Cuba nurture?

All the facts that we ourselves have noted conspire against the solution of such problems, and it is good for the United Nations to take this very much into account, because the Government of Cuba, and the people of Cuba too, are, most justifiably, concerned at the aggressive turn in the American policy regarding Cuba, and it is appropriate and good that we should be up-to-date and well informed.

First of all, the Government of the United States considers it has the right to promote and encourage subversion in my country. The Government of the United States of America is promoting the organization of subversive movements against the Revolutionary Government of Cuba, and we here at the United Nations, in the General Assembly, denounce these movements and this encouragement: and concretely we wish to denounce the following. In a Caribbean Island, a territory which belongs to Honduras and which is known as the Islas Cisnes, the Swan Islands, the Government of the United States has taken over this Island in a military manner.

There are now American infantrymen there. Despite the fact that this territory is Honduran territory, thus violating every international law, despoiling a neighbour country of part of its territory, the Americans have taken over. Violating international treaties and radio treaties, it has set up a very powerful broadcasting station which it has placed at the disposal of the war criminals and the subversive groups that are still being kept and sheltered in this country; and manoeuvres and training are being carried out on that Island to promote subversion in Cuba and to promote the landing of armed forces in our Island.

It might be good for the representative of Honduras to the United Nations General Assembly to stress and claim Honduras' right to that part of its territory. But that is a matter encumbent upon the representative of Honduras only. As far as we are concerned, the fact is that this is part of a neighbour's land, stolen by piracy by the United States Government and used by the Americans as a base for the settling of its subversive movements against our territory. I want careful note taken of this denunciation that we make on behalf of the Government of the people of Cuba.

Does the Government of the United States feel that it has the right to promote and encourage subversion in my country, violating international treaties, violating the air space of my country? Does this mean that the Cuban Government, then, has the right also to promote subversion in the United States of America; that we have the right to violate the air and radio frequencies of the United States of America?

Does this mean, too, that the Government of Cuba has a perfect right to do this? What right have they over us? What right has the American Government: what powers has it over our Island?

Let the United States return the Islas Cisnes to Honduras, because it never had jurisdiction over such Islands.

Yet there are even more alarming circumstances, circumstances that frighten our people even more. We know that because of the Platt Amendment, imposed by force on our people, the Government of the United States took upon itself the right to establish naval bases on our territory, a right that it imposed on us by force and which it has maintained by the same means.

A naval base in the territory of any country is surely reason for just preoccupation and concern. First of all, there is the concern and the fear of a country that has followed an aggressive and warlike policy: possessing a base in the very heart of our Island, that turns our Island into the possible victim of any international conflict. It forces us to run the risk of any atomic conflict without our having even the slightest intervention in the problem — because we have nothing to do with the problems of the United States Government, or the crises that the Government of the United States produces and provokes. Yet there is a base on Cuban soil that is a dire risk for us in the case of any conflict breaking out.

But is that the only danger? Far from it. There is a fear and a danger that is even greater, since it is closer to home. The Revolutionary Government of Cuba has repeatedly expressed its concern at the fact that the imperialist government of the United States of America takes that base in the heart of our national territory as a means of promoting self-aggression, to justify an attack on our country. And I repeat. This may sound complicated, but this is the way they have done it. The Revolutionary Government of Cuba is seriously concerned, and makes known this concern, at the fact that the imperialist government of the United States of America is taking as a pretext a selfaggression in order to try to justify its attack and its assault on my country.

This concern on our part is increasing, and it is increasing because the aggressiveness and the aggressions are increasing and the symptoms become more frightening. For instance, I have here an Associated Press cable which came to my country and which reads as follows:

"Admiral Arleigh Burke, United States Chief of Naval Operations, says that if Cuba should attempt to take the Guantanamo Naval Base by force 'we would fight back.'

"In a copyrighted interview published today in the magazine U.S. News and World Report, Admiral Burke was asked if the Navy is concerned about the situation in Cuba under Premier Fidel Castro.

"'Yes, our Navy is concerned — not about our base at Guantanamo, but about the whole Cuban situation,' Admiral Burke said. He added that all the military services are concerned.

"'Is that because of Cuba's strategic position in the Caribbean?' he was asked.

"'Not necessarily,' Admiral Burke said. 'Here is a country with a people normally very friendly to the United States, people who have liked the people of this country — and we have liked them. Yet, here has come a man with a small, hard core of Communists determined to change all of that. Castro has taught hatred of the United States and he has gone far toward wrecking his country.'

"Admiral Burke said 'we would react very fast' if Castro moved against the Guantanamo base.

"'If they would try to take the place by force, we would fight back,' he added.

"To a question whether Soviet Premier Khrushchev's threat about retaliatory rockets give Admiral Burke 'second thoughts about fighting in Cuba,' the Admiral said:

"'No. Because he's not going to launch his rockets. He knows he will be destroyed if he does — I mean Russia will be destroyed …' (Journal American, September 26, 1960)

First of all, I must emphasize the fact that, for this gentleman, the increase of industrial production in my country by 35 percent, the fact that we have given employment to more than 200,000 new Cubans, the fact that we have solved many of the social problems of our country, all these facts constitute for this Admiral the ruination of our country and, therefore, they take upon themselves the right to set the stage for aggression. Just see how an estimate is made, an estimate which is dangerous, since he intimates that in the case of an attack on us we are to stand alone. This is something that Admiral Burke has not thought up for himself. But suppose for a moment that Admiral Burke is mistaken. Let us imagine for a moment that Admiral Burke, although an Admiral, is wrong. If he is wrong, he is playing irresponsibly with the strongest thing in the world. Admiral Burke and all those of his aggressive militarist bloc are playing, and the stake happens to be the fate of the world. And I think that the fate of each of us warrants some concern. Yet, we only represent the peoples of the world and, as such, we are duty bound to concern ourselves with the fate of the people whom we represent and of the world itself, and it is our duty to condemn all those who play irresponsibly with the fate of the world. They are not playing only with our own people's fate; they are playing with the destiny of their own people too, and also with the entire planet.

Does this Admiral Burke think that we are now fighting with blunderbusses? Does he not realize, this Admiral Burke, that we are living in the atomic age, in an age whose disastrous and cataclysmic destructive forces could not even be imagined by Dante in his seventh circle of hell, or Leonardo, with all their imagination, because this goes further than man has been able to dream of in his worst nightmares. Yet this Admiral Burke — and, naturally, the Associated Press sent this report all over the world — is beginning to prepare his campaign. He is already beginning to whip up hysteria. He is beginning to bruit about the imaginary danger of a Cuban attack against the base at Guantanamo. But this is not the sole factor.

Yesterday a United Press Information Circular appeared containing a declaration by United States Senator Styles Bridges who, I believe, is a member of the Armed Forces Committee of the Senate of the United States. He said:

"Today the United States must be ready, at any expense, to maintain its base at Guantanamo in Cuba. We must go as far as necessary to preserve that base and to defend that gigantic installation of the United States. We have naval forces there; we have military forces and we have the Marines, and if we were attacked we should defend it, for I consider it to be the most important base in the Caribbean area."

This member of the Senate Committee of the Armed Forces did not entirely discard the use of atomic weapons in the case of an attack against the base at Guantanamo. What does this mean? This means that not only is hysteria being whipped up, not only is a systematic preparation of the atmosphere being indulged in, but we are being threatened with the use of atomic weapons. Among the many things that we can think of, one is to ask this Mr. Bridges whether he is not ashamed of himself to threaten anyone with atomic weapons, especially a small country like Cuba.

As far as we are concerned, and with all due respect, I must say that the world's problems are not settled by threatening nor by sowing fear. Our humble people of Cuba is there. It exists, even though they may dislike the idea, and the revolution will go ahead, however much they dislike that. And besides, our humble and small people has to resign itself to its fate. And our people are not afraid. It is not shaken by this threat of the use of atomic weapons.

And what does this mean? There are many countries that have military bases — American military bases. But these bases exist. They are there, but they are not directed against the Governments that granted the concessions — at least, not as far as we know. In our case, we are in the most tragic position because this is a base in our insular territory, pointed at the heart of Cuba and pointed at the heart of the Revolutionary Government of Cuba, in the hands of those who declare themselves enemies of our country, of our revolution and of our people.

In the entire history of bases set up anywhere in the world the most tragic case is that of Cuba — a base thrust upon us in a territory that is a good many miles from the coast of Cuba, a base against the Government of Cuba, imposed by force and a constant threat and a constant fear for our people.

We must say that all this talk of attacks must be intended to create hysteria. It is the preparation of an atmosphere of aggression against our country of which we have never spoken. We have never spoken one single, solitary word of aggression, or any word that might be taken as implying any type of attack on the Guantanamo base, because we are the first in not wanting to give imperialism a pretext to attack us.

We state this categorically and vehemently, but at the same time we also declare that at the moment when that base has become a threat to the security and tranquility of our people, a threat to our people itself, then the Revolutionary Government of Cuba is seriously considering requesting, within the framework of international law, that the naval and military forces of the United States be withdrawn from the Guantanamo base, from that portion of national territory, and there will be no option for the imperialist Government of the United States but to withdraw its forces, because how will it be able to justify itself to the world for leaving this army in an island from which it has been asked to withdraw it?

The island of Cuba belongs to the Cuban people. It is the Cuban people which lives there. How can the Americans justify to the world any right to maintain and to hold sovereignty over a part of our territory? How will they be able to stand before the world and justify such an arbitrary procedure? And since it will be unable to justify itself to the world when our Government requests it, within the framework of international law, the Government of the United States will have no option but to abide by the canons of international law.

But this Assembly has to be up to date and informed regarding the problems of Cuba, because we must be alert against confusion and against misrepresentation, and very clearly these problems have to be laid out because with them go the security and the fate of our country. That is why we want very clear note to be taken of the words I have spoken — especially if note is taken of the fact that there seems to be no chance of correcting the impression that the politicians of this country have regarding the question of Cuba. They seem unable to understand the true facts of the story. Here I have declarations of Mr. Kennedy that would surprise anybody. On Cuba he says, "We must use all the power of the Organization of American States to avoid Castro's interfering in other Latin American countries and force him to return Cuba to freedom." They are going to give freedom back to Cuba.

"We must state our intention", he says, "of not allowing the Soviet Union to turn Cuba into its Caribbean base, and apply the Monroe Doctrine." And this is more than half way through the twentieth century, but it is Kennedy speaking of the Monroe Doctrine. "We must force Prime Minister Castro to understand that we propose to defend our right to the naval base of Guantanamo" — he is the third who speaks of this problem — "and we must show the Cuban people that we agree with its legitimate economic aspirations," — why did they not do this before — "that we know full well their love for freedom, and that we shall never be satisfied until democracy returns to Cuba." What democracy? The democracy made by the monopolists of the United States of America?

"The forces that are struggling for freedom in exile", he says — note this very carefully so that you will understand later why there are planes that fly from American territory over Cuba; note carefully what this gentleman says — "and in the mountains of Cuba must be supplied and assisted, and in other countries of Latin America communism must be confined without allowing it to expand or spread."

If Kennedy were not an illiterate and ignorant millionaire he would understand that it is not possible to carry out a revolution against the peasants in the mountains with the aid of the landowners; he would know how many times imperialism has tried to stir up counter-revolutionary groups which the peasant militia has put hors de combat in the course of a few days. But as far as he is concerned, it seems he has been reading some novels or seeing various Hollywood films — some story about guerilla warfare — and believes it possible, socially speaking, to carry on guerilla warfare in Cuba.

In any case, this is discouraging. And let nobody think, nevertheless, that these opinions on Kennedy's statements indicate that we feel any sympathy for the other one, for Mr. Nixon, who has made similar statements. As far as we are concerned, both of them lack political brains.

THE PRESIDENT: I am sorry to have to interrupt the Prime Minister of Cuba, but I am sure that I am faithfully reflecting the feelings of the Assembly as a whole when I ask him to consider whether it is right and proper that the candidates in the current election in this country be discussed at the rostrum of the Assembly of the United Nations.

I am sure that in this matter the distinguished Prime Minister of Cuba will, on reflection, see my point of view, and I feel that I can rely with confidence on his good-will and co-operation. On that basis I would ask him kindly to continue with his remarks.

MR. CASTR0 (Cuba) (interpretation from Spanish): It is not our intention in the least to infringe upon the rules which determine our behaviour in the United Nations, and the President can depend fully on my co-operation to avoid having words misunderstood. I have no intention of offending anyone. It is somewhat a question of style and, above all, a question of trust in the Assembly. In any case, I will try to avoid wrong interpretation.

Up to this point we have been dealing with the problem of our country, the fundamental reason for our attending this session of the United Nations. But we understand perfectly that it would be somewhat selfish on our part if our concern were to be limited to our specific case alone. It is also true that we have used up the greater part of our time informing the Assembly on the case of Cuba, and that there is not much time left for us to deal with the remaining questions, to which we wish briefly to refer.

Still, the case of Cuba is not an isolated case. It would be an error to think of it only as the case of Cuba. The case of Cuba is the case of all under-developed peoples. It is, as it were, the case of the Congo; it is like the case of Egypt, of Algeria, of West Irian; it is like that of Panama, which wishes to have its Canal; it is like that of Puerto Rico, whose national spirit they are destroying; like that of Honduras, a portion of whose territory has been taken away. In short, although we have not made reference specifically to other countries, the case of Cuba is the case of all the underdeveloped colonial countries.

The problems which we have been describing in relation to Cuba apply perfectly well to all of Latin America. The control of Latin American economic resources by the monopolies — which, when they do not directly own the mines and take charge of the working of them, as in the case of copper in Chile, Peru and Mexico and in the case of zinc in Peru and Mexico, as well as in the case of oil in Venezuela — when this control is not exercised directly it is because they are the owners of the public-service companies, which is the case with the electric services in Argentina, Brazil, Chile, Peru, Ecuador and Colombia, or of the telephonic services, which is the case in Chile, Brazil, Peru, Venezuela, Paraguay and Bolivia. Or, if they do not exploit our products, as is the case with coffee in Brazil, Colombia, El Salvador, Costa Rica and Guatemala, or with the exploitation, marketing and transportation of bananas by the United Fruit Company in Guatemala, Costa Rica and Honduras, or with cotton in Mexico and Brazil, that economic control is exercised by North American monopolies of the most important industries of the country, dependent completely on the monopolies.

Woe betide them on the day when they too shall wish to carry out agrarian reform! They will be asked for immediate, efficient and just payment. And if, in spite of everything, they carry out agrarian reform, the representative of a sister nation who comes to the United Nations will be confined to Manhattan; they will not rent hotel space to him; insults will be poured upon him and he may even, possibly, be mistreated, in fact, by the police themselves.

The problem of Cuba is only an example of what Latin America is. How long must Latin America wait for its development? According to the point of view of the monopolists it will have to wait ad calendas Graecas. Who is going to industrialize Latin America? The monopolists? Certainly not.

There is a report of the Economic Commission of the United Nations which explains how even private capital, instead of going to the countries that need it most, for the setting up of basic industries in order to contribute to the development of those countries are preferably being channeled to the more industrialized countries because there, according to their findings, private capital finds greater security in those more industrialized countries. Naturally the economic secretariat of the United Nations has had to recognize the fact that there is no possible chance of development through investment of private capital — that is, through the monopolies.

The development of Latin America will have to be achieved through public investment planned and granted unconditionally without any political strings attached because, naturally, we all like to be representatives of free countries. None of us likes to represent a country that does not feel itself to be in full possession of its freedom. None of us wants the independence of his country to be subjected to any interest other than that of the country itself. Therefore the assistance must be without any political strings attached.

That help has been denied to us does not matter. We did not ask for it. However, in the interest of and for the benefit of the Latin American peoples we do feel in duty bound, out of solidarity, to stress the fact that the assistance must be given without any political conditions whatsoever. Public investment for economic development, not for social development — this is the latest thing that has been invented to hide the true need for economic development of the countries.

The problems of Latin America are like the problems of the rest of the world: Africa and Asia. The world is divided up among the monopolies; those same monopolies that we see in Latin America are also seen in the Middle East. There the oil is in the hands of monopolistic companies that are controlled by the financial interests of the United States, the United Kingdom, the Netherlands, France, in Iran, in Iraq, in Saudi Arabia, in Kuwait, in Qatar and, finally, in all corners of the world. The same thing happens, for example, in the Philippines. The same thing happens in Africa.

The world has been divided among the monopolistic interests. Who would dare deny this historic truth? The monopolistic interests do not want to see the development of peoples. What they want is to exploit the natural resources of the countries and to exploit the people in the bargain. The sooner they amortize their investments or get them back, the better it is for them.

The problems that the Cuban people have suffered from the imperialist Government of the United States are the same problems that Saudi Arabia would have if it decided to nationalize its oil fields, or if Iran or Iraq decided to do so; the same problems that Egypt had when it quite justifiably and correctly nationalized the Suez Canal; the very same problems that Indonesia had when it wanted to become independent; the same surprise attack that was made against Egypt and on the Congo. Has there ever been a lack of pretexts for the colonialists or imperialists when they wanted to invade a country? They have never lacked pretexts; somehow they have always managed to pull out of the hat the pretext that they wanted. Which are the colonialist countries? Which are the imperialist countries? There are not four or five countries but four or five groups of monopolies which possess the world's wealth.

If a person from outer space were to come to this Assembly, someone who had read neither the Communist Manifesto of Karl Marx nor the cables of the UP or the AP or the other publications of a monopolistic character, and if he were to ask how the world was divided and if he saw on a map of the world that its riches were divided among the monopolies of four or five countries, he would say: "The world has been badly divided up, the world has been exploited." Here in this Assembly, where there is a majority of the under-developed countries, I would say that the great majority of the people you represent are being exploited, that they have been exploited for a long time; the forms of exploitation may have varied, but they are still being exploited. That would be the verdict.

In the statement made by Premier Khrushchev there is a statement that attracted our attention because of its content; it was when he said that the Soviet Union did not have colonies and that the Soviet Union has no investments in any country. How great would our world be today, our world which today is threatened with catastrophe, if all the representatives of all countries could make the same statement: Our country has no colonies and no investments in any foreign country.

But why twist the matter around any further? Why labour it? This is what it all boils down to. This is what even peace boils down to, and war. This is the reason for the arms race. This is the reason for disarmament. On this everything hinges. Wars, since the beginning of humanity, have emerged for one reason, and one reason alone, the desire of some to despoil others of what the others possess. Do away with the philosophy of spoiling, and you will have done away forever with the philosophy of war. Do away with the colonies, wipe out the exploitation of countries by monopolies, and then humanity will have achieved a true period of progress. Until that stage is reached, the world will have to live constantly under the terror and fear of being involved in any crisis and wiped out by an atomic conflagration, because there are those who wish to perpetuate this exploitation and there are those who wish to maintain this philosophy.

We have spoken here of the Cuban case. Our case has taught us, because of the problems we have had to confront with the imperialism that is against us, but, when all is said and done, imperialisms of any nature are all the same, they are all allied. A country exploiting the countries of Latin America or of any part of the world is an ally in its exploitation of the others in the world who do the same thing.

There was one thing that alarmed us considerably in the statement made by the President of the United States of America when he said in the General Assembly:

"In the developing areas, we must seek to promote peaceful change, as well as to assist economic and social progress. To do this — to assist peaceful change — the international community must be able to manifest its presence in emergencies through United Nations observers or forces.

"I should like to see Member countries take positive action on the suggestions in the Secretary-General's report looking to the creation of a qualified staff within the Secretariat to assist him in meeting future needs "for United Nations forces." (A/PV.868, pp. 31-32)

In other words, after considering Latin America, Africa, Asia and Oceania as zones of development, he suggests that there be peaceful changes, and he proposes that in order to bring this about, observers and United Nations forces be used. In other words, the United States is trying to carry out a revolution in the world. The rights of peoples to self-determination, by means of revolutions if necessary, to throw off colonialism or any type of oppression was recognized in Philadelphia by the Declaration of July 4th, 1776, yet today the Government of the

United States of America proposes to use United Nations forces to avoid revolutions and changes. President Eisenhower continued:

"The Secretary-General has now suggested that Members should maintain a readiness to meet possible future requests from the United Nations for contributions to such forces. All countries represented here should respond to this need by earmarking national contingents which could take part in United Nations forces in case of need.

"The time to do it is now — at this Assembly.

"I assure countries which now receive assistance from the United States that we favour use of that assistance to help them maintain such contingents in the state of readiness suggested by the Secretary-General." (A/PV.868, p. 32)

In other words, he proposes to the countries that are receiving technical assistance that he is ready to give them more assistance for the formation of this United Nations emergency force. He continued:

"To assist the Secretary-General's efforts, the United States is prepared to earmark also substantial air and sea transport facilities on a stand-by basis, to help move contingents requested by the United Nations in any future emergency." (Ibid.)

In other words, the United States offers its planes and ships for the use of such emergency forces. We wish to state here that the Cuban delegation does not agree with that emergency force until all peoples of the world can feel sure that these forces will not be used at the disposal of colonialism and imperialism, and especially when any of our countries can at any moment become the victim of the use of such forces against the rights of our people.

There are a number of problems inherent here, and on this much has been said by a number of delegations. For reasons of time, we should like merely to express our opinion.

Firstly, we would refer to the problem of the Congo. Naturally, since we hold an anti-colonialist position against the exploitation of under-developed countries, we condemn the way in which the intervention by the United Nations forces was carried out in the Congo. First of all, these forces did not go there to act against the forces that had intervened and interfered, for which originally they were sent. All necessary time was given for the first dissension to be caused, and when this did not suffice, further time was given and the opportunity was made for the second division to occur in the Congo.

And finally, while the broadcasting stations and the airfields were occupied, further time was given for the emergence of the third man, as he is known; and the saviours who emerge in these circumstances are all too well known to us; because in 1934 in my country this type of saviour also appeared, his name was Fulgencio Batista. In the Congo his name is Mobutu. In Cuba he paid a daily visit to the American Embassy, and it appears that in the Congo the same applies. Not because I say so. You do not have to take my word for it. No, because no less then a magazine which is a major defender of the monopolies, and therefore cannot be against it is the one who says so. Certainly they cannot be in favour of Lumumba, because they are against him and in favour of Mobutu. But it explains who he is, how he devoted himself to his work, and it winds up by saying — this is Time magazine to which I am referring; the latest issue of Time says that"Mobutu became a frequent visitor to the United States Embassy and held long talks with officials there.

"One afternoon last week, Mobutu conferred with officers at Camp Leopold, and got their cheering support. That night he went to Radio Congo" — that Lumumba had not been allowed to use — "and abruptly announced that the army was assuming power." In other words, all this occurred after frequent visits and lengthy conversations with the officials of the United States Embassy. This is Time magazine speaking. Time surely is an advocate and champion of the monopolies. In other words, the hand of the colonialist interests has been obvious and visible in the Congo and therefore our position is frankly that favouritism and favour was shown the colonial interests and that all the facts point to the people of the Congo, and the reason in the Congo, being on the side of the only leader who remained there to defend the interests of his country, and that leader is Lumumba.

If the Afro-Asian countries manage, in view of this situation and in view of the appearance of this mysterious third man in the Congo called upon apparently to overthrow the legitimate Government and the legitimate interests of the Congo, to conciliate all these interests of the people, to strengthen the interests of the Congolese people, so much the better. But if this conciliation is not achieved then law and order will be on the side not only of he who has the support of the people and of the Parliament, but on the side of the one who stood and confronted the interests of the monopolies and who stood shoulder to shoulder with his people.

Regarding the problem of Algeria, I do not think I need say that we are 100 percent on the side of the rights of the people of Algeria for independence. Furthermore, it is ridiculous — many ridiculous things appear and exist in the world, imbued with an artificial life, given it by vested interests — to pretend that Algeria is part of the French community. These efforts were made by other countries when they wanted to keep their own colonies in other times. That is known as integration — and in this sense it was exploded by history. Let us look at the question inversely: suppose Algeria was the metropolitan area and declared that part of Europe formed an integral part of its metropolitan area. This is obviously an idea that is dragged in arbitrarily, that has no sense whatever and it is most ludicrous to maintain. Algeria belongs to Africa, as France belongs to Europe. Yet for a number of years these African people have been struggling heroically against the metropolitan area.

Perhaps even while we are discussing matters here calmly, over villages and hamlets of Algeria bombs may be falling and people may be machine-gunned — bombs dropped and machine guns operated by the Government and the people of France. And men are dying in a fight where there can be no possible doubt as to which side is right, a fight that could be settled, even taking into account the interests of that minority which is the one which is taken as a pretext in order to deny the right of independence to the nine-tenths part of the population of Algeria. And yet we do nothing. We were so quick to go to the Congo and so half-heartedly do we turn to Algeria. And if the Algerian Government, which is a Government because it represents millions of Algerians who are fighting and struggling, asks for United Nations forces to go there, would we go with the same enthusiasm? I wish we would go with the same enthusiasm, but with very different purposes, in other words, that we go to Algeria to defend the interests of the Algerians, and not the interests of the colonizers.

We are on the side of the Algerian people, as we are on the side of the other people of Africa that are still colonies and on the side of those coloured people discriminated against in the Union of South Africa. And as we are on the side of the peoples that wish not only to be politically free — because it is very easy to raise a flag, a standard, sing an anthem and put another colour on the map — but also who would be economically free, because there is a truth which we should all bear in mind as the first of all truths, and that is that there can be no political independence unless there be economic independence. Political independence is a fiction unless there is economic independence, and therefore the aspiration to be economically and politically free is one that we defend; not only the right to have a flag, not only the right to have a shield, a coat of arms and representation in the United Nations.

It is not only a question of the right to have a flag, a coat of arms, representation at the United Nations. We want to raise another right here, a right that was proclaimed by our people at an enormous public manifestation a few days ago. I refer to the right of the under-developed countries to nationalize, without indemnity, the natural resources of and the monopolistic investments in their countries. In other words, we proclaim the nationalization of the natural resources of and foreign investments in the under-developed countries. And if the highly industrialized countries wish to do likewise, we shall not oppose them.

For countries to be truly free politically, they must be truly free economically. They must be assisted. We may be asked: what about the value of the investments? And we shall then ask: what about the value of the profits that have been derived from the colonies and the underdeveloped countries for decades, if not centuries?

We should like to support a proposal made by the head of the delegation of Ghana — namely, the proposal to rid African territory of military bases, and therefore of nuclear weapon bases. In other words, the proposal is to keep Africa free from the dangers of nuclear war. Something has been done so far as Antarctica is concerned. If we want to make progress on the question of disarmament, why do we not proceed on the lines of freeing certain regions of the

earth from the danger of nuclear war. If Africa is to be reborn — that Africa which we are learning to know today, not the Africa that we saw on the maps, not the Africa that we were shown in Hollywood films and about which we read in magazines and novels, not the Africa of semi-naked tribes carrying lances, who were ready to run away at their first encounter with the white hero, the white hero whose heroism increased in proportion to the number of Africans who were killed, not that Africa but the Africa which today stands here represented by Seko Touré and Nkrumah, the Africa of the Arab world — if that Africa, I say, is to be reborn and to reawaken, then this formerly oppressed and exploited Continent, this Continent from which came millions of slaves, this Africa that has suffered so greatly during its history, must be preserved from the danger of destruction; it is our duty so to preserve it.

Let the West somehow repay Africa for all that it has gained from Africa and for all that Africa has suffered. Let the West compensate for Africa's past suffering by ensuring its future safety. Let us declare Africa a free zone. Let no atomic bases be established in Africa. Let that Continent, at least, be kept clean. If we can do nothing else, let us at least keep that Continent as a sanctuary where human life will be preserved. We warmly support that proposal, and on the question of disarmament we entirely support the Soviet proposal. We do not blush when we say this: we openly and warmly support the Soviet proposal. We understand that it is a correct proposal; its terms are precise; it is clearly defined.

We have very carefully read the speech delivered here by President Eisenhower. Basically he did not speak of disarmament; he did not speak of the development of the underdeveloped countries; he did not speak of the problem of colonies. The citizens of this country who are so swayed by propaganda should objectively and carefully read the speech of the President of the United States and the speech of the Prime Minister of the Soviet Union in order to see where there is a true concern for the problems of the world, in order to see where clear and sincere language is used, in order to see who wants disarmament and who does not want disarmament, and why.

The Soviet proposal could not be more clear. Why should there be reservations? When has such a tremendous problem been so clearly discussed?

The history of the world has shown, tragically, that armaments races always lead to war. Yet at no time has war entailed such a dreadful holocaust for humanity as at the present time; never has the responsibility been greater than at the present time. The problem of disarmament is of such great interest to humanity, since its very existence is involved. On this problem the Soviet delegation has presented a proposal for general and complete disarmament. Can anything more be asked? And if anything more is required, then ask for it. If further guarantees are asked for, let those who want them speak out. But the Soviet proposal could not be more clear. It cannot be rejected without assuming the dreadful responsibility for war and all the destruction that war brings with it. Why should the problem be taken away from the General Assembly? The delegation of the United States does not want this problem to be discussed here among all of us. Have we no brains? Do we know nothing about this problem? Are we not supposed to be aware of this problem? Is only a committee to discuss this problem? Why should not the problem be discussed in the most democratic way possible — in the General Assembly? Let each representative here lay his cards on the table so that we may clearly show who stands for disarmament and who does not, who wants to play at war and who does not, who is betraying humanity's aspiration to peace and who is not. Humanity must never be dragged into a holocaust because of egotistical interests.

The reality is that our peoples must be safeguarded from that holocaust. Not *we*. We do not count. It is our *people* who count. All that humanity has created cannot be used to destroy humanity itself.

The Soviet delegation spoke in clear terms — and I am speaking objectively here — I invite you gentlemen to study those proposals, I invite you gentlemen to place all your cards on the table. This is not a question of delegations now. This is a question of world public opinion. The warmongers and the military-minded must be unveiled before the opinion of the world. This is not a problem for the minority. This is a problem for the world itself. And we must strip the masks from those warmongers, those militarists. That is the task for world public opinion. Not only must this be discussed in the plenary of the General Assembly, but it must discussed before all humanity, before the great assembly of the world itself, because in the case of a war it will not be the representatives of countries that will be exterminated; it will be the entirety of humanity. Innocent humanity, which is not to blame, will be exterminated — innocent humanity, represented by those we meet here, or at least some of us, because the world is not complete here yet and it will not be complete until we have the People's Republic of China represented here, too. A quarter of the world is absent from this Assembly. But those of us who are here have a duty to perform. Our duty is to speak frankly and not to pass the buck. This is too serious a problem to silence some and allow others to speak. This is more important than economic assistance and all the other commitments, because this is the commitment which we have — our mission to preserve the life of humanity. All of us have to discuss the problem, we all have to speak about it, and all have to struggle so that peace will prevail in the world — or at least to strip the masks from the militarists and the warmongers of the world. Especially, if we of the under-developed countries want to have some hope that progress will be achieved, give us at least the hope that our peoples will enjoy a better standard of living. Then let us struggle and strive for peace, and let us struggle and strive for disarmament. With one fifth of what the world spends and squanders on armaments, we could promote a development of the under-developed countries, with a rate of growth of ten percent per annum, and the standard of living of our countries could be raised — the standard of living of countries that are wasting their wealth on armaments.

Now, what are the difficulties? Who is interested in being armed? Those who are interested in being armed to the teeth are those who wish to hold on to their colonies, to their monopolies — those who want to hold in their hands the oil of the Middle East, the natural resources of the Middle East and of Asia and of Africa. In order to defend these interests, they need force and might. And, you know, it was because of the right of might that these territories were occupied and colonized. Because of this right of might, millions of men were made slaves. It is might and force that keep this exploitation going in the world. Therefore, the first who do not want disarmament are those who wish to maintain this right of might, those who wish to keep their hands on the wealth of countries and on the cheap labour of under-developed countries.

I said I was going to speak clearly, and I could not refer to truth or voice truth in any other words. The colonialists, then, are those who are opposed to disarmament. Then we will have to fight, with world opinion on our side, to impose disarmament on them. We will impose on them the rights of all peoples to political and economic self-determination. The monopolies are against disarmament because, besides the fact that with arms they can defend their interests, the arms race has always been good business for the monopolies. For example, everybody knows that the great monopolies in these countries doubled their capital during the Second World War. Like vultures, the monopolies feed on the dead of the wars — and war is good business. Let us then strip the masks from those who do business with war, those who enrich themselves by war. Let us open the eyes of the world and show them who is to blame, who are those warmongers playing and trading on the fate of humanity, trading on the dangers of war, when war can be so terrifying as to leave no hope of salvation for anybody.

That is the task to which we, a small underdeveloped country, invite the rest of you, and especially those other countries that are underdeveloped. We would never forgive ourselves for the consequences if, because of an oversight or a lack of determination on our part, the world were to be involved again in the danger of another war.

There is one point remaining which, as I have read in some newspapers, was one of the points that the Cuban delegation wanted to raise. That is the question of the People's Republic of China. A number of delegations have already spoken of this. We merely wish to say that it is a negation of the raison d'être of the United Nations, and of the very essence of the United Nations, that this problem has not even been discussed here. Why? Because of the will of the United States Government not to discuss the matter. Because, for that reason, the General Assembly of the United Nations must renounce its right to discuss this problem.

In recent years, a number of countries have become Members of our Organization. It is to deny an historical reality and a fact, it is to deny the realities of life itself, to oppose the discussion — mind you, the very discussion — of the right of the People's Republic of China to be represented here, in other words, of ninety-nine percent of the inhabitants of one of the most highly populated countries of the world to be represented here. It is preposterous, and it is an absurdity. It is ludicrous to say that this matter should not be discussed. How long are we to play this sad role of not discussing the problem in the United Nations — when there are represented here, for example, the representatives of Franco? Mr. President, will you allow me to express my opinion, with all due respect, on this specific point, without offending anybody?

THE PRESIDENT: I think it is only fair to the Prime Minister to make clear the position of the Chair. The Chair does not think it is in keeping with the dignity of the Assembly or the decorum that we like to preserve in our debates that references of a personal nature should be made to the Heads of States or the Heads of Governments of Member States of the United Nations, whether present here or not. I hope that the Prime Minister will consider that a fair and reasonable rule.

MR. CASTRO (Cuba) (interpretation from Spanish): I merely wanted to make some comments, Sir, on how the United Nations emerged. The United Nations emerged after the struggle against Fascism, after tens of thousands of men had died on the battlefield. From that struggle which took so many lives this Organization emerged as a hope. But there are some extraordinary paradoxes. American soldiers fell in Guam, Guadalcanal, Okinawa and many other islands. On the Chinese mainland too, they fell fighting against the same enemy. Those same men to whom today we deny the very right to discuss their own entry into the United Nations were also fighting. Though the soldiers of the Blue Brigade were fighting to defend Fascism, the Chinese People's Republic is denied entry and is even denied the right to discuss its case in the United Nations. Still, the regime that was born of Italian Fascism and German Nazism that took power thanks to Hitler's armies and Mussolini's blackshirts, received the accolade of membership in the United Nations.

China represents one-fourth of the world. Which Government truly represents that people which is the greatest people in the world? None other than the Government of the People's Republic of China. Yet here we keep another group, in the middle of a civil war that was interrupted by the interference of the United States Seventh Fleet. May we ask here by what right the fleet of one country, and an extracontinental country at that — and let us stress that when so much is spoken here of extracontinental interference — can interfere in a purely domestic affair of China, with the sole purpose of maintaining there a group that was on its side and stopping the entire liberation of the territory? That is an absurd and illegal position, from any point of view, and that is why the Government of the United States does not want the problem of the representation of the People's Republic of China to be discussed here.

We want it to be clearly noted that this is our viewpoint. We support a discussion of that problem here and the seating in the United Nations of the true representatives of the Chinese people. I understand very well that it is somewhat difficult and invidious for anyone here to speak in any but stereotyped terms regarding representatives of nations, but may I say that we came here free of all prejudice and we came here to analyze the problems objectively. Let those who wish to think think. We are not afraid of the consequences of our conduct or our stand. We have been honest and sincere. We have been frank without being Francoist, because we do not want to be accomplices to that injustice perpetrated against many Spaniards who have for more than twenty years been imprisoned in Spain and who fought together with the Americans in the Lincoln Brigade, colleagues of those same Americans who tried to raise the name of that great American, Lincoln, in Spain.

We shall trust in the reason and in the honesty of all. There are aspects of these world problems with regard to which we should like to sum up our views, on which there can be no doubt whatever. We have made known the problem of Cuba, which is part of the world problems. Those who attack us today are those who assist in attacking others elsewhere in the world. The Government of the

United States cannot agree with the people of Algeria, because the United States is an ally of France; it cannot be with the Congolese people, because the United States is an ally of Belgium; it cannot be with the Spanish people, because it is an ally of Franco. It cannot be in favour of the Puerto Rican people, whose nationality it has for fifty years been destroying; it cannot be with the Panamanians, who are claiming their canal. It cannot allow the growth of civic power in Latin America, Germany or Japan. It cannot be on the side of the peasants who want their own lands because it is an ally of the land-owners. It cannot be with the workers who seek better living conditions in any part of the world, because it is an ally of the monopolies. It cannot be with the colonies that wish for liberation, because it is an ally of the colonizing Powers. In other words, it is with Franco, with the colonizers of Algeria, with the colonizers of the Congo. It is in favour of perpetuating its sovereignty and dominion over the Canal. In a word, it is in favour of its own imperialism all over the world.

It is in favour of the resurgence of German militarism and Japanese militarism. The Government of the United States forgets the millions of Jews who died in the concentration camps of Europe at the hands of the Nazis who are today recovering their influence in the German Army.

They forget the French who were murdered and slaughtered there in their heroic struggle against German occupation. They prefer to overlook the American soldiers who landed at Omaha Beach, in the Ruhr, the Ziegfried Line, in the Rhine and on all the fronts of Asia.

The Americans cannot be in favour of integrity or sovereignty of peoples, because they have to limit and amputate the sovereignty of peoples in order to maintain their military bases. And each military base is another dagger stuck into the sovereignty of a nation; each base is another amputated and lopped-off sovereignty.

That is why the United States must be against the sovereignty of the people, because it must constantly limit sovereignty in order to maintain its policy of bases around the Soviet Union.

We understand that the people of the United States do not have these problems clearly explained to them, because suffice it for the people of America to realize, and then what would have happened to their tranquillity if in Cuba, in Mexico or Canada the Soviet Union were to begin to set up a belt of atomic bases? The population certainly would not feel secure; it would not feel tranquil, serene, calm.

World public opinion, including North American public opinion, has to be taught to understand the problems from another point of view, from the other person's point of view, and not always have the under-developed countries shown to it as aggressors, or revolutionaries and aggressors, enemies of the American people.

We cannot be enemies of the American people, because we have seen Americans, such as Waldo Frank, illustrious and distinguished intellectuals, who weep at the thought of the errors that are committed, at the lack of hospitality which was committed particularly against us.

There are many Americans, those humane Americans, those intellectuals, the progressive writers, the most valuable writers, and it is in them that I see the nobility of the true, first pioneers, of the Washingtons, Jeffersons and Lincolns of this country.

I am not using demagogy; I am speaking with the sincere admiration that we feel for those who one day knew how to free their people, destroy colonialism and fight; but not for this country to become today the ally of all the reactionaries of the world, the ally of all the gangsters in the world, the ally of the landowners, the monopolists, the militarists and the fascists of the world, the ally of the most retrograde and reactionary groups of the world.

They struggled for their country to stand ever as a champion of nobility and just ideals. We know full well that what they will be told today, tomorrow and always about us will hoodwink them. It makes no difference. We are fulfilling our duty in expressing our views and expressing these true facts — and expressing them in this historic Assembly.

We proclaim the right of people to nationality, to freedom; and those who know that nationalism means a recuperation of their own goods are aspiring to nationalism and freedom.

In one word, we are in favour of all the noble aspirations of all peoples. That is our position: there we stand. We are on the side of the just; we always will be on the side of the just, against colonialism, exploitation; against monopolies, against war-mongering; against the arms race and against the playing of war. Against those we shall always stand. That will be our position.

In conclusion, fulfilling what we consider to be our duty, we bring to this Assembly the essential part of the Havana Declaration. You know that the Havana Declaration was a reply of the Cuban people to the Costa Rica Letter and Declaration. It was not ten, nor one hundred, nor 100,000; there were more than a million Cubans — and those who doubt it can go and count them at the next concentration, or the general assembly that we hold in Cuba, and you will see a spectacle of a fervent and conscious people that I think you will scarcely have seen elsewhere; a sight that you can only see when the people are truly, fervently defending the most sacred interests.

At that assembly an answer was given to the Costa Rica Declaration. In full consultation with the people, and by acclamation of the people, these principles were proclaimed as the principles of the Cuban revolution. The national general assembly of the people of Cuba condemns land-owning, the source of misery for the peasant and a system of agricultural backwardness and inhumanity; it condemns starvation diets and the iniquitous exploitation by mongrel interests and vested interests; it condemns illiteracy, the absence of teachers, of schools, of doctors and hospitals; it condemns the lack of old-age security which obtains in countries of America; it condemns discrimination against the black and the Indian; it condemns inequality and the exploitation of women; it condemns military and political oligarchies that keep our people in misery and want, hampering their democratic development and the full exercise of their sovereignty; it condemns concessions of natural resources of our countries to foreign monopolies as a treacherous policy handing over the interests of peoples to others; it condemns those Governments that turn deaf ears to the claims of their peoples, who obey foreign orders; it condemns the systematic hoodwinking and lying to peoples by dissemination organs that propagandize imperialism and oppression; it condemns the monopoly over news agencies which are instruments of monopolist trusts, and agents of such interests; it condemns repressive laws that stop workers, peasants, students, intellectuals and the great majorities of each country from organizing and from fighting for their social and patriotic aspirations; it condemns monopolies and imperialist enterprises that constantly sap our wealth, that exploit our workers and peasants and bleed white and maintain our economies in backwardness and submit the policies of Latin America to their designs and interests.

The national general assembly of Cuba condemns exploitation of man by man and the exploitation of under-developed countries by imperialist capital. In consequence, the general assembly of the Cuban people proclaims to America, and proclaims it here to the world, the right of the peasants to own their land; the right of the worker to the fruits of his labour; the right of children to education; the right of the sick to be given medical assistance and hospitalization; the right of youth to work; the right of students to receive free scientific and experimental training and education; the right of the black and the Indian to the full dignity of mankind; the right of women to civic, social and political equality; the right of the old to a secure old age; the right of intellectuals, artists and scientists to fight with the fruits of their labours for a better world, and the right of States to nationalize imperialist monopolies, thus rescuing the national resources and wealth; the right of countries to trade freely with all peoples of the world; the right of nations to their full sovereignty, and the right of peoples to turn their military fortresses into schools and to arm their workers, because in this we too have to be arms conscious, to arm our workers, to defend ourselves against imperialist attack; to arm our workers, our peasants, our students, our intellectuals, the blacks, the Indians, women, youth and the old, and all the oppressed and exploited so that they themselves can defend their rights and their fate.

Some wanted to know the line followed by the Revolutionary Government of Cuba. There you have our line. ❑

The Meeting rose at 8:20 p.m.

UNITED NATIONS

GENERAL ASSEMBLY

Distr. GENERAL A/4537 October 13, 1960 ORIGINAL: ENGLISH

Fifteenth session

LETTER DATED OCTOBER 12, 1960 FROM THE REPRESENTATIVE OF THE UNITED STATES OF AMERICA TO THE UNITED NATIONS ADDRESSED TO THE SECRETARY-GENERAL

On September 26, 1960, the Prime Minister of Cuba, while addressing the General Assembly, made many untrue and distorted allegations against the United States which could not be allowed to stand unanswered. In my brief reply before the Assembly on the following day I stated that the United States would shortly make available a document dealing fully with the issues involved.

On the instructions of the United States Government, therefore, I have the honour to request that the enclosed document, entitled "Facts concerning relations between Cuba and the United States: a reply to allegations against the United States by Prime Minister Fidel Castro of Cuba", be circulated to all Members of the United Nations for their information.

The United States Government, which together with the people of the United States entertains feelings of the warmest friendship and goodwill toward Cuba and her people, deeply regrets that such unfounded and hostile statements should have been made and that it should be necessary to correct the record by means of this reply.

(Signed) James J. WADSWORTH

INTRODUCTION

On September 26, 1960, the Prime Minister of Cuba, Mr. Fidel Castro, addressed the General Assembly at considerable length on the relations between the present Cuban regime and the United States. His speech contained many unfounded accusations, half-truths, malicious innuendoes and distortions of history — all aimed against the historic friendship between Cuba and the United States, a friendship which he seems anxious to destroy.

The most important charges against the United States which Prime Minister Castro made in this address had already been considered and rejected in two meetings of the Organization of American States, consisting of twenty-one Republics of the Western Hemisphere, before he made them in the General Assembly. The Foreign Ministers of the OAS heard and rejected them at their meeting in San Jose, Costa Rica, in August. The delegates to the OAS economic conference in Bogota, Colombia, in September heard essentially the same charges from the representative of Cuba and again rejected them. Now, in view of the repetition of these and other unfounded charges before the General Assembly, and out of respect for the opinions of the entire membership of the United Nations, the United States feels compelled once again to set the record straight.

* * * * * * * * * * *

FACTS CONCERNING RELATIONS BETWEEN CUBA AND THE UNITED STATES

A REPLY TO ALLEGATIONS MADE IN THE UNITED NATIONS AGAINST THE UNITED STATES BY PRIME MINISTER FIDEL CASTRO OF CUBA

1. CUBAN-UNITED STATES RELATIONS SINCE 1898

The charge: That in times past "Cuba was virtually a colony of the United States;" ... "the apple was ripe and the United States Government held out its open hands." That the Platt Amendment, granting the United States the right to intervene and to lease naval bases in Cuba, was "imposed by force" on Cuba. That the "colonization" of Cuba then began with "the acquisition of the best land by United States firms, concessions of Cuban natural resources and mines, concessions of public services for purposes of exploitation, commercial concessions, concessions of all types." That "a greater part of the sugar production, the lion's share of the arable land of Cuba and the most important industries ... belonged to North American companies."

The facts: When the people of Cuba sought independence from Spain toward the end of the 19th century, the American people overwhelmingly sympathized with them. In 1898 the United States became the active ally of the newly independent Cuba. American soldiers fought side by side with Cuban patriots in the war for Cuban independence.

In the years after Cuba became independent the new nation stood in obvious need of political and economic stability and of investment capital. The Platt Amendment, which governed United States relations with Cuba after the withdrawal of United States troops from the island, helped to assure these conditions.

Prime Minister Castro did not mention the fact that the Platt Amendment was abrogated in 1934 — twenty-six years ago — by agreement between the two Governments. This step was taken during the Presidency of Franklin D. Roosevelt, author of the "Good Neighbor" policy, a policy which has remained in effect ever since.

The Prime Minister also neglected to mention that in empowering the use of military forces to assist in the liberation of Cuba the Congress of the United States in 1898 adopted a joint resolution, signed by the President the next day, explicitly disclaiming any intention of the United States to exercise sovereignty, jurisdiction or control over Cuba as an aftermath of this assistance and endorsing the right of Cuba to be free and independent and under the control of its own people.

As regards United States interests in Cuban sugar, it is probably true that at one time American-owned firms owned or leased most of the sugar lands and produced most of the Cuban sugar crop. However, long before Prime Minister Castro came to power United States citizens were reducing their sugar holdings. By 1959 they had an interest in no more than one-third of the sugar lands of Cuba, about 1,210,000 acres on which about one-third of the Cuban sugar crop was produced.

Sugar production accounted for only a minor part of United States investment in Cuba. Only 25 percent of United States investments were devoted to agriculture, and of that more than half represented sugar mills, not the growing cane. The remaining 75 percent were such as to promote not a one-crop economy but a highly diversified economy, with emphasis on industry and manufacturing. The major portion was invested in public utilities — electricity and telephones both indispensable to industrial growth and diversification and both regulated by the Cuban Government. As a result Cuba had the fifth highest rate of electrical consumption in Latin America. In addition, 10 percent of United States investments were directly in manufacturing industries.

2. THE UNITED STATES, ALLEGED ALLY OF MONOPOLY AND REACTION

The charge: "Why does the United States Government not want to speak of development? ... Because the Government of the United States does not want to quarrel with the monopolies, and the monopolies need natural resources ... The Government of the United States cannot propose a plan for public investment, because this would divorce it from the very raison d'être of the United States Government, which is the United States monopolies. That is the true reason why no true program of economic development is planned: to preserve the land of Latin America, of Africa and of Asia, to keep

it the private domain of those who wish to invest their surplus capital." The United States has betrayed its revolutionary origin and has "become today the ally of all the reactionaries of the world, the ally of all the gangsters in the world, the ally of the landowners, the monopolists, the militarists and the fascists of the world, the ally of the most retrograde and reactionary groups of the world."

The facts: The United States does speak of economic development of under-developed countries, and not only speaks of it but contributes increasing sums of money and energy to it, both through the United Nations and through other agencies, including the inter-American system.

In fact, the United States Government contributes more to economic development of other countries than any other Government in the world. Still larger is the outflow of United States private investment — which we believe, as do most other nations, makes a major favourable impact on the economic growth of under-developed countries and on the well-being of their peoples.

As for "monopolies", United States industries are forbidden by law from engaging in monopolistic practices — by the Sherman Anti-Trust Act of 1890 and the Clayton Anti-Trust Act of 1913, both of which are actively enforced by the United States Government. The Marxist idea of "monopolies", applied to the United States, is a hundred years out of date.

The picture of the United States as the ally of "gangsters ... landowners ... monopolists ... militarists ... fascists" is straight out of the mythology of Soviet communism — as are the economic theories quoted above.

The raison d'étre of the United States Government is not "monopolies". It is, in the words of the United States Constitution, "to form a more perfect Union, establish justice, insure domestic tranquility, provide for the common defense, promote the general welfare, and secure the blessings of liberty for ourselves and our posterity."

3. THE U.S. NAVAL BASE AT GUANTANAMO

The charge: That "because of the Platt Amendment, imposed by force on our people, the Government of the United States took upon itself the right to establish naval bases on our territory, a right that it imposed on us by force and which it has maintained by the same means."

The facts: The United States never "took upon itself" or "imposed by force" any right respecting Guantanamo. Nor do United States rights in Guantanamo arise from the now-defunct Platt Amendment.

In 1902 and 1903 the United States conducted diplomatic negotiations with the Republic of Cuba for the purpose of acquiring the right to establish coaling and naval stations on Cuban territory. As a result of these negotiations, two executive agreements were signed in 1903. The first provided for the lease to the United States of certain designated territory at Guantanamo Bay. The second agreement spelled out the terms of the lease.

The validity of these agreements was reaffirmed by Article III of the 1934 Treaty of Relations between the United States and Cuba, which is still in effect and which provides:

"Until the two contracting parties agree to the modification or abrogation of the stipulations of the agreement in regard to the lease to the United States of America of lands in Cuba for coaling and naval stations signed by the President of the Republic of Cuba on February 16, 1903, and by the President of the United States of America on the 23rd day of the same month and year, the stipulations of that agreement with regard to the naval station of Guantanamo shall continue in effect. The supplementary agreement in regard to naval or coaling stations signed between the two governments on July 2, 1903, also shall continue in effect in the same form and on the same conditions with respect to the naval station at Guantanamo."

These instruments were not imposed by force. They were negotiated between sovereign Governments. It is particularly necessary to recall their provisions because Prime Minister Castro has raised a current question concerning Guantanamo (see item 14 page 180).

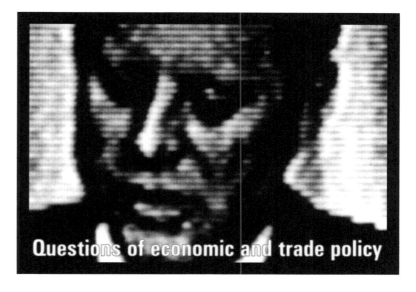

4. THE UNITED STATES ATTITUDE TOWARD THE BATISTA GOVERNMENT

The charge: That "the military group that tyrannized over our country … was based upon the foreign interests that dominated the economy of the country" — meaning those of the United States because it was "the type of government that was chosen and preferred by the monopolists."

The facts: The type of government existing in Cuba is the affair of the Cuban people. Since World War II the United States has maintained normal relations with Cuban Governments of varying political tendencies: Colonel Batista in 1940; Dr. Ramón Grau San Martín in 1944, who promoted social reforms against opposition from both right and left wings, including the Communists; Dr. Carlos Prio Socarras in 1948, who won out over both Communist and Batista forces and sought economic progress for his country; beginning in 1952, the second Batista Government; and, until frustrated by systematic hostility, the present Cuban Government. The idea that leaders of such varying persuasions could have been imposed on the Cuban people by United States "monopolists" is ridiculous, and is an insult to the capacity of the Cuban people to govern themselves.

The United States has a firm policy of nonintervention in Latin American affairs, stemming from the "Good Neighbour" policy of 1934 and in harmony with the United Nations Charter and the Treaty of Rio de Janeiro. The United States regards the principle of non-intervention as one of the cornerstones of the inter-American system.

5. U.S. MILITARY AID TO CUBA

The charge: That "the Batista regime stayed in power with the assistance of tanks, planes and weapons supplied by the Government of the United States;" that the officers of the army under Batista "were instructed and trained by a military mission of the United States;" and the use of this U.S. materiel and training "to fight the Cuban revolutionaries … had received the previous agreement of the Government of the United States."

The facts: The United States military missions in Cuba were established in 1950 and 1951, pursuant to mission agreements between Cuba and the United States. This took place during the Presidency of Dr. Carlos Prio Socarras, not of Colonel Batista. These agreements, like similar agreements with most of the other American Republics, had as their sole purpose co-operation in the military defense of the Western Hemisphere and, in this case, specifically of Cuba and the United States. The function of the missions was to give technical advice, arrange for the admission of Cubans to United States military schools and academies, and to help in the procurement of military equipment and arms needed for the common defense.

Equipment was provided to the Cuban Government under a military assistance agreement for hemisphere defense negotiated with and signed by the Prio Government, prior to the advent of President Batista.

Any use made by the Batista Government of this equipment, or of military training provided by the United States, in order to combat Cuban revolutionaries, was done without the consent of the United States authorities and in disregard of the agreement. The missions had no contact whatever with any military operations against the revolutionaries, trained no personnel for this purpose, and were not present at any time in the zones of operation.

When it became evident that Cuba was undergoing a revolution which had the support of a large part of the Cuban population, the United States showed its determination to stay out of Cuba's internal conflict by suspending all sales and shipments of combat arms to the Batista Government. This suspension was publicly announced in March 1958, ten months before the Castro forces took power. After March 1958 the United States did not make any combat arms available to the Batista Government, either directly or through third countries or in any other way.

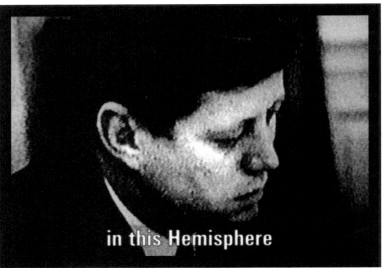

6. CUBA'S BALANCE OF PAYMENTS: "MONOPOLIES ... SUCKING ITS BLOOD"

The charge: That "the balance of payments in the last ten years, from 1950 to 1960, has been favourable for the United States vis-à-vis Cuba to the extent of 1 billion dollars. Thus, that Cuba, "a poor and under-developed country ... was contributing to the economic development of the most highly industrialized country in the world." That the President of the United States did not want this situation changed but rather wanted the new Government to be "true to the monopolies that were exploiting Cuba and sucking its blood."

The facts: These assertions are factually incorrect and the inferences drawn from them are illogical and untrue.

In the decade 1949-1958, the latest for which reliable figures are available, Cuba's exports to the United States earned 4,405 million dollars. (This includes 756 million dollars of premium payments for Cuban sugar sold in the U. S. market, over and above world sugar prices.) In the same decade Cuba imported from the United States goods worth 4,676 million dollars. Thus Cuba's adverse trade balance toward the United States was not one billion dollars in this decade, but about 271 million dollars.

But even this figure does not truly describe Cuba's international trading position. During the same decade her imports from all countries amounted to 6,319 million dollars, while her exports to all countries totaled 6,835 million dollars — a very favourable over-all balance of 516 million dollars for the decade, indicating a healthy trading position.

It is this over-all trading balance that is most significant. Normally a truly free-trading nation does not seek a bilateral trade balance with each and every trading partner, but rather an over-all balance of payments with all countries. Attempts to balance trade bilaterally, as on the barter principle, restrict trade unnecessarily and impede economic growth and the improvement of living standards. Thus, for example, the United States has a favourable balance of trade with some of the American Republics, whereas in others the balance is adverse to the United States by ratios as high as two to one. This principle of balancing trade multilaterally is one of the cornerstones of the General Agreement on Tariffs and Trade, of which both Cuba and the United States are members.

The advantage of this multilateral trading system to Cuba is easily shown. The dollars which Cuba earned for goods sold to the United States could be used freely to import other goods into Cuba from anywhere in the world. The fact that Cubans actually bought from the United States slightly more than they sold to the United States did not result from any artificial barter or quota requirement and was not "blood sucking". It was purely the result of competitive forces and of the free choices of Cuban traders.

Under the present Government, Cuba has artificially reduced imports from the United States by more than one half. There was no economic necessity for this. In the years before Prime Minister Castro came to power Cuban foreign exchange reserves, averaging 270 million dollars, were sufficient to cover temporary fluctuations in Cuba's balance of payments. The only possible conclusion is that the reduction of trade with the United States was artificial and politically motivated.

In exchange for its former dollar earnings, and its freedom to seek the greatest advantage for Cuban traders and consumers in the markets of the world, Cuba has been developing a new system of barter transactions with the Soviet Union. In those transactions Cuba will have no choice as to the country to which it will sell or from which it will buy. It will have no chance to benefit from competition in price, quality or style among various potential trading partners. Its transactions, instead of earning hundreds of millions of dollars a year which can be spent anywhere in the world, will yield only fractional amounts of free currency for Cuba's use in world trade.

7. TERMS OF PAYMENT FOR SEIZED LANDS IN CUBA

The charge: That the United States, in demanding "speedy, efficient, and just" payment for United States-owned lands seized by the Castro regime, was in effect telling Cuba: "Pay now, cash on the spot, and what we ask for our lands" — thus forcing Cuba "to choose between an agrarian reform and nothing ".

The facts: The United States never made such a demand. Several times, it is true, the United States has asked the Cuban Government to make "prompt, adequate and effective compensation" to American citizens whose lands had been taken under the agrarian reform law. But the United States never demanded payment "now, cash on the spot and what we ask", or attempted to impose any other fixed or rigid terms. We sought only to bring about negotiation of the question of compensation, in accordance with accepted principles of international law.

This was the least that could be asked. The laws prevailing in Cuba in the years when the seized lands were originally bought by United States citizens all contained provisions for prior compensation in case of expropriation. Yet, over one year after the Cuban agrarian reform law was passed, not one American owner has received compensation for lands taken under this law. In his United Nations speech, in fact, Prime Minister Castro asserted an alleged right to seize such properties "without indemnity" — a notion which directly flouts international law.

The United States has a long record of co-operation with countries seeking to carry out sound land reform programmes. On June 11th and October 12, 1959 the United States expressed to the Cuban Government its full support for soundly conceived programmes of rural betterment — including badly needed land reform. The implication that the United States sought to interfere with the Cuban land reform programme, either by making unreasonable demands for compensation or in any other way, is groundless.

8. CUBAN SUGAR EXPORTS TO THE UNITED STATES

The charge: That the United States, by reducing in 1960 the quota of Cuban sugar annually imported into the United States at premium prices, committed "economic aggression" against Cuba.

The facts: This charge is absurd. It was Cuba under Prime Minister Castro, not the United States, which first caused drastic reductions in Cuban-United States trade. In the sugar trade alone, months before the United States reduced Cuba's sugar quota, Cuba made firm agreements to export a large part of its present and future sugar crops to the Soviet Union and Communist China. In the interest of its own economy the United States could not remain tied to a source of supply burdened with this new obligation and with many other new uncertainties.

These facts deserve to be set forth in more detail.

In January 1960, seven months before the United States Congress acted to reduce the Cuban sugar quota, the present Cuban Government began a series of steps to obstruct trade with the United States. These steps included:

— New import licensing requirements contrary to Cuba's obligations under the General Agreement on Tariffs and Trade.

— Threats and pressures on traditional Cuban customers of the United States to divert their orders to suppliers in other countries.

— Reduction of the import quota on United States rice by more than 25 percent; severe limits on dollar exchange allowed by the Government for rice imports from the United States; imposition of a new "contribution" (i.e. duty) on all rice imported from the United States; and, meanwhile, duty-free importation of at least 16,500,000 pounds of rice from a third country under a new bilateral trade agreement.

— New surcharges, ranging from 30 percent to 100 percent, on remittances of dollar exchange needed by Cuban importers to pay for certain kinds of commodities normally imported from the United States.

— A new order that all Cuban exporters and other Cubans who earn dollars or other foreign exchange in their business must surrender all this foreign exchange to the Government.

— Refusal to lend money to United States-owned banks in Cuba, forcing them to bring in funds from abroad to meet normal business requirements.

If the aim of these steps has been to reduce Cuban imports from the United States, they have succeeded. There is now an estimated backlog of over 150 million dollars owed to United States citizens for goods shipped to Cuba and for services and earnings. During the first four months of 1960 Cuban imports from the United States were 50 percent below those in the same four months of 1958 and 75 percent below those in the same four months of 1959.

Meanwhile Cuba's export trade to the United States continued to flourish. Cuban exports to the United States in the first four months in 1960 were only slightly below those for the same part of 1958 and well above the figure for the same part of 1959.

Then in 1960 the Cuban Government concluded barter agreements with the Soviet Union and Communist China involving the export of a very large part of its annual sugar crop. The agreements provided for payment not at premium prices, as had been true of Cuban sugar exports to the United States, but at prices at or even below the world market level. Moreover, only a minor portion of the payment was to be in convertible currencies, whereas the entire payment for Cuban sugar imported into the United States has been in dollars which Cuba could spend anywhere in the world.

The present leaders in Cuba have often referred to the sugar quota arrangement with the United States, by which Cuba earned convertible dollars at preferential prices, as a form of "bondage" or "slavery". For instance, on March 2, 1960, Dr. Ernesto Guevara, the president of the National Bank of Cuba and a ranking official of the regime, said of the United States citizens concerned: "They have never stopped to analyze what amount of slavery the three million tons of our sugar which we customarily sell at supposedly preferential prices to the giant of the north has meant and means to the people of Cuba." When the United States Government queried the Cuban Government about these remarks there was no reply. The inference was left that the Cuban rulers regarded the sugar quota as a form of slavery imposed by the United States on the Cuban people.

It is hard to understand how a traditional pattern of Cuban sugar exports paid for in dollars, at prices above the world market, the proceeds of which Cuba was able to use to purchase goods anywhere in the world, can be described as slavery — whereas new barter agreements at lower prices, agreements which tie the Cuban economy to the Sino-Soviet bloc and infringe on Cuba's right to choose the origin, cost and quality of its imports, can somehow be portrayed as "economic freedom".

At all events, it became apparent that the present rulers of Cuba were forcing a radical change in Cuba's entire foreign trade system, and that the motives in their minds in doing this were not economic or commercial but political. This was confirmed when the Foreign Minister of Cuba, Dr. Raul Roa, said in Montevideo, on June 10, 1960, that Cuba had decided to break the structure of its commercial relations with the United States".

It was against this background that the United States Congress and the President of the United States acted in the summer of 1960 to reduce the preferential quota for imports of Cuban sugar. Despite the vindictive attitude of the Cuban leaders over many months, this act by the United States was not an act of retaliation or revenge. Indeed, it would have been strange to take revenge by reducing a quota which Cuban leaders themselves had condemned as a form of bondage. Rather, the reduction in the quota was necessary in defense of the United States economy, which has for many years depended heavily on Cuba as a source of sugar.

Cuba normally has supplied about 71 percent of the sugar import requirements of the United States. In the years 1931–1958 the United States imported from Cuba an average of 2,580,000 tons of sugar — all at preferential prices. Cuba's dollar earnings from this trade rose from a low of 39 million dollars in the depression years of the early 1930's to 100 million dollars in 1936 and 400 million dollars in 1947. In 1959 the earnings were 350 million dollars.

Cuba's preferential position in the United States sugar market goes back to 1902. It was made more secure in 1934 by a quota system which gave Cuba a more stable United States market at the higher United States domestic price and in addition a 20 percent tariff preference as compared with other foreign producers.

This arrangement was a matter of mutual advantage. It helped the Cuban economy by providing a most important source of dollar exchange to pay for imports from all parts of the world. It helped the United States economy by providing a reliable source of needed sugar imports at all times, including times of war and crisis. Thus during both the Korean war and the Suez crisis, when world markets were disturbed, the Cuban sugar industry maintained large stocks which were made available to the United States at fair prices.

This arrangement could last only as long as both parties wanted it to last. The events of early 1960 in Cuba made it doubtful that the Cuban Government was either able or willing to continue it. The highest officials of the Cuban Government made repeated statements describing the supposed political and commercial advantages of selling Cuban sugar elsewhere. On August 13, 1960, the Minister of Finance, Raul Cepero Bonilla, said: "For the next year, it would be much more advantageous to Cuba if the United States did not buy a single grain of sugar." Meanwhile agreements were made committing Cuba to sell a major part of her sugar crop to the Sino-Soviet bloc, and indications appeared that that bloc was prepared to import even larger quantities of Cuban sugar by purchase or barter. Finally, it appears that these new obligations must be met out of a smaller Cuban sugar crop. United States experts estimate that the 1961 Cuban sugar crop may fall as low as 4,900,000 Spanish long tons — as compared with 5,7000,000 Spanish long tons in 1960.

For all those reasons the United States was forced, slowly and reluctantly, to conclude that Cuba is no longer a reliable source of supply for vital United States sugar requirements. This was the reason why the United States reduced the Cuban sugar quota and thus freed itself to turn to other sources of sugar supply.

The conditions leading to this decision were created by the present authorities in Cuba. Their right as a sovereign nation to order their foreign trade as they wish is not in dispute, except when in so doing they violate their agreements. But if they claim that right for themselves, they cannot deny it to others.

There are ample grounds for the belief that the present Government of Cuba set out deliberately to provoke, by its own action and threats, a United States action unavoidable as a matter of economic self-defense — which it could then picture in its propaganda as "economic aggression". Now that it has achieved this dubious success, at a very considerable economic cost to the Cuban people, the cry of "economic aggression" against the United States sounds utterly hollow.

9. PRESENCE OF ANTI-CASTRO CUBANS IN THE UNITED STATES

The charge: "The first unfriendly act perpetrated by the Government of the United States was to throw open its doors to a gang of murderers, bloodthirsty criminals who had murdered hundreds of defenseless peasants, who had never tired of torturing prisoners for many, many years, who had killed right and left".

The facts: The number of people who have fled Cuba and have taken refuge in the United States since the Castro Government came to power does indeed run into the hundreds. In view of the fact that the Castro Government has effectively banned all political opposition or public criticism as "counter-revolutionary", and has sought to brand those who dissent from its policies as "war criminals" and adherents of the deposed Batista regime, it is not surprising that many Cubans who value freedom have gone into exile — some of them in the United States. Here they enjoy the traditional right of political asylum. They do not enjoy protection against criminal charges of murder or any other extraditable crime.

In all cases where the Cuban Government sought extradition of Cuban refugees on criminal charges, the United States Government has given the fullest possible co-operation consistent with its traditional legal safeguards and with the very limited co-operation of the Cuban Government itself.

The provisions for extradition of persons from the United States to Cuba are set forth in the United States-Cuban Extradition Treaty and in United States statutes. Cuba can file extradition proceedings in United States courts without even notifying the executive branch of the United States Government.

All this was explained to the new Cuban authorities when, in January 1959, they raised the question of the return to Cuba of certain Cubans who had taken refuge in the United States. Yet to the best of the knowledge of the Department of State, from that day to this the Cuban Government has never requested extradition for a single one of those persons commonly defined by the Government of Cuba as war criminals from the Batista regime.

In fact, the only extradition case which the Cuban Government has followed through to conclusion is that of Major Pedro Diaz Lanz, a former member of the Castro revolutionary group and chief of the Cuban air force after the Castro Government came to power in 1959. In the case of Major Diaz Lanz a United States. District Court denied extradition on the ground that the Cuban authorities had given insufficient evidence of his alleged "crimes". (Major Diaz Lanz is referred to in item 11 on this page).

In some cases the United States Embassy in Havana has certified extradition papers against certain Cuban refugees, but the Cuban Government has failed to follow up this step. In still other cases Cuban authorities have asked that the United States exercise its "good offices" to detain certain Cubans, but have not taken any step to have them extradited or even indicated the offenses with which they were charged in Cuba.

This record strongly suggests that the Cuban Government has no serious desire to obtain extradition of those whom it has branded as "war criminals", preferring to keep the issue alive as one item in its campaign of anti-United States propaganda.

10. EXPLOSION OF THE MUNITIONS SHIP "LA COUBRE"

The charge: That "a mysterious explosion — an explosion that was too mysterious — took place in the harbor of Havana, an explosion of a ship carrying Belgian weapons to our country, after many efforts made by the United States Government to prevent the Belgian Government from selling weapons to us" — in other words, by clear implication, that the United States Government caused the explosion.

The facts: The explosion of the French vessel La Coubre in Havana harbour on March 4, 1960, while it was discharging ammunition purchased by the Castro Government, resulted in many deaths and injuries and wide-spread damage. The United States Government promptly expressed its condolences to the Government of Cuba over this tragic disaster, the cause of which is unknown to this day.

Within a few hours of the disaster, before any investigation could be carried out, the propaganda agencies of the Cuban Government, including the controlled press and radio, implied that the United States had caused the explosion. No evidence whatever was adduced to support this charge. The following day March 5th, at the public funeral of the victims, Prime Minister Castro directly accused the United States of the responsibility — while in the same breath admitting, "we do not have conclusive evidence". The same charge, only thinly veiled and again completely unsubstantiated, was repeated in a pamphlet entitled Patria o Muerte (Fatherland or Death) issued by the Department of Public Relations of the Cuban foreign ministry. This pamphlet was widely disseminated in Latin America and was distributed by the Cuban representative on the Council of the Organization of American States to all his diplomatic colleagues. Despite repeated United States protests and denials, the charge has now been repeated by the Cuban Prime Minister before the United Nations.

To this day not one piece of evidence, conclusive or otherwise, has been divulged by the Cuban authorities to support this extremely serious charge against the United States. The only possible conclusion is that there is no such evidence, and that the Cuban Government is cynically using this disaster to add fuel to the fire of its propaganda against the United States.

11. CHARGES OF AERIAL BOMBING OF CUBA FROM U.S. TERRITORY

The charge: "A plane manufactured in the United States ... flew over Havana, our capital, dropping pamphlets and a few hand grenades ... The result was more than forty victims, between the grenades dropped and the anti-aircraft fire ... Pirate planes continued to fly over our territory dropping incendiary bombs ... Millions upon millions of pesos were lost in the burning fields of sugar cane ... The American Government was an accomplice in these aerial incursions."

The facts: The United States Government, in endeavoring to prevent unauthorized flights of aircraft from United States soil in the Caribbean area, has imposed upon such flights the most vigorous and elaborate system of controls in its peacetime history. Since there are 75,000 private aircraft in the United States, and 200 airports in Florida alone, the prevention of unauthorized flights is not easy — as Prime Minister Castro and his associates must know very well, having been political exiles in the United States before they came to power in Cuba.

There have been only five unauthorized flights over Cuba concerning which the United States Government possesses any substantial evidence. The Cuban Government has been asked repeatedly to give evidence of other flights so that United States authorities may investigate — but no such evidence has been furnished.

In one of the five known flights, in March 1960, the pilot William Shergalis was, by his own admission, an agent of Fidel Castro — directed to make the flight in order to fabricate evidence of an alleged "United States provocation". Shergalis is now under indictment in the United States District Court of the Southern District of Florida for violating the United States laws applying to agents of a foreign principal and for making an illegal flight.

Another flight, that of Rafael del Pino, on July 25, 1960, is surrounded by circumstances similarly suspicious. Del Pino flew to Cuba in a light, unarmed airplane which he had rented from a private company in Florida. After landing in Cuba, he was attempting to take off when a force of Cuban police opened fire and shot the plane down, wounding Del Pino in the process. The firing took place from ambush and without warning, in circumstances such that the police could not have known the purpose of the flight or the identity of the pilot unless by prior arrangement. The suspicion of prior arrangement is heightened by the fact that Del Pino was a long-time friend of Fidel Castro, knew him at the University of Havana, participated with him in the Bogota riots of 1948, and was with him in Mexico in 1956. Moreover, it is known that Del Pino had been in communication with a member of the Castro family shortly before the flight.

Of the three remaining known flights, the best known is that of Major Pedro Diaz Lanz.

Major Diaz Lanz had fought in the mountains with the Castro revolutionary forces. He had been chief of the Cuban air force under Prime Minister Castro. On June 30, 1959, he broke with the Government of Prime Minister Castro, stating that the Government was under Communist influence and that Communist pressure had forced him out. He thereupon left Cuba.

On October 21, 1959, Major Diaz Lanz eluded the surveillance of United States authorities and made an illegal flight from United States territory over Havana, the Cuban capital. When the United States Government determined the facts on this flight it expressed its regrets and apologies to the Cuban Government. It was in this flight that Prime Minister Castro told the General Assembly that hand grenades were dropped on Havana. The Cuban Government had earlier charged, both in the Security Council and in a pamphlet which was widely distributed, that this plane had dropped bombs and strafed. This charge was false, as the United States demonstrated in the Security Council in July. The converted bomber making this flight had a permanent luggage rack in its bomb bay and had completely sealed gun positions, as revealed by an investigation by United States authorities after it returned to a United States airport. Perhaps this is why the renewed charge, as stated by Prime Minister Castro in his speech to the General Assembly in September, was that the plane had dropped "grenades", not bombs.

In its efforts to establish the facts about the Diaz Lanz flight, the United States Government has had no help from the Cuban Government which has submitted no official information on the subject. The United States possesses no evidence that the plane dropped hand grenades on Havana. A report by the Cuban Government's own police at the time, moreover, attributed the injuries during the incident either to anti-aircraft fire or to grenades or bombs thrown from automobiles by terrorists, not to bombs, strafing or any other objects coming from an airplane.

The foregoing accounts for three of the five known illegal flights.

A fourth illegal flight took place on February 18, 1960. Its apparent purpose was to bomb a sugar mill. The flight failed when the bomb exploded in mid-air, destroying the airplane and killing its occupants. In the case of this flight also, the United States Government offered its regrets and apologies to the Cuban Government — for which it has received no acknowledgment.

The fifth flight, in May 1960, is still under investigation. The United States has asked the Cuban authorities for help in this investigation but has received no reply.

The stream of unsubstantiated charges on this subject by the Cuban authorities caused the United States to propose, at the Seventh Meeting of Foreign Ministers of the American Republics in San Jose in August 1960, that a special committee be created to clarify the facts. The Foreign Ministers approved this proposal but the Government of Cuba has shown no sign of willingness to co-operate with such a committee.

The conclusion is inescapable that the Cuban Government is less interested in preventing these unauthorized flights than it is in keeping the charges alive as a part of its campaign against the United States.

12. ALLEGED PROPAGANDA AND SUBVERSION ON SWAN ISLAND

The charge: That the United States has "taken over" Swan Island, "which belongs to Honduras"; that "There are now American infantrymen there"; that the United States "has set up a very powerful broadcasting station" on the island "which it has placed at the disposal of war criminals … and manoeuvres and training are being carried out on that island to promote subversion in Cuba and to promote the landing of armed forces in our islands".

The facts: The two Swan Islands have been under United States control for almost 100 years. The United States has offered to discuss with Honduras, at an early date, the latter's claim to the islands.

There is a private commercial broadcasting station on the islands, operated by the Gibraltar Steamship Company. The United States Government understands that this station carries programs in Spanish which are heard in Cuba, and that some of its broadcast time has been purchased by Cuban political refugees.

The assertion that manoeuvres and training are being carried out in the Swan Islands with a view to subversion or the landing of armed forces in Cuba is totally false.

13. ALLEGED "RED SMEAR" AGAINST THE GOVERNMENT OF PRIME MINISTER CASTRO

The charge: That United States news agencies told the world that "Cuba was already a communist government, a red peril ninety

miles from the United States, with a government dominated by communists" at a time when the present Cuban Government "had not even had the opportunity of establishing diplomatic and commercial relations with the Soviet Union".

The facts: Unlike the press of a totalitarian country, the press and news services of the United States are free to write and interpret the facts as they see them, without governmental guidance or restraint. It is true that many American newspapermen, even during the early months after the present Government came to power in 1959, reported what they regarded as clear signs of communist influence in the new Government. Far from seeking to "smear" the new Government, however, the Government of the United States — which alone can speak officially for the American people in international affairs — exercised great restraint in commenting publicly on political trends in Cuba.

In fact, on January 26, 1960, over a year after Prime Minister Castro came to power and long after the press reports referred to above, President Eisenhower issued a major restatement of United States policy toward Cuba. In it he reaffirmed the adherence of the United States Government to the policy of non-intervention in the domestic affairs of other countries, including Cuba; he explicitly recognized the right of the Cuban Government and people, in the exercise of their national sovereignty, "to undertake those social, economic and political reforms which, with due regard for their obligations under international law, they may think desirable"; and he expressed the sympathy of the American people for the aspirations of the Cuban people.

Had the United States Government not followed such a policy of restraint, it could have mentioned various developments: the silencing of almost all the anti-Communist forces in Cuba; the consequent flight into exile or many of the leading editors and commentators of the nation; the emergence of the Communist party newspaper Hoy and the increasing influence of its editor, Carlos Rafael Rodriguez, in the governmental machinery of censorship; and the fact that the only political party permitted to function in Cuba is the Communist party.

It is quite true that these developments took place, and were discovered and reported through the free press, long before Prime Minister Castro established formal diplomatic and commercial relations with the Soviet Union. But the point is irrelevant. Diplomatic and commercial relations are not the only means by which outside influence may be exerted.

14. GUANTANAMO: ALLEGED "PRETEXT" FOR AGGRESSION ON CUBA

The charge: That the United States is using the naval base at Guantanamo, Cuba, "as a means of promoting self-aggression, to justify an attack on our country"; that various speculations in the United States about a possible Cuban attack on Guantanamo are published in order "to set the stage for aggression"; that Guantanamo is "pointed at the heart of Cuba and pointed at the heart of the Revolutionary Government of Cuba, in the hands of those who declare themselves enemies of our country, of our revolution and of our people".

The facts: It is not the United States but the Government of Cuba whose responsible officials appear intent on provoking an incident concerning the base at Guantanamo. Prime Minister Castro and his brother Raul Castro have both issued frequent hints and warnings about the possibility that the Cuban Government might reclaim the United States naval base — notwithstanding the legal and binding international agreements which cannot be abrogated except by the mutual consent of both parties.

The idea of a United States threat of aggression against Cuba, whether because of Guantanamo or for any other cause, is a figment of the imaginations of the leaders of the Cuban Government and cannot be substantiated by any action or any statement by the responsible spokesmen of United States foreign policy.

The war of nerves launched against Guantanamo by the Cuban leaders can have no result but to incite Cuban citizens against the United States and against the naval base itself. The personnel and authorities of this base have always enjoyed the best relations with the Cuban people; the base has contributed substantially to the economy of the nation; and it is an important factor in the military security of all the nations of the Western Hemisphere.

The assertion by Prime Minister Castro that the United States authorities who control the Guantanamo base "declare themselves enemies of our country, of our revolution and of our people" is totally false. The command of the Guantanamo naval base has always been, and is still, under orders to stay out of the internal affairs of Cuba. It has done so and will continue to do so. The base is in the hands of the United States, whose Government and people are friends of Cuba, of the Cuban people, and of their just aspirations.

15. UNITED STATES POLICY CONCERNING PUERTO RICO

The charge: That the United States "has destroyed the Puerto Rican nationality"; is destroying Puerto Rico 's "national spirit"; has been destroying Puerto Rico's nationality "for fifty years".

The facts: These assertions can best be answered by quoting two statements. The first statement was made in the General Assembly on November 27, 1953, by the United States Representative, Mr. Lodge, at the time when the United States ceased to report to the Committee on Non-Self-Governing Territories concerning Puerto Rico, which had now attained complete self-government and commonwealth status. It reads:

"I am authorized to say, on behalf of the President, that if at any time the Legislative Assembly of Puerto Rico adopts a resolution in favor of more complete or even absolute independence he will immediately thereafter recommend to Congress that such independence be granted. The President also wishes me to say that in this event he would welcome Puerto Rico's adherence to the Rio Pact and the United Nations Charter."

The second statement is a message by Luis Muñoz Marín, Governor of Puerto Rico, to the President of the General Assembly, dated September 27, 1960, which reads:

"In view of the charges of United States colonialism against Puerto Rico, raised at the General Assembly of the United Nations by the Soviet and Cuban delegations, I have the honor of bringing to your attention the following views of the Commonwealth Government:

"The people of Puerto Rico strongly adhere to the democratic way of life, based on the respect of minority rights, the protection and furtherance of individual freedoms, and the effective exercise of the right to vote in free, unhindered elections. There can be no genuine self-determination unless these conditions are met.

"Puerto Rico has truly and effectively met them and it has freely chosen its present relationship with the United States. The people of Puerto Rico are a self-governing people freely associated to the United States of America on the basis of mutual consent and respect. The policies regarding the cultural and economic development of Puerto Rico are in the hands of the people of Puerto Rico themselves for them to determine according to their best interests.

"The United Nations General Assembly, by Resolution of November 1953, has solemnly recognized that the people of Puerto Rico effectively exercised their right to self-determination in establishing the Commonwealth as an autonomous political entity on a mutually agreed association with the United States. In further regard to the principle of self-determination, the Commonwealth Legislative Assembly has approved this very year a law authorizing another vote on Puerto Rico's status whenever 10 percent of the electors request it.

"More than 13,000 visitors and trainees from all over the world, including thousands from the new states in Africa and Asia now represented at the United Nations, have seen with their own eyes the social and economic achievements of the Commonwealth under free, democratic institutions. As an example of Puerto Rico's great forward strides as a Commonwealth, the rate of growth of the net Commonwealth income in 1959 was 9.4 percent, one of the highest in the entire world.

"The People of Puerto Rico fully support the United Nations as a symbol of a world order, ruled by law and the principle of self-determination, and hope that through the United Nations a militant campaign for peace is developed that would avoid the nuclear extinction of our civilization."

16. CONFINEMENT OF CUBAN DELEGATION TO MANHATTAN

The charge: That the Cuban delegation to the General Assembly was "singled out for … confinement to the island of Manhattan"… and was subjected to "hostility under the pretext of security."

The facts: As host country to the United Nations, the United States is obligated to afford to accredited delegates "any necessary protection to such persons while in transit to or from the Headquarters District". In the case of Prime Minister Castro and his delegation, the United States made extraordinary efforts to fulfill this obligation — efforts made necessary by the fact that the conduct of Prime Minister Castro and his associates, both before and during their visit to New York, created extraordinary difficulties.

For more than a year and a half Prime Minister Castro and his Government have carried on a systematic campaign of defamation against the United States Government in terms which were contrary to known fact and offensive to the American people. In addition, hundreds of Cubans who fled Cuba since the coming to power of Prime Minister Castro have taken up residence in the United States rather than live under the present Cuban Government. Thus, in the interest of Prime Minister Castro's personal safety, and given the heavy demands upon United States security personnel because of the large number of Prime Ministers in the United States, it was necessary to confine his movements to Manhattan. The same decision was made concerning the delegations of the Soviet Union, Hungary, and Albania.

17. CUBAN DIFFICULTIES IN NEW YORK HOTELS

The charge: That notice was given by unnamed persons, presumably United States officials, "to all hotels not to rent rooms to us"; and that, when the Hotel Theresa in Harlem offered to rent rooms to Prime Minister Castro 's party, "an official of the State Department did all in his power to try to stop us from being given rooms in the hotel".

The facts: The United States Government never gave, or caused to be given, notice to any hotel "not to rent rooms" to the Cuban delegation. This is the very reverse of the truth. When the management of the Hotel Shelburne in New York asked the State Department whether he should accept an application for rooms for the Cuban delegation, the Department of State informed him that it hoped he would "accept the request of the Cuban Consul General of New York for accommodations for the Cuban Delegation to the General Assembly of the United Nations". As a result, the management of the Hotel Shelburne agreed to accommodate the Cuban delegation.

Nor was there any attempt by any United States official to prevent the Cuban delegation from moving to the Hotel Theresa. The remoteness of that hotel from the United Nations headquarters placed a greater burden on the already overburdened police whose duty it was to assure the safety of Prime Minister Castro. Nevertheless, to assist Prime Minister Castro, who was at this point at United Nations Headquarters, an immediate security check was undertaken. By 10.30 p.m., September 19th, the United States Mission to the United Nations informed Prime Minister Castro that his party could proceed to the Hotel Theresa. Simultaneously Prime Minister Castro had instructed his own security officers to check the hotel. This investigation was not completed until midnight. The Prime Minister then proceeded under police escort to his new accommodations.

It is also true that a private citizen offered to house the Prime Minister and his party at the Hotel Commodore, only a few blocks from the United Nations, free of charge — an offer which the Cuban delegation rejected.

18. DEATH OF MAGDALENA URDANETA

The charge: That the shooting and subsequent death of a nine-year-old Venezuelan girl, Magdalena Urdaneta, in New York during the Castro visit was "provoked by those who receive support from the systematic campaigns against Cuba and with the connivance of the authorities"; and that "a spokesman from the White

House" in an act of "hypocrisy" made a statement "fixing the guilt on the Cuban delegation".

The facts: On September 21st a large group of Castro supporters assaulted members of a small anti-Castro group while the latter was patronizing a New York City restaurant. During the mêlée, several shots were fired by a pro-Castro combatant, one of which struck Magdalena Urdaneta, a nine-yearold Venezuelan girl, as she sat with her parents having dinner. Miss Urdaneta died shortly afterward.

The following day, the Department of State (not White House) press officer stated that this Venezuelan girl was the innocent victim of an aggressive attack by adherents of the present Cuban Government and that the Department of State wished to express to the parents of Magdalena Urdaneta its deep sympathy and regret over her untimely death.

Francisco Molina, a Cuban national known as "Pancho the Hook", has been identified by a witness as the assailant who fired the shot which took the life of Magdalena Urdaneta. Molina lost his right hand in an industrial accident several years ago and in its place alternately wears a metal hook or flesh colored artificial hand. Molina is known to anti-Castro forces in the New York City area as the head of a group of Castro followers intimidating anti-Castro people.

Assistance was requested of the Federal Bureau of Investigation when it appeared that Molina had fled the State of New York to avoid prosecution for the murder of the Venezuelan girl. The Federal Bureau of Investigation has distributed 140,000 "wanted" flyers on Molina.

19. ALLEGED REFUSAL OF THE UNITED STATES TO RENEGOTIATE WITH CUBA

The charge: That "the Government of Cuba has always been ready to discuss its problems with the Government of the United States, but the Government of the United States has not been ready to discuss these problems with Cuba"; that "the Government of the United States does not deign to discuss matters with the small country of Cuba on the Cuban problems".

The facts: Since the advent of the Government of Prime Minister Castro on January 1, 1959 the United States has officially expressed a willingness to negotiate matters at issue between Cuba and the United States on more than twenty-five separate occasions.

This is the fourth time that the present Government of Cuba has alleged to a responsible international body that the Government of the United States refused to negotiate with the Government of Cuba. Prime Minister Castro 's reference to the Cuban Government's willingness to negotiate presumably relates to the proposal of the Government of Cuba last February to name a commission to conduct negotiations in Washington. Secretary Herter described the actual circumstances of this case at the meeting of Foreign Ministers at San José, Costa Rica on August 26, 1960 in the following words:

"The Cuban Foreign Minister has asserted that the United States Government refused to negotiate with the revolutionary Government of Cuba when, last February, it decided to name a commission to conduct negotiations in Washington. I need not point out that the Government of Cuba, in its proposal, suggested that the Government of the United States should bind both the executive and the Congress to refrain from any action whatever which the Government of Cuba might consider to affect its interests while leaving the Government of Cuba free to negotiate or procrastinate as it chose. It is appropriate to ask, however, why the Government of Cuba deliberately refrained from quoting my government's reply in its entirety. I say deliberately refrained because, Mr. Chairman, this is the third time that the Government of Cuba has trumpeted this note before responsible international bodies to serve its own purpose in completely distorting the position of the U.S. Government in this matter. The fact is that the part of the United States note which Minister Roa has again deleted from his presentation to this body went on to affirm the friendship between the Cuban and American peoples and to welcome any proposals which the Cuban Government might wish to make, the subjects which might be discussed, as well as the manner and the place in which negotiations might be conducted. It may be well to recall to the Foreign

Minister of Cuba the full text of the closing paragraph of the note sent on February 29, 1960, by the U.S. Ambassador in Cuba which he has again found it so convenient to omit:

"'The Government of the United States for its part firmly intends to continue by its conduct and through its utterances to reaffirm the spirit of fraternal friendship which, as Your Excellency so well stated, has bound and does bind our two peoples, and which the United States Government believes is earnestly cherished by them. Prior to the initiation of negotiations and through normal diplomatic channels the United States Government would wish to explore with the Government of Cuba the subjects to be discussed and the manner and place in which negotiations might be conducted. Accordingly, I would welcome, for transmittal to my government, any proposals which Your Excellency might care to submit in these respects.'

"To this date, despite the several subsequent efforts to elicit a reply from the Government of Cuba, none has been forthcoming. When, shortly after the note referred to above was delivered, the revolutionary Government of Cuba designated Dr. José Miró Cardona, who preceded Dr. Castro as Prime Minister of the revolutionary Government, as its Ambassador to Washington, there was high expectation that he would carry forward the negotiations. He never arrived. After months of waiting, he was forced to seek asylum in the Argentine Embassy in Havana after protesting the increasing role of communism in Cuba."

Dr. José Miró Cardona, incidentally, is still in the Argentine Embassy in Havana.

CONCLUSION

The relationship between Cuba and the United States is no mere accident of geography and trade. It is part of our mutual history. Tear the history of either country from that of the other, and there would be a gap making much of the rest inexplicable. It is our belief that such a wrench will never come. Neither the people of the United States nor — we are convinced — the Cuban people would consider it.

Like all the other American Republics, Cuba and the United States began as colonies. Our first English settlement was in Virginia in 1607 and our independence came 169 years later in 1776. Cuba, discovered by Columbus on his second voyage and settled approximately 100 years before Jamestown, was a colony from 1510 to 1898, a period of 388 years.

Both Cuba and the United States were born of revolutions dedicated to the common purpose of independence and freedom. In the United States we are proud to remember that the heart of our people went out to Cuba in the Cuban struggle for liberty. Although we are a peaceful people, we declared war in Cuba's behalf, and the blood of our young men was shed with that of Cuban patriots for Cuban independence.

The great apostle of American liberty was Thomas Jefferson. The great Cuban apostle of liberty was José Martí, a man whose name and ideals are respected in the United States.

On the centenary of Martí's birth the Soviet Union tried to indicate some spiritual tie between Martí and communism. No such tie exists, nor could exist. Martí's opinion of Marxism was expressed in his famous letter to Fermin Valdez Domingues. The Marxian concept has two basic dangers, he said: "that of extraneous, confused, and incomplete interpretations, and that of the pride and dissimulated violence of ambitious men, who in order to raise themselves in the world begin by pretending — in order to have shoulders of other men on which to stand — to be impassioned defenders of the helpless."

Martí perceived correctly the dangers of communist imperialism under a pretense of defending and succoring the oppressed. He perceived correctly that the strength of the Western Hemisphere depends on the fraternal unity of its people. He perceived correctly that the true goal and glory of mankind is brotherhood, peace, dignity; and that unity is the key to strength and progress.

Prime Minister Castro has accused the United States of holding back Cuban development as a free nation. The facts are to the contrary. Cuba has not only consistently received higher prices from the

United States for sugar than any other supplier but has also been a partner with the United States in a mutually preferential tariff with special low import duty rates. In per capita gross national product Cuba ranks third in Latin America. It is quite true that in the Republic of Cuba these developments were not matched, as the United States hoped they would be, by corresponding progress in eliminating corruption in public life, and achieving greater social justice and a more equitable distribution of the national income, in guaranteeing free elections, and ensuring government of, by, and for the people — progress which only the Cuban people could make for themselves.

When Prime Minister Castro came to power in January 1959, with promises to his people seemingly made in all sincerity, the United States hoped he would perfect the revolution by needed internal reforms. The United States tried to show its understanding and sympathy for his stated aims: honest and efficient government, the perfection of democratic processes, and economic development leading to higher living standards and to full employment. On June 11 and October 12, 1959, we expressed officially to the Cuban Government our full support for soundly conceived programmes for rural development. We particularly endorsed its stated desire to do something for land reform.

Not even the shock of the many executions in the first month following the establishment of the revolutionary government, nor the sharp attacks on the United States Government by high officials, could dampen the friendly feeling with which Prime Minister Castro was greeted when he came to the United States in April of 1959. There was a genuine reluctance to believe that Cuba, a country for which the people of the United States have long had a special affection, could be embarked on an unfriendly course.

On January 26, 1960, President Eisenhower issued a major restatement of American policy toward Cuba, reaffirming the adherence of the United States Government to a policy of non-intervention in the domestic affairs of other countries, including Cuba, and explicitly recognizing the right of the Cuban Government and people, in the exercise of their national sovereignty, "to undertake those social, economic and political reforms which, with due regard to their obligations under international law, they may think desirable", and expressing sympathy for the aspirations of the Cuban people.

Unfortunately, these policies of the United States were not reciprocated. The present Government of Cuba has deliberately and consciously sought to exacerbate relations with the United States. For openly announced political reasons Cuba's imports from the United States have been reduced to less than one-half of the level of two years ago. Property is not expropriated, but confiscated without payment, to serve political rather than social ends.

Growing intervention in Cuban affairs by the Soviet Union and Communist China is welcomed by the Government of Cuba. The present Cuban Government itself seeks to intervene in internal affairs of other American States and to undermine the inter-American system.

The present Cuban Government claims to speak for the Cuban people but denies them the right to choose their own spokesman in free elections. It claims to believe in democracy, yet only the Communist party is permitted to function. It speaks of the rights of man, but Cuban jails are crowded with thousands of political prisoners.

It boasts of freedom or expression in Cuba, yet the editors of the great Cuban papers are all in exile while every expression of opposition to the policies of the Government, or to communism, is suppressed as counter-revolutionary. It interferes with the free exercise of religion. It affirms the independence of the judiciary but the right of a fair and impartial trial is denied those who differ with the government in power.

We regret that these things are true, but they are true. The people and Government of the United States, who are friends of the Republic of Cuba, still look to see it again become what the great son Martí declared he would have it be: "A democratic and cultured people zealously aware of her own rights and the rights of others." ❏

—Circulated October 13, 1960.

THE
HASHEESH
EATER

By
FITZHUGH
LUDLOW

C O N T E N T S.

PREFACE.

I LIKE Prefaces as little as my readers can. If this so proverbially unnoticed part of the book catch any eye, the glance that it gives will of course travel no farther to find my apology for making this preface a short one. There is but one thought for which I wish to find place here. I am deeply aware that, if the succeeding pages are read at all, it will be by those who have already learned to love De Quincey. Not that I dare for a moment to compare the manner of my narrative with that most wondrous, most inspired Dreamer's; but in the experience of his life and my own there is a single common characteristic which happens to be the very one for whose sake men open any such book. The path of De Quincey led beyond all the boundaries of the ordinary life into a world of intense lights and shadows—a realm in which all the range of average thought found its conditions surpassed, if not violated. My own career, however far its recital may fall short of the Opium Eater's, and notwithstanding it was not coincident and but seldom parallel with his, still ran through lands as glorious, as unfrequented, as weird as his own, and takes those who would follow it out of the trodden highways of mind. In the most candid and indulgent reader who has come to my story from the perusal of the Confessions, I foresee that there will exist an inevitable tendency to compare the two, to seek resemblances, and perhaps, if such be found, to ascribe them to my at least unconscious imitation of the great, the elder author. How much to my disparagement this would be, my natural desire for the success of this book makes unpleasant to represent even to myself.

If it be possible to forestall such a state of things, let me aim at it by a few brief representations of the manner in which this work has been written.

Frankly do I say that I admire De Quincey to such a degree that, were not imitation base and he imitable, I know no master of style in whose footsteps I should more earnestly seek to tread; but, in the first place, as this book asserts, it is a resumé of experiences which, so far from being fiction, have received at my hands a delineation unsatisfactory to myself from its very inadequacy. The fact of my speaking truths, so far as they can be spoken, out of my actual memory, must shield me, if the assertion be received by any but one who has tasted my cup of Awakening, from the imputation of being a copyist of incidents.

In the second place, to copy *style*, study, care, and frequent references to the proposed model are indispensable. Very well; not one of the pages which make this book has ever been rewritten. It has been printed from the first draft, and that, through necessities of other occupation, illness, and care, compelled to be thrown off, though on its author's part unwillingly, currente calamo. Moreover, out of particular jealousy against the risk of burlesquing the inimitable, I have refrained from looking at the Confessions from the beginning to the end of my undertaking.

My memory, however, tells me that occasionally there are actual resemblances both in incident and method. As an incident-resemblance, I instance the perception, in both experiences, of the inerasible character of the mind's memorial inscriptions—as De Quincey grandly has it—the Palimpset characteristic of memory. Acknowledging the resemblance, I only say that we both saw the same thing. The state of insight which he attained through opium, I reached by the way of hasheesh. Almost through the very same symbols as De Quincey, a hasheesh-maenad friend of mine also saw it, as this book relates, and the vision is accessible to all of the same temperament and degree of exaltation. For a place, New York for instance, a stranger accounts, not by saying that any one of the many who testify to its existence copied from another, but by acknowledging "there is such a place." So do I account for the fact by saying "there is such a fact."

As a resemblance in method, by which I mean mechanical arrangement, I am aware only of this, viz., that I divide my narrative into use and abandonment of hasheesh, and speculations upon the phenomena after abandonment, which latter, for the sake of anticipating the change, I say might perhaps be compared as to its order with the Suspiria; but the most perfect Zoilus among hypercritics would be aware that in this arrangement I follow Nature, who begins, goes on, and finishes, and reflects the past in her progress, so that I should seem no copyist on that score.

But, at any rate, if influenced by the memory of the great Visionary's method in any sense (and it is true that I might have made my course more dissimilar by neglecting the order of time), I feel that the influence must necessarily have been beneficial to my own efforts.

As the bard who would sing of heroes follows the blind old harper of Ionia along that immortal corridor of resounding song which first made Greece imperishable, and tells his battles in the Epic, not the Elegy, so must every man hereafter, who opens the mysteries of that great soul within him, speak, so far as he can, down the channels through which Thomas de Quincey has spoken, nor out of vain perversity refuse to use a passage which the one grand pioneer has made free to all.

If in any way, therefore, except servilely, I seem to have followed De Quincey, I am proud of it. If there be any man who does not feel the grace which the mantle of that true poet's influence confers upon every thinker and scholar who loves truth, beauty, and the music of the English tongue, I ask that he will transfer unto me his share thereof, and at once the Preface and the Prayer of

THE HASHEESH EATER, THE SON OF PYTHAGORAS, are ended.

INTRODUCTION.

THE singular energy and scope of imagination which characterize all Oriental tales, and especially that great typical representative of the species, the Arabian Nights, were my ceaseless marvel from earliest childhood. The book of Arabian and Turkish story has very few thoughtful readers among the nations of the West, who can rest contented with admiring its bold flights into unknown regions of imagery, and close the mystic pages that have enchanted them without an inquiry as to the influences which have turned the human mind into such rare channels of thought. Sooner or later comes the question of the producing causes, and it is in the power of few—very few of us—to answer that question aright.

We try to imitate Eastern narrative, but in vain. Our minds can find no clew to its strange, untrodden by-ways of speculation; our highest soarings are still in an atmosphere which feels heavy with the reek and damp of ordinary life. We fail to account for those storm-wrapped peaks of sublimity which hover over the path of Oriental story, or those beauties which, like rivers of Paradise, make music beside it. We are all of us taught to say, "The children of the East live under a sunnier sky than their Western brethren; they are the repositors of centuries of tradition; their semi-civilized imagination is unbound by the fetters of logic and the schools." But the Ionians once answered all these conditions, yet Homer sang no Eblis, no superhuman journey on the wings of genii through infinitudes of rosy ether. At one period of their history, France, Germany, and England abounded in all the characteristics of the untutored Old-world mind, yet when did an echo of Oriental music ring from the lute of minstrel, minnesinger, or trouvére? The difference can not be accounted for by climate, religion, or manners. It is not the supernatural in Arabian story which is inexplicable, but the peculiar phase of the supernatural both in beauty and terror.

I say inexplicable, because to me, in common with all around me, it bore this character for years. In later days, I believe, and now with all due modesty assert, I unlocked the secret, not by a hypothesis, not by processes of reasoning, but by journeying through those self-same fields of weird experience which are dinted by the sandals of the glorious old dreamers of the East. Standing on the same mounts of vision where they stood, listening to the same gurgling melody that broke from their enchanted fountains, yes, plunging into their rayless caverns of sorcery, and imprisoned with their genie in the unutterable silence of the fathomless sea, have I dearly bought the right to come to men with the chart of my wanderings in my hands, and unfold to them the foundations of the fabric of Oriental story.

The secret lies in the use of hasheesh. A very few words will suffice to tell what hasheesh is. In northern latitudes the hemp plant (Cannabis Sativa) grows almost entirely to fibre, becoming, in virtue of this quality, the great resource for mats and cordage. Under a southern sun this same plant loses its fibrous texture, but secretes, in quantities equal to one third of its bulk, an opaque and greenish resin. Between the northern and the southern hemp there is no difference, except the effect of diversity of climate upon the same vegetable essence; yet naturalists, misled by the much greater extent of gummy secretion in the latter, have distinguished it from its brother of the colder soil by the name Cannabis Indica. The resin of the Cannabis Indica is hasheesh. From time immemorial it has been known among all the nations of the East as possessing powerful stimulant and narcotic properties; throughout Turkey, Persia, Nepaul, and India it is used at this day among all classes of society as an habitual indulgence. The forms in which it is employed are various. Sometimes it appears in the state in which it exudes from the mature stalk, as a crude resin; sometimes it is manufactured into a conserve with clarified butter, honey, and spices; sometimes a decoction is made of the flowering tops in water or arrack. Under either of these forms the method of administration is by swallowing. Again, the dried plant is smoked in pipes or chewed, as tobacco among ourselves.

Used in whatever preparation, hasheesh is characterized by the most remarkable phenomena, both physical and spiritual. A series of experiments made with it by men of eminent attainments in the medical profession, principally at Calcutta, and during the last ten years, prove it to be capable of inducing all the ordinary symptoms of catalepsy, or even of trance.

However, from the fact of its so extensive daily use as a pleasurable stimulus in the countries where experiments with it have been made, it has doubtless lost interest in the field of scientific research, and has come to be regarded as only one more means among the multitude which mankind in all latitudes are seeking for the production of a sensual intoxication. Now and then a traveler, passing by the bazar where it was exposed for sale, moved by curiosity, has bought some form of the hemp, and made the trial of its effects upon himself; but the results of the experiment were dignified with no further notice than a page or a chapter in the note-book of his journeyings, and the hasheesh phenomena, with an exclamation of wonder, were thenceforward dismissed from his own and the public mind. Very few even of the permanently domesticated foreign residents in the countries of the East have ever adopted this indulgence as a habit, and of those few I am not aware of any who have communicated their experience to the world, or treated it as a subject possessing scientific interest.

My own personal acquaintance with this drug, covering as it did a considerable extent of time, and almost every possible variety of phenomena, both physical and psychological, proper to its operation, not only empowers, but for a long time has been impelling me to give it a publicity which may bring it in contact with a larger number of minds interested in such researches than it could otherwise hope to meet. As a key to some of the most singular manifestations of the Oriental mind, as a narrative interesting to the attentive student of the human soul and body, and the mysterious network of interacting influences which connect them, I therefore venture to present this experience to the investigation of general readers, accompanying it with the sincere disavowal of all fiction in my story, and the assurance that whatever traits of the marvelous may appear in its gradual development are inherent in the truth as I shall simply delineate it. I am aware that, without this disavowal, much—nay, even most that I shall say, will be taken "cum grano salis." I desire it, therefore, to be distinctly understood at the outset that my narrative is one of unexaggerated fact, its occurrences being recorded precisely as they impressed themselves upon me, without one additional stroke of the pencil of an after-fancy thrown in to heighten the tone or harmonize the effect. Whatever of the wonderful may appear in these pages belongs to the subject and not to the manner.

The progress of my narration will be in the order of time. I shall begin with my first experiment of the use of hasheesh, an experiment made simply from the promptings of curiosity; it will then be my endeavor to detail the gradual change of my motive for its employment from the desire of research to the fascinated longing for its weird and immeasurable ecstasy; I shall relate how that ecstasy by degrees became daily more and more flecked with shadows of as immeasurable pain, but still, in this dual existence, assumed a character increasingly apocalyptic of utterly unpreconceived provinces of mental action. In the next succeeding stage of my experience, torture, save at rare intervals, will have swallowed up happiness altogether, without abating in the least the fascination of the habit. In the next and final one will be beheld my instantaneous abandonment of the indulgence, the cause which led to it, and the discipline of suffering which attended the self-denial.

The aim of this relation is not merely aesthetic nor scientific: though throughout it there be no stopping to moralize, it is my earnest desire that it may teem with suggestions of a lesson without which humanity can learn nothing in the schools. It is this: the soul withers and sinks from its growth toward the true end of its being beneath the dominance of any sensual indulgence. The chain of its bondage may for a long time continue to be golden —many a day may pass before the fetters gall—yet all the while there is going on a slow and insidious consumption of its native strength, and when at last captivity becomes a pain, it may awake to discover in inconceivable terror that the very forces of disenthralment have perished out of its reach.

THE HASHEESH EATER.

I.

The Night Entrance.

ABOUT the shop of my friend Anderson the apothecary there always existed a peculiar fascination, which early marked it out as my favorite lounging-place. In the very atmosphere of the establishment, loaded as it was with a composite smell of all things curative and preventive, there was an aromatic invitation to scientific musing, which could not have met with a readier acceptance had it spoken in the breath of frankincense. The very gallipots grew gradually to possess a charm for me as they sat calmly ranged upon their oaken shelves, looking like a convention of unostentatious philanthropists, whose silent bosoms teemed with every variety of renovation for the human race. A little sanctum at the inner end of the shop, walled off with red curtains from the profane gaze of the unsanative, contained two chairs for the doctor and myself, and a library where all the masters of physic were grouped, through their sheep and paper representatives, in more friendliness of contact than has ever been known to characterize a consultation of like spirits under any other circumstances. Within the limits of four square feet, Pereira and Christison condensed all their stores of wisdom and research, and Dunglison and Brathwaite sat cheek by jowl beside them. There stood the Dispensatory, with the air of a business-like office, wherein all the specifics of the materia medica had been brought together for a scientific conversazione, but, becoming enamored of each other's society, had resolved to stay, overcrowded though they might be, and make an indefinite sitting of it. In a modest niche, set apart like a vestibule from the apartments of the medical gentlemen, lay a shallow case, which disclosed, on the lifting of a cover, the neatly-ordered rank of tweezers, probe, and lancet, which constituted my friend's claim to the confidence of the plethoric community; for, although unblessed with metropolitan fame, he was still no

"Cromwell guiltless of his country's blood."

Here many an hour have I sat buried in the statistics of human life or the history of the make-shifts for its preservation. Here the details of surgical or medical experiment have held me in as complete engrossment as the positions and crises of romance; and here especially, with a disregard to my own safety which would have done credit to Quintus Curtius, have I made upon myself the trial of the effects of every strange drug and chemical which the laboratory could produce. Now with the chloroform bottle beneath my nose have I set myself careering upon the wings of a thrilling and accelerating life, until I had just enough power remaining to restore the liquid to its place upon the shelf, and sink back into the enjoyment of the delicious apathy which lasted through the few succeeding moments. Now ether was substituted for chloroform, and the difference of their phenomena noted, and now some other exhilarant, in the form of an opiate or stimulant, was the instrument of my experiments, until I had run through the whole gamut of queer agents within my reach.

In all these experiences research and not indulgence was my object, so that I never became the victim of any habit in the prosecution of my headlong investigations. When the circuit of all the accessible tests was completed, I ceased experimenting, and sat down like a pharmaceutical Alexander, with no more drug-worlds to conquer.

One morning, in the spring of 185-, I dropped in upon the doctor for my accustomed lounge.

"Have you seen," said he, "my new acquisitions?"

I looked toward the shelves in the direction of which he pointed, and saw, added since my last visit, a row of comely pasteboard cylinders inclosing vials of the various extracts prepared by Tilden & Co. Arranged in order according to their size, they confronted me, as pretty a little rank of medicinal sharpshooters as could gratify the eye of an amateur. I approached the shelves, that I might take them in review.

A rapid glance showed most of them to be old acquaintances. "Conium, taraxacum, rhubarb—ha! what is this? Cannabis Indica?"

"That," answered the doctor, looking with a parental fondness upon his new treasure, "is a preparation of the East Indian hemp, a powerful agent in cases of lock-jaw." On the strength of this introduction, I took down the little archer, and, removing his outer verdant coat, began the further prosecution of his acquaintance. To pull out a broad and shallow cork was the work of an instant, and it revealed to me an olive-brown extract, of the consistency of pitch, and a decided aromatic odor. Drawing out a small portion upon the point of my pen-knife, I was just going to put it to my tongue, when "Hold on!" cried the doctor; "do you want to kill yourself? That stuff is deadly poison." "Indeed!" I replied; "no, I can not say that I have any settled determination of that kind"; and with that I replaced the cork, and restored the extract, with all its appurtenances, to the shelf.

The remainder of my morning's visit in the sanctum was spent in consulting the Dispensatory under the title "Canabis Indica." The sum of my discoveries there may be found, with much additional information, in that invaluable popular work, Johnston's Chemistry of Common Life. This being universally accessible, I will allude no further to the result of that morning's researches than to mention the three following conclusions to which I came.

First, the doctor was both right and wrong; right, inasmuch as a sufficiently large dose of the drug, if it could be retained in the stomach, would produce death, like any other narcotic, and the ultimate effect of its habitual use had always proved highly injurious to mind and body; wrong, since moderate doses of it were never immediately deadly, and many millions of people daily employed it as an indulgence similarly to opium. Second, it was the hasheesh referred to by Eastern travelers, and the subject of a most graphic chapter from the pen of Bayard Taylor, which months before had moved me powerfully to curiosity and admiration. Third, I would add it to the list of my further experiments.

In pursuance of this last determination, I waited till my friend was out of sight, that I might not terrify him by that which he considered a suicidal venture, and then quietly uncapping my little archer a second time, removed from his store of offensive armor a pill sufficient to balance the ten grain weight of the sanctorial scales. This, upon the authority of Pereira and the Dispensatory, I swallowed without a tremor as to the danger of the result.

Making all due allowance for the fact that I had not taken my hasheesh bolus fasting, I ought to experience its effects within the next four hours. That time elapsed without bringing the shadow of a phenomenon. It was plain that my dose had been insufficient.

For the sake of observing the most conservative prudence, I suffered several days to go by without a repetition of the experiment, and then, keeping the matter equally secret, I administered to myself a pill of fifteen grains. This second was equally ineffectual with the first.

Gradually, by five grains at a time, I increased the dose to thirty grains, which I took one evening half an hour after tea. I had now almost come to the conclusion that I was absolutely unsusceptible of the hasheesh influence. Without any expectation that this last experiment would be more successful than the former ones, and indeed with no realization of the manner in which the drug affected those who did make the experiment successfully, I went to pass the evening at the house of an intimate friend. In music and conversation the time passed pleasantly. The clock struck ten, reminding me that three hours had elapsed since the dose was taken, and as yet not an unusual symptom had appeared. I was provoked to think that this trial was as fruitless as its predecessors.

Ha! what means this sudden thrill? A shock, as of some unimagined vital force, shoots without warning through my entire frame, leaping to my fingers' ends, piercing my brain, startling me till I almost spring from my chair.

I could not doubt it. I was in the power of the hasheesh influence. My first emotion was one of uncontrollable terror—a sense of getting something which I had not bargained for. That moment I would have given all I had or hoped to have to be as I was three hours before.

No pain any where—not a twinge in any fibre—yet a cloud of unutterable strangeness was settling upon me, and wrapping me impenetrably in from all that was natural or familiar. Endeared faces, well known to me of old, surrounded me, yet they were not with me in my loneliness. I had entered upon a tremendous life which they could not share. If the disembodied ever return to hover over the hearth-stone which once had a seat for them, they look upon their friends as I then looked upon mine. A nearness of place, with an infinite distance of state, a connection which had no possible sympathies for the wants of that hour of revelation, an isolation none the less perfect for seeming companionship.

Still I spoke; a question was put to me, and I answered it; I even laughed at a bon mot. Yet it was not my voice which spoke; perhaps one which I once had far away in another time and another place. For a while I knew nothing that was going on externally, and then the remembrance of the last remark which had been made returned slowly and indistinctly, as some trait of a dream will return after many days, puzzling us to say where we have been conscious of it before.

A fitful wind all the evening had been sighing down the chimney; it now grew into the steady hum of a vast wheel in accelerating motion. For a while this hum seemed to resound through all space. I was stunned by it—I was absorbed in it. Slowly the revolution of the wheel came to a stop, and its monotonous din was changed for the reverberating peal of a grand cathedral organ. The ebb and flow of its inconceivably solemn tone filled me with a grief that was more than human. I sympathized with the dirge-like cadence as spirit sympathizes with spirit. And then, in the full conviction that all I heard and felt was real, I looked out of my isolation to see the effect of the music on my friends. Ah! we were in separate worlds indeed. Not a trace of appreciation on any face.

Perhaps I was acting strangely. Suddenly a pair of busy hands, which had been running neck and neck all the evening with a nimble little crochet needle over a race-ground of pink and blue silk, stopped at their goal, and their owner looked at me steadfastly. Ah! I was found out—I had betrayed myself. In terror I waited, expecting every instant to hear the word "hasheesh." No, the lady only asked me some question connected with the previous conversation. As mechanically as an automation I began to reply. As I heard once more the alien and unreal tones of my own voice, I became convinced that it was some one else who spoke, and in another world. I sat and listened; still the voice kept speaking. Now for the first time I experienced that vast change which hasheesh makes in all measurements of time. The first word of the reply occupied a period sufficient for the action of a drama; the last left me in complete ignorance of any point far enough back in the past to date the commencement of the sentence. Its enunciation might have occupied years. I was not in the same life which had held me when I heard it begun.

And now, with time, space expanded also. At my friend's house one particular arm-chair was always reserved for me. I was sitting in it at a distance of hardly three feet from the centre-table around which the members of the family were grouped. Rapidly that distance widened. The whole atmosphere seemed ductile, and spun endlessly out into great spaces surrounding me on every side. We were in a vast hall, of which my friends and I occupied opposite extremities. The ceiling and the walls ran upward with a gliding motion, as if vivified by a sudden force of resistless growth.

Oh! I could not bear it. I should soon be left alone in the midst of an infinity of space. And now more and more every moment increased the conviction that I was watched. I did not know then, as I learned afterward, that suspicion of all earthly things and persons was the characteristic of the hasheesh delirium.

In the midst of my complicated hallucination, I could perceive that I had a dual existence. One portion of me was whirled unresistingly along the track of this tremendous experience, the other sat looking down from a height upon its double, observing, reasoning, and serenely weighing all the phenomena. This calmer being suffered with the other by sympathy, but did not lose its self-possession. Presently it warned me that I must go home, lest the growing effect of the hasheesh should incite me to some act which might frighten my friends. I acknowledged the force of this remark very much as if it had been made by another person, and rose to take my leave. I advanced toward the centre-table. With every step its distance increased. I nerved myself as for a long pedestrian journey. Still the lights, the faces, the furniture receded. At last, almost unconsciously, I reached them. It would be tedious to attempt to convey the idea of the time which my leave-taking consumed, and the attempt, at least with all minds that have not passed through the same experience, would be as impossible as tedious. At last I was in the street.

Beyond me the view stretched endlessly away. It was an unconverging vista, whose nearest lamps seemed separated from me by leagues. I was doomed to pass through a merciless stretch of space. A soul just disenthralled, setting out for his flight beyond the farthest visible star, could not be more overwhelmed with his newly-acquired conception of the sublimity of distance than I was at that moment. Solemnly I began my infinite journey.

Before long I walked in entire unconsciousness of all around me. I dwelt in a marvelous inner world. I existed by turns in different places and various states of being. Now I swept my gondola through the moonlit lagoons of Venice. Now Alp on Alp towered above my view, and the glory of the coming sun flashed purple light upon the topmost icy pinnacle. Now in the primeval silence of some unexplored tropical forest I spread my feathery leaves, a giant fern, and swayed and nodded in the spice-gales over a river whose waves at once sent up clouds of music and perfume. My soul changed to a vegetable essence, thrilled with a strange and unimagined ecstasy. The palace of Al Haroun could not have brought me back to humanity.

I will not detail all the transmutations of that walk. Ever and anon I returned from my dreams into consciousness, as some well-known house seemed to leap out into my path, awaking me with a shock. The whole way homeward was a series of such awakings and relapses into abstraction and delirium until I reached the corner of the street in which I lived.

Here a new phenomenon manifested itself. I had just awaked for perhaps the twentieth time, and my eyes were wide open. I recognized all surrounding objects, and began calculating the distance home. Suddenly, out of a blank wall at my side a muffled figure stepped into the path before me. His hair, white as snow, hung in tangled elf-locks on his shoulders, where he carried also a heavy burden, like unto the well-filled sack of sins which Bunyan places on the back of his pilgrim. Not liking his manner, I stepped aside, intending to pass around him and go on my way. This change of our relative position allowed the blaze of a neighboring street-lamp to fall full on his face, which had hitherto been totally obscured. Horror unspeakable! I shall never, till the day I die, forget that face. Every lineament was stamped with the records of a life black with damning crime; it glared upon me with a ferocious wickedness and a stony despair which only he may feel who is entering on the retribution of the unpardonable sin. He might have sat to a demon painter as the ideal of Shelley's Cenci. I seemed to grow blasphemous in looking at him, and, in an agony of fear, began to run away. He detained me with a bony hand, which pierced my wrist like talons, and, slowly taking down the burden from his own shoulders, laid it upon mine. I threw it off and pushed him away. Silently he returned and restored the weight. Again I repulsed him, this time crying out, "Man, what do you mean?" In a voice which impressed me with the sense of wickedness as his face had done, he replied, "You shall bear my burden with me," and a third time laid it on my shoulders. For the last time I hurled it aside, and, with all my force, dashed him from me. He reeled backward and fell, and before he could recover his disadvantage I had put a long distance between us.

Through the excitement of my struggle with this phantasm the effects of the hasheesh had increased mightily. I was bursting with an uncontrollable life; I strode with the thews of a giant. Hotter and faster came my breath; I seemed to pant like some tremendous engine. An electric energy whirled me resistlessly onward; I feared for myself lest it should burst its fleshly walls; and glance on, leaving a wrecked frame-work behind it.

At last I entered my own house. During my absence a family connection had arrived from abroad, and stood ready to receive my greeting. Partly restored to consciousness by the naturalness of home-faces and the powerful light of a chandelier which shed its blaze through the room, I saw the necessity of vigilance against betraying my condition, and with an intense effort suppressing all I felt, I approached my friend, and said all that is usual on such occasions. Yet recent as I was from my conflict with the supernatural, I cast a stealthy look about me, that I might learn from the faces of the others if, after all, I was shaking hands with a phantom, and making inquiries about the health of a family of hallucinations. Growing assured as I perceived no symptoms of astonishment, I finished the salutation and sat down.

It soon required all my resolution to keep the secret which I had determined to hold inviolable. My sensations began to be terrific— not from any pain that I felt, but from the tremendous mystery of all around me and within me. By an appalling introversion, all the operations of vitality which, in our ordinary state, go on unconsciously, came vividly into my experience. Through every thinnest corporeal tissue and minutest vein I could trace the circulation of the blood along each inch of its progress. I knew when every valve opened and when it shut; every sense was preternaturally awakened; the room was full of a great glory. The beating of my heart was so clearly audible that I wondered to find it unnoticed by those who were sitting by my side. Lo, now, that heart became a great fountain, whose jet played upward with loud vibrations, and, striking upon the roof of my skull as on a gigantic dome, fell back with a splash and echo into its reservoir. Faster and faster came the pulsations, until at last I heard them no more, and the stream became one continuously pouring flood, whose roar resounded through all my frame. I gave myself up for lost, since judgment, which still sat unimpaired above my perverted senses, argued that congestion must take place in a few moments, and close the drama with my death. But my clutch would not yet relax from hope. The thought struck me, Might not this rapidity of circulation be, after all, imaginary? I determined to find out.

Going to my own room, I took out my watch, and placed my hand upon my heart. The very effort which I made to ascertain the reality gradually brought perception back to its natural state. In the intensity of my observations, I began to perceive that the circulation was not as rapid as I had thought. From a pulseless flow it gradually came to be apprehended as a hurrying succession of intense throbs, then less swift and less intense, till finally, on comparing it with the second-hand, I found that about 90 a minute was its average rapidity. Greatly comforted, I desisted from the experiment. Almost instantly the hallucination returned. Again I dreaded apoplexy, congestion, hemorrhage, a multiplicity of nameless deaths, and drew my picture as I might be found on the morrow, stark and cold, by those whose agony

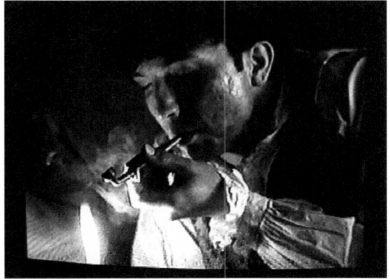

would be redoubled by the mystery of my end. I reasoned with myself; I bathed my forehead—it did no good. There was one resource left: I would go to a physician.

With this resolve, I left my room and went to the head of the staircase. The family had all retired for the night, and the gas was turned off from the burner in the hall below. I looked down the stairs: the depth was fathomless; it was a journey of years to reach the bottom! The dim light of the sky shone through the narrow panes at the sides of the front door, and seemed a demon-lamp in the middle darkness of the abyss. I never could get down! I sat me down despairingly upon the topmost step.

Suddenly a sublime thought possessed me. If the distance be infinite, I am immortal. It shall be tried. I commenced the descent, wearily, wearily down through my league-long, year-long journey. To record my impressions in that journey would be to repeat what I have said of the time of hasheesh. Now stopping to rest as a traveler would turn aside at a wayside inn, now toiling down through the lonely darkness, I came by-and-by to the end, and passed out into the street.

II.

Under The Shadow Of Esculapius.

ON reaching the porch of the physician's house, I rang the bell, but immediately forgot whom to ask for. No wonder; I was on the steps of a palace in Milan—no (and I laughed at myself for the blunder), I was on the staircase of the Tower of London. So I should not be puzzled through my ignorance of Italian. But whom to ask for? This question recalled me to the real bearings of the place, but did not suggest its requisite answer. Whom shall I ask for? I began setting the most cunning traps of hypothesis to catch the solution of the difficulty. I looked at the surrounding houses; of whom had I been accustomed to think as living next door to them? This did not bring it. Whose daughter had I seen going to school from this house but the very day before? Her name was Julia—Julia—and I thought of every combination which had been made with this name from Julia Domna down to Giulia Grisi. Ah! now I had it—Julia H.; and her father naturally bore the same name. During this intellectual rummage I had rung the bell half a dozen times, under the impression that I was kept waiting a small eternity. When the servant opened the door she panted as if she had run for her life. I was shown up stairs to Dr. H.'s room, where he had thrown himself down to rest after a tedious operation. Locking the door after me with an air of determined secrecy, which must have conveyed to him pleasant little suggestions of a design upon his life, I approached his bedside.

"I am about to reveal to you," I commenced, "something which I would not for my life allow to come to other ears. Do you pledge me your eternal silence?"

"I do; what is the matter?"

"I have been taking hasheesh—Cannabis Indica, and I fear that I am going to die."

"How much did you take?"

"Thirty grains."

"Let me feel your pulse." He placed his finger on my wrist and counted slowly, while I stood waiting to hear my death-warrant. "Very regular," shortly spoke the doctor; "triflingly accelerated. Do you feel any pain?" "None at all." "Nothing the matter with you; go home and go to bed." "But—is there—is there—no—danger of—apoplexy?" "Bah!" said the doctor; and, having delivered himself of this very Abernethy-like opinion of my case, he lay down again. My hand was on the knob, when he stopped me with, "Wait a minute; I'll give you a powder to carry with you, and if you get frightened again after you leave me, you can take it as a sedative. Step out on the landing, if you please, and call my servant."

I did so, and my voice seemed to reverberate like thunder from every recess in the whole building. I was terrified at the noise I had made. I learned in after days that this impression is only one of the many due to the intense susceptibility of the sensorium as produced by hasheesh. At one time, having asked a friend to check me if I talked loudly or immoderately while in a state of fantasia among persons from whom I wished to conceal my state, I caught myself shouting and singing from very ecstasy, and reproached him with a neglect of his friendly office. I could not believe him

when he assured me that I had not uttered an audible word. The intensity of the inward emotion had affected the external through the internal ear.

I returned and stood at the foot of the doctor's bed. All was perfect silence in the room, and had been perfect darkness also but for the small lamp which I held in my hand to light the preparation of the powder when it should come. And now a still sublimer mystery began to enwrap me. I stood in a remote chamber at the top of a colossal building, and the whole fabric beneath me was steadily growing into the air. Higher than the topmost pinnacle of Bel's Babylonish temple—higher than Ararat—on, on forever into the lonely dome of God's infinite universe we towered ceaselessly. The years flew on; I heard the musical rush of their wings in the abyss outside of me, and from cycle to cycle, from life to life I careered, a mote in eternity and space. Suddenly emerging from the orbit of my transmigrations, I was again at the foot of the doctor's bed, and thrilled with wonder to find that we were both unchanged by the measureless lapse of time. The servant had not come.

"Shall I call her again?" "Why, you have this moment called her." "Doctor," I replied solemnly, and in language that would have seemed bombastic enough to any one who did not realize what I felt, "I will not believe you are deceiving me, but to me it appears as if sufficient time has elapsed since then for all the Pyramids to have crumbled back to dust." "Ha! ha! you are very funny to-night," said the doctor; "but here she comes, and I will send her for something which will comfort you on that score, and reestablish the Pyramids in your confidence." He gave the girl his orders, and she went out again.

The thought struck me that I would compare *my time* with other people's. I looked at my watch, found that its minute-hand stood at the quarter mark past eleven, and, returning it to my pocket, abandoned myself to my reflections.

Presently I saw myself a gnome imprisoned by a most weird enchanter, whose part I assigned to the doctor before me, in the Domdaniel caverns, "under the roots of the ocean." Here, until the dissolution of all things, was I doomed to hold the lamp that lit that abysmal darkness, while my heart, like a giant clock, ticked solemnly the remaining years of time. Now, this hallucination departing, I heard in the solitude of the night outside the sound of a wondrous heaving sea. Its waves, in sublime cadence, rolled forward till they met the foundations of the building; they smote them with a might which made the very topstone quiver, and then fell back, with hiss and hollow murmur, into the broad bosom whence they had arisen. Now through the street, with measured tread, an armed host passed by. The heavy beat of their footfall and the grinding of their brazen corslet-rings alone broke the silence, for among them all there was no more speech nor music than in a battalion of the dead. It was the army of the ages going by into eternity. A godlike sublimity swallowed up my soul. I was overwhelmed in a fathomless barathrum of time, but I leaned on God, and was immortal through all changes.

And now, in another life, I remembered that far back in the cycles I had looked at my watch to measure the time through which I passed. The impulse seized me to look again. The minute-hand stood half way between fifteen and sixteen minutes past eleven.

The watch must have stopped; I held it to my ear; no, it was still going. I had traveled through all that immeasurable chain of dreams in thirty seconds. "My God!" I cried, "I am in eternity." In the presence of that first sublime revelation of the soul's own time, and her capacity for an infinite life, I stood trembling with breathless awe. Till I die, that moment of unveiling will stand in clear relief from all the rest of my existence. I hold it still in unimpaired remembrance as one of the unutterable sanctities of my being. The years of all my earthly life to come can never be as long as those thirty seconds.

Finally the servant reappeared. I received my powder and went home. There was a light in one of the upper windows, and I hailed it with unspeakable joy, for it relieved me from a fear which I could not conquer, that while I had been gone all familiar things had passed away from earth. I was hardly safe in my room before I doubted having ever been out of it. "I have experienced some wonderful dream," said I, "as I lay here after coming from the parlor." If I had not been out, I reasoned that I would have no powder in my pocket. The powder was there, and it steadied me a little to find that I was not utterly hallucinated on every point. Leaving the light burning, I set out to travel to my bed, which gently invited me in the distance. Reaching it after a sufficient walk, I threw myself down.

III.

The Kingdom of the Dream.

THE moment that I closed my eyes a vision of celestial glory burst upon me. I stood on the silver strand of a translucent, boundless lake, across whose bosom I seemed to have been just transported. A short way up the beach, a temple, modeled like the Parthenon, lifted its spotless and gleaming columns of alabaster sublimely into a rosy air—like the Parthenon, yet as much excelling it as the godlike ideal of architecture must transcend that ideal realized by man. Unblemished in its purity of whiteness, faultless in the unbroken symmetry of every line and angle, its pediment was draped in odorous clouds, whose tints outshone the rainbow. It was the work of an unearthly builder, and my soul stood before it in a trance of ecstasy. Its folded doors were resplendent with the glory of a multitude of eyes of glass, which were inlaid throughout the marble surfaces at the corners of diamond figures from the floor of the porch to the topmost moulding. One of these eyes was golden, like the midday sun, another emerald, another sapphire, and thus onward through the whole gamut of hues, all of them set in such collocations as to form most exquisite harmonies, and whirling upon their axes with the rapidity of thought. At the mere vestibule of the temple I could have sat and drunk in ecstasy forever; but lo! I am yet more blessed. On silent hinges the doors swing open, and I pass in.

I did not seem to be in the interior of a temple. I beheld myself as truly in the open air as if I had never passed the portals, for whichever way I looked there were no walls, no roof, no pavement. An atmosphere of fathomless and soul-satisfying serenity surrounded and transfused me. I stood upon the bank of a crystal stream, whose waters, as they slid on, discoursed notes of music which tinkled on the ear like the tones of some exquisite bell-glass. The same impression which such tones produce, of music refined to its ultimate ethereal spirit and borne from a far distance, characterized every ripple of those translucent waves. The gentle sloping banks of the stream were luxuriant with a velvety cushioning of grass and moss, so living green that the eye and the soul reposed on them at the same time and drank in peace. Through this amaranthine herbage strayed the gnarled, fantastic roots of giant cedars of Lebanon, from whose primeval trunks great branches spread above me, and interlocking, wove a roof of impenetrable shadow; and wandering down the still avenues below those grand arboreal arches went glorious bards, whose snowy beards fell on their breasts beneath countenances of ineffable benignity and nobleness.

They were all clad in flowing robes, like God's high-priests, and each one held in his hand a lyre of unearthly workmanship. Presently one stops midway down a shady walk, and, baring his right arm, begins a prelude. While his celestial chords were trembling up into their sublime fullness, another strikes his strings, and now they blend upon my ravished ear in such a symphony as was never heard elsewhere, and I shall never hear again out of the Great Presence.

A moment more, and three are playing in harmony; now the fourth joins the glorious rapture of his music to their own, and in the completeness of the chord my soul is swallowed up. I can bear no more. But yes, I am sustained, for suddenly the whole throng break forth in a chorus, upon whose wings I am lifted out of the riven walls of sense, and music and spirit thrill in immediate communion. Forever rid of the intervention of pulsing air and vibrating nerve, my soul dilates with the swell of that transcendent harmony, and interprets from it arcana of a meaning which words can never tell. I am borne aloft upon the glory of sound. I float in a trance among the burning choir of the seraphim. But, as I am melting through the purification of that sublime ecstasy into oneness with the Deity himself, one by one those pealing lyres faint away, and as the last throb dies down along the measureless ether, visionless arms swiftly as lightning carry me far into the profound, and set me down before another portal. Its leaves, like the first, are of spotless marble, but ungemmed with wheeling eyes of burning color.

Before entering on the record of this new vision I will make a digression, for the purpose of introducing two laws of the hasheesh operation, which, as explicatory, deserve a place here. First, after the completion of any one fantasia has arrived, there almost invariably succeeds a shifting of the action to some other stage entirely different in its surroundings. In this transition the general character of the emotion may remain unchanged. I may be happy in Paradise and happy at the sources of the Nile, but seldom, either in Paradise or on the Nile, twice in succession. I may writhe in Etna and burn unquenchably in Gehenna, but almost never, in the course of the same delirium, shall Etna or Gehenna witness my torture a second time.

Second, after the full storm of a vision of intense sublimity has blown past the hasheesh-eater, his next vision is generally of a quiet, relaxing, and recreating nature. He comes down from his clouds or up from his abyss into a middle ground of gentle shadows, where he may rest his eyes from the splendor of the seraphim or the flames of fiends. There is a wise philosophy in this arrangement, for otherwise the soul would soon burn out in the excess of its own oxygen. Many a time, it seems to me, has my own thus been saved from extinction.

This next vision illustrated both, but especially the latter of these laws. The temple-doors opened noiselessly before me, but it was no scene of sublimity which thus broke in upon my eyes. I stood in a large apartment, which resembled the Senate-chamber at Washington more than any thing else to which I can compare it. Its roof was vaulted, and at the side opposite the entrance the floor rose into a dais surmounted by a large armchair. The body of the house was occupied by similar chairs disposed in arcs; the heavy paneling of the walls was adorned with grotesque frescoes of every imaginable bird, beast, and monster, which, by some hidden law of life and motion, were forever changing, like the figures of the kaleidoscope. Now the walls bristled with hippogriffs; now, from wainscot to ceiling, toucans and maccataws swung and nodded from their perches amid emerald palms; now Centaurs and Lapithae clashed in ferocious tumult, while crater and cyathus were crushed beneath ringing hoof and heel. But my attention was quickly distracted from the frescoes by the sight of a most witchly congress, which filled all the chairs of that broad chamber. On the dais sat an old crone, whose commanding position first engaged my attention to her personal appearance, and, upon rather impolite scrutiny, I beheld that she was the product of an art held in preeminent favor among persons of her age and sex. She was *knit* of purple yarn! In faultless order the stitches ran along her face; in every pucker of her reentrant mouth, in every wrinkle of her brow, she was a yarny counterfeit of the grandam of actual life, and by some skillful process of stuffing her nose had received its due peak and her chin its projection. The occupants of the seats below were all but reproductions of their president, and both she and they were constantly swaying from side to side, forward and back, to the music of some invisible instruments, whose tone and style were most intensely and ludicrously Ethiopian. Not a word was spoken by any of the woolly conclave, but with untiring industry they were all knitting, knitting, knitting ceaselessly, as if their lives depended on it. I looked to see the objects of their manufacture. They were knitting old women like themselves! One of the sisterhood had nearly brought her double to completion; earnestly another was engaged in rounding out an eyeball; another was fastening the gathers at the corners of a mouth; another was setting up stitches for an old woman in petto.

With marvelous rapidity this work went on; ever and anon some completed crone sprang from the needles which had just achieved her, and, instantly vivified, took up the instruments of reproduction, and fell to work as assiduously as if she had been a member of the congress since the world began. "Here," I cried, "here, at last, do I realize the meaning of endless progression!" and, though the dome echoed with my peals of laughter, I saw no motion of astonishment in the stitches of a single face, but, as for dear life, the manufacture of old women went on unobstructed by the involuntary rudeness of the stranger.

An irresistible desire to aid in the work possessed me; I was half determined to snatch up a quartette of needles and join the sisterhood. My nose began to be ruffled with stitches, and the next moment I had been a partner in their yarny destinies but for a hand which pulled me backward through the door, and shut the congress forever from my view.

For a season I abode in an utter void of sight and sound, but I waited patiently in the assurance that some new changes of magnificence were preparing for me. I was not disappointed. Suddenly, at a far distance, three intense luminous points stood on the triple wall of darkness, and through each of them shot twin attenuated rays of magic light and music. Without being able to perceive any thing of my immediate surroundings, I still felt that I was noiselessly drifting toward those radiant and vocal points. With every moment they grew larger, the light and the harmony came clearer, and before long I could distinguish plainly three colossal arches rising from the bosom of a waveless water. The mid arch towered highest; the two on either side were equal to each other. Presently I beheld that they formed the portals of an enormous cavern, whose dome rose above me into such sublimity that its cope was hidden from my eyes in wreaths of cloud. On each side of me ran a wall of gnarled and rugged rock, from whose jutting points, as high as the eye could reach, depended stalactites of every imagined form and tinge of beauty, while below me, in the semblance of an ebon pavement, from the reflection of its overshadowing crags, lay a level lake, whose exquisite transparency wanted but the smile of the sun to make it glow like a floor of adamant. On this lake I lay in a little boat divinely carved from pearl after the similitude of Triton's shelly shallop; its rudder and its oarage were my own unconscious will, and, without the labors of especial volition, I floated as I list with a furrowless keel swiftly toward the central giant arch. With every moment that brought me nearer to my exit, the harmony that poured through it developed into a grander volume and an intenser beauty.

And now I passed out.

Claude Lorraine, freed from the limitations of sense, and gifted with an infinite canvas, may, for aught I know, be upon some halcyon island of the universe painting such a view as now sailed into my vision. Fitting employment would it be for his immortality were his pencil dipped into the very fountains of the light. Many a time in the course of my life have I yearned for the possession of some grand old master's soul and culture in the presence of revelations of Nature's loveliness which I dared not trust to memory; before this vision, as now in the remembrance of it, that longing became a heartfelt pain. Yet, after all, it was well; the mortal limner would have fainted in his task. Alas! how does the material in which we must embody the spiritual cramp and resist its execution! Standing before windows where the invisible spirit of the frost had traced his exquisite algae, his palms and his ferns, have I said to myself, with a sigh, Ah! Nature alone, of all artists, is gifted to work out her ideals!

Shall I be so presumptuous as to attempt in words that which would beggar the palette and the pencil of old-time disciples of the beautiful? I will, if it be only to satisfy a deep longing.

From the arches of my cavern I had emerged upon a horizonless sea. Through all the infinitudes around me I looked out, and met no boundaries of space. Often in after times have I beheld the heavens and the earth stretching out in parallel lines forever, but this was the first time I had ever stood "un-ringed by the azure world," and I exulted in all the sublimity of the new conception. The whole atmosphere was one measureless suffusion of golden motes, which throbbed continually in cadence, and showered radiance and

harmony at the same time. With ecstasy vision spread her wings for a flight against which material laws locked no barrier, and every moment grew more and more entranced at further and fuller glimpses of a beauty which floated like incense from the pavement of that eternal sea. With ecstasy the spiritual ear gathered in continually some more distant and unimaginable tone, and grouped the growing harmonies into one sublime chant of benediction. With ecstasy the whole soul drank in revelations from every province, and cried out, "Oh, awful loveliness!" And now out of my shallop I was borne away into the full light of the mid firmament; now seated on some toppling peak of a cloud-mountain, whose yawning rifts disclosed far down the mines of reserved lightning; now bathed in my ethereal travel by the rivers of the rainbow, which, side by side, coursed through the valleys of heaven; now dwelling for a season in the environment of unbroken sunlight, yet bearing it like the eagle

with undazzled eye; now crowned with a coronal of prismatic beads of dew. Through whatever region or circumstances I passed, one characteristic of the vision remained unchanged: peace—everywhere godlike peace, the sum of all conceivable desires satisfied.

Slowly I floated down to earth again. There Oriental gardens waited to receive me. From fountain to fountain I danced in graceful mazes with inimitable houris, whose foreheads were bound with fillets of jasmine. I pelted with figs the rare exotic birds, whose gold and crimson wings went flashing from branch to branch, or wheedled them to me with Arabic phrases of endearment. Through avenues of palm I walked arm-in-arm with Hafiz, and heard the hours flow singing through the channels of his matchless poetry. In gay kiosques I quaffed my sherbet, and in the luxury of lawlessness kissed away by drops that other juice which is contraband unto the faithful. And now beneath citron shadows I laid me down to sleep. When I awoke it was morning—actually morning, and not a hasheesh hallucination. The first emotion that I felt upon opening my eyes was happiness to find things again wearing a natural air. Yes; although the last experience of which I had been conscious had seemed to satisfy every human want, physical or spiritual, I smiled on the four plain white walls of my bedchamber, and hailed their familiar unostentatiousness with a pleasure which had no wish to transfer itself to arabesque or rainbows. It was like returning home from an eternity spent in loneliness among the palaces of strangers. Well may I say an eternity, for during the whole day I could not rid myself of the feeling that I was separated from the preceding one by an immeasurable lapse of time. In fact, I never got wholly rid of it.

I rose that I might test my reinstated powers, and see if the restoration was complete. Yes, I felt not one trace of bodily weariness nor mental depression. Every function had returned to its normal state, with the one exception mentioned; memory could not efface the traces of my having passed through a great mystery. I recalled the events of the past night, and was pleased to think that I had betrayed myself to no one but Dr. H. I was satisfied with my experiment.

Ah! would that I had been satisfied! Yet history must go on.

IV.
Cashmere and Cathay by Twilight.

"You will never take it again, will you?"

"Oh no, I never expect to; I am satisfied with my one successful experiment."

It was the fair lady of the crochet-needle who asked me the question as, a few days after my first practical acquaintance with hasheesh, I gave her the recital contained in the preceding pages. In my answer I spoke truly; I did suppose that I never should repeat my experiment. The glimpse which I had gained in that single night of revelation of hitherto unconceived modes and uncharted fields of spiritual being seemed enough to store the treasure-house of grand memories for a lifetime. Unutterably more, doubtless, still remained unveiled, but it contented me to say,

"In Nature's infinite book of secrecy, a little I can read,"

when that little swept a view whose faintest lineament outshone all the characters upon the scroll of daily existence. No, I never should take it again.

I did not know myself; I did not know hasheesh. There are temperaments, no doubt, upon which this drug produces, as a reactory result, physical and mental depression. With me, this was never the case. Opium and liquors fix themselves as a habit by becoming necessary to supply that nervous waste which they in the first place occasioned. The lassitude which succeeds their exaltation demands a renewed indulgence, and accordingly every gratification of the appetite is parent to the next. But no such element entered into the causes which attached me to hasheesh. I speak confidently, yet without exaggeration, when I say that I have spent many an hour in torture such as was never known by Cranmer at the stake, or Gaudentio di Lucca in the Inquisition, yet out of the depths of such experience *I* have always come without a trace of its effect in diminished strength or buoyancy.

Had the first experiment been followed by depression, I had probably never repeated it. At any rate, unstrung muscles and an enervated mind could have been resisted much more effectually when they pleaded for renewed indulgence than the form which the fascination actually took. For days I was even unusually strong; all the forces of life were in a state of pleasurable activity, but the memory of the wondrous glories which I had beheld wooed me continually like an irresistible sorceress. I could not shut my eyes for midday musing without beholding in that world, half dark, half light, beneath the eyelids, a steady procession of delicious images which the severest will could not banish nor dim. Now through an immense and serene sky floated luxurious argosies of clouds, continually changing form and tint through an infinite cycle of mutations.

Now, suddenly emerging from some deep embowerment of woods, I stood upon the banks of a broad river that curved far off into dreamy distance, and glided noiselessly past its jutting headlands, reflecting a light which was not of the sun nor of the moon, but midway between them, and here and there thrilling with subdued prismatic rays. Temples and gardens, fountains and vistas stretched continually through my waking or sleeping imagination, and mingled themselves with all I heard, or read, or saw. On the pages of Gibbon the palaces and lawns of Nicomedia were illustrated with a hasheesh tint and a hasheesh reality; and journeying with old Dan Chaucer, I drank in a delicious landscape of revery along all the road to Canterbury. The music of my vision was still heard in echo; as the bells of Bow of old time called to Whittington, so did it call to me— "Turn again, turn again." And I turned.

Censure me not harshly, ye who have never known what fascination there is in the ecstasy of beauty; there are baser attractions than those which invited me. Perhaps ye yourselves have turned from the first simple-mindedness of life to be led by the power of a more sordid wooing. The hope of being one day able to sleep lazily in a literally golden sun, the lazzaroni of fortune; of securing a patient hearing for some influential and patriotic whisper in the ear of the "mobilium turba Quiritium"; of draining any cup which drugs the soul and leaves the body to rifle it of its prerogative—each and all of these are lower fascinations than that to which I yielded.

And ye better, wiser, and therefore gentler ones, who decry not another's weakness because it is not your own, who are free from all bondage, be it of the sordid or the beautiful, be kindly in your judgment. Wherein I was wrong I was invited as by a mother's voice, and the blandishments which lulled me were full of such spiritual sweetness as we hear only twice in a lifetime—once at its opening, once at its close; the first time in the cradle-hymn that lulls innocence to slumber, the last in that music of attendant angels through which the soul begins to float upward in its euthanasia toward the restoration of primeval purity and peace. I yielded to no sensual gratification. The motives for the hasheesh-indulgence were of the most exalted ideal nature, for of this nature are all its ecstasies and its revelations—yes, and a thousand-fold more terrible, for this very reason, its unutterable pangs. I yielded, moreover, without realizing to what. Within a circle of one hundred miles' radius there was not a living soul who knew or could warn me of my danger. Finally, I yielded without knowing that I yielded, for I ascribed my next indulgence to a desire of research.

One day, about the hour of noon, a little more than a week after my first experiment, I rolled twenty grains of hasheesh into a pill and swallowed it, saying as I did so, "Here is the final test for the sake of science." The afternoon lay before me unoccupied by any especial appointment, and, after dining, I threw myself down upon a lounge to await the result of the dose. The day was soft and hazy, and its influence lay so nepenthe-like upon my eyelids, that before long, without knowing it, I fell asleep. It was tea-time when I awoke, and I had not experienced any visions. A friend of mine joined me at the table, and when we pushed back our chairs, he proposed that we should take a walk. Every thing above, below, around us united in the invitation. It was one of those evenings when the universal sense of balminess makes all outdoors as homelike and delicious as the cheeriest winter fireside can be, with its enlivenment of ruddy blaze, and its charm of sheltered privacy. The very soul seems turned inside out for an airing, and we are almost ashamed of ourselves for ever preferring rafters to the sky, and fleeing from the presence of Nature to find a home.

Through all the streets that ran toward the west the sun was sending a thrill of light from his good-by place on the horizon, and the pavements were a mosaic of dancing leaf-shadows and golden polygons, forever shifting as the trees quivered over us in the gentlest of southern winds. Arm-in-arm with Dan, I strolled down the checkered avenue, and more and more luxuriant grew the sunset as we came gradually out of the environment of houses and breathed the air of the open country. The suburbs of P— are very beautiful. If the stranger knows it and remarks it, it is not because he is smitten with the mere novelty of his view. There are few landscapes which will bear so frequent beholding—few whose admirers so soon and lastingly become their lovers. Were there any jealousy in my love for that, my own home-scenery, I know no season which would ever have given me more pangs for fear of a rival than the other of which I speak, for the earth and sky were fair around us, even with a human fascination. Of my companion let me say that which any man of varying moods will realize to be one of the highest eulogies that can be passed upon a friend. Dan was one of those choice spirits whom you are always glad to have beside you, whatever may be your feeling. He belonged to that rare and sensitive order of beings who can never become uncongenial to one who has once been in sympathy with them. How many a time, most valued and longed-for one, have I tested this in thee! How often, in this very intuitive perception of our accordance, have I felt the proof that friendship is as inborn a principle in hearts as the quality of their harmony in tones of a chord.

There is a road running south from the suburbs of P—— which in many respects affords one of the most delightful walks which can be imagined. On the one hand, for a long distance, a terraced embankment rises luxuriantly green through all the days of summer, and crowned with picturesque suburban cottages. On the other, a broad table-land stretches away to the abrupt banks of the Hudson, dotted over all its surface with clumps of healthful trees and embowered villas. Here and there, through the fringes of shade which skirt the brink, delicious views of the river break upon the eye, with a background of mountains, still unsubdued by labor, rising in primeval freshness from the other side. Under the tutelar protection of their evening shadows the farther water lay, at the season of which I speak, like a divine child asleep, watched by an eternal muse.

Along this road we traveled arm-in-arm, so filled and overcome with the beauty of the view that we read each other's feelings and went silently. Perhaps we had come half a mile from the town when, without the smallest premonition, I was smitten by the hasheesh thrill as by a thunderbolt. Though I had felt it but once in life before, its sign was as unmistakable as the most familiar thing of daily life. I have often been asked to explain the nature of this thrill, and have as often tried to do it, but no analogue exists which will represent it perfectly, hardly even approximately. The nearest resemblance to the feeling is that contained in our idea of the instantaneous separation of soul and body. Very few in the world have ever known before absolute death what state accompanies this separation, yet we all of us have an idea more or less distinct of that which it must be when it arrives. Even on this vague conception I throw myself for the sake of being understood with more confidence than I would dare to give to the most thorough description that I could elaborate.

The road along which we walked began slowly to lengthen. The hill over which it disappeared, at the distance of half a mile from me, soon came to be perceived as the boundary of the continent itself. But for the infinite loveliness of the sky, and waters, and fields, I should have been as greatly terrified with the increasing mystery of my state as I had been at the commencement of my first experience. But a most beautiful sunset was dying in the west, the river was tinged by it, the very zenith clouds were bathed in it, and the world beneath seemed floating in a dream of rosy tranquility. My awakened perceptions drank in this beauty until all sense of fear was banished, and every vein ran flooded with the very wine of delight. Mystery enwrapped me still, but it was the mystery of one who walks in Paradise for the first time.

Could I keep it from Dan? No, not for a moment. I had no remembrance of having taken hasheesh. The past was the property of another life, and I supposed that all the world was reveling in the same ecstasy as myself. I cast off all restraint; I leaped into the air; I clapped my hands, and shouted for joy. An involuntary exclamation

raised the mustache of the poet beside me. "What in the world," he cried, "is the matter with you?" I could only answer, "Bliss! bliss! unimagined bliss!" In an instant he saw all, for he knew my former experience, and as quickly formed the resolution of humoring me to the utmost in all my vagaries.

I glowed like a new-born soul. The well-known landscape lost all of its familiarity, and I was setting out upon a journey of years through heavenly territories, which it had been the longing of my previous lifetime to behold. "My dear friend," I said, "we are about to realize all our youthful dreams of travel. Together you and I will wander on foot at our will through strange and beauteous countries; our life spreads before us henceforward unoccupied by cares, and the riches of all nature stretch onward through the immense domain we see in exultant expectancy to become the food for our thought and the fountains of our delight. To think that we should have been spared until this day—spared to each other, spared for such glorious scenes! My friend, we shall travel together, linked soul to soul, and gaining ecstasy by impartition. At night, beneath the shade of zephyr-fanned mimosas, we shall lay ourselves down to sleep on the banks of primeval Asian rivers, and Bulbul shall sing us to sleep with his most delicious madrigals. When the first auroral tinges are glassed back from the peaks of Himmaleh, we will arise, and, bathing ourselves in rock-o'ershadowed fountains, will start again upon our immortal way. Sleep shall repeat the echoes of the day to another and unfatigued inner sense of dreams, and awaking shall be a repetition of birth into newer and still more enchanting life. On! on!"

"I will go," said my friend, "with delight." Not a shadow of incredulousness or inappreciation passed over his face, and, drawing his arm still closer through my own, I hastened onward, as delighted with his consent as I was thoroughly convinced of the reality of the presence of grand old Asia.

The peculiar time of hasheesh, already so frequently mentioned, added one more most rapturous element to my enjoyment. Through leagues of travel the shadows did not deepen around us, but the same unutterable sunset peace and beauty transfused the earth unchangeably. In watching the glories of the west at sunset in our ordinary state, they pass away from us as soon that the dying lustres have become to us almost the synonym for transition and decay. The golden masses become ruddy, the ruddy fall away to purple, the purple speedily grow black, and all this transmutation occupies no longer time than we may lean our foreheads, unfatigued, against a window-pane. In my present state of enlarged perception, Time had no kaleidoscope for me; nothing grew faint, nothing shifted, nothing changed except my ecstasy, which heightened through interminable degrees to behold the same rose-radiance lighting us up along all our immense journey. I might style my present chapter "Notes of Travel through the Champaigns of Perpetual Sunset."

From he road along which we traveled another leads back into P—, across a more precipitous hill than any we had already ascended. Into this second road we turned. Yet, from the absence of all familiar appearances in the world around me, I did not suppose that we were returning to the town, but merely that we were continuing our journey through a new and less frequented by-path. Presently we struck a plank walk, and began mounting the hill of which I have spoken.

The moment that the planks began to resound beneath our feet I realized in what part of Asia we were journeying. We were on the great wall of China. Below us stretched into grand distances the plaints of Thibet. Multitudinous were the flocks that covered them; countless groups of goats and goatherds were dispersed over the landscape as far as the eye could reach. The banks of innumerable streams were dotted with picturesque tents, and every minutest detail of the view in all respects harmonized with the idea of Asiatic life. Beyond Thibet, as with clairvoyant eyes, I looked straight through and over Hindoo Koosh, and beheld Cashmere sleeping in grand shadows. The fountains of the Punjaub were unveiled, and among their spicy outflowings there gamboled, in Old-world freshness of heart, children of a primitive race whom prodigal nature had put beyond the necessity of labor. Through greenest valleys roved pairs of Oriental lovers, while above them flashed golden light from the fruit that hung in a Vallambrosa of citron-branches. Distance did not dim either scenery or countenances; every living thing was audible and visible in its rejoicing through leagues of light and shadow stretched between us. Again I leaped into the air and shouted for joy.

Along the road that skirted the outside of my Chinese wall a carriage came, drawn by a span of richly-caparisoned white horses. In it a young man and a maiden were sitting, and as they drew nearer they bowed to myself and my fellow-traveler. "Who are those?" asked Dan. "An eminent mandarin of the interior," I replied, "of the order of the Blue Button, and by name Fuh-chieng, who, with his sister, at this season every year takes the tour of the provinces, dispensing justice and examining into the state of the public works. Verily, an estimable youth. Having known him during the summer we spent together at Pekin, I feel constrained to speak with him." With a choice compliment upon my lips, worded in the most courtly Chinese with which I was conversant, I was about to rush up to the carriage and make my kow-tow, which my friend, grasping my arm, entreated me to desist, begging to know whether I were not aware that, since the year 580 B.C., when Ching-Chong was assassinated in his palanquin, it had been a criminal offense to approach within ten paces of a mandarin on his travels. "My dearest friend," I replied, "you have saved me! I am astonished at your knowledge of Chinese law, this title of which had entirely escaped my mind. With thankfulness I yield to your suggestion, and will suffer the young man to pass on." It was well that I did so, as my acquaintance in the carriage might otherwise have been terrified beyond measure by the singularity, if not by the sublimity of the dialect in which I should have addressed them.

It is possible for a man of imaginative mind, by mere suggestions of rich veins of thought, to lead a companion in the hasheesh state through visions of incomparable delight. This fact Dan had discovered in the good grace with which I instantly received his advice as to the mandarin. In our journeying we came to a tall gate-post of granite, which stood at the entrance to a lawn in front of one of the suburban residences of which I have spoken. Making his manner Oriental, to suit our supposed surroundings, he said to me, "Seest thou that tower that rises into the rosy air?" In an instant I beheld the tower with such conviction of reality that I did not even think of it as a metamorphose from something else. From the battlements flaunted yellow flags gorgeous with crimson dragons, and over each corner of the turret glared a rampant hippogriff, flaming, from his forked tongue even to his anomalous tail, with scales of dazzling gold. There was revelry within; its ecstasy worded in Shemitic monosyllables, and accompanied by the mellifluous flights of gong and tom-tom. We passed on through Asia.

We now reached the summit of the hill. The broadest scope of vision which was possible was now ours. My ecstasy became so great that I seemed to cast off all shackles of flesh. The lover of beauty who should, for the first time, drink in the richness of this exalted view through the channels of the soul which are ordinarily opened, might well burst forth into singing were not reverence the stronger feeling. But when, with me, that flow of loveliness broke in through doors in the spiritual nature to which no open sesame had ever before been granted, I felt, I cried out, "Why need we, in our journey, touch the earth at all? Let us sweep through air above this expanse of beauty, and read it like the birds."

I was about to fly heavenward, chanting a triumphant hymn, when I turned and looked at Dan. He was standing sorrowfully, without means of flight. I was filled with contrition. "Dear brother of my pilgrimage," I said, "did I speak of tempting the air, forgetful that thou wast not like unto myself? Forgive me—I will not leave thee; yet, oh that thou couldst also fly! through what abysses of sublimity would we float!" Restoring myself to contentment with the airy tread of feet which hardly seemed to touch the ground, and my wish to oblivion, I again took his arm, and we voyaged as before.

Now we went singing, and I question whether Mozart ever rejoiced in his own musical creations as I did in that symphony we sang together. The tune and the words were extemporaneous, yet, by a close sympathy, he sang an accordant base to my air, and I heard delicious echoes thrown back from the dome of heaven. We sang the primal simplicity of Asia, the cradle of the nations, the grand expectancy of the younger continents, looking eastward to their mysterious mother for the gift of races still treasured in her womb. On our paean were borne the praises of the golden days of Foh and the serene prophecies of Confucius; we spoke of the rivers that for numberless centuries bore down to the eternal ocean no freight but the sere leaves of uninhabited wildernesses, whose shadows they glassed, and of fountains upon whose face no smile had rested save that of Hesper and the rising sun. I lived in what we sang: our music seemed a wondrous epic, whose pages we illustrated, not with pictures, but with living groups; the ancient days were restored before my eyes and to my ears, and I exulted in the perception with such conviction of reality that I ascribed it to no power of my own, but knew it as an exterior and universal fact.

This will be realized, perhaps, by very few who read my recital. The word for every strange phenomenon with all the world is "only imagination." Truly, this was imagination; but to me, with eyes and ears wide open in the daylight, an imagination as real as the soberest fact.

It will be remembered that the hasheesh states of ecstasy always alternate with less intense conditions, in which the prevailing phenomena are those of mirth or tranquility. In accordance with this law, in the present instance, Dan, to whom I had told my former experience, was not surprised to hear me break forth at the final cadence of our song into a peal of unextinguishable laughter, but begged to know what was its cause, that he might laugh too. I could only cry out that my right leg was a tin case filled with stair-rods, and as I limped along, keeping that member perfectly rigid, both from fear of cracking the metal and the difficulty of bending it, I heard the rattle of the brazen contents shaken from side to side with feelings of the most supreme absurdity possible to the human soul. Presently the leg was restored to its former state, but in the interim its mate had grown to a size which would have made it a very respectable trotter for Brian Borru or one of the Titans. Elevated some few hundred feet into the firmament, I was compelled to hop upon my giant pedestal in a way very ungraceful in a world where two legs were the fashion, and eminently disagreeable to the slighted member, which sought in vain to reach the earth with struggles amusing from their very insignificance. This ludicrous affliction

being gradually removed, I went on my way quietly until we again began to be surrounded by the houses of the town.

Here the phenomenon of the dual existence once more presented itself. One part of me awoke, while the other continued in perfect hallucination. The awakened portion felt the necessity of keeping in side streets on the way home, lest some untimely burst of ecstasy should startle more frequented thoroughfares. I mentioned this to Dan, who drew me into a quiet lane, by the side of which we sat down together to rest on a broad stone. By this time the sunset had nearly faded, while my attention was directed to other things, and its regency of all the beauties of the sky was replaced by that of the full moon, now at the zenith. A broad and clearly-defined halo surrounded her, and refracted her rays in such a manner as to shower them from its edge in a prismatic fringe. That vision of loveliness was the only possible one which could have recompensed me for the loss of my sunset. I gazed heavenward, as one fascinated by mystical eyes. And now the broad luminous belt began to be peopled with myriads of shining ones from the realm of Faëry, who plunged into the translucent lake of ether as into a sea, and, dashing back its silvery spray from their breasts, swam to the moon and ascended its gleaming beach.

Between this moon-island and the shore of halo now growing multitudes endlessly passed and repassed, and I could hear, tinkling down through the vacant spaces, the thrill of their gnome-laughter. I could have kept that stony seat all night, and looked speechlessly into heaven, unmoved though an armed host had passed by me on the earth, but unconsciously I closed my eyes, and was in a moment whirling on through a visionary dance, like that in which I had been borne as soon as I lay down at the time of my first experiment. Temples and gardens, pyramids and unearthly rivers, began to float along before the windows of my sense, when Dan, looking around, saw that I would become unconscious, and aroused me. Again we walked on.

And now that unutterable thirst which characterizes hasheesh came upon me. I could have lain me down and lapped dew from the grass. I must drink, wheresoever, howsoever. We soon reached home—soon, because it was not five squares off from where we sat down, yet ages, from the thirst which consumed me and the expansion of time in which I lived. I came into the house as one would approach a fountain in the desert, with a wild bound of exultation, and gazed with miserly eyes at the draught which my friend poured out for me until the glass was brimming. I clutched it—I put it to my lips. Ha! a surprise! It was not water, but the most delicious metheglin in which ever bard of the Cymri drank the health of Howell Dda. It danced and sparkled like some liquid metempsychosis of amber; it gleamed with the spiritual fire of a thousand chrysolites. To sight, to taste it was metheglin, such as never mantled in the cups of the Valhalla.

The remainder of that evening I spent in a delirium which, unlike all that had preceded it, was one of unutterable calm. Not the heavy sleep of a debauch, not the voluntary musing of the visionary, but a clarifying of all thought, and the flowing in of the richest influences from the world around me, without the toil of selecting them. I looked at the stars, and felt kindred with them; I spoke to them, and they answered me. I dwelt in an inner communion with heaven—a communion where every language is understood, rather where all speak the same language, and deeply did I realize a voice which seemed to say, as in my waking dreams I had faintly heard it murmur upon earth,

Πολλαι μεν θυητοις γλωττα, μιαδ᾽αθ᾽ανατοισιν.

V.

The Hour and the Power of Darkness.

IT may perhaps be not altogether a fanciful classification to divide every man's life into two periods, the locomotive and the static. Restless fluidity always characterizes the childish mind in its healthy state, exemplifying itself in the thousand wayward freaks, hair-breadth experiments, and unanswerable questions which keep the elder portions of a family in continual oscillation between mirth and terror. There is not always a thorough solidification of the mental nature, even when the great boy has learned what to do with his hands, and how to occupy his station at maturer tea-parties with becoming dignity and resignation. No longer, to be sure, does he gratify experimental tendencies by taking the eight-day clock to pieces to look at its machinery; no longer does he nonplus grave aunts and grandmothers with questions upon the causes of his own origination, but the same dynamic propensities exist expanded into a larger and more self-conscious sphere. His restlessness of limb has now become the desire of travel, his investigation into the petty matters of household economy has grown into a thirst for research whose field is the world and whose instruments are the highest faculties of induction.

With some men this state remains unchanged through a long life, but to most of us there comes, sooner or later, a period when the longing for change dies out, and a fixed place and an unalterable condition become the great central ideas of existence. We look back with a wonder that is almost incredulousness upon the time when a ride by railway was the dream of weeks preceding, and try in vain to realize the supernatural freshness which the earth put on when for the first time we discovered that we were near-sighted, and looked through some friend's spectacles. Motion, except for the rare purpose of recreation, becomes an annoyance to us beyond a circumscribed territory, and we have emerged into the static condition of life before we are aware.

Much earlier than the usual period did this become the case with me. A feeble childhood soon exhausted its superfluous activities, and into books, ill health, and musing I settled down when I should have been playing cricket, hunting, or riding. The younger thirst for adventure was quenched by rapid degrees as I found it possible to ascend Chimborazo with Humboldt lying on a sofa, or chase hartebeests with Cumming over muffins and coffee. The only exceptions to this state of imaginative indolence were the hours spent in rowing or sailing upon the most glorious river of the world, and the consciousness that the Hudson rolled at my own door and only contributed to settle the conviction that there was no need of going abroad to find beauties in which the soul might wrap itself as in a garment of delight. Even at these seasons exercise was not so much the aim as musing. Many a time, with the handles of my sculls thrust under the sidegirders, and the blades turned full to the wind, have I sat and drifted for hours through mountain-shadows, and past glimpses of light that flooded the woody gorges, with a sense of dreamy ecstasy which all the novelties of a new world could never have supplied.

Oh, most noble river, what hast thou not been to me? In childhood thy ripples were the playmates of my perpetual leisure, dancing up the sandy stretches of thy brink, and telling laughing tales of life's beamy spray and sunshine. In after years, the grand prophet of a wider life, thine ebb sang chants to the imperial ocean, into whose pearly palaces thou wast hastening, and thy flood brought up the resounding history of the infinite surges whence thou hadst returned. It is not thine to come stealing from unnamed fountains of mystery, nor to crown thy sublime mountains with the ruined battlements of a departed age; but more than Nile hath God glorified thee, and Nature hath hallowed thy walls with her own armorial bearings till thou art more reverend than Rhine. On thy guarding peaks Antiquity sits enthroned, asking no register in the crumbling monuments of man, but bearing her original sceptre from the hand of Him who first founded her domain beside thy immortal flow.

Gradually the Hudson came to supply all my spiritual wants. Were I sad, I found sympathy in the almost human murmurs of his waters, as, stretched upon the edge of some rocky headland, I heard them go beating into the narrow caves beneath me, and return sighing, as if defrauded of a hiding-place and a home. Were I merry, the white-caps danced and laughed about my prancing boat, and the wind whistled rollicking glees against my stays. In weariness, I leaped into the stream; his cool hand upbore and caressed me till I returned braced for thought, and renewed as by a plunge into El Dorado. In the Hudson I found a wealth which satisfied all wishes, and my supreme hope was that on his banks I might pass all my life. Thus supplied with beauty, consolation, dreams, all things, every day I became more and more careless of the world beyond, and in my frame grew even *hyperstatic.*

It was in this state that hasheesh found me. After the walk which I last recorded, the former passion for travel returned with powerful intensity. I had now a way of gratifying it which comported both with indolence and economy. The whole East, from Greece to farthest China, lay within the compass of a township; no outlay was necessary for the journey. For the humble sum of six cents I might purchase an excursion ticket over all the earth; ships and dromedaries, tents and hospices were all contained in a box of Tilden's extract. Hasheesh I called the "drug of travel," and I had only to direct my thoughts strongly toward a particular part of the world previously to swallowing my bolus to make my whole fantasia in the strongest possible degree topographical. Or, when the delirium was at its height, let any one suggest to me, however faintly, mountain, wilderness, or market-place, and straightway I was in it, drinking in the novelty of my surroundings in all the ecstasy of a discoverer. I swam up against the current of all time; I walked through Luxor and Palmyra as they were of old; on Babylon the bittern had not built her nest, and I gazed on the unbroken columns of the Parthenon.

Soon after my pedestrian journey through Asia I changed my residence for a while, and went to live in the town of Schenectady. It was here that the remainder of my hasheesh-life was passed, and here, for many days, did I drain alternately cups of superhuman joy and as superhuman misery. At Union College, of which I was a resident, I had a few friends to whom I communicated my acquaintance with the wondrous drug which was now becoming a habit with me. Some of them were surprised, some warned me, and as they will most of them be introduced into the narrative which I am writing, I now mention them thus particularly, lest it may be thought strange that, in an ordinary town of small size, there should be found by one man a sufficient number of congenial persons to vary the dramatis personae of a story as mine will be varied.

Having exhausted the supply of hasheesh which I had originally obtained from the shelves of my old lounging-place at the shop of the doctor, I procured a small jar of a preparation of the same drug by another chemist, which, I was told, was much weaker than the former. Late in the evening I took about fifty grains of the new preparation, arguing that this amount was a rational equivalent for the thirty which had before been my maximum dose.

It is impossible, however, to base any calculation of the energy of hasheesh upon such a comparison. The vital forces upon which this most magical stimulant operates are too delicate, too recondite to be treated like material parts in a piece of mechanism whose power of resistance can be definitely expressed by an equation. There are certain nerves, no doubt, which the anatomist and the physician will find affected by the cannabine influence—certain functions over which its essence appears to hold peculiar regency; but we must have proceeded much farther in the science which treats of the connection between matter and mind, must know much more of those imponderable forces which, more delicate than electricity and more mysterious than the magnetic fluid, weave the delicate interacting network that joins our human duality, before we can treat that part of us affected by hasheesh as a constant in any calculation.

There are two facts which I have verified as universal by repeated experiment, which fall into their place here as aptly as they can in the course of my narrative: 1st. At two different times, when body and mind are apparently in precisely analogous states, when all circumstances, exterior and interior, do not differ tangibly in the smallest respect, the same dose of the same preparation of hasheesh will frequently produce diametrically opposite effects. Still further, I have taken at one time a pill of thirty grains, which hardly gave a perceptible phenomenon, and at another, when my dose had been but half that quantity, I have suffered the agonies of a martyr, or rejoined in a perfect phrensy. So exceedingly variable are its results, that, long before I abandoned the indulgence, I took each successive bolus with the consciousness that I was daring an uncertainty as tremendous as the equipoise between hell and heaven. Yet the fascination employed Hope as its advocate, and won the suit. 2d. If, during the ecstasy of hasheesh delirium, another dose, however small—yes, though it be no larger than half a pea—be employed to prolong the condition, such agony will inevitably ensue as will make the soul shudder at its own possibility of endurance without annihilation. By repeated experiments, which now occupy the most horrible place upon my catalogue of horrible remembrances, have I proved that, among all the variable phenomena of hasheesh, this alone stands

unvarying. The use of it directly after any other stimulus will produce consequences as appalling.

But to return from my digression. It was perhaps eight o'clock in the evening when I took the dose of fifty grains. I did not retire until near midnight, and as no effects had then manifested themselves, I supposed that the preparation was even weaker than my ratio gave it credit for being, and, without any expectation of result, lay down to sleep. Previously, however, I extinguished my light. To say this may seem trivial, but it is as important a matter as any which it is possible to notice. The most direful suggestions of the bottomless pit may flow in upon the hasheesh-eater through the very medium of darkness. The blowing out of a candle can set an unfathomed barathrum wide agape beneath the flower-wreathed table of his feast, and convert his palace of sorcery into a Golgotha. Light is a necessity to him, even when sleeping; it must tinge his visions, or they assume a hue as sombre as the banks of Styx.

I do not know how long a time had passed since midnight, when I awoke suddenly to find myself in a realm of the most perfect clarity of view, yet terrible with an infinitude of demoniac shadows. Perhaps, I thought, I am still dreaming; but no effort could arouse me from my vision, and I realized that I was wide awake. Yet it was an awaking which, for torture, had no parallel in all the stupendous domain of sleeping incubus. Beside my bed in the centre of the room stood a bier, from whose corners drooped the folds of a heavy pall; outstretched upon it lay in state a most fearful corpse, whose livid face was distorted with the pangs of assassination. The traces of a great agony were frozen into fixedness in the tense position of every muscle, and the nails of the dead man's fingers pierced his palms with the desperate clinch of one who has yielded not without agonizing resistance. Two tapers at his head, two at his feet, with their tall and unsnuffed wicks, made the ghastliness of the bier more luminously unearthly, and a smothered laugh of derision from some invisible watcher ever and anon mocked the corpse, as if triumphant demons were exulting over their prey. I pressed my hands upon my eyeballs till they ached, in intensity of desire to shut out the spectacle; I buried my head in the pillow, that I might not hear that awful laugh of diabolic sarcasm.

But—oh horror immeasurable! I beheld the walls of the room slowly gliding together, the ceiling coming down, the floor ascending, as of old the lonely captive saw them, whose cell was doomed to be his coffin. Nearer and nearer am I borne toward the corpse. I shrunk back from the edge of the bed; I cowered in most abject fear. I tried to cry out, but speech was paralyzed. The walls came closer and closer together. Presently my hand lay on the dead man's forehead. I made my arm as straight and rigid as a bar of iron; but of what avail was human strength against the contraction of that cruel masonry? Slowly my elbow bent with the ponderous pressure; nearer grew the ceiling—I fell into the fearful embrace of death. I was pent, I was stifled in the breathless niche, which was all of space still left to me. The stony eyes stared up into my own, and again the maddening peal of fiendish laughter rang close beside my ear. Now I was touched on all sides by the walls of the terrible press; there came a heavy crush, and I felt all sense blotted out in darkness.

I awaked at last; the corpse was gone, but I had taken his place upon the bier. In the same attitude which he had kept I lay motionless, conscious, although in darkness, that I wore upon my face the counterpart of his look of agony. The room had grown into a gigantic hall, whose roof was framed of iron arches; the pavement, the walls, the cornice were all of iron. The spiritual essence of the metal seemed to be a combination of cruelty and despair. Its massive hardness spoke a language which it is impossible to embody in words, but any one who has watched the relentless sweep of some great engine crank, and realized its capacity for murder, will catch a glimpse, even in the memory, of the thrill which seemed to say, "This iron is a tearless fiend," of the unutterable meaning I saw in those colossal beams and buttresses. I suffered from the vision of that iron as from the presence of a giant assassin.

But my senses opened slowly to the perception of still worse presences. By my side there gradually emerged from the sulphurous twilight which bathed the room the most horrible form which the soul could look upon unshattered—a fiend also of iron, white hot and dazzling with the glory of the nether penetralia. A face that was the ferreous incarnation of all imaginations of malice and irony looked on me with a glare, withering from its intense heat, but still more from the unconceived degree of inner wickedness which it symbolized. I realized whose laughter I had heard, and instantly I heard it again. Beside him another demon, his very twin, was rocking a tremendous cradle framed of bars of iron like all things else, and candescent with as fierce a heat as the fiend's.

And now, in a chant of the most terrific blasphemy which it is possible to imagine, or rather of blasphemy so fearful that no human thought has ever conceived of it, both the demons broke forth, until I grew intensely wicked merely by hearing it. I still remember the meaning of the song they sang, although there is no language yet coined which will convey it, and far be it from me even to suggest its nature, lest I should seem to perpetuate in any degree such profanity as beyond the abodes of the lost no lips are capable of uttering. Every note of the music itself accorded with the thought as symbol represents essence, and with its clangor mixed the maddening creak of the forever-oscillating cradle, until I felt driven into a ferocious despair. Suddenly the nearest fiend, snatching up a pitchfork (also of white-hot iron), thrust it into my writhing side, and hurled me shrieking into the fiery cradle. I sought in my torture to scale the bars; they slipped from my grasp and under my feet like the smoothest icicles. Through increasing grades of agony I lay unconsumed, tossing from side to side with the rocking of the dreadful engine, and still above me pealed the chant of blasphemy, and the eyes of demoniac sarcasm smiled at me in mockery of a mother's gaze upon her child.

"Let us sing him," said one of the fiends to the other, "the lullaby of Hell." The blasphemy now changed into an awful word-picturing of eternity, unveiling what it was, and dwelling with raptures of malice upon its infinitude, its sublimity of growing pain, and its privation of all fixed points which might mark it into divisions. By emblems common to all language rather than by any vocal words, did they sing this frightful apocalypse, yet the very emblems had a sound as distinct as tongue could give them. This was one, and the only one of their representatives that I can remember. Slowly they began, "To-day is father of to-morrow, to-morrow hath a son that shall beget the day succeeding." With increasing rapidity they sang in this way, day by day, the genealogy of a thousand years, and I traced on the successive generations, without a break in one link, until the rush of their procession reached a rapidity so awful as fully to typify eternity itself; and still I fled on through that burning genesis of cycles. I feel that I do not convey my meaning, but may no one else ever understand it better!

Withered like a leaf in the breath of an oven, after millions of years I felt myself tossed upon the iron floor. The fiends had departed, the cradle was gone. I stood alone, staring into immense and empty spaces. Presently I found that I was in a colossal square, as of some European city, alone at the time of evening twilight, and surrounded by houses hundreds of stories high. I was bitterly athirst. I ran to the middle of the square, and reached it after an infinity of travel. There was a fountain carved in iron, every jet inimitably sculptured in mockery of water, yet dry as the ashes of a furnace. "I shall perish with thirst," I cried. "Yet one more trial. There must be people in all

these immense houses. Doubtless they love the dying traveler, and will give him to drink. Good friends! water! water!" A horribly deafening din poured down on me from the four sides of the square. Every sash of all the hundred stories of every house in that colossal quadrangle flew up as by one spring. Awakened by my call, at every window stood a terrific maniac. Sublimely in the air above me, in front, beside me, on either hand, and behind my back, a wilderness of insane faces gnashed at me, glared, gibbered, howled, laughed horribly, hissed, and cursed. At the unbearable sight I myself became insane, and, leaping up and down, mimicked them all, and drank their demented spirit.

A hand seized my arm—a voice called my name. The square grew lighter—it changed—it slowly took a familiar aspect, and gradually I became aware that my room-mate was standing before me with a lighted lamp. I sank back into his arms, crying "Water! water, Robert! For the love of heaven, water!" He passed across the room to the washstand, leaving me upon the bed, where I afterward found he had replaced me on being awakened by hearing me leap frantically up and down upon the floor. In going for the water, he seemed to be traveling over a desert plain to some far-off spring, and I hailed him on his return with the pitcher and the glass as one greets his friend restored after a long journey. No glass for me! I snatched the pitcher, and drank a Niagara of refreshment with every draught. I reveled in the ecstasy of a drinker of the rivers of Al Ferdoos.

Hasheesh always brings with it an awakening of perception which magnifies the smallest sensation till it occupies immense boundaries. The hasheesh-eater who drinks during his highest state of exaltation almost invariably supposes that he is swallowing interminable floods, and imagines his throat an abyss which is becoming gorged by the sea. Repeatedly, as in an agony of thirst I have clutched some small vessel of water and tipped it at my lips, I have felt such a realization of an overwhelming torrent that, with my throat still charred, I have put the water away, lest I should be drowned by the flow.

With the relighting of the lamp my terrors ceased. The room was still immense, yet the iron of its structure, in the alembic of that heavenly light, had been transmuted into silver and gold. Beamy spars, chased by some unearthly graver, supported the roof above me, and a mellow glory transfused me, shed from sunny panels that covered the walls. Out of this hall of grammarye I suddenly passed through a crystal gate, and found myself again in the world outside. Through a valley carpeted with roses I marched proudly at the head of a grand army, and the most triumphant music pealed from all my legions. In the symphony joined many an unutterable instrument, bugles and ophicleides, harps and cymbals, whose wondrous peals seemed to say, "We are self-conscious; we exult like human souls." There were roses every where—roses under foot, roses festooning the lattices at our sides, roses showering a prodigal flush of beauty from the arches of an arbor overhead. Down the valley I gained glimpses of dreamy lawns basking in a Claude Lorraine sunlight. Over them multitudes of rosy children came leaping to throw garlands on my victorious road, and singing paeans to me with the voices of cherubs. Nations that my sword had saved ran bounding through the flowery walls of my avenue to cry "Our hero—our savior," and prostrate themselves at my feet. I grew colossal in a delirium of pride. I felt myself the centre of all the world's immortal glory. As once before the ecstasy of music had borne me from the body, so now I floated out of it in the intensity of my triumph. As the last cord was dissolved, I saw all the attendant splendors of my march fade away, and became once more conscious of my room restored to its natural state.

Not a single hallucination remained. Surrounding objects resumed their wonted look, yet a wonderful surprise broke in upon me. In the course of my delirium, the soul, I plainly discovered, had indeed departed from the body. I was that soul utterly divorced from the corporeal nature, disjoined, clarified, purified. From the air in which I hovered I looked down upon my former receptacle. Animal life, with all its processes, still continued to go on; the chest heaved with the regular rise and fall of breathing, the temples throbbed, and the cheek flushed. I scrutinized the body with wonderment; it seemed no more to concern me than that of another being. I do not remember, in the course of the whole experience I have had of hasheesh, a more singular emotion than I felt at that moment. The spirit discerned itself as possessed of all the human capacities, intellect, susceptibility, and will—saw itself complete in every respect; yet, like a grand motor, it had abandoned the machine which it once energized, and in perfect independence stood apart. In the prerogative of my spiritual nature I was restrained by no objects of a denser class. To myself I was visible and tangible, yet I knew that no material eyes could see me. Through the walls of the room I was able to pass and repass, and through the ceiling to behold the stars unobscured.

This was neither hallucination nor dream. The sight of my reason was preternaturally intense, and I remembered that this was one of the states which frequently occur to men immediately before their death has become apparent to lookers-on, and also in the more remarkable conditions of trance. That such a state is possible is incontestably proved by many cases on record in which it has fallen under the observation of students most eminent in physico-psychical science.

A voice of command called on me to return into the body, saying in the midst of my exultation over what I thought was my final disenfranchisement from the corporeal, "The time is not yet." I returned, and again felt the animal nature joined to me by its mysterious threads of conduction. Once more soul and body were one.

VI.

The Mysteries of the Life-sign Gemini.

IN this vision the conception of our human duality was presented to me in a manner more striking than ever before. Hitherto it had been more a suggestion than a proof; now it appeared in the light of an intuition. A wonderful field of questions is opened by such an experience, and I am constrained to sketch a few of them as they have occurred to myself.

1st. Are the animal and spiritual conjoint parts of the same life, or two different lives which intensely interact, yet are not altogether dependent upon each other for their continuance?

That the soul is dependent upon aught that we call material for the preservation of its highest functions, very few men will feel disposed to assert. Yet we are all exceedingly loth to concede that the animal has a distinct life of its own, which, for some time after the dissolution of the ties which bind it to the spiritual, might continue to throb on unimpaired. Your critic, who aims altogether at uses comprehended in bread, meat, and broad-cloth, may ask, "If it be so, of what practical utility would it be to discover it?" A sufficient answer lies in the fact that men would know one more truth. A truth tested and established may lie for centuries, mildewed and rusted, in the armory of knowledge, until some great soul comes along, draws it out of the rubbish, buckles it on, rushes into the conflict, and with it pries open the portals of one more promised land of blessing for the human race. Gunpowder is a truth; wise men sneer at the monk's obstreperous plaything. The years float calmly on; that plaything strikes the cliffs of Dover, and as they go toppling down to leave a highway for the nations, contemned truth vindicates her uses with a triumphant voice of thunder.

But there is also a tangible utility in this discovery of an independent animal life (supposing it to be made) which arises out of the fact that we should thus possess much higher notions of the spiritual than we have at present. In the desire to make the body entirely dependent on the soul for all its processes, we have linked the two in so close a marriage that the soul itself has become materialized by contact in our conceptions. What we call spirit is, after all, when its vague and variable boundaries are somewhat accurately drawn, nothing but an exceedingly rarefied mist, capable, to be sure, of self-conscious phenomena, but nevertheless subject to most of the conditions of matter. We grant, indeed, that after death the interior eyes may see without the mediation of our present lens and retina, but scout the idea that those eyes, in this world, ever employ a power which, after a few years, they shall keep in constant activity forever. Now, if we can more definitely mark the line between the spiritual and the animal as between two independent lives hinged on each other, yet not interpenetrating, we shall have done much to glorify the soul and reinstate it in its proper reverence.

Not to assert the separate existence of the animal life as proven, let us look at some singular phenomena which, by such an hypothesis, would be explained, and (as it seems to me) by such a one only.

1st. In surgical operations performed while the patient lay under the influence of an anaesthetic, as chloroform or ether, I have witnessed contortions of the whole muscular system, and heard outcries so fearful that it was impossible to persuade the lookers-on that the application of the instrument was not causing the severest agony. Upon one occasion I myself stood by a man who was to suffer a difficult dental operation, and with my own hands administered chloroform to him. All the usual symptoms of complete anaesthesia ensuing, I signaled the dentist to begin his work. The moment that the instrument came into successful operation, the patient uttered a harrowing cry of pain and struggled convulsively, at the same time entreating the operator to stop. I was persuaded, from former cases of a similar nature, that the man had no consciousness of pain, and so advised the dentist. From motives of humanity, however, the latter desisted when his work was but partly accomplished, and, having extracted a single tooth instead of the several which were to be drawn, permitted the seeming sufferer to return to his natural state. He presently awoke, as from a dream; and on being asked whether he endured great torture, he laughed at the idea, denying that he had even been aware of the application of the forceps, although fully self-conscious internally during the whole effect of the anaesthesia.

I believe I am only stating one of many cases which fall under the almost daily observation of men of wide experience in the surgical profession. Although far from being an expert myself, I have been an eye-witness to two such instances.

Now what is it, or who is it that is suffering tortures so great that the face, the lips, the limbs must give vent to them in such intensity of expression? The soul has been all the time lying in a delicious calm of meditation, or gliding through a succession of strange images, whose order was not once broken by the thrill of pain. It frequently remembers its visions, and can repeat them coherently; it would certainly have recollected, if it had ever known them, some traits of an experience so utterly discordant as suffering.

An inference directly suggests itself. Where all the outer phenomena of torture have been witnessed, the anaesthetic has not so much affected the body as the ties which unite it with the soul. A temporary disjunction has taken place between the two, and the animal nature has been suffering while the spiritual, completely insulated, was left to its own free activity.

2d. I believe it is gradually becoming conceded that the agonies which universal belief once attached to the idea of death are rather imaginary than real. Yet the hour of dissolution is almost invariably accompanied by groans and contortions, which tell tales of the bitter pang felt somewhere in the depths of that mysterious being which is becoming disjoined. While the dying man, if still fully conscious, frequently asserts that he is in ecstasy beyond compare, tense muscles and writhing limbs are telling another story. What is it that is suffering?

3d. There have been instances of the trance state which throw an additional light upon this question, or involve it in deeper mystery, according to the mental temperament of the man who considers them. It is needless to quote the case of Tennant in our own country, and many cataleptic and hypnotic states which have fallen under private notice, when an argument *à fortiori* may be drawn from the remarkable phenomena which but a few years ago transpired under the eye-witness of many eminent men of the medical and other professions in India (See Appendix, note A). So important a field of inquiry did these phenomena seem to open, that Dr. Braid, of Edinburgh, a physician of considerable fame, made it the groundwork of a book, condensed, yet valuable for its research, upon the trance condition, and the scientific mind through out Great Britain took a lively interest in the subject. A fakeer presented himself at one of the Company's stations, and proffered the singular request that he might be buried alive. Though not much astonished at any possible petition coming from one of an order of men so wildly fanatic as

those who infest India with their monstrous devotions and insatiable alms-begging, the servants of the Company still treated him as insane, and answered his request with corresponding neglect. Still, the fakeer insisted upon their compliance, asserting that he possessed the power of separating soul and body at will, and was able to live without air or food for the space of thirty days. Upon his producing native witnesses who fully corroborated his statement, he obtained a more deferential attention to his demand. As his reason for asking sepulture, he stated the desire for a more complete abstraction of soul than he could attain above ground and among the things of sense, positively assuring his questioners that this abstraction, as he had tested by repeated experiments, was in no danger of proving fatal to the body.

At last, then, his petition was granted. By an effort of will he threw himself into the ecstatic or trance state, and when the vital processes had become absolutely imperceptible, and he lay to all appearance dead, he was closely wrapped in a winding-sheet, and, for fear of imposition, buried in a tightly-masoned tomb. The opening was then filled with earth, and the mound thus raised above him thickly sown with barley. A Mohammedan guard (the last in the world which would be likely to connive at the cheat of a disciple of Brahm) was stationed about the grave night and day. The barley grew up undisturbed till the month was accomplished, and, at the expiration of that time, hundreds of people thronged to be present at the disentombing of the fakeer. Among them were grave men, men of calm and scientific minds, and many utterly incredulous of the possibility that human life could have been sustained from inner sources through so long a period. Every test was thus present which could make evidence of any fact conclusive beyond doubt.

The body of the fakeer was found unaltered by decay, yet shriveled to a mummy. Means of restoration were used very similar to those employed in bringing a cataleptic patient to consciousness. Presently the seemingly dead man began to breathe, his color returned, and before the close of the day, as the nutriment which was given him was assimilated, all his functions were in their ordinary activity.

A more complete separation of the animal and spiritual probably never existed without death, yet the two lives, through the whole period of sepulture, were sustained apart without the slightest consciousness in the soul that the body was growing emaciated, convulsed, and juiceless. Many of the eye-witnesses to this wonderful experiment are living to the present day.

Upon the theory of these independent existences it may be asked, "How is death possible at all to the animal?" We reply, In most cases, doubtless, the animal dies first, and the spiritual deserts it afterward; but, wherever the spiritual is the more powerfully agonized of the two, in the very shock of its exertions to depart it may bear the animal away with it, which, not being immortal, has no possible residence outside of the body, but instantly perishes. Yet when, as by the gentle disentanglement of patient fingers, the ligaments of the corporeal life are unwound from about the soul, the latter, undestroyed, may still remain through its allotted day of endurance. If this be more than mere visionary conjecture, it accounts for the unchanged appearance of bodies disentombed after a hundred years, and the relics unconsumed by time, which, in the world's reaction from hyper-credulity, we have so long been apt to classify with the other legends of the *Vita Sanctorum*.

2d. Another question suggested by the experience of my own duality is this: If the two existences are independent, may not the fact account for that blind feeling which almost every man has experienced, that he has lived previously to his present form in other and entirely different states? The idea of the metempsychosis was never, indeed, made the central one of any system of philosophy until the time of Pythagoras. He was the first of whom we have historic mention to scale off from the original gem the laminae of grosser Egyptian and Indian fable, which covered it like a later deposit (and he had reasons for doing so, which we think will be proved, to a strong probability at least, in a future portion of this narrative); yet, after all, metempsychosis, as a fact, has been dimly felt by universal humanity, and even at the present day presents itself at times so strongly to many a mind as almost to carry the conviction of an intuition.

But, upon our hypothesis, can the idea be accounted for? Let us see.

Except in the prerogative of the peculiar quality of that life which animates it, the body has no more claims to reverence than the same number of pounds of alkali, water, iron, and other chemicals composing it, in any other form.

But for the energizing, vital element of the particular rank in the scale of vitality which energizes man, he would be worthy of quite as much consideration were he sealed up in carboys, poured into pitchers, blown into bladders, and tied up in brown paper parcels. His body has not the faintest stamp of originality. As bovine muscle he existed long ago in the food which nourished his parents; still farther back he was eaten by an ox in the form of some succulent weed of the pasture, and that very weed educed him from the soil through microscopic tubes by capillary attraction. Wash this soil, and he will be deposited in the form of a precipitate; yet, after all this investigation of his material genealogy, we have only arrived at the same result which could be attained by any skillful chemist who would undergo the labor of taking him to pieces in his present state, and subject him to adequate tests. The man of visionary mind may sit down before one solitary cabbage, and find food for his thought, if not for his palate, in the reflection, "Truly thou mightest have been my brother."

Now, without the least shadow of a wish to prove matter self-conscious, may we not hold it possible that the particles entering into our corporeal composition still preserve some subtile properties (not memory, be it understood) of the other bodies through which they have passed, which, being felt by our own animal nature, are suggested by it to the spiritual as a ground for the idea of metempsychosis? The body will then be that part of us which has really transmigrated, while the soul is original.

The idea that the soul has ever transmigrated leads us into painful, disgusting, irrational, and irreligious conclusions. But grant that, in the animal life, a blind perception exists of peculiar qualities in the corporeal particles, arising out of former conditions through which they have passed, and we can then see how it may be possible for the spiritual to sympathize with the animal to such a degree as to etherealize these perceptions into a dreamy echo of its own former being. The problem, therefore, stands thus: Both for the sake of right and reason we must utterly disown the idea of spiritual metempsychosis. How, then, can we explain the fact of its universality among the race? We offer our hypothesis.

VII.

The Night of Apotheosis.

It may be thought strange that, after that experience of infinite agony which I have last related, I should ever take hasheesh again. "Surely," it will be said, "another experiment with the drug would be a daring venture into the realms of insanity and death. The gentlest name that could be applied to it is foolhardiness."

The morning immediately succeeding my night of horror found me as vigorous and buoyant as I ever was in my life. No pain, no feeling of lassitude remained, and on my face there was not the faintest record of the tortures through which I had passed. In the midst of the very astonishment with which I noted this fact, I felt assured that I had done myself no injury. Yet, mentally, I had the conception of being older by many years than on the night previous; all past experiences in life seemed separated from me by a measureless gulf of duration, and when the demon faces or the hellish songs of my vision flashed up into memory, I shuddered and turned my head as if they were close at hand. Quietly I made a resolve that I would experiment with the drug of sorcery no more, for I dreaded another plunge into the abyss of terror as I dreaded hell itself.

Slowly passed away from my mind the image of my sufferings. The elastic force of thought threw off the weight of all direful remembrances, and whenever I recalled my last night of vision it was only to dwell with tenderness upon the roses of my valley, and exult in the echo of the paeans which had glorified my march. So beautiful did such memories make the inner world, that I wearied of the outer till it became utterly distasteful, like a heavy tragedy seen for the fortieth time. I tried in vain to detect in the landscape that ever-welling freshness of life which hasheesh unveils; trees were meaningless wood, the clouds a vapory sham. I thirsted for insight, adventure, strange surprises, and mystical discoveries. I took hasheesh again.

I was sitting at the tea-table when the thrill smote me. I had handed my cup to Miss M'Ilvaine to be replenished for the first time, and she was about restoring it to me brimming with that draught "which cheers but not inebriates." I should be loth to calculate the arc through which her hand appeared to me to travel on its way to the side of my plate. The wall grew populous with dancing satyrs; Chinese mandarins nodded idiotically in all the corners, and I felt strongly the necessity of leaving the table before I betrayed myself.

I rose and hurried from the room. A friend of mine, thinking that I had been taken suddenly ill, immediately followed me. The look of wild delight with which I greeted him would have revealed my secret, even had I not spontaneously imparted it to him.

In the first stages of his singular life, the hasheesh-eater finds so much that is strange, beautiful, or appalling, that he can restrain neither his outbursts of enthusiasm nor of pain. He is big with infinite arcana, which he feels he must disclose or perish. Gradually self-control becomes with him more of a possibility, and finally it is stereotyped into a habit. In my earlier experience I found it beyond my power, even with the most agonizing efforts, to keep back the wonders which I saw, and accordingly, the moment that I found my brain expanding into the hasheesh-dome, I made it my wont to rush from the presence of all who ought not to share my secret. When many days had taught me lessons of self-retention, I sat frequently for hours charred in demoniac flames, or lifted into the seventh heaven of ecstasy, with a throng around me who could not have gained the faintest intimation from my manner of the processes which were going on within.

When Sam joined me I was on the eve of another journey through vast territories. I say "Sam," for I shall take the liberty of calling all my friends by those familiar names which imbody to me all that is loving, genial, and belonging to idiosyncrasy in my remembrance of them. Doubtless such a practice is discordant with courtly style in the most eminent degree. It would be much more polite to say Villiers where I meant Joe, and Cholmondeley instead of Harry; for in this way I should much more readily and thoroughly conciliate those minds which, enervated by the spicy feasts of high-life literature, are unable to find the least sapidity in the vocabulary of daily affections.

Southey, discoursing of the Doctor, has made that mirror of true-heartedness, as well as true courtesy, remark (I quote from memory), that among the most painful, though quiet and unnoticed losses which a man sustains in his passage from the infant to the gray-beard, is the gradual divestment of his right to be called by the name which he heard in the nursery and on the play-ground. "Now," said Daniel Dove, with a gentle sigh, "even my wife speaks of me as 'the Doctor.'" Most genial men have felt the same thing with sorrow as the "toga virilis" slowly wrapped them closer and closer into the reserve of middle life, hiding those earlier insignia of frankness and good-fellowship which no longer give them a claim to be hailed with affectionate intimacy, yet which every true man will still bear with lively remembrance upon his heart of hearts.

I have always entertained a deep grudge against the cold and courtly Cicero for that unworthy sneer launched at the friendship between Catiline and Tongilius, "Quem amare in praetexta coeperat." It was in the style of Cicero, indeed, yet not in the style of the truly noble man, nor of one who holds in fitting reverence the bond of our earlier humanities. It seems impossible to conceive how any one dignified with the better and deeper feelings of our nature should become aware, with any other sentiment than pain, that he is surviving the days when a more intimate confidence and unworldly simplicity gave genial friends a right to address him and treat him as a brother.

I shall therefore, without any apology, unless this digression may be styled so, call all the nearer and dearer companions of my youth by those names which sound as the sweetest echoes of the Past in the chambers of my memory, since the strings with which they vibrate in unison can not too long be kept thrilling in any heart that would not neglect all music beyond that with which the march of our dusty life in the exterior keeps step.

I have said that when Sam joined me I was once more filled with the phrensy of travel. I besought him to go with me, painting in the most glowing tints the treasures which such a gigantic tour as I had laid out would add to his acquaintance with the grand Kosmos. He

consented to become my compagnon de voyage for a few hundred miles, at any rate, and directly we set out. Our way led through a broad meadow, at that season beautifully green, and before my gaze it grew into a tremendous Asiatic plateau thronged with innumerable Tartars. As if assembling for a foray, they rushed past me in mad haste, their oblique eyes snapping with a ferocious light, and plumes of horse-hair streaming from their tufted caps. It is not possible to convey to a mind in its ordinary state the effect produced by beholding a field which one has been accustomed to see vacant suddenly bristling with weird and foreign forms, which by perfect distinctness of outline equal in reality, while they surpass in impressiveness the most usual objects of daily sight.

Sam was a man unexcelled by any of his age that I have ever met for the breadth of his historic, geographical, and political knowledge. Mention a fact in the Saracen annals, and straightway he would give you its date, and run its parallel of chronological latitude through all the empires and dynasties of the world. The name of the most inconsiderable place suggested to him every thing of note that had ever been transacted in its neighborhood, and on the factious efforts of an Athenian demagogue he would build you in an instant the intricate fabric of all the coups d'état, revolutions, and strokes of diplomacy up to the present day. It is not to be wondered at, such being the case, that some incongruous remark of my own, which confounded two utterly distinct tribes of Tartary, should grate on his historic taste to such a degree as to force from him a mild correction.

"It is impossible," said Sam, "that the tribe of which you speak should occupy this territory through whose boundaries you inform me we are traveling."

The instantaneous thrill of pain which this slight contradiction darted through me can not be imagined by any one who does not know the intense sensitiveness of the hasheesh state. In a tone of deepest reproach I said, "Alas! my friend, I see you do not sympathize with me. Let us travel apart."

So saying, I wandered from his side and walked alone, feeling hurt in the very centre of my pride and self-respect. But Sam, who now saw that he must humor my hallucination, followed me, and appeasing my indignation upon the delicate subject of the Ukraine Tartars, took my arm, and we walked together as before.

With all the delicious ecstasy of a traveler who looks for the first time upon the gorgeous piles of mediaeval architecture, I saw far in the distant east a palace rise sublimely above its emerald terraces. We walked for hours and through leagues, yet it grew no nearer, and I enjoyed the luxury of anticipation indefinitely prolonged, yet growing sweeter by delay. The wind came to me freighted with spicy odors; it whispered of dalliance with citron blossoms, and reeled in playful circles, new-flown from its deep draught among the vines of Muscat. In my ears it sang promises of immortal youth, and added its own wings to my already superhuman lightness.

What mattered it that my far-off battlements were the walls of college, my mighty plain a field, and my wind of balm but an ordinary sunset breeze? To me all joys were real—yes, even with a reality which utterly surpasses the hardest facts of the ordinary world.

Hasheesh is indeed an accursed drug, and the soul at last pays a most bitter price for all its ecstasies; moreover, the use of it is not the proper means of gaining any insight, yet who shall say that at that season of exaltation I did not know things as they are more truly than ever in the ordinary state? Let us not assert that the half-careless and uninterested way in which we generally look on nature is the normal mode of the soul's power of vision. There is a fathomless meaning, an intensity of delight in all our surroundings, which our eyes must be unsealed to see. In the jubilance of hasheesh, we have only arrived by an improper pathway at the secret of that infinity of beauty which shall be beheld in heaven and earth when the veil of the corporeal drops off, and we know as we are known. Then from the muddy waters of our life, defiled by the centuries of degeneracy through which they have flowed, we shall ascend to the old-time original fount, and grow rapturous with its apocalyptic draught.

But for this reflection I had never abandoned hasheesh. Yet, through all the long agonies which attended its abjurement, I consoled myself with the knowledge that the infinite glories of the past should beam on me again. I had caught a glimpse through the chinks of my earthly prison of the immeasurable sky which should one day overarch me with an unconceived sublimity of view, and resound in my ear with unutterable music. Then I stayed myself upon the hope, and grew into calm endurance.

We may depend upon it, we have not read the world within or the world without. Some mystic wind, like that of hasheesh, now and then just flutters the leaves of those shut books as it passes by, and the gleam of the divine characters for an instant ravishes us. As from children too young to bear them, they are kept against that day when, grown into perfect men, the props, and helps, and screens of the earthly shall be removed from us, and "the books shall be opened."

Presently we reached the doors of college. I do not remember whether I have yet mentioned that in the hasheesh state an occasional awaking occurs, perhaps as often as twice in an hour (though I have no way of judging accurately, from the singular properties of the hasheesh time), when the mind returns for an exceedingly brief space to perfect consciousness, and views all objects in their familiar light. Such an awaking occurred to me as we drew near the steps of the building, and I took advantage of it to request of Sam that he would conduct me to the room of another friend of mine, if he were unable to remain longer with me himself. He answered that he was obliged to leave me, and accordingly led me to the place I had mentioned. The hasheesh fantasia having returned directly after I had made my request, I might never have been able to find it alone.

Repeatedly have I wandered past doors and houses which, in my ordinary condition, were as well known as my own, and have at last given up the search for them in utter hopelessness, recognizing not the faintest familiar trace in their aspect. Certainly, a hasheesh-eater should never be alone.

I found Sidney in his room: in his charge Sam left me, after apprising him of my state, and I easily persuaded him to go with me on my travels.

Back of the buildings a very large domain of woods and fields extends toward the east. From the door of one of the entries a continuous path leads to the further extent of these grounds, and into this path we struck. The evening shadows were deepening, yet the woods had not yet become so sombre as to wear that terrible air of mystery which, among them, in my after hasheesh-life, oppressed me to an unbearable degree, even in the daylight. Our way skirted the banks of a little stream, which, tinkling over its rocky bed, makes music through all those shades from boundary to boundary. Coming to a convenient place, we crossed it on broad stepping-stones a pebble's throw from a low waterfall, which, higher up the bed, was now swollen by recent rains. An instantaneous dart of exultation shot through me. Could it be possible? Yes, true, beyond doubt! I clapped my hands and cried, "The Nile! the Nile! the eternal Nile!" Lo, now I was Bruce, and beside me walked Clapperton. "Companion of my journey," I exclaimed, "see you yonder cataract? Above it lie the sources. Out of that gleaming chasm which you behold toward the east, this mystery-veiled river has poured his floods since God first awakened the years. I drink in the ecstasy of his maternal fount now for the second time. Through lonely pilgrimages I toiled, foot-sore, in the desert; my life hung, many a night of sleeplessness and many a day of famine, upon the mood of ferocious men; I did all things, I suffered all things; and one day, at even, the sources broke upon me. Oh, that unshared view was glory enough for a lifetime!" "But why," asked Clapperton, "has the world never known the discovery of yours? In all my wanderings (and, as you are aware, they have been only exceeded by your own), I have never heard of your visit to this fountain before."

"I died in the desert on my way homeward. As I felt the unmistakable signs of death come upon me, I gathered strength to trace upon a small piece of paper a few words, simply stating the fact of the discovery, and the bearings of the sources. This I committed to my guide, extorting from him a reluctant promise never to part with it until he had carried it to my friends at Alexandria."

"Why reluctant?"

"Because he declared that it was sacrilege to unveil the forehead of the Nile, and that he dreaded some fearful recompense for his impiety."

"Where is that paper now? Did he fulfill his promise?"

"No. He carried the writing as far as Alexandria, and there, being overcome by the terrors of his superstition, burned it, and forever

deprived me of the triumph of my labors. Yet with you, Clapperton—you, who so well know my toils—I rejoice as if the world were applauding me. Glory, glory in the highest, that I behold again—that I behold with *you*—the Nile, the eternal Nile!"

My eyes ran tears of ecstasy. I clasped Clapperton to my bosom in speechless joy. I heard the river in its upper caverns hymning such invitations as float down to the seer, entranced, from the lips of angels. Bruce revisiting earth felt such exultation as can only be excelled by that of Bruce first freed from earth.

Leaving the banks of the Nile, we struck deeper into the dense shade of pines and chestnuts, which, to my sense, were spice-trees of the African wilderness. On a stile over which our way led sat two students repeating Shakespeare to each other. To avoid their beholding my rejoicing, Sid gently took me into another path, yet we came near enough to hear one sentence:

"With this, farewell; I'm on my way to Padua."

(Not exactly Shakespeare, but they meant it to be, and I was not in a mood to cavil.)

In an instant, like the shifting of a scene, all the thoughts and images of Africa vanished. Italy, the glad, the sunny, took its place, and the wood grew dense with palaces and fountains. In a broad piazza we sauntered up and down, transfused with a dreamy summer languor, or strolled from portico to portico, on all sides surrounded by the most beautiful creations of Art.

At first I had a dim conception of the unreality of this vision, for I saw its groundwork in certain material things, remembered as once existing in other forms. For instance, I sometimes perceived the development of an arch in its transition state from two curved branches which locked over us, and now and then a new column grew up gradually from the vacant light-spaces between two trunks of trees. But in a very short time, of course, much shorter than I supposed, every suspicion of the imaginary utterly vanished from

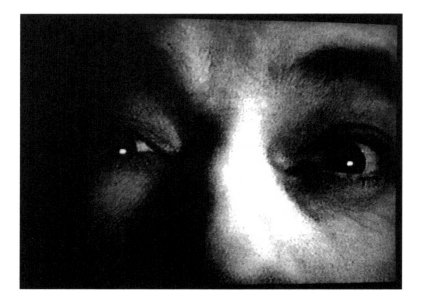

my mind, and I no more doubted our being in some fair Italian city than I doubted my own existence.

The effect of the hasheesh increased, as it always does, with the excitement of the visions and the exercise of walking. I began to be lifted into that tremendous pride which is so often a characteristic of the fantasia. My powers became superhuman; my knowledge covered the universe; my scope of sight was infinite. I was invested with a grand mission to humanity, and slowly it dawned upon me that I was the Christ, come in the power, and radiance of his millennial descent, and bearing to the world the restoration of perfect peace. I spoke, and it was done: with a single sentence I regenerated the Creation. A smile of exultation beamed from the awakened earth. I could hear her low music of rejoicing as she perceived that the fullness of the times with which, for centuries, she had travailed in woe, had at length been brought forth. All men once more lived in love to God and their neighbor, and, secure in an eternal compact, began marching on harmoniously to the sublime end of spiritual greatness. The nature of all beasts grew mild; the satyr walked down from his mountain fastness, and led his young fearlessly into the presence of his old foe, the leopard; the kite and the dove imped their wings upon the same branch; out of the depths of the jungle the tiger stepped forth and gently drew near to fawn upon his king. The terrible lustre of his eyes was dissolved into the serene light of love, and as I caressed his spotted hide, he returned the kindness with a thankful purr.

My mission being accomplished, we passed on. Returning to the college, a most singular phenomenon presented itself. The faces of all that I met were metamorphosed into appearances which symbolized some inner attribute, or some speciality of manners and habits. One of my friends was an admirable whist-player, noted for his accurate observance and employment of the times and seasons for returning leads, finessing, and crying privilege. His face was changed to a fan-like display of cards, which winked at me with a quiet and balmy air of exultation, as in the consciousness of being

> "Quite irresistible,
> Like a man with eight trumps in his hand at a whist-table."

Another, famous for his studently habits, a great reader, and fond of research, looked at me for a moment, and his visage immediately turned into a book-case bristling with encyclopedias. I stretched forth my hand to take one from its shelf, and, by a sudden outcry, became aware that I had performed that amiable office known among mortals as pulling one's nose.

But this vision of the ludicrous was soon dissipated by the return of the former ecstasy of pride. Now braced for its exaltation by the few moments of jocose refreshment, I towered into all the sublimity of self-adulation. Pacing the floor, which, for my display, had been changed into that of the Senate, as Webster revivified, I rolled a thunder-cloud of colossal argument over the head of a mythical opponent, and brought all-time to the witness-stand with testimony against the direful results of some intemperate measure.

And now, the hallucination changing, I was exhaustlessly rich, and as exhaustlessly benevolent. Through long avenues I walked between kneeling files of poor, and scattered handfuls of gold into their bosoms. "Be comfortable, be opulent, be luxurious," I cried; and as the metallic rain dripped from my thrilling fingers, again the plaudits of my march poured in upon me, and the famine-stricken shouted, "Our savior!" I rejoiced in the measureless pride of bounteousness.

Awaking on the morrow after a succession of vague and delicious dreams, I had not yet returned to the perfectly natural state. I now began to experience a law of hasheesh which developed its effects more and more through all the future months of its use. With the progress of the hasheesh life, the effect of every successive indulgence grows more perduring until the hitherto isolated experiences become tangent to each other; then the links of the delirium intersect, and at last so blend that the chain has become a continuous band, now resting with joyous lightness as a chaplet, and now mightily pressing in upon the soul like the glowing hoop of iron which holds martyrs to the stake. The final months of this spell-bound existence, be it terminated by mental annihilation or by a return into the quiet and mingled facts of humanity, are passed in one unbroken yet checkered dream.

In the morning the ludicrous side of the hasheesh sphere alone was turned toward me. I was whirled through the progress of an infinite number of strange transmutations. Now, as a powerful saw in some mill of a northern lumber region, I darted up and down at the imperative instigation of an overshot wheel, and on either side of me the planks flew off in the utmost completeness of manufacture. Now, changed to a bottle of soda-water, I ran hither and thither with intricate and rapid involutions, pursued by an army of publicans, who, with awl in hand, were trying to break the wires which kept in my vital effervescence. Weak with laughter, for I was strangely reckless of the peril which my life sustained, I sat down to rest, having distanced the whole troop of my persecutors. Suddenly the sentiment of an intense mortification overcame me. "Is it possible," I soliloquized, "that thou, the descendant of an ancient and glorious line, canst be so utterly dishonored as to merge thy being in one of society's grossest and basest potables? Child worthy of a better destiny, I will implore the gods for thee, that in their condescension they may elevate thee to some more spiritual essence." No sooner said than done. My neck grew longer, my head was nightcapped with snowy kid, ethereal odors of delight streamed through my brain, and, exultant with apotheosis, I beheld my patent of nobility stamped on my crystal breast in these golden characters:

EAU DE COLOGNE.
jean maria de farina

A lordly hippopotamus, I wandered in from the wilderness, and with my fore-foot knocked at the door of a friend of mine celebrated for wasting the midnight burning-fluid in the pursuit of classical and mathematical researches. "Tidings!" I cried; "tidings from the interior of Africa!" With a look of astonishment and half terror, for he had never seen me in the hasheesh state before, the lover of books opened unto me, and I passed in.

An unceremonious hippopotamus, I sat down, with the most incongruous disregard of the breadth of beam proper to my species, in the nearest chair, without explanation or apology. A poetical hippopotamus, I soared into a sublime description of equatorial crags, medio-terrene lakes, and marshy jungles. I expatiated upon the delights of an Ethiopian existence; I grew rapturous over the remembered ecstasy of mud-baths and lunches upon succulent lotus-stems by riversides where Nature kept free restaurant for pachydermatous gentlemen forever.

Ed was a man of strong social impulses, most kindly heart, and high appreciation of the beautiful. Yet at that moment, being ensconced in a tremendous munition of tomes, and supplied with stores of reading which might sustain the most protracted siege, pleaded preoccupation, and begged me to defer my lecture on the African far niente. I consented, with some indignation, however, at his lack of taste. I opened the door to leave his room for the sake of finding a more respectful auditor, when lo! to my shame, I had altogether mistaken my species for I was the tallest giraffe that ever dallied amorously with a palm-bud. Abasing my exalted head to suit the dimensions of the door, I passed out, and was again restored to human semblance.

VIII.

Vos non vobis—wherein the Pythagorean is a By-stander

THE judgment that must be passed upon the hasheesh life in retrospect is widely different from the one which I formed during its progress. Now the drug, with all its revelation of interior mysteries, its glimpses of supernatural beauty and sublimity, appears as the very witch-plant of hell, the weed of madness. At the time of its daily use, I forgave it for all its pangs, for its cruel exercise of authority, its resistless fascination, and its usurpation of the place of all other excitement, at the intercession of the divine forms which it created for my soul, and which, though growing rarer and rarer, when they were present retained their glory until the last. Moreover, through many ecstasies and many pains, I still supposed that I was only making experiments, and that, too, in the most wonderful field of mind which could be opened for investigation, and with an agent so deluding in its influence that the soul only became aware that the strength of a giant was needed to escape when its locks were shorn.

In accordance with these facts, I did not suppose that I was imperiling any friend of mine by giving him an opportunity to make the same experiment which he beheld producing in me phenomena so astonishing to a mind in love with research. Several of my intimate associates applied to me for the means of experimentally gratifying their curiosity upon the subject, and to some of them, as favorable opportunities presented themselves, I administered hasheesh, remaining by their side during the progress of the effects. In no other experience can difference of temperament, physical and mental, produce such varieties of phenomena; nowhere can we attain so well defined an idea of this difference. I shall, therefore, devote this chapter to the relation of some of the more remarkable of these cases.

Upon William N— hasheesh produced none of the effects characteristic of fantasia. There was no hallucination, no volitancy of unusual images before the eye when closed. Circulation, however, grew to a surprising fullness and rapidity, accompanied by the same introversion of faculties and clear perception of all physical processes which startled me in my first experiment upon myself. There was stertorous breathing, dilatation of the pupil, and a drooping appearance of the eyelid, followed at last by a comatose state, lasting for hours, out of which it was almost impossible fully to arouse the energies. These symptoms, together with a peculiar rigidity of the muscular system, and inability to measure the precise compass and volume of the voice when speaking, brought the case nearer in resemblance to those recorded by Dr. O'Shaughnessy, of Calcutta, as occurring under his immediate inspection among the natives of India than any I have ever witnessed.

In William N— I observed, however, one phenomenon which characterizes hasheesh existence in persons of far different constitutions—the expansion of time and space. Walking with him a distance not exceeding a furlong, I have seen him grow weary and assume a look of hopelessness, which he explained by telling me that he never could traverse the immensity before him. Frequently, also, do I remember his asking to know the time thrice in as many minutes, and when answered, he exclaimed, "Is it possible? I supposed it an hour since I last inquired." His temperament was a mixture of the phlegmatic and nervous, and he was generally rather unsusceptible to stimulus. I was anxious at the time that he should be favorably affected, since he had been, and afterward was still more so, in an eminent degree, the kind-hearted assuager of my sufferings and increaser of my joys in many an experience of hasheesh. To him I ran, many a time, for companionship in my hasheesh journeyings, and always found in him full appreciation and sympathy.

I am now glad that he learned none of the fascination of the drug, for Heaven only, and not the hasheesh-eater in any wise, knows where it will lead him.

One of my friends in college was a man to whom it would have been physically, spiritually, and morally impossible ever to have borne any other name than Bob, the name by which he was called among all his intimates, and which has an air eminently expressive of his nature. Impulsive, enthusiastic in his affections, generous to a fault; excitable, fond of queer researches and romantic ventures, there is no other cognomen which would so typify him as to give more than a shadowy image of his constitution—none which would so incarnate him as not to leave some elbow of his inner being sticking out in the improper place. It is not surprising that a person of his temperament found much in the hasheesh condition that was strikingly attractive.

At half past seven in the evening, and consequently after supping instead of before, as I should have preferred, he took twenty-five grains of the drug. This may seem a large bolus to those who are aware that from fifteen grains I frequently got the strongest cannabine effect; but it must be kept in mind that, to secure the full phenomena, a much greater dose is necessary in the first experiment than ever after. Unlike all other stimuli with which I am acquainted, hasheesh, instead of requiring to be increased in quantity as existence in its use proceeds, demands rather a diminution, seeming to leave, at the return of the natural state (if I may express myself by rather a material analogy), an unconsumed capital of exaltation for the next indulgence to set up business upon.

From the untoward lateness of the hour at which the dose was administered, it was now half past ten o'clock before any effects began

to show themselves in this case. At that time Bob, and Edward, the reading man, to whose favorable notice I had presented myself under the guise of a hippopotamus, were both seated, together with myself, in a well-lighted room, conversing. Suddenly Bob leaped up from the lounge on which he had been lying, and, with loud peals of laughter, danced wildly over the room. A strange light was in his eyes, and he gesticulated furiously, like a player in pantomime. I was not in the least surprised by these symptoms, for I realized precisely the state of mind through which he was passing; yet my other companion was astonished even to terror with the idea that the experimenter would permanently lose his sanity. Suddenly he stopped dancing, and trembling, as with an undefinable fear, he whispered, "What will become of me?" This question distinctly recalled all the horrible apprehensions of my first experiment; and, though satisfied of the perfect harmlessness of the result, I saw the necessity of steadying the sufferer's mind upon my own firm assurance of his safety, for the sake of giving him quiet and endurance. I replied, "Trust me, however singularly you may feel, you have not the slightest cause for fear. I have been where you are now, and, upon my honor, guarantee you an unharmed return. No evil will result to you; abandon yourself to the full force of your feelings with perfect confidence that you are in no danger." Entirely new and unconceived as is the hasheesh-world, viewed for the first time, the man of greatest natural courage is no more capable of bearing its tremendous realities, unbraced by some such exterior support, than the most feeble woman.

The delirium, now rapidly mounting to its height, made it better that Bob should exert the supernatural activity with which he was endued out of doors, where the air was freer and less constraint was necessary. Clothing my words in as imaginative a garb as I was master of, I therefore proposed to him that we should set out on a journey through the wonderful lands of vision. We were soon upon the pavement, he leaping in unbounded delight at the prospect of the grand scenery to come, I ready to humor to the utmost any pleasing fantasy which might possess him; and in the absence of such, or the presence of the contrary, to suggest fine avenues for his thought to follow up.

It will of course be perceived that I labor under a great disadvantage from being compelled to relate the progress of subjective states from an objective point of view. My authority for all that I shall give in this case will be my own observation of outward phenomena and my friend's statement of interior ones, which he gave to me upon returning to consciousness. These latter were expressed with a height of ideality which I feel myself incompetent to give, and gave evidence of as remarkable an inner condition as I have ever known hasheesh to produce.

On our first leaving the steps of the building, a grand mosque rose upon his vision in the distance, its minarets flaunting with innumerable crescent-emblasoned flags. A mighty plain, covered with no other than a stinted grass, stretched between him and the mosque. Mounted upon Arab horses, with incredible swiftness we sped side by side toward the structure; and I knew when this imagination took place by the answers which he returned me upon my inquiry into the reasons of his prancing as we went. Before we reached the walls, arch and minaret had vanished, and, metamorphosed into an ostrich, he scoured the desert reaches, now utterly void of any human sign. Of this fact also I became aware at the moment from his own lips; for, although in perfect hallucination, the dual existence, as in me, was still capable of expressing its own states.

It is not one of the least singular facts of hasheesh that its fantasia almost invariably takes an Oriental form. This can not be explained upon the hypothesis that the experimenter remembers it as an indulgence in use among the people of the East, for at the acme of the delirium there is no consciousness remaining in the mind of its being an unnatural state. The very idea of the drug is utterly forgotten, and present reality shuts out all inquiry into grounds for belief. The only supposition which at all accounts for the fact to my own mind is that the hasheesh is the antecedent instead of the result of the peculiar characteristics of Oriental mind and manners. The Turk and the Syrian are indeed situated amid surroundings well calculated to stimulate the imaginative nature. A delicious sky, a luxuriant vegetation, and scenery like that of the Bosphorus and Damascus are eminently calculated for fascination to dreams and poesy, but then hasheesh comes bearing an unutterably grander and richer gratification to the same music and odor haunted sense, and makes the highest tone in a harmony already beautiful almost beyond all that earth possesses.

To us, of a mistier atmosphere, yet far more lively perceptions of the very principle of beauty, the drug brings a similar wealth of visions, and, conjoining its influence with a greater scope of sight and strength of thought than the Oriental ever possesses, fills up all deficiencies of exterior sun and landscape by borrowing from the activities of the experimenter.

Eastern architecture, and, in fine, the sum total of Eastern manners, are all the embodiment and symbol of Eastern mind. That mind, or at least its speciality of condition, is very much the product of those stimulants which are in use throughout that portion of the world, and among these hasheesh holds the regency, as swaying the broadest domain of mind, and most authoritatively ruling all faculties within it. It is therefore the case that, wherever this drug comes in contact with a sensitive organization, the same fruit of supernatural beauty or horror will characterize the visions produced. It is hasheesh which makes both the Syrian and the Saxon Oriental.

That this hypothesis is more than mere vagary, it appears to me, may be proved by numerous parallels running through other nations than the Eastern. It is not mere murky weather, chill winds, and sudden changes of temperature which have built up the walls of reserve in manner and masonry in architecture around the Englishman. His national stimulus is beer, mildly toned by the moderate use of tobacco; his mental result is reticence, solidity, reflectiveness.

Nor does the newness of his country, the peculiarities of his climate, and the demand of his age for rapidity of action alone erect for the American his airy structures, rising with a fungus-vitality from basement to cope in a fortnight, and the pale fence of frankness, which permits insight into all his thoughts. His infants stretch supplicating hands from the cradle toward their father's tobacco-box; the olive-plants around his table are as regularly fumigated as if they were in a green-house; his gray-beard uncle (whenever an American takes time to live so long) through all the house continually pipes a fragrant music, to which the remainder of the household do not refuse to dance, and from this most catholic transfusion of nicotine he results in that very anomalous, yet, on the whole, laudable product, our National Man. This man is a singular compound of the visionary and the actual: visionary, because (with other causes, to be sure) his stimulant makes him so; actual, because the necessity of hard work in this New World of intense activity demands it of him. His mind incarnates itself in structures whose decoration and rapidity of finish are accomplished at the risk of safety, permanence, and health, and in manners which caution and reserve only characterize when hard knocks against projecting angles of humanity have taught him the lesson of their needfulness.

His town house is the embodiment of the cigar, as the Briton's is that of the tankard, and the modes of living of both of them symbolize to a great degree the essence of their several stimulants.

In all civilized nations, the public works of architecture are an exception to this rule, for the design of the pile being more cosmopolitan, national idiosyncrasies are merged in the more comprehensive plan which contains within itself the garnered excellence of all worldly art. With the Turk it is not so; uncatholicized as is his nature, his mosque and his sultan's seraglio are as definite incarnations of generic peculiarity as his kiosk.

Excusing myself for this digression, I return to the details of the vision which I had commenced.

The night was much darker than it should have been for a hasheesh-eater's walk, who, it will be remembered, calls imperatively for light to gine his visions. The hallucination of the ostrich still remaining, we passed out into the street through the stone gateway at the end of the college terrace. The sky above us was obscured by clouds, but the moon, now at her full, was about three breadths of her disk above the western horizon. I pointed through the trees to her radiant shield, and called Bob's attention to the peculiar beauty of the view. He clapped his hands in ecstasy, exclaiming, "Behold the eternal kingdom of the moonlight!" From that moment until the planet set, in this kingdom he walked. A silvery deliciousness transfused all things to his sight; his emotions rose and fell like tides with the thrill of the lunar influence. All that in past imaginings he had ever enjoyed of moonlit river views, terraces, castles, and slumberous gardens, was melted into this one vision of rapture.

At length the moon sank out of sight, and a thick darkness enveloped us in the lonely street, only relieved by the corner lamps, which dotted the long and drear prospective. For a while we walked silently. Presently I felt my companion shudder as he leaned upon my arm. "What is the matter, Bob?" I asked. "Oh! I am in unbearable horror," he replied. "If you can, save me!" "How do you suffer?" "This shower of soot which falls on me from heaven is dreadful!"

I sought to turn the current of his thoughts into another channel, but he had arrived at that place in his experience where suggestion is powerless. His world of the Real could not be changed by any inflow from ours of the Shadowy. I reached the same place in after days, and it was then as impossible for any human being to alter the condition which enwrapped me as it would have been for a brother on earth to stretch out his hands and rescue a brother writhing in the pangs of immortality. There are men in Oriental countries who make it their business to attend hasheesh-eaters during the fantasia, and profess to be able to lead them constantly in pleasant paths of hallucination. If indeed they possess this power, the delirium which they control must be a far more ductile state than any I have witnessed occurring under the influence of hasheesh at its height. In the present instance I found all suggestion powerless. The inner actuality of the visions and the terror of external darkness both defeated me.

Again, for a short distance, we went without speaking. And now my friend broke forth into a faint, yet bitter cry of "Pray for me! I shall be lost!" Though still knowing that he was in no ultimate danger, I felt that it was vain to tell him so, and, granting his request, ejaculated, "Oh best and wisest God, give peace unto this man!" "Stop! stop!" spoke my friend; "that name is terrible to me; I can not hear it. I am dying; take me instantly to a physician."

Aware that, though no such physical need existed, there was still a great spiritual one if I would make him calm, I immediately promised him that I would do as he asked, and directed our course to the nearest doctor. Now, denominate shapes clutched at him from the darkness, cloaked from head to foot in inky palls, yet glaring with fiery eyes from the depths of their cowls. I felt him struggling, and by main force dragged him from their visionary hands. The place wherein he seemed to himself to be walking was a vast arena, encircled by tremendous walls. As from the bottom of a black baranthrum, he looked up and saw the stars infinitely removed; they glazed mournfully at him with a human aspect of despairing pity, and he heard them faintly bewailing his perdition. Sulphurous fires rolled in the distance, upbearing on their waves agonized forms and faces of mockery, and demon watch-fires flared up fitfully on the impenetrable battlements around him. He did not speak a word, but I heard him groan with a tone that was full of fearful meaning.

And now, in the midst of the darkness, there suddenly stood a wheel like that of a lottery, surrounded by one luminous spot, which illustrated all its movements. It began slowly to revolve; its rapidity grew frightful, and out of its opening flew symbols which indicated to him, in regular succession, every minutest act of his past life: from his first unfilial disobedience in childhood—the refusal upon a certain day, as far back as infancy, to go to school when it was enjoined upon him, up to the latest deed of impropriety he had committed—all his existence flew before him like lightning in those burning emblems. Things utterly forgotten—things at the time of their first presence considered trivial—acts as small as the cutting of a willow wand, all fled by his sense in arrow-flight; yet he remembered them as real incidents, and recognized their order in his existence.

This phenomenon is one of the most striking exhibitions of the state in which the higher hasheesh exaltation really exists. It is a partial sundering, for the time, of those ties which unite soul and body. That spirit should ever lose the traces of a single impression is impossible. De Quincey's comparison of it to the palimpsest manuscripts, while it is one of the most powerful that even that great genius could have conceived, is not at all too much as to express the truth. We pass, in dreamy musing, through a grassy field; a blade of the tender herbage brushes against the foot; its impression hardly comes into consciousness; on earth it is never remembered again. But not even that slight sensation is utterly lost. The pressure of the body dulls the soul to its perception, other external experiences supplant it; but when the time of the final awaking comes, the resurrection of the soul from its charnel in the body, the analytic finger of inevitable light shall search out that old inscription, and to the spiritual eye no deep-graven record of its earthly triumphs shall be clearer.

The benumbing influences of the body protect us here from much of remorse and retrospective pining. Its weight lies heavily upon the inner sense, and deadens it to perception of multitudes of characters which, to be read, require acutest powers of discernment. When the body is removed, the barrier to the Past goes also.

This fact may perhaps be one of the final causes why the body exists at all. Why are we not born directly into the spiritual world, without having to pass through a weary preliminary experience hemmed in by the gross corporeal nature? May not the answer be something like this? Were the soul, at its first creation, introduced directly into the world where truth is an intuition, and stands in the dazzling light of its own essence, the dreadful sublimity of the view might prove its annihilation. We accordingly pass first through an apprenticeship, in which we have nothing colossal either to learn or to do; and eternal verities dawn on us slowly, instead of breaking in like lightning. The Phenomenal is at first all that we know; we have qualities and quantities, and through the period of infancy are content with novel acquisitions in this field. Next, we become aware of certain faculties of induction, investing us with the power of apprehending the Notional, which never comes within the grasp of Sense: we learn relations which exist only to the thought, yet are deemed still as valid experiences as if they were tasted or handled. Last of all, we mount into the Intuitional domain, and, without the props of Sense in any way to steady us, either by sensations perceived or suggesting relations, we know universal principles of Being face to face. Up this gradual stairway of Sense, Understanding, Intuition, we mount to that height from which we are able to behold, with some degree of calmness, the infinite field of intuitive Beauty and Truth, when the screen of the bodily is removed, and the scope of vision belonging to our highest faculty is realized to be immeasurably beyond all that our most rapturous visions ever conceived it. Without this slow indoctrination, the soul might have flamed out in dazzling momentary irradiance, and then been extinguished in eternal nothingness.

If it be true that the bodily is thus our shield from the lethal glories of the purely spiritual world, and also from the full force of painful memories in the past, we can easily see how a most terrible retribution might be wreaked upon the soul by permitting it to stand through eternity without any covering to dim the events of its earthly time. Doubtless the spirit, interiorly in a state harmonious to the celestial concourse, will be invested with a spiritual body—a body which, while it does not press heavily, like ours of the earthy, will still so condition states of mind as to permit no inflow but that of delightful impressions. But let the soul to which such societies and such garments are uncongenial, from the evils which he loves, stand bare in the presence of the Nemesis of his past life, with the wondrous light of the New World irradiating the terrors of her countenance, and all the symbols of fire and scorpion-stings will but faintly image the agonies of the view. Well then, does Paul pray, "Not that I may be unclothed, but clothed upon."

I left the narration of my story while we were still walking toward the doctor's. At length, reaching there, we found him still sitting in his office, although it was now eleven o'clock.

I tried in vain to obtain the first word with him; for Bob, who seemed, according to the frequent nature of the hasheesh hallucination, suspicious of some wrong about to be done him, would not allow me to say any thing which might tinge the opinion of the physician. He persisted in affirming that he was at the point of death, although denying that he felt pain in any place which he could touch. He was totally unable to inform the doctor of the cause of his condition; but I at last managed to tell him myself. Like the great majority of practitioners, he knew nothing of the nature of the drug, and could only shake his head and presage evil from observing the singular phenomena which characterized his patient's outward conduct. He told Bob that he was very foolish to have made the experiment; was in imminent danger—might die; would give him a powder—ahem!

With such pre-eminent consolation he was poulticing the poor fellow's excited mind, when I took advantage of his going out for a dose of ipecac to follow him unostentatiously, feigning the intention of helping him to prepare the dose. The moment that we were in another room, I said, with as much vehemence as was possible without Bob's overhearing it, "For Heaven's sake, if you have any mercy, tell that man that he is in no danger! He *is* in none whatever. I have made the same experiment repeatedly, and I assure you that all he wants is the calm assurance of his safety."

My earnest manner satisfied him of my truth, and he accordingly went into the room where Bob was still sitting, and comforted him very much in the same manner that my doctor used with me when I was terrified in my first experiment. He told him, laughingly, to be in no apprehension whatever for results, as he would certainly recover from his present feelings intact.

In an instant Bob became perfectly calm, and the former state of happiness succeeded his agonies. We passed out of the doctor's office and began returning home. On the way he supposed himself a Mandarin freshly come from some triumph over invading tribes. Like myself, in the vision of my victorious march, he heard anthems of land and glory pealing in his ears; but he did still more—he played one of the instruments himself. Always a man of fine musical imagination, and quite a brilliant pianist, he now possessed a power of melodious creation unknown in his highest natural states. Setting his lips so as to send forth sounds in imitation of a bugle, he played in my hearing a strain of his own impromptu composition so beautiful that it would have done credit to any player upon wind instruments that ever obtained celebrity. For a quarter of a mile I enjoyed this unexpected rapture of music, in the utmost astonishment at a phenomenon I had never conceived of before.

We reached home. The experimenter lay down, and through all the night he was wrapped in visions of the utmost ecstasy. I sat beside his bed for hours, and always became aware of the moment of his

highest exaltation by some strain after the manner of that which had cheered our way up the dark and lonely hill, bursting from his lips, even in sleep, with delicious melody. In the morning he awoke at the usual time; but, his temperament being perhaps more sensitive than mine, the hasheesh delight, without its hallucination, continued for several days. Bob never took it again.

The next case which I shall mention is that of my friend Fred W—, who, although now having abandoned hasheesh forever, still from the first experiment he made with it, was so delighted with the spell that for several months he made trial of its powers, as successfully, if never to the same extent, as myself. His temperament was the sanguine and nervous commingled; his taste for the arts amounted to a passion. The initiatory test of hasheesh which he made gave him only its space and time expanding effects, but he had obtained a sufficient glimpse of its weirdness to make him try again.

Upon many a bright moonlight night have I walked with him through streets made balmy by the breath of the summer night, or rowed our boat along the silvery river while he lay in ecstatic musing upon the stern seat. In the dreams of such a man as he or the last one whom I mentioned, by sympathy I lived almost as delicious a hasheesh life as in my own. Once do I remember well, while we were floating noiselessly between those twin welkins, the glorious sky above us, and its image mirrored in the stream below, his beholding in the clouds that lifted their beamy masses on the western horizon a resplendent city, built amphitheatrically like Algiers, yet in every dome and architrave beautiful with the taintless lustre of marble. And now he cried, "Sing! my mood is congenial to the ethereal spirit of music." I softly hummed "Spargi d'amaro pianto." "That is ecstasy!" he broke forth once more. "Do you remember those words, 'Architecture is frozen music?' With your ascending notes I saw grand battlements rise immensely into the sky; with the descending tones they sank again, and through all your song I have sat enamored of one delicious dance of Parian marble."

But his most wonderful experience—wonderful for its exceeding beauty, but still more so for the glimpse which it gave him of the mind's power of sympathetic perception, was a vision which he had after that which I have just related. Having taken hasheesh and felt its influence already for several hours, he still retained enough of conscious self-control to visit the room of a certain excellent pianist without exciting the suspicion of the latter. Fred threw himself upon a sofa immediately on entering, and asked the artist to play him some piece of music, without naming any one in particular.

The prelude began. With its first harmonious rise and fall the dreamer was lifted into the choir of a grand cathedral. Thenceforward it was heard no longer as exterior, but I shall proceed to tell how it was internally embodied in one of the most wonderful imaginative representations that it has ever been my lot to know.

The windows of nave and transept were emblazoned, in the most gorgeous coloring, with incidents culled from saintly lives. Far off in the chancel, monks were loading the air with essences that streamed from their golden censers; on the pavement, of inimitable mosaic, kneeled a host of reverent worshippers in silent prayer.

Suddenly, behind him, the great organ began a plaintive minor like the murmur of some bard relieving his heart in threnody. This minor was unjoined by a gentle treble voice among the choir in which he stood. The low wail rose and fell as with the expression of wholly human emotion. One by one the remaining singers joined in it, and now he heard, thrilling to the very roof of the cathedral, a wondrous miserere. But the pathetic delight of hearing was soon supplanted by, or rather mingled with, a new sight in the body of the pile below him. At the farther end of the nave a great door slowly swung open and a bier entered, supported by solemn bearers. Upon it lay a coffin covered by a heavy pall, which, being removed as the bier was set down in the chancel, discovered the face of the sleeper. It was the dead Mendelssohn!

The last cadence of the death-chant died away; the bearers, with heavy tread, carried the coffin through an iron door to its place in the vault; one by one the crowd passed out of the cathedral, and at last, in the choir, the dreamer stood alone. He turned himself also to depart, and, awakened to complete consciousness, beheld the pianist just resting from the keys. "What piece have you been playing?" asked Fred. The musician replied it was "Mendelssohn's Funeral March!"

This piece, Fred solemnly assured me, he had never heard before. The phenomenon thus appears inexplicable by any hypothesis which would regard it as a mere coincidence. Whether this vision was suggested by an unconscious recognition of Mendelssohn's style in the piece performed, or, by the awaking of some unknown intuitional faculty, it was produced as an original creation. I know not, but certainly it is as remarkable an instance of sympathetic clairvoyance as I ever knew.

Dan, the partner of my hasheesh-walk mentioned as occurring in the town of P—, was, at the same time as myself, a member of the college. The Coryphaeus of witty circles, and the light of all our festivals, he was still imaginative in higher spheres, and as worthily held the rostrum and the bard's chair as his place by the genial fireside or generous table. A poet, and an enthusiastic lover as well as performer of music, I supposed that the effect of hasheesh upon his susceptible temperament would be delightful in the extreme. But to such a result, the time at which he took the drug was one of the most unfavorable in the world—when his nervous system was in a state of even morbid excitability. We had started together on a walk when the thrill came on. And such a thrill—or, rather, such a succession of thrills—it is wonderful how a human organism could sustain. At first a cloud of impenetrable mystery inwrapt him; then upon the crown of his head a weight began to press. It increased in gravity without gaining bulk, and at last, breaking through the barrier of the skull, it slid down the spinal column like lightning, convulsing every nerve with one simultaneous shudder of agony.

This sensation was repeated again and again, until, with horror, he called on me to return, as assured as I had ever been in my first experiments that death was soon to be the result of the shock. I instantly obeyed his wish, and on reaching his room he lay down. Of a sudden all space expanded marvelously, and into the broad area where he reclined marched a multitude of bands from all directions, discoursing music upon all sorts of instruments, and each band playing a different march on a different key, yet all, by some scientific arrangement, preserving perfect harmony with each other, and most exquisitely keeping time. As the symphony increased in volume, so also did it heighten in pitch, until at last the needle-points of sound seemed to concentre in a demon music-box of incredible upper register, which whirled the apex of its scream through the dome of his head, inside of which it was playing.

Now, on the wall of the room, removed to a great distance by the hasheesh expansion, a monstrous head was spiked up, which commenced a succession of grimaces of the most startling yet ludicrous character. First its ferociously bearded under jaw extended forward indefinitely; and then, the jaw shooting back, the mouth opened from ear to ear. Now the nose spun out into absurd enormity, and now the eyes winked with the rapidity of lightning.

Yet suffering in Dan bore an excessive over-ratio to mirth. In his greatest pain he had framed a withering curse against some one who had entered the room, but when he tried to give it utterance his lips failed in their office as if paralyzed. I gave him water when his thirst had become extreme, and the same sensations of a cataract plunging down his throat which I have before described occurred so powerfully that he set the glass down, unwilling to risk the consequences of his draught.

Returning to consciousness, he did not, however, recover from the more moderate hasheesh effects for months. The nervous thrills which I have related reappeared to him at intervals, and his dreams constantly wore a hasheesh tint. Indeed, in all cases which I have known, this drug has retained a more enduring influence than any stimulant in the whole catalogue.

A number of experiments made upon other persons with more or less success, yet none of them characterized by any phenomena differing from those already detailed, prove conclusively that upon persons of the highest nervous and sanguine temperaments hasheesh has the strongest effect; on those of the bilious occasionally almost as powerful a one; while lymphatic constitutions are scarcely influenced at all except in some physical manner, such as vertigo, nausea, coma, or muscular rigidity. Yet to this statement there are striking exceptions, arising out of the operation of some latent forces of vitality which we have not yet included in our physical or psychical science. Until the laws which govern these are fully apprehended, hasheesh must ever remain a mystery, and its operation in any specific case an uncertainty.

IX.

The Shadow of Bacchus, the Shadow of Thanatos, and the Shadow of Shame.

ONCE more at the table I was seized by the hand of the hasheesh genie. Dinner was nearly over, and I escaped into the street without being suspected.

Street did I say? Ah no! That conventional synonym of all dust, heat, and garbage is unheard upon the sunny slopes of Mount Bermius, where I wandered Bacchus-smitten among the Maenades. Through the viny shades that embowered our dance of rapture, Haliacmon threw the gleam of his sky-bright waters, and the noon rays, sifted through leaves and clusters, fell on us softened like gold into the lap of Danae. Grapes above us, grapes around us, grapes every where, made the air fragrant as a censer. They dropped with the burden of their own sweetness; they shed volatile dews of ecstasy on every sense. Constellations of empurpled orbs, they dissolved the outer light of heaven by their own translucency; and from their hemispheres of silver down, which looked toward the sun, to those hemispheres which turned in upon our dance a gaze half of jet, half of sapphire, they transmitted the gentle radiance, until it bathed our cheeks and foreheads in the hue of autumn sunsets. Together with troops of Bacchantes I leaped madly among the clusters; I twirled my thyrsus, and cried Evoë Bacche with the loudest. On a delicious wind of fragrance the fawn-skin floated backward from my shoulders, and the viny leaves and tendrils of my garland caressed my temples lovingly. I drank the blood of grapes like nectar; I sang hymns to the son of Semele; I reeled under the possession of the divine afflatus. Around me in endless mazes circled beauteous shapes of men and women; with hands enclasped we danced and sang, and the Maenad houris overshadowed me with their luxuriant disheveled hair.

Now, wandering from their throng in a rapture which, too high to be imparted, sought some solitude where it could shed itself forth unheard, I passed through the college gateway, and began traveling up the long walk which finally led into the woods toward the east—finally, I say, for I remember even now the measureless stretch of the journey.

At length, reaching the borders of the stream which had before become to me the Nile, and which, through my whole hasheesh life, witnessed many a delirium of joy and torture, I sat down upon a high, precipitous bank which overhung the water, and gave myself up to my fantasia. The stream broadened and grew glorified: it was the Amazon, and on a towering bluff I was gazing down the liquid sweep toward the sea. Now a great ship came gliding past, lifting its top-gallant far above my post of observation, and men ran up the shrouds to peer curiously at me. With her long pennant flying and every inch of her courses shaken out, she passed me majestically, and I climbed down to the brink of the river to catch the last look at her, and see it returned from another inquisitive gazer at the taffrail.

I wandered completely through the woods, and came out into a broad field upon the farther side. Before me rose the buildings of a grand square, in some city whose name, whose nation I could not even imagine, so utterly foreign did it appear to any thing in the world of modern days. In the centre of the square a mighty host had assembled to inaugurate the equestrian statue of a hero, which, exquisitely carved in a rose-tinted marble, rose on its colossal pedestal far above their heads. I was drawn toward them by an irresistible impulse, for sculpture and architecture had reached, in that city, the highest ideal of art. I thought of the hero, and seemed to share the glory of his triumph.

Then out of the borders of the dense wood front which I had just emerged came a hot and hissing whisper, "Kill thyself! kill thyself!" Shuddering, I turned to see who spoke. No one was visible. Again, with still intenser earnestness, the whisper was repeated; and now unseen tongues syllabled it on all sides and in the air above me. To these words soon arguments were added, until the atmosphere seemed all aglow with fierce breathings of "Thou shalt be immortal; thou shalt behold the hidden things of God. The Most High commands thee to kill thyself." "My God!" I cried, "can this be true? I will obey thee, and drink in the eternities."

Feeling myself as mightily pressed on to do the deed as by a direct behest of Deity; daring not, for my soul's sake, to resist the utterances; and immeasurably exalted with the prelibation of the glories that, in a moment, were to flow in upon me, in frantic fury I drew forth my knife, opened it, and placed it at my throat. Another heart-throb, and all would have been over.

It was just then that I felt the blow of some invisible hand strike my arm; my hand flew back, and, with the force of the shock, the knife went spinning away into the bushes. The whispers ceased. I looked up into heaven, and lo! from zenith to horizon, an awful angel of midnight blackness floated, with poised wings, on the sky. His face looked unutterable terrors into me, and his dreadful hand, half clenched, was hollowed above my head, as if waiting to take me by the hair. Across the firmament a chariot came like lightning; its wheels were rainbow-suns that rolled in tremendous music; no charioteer was there, but in his place flashed the glory of an intense brightness. At its approach the sable angel turned and rushed downward into the horizon, that seemed to smoke as he slid through it; and, thank God! from Azrael I was saved.

How many a temptation, which the ordinary grossness of the ear prevents us from ascribing to its true external source, and which we would fain persuade ourselves is nothing but our own thought, would come to us thus in a real demon-voice were the bands of the body but a little loosened! In how many attractions toward good and repulsions from evil would we then feel the touch of angel hands! The world at present is, to a great degree, Sadducee; it scoffs at the Spiritual, which for blindness it can not discern, and lives in meat and bone. The best men conservatively go half way to shake hands with the most unspiritual skeptic, and acknowledge with him that the most reasonable way to account for our wooings and our warnings is the reaction of soul upon itself. What these poor lovers of the earthy will do when they arrive among the realities of another world, it is hard to say. When this poor, mouldy, moth-eaten, time-tattered cloak of the corporeal, which for years has flapped about their heads in the gusts of worldly fortune, or tangled in its wet rags the feet of the soul that were trying to climb higher—when this poor cloak falls off, and they stand transformed into that most dreaded bugbear of their previous lives, spirit—we may, perhaps, hear them cry out in agony, "Oh, my beloved garment! my best suit! what will become of thee?" and see them diving headlong off of the battlements of light to recover the only part of their human wardrobe in which they can feel comfortable.

After my escape from death I returned to the border of the brook, and began pacing back and forth upon a long flat stone around which the shelve of the bank curved. My surroundings instantly became theatrical; the woods behind me changed into a back scene, and on a grand stage I was holding entranced a great audience, whom I beheld before me rising in colossal tiers from earth to sky. The part I was acting was that of a victorious soldier in some tragedy whose words I improvised, and, growing rapidly into the interest of my speech, I poured forth words—now in prose and now in verse—

which swayed the hearers like a whirlwind. As my manner increased in earnestness, I saw a strange and dreadful look of suspicion overshadowing every face of the thousands in my audience. From the searching stare of the pit I sought relief in turning my face toward the boxes. The same stony glance from under eyebrows met me still, and when I raised my despairing countenance to the galleries, the same quenchless scrutiny poured down upon me. "Can it be?" I asked myself. "Oh! they know my secret!" and at that instant one maddening chorus broke from the whole theatre: "Hasheesh! hasheesh! he has eaten hasheesh!" Then, with one tumultuous uprising, the concourse fled. From the stage I crept away, consumed by an unutterable shame. I sought a place upon the bank of the stream still lower down, where a large hazel-bush leaned over the water, and beneath its branches I crouched. The helmet and corslet were gone. I looked at my garments, and beheld them foul and ragged as a beggar's. From head to foot I was an incarnation of the genius of squalidity.

Alas! even here I could not hide. I had chosen my asylum on the very pavement of a great city's principal thoroughfare. Children went by to school, and pointed at me in derision; loungers stood still, and searched me with inquisitive scorn. The multitude of man and beast all eyed me; the very stones of the street mocked me with a human raillery as I cowered against a side wall in my bemired rags.

Now, mixing with the throng of passers-by, and no more real than they, two of my college friends came strolling along the brook. They saw and knew me, and my shame reached its unbearable height when I saw them approach me with looks which I thought also of sarcasm. But, as they drew nearer, they spoke to me kindly, and asked what was the matter with me, and why I sat hiding behind the hazel-branches. I hesitated for a moment, but, on their promise of secrecy, told them my latest experience. They sat down beside me, and in the diversion of talking the hallucination passed away.

Suddenly an unconquerable apprehension possessed me. There were certain secrets which for my right arm I would not have betrayed, and yet I felt imperatively called upon to speak them. I struggled against the impulse with the thews of a spiritual Titan. I was determined to conquer it, yet, that I might provide against a failure, I conceived this expedient. Picking up a withered leaf from the bank of the stream, I called the two to hold it, each by a portion of the rim, while I grasped it by the stem. In this way we raised the leaf toward heaven, and with our hands clasped in each other, I solemnly repeated this adjuration: "As this leaf shall be withered in the fiery breath of the final day, so may we be withered in the vengeance of the Eternal if aught that may be here said pass our lips without the consent of us all three." Here we all said "Amen," and once more I was at ease. I did not betray my own secrecy.

When I became calm the two left me and returned to their rooms. I wandered back to my old station on the high ledge, where I had seen the ship sweep by me, and sat down. When I looked into the sky between the tree-tops, the sun seemed reeling from his place, and the clouds danced around him like a chorus. I turned my eyes downward, and found that I was surrounded by warriors, who had come to bear me an invitation to the coronation of Charlemagne. "In a moment I will go with you," was my reply, "but first I must drink; I am dreadfully athirst." The stream was rattling away directly below me; my distance from it by the most easy roundabout descent was not more than fifty feet, yet I must relate, even at the risk of saying too much of the hasheesh expansion of distance, that in going to it I seemed passing down the league-long ridge of a mountain. I walked, I roamed, I traveled before reaching it, and at last, lying down upon the water's brim, I drank such streams of refreshment as appeared to lower the flood. On my return, after toiling up the weary steep, my escort had gone, and I certainly could not blame them, if the length of my unceremonious absence seemed to them half as great as it did to me.

Wandering through jungle, heather, brake, and fern—through savanna, oak-opening, and prairie—through all imagined and unimaginable countries—now despairing of my ability ever to find my way, and now plucking heart to press on—through many a day, or rather through one boundless perpetual day of journeying, I went until I reached home.

Throwing myself down upon a bed, I was immediately compensated for all past sufferings. In the middle of a vast unpeopled plain I stood alone. With one quick ravishment I was borne upward, as on superhuman wings, until, standing on the very cope of heaven, I looked down and saw beneath me all the worlds that God has made, not wheeling upon their beamy paths through ether, nor yet standing without significance like orbed clods.

By an instantaneous revealing I became aware of a mighty harp which lay athwart the celestial hemisphere, and filled the whole sweep of vision before me. The lambent flame of myraid stars was burning in the azure spaces between its strings, and glorious suns gemmed with unimaginable lustre all its colossal framework. While I stood overwhelmed by the vision, a voice spoke clearly from the depths of the surrounding ether: "Behold the harp of the universe."

In an instant I realized the typifaction of the grand harmony of God's infinite creation, for every influence, from that which nerves the wing of Ithuriel down to the humblest force of growth, had there its beautiful and peculiar representative string.

As yet the music slept, when the voice spake to me again, "Stretch forth thine hand and wake the harmonies." Trembling, yet daring, I swept the harp, and straightway all heaven thrilled with an unutterable music. My arm strangely lengthened, I grew bolder, and my hand took a wider range. The symphony grew more intense; overpowered, I ceased, and heard tremendous echoes coming back from the infinitudes. Again I smote the chords, but, unable to endure the sublimity of the sound, I sank into an ecstatic trance, and was thus borne off unconsciously to the portals of some new vision.

X.

Nimium—the Amreeta Cup of Unveiling.

It was shortly after the last vision which has been related that I first experienced those sufferings which are generated by a dose of hasheesh taken to prolong the effects of a preceding one.

Through half a day I had lain quietly under the influence of the weed, possessed by no hallucination, yet delighted with a flow of pleasant images, which passed by under my closed eyelids. Unimaginable houris intoxicated the sense with airy ballet-dances of a divine gracefulness, rose-wreathed upon a stage of roses, and flooded with the blush of a rosy atmosphere. Through grand avenues of overarching elms I floated down toward the glimpse of an impurpled sky, caught through the vista, or came glancing through the air over gateway of syenite, rose-tinted by the atmosphere, and in Egypt walked among the Caryatides. Up mystic pathways, on a mountain of evergreens, the priests of some nameless religion flocked, mitre-crowned, and passed into the temple of the sun over the threshold of the horizon. Now, "ringed with the azure world," I stood, a lonely hemisphere above me, a calm and voiceless sea beneath me; suddenly an island of feathery palms floated into the centre of the watery expanse, and gauze-winged sprites dropped down upon its shore. Now landscapes of strange loveliness slowly slid before me, but stopped at my will, that I might wander far up their music-haunted bays, and sit, bathed in sunlight, on the giant rock-fragments which lay around their unpeopled shores.

But once did I open my eyes and leap up in fear; for into the gardens of the Grecian villa where I walked among statues and fountains, an incongruous horde of Indian braves burst whooping, in their war-dance; and writhing in savage postures, with brandished club and tomahawk, they called upon my name, and looked for me through the olive-trees. Lying down again, I soared into the dome of St. Peter's, and, lighting on the pen of the apostle, laid my hand upon the angel's shoulder. A mighty stretch of arm indeed; yet, to the hasheesh-eater, all things are possible.

About the hour of noon I found the effects of my first dose rapidly passing off. It had been a small one, possibly fifteen grains, and, as I have said, produced no hallucination; yet so enamored had I become of the procession of pleasing images which it set in motion, that, for the sake of prolonging it, I took five grains more.

Hour after hour went by; I returned to the natural state, and gave up all idea of any result from the last dose. At nine o'clock in the evening I was sitting among my friends writing, while they talked around me. I became aware that it was gradually growing easier for me to express myself; my pen glanced presently like lightning in the effort to keep neck and neck with my ideas. At first I simply wondered at the phenomenon, without in the least suspecting the hasheesh which I had eaten nine hours before. At last, thought ran with such terrific speed that I could no longer write at all. Throwing down my pen, I paced the room, chafed my forehead, and strove to recover quiet by joining in the conversation of those about me.

In vain! intense fever boiled in my blood, and every heart-beat was the stroke of a colossal engine. Within me I felt that prophecy of dire suffering which the hasheesh-eater recognizes as unmistakably as were it graven by the finger of light, but whose signs, to all but him, are incommunicable. In agony of spirit I groaned inwardly, "My God, help me!"

The room grew unbearable with a penetrating glory of light. I mounted into it, I expanded through it, with a blind and speechless pain, which, in my very heart's core, was slowly developing itself into something afterward to burst forth into demoniac torture. I felt myself weeping, and ran to a looking-glass to observe the appearance of my eyes. They were pouring forth streams of blood! And now a sudden hemorrhage took place within me; my heart had dissolved, and from my lips the blood was breaking also.

Still, with that self-retent which a hasheesh-eater acquires by many a bitter discipline, I withheld from my friends the knowledge of my torture, averting my face until the hallucination passed by. Indeed, as often occurs at such times, a paralysis of speech had taken place, which prevented me from communicating with others: not physical, but spiritual; for the recital of such pain seems to increase it tenfold by drawing its outlines more distinctly to the perception, and therefore I did not dare to give it utterance.

And now a new fact flashed before me. This agony was not new; I had felt it ages ago, in the same room, among the same people, and hearing the same conversation. To most men, such a sensation has happened at some time, but it is seldom more than vague and momentary. With me it was sufficiently definite and lasting to be examined and located as an actual memory. I saw it in an instant, preceded and followed by the successions of a distinctly-recalled past life.

What is the philosophy of this fact? If we find no grounds for believing that we have ever lived self-consciously in any other state, and can not thus explain it, may not this be the solution of the enigma? At the moment of the soul's reception of a new impression, she first accepts it as a thing entirely of the sense; she tells us how large it is, and of what quality. To this definition of its boundaries and likeness succeeds, at times of high activity, an intuition of the fact that the sensation shall be perceived again in the future unveiling that is to throw open all the past. Prophetically she notes it down upon the indestructible leaves of her diary, assured that it is to come out in the future revelation. Yet we who, from the tendency of our thought, reject all claims to any knowledge of the future, can only acknowledge perceptions as of the present or the past, and accordingly refer the dual realization to some period gone by. We perceive the correspondence of two sensations, but, by an instantaneous process, give the second one a wrong position in the succession of experiences. The soul is guarded as the historian when she is in reality the sibyl; but the misconception takes place in such a microscopic portion of time that detection is impossible. In the hasheesh expansion of seconds into minutes, or even according to a much mightier ratio, there is an opportunity thoroughly to scrutinize the hitherto evanescent phenomena, and the truth comes out. How many more such prophecies as these may have been rejected through the gross habit of the body we may never know until spirit vindicates her claim in a court where she must have audience.

At length the torture of my delirium became so great that I could no longer exist unsustained by sympathy. To Bob, as possessing, from his own experience, a better appreciation of that which I suffered, I repaired in preference to all others. "Let us walk," said I; "it is impossible for me to remain here."

Arm-in-arm we passed down the front steps. And now all traces of the surrounding world passed away from before me like marks wiped from a slate. When we first emerged from the building, I noticed that the night was dark, but this was the last I knew of any thing external. I was beyond all troubles from earth or sky; my agonies were in the spiritual, and there all was terrific light. By the flame of my previous

vision the corporeal had been entirely burned off from about the soul, and I trod its charred ruins under foot without a remembrance that they had ever been sensitive or part of me. A voice spoke to me, "By the dissolution of fire hast thou been freed, to behold all things as they are, to gaze on realities, to know principles, to understand tendencies of being."

I now perceived that I was to pass through some awful revelation. It proved to be both Heaven and Hell, the only two states in the universe which together comprehend all free-agent creatures, whether in the Here or the Hereafter. Of both I drank tremendous draughts, holding the cup to my lips as may never be done again until the draught of one of them is final.

Over many a mountain range, over plains and rivers, I heard wafted the cry of my household, who wept for me with as distinct a lamentation as if they were close at hand. Above all the rest, a sister mourned bitterly for a brother who was about to descend into hell!

Far in the distance rolled the serpentine fires of an infinite furnace; yet did this not seem to be the place to which I was tending, but only the symbol of a certain spiritual state which in this life has no representative. And now the principles of being, which the prophetic voice had foretold that I should see, suddenly disclosed themselves. Oh, awful sight! Iron, for they were unrelenting; straight as the ideal of a right line, for they were unalterable; like colossal railways they stretched from the centre whereon I stood. Yet more were they to me than their mere material names, for they embodied an infinity of sublime truth. What that truth was I strove to express to my companion, yet in vain, for human language was yet void of signs which might characterize it. "Oh God!" I cried, "grant me the gift of a supernatural speech, that I may, if ever I return, come to humanity like a new apostle, and tell them of realities which are the essence of their being!" I perceived that this, also, was impossible. But vaguely, then, like some far-sighted one who points his brethren through the rack and tempest to a distant shore, should I ever be able to disclose what I had seen of the Real to men who dwelt amid the Shadowy.

For days afterward I remembered the unveiling. I myself knew that which it disclosed, yet could not tell it; and now all the significance of it has faded from my mind, leaving behind but the bare shard and husk of the symbols.

The railway which I saw appeared twofold: one arm led toward the far fires of my torture, the other into a cloudy distance which veiled its end completely from my sight. Upon the first I traveled, yet not on wheels, for I felt my feet still upbearing me through all the stages of an infinitely rapid progress.

Symbols—symbols everywhere. All along my journey they flashed forth the apocalypse of utterly unimagined truths. All strange things in mind, which had before been my perplexity, were explained—all vexed questions solved. The springs of suffering and of joy, the action of the human will, memory, every complex fact of being, stood forth before me in a clarity of revealing which would have been the sublimity of happiness but for their relation to man's tendencies toward evil. I was aware at the time (and I am no less so now) that, to

a mind in its natural state, the symbols by which I was taught would be marrowless and unmeaning; yet so powerfully were they correspondences to unpreconceived spiritual verities, that I can not refrain from giving one or two of them in this recital.

Hanging in a sky of spotless azure, within the walls of my own heart, appeared my soul as a coin flaming with glories, which radiated from the impress of God's face stamped upon it. This told me an unutterable truth of my being. Again the soul appeared as a vast store of the same coin shed prodigally upon the earth. Through clefts in the rocky wall which rose beside my way were thrust, in a manner expressive of wondrous craft, barbed talons, which, grasping the coin one by one, as a fish-hook holds the prey, drew them slowly in, while I stood helpless, shrieking in the desert loneliness. As each piece of my treasure slid through the crevices, I heard it fall, with a cruel metallic ring, upon the bottom of some invisible strong-box, and this ring was echoed by a peal of hollow laughter from within. Another truth, though not the most evident one which now suggests itself, but far more dreadful, was taught me by this symbol.

Again, my heart was a deep well of volatile blood, and into it buckets perpetually descended to be drawn up filled, and carried away by viewless hands to nurture the flames which writhed in the distant furnace. Through all this time I was witnessing one more tremendous truth. But one of the representatives still retains its full significancy to my mind, and is communicable also to others.

Standing upon a mountain peak appeared a serene old prophet, whose face was radiant with a divine majesty. In his look, his form, his manner, was embodied all that glorifies the sage; wonderfully did he typify the ideal of the bard—

" His open eyes desire the truth;
    The wisdom of a thousand years
    Is in them."

All that science, art, and spotless purity of life can do to ennoble humanity, had ennobled him, and I well-nigh knelt down before him in an ecstasy of worship. A voice spoke to me from the infinitudes, "Behold man's soul in primeval grandeur, as it was while yet he talked with God."

Hurried away through immensity, I came, somewhere in the universe, upon a low knoll, flaunting in a growth of coarse and gaudy flowers. Half way down its slope sat a hideous dwarf, deformed in body, but still much more terrible in the soul, which ogled me through his leaden eyes, or broke in ripples of idiotic laughter over his lax and expressionless lip. One by one he aimlessly plucked the flowers among which he was sitting; he pressed them to his bosom, and leered upon them, as a maniac miser looks upon his treasures, and then, tearing to pieces their garish petals, tossed them into the air, and laughed wildly to see them whirling downward to strew his lap. In horror I averted my face, but a strange fascination drew it back to him again, when once more the terrible voice sounded over my shoulder, "Behold thine own soul!" In an agony I cried, "Why, oh why?" Sternly, yet without a thrill of passion, the voice replied, "Thou hast perverted thy gifts, thou hast squandered thine opportunities, thou hast spurned thy warnings, and, blind to great things, thou playest with baubles. Therefore, behold thyself thus!"

In speechless shame I hid my face and turned away. Now, as with the descent of a torrent, all my violations of the principles which I saw revealed fell down upon my head from the heights of the Past. It was no bewailing over the inexpediency of any deed or thought which I then uttered; from the abysses of my soul a cry of torture went up for discords which I had caused in the grand harmony of universal law. The importance to mere temporal well-being of this act or that, made no difference in the inconceivable pain which I felt at its clear remembrance. Whether, in the Past, I was confronted with a deliberate falsehood or a fictitious addition, for the sake of symmetry, to an otherwise true recital, the horror was the same. It was not consequences to happiness that troubled me, but something of far mightier scope, for I looked upon some little pulse of evil which, at its time, had seemed to die away in the thought, and lo, in all the years since then it has been ceaselessly waving onward in consecutive circles, whose outer rim touched and invaded the majestic symphony of unalterable principles of Beauty and Truth. Before the presence of that beholding there was no such thing as a little wrong in all the universe.

And now, in review, there passed before my mind all those paradoxes of being which, to our natural sense, forever perplex the relations between God and Man—God, the omnipotent; Man, the free agent, the two concentric wheels of self-determining will which turn the universe. How can these things be?

In an instant I saw that hitherto unattainable How. Out of the depths of mystery it broke forth and stood in grand relief upon its midnight veil. Between truths there was no longer any jar; as on a map, illustrated by eternal light, I beheld all their relative bearings, and in the conviction of an intuition cried out, "True, true, divinely true!"

Do you ask me to give the process? As well might I attempt to define sight to a being born without eyes as to image, even to myself, at this moment, the mode of that apocalypse. Had memory of it as aught else than a fact remained to me, I had long since been consumed, as a red-hot needle dissolves away in oxygen. As it is, I remember not the manner, except that it was Sight; at the moment it was incommunicable by any human language. Yet the stamp of the intuition remains so indelibly upon my soul, that there is no self-evident truth which I could not more easily abjure than the undimmed and perfect harmony which, in that dreadful night, I beheld as an intuition.

After this I suffered hellish agonies, prolonged through an infinite duration. As they were all embodied in symbols, I recall them dimly, and the endeavor to relate them would be painful and profitless.

At the end of my representative road, arriving through growing distances, times, and tortures, God-drawn, I was hurried back to be launched forward in the direction of the other, the celestial tendency. The music of unimaginable harps grew clearer with every league of speed; symbols were turned to their most ravishing uses; the gleam of crystal grates and empyrean battlements flashed on me with increasing radiance; the sky breathed down a balm which signified love, love—quenchless love. At the end of this journey I arrived also; and, between towers of light, was about to pass through into a land resounding with infinite choruses of joy. I was detained. Again the voice spake to me, "The thing is too great for thee; seek not to enter. As thou wast preserved at the end of thy former way from going into the fires to which it led, so also now do I guard thee from beholding the fatal glories of the Divine face to face." With inconceivable grief I hid my face in my hands and returned, weeping bitterly.

At this moment, for the first time since coming from my room, I became aware of the external world. My friend still walked by my side, supporting me through the darkness. We had not come half a mile while I passed through all that awful vision!

Presently we came to a short bridge. Little conceiving the state of mind from which I had just emerged, Bob said to me, with the impression that the novelty of the idea would give me an attractive suggestion of adventure, "See the Styx." Groaning in spirit, I looked down upon that dark and sullen water which rolled below me, and saw it mightily expanded beneath horrible shadows toward a shore which glowed with the fires of my earlier vision. "My God!" I cried, "am I again journeying toward the Infernal?" Yes, it must be so; for even this man, who has learned nothing of my past tortures, knows and tells me this is one of the rivers of Hell!"

Bob caught a glimpse of the pain he had innocently caused me, and assured me, for the sake of my peace, that he had only been jesting. "This is not the Styx at all," said he, "but only a small stream which runs through Schenectady." By pointing out to me familiar surroundings, by persuasion, by entreaty, he at length prevailed upon me to cross the bridge; yet I only did so by concealing my eyes in his bosom and clasping his hands with the clutch of a vice.

Supposing that light and the restorative influence of wine would relieve me, he led me to a restaurant, and there, sitting down with me to a table, called for a glass of Port. In the unnatural shadow which inwrapped all things and persons, a man was standing near the door, and in the conversation which he was carrying on with another I heard him use the word "damn."

In an instant my mind, now exquisitely susceptible, took fire from that oath as tinder from steel. "There is, indeed," I soliloquized, "such a thing as damnation, for I have seen it. Shall I be saved?" This dreadful question forced me to determine it with an imperative fascination. I continued, "Oh thou Angel of Destiny, in whose book all the names of the saved are written, I call on thee to open unto me the leaves!"

Hardly had I spoken when upon a sable pedestal of clouds the dread registrar sat before me, looking immeasurable pity from his superhuman eyes. Silently he stretched out to me the great volume of record, and with devouring eyes I scanned its pages, turning them over in a wild haste that did not preclude the most rigid scrutiny. Leaf after leaf flew back; from top to bottom I consumed them in my gaze of agony. Here and there I recognized a familiar name, but even my joy at such revelations took nothing from the cruelty of the suspense in which I looked to find my own. With a face cold as marble I came to the last page, and had not found it yet. Drops of torture beaded my brow as with eye and finger I ran down the final column. One, two, three—I came to the bottom—the last. It was not there!

My God! nothing but thine upbearing arms at that moment kept me from eternal annihilation. In stony horror I sat dumb.

After the Angel of Destiny took back his book and shut it with the echo of doom, I know not what time elapsed while I dwelt in that unfathomable abyss of despair. I saw Eternity, like a chariot out of which I had fallen, roll out of sight upon the bowed and smoking clouds to leave me, a creature of perdition, in an inanity of space and out of the successions of duration. Familiar faces were around me, yet the thought of obtaining relief from them never crossed my mind. They were powerless to help a sufferer of the immortal pangs.

If, as I sat at the table, a caldron of boiling lead had been brought in and set beside me, I would have leaped into it with exultant haste, to divert my mind from spiritual to physical sufferings. Through a period which the hasheesh-eater alone can know, I sat speechlessly beside my friend.

Suddenly upon the opposite wall appeared a cross, and Christ the Merciful was nailed thereon. I sprang from my seat; I rushed toward him; I embraced his knees; I looked intensely into his face in voiceless entreaty. That sad face sweetly smiled upon me, and I saw that my unspoken prayer was granted. Through my soul, as through a porous film, swept a wind of balm, and left it clean. The voice that had attended me through all past journeyings, now changed from stern upbraiding to unimaginable love, spoke gently, "By the breath of the Spirit thine iniquities are borne utterly away." To colossal agonies peace as great succeeded, and, thus sustained, I returned to my room.

Yet all my sufferings had not yet been fulfilled. The moment that I reached home I threw myself down upon my bed. Hardly had I touched it when, from all sides, devouring flame rolled upward and girt me in with a hemisphere of fire. Shrieking, I leaped up and ran to my friends, who cared for me till the wrathful hallucination was overpast.

At this day it seems to me almost incredible that I ever survived that experience at all. Yet, inexplicable as it may be, when I awoke on the next morning, I was as free from all traces of suffering as if I had been, all the evening previous, cradled in a mother's arms.

XI.

The Book of Symbols.

OF all experiences in the hasheesh state, my indoctrination into spiritual facts through means of symbols was the most wonderful to myself. In other visions I have reveled in more delicious beauty, and suffered horrors even more terrible; but in this I was lifted entirely out of the world of hitherto conceivable being, and invested with the power of beholding forms and modes of existence which, on earth, are impossible to be expressed, for the reason that no material emblems exist which even faintly foreshadow them.

Among men we communicate entirely by symbols. Upon any thought which has not its symbol in the Outer, "untransferable" is stamped indelibly. A certain relation between two thoughts is beheld by one human mind. How shall the man inform his neighbor of this relation? There is no meatus for it through any of the labyrinths of material sense; it can not be seen, heard, felt, smelt, or tasted. What is to be done?

A flock of cranes are assembling from the four quarters of heaven to hold their aerial council on some tall crag above him. Into our thinker's mind flashes a bright idea. Those birds shall mediate for his relation a passage into his brother's understanding. The cranes (grues) are coming together (con), and in this visible symbol he embodies his invisible relation, and the name henceforth that passes for it among men is "congruous."

Yet there is one condition beyond the mere discovery of an apt symbol which is necessary before that symbol can be circulated as the bank-note which bases its security on the intangible coin within the spiritual treasury. That coin must be universally felt to exist, or the bill will be good for nothing. In the present instance, the idea of the relation expressed by "congruous" must already have been perceived by the communicatee, or the communicator will be unable to express himself intelligibly. Rather should we say, the idea of the possibility of this relation must exist before the former can perceive it; for, if he recognizes such a possibility, then, by virtue of this very capacity, he will immediately actualize the possible, and on the communication of the symbol perceive the idea of "congruity," though it be for the first time.

The question now arises, What state of mind lies back of, and conditions the capacity to recognize, through symbols, the mental phenomena of another? Plainly this: the two who are in communication must be situated so nearly upon the same plane of thought that they behold the same truths and are affected by the same emotions. In proportion as this condition is violated will two men be unappreciating of each other's inner states.

Now in hasheesh it is utterly violated. In the hasheesh-eater a virtual change of worlds has taken place, through the preternatural scope and activity of all his faculties. Truth has not become expanded, but his vision has grown telescopic; that which others see only as the dim nebula, or do not see at all, he looks into with a penetrating scrutiny which distance, to a great extent, can not evade. Where the luminous mist or the perfect void had been, he finds wondrous constellations of spiritual being, determines their bearings, and reads the law of their sublime harmony. To his neighbor in the natural state he turns to give expression to his visions, but finds that to him the symbols which convey the apocalypse to his own mind are meaningless, because, in our ordinary life, the thoughts which they convey have no existence; their two planes are utterly different.

This has not only occurred in my own case, but in several others—in persons upon whom I have experimented with hasheesh. At their highest exaltation, so earnest has been the desire to communicate the burden which overpowered them, that they have spoken forth the symbols presented to their minds; yet from these symbols men around them, in the unexalted state, drew an entirely different significance from the true one, or, perceiving none at all, laughed at what was said as an absurdity, seeing nothing in the name of some ordinary thing or mode of being to excite such emotions of terror or of ecstasy as were produced in the hasheesh-eater. Yet many a time, as I stood near, by these symbols thus expressed, have I been able to follow the ecstatic wanderer, and recognize the exact place in his journey at which he had arrived as something which I had once seen myself.

It is this process of symbolization which, in certain hasheesh states, gives every tree and house, every pebble and leaf, every footprint, feature, and gesture, a significance beyond mere matter or form, which possesses an inconceivable force of tortures or of happiness.

Perhaps one of the most difficult things to convey to a mind not in the hasheesh delirium, by the symbols which there teach the manner of its process, or by any others, is the interchange of senses. The soul is sometimes plainly perceived to be but one in its own sensorium, while the body is understood to be all that so variously modifies impressions as to make them in the one instance smell, in another taste, another sight, and thus on, *ad finem*. Thus the hasheesh-eater knows what it is to be burned by *salt* fire, to *smell* colors, to *see* sounds, and, much more frequently, to *see* feelings. How often do I remember vibrating in the air over a floor bristling with red-hot needles, and, although I never supposed I came in contact with them, *feeling* the sensation of their frightful pungency through *sight* as distinctly as if they were entering my heart.

In the midst of sufferings unfathomable or raptures measureless, I often thought of St. Paul's God-given trance, and the "—." Never was I more convinced of any thing in my life than that our translation, "which it is not lawful for a man to utter," is wholly inadequate. It should be, "which it is impossible to utter to man"; for this alone harmonizes with that state of intuition in which the words are "speechless words," and the truths beheld have no symbol on earth which will embody them. Though far from believing that my own ecstasy, or that of any hasheesh-eater, has claim to such inspiration as an apostle's, the states are still analogous in this respect, that they both share the nature of disembodiment, and the soul, in both, beholds realities of greater or less significance, such as may never be apprehended again out of the light of eternity.

There is one thought suggested by the symbolization of hasheesh which I can not refrain from introducing here. In some apocalyptic states of delirium like that which I have mentioned, and others succeeding it, there were symbols of an earthly nature used, which not only had never before conveyed to me such truth as I then saw, but never had expressed any truth at all. Things the least suspected of having any significance beyond their material agency were perceived to be the most startling illustrations and incarnations of spiritual facts.

Now where, among created things, shall we set the boundaries to this capacity for symbolizing. In view of that which I saw, especially upon the last detailed memorable night, I felt, and still feel, forced to the conclusion that there is no boundary. If, as the true philosopher must believe, the material was created for the spiritual, as the lower for the higher, the means for the end, it is impossible that any minutest lichen should exist as mere inert matter, lessonless to the soul of all creation's viceroy—man.

What a world of symbols, then, lie sleeping in expectancy of the approaching times which shall bring some translator to their now unnoticed sermons, and bid them speak of unconceived beauties and truths!

Following out the perverted tendencies of a pseudoscience, we are now forever seeking some reason for the existence of the outer world as it is, which will utterly insphere it within the ends of material well-being. Plainly perceiving that respect for the Creative Wisdom will not permit us to suppose that any thing, however microscopic, has been made aimlessly, we belabor our brains with attempts to find out some physical good arising out of the being of every object in all the terrene kingdoms. Such a thing was created that man might be cured of the headache; such another, that his food might be varied; still another, that a convenient circulating medium might be in his power. Doubtless such corporeal goods were among the final causes of some portions of the creation. Our trouble is not our activity in the discovery of these, but that beyond their petty circle discovery does not dare to set her foot, for fear of being called visionary.

Doubtless, when God has lent us a tenement to lodge in, albeit for a few days and nights, it is our duty to find out and apply all those materials of repair which will keep it in good order till we pass finally from its low door-step into our palace; as honorable tenants, and for the sake of our own better preservation, this is both duty and right, so far as it may be done without bespangling and frescoing our wayfaring house as if it were to be our perpetual home. Yet what effort can be meaner, what more unworthy of Spirit, than studiously to degrade the whole sublime Kosmos into one colossal eating-house, wardrobe, or doctor's shop for the body? Good men, perhaps wise men, are forever looking for something medicinal in the scorpion, or edible in the fungus, to vindicate God's claim to an intention. Most ingeniously do they fabricate suppositious purposes for outer things; hopelessly writhe in the folds of perplexity when, with all their far-fetched hypotheses, they can not see what material good is to come out of some obstinate resistance to their analysis.

Blind philosophers! Nature refuses to cramp herself within your impossible law; she rejects your generalizations; she throws off the shackles of your theory! For the sake of mere physical well-being, it had doubtless been far better that never a centipede had been created; that the most formidable snake had been the harmless garter; that the euphorbus had never put forth a leaf, nor the seleniuret a vapor. Yet this is not the grand aim of the system of things, but that man might, for the present, have symbols for the communication of manly thought; that God himself, for the future, might

have symbols for the revelation of Divine Truth, when, in the grand unveiling, rocks, trees, and rivers—yea, the smallest atom also—shall come thronging up along all the ways of the Universe to unseal their long-embosomed messages, and join in the choral dance of the Spiritual—the only science—to the Orpheus-music of the awakened soul.

XII.
To-day, Zeus; To-morrow, Prometheus.

AT what precise time in my experience I began to doubt the drug being, with me, so much a mere experiment as a fascinating indulgence, I do not now recollect. It may be that the fact of its ascendency *gradually* dawned upon me; but, at any rate, whenever the suspicion became definite, I dismissed it by so varying the manner of the enjoyment as to persuade myself that it was experimental still.

I had walked, talked, and dreamed under the hasheesh influence; I would now listen to music and see acting, that, under such circumstances, I might note the varying phenomena, if any occurred.

To reach New York for the purpose I would go by water, sailing down the glorious Hudson under the full moon; and this would still be another opportunity for experimenting.

Upon one of the largest and most beautiful of the steamers which ever glided down the shining pathway of the river upon a moonlight night of summer, I stepped, at eight o'clock in the evening, accompanied by several of my friends, and carrying in my pocket a box of boluses. The gangplank was drawn in, and we were on our way.

In the few moments which elapsed before the steward appeared, brandishing his noisy harbinger of things edible, I managed to swallow, unseen, a number of the spheroids contained in my box.

On regaining the deck from that savory, subaqueous cavern where, amid sepulchral lights, five hundred Americans of us had, for the incredible space of fifteen minutes, been fiercely elbowing each other in insane haste to secure that grand national end, indigestion, we found in the broad disk of the moon just above the horizon, and, on arm-chairs taken forward, sat down, with our toes thrust into the bulwark-netting, for our post-coenatial smoke. Cigars and studently habits of thinking impelled us toward song, and for two hours, at least, the low rocks which skirt the upper channel echoed with "There is music in the air," "Co-ca-che-lunk," and other collegiate harmonies.

The Opera, with its glory of lights, passionate song, orchestral crashes, and scenery, whirls the soul on with it, indeed, in a bewildering dance of delight; the ballad we love, sung feelingly by the woman we love, at that hour when to lift the curtains would only let in more twilight, is a calm rapture which is good for the heart; if it be not too near, the bugle discourses rich melody and spirit-stirring among the mountains of its birth; yet, beyond all other music, grant me a song trolled from manly throats, which keep good chord and time, and first learned within those homely walls which, to the true American collegian, are dearer than all the towers of Oxford.

Reverend Union! it is not thine to deck thyself in the trappings of feudal pomp; not even is it thine to bear upon thy brow the wrinkles of unnumbered years, though long before thou lackest such prestige its sign shall come upon thee. Thou hast no high places for lineage nor fat tables for gold; thou art beautiful neither in marble nor carved workmanship. Yet art thou the mother of thinkers and workers—high souls and brave hearts, which make their throb felt in the giant pulses of a great nation. To these Gracchi of thine dost thou point and say, "Behold my jewels." With the love of thy sons thou art crowned more royally than turrets might crown thee; and better than all the remembrance of coronets upon thy calendar and ermine in thy halls is the thought that, grasping thy protectress hand, merit hath so often struggled up to fame out of the oblivion of namelessness and the clutch of poverty.

It is in the American college, with its freedom from fictitious distinctions, its rejection of all odious badges, which set genealogy and money over mind and heart; its inculcation of manly self-government rather than the fear of tyrannic espionage; its unrestrained intercourse between congenial souls, and its grouping of congenialities by society bonds, that the most perfect development of the social and individual man takes place. Here it is that, by attrition of minds, unworthy eccentricities are rubbed off, while the personal and characteristic nature of the man is solidified and polished into higher symmetry. And here, last, though far from least, among all the true purposes of education, the heart gets its due in the attainment of those unworldly associations which, many a year after the actual presences which they symbolize have dropped down into the "long ago," send up the hallowed savor of friendship and disinterestedness through the dust and cobwebs which choke well-nigh every other memory.

It is not wonderful that, out of such free and intimate converse among young men as we find in our colleges, song should spring up as a most legitimate and accredited progeny. He who should collect the college carols of our country, or, at least, those of them whose spice would not be wholly lost in the transplantation from their original time and place, would be adding no mean department to the national literature. Piquant, fresh-imaged, outwelling, and sitting snug to their airs, they are frequently both excellent poetry and music. Whether they ring through the free air of a balmy summer evening from a row of sitters on a terrace or a green, who snatch fragrant puffs of old Virginia between staves, or gladden a college room through the long evenings of winter, they are always inspiriting, always heart-blending, and always, I may add, well sung.

I have rambled round the complete circle of my digression to the place where I left my friends seated upon the forward deck and singing in the incipient moonlight. By the time that we had grown tired of singing, the river was very beautiful with the clear reflection of the sky, turning the spray of our prow to silver beads, and giving still snowier lustre to our wake. The excitement of music had put off that of hasheesh, but I was not surprised to feel the well-known thrill as our voices died away.

In a moment I became the fairy monarch. Etherealized and beautiful, I was gliding upon my willborne pleasure-vessel through the moonlit kingdom over which I was supreme. Now whippoorwills chanted me a plaintive welcome from the dreamy, wooded shores; fire-flies illuminated, with triumphal lights, their palace fronts among the shadowy elms; and the little moon-glorified islands, that caught our waves upon their foreheads, sent back a delicious voice of laud and joy.

In this ecstasy I sat reviewing my domain until the moon stood at the zenith, and then pacing through the long saloons, I reveled in the ownership of gorgeous tapestry and panelings, and from the galleries looked proudly upon my retinue of beautiful women and brave men who sat or walked below.

When I shut my eyes I dwelt in a delicious land of dreams. Charging at the head of ever-victorious legions, I drove millions of laughing foes in playful rout through an illimitable field of roses. Down the mountains of Congo a whole universe of lithe and shapely negro children ran leaping, with their arms full of elephants' tusks, boxes of gold-dust, and fresh cocoanuts, to be the purveyors of my palace. On the wings of a speechless music I floated through the air, and in the cloud-valleys played hide-and-seek with meteors.

A little after midnight I felt the hasheesh effects decreasing, and not having yet recognized that law of the drug which forbids prolonging its dreams by a second dose (nor, indeed, did I recognize it until several bitter experiences had taught me), I took five grains more.

Gradually more and more the hasheesh influence wore off. I went to my state-room, and now, perfectly restored to the natural state, lay down, and all night slept quietly.

Upon awaking with the early sunlight I found that we were midway past the Palisades. Upon the eastern bank of the river the signs of suburban life had become visible in terraces, lawns, and verandas, and bells were audible down the bay.

It was not until we reached the pier that I felt the effect of my last bolus. I stepped ashore, and, for the first time, separated for a season from my fellow voyagers. The morning already gave most earnest promise of a day which was to be one of the hottest of summer, and as I walked up that unsheltered quay alone, and with the sun streaming full upon me, I suddenly felt my heart catch fire. There was no premonitory, no mystery, no thrill; and this gave a more terrible tone to my suffering, for I burned among acknowledged and familiar realities without the possibility of remembering any former state of a calmer nature upon which to steady myself.

Most fully did I then realize the hell of Eblis and its inextinguishable pangs, as, walking through the thronged streets of the great city, I laid my hand upon my heart to hide its writhings, and saw in every face of the vast multitude who hurried past tokens of something despairing and diabolic. The well-known long rows of palatial shops and gaudy windows swept by me as I paced along. The hurrying crowds of men upon the pavement who went to their business, and the fluctuating stream of carriages and omnibusses which rolled down the street, seemed, in their mere matter, nothing unusual to me. Yet the spirit which pervaded all things was that of the infernal. I wandered through a colossal city of hell, where all men were pursuing their earthly tendencies amid pomp and affluence as great as ever, yet stamped upon their foreheads with the dreadful sign of all hope of better things forever lost.

At all times the thoroughfare of a large town is a wilderness to me. In desert loneliness, on mountain tops, or by the side of an unfrequented stream, there is no such hermit conceivable as the hermit of a crowd. The study of character in faces, of universal human nature in its elbowings and windings toward its aim, may be pursued upon a city's pavé to the greatest advantage; yet overtopping all the external aspects of society found there is the solitude which insphere the wanderer within himself, as he perceives not one being within the distance of miles to whom he is bound by any dearer interest than our common humanity.

But at this time how singularly, how especially was I a hermit! Still conscious of retaining some of the attributes of a man, I was surrounded by infernal forms and features, shaped, indeed, like my own, but with the good-will, the hope, the confidence of our common life forever evaporated from them. Every one of the begins that hastened by me in hum and tumult looked under his eyebrows, with dreadful suspicion, at his neighbor and at me. The ideal of hell, where all faith hath perished, and in endless mutation of couples the wretched sneer and glare at each other continually, was realized in that scene.

I could not bear the pavement, and so stepped into an omnibus, that I might behold less of that terrible ebb and flow of Life in Death. As we rolled heavily over the stones of the street, I felt my heart transferred to some flinty road-bed, a fathom below the surface, where it writhed beneath the jar of wheels, and the puncture of the cruel rock-fragments yet communicated all its sufferings to me by slender cords of conduction, whose elastic fibre stretched more and more as we rode on, and grew tenser with an unutterable pain. At the same time, all my fellow-passengers in the omnibus seemed staring at me with hot and searching eyes; in one corner I cowered from their glance, and sat with my hand upon my face. They whispered; it was myself of whom they talked; and I distinctly heard them use the word "hasheesh."

I got out of the omnibus and again took the pavement, realizing that there was nowhere any relief for my pangs. It would be vain to detail all the horrors through which I passed before I took shelter in the house of a friend. Among them not the least were a heart on fire, a brain pierced by a multitude of revolving angers, and the return, amid dim inner flames, of the fearful symbolization and the demon-songs of former visions.

Arriving at my friend's, I pleaded fatigue, and lay down. Hours were wretchedly passed in failing asleep, and then darting up in terror at some ideal danger. Sometimes a gnashing maniac looked at me, face to face, out of the darkness; sometimes into rayless caverns I fell from the very heavens; sometimes the lofty houses of an unknown city were toppling over my head in the agonies of an earthquake. Agonies, I say, for their throes seemed like human sufferings.

Out of this woe I emerged entirely by noon, but began to be aware that I should never again, in the hasheesh state, be secure in the certainty of unclouded visions. The cup had been so often mingled, that its savor of bitterness would never wholly pass away. Yet ascribing all the pain which, in this instance, I had endured, to some unfavorable state of the body (I had not yet realized the law of a second dose), I supposed that, by preserving a general healthy tone of the system, hasheesh might be used harmlessly.

Eidola Theatri and the Prince of Whales.

WAITING until the next day at evening, I took a moderate bolus, say twenty-five grains, and repaired to the theatre.

In the action of the pieces which were performed I lived as really as I had ever lived in the world. With the fortunes of a certain adventurer in one of the plays my mind so thoroughly associated me that, when he was led to the block and the headsman stood over him, I nerved myself for the final stroke, and waited to feel the steel crash through my own neck. He was reprieved, and, in his redemption, it was I who exulted.

The effect of some rich-toned frescoing above the stage was to make me imagine myself in heaven. Yet "imagine" is not the proper word, for it does not express the cloudless conviction of reality which characterized this vision. There were no longer any forms or faces visible below me, but out of the wondrous rosy perspective of the upper paneling angels came gliding, as through corridors hewn of ruby, and showered down rays of music, which were also beheld as rays of color.

A most singular phenomenon occurred while I was intently listening to the orchestra. Singular, because it seems one of the most striking illustrations I have ever known of the preternatural activity of sense in the hasheesh state, and in an analytic direction.

Seated side by side in the middle of the orchestra played two violinists. That they were playing the same part was evident from their perfect uniformity in bowing; their bows, through the whole piece, rose and fell simultaneously, keeping exactly parallel. A chorus of wind and stringed instruments pealed on both sides of them, and the symphony was as perfect as possible; yet, amid all that harmonious blending, I was able to detect which note came from one violin and which from the other as distinctly as if the violinists had been playing at the distance of a hundred feet apart, and with no other instruments discoursing near them.

According to a law of hasheesh already mentioned, a very ludicrous hallucination came in to relieve the mind from its tense state. Just as the rapture of music, lights, and acting began to grow painful from excess, I felt myself losing all human proportions, and, spinning up to a tremendous height, became Cleopatra's Needle.

A man once remarked to young Dumas, "My poor friend, M. Thibadeau, returned home, took off his spectacles, and died." "Did he take off his spectacles first?" asked Dumas. "Yes, truly," replied the other; "but why?" "Merely how delightful it must have been to him to be spared the grief of seeing himself die!"

About as absurd a duality as that inferred for Monsieur Thibadeau, if he had kept on his spectacles, was the duality with which I looked up and saw my own head some hundred feet in the air. Suddenly a hasheesh-voice rang clearly in my ear, "Sit still upon thy base, Eternal Obelisk!" Ah me! I had not realized till then how necessary it was that I should preserve the centre of gravity. What if I should go over? One motion on this side or that, and dire destruction would overwhelm the whole parquette. From my lofty top I looked down upon responsible fathers of families; innocent children; young maidens, with the first peach-bloom of womanhood upon their cheeks; young men, with the firelight of ambitious enterprise new-kindled in their eyes. There was absolutely no effort which I was unwilling to make to save them from destruction. So I said to myself, "Be a good obelisk and behave yourself, old fellow; keep your equilibrium, I entreat you. You don't want to clothe all the families of New York in mourning, I know you don't; control yourself, I beg." Bolt upright and motionless I sat, until it pleased the gods to alter my shape, most opportunely, when I was just giving out, to the far more secure pyramid, after which all hallucinations gently passed away.

The hasheesh state, in its intensest forms, is generally one of the wildest insanity. By this I do not mean to say that the hasheesh-eater at such a season necessarily loses his self-control, or wanders among the incoherent dreams of a lawless fancy, for neither of these propositions is true. As I have heretofore remarked, self-government during the delirium, from being at first apprehended as a necessity, grows up at length in a habit, and the visions that appear before the shut or open eyes of the ecstatic have an orderly progress and a consistent law according to which they are informed, which elevate them above the prodigal through meaningless displays of fancy into the highest sphere of imagination.

Yet, after all, there are reasons for calling the state an insanity, and a wild insanity, which will defend the name to all who can realize them from a description, and far more completely to those who have known them by experiment.

In the first place, when self-control has reached its utmost development, and the tortured or exultant spirit restrains itself from all eruptive paroxysms of communication among those people to whom its secret would be unwisely imparted, there is still a sense of perfect passivity to some Titanic force of life, which, for good or evil, must work on through its seeming eternity. Hurried through sublimest paths, or whirled downward through ever-blackening infinitudes, longing for a Lemnos where the limbs may rebound from solid ground, even though shattered by the shock, there is no relief for the soul but to endure, to wait, and through a time of patience but faintly imaged by the nine days of the headlong Hephaestus. When the Afreet who was of old your servant becomes your lord, he is as deaf to petitions as you were avaricious in your demand for splendors.

Again: at the moment of the most rapturous exultation, the soul hears the outcry of the physical nature pouring up to its height of vision out of the walls of flesh, and the burden of that cry is, "I am in pain; I am finite, though thou art infinite!" The cords which bind the two mysterious portions of our duality together have been stretched to their ultimate tensity, and the body, for the sake of its own existence, calls the soul back into the husk which it can not carry with it. Oftentimes, in the presence of the most ravishing views, have I felt these cords pulling me downward with as distinct a sensation as if they were real sinews, and, compelled to ask the question "Is this happiness or torture?" soul and body have returned opposite verdicts.

These two facts constitute hasheesh a most tremendous form of insanity.

At intervals, however, in the enchanted life which I led under the influence of the drug, there occurred seasons of a quieter nature than the ravishment of delirium, where my mind, with a calm power of insight, penetrated into some of its own kingdoms, whose external boundaries only it had known before, reflected, marveled, and took notes as serenely as a philosophic voyager.

In the department of philological discovery I sometimes reveled for hours, coming upon clews to the genealogy of words and unexpected affinities between languages, which, upon afterward recalling them (though only in a few cases was I able to do this), I generally found substantiated by the authorities of science, or, if they had not before been perceived by any writers whom I had at hand, at least bearing the stamp of a strong probability of correctness.

I mention but one of them as with me merely conjectural, for it bases its plausibility upon a root in the Sanscrit, with which language I do not pretend to be acquainted.

I remembered during one of these calm, suggestive states that the Latin *cano* (to sing) and *candeo* (to shine) were supposed to derive their origin from a common Sanscrit root, whose signification was "to dart forth, as the sun his rays of light." The thought struck me, might not other vocal utterance than singing be found cognate with the out-darting of light also? I would see. The Latin "fari," "to speak," referred me back to its Greek equivalent $\phi\acute{\alpha}\nu\alpha\iota$. The verb "to shine" was "$\phi\alpha\acute{\iota}\nu\epsilon\iota\nu$." So far, in sound at least, the two were affiliated. It now occurred to me that "$\phi\omega\zeta$" was both "a light" and "man," in his prerogative of speech, with a slight variation of accent in the different cases. I had here four words (dividing the last by its two meanings), all of whose original roots must have been something very nearly like $\phi\alpha-$. On referring to authorities, I found that the fountain-head of the Greek "$\phi\alpha\acute{\iota}\nu\omega$," is supposed to be the Sanscrit "bhâ," "to shine forth." Following out the result of my previous argument, I connected all the words with this root, and in this conjecture saw both light and speech as effluences from Brahm, the great giver of all radiance, and man not merely an effluence from him, but, in virtue of speech, a "shiner" also, a reflector of Him from whose radiance he came, and

into whose glory he should be absorbed. Now all this process (be its result true or false) was accomplished internally in a hundredth part of the time which it will take to read it—nay, almost instantaneously, and with a sense of delight in the mental activity which carried it on such as the creation of his highest ideal by an artist gives him when he stands mute before his marble.

Another field through which I sometimes wandered was sown with those sound-relations between words which constitute the pun. For hours I walked aching with laughter in this land of Paronomasia, where the whole Dictionary had arrayed itself in strophe and antistrophe, and was dancing a ludicrous chorus of quirk and quibble. If Hood had been there, the notes which he would have taken had supplied him with materials for the Comic Annuals of a cycle. Rarely did the music of a deeper wit intermingle with the rattling fantasies of the pun-country; never was any thing but the broad laugh heard there, and the very atmosphere was crazy with oxygen. Were it possible to transport to a country such as this those grave professors of the moralities who have been convicted of contempt of the court of Mirth, and high treason to the King of Misrule, how delightful would it be to behold their iron diaphragms vibrating perforce, and the stereotyped downward curves at the corners of their mouths reversed until they encroached upon the boundaries of their juiceless cheeks! But, in hasheesh states, temperament and previous habit so much decide tendencies, that the transport-ship which bore these convicts would float inevitably to the mouth of Acheron, or strand midway upon some reef upraised by a million of zoophytic Duns Scotuses.

Out of the number of double-entendres which appeared to me (and they probably amounted to thousands), I recollect but very few. To recall them all would be nearly, if not quite as difficult as to remember the characteristics of each separate wheat-head in a large harvest-field after having but once passed through it. I give two of them.

A youth, not at all of that description which "maketh a glad father," was seen standing at the counter of a gaudy restaurant. Glass after glass of various exhilarating compounds was handed to him by the man in waiting, and as quickly drained. I did not observe that the genius of decanters received any compensation for the liquors consumed from the young man who demanded them, and modestly asked him how he had been induced to purvey to the drinker's thirst on so liberal a scale. With arms akimbo, and casting upon me a most impressive look, the official replied, "Like the man in Thanatopsis, I am

" 'Sustained by an unfaltering trust.' "

Upon the steps of the post-office stood another young man who had been disappointed in a remittance from the parental treasury. "What are you doing there?" I asked. "I am waiting patiently until my *change* come."

Occasionally there intervened between the vagaries of pun and double-entendre some display of comic points in human nature, which were as amusing as the puns themselves. For instance, I remember the representation to me of a man of remarkable self-esteem, who happened, as he sat in my presence, to appease the irritation of his scalp with his digit. Just then a peal of thunder shook the sky above us. "Heavens!" cried our friend, "to think that it should thunder because a man scratched his head!"

I feel that these things lose very much of their original effervescence in the relation, for at the time they none of them seemed so much told to me as acted before me; nor was it the action of a stage, but of a vivified picture, where fun, in all its myriad mutations, was embodied to sight, and the joke was as much apprehended by the eye as by the feeling. Every gesture of the figures that passed before me told more of raillery than tongue could utter, and it was this fact that sometimes made pantomime upon the stage a perfect feast of mirth to me as I sat seeing it in the appreciative state induced by hasheesh. At such seasons, not the faintest stroke of humor in look or manner escaped me, and I no doubt often committed that most gross error in any man, laughing when my neighbors saw fit not to be moved.

At one time, in my ramble through the realm of incongruities, I came to the strand of the Mediterranean, and beheld an acquaintance of mine standing close beside the water. With a tourist's knapsack upon his back, and a stout umbrella in his hand, to serve the double purpose of a walking-stick, he drew near and accosted me.

"Will you go with me," said he, "to make a call upon a certain old and valued friend?"

"Most willingly, if you will let me know his name."

"It is the Prophet Jonah, who still occupies submarine lodgings in a situation, to be sure, rather cold and damp, yet commanding a fine water privilege." "There is nothing," I replied, "which would please me more; but how is it to be accomplished?" "Be patient, and you shall see." Just then a slight ripple ridged the surface of the sea, bubbles appeared, and then there followed them the black muzzle of Leviathan, who, with mighty strokes, pushed toward the shore. Arriving there, his under jaw slid half way up the beach, and his upper jaw slowly rose like a trapdoor, disclosing a fearful chasm of darkness within. I looked down the throat of the beast, and beheld descending it a rickety wooden staircase, which was evidently the only feasable access to interior apartments. Hardly would I have dared to trust myself to the tumble-down passage but for the importunate hand of my companion, which pressed me along beside him through the doorway and down the steps. The monster let down his grisly portcullis behind us, and in total darkness we groped to the bottom of our way, where we emerged into the most shabby room that ever dawned upon the eyes of the visiting committee of a benevolent association.

The central figure was an unutterably lean and wobegone looking man, who, on a rush-bottomed chair, the only one in the room, sat mending his sole pair of unmentionables by the aid of a small needle-book which I was informed his mother had given him on leaving home.

"Mr. Jonah, Mr. Fitz-Gerald," said my friend, sententiously. "Very happy to know Mr. Fitz-Gerald," returned the seer; though, as I took his lank and ghostly fingers in mine, he looked the very antipodes of happy. Decayed gentleman as he was, he shuffled around to do the honors of his mansion, and offered us the chair in which he had been sitting. We refused to dispossess him, and took our seats upon the shaky pine table, which, with one battered brazen candlestick, holding an inch of semi-luminous tallow, and a dog's-eared copy of Watts's Hymns, also a gift from his mother, completed his inventory of furniture.

"How do you like your situation?" asked my friend.

"Leaky," replied Jonah; "find the climate don't agree with me. I often wish I hadn't come."

"Can't you leave here when you want to? I should think you would clear out if you find it uncomfortable," said I to our entertainer.

"I have repeatedly asked my landlord to make out his bill and let me go," replied the gentleman; "but he isn't used to casting up his prophets, and I don't know when I *shall* get off."

Just then Leviathan, from the top of the stairs, by a strange introversion looked down into his own interiors, and in a hoarse voice called out to know whether we were going to stay all night, as he wanted to put down the shutters.

"Be happy to give you a bed, gentlemen, but I sleep on the floor myself," woefully murmured the poor seer. "You mustn't neglect to call on me if you ever pass through Joppa, and—and—I ever get back myself." We wrung Jonah's hand convulsively, rattled up the crazy stairs, and ran out upon the sand just as Leviathan was about shoving off into deep water.

It may, perhaps, be hard to conceive how this incongruous element of the hasheesh visions should comport with all I have said upon the subject of those delicious raptures of beauty and sublime revealings of truth which break upon the mind under the influence of the drug.

How, it will be asked, as oftentimes it has been asked me already, can you put any confidence in discoveries of unsupposed significancy in outer things, and wonderful laws of mental being, attained during the hasheesh state, when you have also beheld vagaries of fancy which Reason instantly pronounced absurd? You do not believe that you really saw Jonah; how, then, can you believe that you saw truth?

I would answer thus: The domains of intuition and those of a wild fancy were always, in my visions, separated from each other by a clearly-defined and recognized boundary. The congruous and the incongruous might alternate, but they never blended. The light which illustrated the one was as different from that shed upon the other as a zenith sun is from lamplight. Moreover, at the time of each specific envisionment, I beheld which faculty of mind was working as distinctly as in the simplest tests of his laboratory the chemist knows whether cobalt or litmus is producing a certain change of color. The conviction of truth in the one case was like that of an axiom; in the other, such only as is drawn inferentially from mere sense.

We very little realize in our daily life that there are two species of conviction felt at various times by every man, yet a moment's reflection will show that it is so. I look, for example, at a piece of silk, and pronounce it black; if I were now to turn away without any further inspection, I should not be at all astonished to hear afterward, from some one who had examined the fabric more closely and in a better light, that it was not black, as I had pronounced it, but a dark shade of blue. I would be very willing to abjure my previous conviction, and, in this willingness, would show that I ascribed no absolute infallibility to the proofs of sense. Yet if the same man should assure me that the silk was both wholly black and wholly blue at the same time, I should instantly reject his assertion as absurd, for the reason that it was a violation of the very law of possibility. There would be no need of going back to test his truth, for it is denied by an entirely different conviction from that of sense—the conviction arising from an insight into necessary and universal law.

Between the convictions of reality in the different hasheesh states, the boundary-lines are drawn even more distinctly than in the natural; and not only so, but the hasheesh-eater beholds those lines and acknowledges them, as the ordinary observer never does, from the fact that the practical wants of life make it convenient, nay, even imperative, that the data of sense should be treated as valid for the basis of action. We have neither time nor power in our present daylabor to secure the same unerring verdict upon objects of sense which the axiom gives us upon objects of intuition.

Nor is it necessary that in this life such a power should be possible. In a former part of these pages we have suggested a reason why it would not be best for the soul, thus early in its career, to have its intuitional domain enlarged. We may here, by another process, get at some of the final causes why this domain is just so large as it is. We have a sufficient scope of intuition for all our earthly purposes. Those truths are imparted to us as axioms which are necessary for the shaping of our habitual conduct. In the thousands of constantly-recurring cases where, to direct our course wisely, it is necessary to know that a straight line is the shortest distance between two given points, that the whole is equal to its parts, and numerous similar facts, it would greatly hinder action were it necessary to take the rule and the balance into each specific consideration, and make a measurement according to sense. These truths, therefore, stand before every man in a light which shows them to be universal and necessary; they are every where assented to upon their mere statement. The animal is not God's grand laborer, but man's; *he*, therefore, needs no such faculty as intuition, the work of his little day requiring neither dispatch nor accuracy; and when he is impressed for human uses into the harness or the mill, the intuitions of his master guide him through the rein and the halter.

Doubtless, as our field of action widens, our intuitional eyesight shall be increased also; not only because otherwise we should be mortified and saddened by our purblindness and the sense of making no progress proportional to the pace of our circumstances, but because God will never leave the workmen of his purposes hampered in their action among the colossal plans of the eternal building.

There is one more fact for which I would advert in this rather rambling portion of my narrative, which characterizes the hasheesh state at times when it does not reach the height of delirium. I refer to a lively appreciation of the feelings and manners of all people, in whatever lands and ages—a catholic sympathy, a spiritual cosmopolitanism. Not only does this exhibit itself in affectionate yearnings toward friends that are about one, and an extraordinary insight into the excellencies of their characters, but, taking a wider sweep, it can understand and feel with the heroism of philanthropists and the enthusiasm of Crusaders. The lamentation of the most ancient Thracian captive is a sincere grief to the dreamer, and the returning Camillus brought no greater joy to Rome, as he threw his defiant sword into the scale, than over the chasm of ages he sends thrilling into the hasheesh-eater's heart. Whether it is the Past or the Present that is read or heard, he sorrows in all its woes and rejoices in all its rejoicings. He understands all feelings; his mind is malleable to all thoughts; his susceptibilities run into the mould of all emotions.

Sitting in this fused state of mind, I have heard the old ladies of the Latin time, as they sat gossiping over spindle and distaff, keep up their perpetual round of "inquit" and "papae" with as distinct and as kind appreciations as were they our own beloved American aunts and grandmothers, knitting after tea amid the interchange of "says he" and "do tell." For Epaminondas, coming glorious from Leuctra, I could have hurrahed as enthusiastically as any Theban of them all, or hobnobbed with Horace over his

"Pocula veteris Massici"

with a true Roman zest and full-heartedness. At such times no anachronism seems surprising; time is treated as an insignificant barrier to those souls who, in the element of their generous humanity, possess the only true bond of conjunction, and a bond which, though now so elastic that it permits years and leagues to keep souls apart, shall one day pull with a force strong enough to bring all congenialities together, in place as well as in state, and every man shall be with those whom, for their inner qualities, he has most deeply loved through all his life.

XIV.

Hail ! Pythagoras.

THE hemisphere of sky which walls us in is something more than a mere product of the laws of sight. It is our shield from unbearable visions. Within our little domain of view, girt by the horizon and arched by the dome of heaven, there is enough of sorrow, enough of danger, yes, enough of beauty and of mirth visible to occupy the soul abundantly in any one single beholding. That lesser and unseen hemisphere which bounds our hearing is also amply large, for within it echo enough of music and lamentation to fill all susceptibility to the utmost. In this world we are but half spirit; we are thus able to hold only the perceptions and emotions of half an orb. Once fully rounded into symmetry ourselves, we shall have strength to bear the pressure of influences from a whole sphere to truth and loveliness.

It is this present half-developed state of ours which makes the infinitude of the hasheesh awakening so unendurable, even when its sublimity is the sublimity of delight. We have no longer any thing to do with horizons, and the boundary which was at once our barrier and our fortress is removed, until we almost perish from the inflow of perceptions.

One most powerful realization of this fact occurred to me when hasheesh had already become a fascination and a habit. In the broad daylight of a summer afternoon I was walking in the full possession of delirium. For an hour the expansion of all visible things had been growing toward its height; it now reached it, and to the fullest extent I apprehended what is meant by the infinity of space. Vistas no longer converged; sight met no barrier; the world was horizonless, for earth and sky stretched endlessly onward in parallel planes.

Above me the heavens were terrible with the glory of a fathomless depth. I looked up, but my eyes, unopposed, every moment penetrated farther and farther into the immensity, and I turned them downward, lest they should presently intrude into the fatal splendors of the Great Presence. Unable to bear visible objects, I shut my eyes. In one moment a colossal music filled the whole hemisphere above me, and I thrilled upward through its environment on visionless wings. It was not song, it was not instruments, but the inexpressible spirit of sublime sound—like nothing I had ever heard—impossible to be symbolized; intense, yet not loud; the ideal of harmony, yet distinguishable into a multiplicity of exquisite parts.

I opened my eyes, but it still continued. I sought around me to detect some natural sound which might be exaggerated into such a semblance; but no, it was of unearthly generation, and it thrilled through the universe an inexplicable, a beautiful, yet an awful symphony.

Suddenly my mind grew solemn with the consciousness of a quickened perception. And what a solemnity is that which the hasheesh-eater feels at such a moment! The very beating of his heart is silenced; he stands with his finger on his lip; his eye is fixed, and he becomes a very statue of awful veneration. The face of such a man, however little glorified in feature or expression during his ordinary states of mind, I have stood and looked upon with the consciousness that I was beholding more of the embodiment of the truly sublime than any created thing could ever offer me.

I looked abroad on fields, and waters, and sky, and read in them a most startling meaning. I wondered how I had ever regarded them in the light of dead matter, at the farthest only *suggesting* lessons. They were now, as in my former vision, grand symbols of the sublimest spiritual truths—truths never before even feebly grasped, and utterly unsuspected.

Like a map, the areana of the universe lay bare before me. I saw how every created thing not only typifies, but springs forth from some mighty spiritual law as its offspring, its necessary external development—not the mere clothing of the essence, but the essence incarnate.

I am aware that, in this recital, I may seem to be repeating what I have said before of my dreadful night of insight; but between the two visions there was this difference, the view did not stop here. While that music was pouring through the great heavens above me, I became conscious of a numerical order which ran through it, and in marking this order, I beheld it transferred to every moment of the universe. Every sphere wheeled on in its orbit, every emotion of the soul arose and fell, every smallest moss and fungus germinated and grew according to some peculiarity of numbers which severally governed them, and was most admirably typified by them in return. An exquisite harmony of proportion reigned through space, and I seemed to realize that the music which I heard was but this numerical harmony making itself objective through the development of a grand harmony of tones.

The vividness with which this conception revealed itself to me made it a thing terrible to bear alone. An unutterable ecstasy was carrying me away, but I dared not abandon myself to it. I was no seer who could look on the unveiling of such glories face to face.

An irrepressible yearning came over me to impart what I beheld, to share with another soul the weight of this colossal revelation. With this purpose I scrutinized the vision; I sought in it for some characteristic which might make it translatable to another mind. There was none. In absolute incommunicableness it stood apart. For it, in spoken language, there was no symbol.

For a time—how long a hasheesh-eater alone can know—I was in an agony. I searched every pocket for my pencil and note-book, that I might at least set down some representative mark which would afterward recall to me the lineaments of my apocalypse. They were not with me. Jutting into the water of the brook along which I then wandered, and which, before and afterward, was my sole companion through so many ecstasies, lay a broad, flat stone. "Glory in the highest!" I shouted, exultingly; "I will at least grave on this tablet some hieroglyph of what I feel. Tremblingly I sought for my knife; that, too, was gone! It was then that, in a phrensy, I threw myself prostrate on the stone, and with my nails sought to make some memorial scratch upon it. Hard, hard as flint! In despair I stood up.

Suddenly there came a sense as of some invisible presence walking the dread paths of the vision with me, yet at a distance, as if separated from my side by a long flow of time. Taking courage, I cried, "Who has ever been here before me? who, in years past, has shared with me this unutterable view?" In tones which linger with me to this day, a grand, audible voice responded "Pythagoras!" In an instant I was calm. I heard the footsteps of that sublime sage echoing upward through the ages, and in celestial light I read my vision unterrified, since it had burst upon his sight before me.

For years previous I had been perplexed with his mysterious philosophy. I saw in him an isolation from universal contemporary mind for which I could not account. When the Ionic school was at the height of its dominance, he stood forth alone the originator of a system as distinct from it as the antipodes of mind.

The doctrine of Thales was built up by the uncertain processes of an obscure logic; that of Pythagoras seemed informed by intuition. In his assertions there had always appeared to me a grave conviction of truth, a consciousness of sincerity which gave them a great weight, though I saw them through the dim refracting medium of tradition, and grasped their meaning imperfectly. It wa snow given to see, in their own light, the truths which he set forth. I also saw, as to this day I firmly believe, the source whence their revelation flowed.

Tell me not that from Phoenicia he received the wand at whose signal the cohorts of the spheres came trooping up before him in review, unveiling the eternal law and itinerary of their revolutions, and pouring on his spiritual ear that tremendous music to which they marched through space. No. During half a lifetime spent in Egypt and in India, both mother-lands of this nepenthe, doubt not that he quaffed its apocalyptic draught, and awoke, through its terrific quickening, into the consciousness of that ever-present and all-pervading harmony "which we hear not, because the coarseness of the daily life hath dulled our ear." The dim penetralia of the Theban Memnonium, or the silent spice-groves of the upper Indus, may have been the gymnasium of his wrestling with the mighty revealer; a priest or a gymnosophist may have been the first to anoint him with the palaestric oil, but he conquered alone. On the strange intuitive characteristics of his system; on the spheral music; on the government of all created things, and their development according to the laws of numbers; yes, on the very use of symbols, which could alone have force to the esoteric disciple (and a terrible significancy, indeed, has the simplest form to a mind hasheesh-quickened to read its meaning)—on all of these is the legible stamp of the hasheesh inspiration.

It would be no hard task to prove, to a strong probability, at least, that the initiation to the Pythagorean mysteries, and the progressive instruction that succeeded it, to a considerable extent consisted in the employment, judiciously, if we may use the word, of hasheesh, as giving a critical and analytic power to the mind, which enabled the neophyte to roll up the murk and mist from beclouded truths till they stood distinctly seen in the splendor of their own harmonious beauty as an intuition.

One thing related of Pythagoras and his friends has seemed very striking to me. There is a legend that, as he was passing over a river, its waters called up to him, in the presence of his followers, "Hail! Pythagoras." Frequently, while in the power of the hasheesh delirium, have I heard inanimate things sonorous with such voices. On every side they have saluted me, from rocks, and trees, and waters, and sky; in my happiness filling me with intense exultation as I heard them welcoming their master; in my agony heaping nameless curses on my head as I went away into an eternal exile from all sympathy. Of this tradition of Iamblichus I feel an appreciation which almost convinces me that the voice of the river was indeed heard, though only by the quickened mind of some hasheesh-glorified esoteric. Again, it may be that the doctrine of the metempsychosis was first communicated to Pythagoras by Theban priests; but the astonishing illustration which hasheesh would contribute to this tenet should not be overlooked in our attempt to assign its first suggestion and succeeding spread to their proper causes.

A modern critic, in defending the hypothesis that Pythagoras was an impostor, has triumphantly asked, "Why did he assume the character of Apollo at the Olympic games? Why did he boast that his soul had lived in former bodies, and that he had first been Aethalides, the son of Mercury, then Euphorbus, then Pyrrhus of Delos, and at last Pythagoras, but that he might more easily impose upon the credulity of an ignorant and superstitious people?" To us these facts seem rather an evidence of his sincerity. Had he made these assertions without proof, it is difficult to see how they would not have had a precise contrary effect from that of paving the way to a more complete imposition upon popular credulity. Upon our hypothesis it may be easily shown, not only how he could fully have believed these assertions himself, but also have given them a deep significance to the minds of his disciples.

Let us see. We will consider, for example, his assumption of the character of Phoebus at the Olympic games. Let us suppose that Pythagoras, animated with a desire of alluring to the study of his philosophy a choice and enthusiastic number out of that host who, along all the radii of the civilized world, had come up to the solemn festival at Elis, had, by the talisman of hasheesh, called to his aid the magic of a preternatural eloquence; that while he addressed the throng, whom he had chained into breathless attention by the weird brilliancy of his eye, the unearthly imagery of his style, and the oracular insight of his thought, the grand impression flashed upon him from the very honor he was receiving, that he was the incarnation of some sublime deity. What wonder that he burst into the acknowledgment of his godship as a secret too majestic to be hoarded up; what wonder that this sudden revelation of himself, darting forth in burning words and amid such colossal surroundings, went down with the accessories of time and place along the stream of perpetual tradition?

If I may illustrate great things by small, I well remember many hallucinations of my own which would be exactly parallel to such a fancy in the mind of Pythagoras. There is no impression more deeply stamped upon my past life than one of a walk along the brook which had so often witnessed my wrestlings with the hasheesh-effect, and which now beheld me, the immortal Zeus, descended among men to grant them the sublime benediction of renovated life. For this cause I had abandoned the serene seats of Olympus, the convocation of the gods, and the glory of an immortal kingship, while by my side Hermes trod the earth with radiant feet, the companion and dispenser of the beneficence of Deity. Across lakes and seas, from continent to continent we strode; the snows of Haemus and the Himmalehs crunched beneath our sandals; our foreheads were bathed with the upper light, our breasts glowed with the exultant inspiration of the golden ether. Now resting on Chimborazo, I poured forth a majestic blessing upon all my creatures, and in an instant, with one omniscient glance, I beheld every human dwelling-place on the whole sphere irradiated with an unspeakable joy.

I saw the king rule more wisely; the laborer return from his toil to a happier home; the park grow green with an intenser culture; the harvest-field groan under the sheaves of a more prudent and prosperous husbandry. Adown blue slopes came new and more populous flocks, led by unvexed and gladsome shepherds; a thousand healthy vineyards sprang up above their new-raised sunny terraces; every smallest heart glowed with an added thrill of exultation, and the universal rebound of joy came pouring up into my own spirit with an intensity which lit my deity with rapture.

And this was but a lay hasheesh-eater, mysteriously clothed in no Pallas-woven, philosophic stole, who, with his friend, walked out into the fields to enjoy his delirium among the beauties of a clear summer afternoon. What, then, of Pythagoras?

It was during this walk that one of the strangest phenomena of sight which I have ever noticed appeared to me. Every sunbeam was refracted into its primitive rays; wherever upon the landscape a pencil of light fell, between rocks or trees, it seemed a prismatic pathway between earth and heaven. The atmosphere was one network of variegated solar threads, tremulous with radiance, and distilling rapture from its fibres into all my veins.

It is singular in how many ways, during the hasheesh life, the harmony of creation was typified to me. The harp of the universe, which I have already mentioned, was itself once repeated in vision; other representations, on a scale perhaps even as grand, have left but a dim outline upon my memory; yet there is one which, though at least thrice repeated, lost no glory by growing familiar, but more and more deepened its first impress of awe and rapture. The first time that it occurred to me was when, at the close of my walk amid the majesty of apotheosis, I sat quietly at the window of my room looking out upon the sunset which bathed the gigantic landscape before me. As yet the magnifying effect of the drug had not begun to decrease, and I gazed with fascinated eyes upon mountains which scaled heaven, and a river which was oceanic, in a breathless exultancy which vibrated on the diamond edge of pain.

Suddenly the landscape floated out of sight, and in its place there sat on the trembling ether a tremendous ship, which within itself included every portion of created being. Not a God-born essence, not a microscopic atom, but was builded up into some bulwark, beam, or spar of the colossal vessel. Its marked outline was traced with the more glorious things of creation, the baser formed its inner and hidden parts. Its sides, its stern, its bow were wrought of mighty stars whose rays interlaced; its masts were similar constellations, that at their heads, a million leagues above me, yet still distinctly radiant, bore systems of suns for lanterns. Like lanterns flashed far off upon the prow, and dazzling clouds and nebulae, filled out with the breath of an omnipotent will, strained the crystal yards upon which they hung.

Now I was transferred to the deck of this infinite ship; her name was whispered in my ear, "The Ship of the Universe," and the helm was put into my hand. With unutterable symphonies we floated out upon the boundless space, and on the distant bows there broke in music the waves of resplendent ether. It was at this post of pilotage, steering out into the unknown void, that I felt human nature within me grow godlike to an insane excess. The helmsman, the master of all being but the Divine, I burst into a chant of triumph, which shook the starry lights above me till their clusters rained glory like wine.

I bethought me, forgetful of the infinity of the ocean we were traveling, that I might mark the rate of our progress, and so drew out my watch. Its second-hand had stopped. I held it to my ear and heard it tick. Again I looked at it; the hand was motionless. Continuing my gaze, I saw it at length move slowly through one of the second-spaces, when it stopped once more. Still I looked, and at last became aware that, by the hasheesh expansion of time, I was enabled to realize as a quite prolonged and definite period—a period as great as in our ordinary state a whole minute, at least, would appear—that almost infinitesimal instant during which a second-hand actually is motionless at the end of its vibration between two consecutive ticks.

XV.

"Then Seeva Opened on the Accursed One his Eye of Anger."

In the agonies of hasheesh, which now became more and more frequent, a new element began to develop itself toward a terrible symmetry, which afterward made it effective for the direst spiritual evil. This was the appearance of Deity upon the stage of my visionary life, now sublimely grand in very person, and now through the intermediation of some messenger or sign, yet always menacing, wrathful, or avenging, in whatever form or manner the visitation might be made. The myriad voices which, earlier in my enchanted life, I had heard from Nature through all her mysterious passages of communication, now died down forever, or, rather, became absorbed into one colossal and central voice, which spoke with the forces of a fiat, and silenced my own faint replies like the sentence of inevitable doom.

At first I was calmly warned. Repeatedly, as I sat in an elysium of rosy languor, banqueting upon all that could exalt the inner sense into the serenest ecstasy, the hand that wrote upon the wall has invaded the sanctity of my feast, and its dread tracery has made me suddenly afraid. In characters of light I have seen in written, "Beware how thou triflest with a mysterious power of the Most High!" and an audible voice, whose divinity at the moment I no more doubted than my own humanity, has added its injunction, "Beware! beware!" Anticipating nothing but an uninterrupted procession of sublime images and the choral music which had so often ravished me out of the walls of sense, I have in an instant shuddered with unutterable terror as I felt the unlooked-for finger of some awful presence marking out downward channels for my upwelling thought, and solemnly forcing its streams into them with a power which bore no doubtful tokens of irresistibleness, but commanded even my own assent to the impossibility of escape.

At length the reasons of my punishment were shown me. Here again, as audibly as man talks with man, I was told, "Thou hast lifted thyself above humanity to peer into the speechless secrets before thy time; and thou shalt be smitten—smitten—smitten." As the last echo of the sentence died away, it always began its execution in Promethean pangs. At last even the faintest suggestion of the presence of Deity possessed a power to work me ill which hardly the haunting of demons had been able to produce before. At one time I well remember beholding a colossal veiled figure part the drapery of sombre clouds which hung over the horizon, and appear upon a platform which I supposed to be the stage of the universe. No sound, no radiance issued from behind the veil, yet when the mysterious figure lifted his hands, I cried, "It is the Day of Judgment, and my doom is being pronounced!" Then I fled for my soul, and cowered in the darkest spot that I could find.

One tremendous vision occurred to me during the progress of one of these peculiar states, which, while it filled me with the agony of despair for my own fate, still gave me an inconceivable pain for another being. In the heavens I heard a voice of weeping; no plaintive wail like that of woman in affliction, no passionate cry like that of a strong man riven by distress, but some nameless agony, foreshadowed by a solemn voice of woe, which spoke of universal creation suffering fearfully at its centre, life drying up at its fountainhead of being. "Who weeps?" I cried in terror. And the answer was returned to me out of the viewless air, "The Mighty One, who was of old held supreme, hath discovered that his supremacy is void. Fate, blind Fate, that hath no ear for thy yearnings, sits mover of the spring of all things, and He to whom thou prayest is a discrowned King." Ah! well might there be such weeping in the heavens! After all, we had no Lord, no God but Destiny. And I saw dynasties rush down in aimless ruin; good and evil met in eternal shock; there should be no prevalence to Right; the souls of all humanity were but atoms hurled onward through an infinite, lawless Chaos. In my own spirit there sounded an echo to the celestial groaning, and with tearless horror I went straying through the rayless abyss of accident, a tortured creature without a goal. "My God," I whispered, "annihilate me!" Words of accursed folly! God no longer lived.

I threw myself upon the earth, and clutched its dead, ungoverned dust in my writhing fingers. I called no longer upon God, and was dumb because Fate was deaf. I cursed the day that I was born—meaningless, still meaningless, since there was no power who could authenticate me. I lay balancing the chances of being blotted out. Somewhere in the eternities a crash might end me. Forever? What if my disrupted being should float together in cycles measurelessly on? Reunited, I should wander once more a godless wretch!

From horizon to horizon there flashed a quick glory; heaven rang through all its dome with a multitude of tremendous bands, and a sound of chanting joined in the symphony. "Ah! what is this?" I said, and started up. "I hear a harmony, and Fate knows only discords." Again the aerial voice responded, but now in a triumphant song, "After all, there is a Supreme; he rules whose right it is; there is no destiny but God, and he is over all forever." I leaped into the air—I shouted for joy. The hope of the ages was sure—there was a God!

Yet few of my visions of the Divine, as bitterly I tested in many a trial of fire, were to have an issue so blessed as this.

Through the watches of a long and lonely night I had been sitting, with no other companion than my crusted lamp, and the shapes of strange men and things passed by me ceaselessly in tides of pain and pleasure. At length I found myself in the highest story of an unknown and desolate house, surrounded by blank walls, and lighted by a single narrow window. "This room," spoke the hasheesh voice, "is that which thou called Time. Outside the whirl the resistless, the unbounded winds of Eternity."

I went to the window, and, looking out, saw nothing; but the heavy roar of a storm-lashed atmosphere shook the panes. A strange fascination tempted me to draw nearer to the tempest. I threw up the sash; in one moment the wind of eternity came rushing in; the foundations of my building shook, and straightway, by those stormy wings, every atom of it was winnowed out of sight, and, houseless, I found myself alone among the infinitudes. For a while I was blown hither and thither unconsciously. Then, coming to myself, I found that I had been wafted to the door of a certain friend of mine, who doubtless would care for me in my bewilderment of suffering.

It was now four o'clock of a midsummer morning, and the western hills, that I could see through a hall window, began to be impurpled by reflection from the opposite horizon of the dawn. My friend was an early riser, and he would, perhaps, be willing to walk with me, for I could not endure to sit still for a moment. "Baldwin!" I cried; "Baldwin, it is necessary that I should speak with you," at the same time knocking stoutly until I aroused him from sleep.

It was at first very difficult for me to persuade him how intensely I was suffering, for my habit of self-control subdued even my face. At last we were in the open air, and I walked clinging to Baldwin's arm. I said little, for I had no power to speak above a whisper, and in disjointed sentences. Coming to the steps which led from my own entry, we sat down for a few moments' rest. All familiarity of appearance was utterly dissipated from the place, and the buildings in view had become to me the temples and pylons of disentombed Memphis. Awful Egyptian gateways frowned down upon me with a wrathful meaning, which they had not lost in all their centuries of sepulchral dust since the Pharaohs, and the grisly stare of Sphinx and Caryatid appalled me, on all sides shutting out relief through change of view. But, worse horror yet, beneath pedestal and foundation, under the lowest stone of the deepest-based temple of all the adamantine group, supporting its weight, bursting with a torture in which it could not writhe, lay my own, my living heart, unreached and never to be reached by the instrument of the resurrectionist of ages!

It was the wrath of God which had whelmed that city; my heart, therefore, lay under that wrath. Yet I would appeal submissively to the Supreme, that he might perchance have mercy on me. I looked heavenward, but what a vision there unveiled itself! In the most intimate recess of a sable, cloudy cavern flamed vengefully two burning, soul-penetrating eyes. Their gaze dissolved me, and, turning away, I hid my face in my friend's lap.

When he sought the cause of my pain, I could not tell him. At that moment I would not have embodied in words the infinity of wrathful meance which I had seen on high for the endowment of coined worlds.

When at length I dared to look out from my lurking-place, my sight chanced to fall upon the vapory banks which skirted the gleaming western horizon. In mercy my vision was here changed to one of peace. As if to heal the pangs of my spirit, I saw, flowing down to me through a rift in the clouds, a silvery river of unutterable balm. Unknown trees drooped, prodigal of wondrous fruit and odors, over its enameled margin; and rare beings floated, with their beaming girdles streaming on the breeze, above the crystal waters, or stooped to drink of them along the edge; and the hasheesh voice whispered me, "The River of the Water of Life." If heaven be like that, the stake and the rack are worth while to bear on the way to it!

Slowly the celestial aspect of the vision passed away. The river still remained, but on its banks a great city lifted her walls, and I knew that the river was Simois, and the city Troy. As yet the inner citadel rose fair and vast, and the broad gates stood firm.

Upon the bank of the stream I saw a dead face turned up toward the morning sky. The agony of the death-struggle had plowed no furrows upon brow or cheek, and a mysterious, matchless loveliness slept in the features chiseled without fault. More than I had ever been with life was I ravished with death—nay, I had given my own life to print a kiss upon the serene lips of the sleeper, or to pluck a lock from the wavy wealth which flowed out of his helmet, whose clasps, now unbound, hung idly to the earth beside him.

A warrior still living came into my view. With shield thrown on the ground and spear trailing through his arm in all the negligence of grief, with bowed crest and hands intensely clasped, he stood silently gazing upon the dead, and his look was so instinct with a superhuman grief that I wept in sympathy with him.

Again the hasheesh voice spoke to me, "This is Achilles standing over the slain Patroclus," and my grief was changed into a sublime awe of mystery as I beheld that some unknown power had borne me over the bridgeless abyss of three thousand years to sorrow in the sorrowing of one of the grandest children of the epic Past.

I have sometimes lamented that in my hasheesh experience visions of ecstasy almost always followed those of pain, and, indeed, generally concluded the trance, whether I walked or slept. With opium-eaters or drinkers of liquor the case is ordinarily different. Their happiness comes first, and the depression that follows brings with it shame, repentance, and at least a feeble aim at some new life. When they have become satiated with their pleasure, they have to pay for it, and of all things which it is odious to pay for, a luxury enjoyed in the past is the most so. If, in my own experience, such a disgust and loathing, such reaction of body and spirit, had succeeded the hasheesh indulgence, I had possessed much stronger motives for renouncing it. But with me ecstasy had always the last word, and, on returning to the natural state, I remembered great tortures to be sure, but only as the unnecessary adjuncts to a happiness which I fondly persuaded myself was the legitimate effect of the drug. I said, I have suffered, but only because certain unfortunate circumstances came in to pervert my condition, and I will, in the future, avoid them. In the instance just related this fact fully obtained. For days afterward I never looked toward a certain quarter of the heavens without shuddering, as I remembered that it was there I met the gaze of the burning eyes, and my hand involuntarily went to my heart as I saw the site of the disentombed city, in imagination, once more occupied by its ponderous and cruel piles of granite. But from such memories as these my mind glanced with an elasticity as yet undiminished by its many shocks to the healing waters of the celestial river, or the face of mortal loveliness which has never, even now, passed thoroughly from my dreams.

After this, therefore, I took hasheesh many times; nay, more, life became with me one prolonged state of hasheesh exaltation—a very network, singularly varied, of golden and iron strands, and throughout this life I ever and anon bore hours of wretchedness from superhuman threatenings such as I would not, if I could, transcribe entire, unless called by most imperative duty to hand down a legacy of admonition to all who may seek by other than the appointed means to mount into a life above the utterly material. I shall not, therefore, detail in their order of time all the visitations of horror which afflicted me, but will endeavor here and there to cull those which may most graphically foreshadow that "last state of a man which is worse than the first."

Repeatedly, as I have said, was I menaced by voices. Yet the threatening sometimes took other forms, and none of them were more terrific than the exhibition to me, as frequently occurred, of all nature abominating me, sometimes for the reason clearly set forth that I had tampered with a mystery which encroached on the prerogative of God, and sometimes for the sake of a nameless crime—nameless because too horrible to be named—whose nature or aggravation I did not know, but which lurked for me in some covert by the wayside, ready to spring upon me with the sword of Nemesis as I came by.

Through the whole of one breezy summer afternoon I had been wandering through the woods which I have so often mentioned, happy to delirious excess, and sustained by the arm and the conversation of a congenial friend, whom I now found it wisest to take with me as a precaution against wild vagaries, whenever I walked in the hasheesh state. Our pathway led over a thick carpet of fallen pine leaves, and my delight was heightened by the aromatic odors which exhaled from them in the warm winds which fanned us as we went. In this perfume was luxuriant suggestion of Indian spice-groves, and nothing more marked than such a mere suggestion does the hasheesh-eater need to build up for him the fabric of a most amazing and odorous dream. Straightway a grand procession of Burmese priests wound down the slope of a distant hill; solemnly, yet joyously, they approached me with music, and the air was loaded with the breath of their swinging censers. At a vast distance above me I could catch glimpses through the treetops of a radiant sapphire sky, and rose-tinged clouds floated dreamily therein, yet the incense vapors reached and blended with them even at that grand height. I stopped the foremost of the sacerdotal train, and spoke with him in his own language. He answered me, and we understood each other through a prolonged conversation, while my friend stood waiting by my side, in speechless marvel at an exhibition of my delirium for which he could not see even as much cause as usually explains conduct in the hasheesh state.

Our conversation over, the procession passed on. I now felt, as suddenly as if it had fallen upon me from heaven, and as assuredly as if Heaven had spoken it, that that priestly multitude were the last of

human kind that should ever endure my presence. My companion
abhorred me, and nothing but his sense of duty forced him to accede
to my request that he should lead me to my room. On the way back
we passed a radiant and balmy knoll, whereon, amid a tropical excess
of flowers and foliage, a group of Burmese children were dancing to
stringed instruments. They saw me, and instantly rushed out of sight
in precipitate agony of loathing.

Reaching home, I entered my room. Wherever upon tables or
chairs, on the bed or on the floor, there was any possible space, stood
a coffin, with lid let down, disclosing the face of some one among the
well-remembered dead. Though I never feared death, I always knew
well the feeling of our ancient sire, who prayed the sons of Heth, saying, "Give me a burying-place with you, that I may bury the dead out
of my sight." Yet at this moment I crouched between the coffins as in
an asylum, a demon, indeed, in nature, yet exulting in the security of
possessing a hiding-place among the ruins which had once held holy
souls. My God! could the dead still know me and my dreadful state?
Over every one of those cold faces passed a ripple of dire agony!
They feared me, after having been lifeless for many years! Distinctly
I saw them convulsed with a tremendous shudder. One by one they
turned upon their faces, and eagerly snatched with their hands
behind them to close the lids which let in my accursed sight.

And now the two most loving friends who remain to me alive came
walking toward me with tears streaming from their eyes. They had
come on foot from a far city to fall upon their knees and beseech me,
by all that I held sacred in the dearness of our relation, by the most precious future of my soul, to abandon hasheesh. The moment that their
faces met my own, with a piercing cry of pain they fled out of my sight.

I ran out of my room and came to the house of an old and intimate
companion. In a work-shop which he had fitted up as the place for
his recreation he was busily engaged, as I came in, upon some
mechanical contrivance, commenced when I had last seen him. His
back was turned, and, to attract to his attention, I called him by
name, "Edward!"

Suddenly he faced me, smiling to recognize my voice; but, as the
change of horror came over his features, he flung the hammer which
he held in his hand at my head. It just missed its aim, and I saw that he
had delivered the weapon, not in anger, but as the last boon he could
give me to deprive me of my infernal life. The next moment he leaped
through the lofty window of the room, and fathoms below I heard him
crushed upon the pavement.

In a former agony I had suddenly obtained relief from the view of
a certain name written in soft tints upon the sky. It was the name of
a beautiful, good, and beloved girl; and as I saw it, it represented to
me such lovely qualities of innocence, that beneath if I took sweet
refuge as under an aegis. In an instant I grew calm, and the devil-
voices that boomed after me died away.

Remembering this, I now bethought me to image that protectress'
name in the same way as before, and therefrom promised myself
speedy comfort. I sought to picture it before me, a name as simple as
it was beautiful both in itself and its associations. It was "Mary," and
I fled to it as never hunted murderer fled to grasp the skirts of Our
Lady, the holy namesake of this most pure child.

In the first place, I tried to set the whole word before my eyes. This
I found impossible. Then my endeavor was, letter by letter, to behold
it in succession. I tried to get the first letter. And now came the inexplicable affliction of a perfect capability to think of the one which I
wanted without being able to represent its form even to my inner
sight. Backward and forward I boxed the whole alphabet. With
inconceivable rapidity, every character beginning with A flew past
me, but when the flight came to L there was one inevitable void
between it and N. At Z I took the trail of the alphabetic whirl; in the
same way, from N the letters leaped to L. At length, after a countless
multitude of trials, I madly dashed myself upon the ground before
that rushing demon font of type, and cried to Heaven, "An M! an M!
for the love of my soul, grant me an M!"

My prayer was not heard, but without warning I was lifted from the
earth, and on a burning wind wafted like a dry leaf into the sky.
Whither and wherefore I was going I knew not until a dreadful voice
hissed close beside my ear, "On earth thou didst triumph in superhuman joys—now shalt thou ring their knell. It is thine to toll the
summons to the Judgment."

I looked, and lo! all the celestial hemisphere was one terrific grazen ball, which rocked upon some invisible admantine point in the infinitudes above. When I came it was voiceless, but I soon knew how it was to sound. My — were quickly chained fast to the top of heaven, and, swinging with my head downward, I became its tongue. Still more mightily swayed that frightful bell, and now, tremendously crashing, my head smote against its side. It was not the pain of the blow, though that was inconceivable, but the colossal roar that filled the universe, and rent my brain also, which blotted out in one instant all sense, thought, and being. In an instant I felt my life extinguished, but knew that it was by annihilation, not by death.

When I awoke out of the hasheesh state I was as overwhelmed to find myself still in existence as a dead man of the last century could be were he now suddenly restored to earth. For a while, even in perfect consciousness, I believed I was still dreaming, and to this day I have so little lost the memory of that one demoniac toll, that, while writing these lines, I have put my hand to my forehead, hearing and feeling something, through the mere imagination, which was an echo of the original pang. It is this persistency of impressions which explains the fact of the hasheesh state, after a certain time, growing more and more every day a thing of agony. It is not because the body becomes worn out by repeated nervous shocks; with some constitutions, indeed, this wearing may occur; it never did with me, as I have said, even to the extent of producing muscular weakness, yet the universal law of constantly accelerating diabolization of visions held good as much in my case as in any others. But a thing of horror once experienced became a "κτ´ημα ¨εζ ᾽αε´ι," an inalienable dower of hell; it was certain to reproduce itself in some—to God be the thanks if not in all—future visions. I had seen, for instance, in one of my states of ecstasy, a luminous spot on the firmament, a prismatic parhelion. In the midst of my delight in gazing on it, it had transferred itself mysteriously to my own heart, and there became a circle of fire, which gradually ate its way until the whole writhing organ was in a torturous blaze. That spot, seen again in an after vision, through the memory of its former pain instantly wrought out for me the same accursed result. The number of such remembered fagots of fuel for direful suggestion of course increased proportionally to and prolonging of the hasheesh life, until at length there was hardly a visible or tangible object, hardly a phrase which could be spoken, that had not some such infernal potency as connected with an earlier effect of suffering.

Slowly thus does midnight close over the hasheesh-eater's heaven. One by one, upon its pall thrice dyed in Acheron, do the baleful lustres appear, until he walks under a hemisphere flaming with demon lamps, and upon a ground paved with tiles of hell. Out of this awful domain there are but three ways. Thank God that over its alluring gateway is not written,

"Lasciate ogni speranza voi ch' entrate!"

The first of these exits is insanity, the second death, the third abandonment. The first is doubtless oftenest trodden, yet it may be long ere it reaches the final escape in oblivion, and it is as frightful as the domain it leaves behind. The second but rarely opens to the wretch unless he pries it open with his knife; ordinarily its hinges turn lingeringly. Toward the last let him struggle, though a nightmare torpor petrify his limbs—though on either side of the road be a phalanx of monstrous Afreets with drawn swords of flame—though demon cries peal before him, and unimaginable houris beckon him back—over thorns, through furnaces, but into—Life!

XVI.

An Oath in the forum of Madness.

HAVING been threatened many times with an utter isolation from human kind, it now became my practice, the moment that I began to feel the hasheesh change come over me, to run for sympathy to some congenial friend, and thus assure myself that the sentence had not yet been carried out. I entered his room. I told him of my state; and, before increasing delirium had any power to pervert my thoughts, pledged him to care for me, never to leave me, always to interest himself in my welfare to the end. Frequently this step prevented any under-current of horror from breaking up through my delightful

tides of vision. Frequently, when I beheld the fearful Afreet invade the sanctity of my rejoicing with drawn cimeter, was that remembered pledge to me as the ring of Abdaldar, and straightway

"There ceased his power; his lifted arm,
Suspended by the spell,
Hung impotent to strike."

The penal renunciation of me by God and man was the grand prevailing shadow which now lowered about the horizon of my visions, and thrice happy was I when, in this way, I could keep it from blackening the whole sky. I mean more by this word "blackening" than mere metaphor, for, fully awake and at unclouded noonday, I have seen both heavens and air grow sable suddenly with a supernatural eclipse, and I walked by no beacon save that of fiery eyes which "glared upon me through the darkness."

Yet the spell was not always powerful. There occurred seasons when I was beyond the power of man, and, as I thought, also an outcast from man's league with God. Man could not, God would not, keep faith with me.

In the ecstasy of a serene uplifting I came one afternoon to the room of an acquaintance who had often expressed a wish to witness the hasheesh state in some walk with me while I was under the influence of the drug. By the pledge of sympathy I bound him, and felt assured —doubly assured; for, as he prepared to accompany me out, without premonition there flashed into my mind that grand line of Festus,

" 'Tis not my will that evil be immortal."

Not only did this line suggest to me a great future of good and happiness throughout my hasheesh eternity, but I saw the triumphant reign of right established forever among men. A sublime emancipation from the thraldom of the ages had been declared to earth, and in visible and audible joy Creation leaped and sang. Should I not, then, be happy, since God had pronounced it? I had no fears. Taking the arm of my friend, I passed into the open air.

We had hardly gone fifty feet when I heard the dreadful voice distinctly speak to me: "This is an imaginative man; if you are happy, he will powerfully sympathize with you; he will be fascinated, he will become like yourself a hasheesh-eater. To save him from this, it is necessary that you should become an exemplar of agony. Are you content?" Knowing well what should ensue, aware of the tortures that lay prepared in the intimate abyss of the hasheesh hell, could I, as aught less than a God, say "Yes"? Unable to bring myself to this height of superhuman heroism, I only forced my lips to murmur, "The will of God be done."

Then the voice answered, "Horribly shalt thou suffer, suffer, suffer, more than tongue can tell, more than thou hast dreamed."

I clenched my fists, I shut my teeth, I nerved my whole being for the flood of agony which was about to pour upward on me from the depths. I felt within me the prophecy of such pangs as would bring me to the very portals of nothingness.

The sentence began to be fulfilled. From the fence beside which we walked came hot blasts, as from a furnace, and, looking at its base, I saw fiery rifts in the ground whence the tornado issued. I withered to a parchment sack, which bound in my heart as the sensitive fuel for more torments.

And now through that heart glided a delicate saw, of innumerable blades, each sharpened to the ultimate thinness of steel, and each glowing with a red heat. Slowly as a marble-saw the dreadful engine passed back and forth, hissing through the writhing muscle, and, as I pressed my hand upon my breast, it was scorched by the intense heat of the laminae. From the walls of houses, black talons darted forth to clutch my skirts; they left a scar like the touch of moxa. And still I burned unquenchably.

For a while I kept silence, shutting my mouth with Promethean self-control. Not only did my acquired habit of suffering speechlessly restrain me, but my pride could not endure the thought of acknowledging to him who walked by my side the vengeful infliction which had fallen upon me, in place of the mantle of rapture which my promise had prepared him to see.

The voice then said, "Confess, confess!" In desperation, I set my lips like a vice, and in my soul replied, "No! I will not!"

"Wilt thou not confess?" wrathfully the voice returned.

"Thou shalt then know bitterer agonies."

Now in my brain, moved by the same hellish machinery which was driving the saws through my heart, a murderous red-hot anger began turning round. Its speed increased, and with it a tremendous roar that shook my being. In every nerve I was agonized with an agony such as no martyr can ever have known. Head and heart both flaming, both riven by steel, the heavens looking wrathfully down, the earth opening up dreadful views of her demon-peopled deeps. Oh, here was a hell in which how could I live!

To the man at my side I whispered my confession. I told him all. I revealed to him the reasons of my punishment. I adjured him by all my own immortal tortures never to tamper with the insane spell.

And then, in piteous accents, I besought him to put out my fire.

To the first restaurant at hand we hastened. Passing in, I called for that only material relief which I have ever found for these spiritual sufferings—something strongly acid. In the East the form in use is sherbet; mine was very sour lemonade. A glass of it was made ready, and with a small glass tube I drew it up, not being able to bear the shock of a large swallow. Relief came but very slightly—very slowly. Before the first glass was exhausted I called most imperatively for another one to be prepared as quickly as possible, lest the flames should spread by waiting. In this way I kept a man busy with the composition of lemonade after lemonade, plunging my tube over the edge of the drained tumbler into the full one with a precipitate haste for which there were mortal reasons, until six had been consumed.

And now, almost entirely restored, I assured myself that I had expiated my full penal term, and passed out rejoicing. Baseless hope! In a moment my heart caught fire again, and now it was a huge cathedral organ wrapped in a garment of flame, and played upon mysteriously by the fingers of the element which was burning it up. Every stop that could sound like the despairing shrieks and groans of a human soul was open; nay, it was human; it lived in this slow and cruel death, and I felt its torture. A devil-choir sang anthems of mockery to its accompaniment, and I grew phrensied as I recognized the voices which ages back in the measureless past had blasphemed over my white-hot cradle and rocked me with the lullaby of hell. As we came along the broad terrace which extends before the colleges, I looked into heaven, and lo! upon rosy coursers serene angels were riding like an army, with incredible swiftness, upon some expedition of succor. Behind them trailed on winds that blew from the gates of Paradise resplendent garments of cloud ermine dotted with stars. In an ecstasy which upbore me above my demoniac pangs, I clasped my hands and shouted, "It is I whom they are coming to save!"

Just then a black hand parted the top of heaven and shook at me menacingly. Talk not to me of faces instinct with spiritual expression; that hand, slowly brandished and then withdrawn, held more expression than the most facile face. It told me all things of terror and of doom.

Until we arrived at the door of my entry I was speechless. Here my companion left me, and once more I gathered strength to burst into a bitter cry, "O God, if it be possible, let this cup pass from me." I used the prayer of the Divine One with a most reverent soul, and hoping that the remembered words of his Son might move the heart of the Father.

I added also a promise, "Save me, and I will never take hasheesh again." Once more the voice spoke and answered me, "Many a time hast thou promised this before. Speak! how hast thou kept thy vow?"

This was true. Repeatedly during the seasons of my suffering I had resolved, yes, sworn, that if I ever escaped with life and reason from the then present delirium, I would abjure the weed of madness forever. On returning to the natural state I always recollected having made the promise, but regarded it as the act of an unphilosophic fear in irresponsible circumstances, and moved by a suffering which it was perfectly possible to prevent by sufficient attention to general health and spirits as elements materially modifying the effect of the drug. Holding it, therefore, not at all binding, I had broken it as I would if it had been made in some terrific dream. Yet always when the hasheesh suffering brought me into the same court before whose awful bar I had bound myself at my last similar trial, I was charged by the prosecuting voice with my breach of faith, convicted, sentenced

by my own soul, and after that the pangs were sharp with the blade of Nemesis. I writhed not under affliction, but under penalty.

At this moment I answered the voice, "I have not kept my vow, but for this once be merciful, and I will sin no more."

Again my accuser spoke: "Once more shalt thou go free—remember—once!"

I accepted this promise as the safe-conduct of Deity; my pain ceased, and I walked fearlessly.

But, oh unbearable! In an instant it seized me again, and I groaned out, "Hath even faith perished in the Divine? O God, hast *thou* broken faith with me?" I received no reply. For a few moment I paced up and down an empty room into which I had entered, with my hand upon my struggling heart, and feeling its mighty beats blend with the throbs of the devilish enginery.

Then I came out into the entry. From the opposite door a man was approaching me. I stood still, and he also stopped. I walked forward, and he came to meet me. I turned away, and he followed behind me. I faced him—we were foot to foot—it was myself! Yes, there stood my double, resembling me as face answereth to face in water. Another being for whose crimes I had to answer, whose wrathful portion I should suffer! It was too much to endure. I fell upon my knees, and called out to Heaven, "Oh! do I not dream? Tell me, tell me, am I indeed more than one?" I was answered, "Thou art Legion!" I looked away toward the stairs. Crouching upon a step, glaring upon me between the posts of the balustrade, clutching at me like a tiger-cat, sat—myself again! I rushed toward the door of another room; I would lock myself in from my multitude of being. At that door, tearing his hair, gnashing his teeth, smiling with a maniac smile of pain, stood once more myself!

The remainder of my personalities I was spared from seeing. One more would have driven me forever mad.

For the last time I cried to Heaven, "How shall I be saved?" I was now finally answered, "Thy goodness extendeth not to God. To man must thou repay thy fault in that thou hast sought to lift thyself above humanity. Go find a man who will believe thy promise, and thou shalt be saved."

Hard condition. So many of my friends had known the former vows, and seen how I had kept them, that I bitterly feared I should never be able to fulfill it.

But as in this lay my last hope, I rushed up the staircase to find the man who would accept my security. The first I met was at the top of the farthest stairs. There he was sitting, as if in anticipation that I should come, on the throne of a solemn tribunal.

Yet not a tribunal of severe and unrelenting justice. The courtly appanage of the scene which surrounded him was necessary for my very sense of security, since, in bringing my case to any other than the most august judication, I should have felt that I was trifling with immeasurable destiny.

Moreover, the man was my bosom friend. In his truthful and serene eyes nothing but love for me had ever sat, nothing but most brotherly pity was in them now. I loved him for himself—I reverenced him for what he was, the calm, the thoughtful, the wise, the sincere. Heaven had sent him now to hear me, and both in his affection and his character I put my trust.

"Robb, my dear, my priceless friend, have pity on me. Accept my pledge. I will take hasheesh no more."

I spoke to him as if he knew what he did not know, my previous suffering. So he replied sadly, "Ah! you have said that many times before." I began to fear he might refuse me. I looked around, and standing not three paces off stood a cold shadow, and with its lip and finger it mocked me, saying plainly without words, "You are mine; he will not believe you." It was Insanity.

Once more I turned, and looking at him as such a sight alone could make one look, I simply said, "*Believe me!*" This was all, but the intensity of that one expression contained in it enough meaning to show what a dire spiritual necessity there was that he should grant my request. With emphasis he answered, "I *do* believe you." With a look of baffled hellish malice the shadow fled away.

After this I was but once more in pain. As a great chimney, I had grown hundreds of feet into the air; with pitch and fagots of wood, with all things inflammable, I was completely filled. Suddenly some one approached and held a lighted torch to the draught below.

In an instant, from basement to cope, with a tremendous roaring whirl, I took fire. Out of every pore shot spiral jets, my head was crowned with flame and plumed with smoke, and far down in the middle of the blazing mass my heart lay cracking and singing in agony.

"Water!" I shouted; "I am on fire! Help, for the love of heaven!" They tore my clothes from me in the most precipitous haste. From head to foot they deluged me with water. I heard within me the coals hiss and the cinders fall down dead into the grate below, as in extinguished furnace.

And then I grew calm.

XVII.

Down with the Tide.

FOR days after the last-mentioned suffering I adhered sacredly to my vow. Fortified by the sympathy of my friends, nerved by the images of a fearful memory, staying myself on the Divine, I battled against the fascinations of the drug successfully. At last there came a time when nothing but superhuman endurance could withstand and conquer.

As I have frequently said, I felt no depression of body. The flames of my vision had not withered a single corporeal tissue nor snapped a single corporeal cord. All the pains induced by the total abandonment of hasheesh were spiritual. From the ethereal heights of Olympus I had been dropped into the midst of an Acherontian fog. My soul breathed laboriously, and grew torpid with every hour. I dreaded an advancing night of oblivion. I sat awaiting extinction. The shapes which moved about me in the outer world seemed like galvanized corpses; the living soul of Nature, with which I had so long communed, had gone out like the flame of a candle, and her remaining exterior was as poor and meaningless as those wooden trees with which children play, and the cliffs and chalets carved out of box-wood by some Swiss in his winter leisure.

Moreover, actual pain had not ceased with abandonment of the indulgence. In some fiery dream of night, or some sudden thrill of daylight, the old pangs were reproduced with a vividness only less than amounting to hallucination. I opened my eyes, I rubbed my forehead, I arose and walked: they were then perceived to be merely ideal; but the very necessity of this effort to arouse myself, a necessity which might occur at any time and in any place, became gradually a grievous thraldom.

But harder to endure than all these was a sudden flash of that supernatural beauty which had so often tinged my past experience— a quick disclosure of the rosy hasheesh sky let in upon me by some passing wind which fanned aside the dense vapors of my present life—a peal of the remembered mighty music pouring through the gratings of my voiceless prison, and dying sadly away against its granite walls. Ah! well may the most rigid moral critic forgive me, if, looking upward to my former peak of vision, I spoke to my past self as if it were still sitting there.

> " So mayst thou watch me where I weep,
>   As unto vaster motions bound,
>   The circuits of thine orbit round
>   A higher height, a deeper deep."

Like Eblis, I refused to worship earth when I had seen heaven, and once more dared to assume his pride even with his pangs.

I returned to hasheesh, but only when I had become hopeless of carrying out my first intention—its utter and immediate abandonment. I now resolved to abandon it gradually—to retreat slowly from my enemy, until I had passed the borders of his enchanted ground, whereon he warred with me at vantage. Once over the boundaries, and the nightmare spell unloosed, I might run for my life, and hope to distance him in my own recovered territory.

This end I sought to accomplish by diminishing the doses of the drug. The highest I had ever reached was a drachm, and this was seldom necessary except in the most unimpressible states of the brain, since, according to the law of the hasheesh operation which I have stated to hold good in my experience, a much less bolus was ordinarily sufficient to produce full effect at this time than when I commenced the indulgence. I now reduced my daily ration to ten or fifteen grains.

The immediate result of even this modified resumption of the habit was a reinstatement into the glories of the former life. I came out of my clouds; the outer world was reinvested with some claim to interest, and the lethal torpor of my mind was replaced by an airy activity. I flattered myself that there was now some hope of escape by grades of renunciation, and felt assured, moreover, that since I now seldom experienced any thing approaching hallucination, I might pass through this gradual course without suffering on the way.

I did not reveal to my friends the fact of my once more eating hasheesh. To no one who had not participated in my sufferings could I have shown adequate reasons for doing so. I should have pleaded an excuse which none but myself could feel; I should have been answered by the earnest entreaty to cleave to my first purpose— perhaps by the expressed or tacit distrust of my intention to abjure the indulgence at all. But I felt no danger of betraying myself, since from the meditations and the ecstasies in which I now sat I could arouse myself at need, talk and act naturally, or perform any of the duties to which I might be called. I do not think there was a person beside myself who once suspected, at this time, my return to the indulgence. I was not even questioned upon the subject.

Once, and once only, was I in peril of making known my secret. With two or three of my friends I had made an agreement that on a certain afternoon, as was our wont, we should speak in turn, and subject to each other's criticism, for the sake of improvement in oratory. When the time arrived, I found myself not only adequate to any amount of speech-making, but liable to adorn my sentences with an Oriental luxuriance of imagery which would infallibly disclose the fact of my having taken hasheesh two hours before, for the dose, although not extending in size beyond the boundary I had set myself, had still operated with an unusual power.

When my friends called for me I knew not what to do. There was no sickness to plead—the animation with which every word was uttered would have belied that; other engagement I had not, for the appointment had been made unconditionally and some time before. If I went with them, it amounted almost to a physical certainty that I would break forth into some rapture which would let me out. Yet there was no time to be lost. I resolved to go, and giving into the hand of Will the curb of Passion, started with them down the street.

The struggle which I made to keep silent, or, at furthest, to talk in a practical way, was among the hardest of my lifetime. There is a game of forfeits, to most of my readers no doubt well enough known, which consists in walking three times diagonally across a room, bearing a lighted candle, and repeating the most absurd formula to a person who meets you similarly furnished, without moving a muscle of the face. There is also a legend, woven into the Arabian Nights, of a young man who, in fulfillment of some enterprise, descended through a demon-haunted cavern where, though assailed on every side by sights of astoundment most provocative of speech, he was compelled to seal his lips under pain of a terrible retribution.

The nature only, and not the degree of self-control demanded by my circumstances, is foreshadowed by these illustrations. I was assailed with every possible temptation to laughter and to open amazement. At the very commencement of my walk, for the first time in several months I was in China. All the roofs turned up at the corners, and amorphous dragons flaunted in red, green, and gold from their peaks. The air smelt of orange-blossoms, and boys hawked fruit about the streets in the dialect of Whampoa.

But the Chinese hallucination did not long continue. I presently remembered the old familiar town in which I was walking, yet what a singular change in manners had passed over it! Every house had been to dancing-school, and returned educated into the most excruciating politeness. They were all paying me their salutations as I passed with a knowledge of good-breeding absolutely overwhelming.

A spruce brick tenement, evidently a new-comer, and, on account of the insecurity of his social position, particularly anxious to ingratiate himself with the habitués, made me a profound bow, even unto his doorstep.

A respectable old house, that had been there since the last war, looked stiffly over the walls which flanked his chimneys, and slightly inclined himself with a rigid courtliness—a very Roger de Coverley in stone and mortar.

A fast-looking house of a particularly vivid color, conscious of containing all the modern improvements, and profusely ornamented in gingerbread-carved workmanship, took upon himself to be easy in his address as a *soi-disant* fashionable, and nodded to me familiarly, at the same time saying at his front door, "How are you, old fellow?" "Curse his impudence!" said I to myself, and walked on.

The next was a maidenly little cottage, who modestly dropped her second-story window-sashes, and blushed up to her eaves-trough as we came by, at the same time courtseying clear into her back yard.

A church smiled condescendingly on me from its belfry, bowed forward, and immediately took it back by making another bow backward, with a look which said, "I hope you take care of yourself, young man."

A shop bowed blandly and inquiringly, with a what-d'ye-buy air, and even a poor little lawyer's office abased its cornice cautiously, as if it feared to commit itself. In all these salutations there was something which gave me a half-consciousness that after all it was only an emblematical show, yet it required all my self-constraint to refrain from returning the compliment in a succession of bows. I mentally represented to myself my circumstances as nearly as I could make them natural. I painted the necessity of keeping still with all the picturesqueness of which I was capable, and so succeeded in controlling all outbreaks of my feeling.

At length we arrived at the place of our appointment (a church to which we had the key), and one after another my friends spoke, and I listened quietly until my own turn came. With a terrible effort I held myself in, and walked to the platform still guiltless of my own betrayal. If I could resist a few moments more, I was safe.

Hardly had I uttered my first sentence before I awakened to the consciousness that I was Rienzi proclaiming freedom to enthralled Rome. I portrayed the abased glories of the older time; I raised both the Catos from their graves to groan over the present slavery; I hurled fiery invective against the usurpations of Colonna, and pointed the way through tyrant blood up to an immortal future. The broad space below the tribune grew populous with a multitude of intense faces, and within myself there was a sense of towering into sublimity, as I knew that it was my eloquence which swayed that great host with a storm of indignation, like the sirocco passing over reeds.

Strange to say, I did not even here reveal my state. That vigilant portion of my duality which had controlled me hitherto, guarded me from any unwarrantable excess even in the impassioned character of Rienzi.

For a number of weeks I continued this moderate employment of hasheesh, sometimes diminishing the doses, then returning to the boundary, but never beyond it. As the diminutions went on by a tolerably regular but slow ratio, I flattered myself that I was advancing toward a final and perfect emancipation. But the progress was not that painless one with which I had flattered myself. There was much less to endure than in the worst part of the former period of indulgence, yet it could have been many times diminished in intensity without descending to the plane of ordinary physical or spiritual suffering.

One of the most bitter experiences of hasheesh occurred to me about this time, and since it is the only one which in my memory stands in peculiar distinctness of outline from the vague background of alternating lights and shadows, I give it as a powerful and recompensing contrast to the formerly-detailed vision in which I triumphed as the millennial king.

It was now with Christ the crucified that I identified myself. In dim horror I perceived the nails piercing my hands and my feet, but it was not this which seemed the burden of my suffering. Upon my head, in a tremendous and ever-thickening cloud, came slowly down the guilt of all the ages past and all the world to come. By a dreadful quickening, I beheld every atrocity and nameless crime coming up from all time on lines that centred in myself. The thorns clung to my brow, and bloody drops stood like dew upon my hair, yet these were not the instruments of my agony. I was withered like a leaf in the breath of a righteous vengeance. The curtain of a lurid blackness hung between me and heaven; mercy was dumb, and I bore the anger of Omnipotence alone. Out of a fiery distance demon chants of triumphant blasphemy came surging on my ear, and whispers of ferocious wickedness ruffled the leaden air about my cross. How long I bore this vicarious agony I have never known; from the peculiarity of the time in such states, it would be impossible to know.

But, in general, while feeling the full effect of the dose, I sat in solitude, with closed eyes, enjoying the tranquil procession of images, especially those of scenery, which I could dispel at will, since they did not reach the reality of hallucination. Or, if my quiet was broken by the entrance of others, by an effort conversation was possible with them, so long as care was taken to prevent the introduction of any powerfully-agitating subject. This care I found to be extremely necessary, as the peculiar sensitiveness to impression which is induced by hasheesh made sympathy so deep as to be painful. In one instance this fact discovered itself with sufficient clearness to warn me ever afterward. To comply with the request of a friend, I read him some verses of a piece upon doubts of human immortality. Upon arriving at a passage where one of our primeval fathers is introduced as speaking in agony of his dread of advancing death, I felt that agony becoming, by sympathy, so strongly my own emotion, that, lest I should completely identify myself with the sufferer, I was forced to lay down the manuscript, and plead some excuse for not continuing the reading.

XVIII.
My Stony Guardian.

IT was during this period that I spent a short time at Niagara. In the hurry of setting out upon my journey thither, I left behind that traveling companion, which was more indispensable than any article or all possible articles of luggage, my box of boluses. Too late to repair the error, too late for my own serenity, I found out that my staff of life was out of reach at a place on Lake Ontario where the most concentrated cannabine preparation is the jib-stay of a fore-and-after.

At the Falls, however, and once grown enthusiastic, I fared much better than I had expected. The only trace of suffering at first perceptible was left in the shape of a somewhat nervously-written name on the entry-book of the hotel. The excitement of a sublimity which, to say the least, is extra-natural, for a while sustained me above pain for the loss of the supernatural.

Moreover, a material support came in to augment the spiritual. As lemon-juice had been sometimes an effectual cure for the sufferings of excess, I now discovered that a use of tobacco, to an extent which at other times would be immoderate, was a preventive of the horrors of abandonment. Making use of this knowledge, I smoked incessantly when out of the immediate presence of the waters—never could I bring myself, however needy, to puff in the face of Niagara—a blasphemy of deed only second to one of word which came to my notice during this visit.

For an hour of one glorious morning I had been looking down from the balcony of the Goat Island tower upon the emerald crown in all the luxury of solitude. A heavy footstep from within sounded upon the staircase, breaking up my dream, and the next moment flashed upon the platform a man who had come to "do" the falls, with the odors of the metropolis still cleaving to his garments, and rotund in all the plenitude of corporeal well-being— an Omphalopsychite by necessity, since he found it impossible to look down at all without resting his eyes upon that portion of his individuality tangent to the lower border of the waistcoat. The utmost that I could ask from this adipose formation was to keep silence; he did not even do that. Turning his face toward the wind to get its full tonic effect, for a while he drank it in copious draughts, and then enthusiastically broke forth to me, "What a splendid thing to give a man appetite for his dinner!" Sensitive as my state made me at that moment, I so far controlled myself as to answer nothing. It was well that I had not been hasheesh-glorified when he made his assault, or, notwithstanding he no way lacked in the bodily, he might not have been heard of again till he was fished out of Ontario.

It has always been surprising to me that the Falls are so much the theme of lovers of the sublime to the almost entire exclusion of the Rapids. The Rapids have a majesty of their own, which, to my own mind, has never yielded at all to the very different one of the Falls. Trying to resolve this difference by an analysis, it seems to be this:

in the precipitous brink over which takes place the final leap of the waters, we find a reason for the grand power of the descent. Higher up the river the slope of the flood is comparatively imperceptible; the headlong crash of the waves becomes to us a result of some inner will rather than of soulless gravity; and by the putting forth of power from this mysterious will we are overwhelmed, seeming to find our cause in spirit and not in matter. Quite as holy a place does the upper point of the Island appear to me, looking forth, as it does, upon the oceanic wrath of that resistless billowy soul, from the silent eddy where it cleaves itself for the last maddening throes, far up to the line of its trembling in the first consciousness of ingathered strength against the farther sky, quite as holy as any station beside the shifting pavement of flecked and molten porphyry below the Fall, where the spray is forever floating back upon the headlong wall like marble-dust wind-driven from the floor of the Great Sculptor.

There is still another element in the sublimity of the place too little to notice, or noticed only as a curiosity. This is the Profile Rock, in the edge of the American Fall nearest to Goat Island. So little is it known, that many persons go there unaware of its existence, and come away without having had it pointed out to them. Indeed, by a mere superficial looker at, and not a student of Niagara, it would be, in all probability, passed over. Were I not near-sighted, I should be ashamed to confess that I did not see it myself until my eyes were called to it by a most sincere and ardent lover of all that is noble in nature, a very near and dear friend, whom I was so fortunate as to have beside me in most of my walks.

Sustaining the weight of those vast waters upon his half-bowed head, the stony figure stands, visible under the veil, or visible at least above the waist, yet no more is needed than the face, with its look of calm endurance, to suggest for him a whole history of Fate. At that time of which I have been speaking, I myself felt enough need of fortitude to give me an intense yearning toward this emblem of heroic patience, and as I looked upon him I more and more felt myself loving him even humanly. In many a vision afterward did he appear to me as a silent consoler, when Niagara itself had become an affliction to my memory; and as side by side we stood, he under his flood, I under mine, I gathered strength from his moveless eye to bear unto the end of all which should finally be given to the triumph of resignation.

Alone and unable to sleep, though the late night heard nothing to break its stillness but the ceaseless rush of the river, I felt myself thus "flowing in words" to that mute face of forbearance:

Niagara! I am not one who seeks
To lift his voice above thine awful hymn;
Mine be it to keep silence where God speaks,
Nor with my praise to make his glory dim.

Yet unto thee, shape of the stony brow,
Standing forever in thine unshared place,
The human soul within me yearneth now,
And I would lay my head beside thy face

King, from dim ages of God set apart
To bear the weight of a tremendous crown,
And feel the robes that wrap thy lonely heart
Deaden its pulses as their folds flow down;

What sublime years are written on the scroll
Of thine imperial, dread inheritance
Man shall not read until its lines unroll
In the great hand that set thy stony trance.

Perchance thy moveless adamantine look
For its long watch o'er the abyss was bent
Ere the thick gates of primal darkness shook,
And light broke in upon thy battlement.

And when that sudden glory lit thy crown,
And God lent thee a rainbow from His throne,
E'en through thy stony breast flashed there not down
Somewhat of His joy also made thine own?

Who knoweth but He gave thee to rejoice
Till man's hymn sounded through the time to be,
And when our choral coming hushed thy voice,
Still left thee something of humanity?

Still seemest thou a priest—still the veil streams
Before thy reverent eyes, and hides His light,
And thine is as the face of one who dreams
Of a great glory now no more his right.

Soon shall I pass away; the mighty psalm
Of thine o'ershadowing waters shall be heard
In memory only; but thy speechless calm
Hath lessons for me more than many a word,

Teaching the glory of the soul that bears
Great floods, a veil between him and the sun,
And, standing in the might of Patience, dares
To bide His finishing who hath begun.

I have said that Niagara itself became an affliction to me. More especially was this the case after my total abandonment of hasheesh; but I must not anticipate. Every one of sensitive mind has noticed the permanency of impressions left by grand scenery, of none more so than Niagara. Indeed, I have acquaintances who for months, in all their day-dreams as well as those of sleep, were haunted by the Falls in a manner almost like optical illusion. Their visions were always delightful. Fancy now a mind naturally very impressible by scenery, rendered numberless times more sensitive by a process which left it a perfect photographic plate, and then exposed to such lights as those reflected from that supernatural river: you will then have the condition in which I left Niagara—a condition continuing for many a month afterward. So slowly did the traces of that imagery fade on my mind, that I have never, even now, wholly lost them. At times the terrors of the brink and the cataract still echo in dreams with a hasheesh mystery, and appall me as the presence of their real danger could hardly appall.

Upon returning to a place where hasheesh was within reach, I fled to it for relief as into an ark. By considerable self-government, I conquered the tendency to excess produced by long deprivation of the stimulus, and indulged in it within my stated boundaries only.

I now began to find that gradual was almost as difficult as instant abandonment. The utmost that could be done was to keep the bolus from exceeding fifteen grains. From ten and five, which at times I tried, there was an insensible sliding back to the larger allowance, and even there my mind rebelled at the restriction. While there was no suffering from absolute intellectual lassitude, there still, ever and anon, arose a longing more or less intense for the former music and ecstatic fantasia, which could not be satisfied by a mere panoramic display of internal images, however beautiful, dissolved in a moment by opening my eyes.

Yet I struggled strenuously against the fascination to a more generous ration, and hoped against hope for some indefinite time at which the dangerous spell might be entirely unbound.

XIX.

Resurgam!

ONE morning, having taken my ordinary dose without yet feeling its effect, I strolled into a bookseller's to get the latest number of Putnam's. Turning over its leaves as it lay upon the counter, the first article which detained my eyes was headed "The Hasheesh Eater." None but a man in my circumstances can realize the intense interest which possessed me at the sight of these words.

For a while I lingered upon them with an inexplicable dread of looking further into the paper. I shut the book, and toyed with my curiosity by examining its cover, as one who receives a letter directed in some unfamiliar hand carefully scrutinizes the postmark and the envelope, and dallies with the seal before he finally breaks it open. I had supposed myself the only hasheesh-eater upon this side of the ocean; this idea of utter isolation had been one element in many of my horrors. That some one among my acquaintance had been detailing a fragment of my own experience, as viewed by him from without, was my first hypothesis. Although, in itself considered, there was nothing very improbable in the acquirement of the habit by another person, the coincidence of my having fallen upon this article, with the hasheesh force still latent within me, seemed so remarkable that I could not believe it. Then I said to myself, I will not read this paper now. I will defer it until another time; for, if its

recital be one of horrors, it may darken the complexion of my awaited vision. In pursuance of this purpose, I passed out of the shop and went down the street.

I was not satisfied. Whichever way I turned I was followed by a shadow of fascination. By an irresistible attraction I was drawn back to the counter. If the worst were there, I must know it. I returned, and there, as before, lay the unsealed mystery. With a trembling hand I turned to the place; again I scrutinized the caption, to see if some unconscious illusion of a hasheesh state, which had ensued before I was aware, had not made objective the words which so many a day had stamped upon my brain. No; plainly as eyes could read them, they stood upon the page. I would read the article from beginning to end. This resolution, once formed, was shaken, but not broken, by an unavoidable glance ahead, which told me that the recital was one of agonies.

It was only a moment before I found that I was not this hasheesh-eater. Yet as, with the devouring gaze of a miser, I read, dwelt upon, and re-read every line, I found such startling analogies to my own past experience that cold drops started upon my forehead, and I exclaimed, "This man has been in my own soul." We both had been abandoned of Heaven; had climbed up into the prerogatives of Deity, thence to be cast down; had drawn the accursed knife at the whispers of a frightful temptation; had been the disowned, the abominated, the execrated of men. Should I carry the parallel further? *He had forever abandoned hasheesh.* How terribly this question shook my soul! In an instant, like some grand pageant, the glories of the enchantment streamed before my eyes. Out of the past came Memory, swinging delicious censers; upon the fragrant vapor, as it floated upward, was traced a sublimer heaven, a more beauteous earth, from the days gone by, than ever Sorcery painted upon the Fate-compelling smoke for a rapt gazer into Futurity. There the pangs of the old time had no place; all was serenity, ecstasy, revelation. Should I forego all this forever?

So help me God, I would!

The author of that article I did not know. Of his name I had not even the faintest suspicion. Yet for him I felt a sympathy; yes, though it be unworldly, an affection such as would move me to the highest office of gratitude. Into my hitherto unbroken loneliness he had penetrated; unconscious of each other's presence, we had walked the valley of awful shadows side by side. As no other man upon the earth could feel for me, he could feel. As none other could counsel me, he might counsel. For the first time in all the tremendous stretch of my spell-bound eternity heard I the voice of sympathy or saw I an exemplar of escape. Though I might never look upon his face on earth, disenthralled from the bodily I should know him immediately, for I was bound to him by ties spun from the distaff of a supernatural hand.

I returned homeward, bearing in my mind almost the exact words of that vivid and most truthful recital. So powerfully did its emotion possess me as to supplant entirely that of the drug, which did not once render itself perceptible.

There is a rich lesson of deep springs of human action taught by the old history, wherein he who in after years was to make the name of Carthage glorious among the peoples uplifted his hand of adjuration in the presence of his father. From him out of whose original fount he came, and in whose depths his earliest waves of being found their noblest, their truest echo of response, most naturally did he draw that full tide of strength which through all barriers was to bear him on until he whelmed in the deluge of inherited vengeance the territory of his foe.

No Hannibal was I, but the struggling sufferer under long soldered thrall of sorcery, groaning for a deliverance which I just dared to tempt; no Hamilcar wert thou, my father, for the hands with which thou supportedst mine in their final vow of liberty were wet, not with the blood of war, but the tears of a most precious compassion; and as before thee, on that last night of my bondage, I took the oath which opened up my prison-doors, from thy presence I won a sustaining force of will which, through many a day of fray and weariness, was to press me on (in all reverence to the majestic memorials of past time) against a mightier, a subtler enemy than Rome!

After thus sealing my deliverance, my next step was to discover the author of the article in Putnam's, which had determined me to it at first. This, through the kind courtesy of some of its presiding minds,

I was in a few days enabled to do. To the author I then wrote, trusting to no other introduction than that of our common ground and the sympathies of human nature. I asked counsel upon the best means of softening the pathway of my escape, for I had seen enough in my former effort to assure me that it would be a very hard one. Moreover, the simple possession of a letter from one who had been so instrumental in originally effecting my release would be a powerful aid toward rendering it permanent.

A very short time elapsed before I received an answer to my inquiries. My anxiety could not have made it more full than it was of information and assistance; my gratitude could not have exaggerated the value of its sympathy and encouragement. But for the sacredness which to a mind of any refinement invests a correspondence of such nature, I could not refrain from here giving it publicity. It strengthened my resolution, it opened for me a cheering sky of hope, it pointed me to expedients for insuring success, it mitigated the sufferings of the present. It is, and ever will be, treasured among the most precious archives of my life.

Thus supported humanly, and feeling the ever-near incitement and sustenance of a Presence still higher, I began to feel my way out of the barathrum of my long sojourn, and its jaws closed behind me, never since then, never hereafter till there be no more help in heaven, to open for my ingress. Out of its tremendous Elysium, its quenchless Tartarus, its speechless revelations, I came slowly into a land of subdued skies and heavier atmosphere. The jet of flame and fountain grew dimmer behind me in the mists of distance; broader, in the land from which I had long wandered, before me grew the shadows of the present life. Yet among all the lights which, unobscured by vapor, from afar led me on my way, was one which gleamed with a promise that in the days hereafter, the soul, purified from the earthy, should once more, painlessly, look on the now abandoned glories of its past apocalypse.

XX.

Leaving the Schoolmaster, the Pythagorean Sets Up for Himself.

DURING the progress of the events which have hitherto occupied my narrative, I had become a graduate of my college. Willing for a while to defer the prosecution of more immediately professional studies, I cast about for some employment which for a year might engage a portion of my efforts, and leave, at the same time, a reasonable amount of leisure for private reading. As is the case with so many of our newly-fledged American alumni, my choice fell upon the assumption of the pedagogic purple. There were doubtless, somewhere in the States, candidates for induction into the mysteries of the Greek and Latin tongues—some youths of promise who burned for an acquaintance with the arts of address, and who would not scorn to receive, even from the hands of an own countryman, the crumbs of literature which fall from the Gallic table. If my horoscope had not failed me, I could find them out.

Accordingly, at the bar of my college, whither petitions for instruction very frequently came in from the benighted world, I lodged an application for the most eligible situation of the kind above stated which should present itself. Before long a letter reached me, offering a post of teachership, situated somewhere between the Hudson and Fort Laramie, in a village glorified with some name of Epic valor, mighty in the appanage of ten dwelling-houses and a post-office, and, like all places sanctified by the presence of the educational genius, "refined, salubrious, and highly religious." As to the first item in this latter statement, there was every reason to be satisfied of its truth, since the writer of the letter was evidently a gentleman, and, to judge from the size of the place, he was a very large integral portion of its population. Upon the second point it was rather more difficult to be assured, since any number of deaths possible to the dimensions of the village might have occurred there without their wave of agitation reaching the shore that acknowledges the jurisdiction of bills of mortality. Finally came the question of "highly-religiousness." On this head, nothing could have given my doubts a more decisive quietus than the fact that the community wanted a teacher, since, just then looking through the Lorraine-glass of enthusiasm for a chosen occupation, I saw a peculiar force and beauty in the words, "Science, the handmaid of Religion." Yet one thing there was which stood as a slight obstacle in the way of accepting the position. I had determined, for the year to come, to be independent for a support of all aid save my own exertions. Entire self-sustenance was a very dear project with me. Could I hope for it there?

My correspondent informed me that no very great pecuniary inducements could be offered, but seductively added that, to a young man of excellent principles, who desired to establish himself as a moral centre in the community, no opening could be more promising. As he did not go on to advise me whether, in his portion of the country, "moral centres" were gratuitously fed, lodged, and clothed, besides being generously presented, as a slight token of popular esteem, with their laundry-bills, fuel, lights, and stationery, I concluded not to close with his offer, thus forever losing, for the basest of earthly considerations, the priceless opportunity of radiating circular waves of an unctuous excellence through it is impossible to tell how large an area of uninhabited timber-region. Whether any sufficiently self-sacrificing incumbent has been found to fill the rejected vacancy, from want of data is uncertain; if not, the place with the Homeric name wanders in heathen ignorance to this day.

Another application which came to me, seeming in all points satisfactory, was accepted. In the town of W—, in the State of New York, a cry had gone up for a teacher, who might be absorbent as well as radiant, and one, moreover, who might indulge the hope of moderate leisure for his own self-disciplinary purposes.

There, as I began arranging matters for my departure from home, I flattered myself that a stated occupation should absorb me from regrets over the loss of my old indulgence; quiet, books, and a regular life should create in me a new stimulus and energy. The department of pedagoguery over which I was to be installed was congenial to long-consolidated tastes—the ancient and the English classics. Thus I should gradually emerge out of shadows into a being with new motives, and by moderate cares blunt the pains of progress. How far I harvested my hope the sequel will show.

Having reached the scene of my labors, I found myself associated with a teacher who, like myself, was a new-comer, yet not, like myself, a neophyte in the profession, for he had grown venerable in the priesthood of Minerva, having, in all probability, during his previous life, offered up numerous hecatombs of youthful victims, both male and female, upon her altar. At the same time that I congratulated myself upon possessing the aid of his experience, I discovered that I must look elsewhere for congenial sympathies, since he was one of those persons whose metal is not annealed. In youth he had indulged a happy disposition, but now saw the folly of it. Through some fault of my own early training, I was unable to discover the necessary connection between sanctity and acridity, a heart like Enoch and a face like Sphinx.

Yet upon external sympathy I did not expect to be very dependent. The institution in which I was resident offered that invaluable advantage, a large and well-selected library, where I hoped to find all those choice attachments which from without my position might deny me.

In a good library how swiftly time melts away! Not merely in the sense of its rapid passage through our absorption in other interests, but as an element in any consideration, it becomes entirely neglected. In practical business the present is our only actuality; the past has been cast down like a ladder whose rounds have helped us up to a height whence we never again expect to descend. Among books, all temporal successions are obliterated; Plato and Coleridge walk arm-in-arm; genial Chaucer and loving Elia shake hands; with them, with all, we stand enraptured upon the same plane of time, in one age, the ceaseless age of the communion of souls. Well did Heinsius say, as he locked himself into the library of Leyden, *Nune sum in gremio saeculorum!*— "Now I am in the lap of eternity!"

But gradually the increasing pressure of duties connected with my new vocation more and more deprived me of leisure for enjoying any other literature than that of text-books. Long after the last noisy foot had pattered down the front steps of the school building did my table groan with incorrigible exercises which demanded correction, one leaf of which, laid upon the grave of any worthy—Molière, for instance—who spoke the language which it assassinated, would have brought up as deep a groan from the depths below as when the mandrake is uprooted.

I had promised myself regular habits; but the wanderer who was so unfortunate or so eccentric as to be shelterless at that hour, might have seen, at two or three o'clock of almost every morning, the light of my lamp shining through one of the tall windows that looked upon the street. Not that I rose early, but that I retired early—in the morning. It was not the mere sense of duty and responsibility which impelled me to such labors for the school, although, indeed, these had their just, perhaps their exorbitant weight with me. An element more selfish entered into the consideration—the dread of being haunted on the morrow by unappeased ghosts of business. The accumulative nature of work distressed me; the slightest thing left unfinished at the close of one day added itself to the labors of the next, and it had grown mightily during the night. There are some people so constituted that they can not slur matters if they would. No one else may notice the mint, anise, and cumin which they have forborne to tithe, but they can no more themselves overlook the deficiency than if they had neglected the weightier matters of the law.

It will be easily understood that late hours, hard work, and an almost total cessation from bodily exercise were not the best means that could have been taken to restore tone and elasticity to a mind struggling with the horrors of an abandoned stimulus. Without cares of some kind, I had doubtless been at this time a most unhappy being; yet, under such pressure as I then felt, an overtasked mind had no opportunity to recover itself, but rather grew sensitive daily to the loss of its former support. Perhaps, however, even such a state of things was better than an absence of all absorbing employment; for, although I dreaded a return to hasheesh as an upright man dreads the violation of his most sacred oath, I had not reached a point at which I could utterly execrate the drug. The only feat of righteous indignation which was then possible was to think ill of it, as the lover of a faithless mistress whom he must abandon, or as the patriot of his fatherland, swayed by vile rulers, when, "fallen upon evil times," he flies it in voluntary exile. Unemployed with daily and perplexing duties, I might have heard the former siren-voice floating into my careless quiet, and, step by step, have been almost unconsciously led back into the old snares.

As it was, the fascinations of the past were hard enough to resist. If ever for a moment I granted myself leisure to sit still and think—if, especially, I resigned myself with closed eyes to the train of meditations set in motion by good music, I was infallibly borne back into the hasheesh world, and placed face to face with its now irretrievable glories. In quick flashes the old empurpled heights for a moment broke upon me, or amid cloud battalions in their rainbow armor I floated through a tremendous heaven. Or the far windings of some wondrous river allured me into the luxuriant shadows which trembled over its brink, and I sighed for an instant with an unutterable yearning as I thought that its waves were never more to upbear my shallop of gramarye. The embodied temptation of exquisite houris swam in ethereal dance down a garden of Gul: never more were their rosy arms to embrace me. Grand temples reared their spotless pediments into a sapphire sky; a lake that answered back in its own hue the look

of heaven, kissed, dimpling with a fairy laughter, the steps that ascended to their portals—portals eternally barred on me. And sometimes, more solemnly alluring than all these, for an instant I caught a view of that light wherein I had of old read the sublime secrets of things by unbearable apocalypse. At such a season, well— oh! unspeakable well was it that hundreds of miles stretched between me and the nearest box of hasheesh, for, had I possessed the means, I should have rushed to the indulgence, though it were necessary to swim a whirlpool on the way.

I made acquaintances at W— who could play cunningly upon an instrument, that universal one, the piano, especially. Knowing that there was no possibility of yielding to the allurement, I, often as possible, had them play for me, while I sat almost unconscious of any thing outward, abandoning myself to music-inspired visions. Yet even then, perfectly assured that I had no power to gratify the hasheesh appetite, I have started up from my seat to dispel by walking and the sight of familiar objects a rapture which was enchanting me irresistibly.

Constantly, notwithstanding all my occupation of mind, the cloud of dejection deepened in hue and in density. My troubles were not merely negative, simply regrets for something which was not, but a loathing, a fear, a hate of something which was. The very existence of the outer world seemed a base mockery, a cruel sham of some remembered possibility which had been glorious with a speechless beauty. I hated flowers, for I had seen the enameled meads of Paradise; I cursed the rocks because they were mute stone, the sky because it rang with no music; and earth and sky seemed to throw back my curse.

An abhorrence of speech or action, except toward the fewest possible persons, possessed me. For the sake of not appearing singular or ascetic, and so crippling my power for whatever little good I might do, I at first mingled with society, forcing myself to laugh and to talk conventionalities. At last associations grew absolutely unbearable; the greatest effort was necessary to speak with any but one or two to whom I had fully confided my past experience. A footstep on the stairs was sufficient to make me tremble with anticipations of a conversation; every morning brought a resurrection into renewed horrors, as I thought of the advancing necessity of once more coming in contact with men and things. Any man who has felt the pangs of some bitter bereavement can understand this experience when he remembers how many a time he awoke after his affliction, and for a moment remained forgetful that it had fallen upon him. Then suddenly gathering a fearful strength, the knowledge of the reality flashed upon him, and he groaned aloud as if some fresh arrow had entered his soul. At times the awakening was so terrible an experience to me that from any other than my own hand I would have courted death as a mercy. The death which was but another birth and possible, the death which was utter extinction and an impossibility, seemed either of them preferable to that illusion into which the light aroused me, which men called life, but which was, after all, but death in its most horrible form, death vivified, stalking about in hollow pageantry, breathing meaningless utterances, interchanging salutations, mocking spirit by gestures without spirit, and unable to return to its legitimate corruption.

Aware as I was that this terrible state was the revenge of the rejected sorceress, and feeling it grow bitterer every day to bear, I began to struggle against two temptations, yielding to either of which seemed to offer some change of suffering, if not a permanent relief. One of these was self-destruction, the other return to hasheesh, and I can hardly pronounce which of the two was the most abhorrent idea. My argument with myself was, that there must be some turning point, some lowest depth to the abyss which I was descending; the hope I could not see, but faith clung to it desperately, and ever kept repeating,

> "Behold! we know not any thing;
> I can but trust that good shall fall
> At last—far off—"

But, though day was terrible, night was often as much so. While indulging in hasheesh, none of its images had ever been reproduced in dreams, provided that I retired to sleep thoroughly restored from the last dose. Indeed, it is a singular fact, that although, previously to acquiring the habit, I never slept without some dream more or less vivid, during the whole progress of the hasheesh life my rest was absolutely dreamless. The visions of the drug entirely supplanted those of nature.

Now the position of things was transposed. Day was a rayless blank, night became frightful with fire. The first phenomenon which I began to notice, as I entered this condition, was the peculiar susceptibility of the brain to its last impression before my chamber was darkened. Did I look at the flame of the lamp before putting it out?—for an hour afterward I lay tossing and sleepless, because one fiery spot burned unquenchably upon the surrounding blackness. Did I shut the pages of a book immediately before lying down?—the last sentence I had read was as distinctly printed on the dark as it could have been upon a scroll, and there for half the night I read it till it grew maddening. Well was it for me if the words were not of gloomy import, for I could endure with measurable patience even the wearily monotonous assurance of good cheer; but one night I was forced to rise and relight my lamp to blot out the sight of such an awful sentence as this:

"Depart, ye cursed!"

At length, I used the habitual precaution, borrowed from my former usage in the hasheesh state, of keeping one wick of my lamp burning while I slept. At first this was very painful to my eyes; but so much better was any pain than the horror of that permanency of the final impression, that I bore it willingly.

Gradually my rest began to be broken by tremendous dreams, that mirrored the sights and echoed the voices of the former hasheesh life. In them I faithfully lived over my past experience, with many additions, and but this one difference. Out of the reality of the hasheesh state there had been no awakening possible; from this hallucination of dreams I awoke when the terrors became too superhuman.

What has been said in an earlier part of this narrative upon the indelible characteristic of all the impressions of our life seemed to find illustration here. Doomed to re-read the old, yet, though sometimes forgotten, never obliterated inscriptions, I wandered up and down the halls of sleep with my gaze fixed upon the mind's judicial tablets. Not always were the memories in themselves painful; where of old I had felt ecstasy, in the same place I rejoiced wildly now; yet the close of that season of rejoicing was often tinged with most melancholy dye, for, from my recollection of the former order of succession, I could infallibly tell what was coming next, and many a time was it a vision of pain.

All the facts of a recalled experience took their regular relative position save one—I never dreamed of taking hasheesh. I was always seized suddenly by the thrill; it came upon me unexpectedly, while walking with friends or sitting alone. This ignorance of any time when I took the dose did not, however, absolve me from self-convicting pangs. Invariably my first cry was, "I have broken my vow! Alas! alas!" Then followed furious exultancy I rushed like a Maenad through colossal scenery; I leaped unhurt down measureless cataracts; I whirled between skies and oceans, both shining in fiery sapphire; I stood alone and amid ruined piles as vast as the demon-built palaces of Baly. Then an undefined horror seized me. I fled from it to find my friends, but there were none to comfort me. Finally, reaching the climax of pain, I caught fire, or saw the approach of awful presences.

Then I awoke. But not always into the delicious comfort of a calm reality—I may almost say, never; ordinarily to cry out to Heaven for the boon of an unpeopled darkness; always to find the beating of my heart either totally stopped, or so swift and loud that I could hear it with the utmost distinctness, like a rapid, muffled hammer; frequently to discover that the idea of fire had some ground in a raging fever, which parched my lips, and swelled the veins upon my forehead till they projected in relief. At such times my course was to rise and walk the floor for an hour, if need were, at the same time bathing my head until the heat was assuaged.

If memory, still blunted by the body, could thus clearly and faithfully read her old records, in what astonishing apocalypse shall they stand forth at the unerring wand of the disembodying change!

I have spoken of additions to the original scroll of visions. It remains to mention some of them.

The region about W— is a limestone formation, tunneled in one place by a rather extensive and remarkable cave. I have never found there any of those lofty halls and vast stalactites which render certain other caverns famous; the calcareous depositions are very much in miniature, but some of them of a most delicate beauty. One, in particular, is a most perfect statuette (if the term may be allowed in such a connection) of Niagara Falls; the Rapids, Goat Island, with its precipitous battlement toward the lower river, the American Fall, the Horse-shoe, all are there, exquisitely carved, on a scale of not quite an inch to the foot. Another is a Gothic monastery, with its shrine and Madonna just outside the grille, and a cresset hanging from the point of the portal's arch. The chambers are often narrow and sinuous; there is nothing there to astound any one who has visited Weyer's Cave or the Mammoth; but as this was the only one that I had ever seen, it was there that I found my cavernous ideal.

My guide through it was a young man of the neighborhood, whose gratification in obliging a stranger was the only recompense which he would not refuse; yet dear enough was the price which I paid for my visit.

It was no less than the punishment of being cavern-haunted for weeks. Nightly was I compelled to explore the most fearful of subterraneous labyrinths alone. Now climbing crags which gave way behind me, hanging to round projections of slippery limestone, while I heard the dislodged débris go bounding down from ledge to ledge of a yawning pit of darkness and reaching no bottom. Now crawling painfully like a worm, pushed on through winding passages no wider than a chimney, by a Fate whose will I doubted ever to bring me back. Now beholding far above my head the rifted ceiling tremble with the echo of my least footstep, in momentary agony to see it fall. Now joyfully hastening toward a glimpse of daylight, coming up to it, and falling backward just in time to save myself from plunging down some sheer wall of measureless height, upon which the labyrinth opened.

From that visit to the W— cave I suffered that which only the hasheesh-eater and a soul in the other hell can suffer. In time, however, I slowly outgrew its memory, but only to replace it by others almost as fearful. I cite but one more in this place.

I had been sitting upon the window-sill one day, with my body partly outside, for the purpose of performing some repair upon the sash. My sleep thereafter was scared by a vision of a house supernaturally high, upon whose topmost window-sill I stood, holding on by a projecting cornice with one hand, while the other I sought to perform some impossible purpose, which I prevented it from assisting its mate. Still the cornice kept crumbling. I grasped it by a fresh projection. That also gave way; another, and that was broken by my grasp. This position was brought to a crisis in several ways. Sometimes by a powerful impulse I swayed myself inside, and the current of the dream changed. Sometimes, without my knowing how, the vision passed utterly away. Once the whole building on whose side I stood from basement to cap-stone took fire in an instant; I leaped to the more merciful, to avoid the more cruel death, and, awaking, found myself upon the floor in one of those feverish states of which I have spoken.

That night I slept no more. At dawn I laid myself down for an hour of disturbed slumber, to awake again to a day which was as much to be dreaded as the night.

XXI.

Concerning the Doctor; Not Southey's, but Mine.

AT the time of my greatest need, I was so fortunate as to make the acquaintance of one man whose sympathy was, for months of trial, one of my strongest supports. Half discouraged in my attempts at self-rescue, I passed an hour in conversation with him, and fortitude came to me anew; for soul and its connection with the body had so long been his study that he knew how, with the utmost delicacy, to turn thought out of unwholesome channels; moreover, he had the heart as well as the brain for doing good. I need not say that he was a doctor.

I can not resist the temptation to a digression in this place for the purpose of giving my testimony, for the highest that it is worth, to one fact of past experience. It is this: if I have ever met a man before unknown to me, whose sympathies flowed instinctively toward distress, whose self-sacrifice had become an inseparable part of nature, whose comprehensive interest in all that might ennoble our kind was equaled only by his loving patience with its present infirmities, I have called him "doctor," and, nine times in ten, have not been mistaken.

Society has now grown old enough, for the sake of self-respect at least, to despise and abandon those stale jokes upon doctors which tickled her childish ear. With her superstition of the value of a horse-shoe as prophylactic against witches, let her also put aside the inanities which she talks, in her less sombre mood, of the physician in league with the sexton, and the solemnity of mock-learning which reigns over a circle of gold-headed canes. When frightened, she is ever ready to send for the doctor; she stops joking as soon as she is parturient, apoplectic from last night's surfeit, or appalled at the consequences of having swallowed a button.

True, there are empirics in medicine. There are men who tamper with the delicate springs of life upon no other authority than that of a

"possunt quia posse videntur."

We have all seen the advertisement of one "whose sands of life have nearly run out," and as we marvel at the length of time during which those sands have been just on the verge of their final down-flow, we are led to ask if, for the sake of that world upon which an incalculable benefit in cases of consumption may be conferred for the price of one shilling, the benevolent possessor of the recipe may not occasionally have tipped up his hour-glass or diminished its aperture.

We all know the quack in medicine. We are not blind to the thousand astonishing cures of as many desperate maladies, to the placards on the highways, the columns of the press, the almanacs, the guides, the angels that come down in a hurry from heaven, calling through a trumpet to the moribund to hold on till they get there, with a bottle of sirup under each arm which shall restore peace to his afflicted family.

All these things we know; yet are there no other quacks than quacks in medicine? Are there no quacks of divinity? no quacks at law? no political quacks, that dose a diseased nation? no literary quacks, who break down the aesthetic constitution of the people? But, because Brigham Young points out the road to future blessedness through a phalanstery of wives, shall we no more go to church? Because Jeffreys was a villain, must no more causes be adjudicated? And are we to abjure all faith in the science of government inasmuch as some placeman theorizes to the mob in fustian during a campaign, or anathematize all authors in that somebody has befouled the pool of reading-mind by a volume of the Rag-picker's Nephew?

If we hold faith in gold, notwithstanding base metal, let us be assured that nowhere is that gold found at a higher percentage of purity than among doctors. Where one Faun hath stolen the mantle of Esculapius, as the good sire lay sleeping, there are a hundred upon whom he has dropped it as upon worthy children.

Of all men, the doctor is to be peculiarly cherished. Let us not forget that there was one season, very early in all our lives, when

without him we might not have been. Let us remember how often, uncomplainingly, he has deprived himself of sleep, of meat and drink, of all those social endearments which beautify the world to us, that we might be set at ease upon some whimsical ailment, some pulse too little or too much. When the hour of a real need calls for him, with what anxiety he watches every flush of cheek and wandering of eye, with what strategic skill he brings to an issue the battle between the forces of life and death, with what calm earnestness he throws his own energy upon our side, how with very parental anxiety he watches hour after hour at the painful bed, with what eye of suspense he beholds the crisis come, and now, when he knows that a Greater than he has come silently into the consultation, waits until an unseen finger has touched the clogged fount of life, and given him reason to rejoice with them that do rejoice.

In a deep sympathy, in tenderness, in allowance for human frailties, there is no man who meets us on the ways of life that more resembles that mightier Physician whose cures are felt in all the arteries of the world. Like Him, the doctor is compassionate, because, measurably with Him, "he knoweth our frame, he remembereth that we are dust." And, last of all, yet not least, be it not forgotten that there is waiting for us an hour of shadow in the Hereafter, when, all medicine failing us, save that grand one which is to cure us of the body which hath afflicted for years, the voices of farewell, mixed with weeping, that shall be heard around our pillow, will not lack one tone which hath cheered us on through so many remediable distresses, but among the last whom our closing eye shall gather in before it looks on the grand mysteries will be he who, yielding us up unwillingly to the Stronger, remains to help the beloved whom we can help no more—the doctor.

It is hard to understand how any man who, like the physician, from morning till night, and often from night till morning again, is occupied with enginery and the repair of this complicated system of forces, the body, should rest contented with a mere external survey of the levers and pulleys of its machine, or the chemical phenomena of its laboratory. If he be the true man of science which his profession imperatively demands, he can not help perceiving, in a multitude of instances, that some intangible agent is working out processes for good or ill which do not array themselves under any material classification. Changes are taking place which do not seem to originate in the specific function operated upon; new elements enter the consideration of death or cure which can not be referred to food or medicine. The true physician will not be contented until he has gone back of the wheels, and investigated the nature of that strange imponderable force which is energizing them. To him the spiritual in his art is of even more importance than the bodily.

I have not, after all, been making a very wide digression, since it has just led me into the description of my friend the doctor—to me, the doctor by eminence, since, spiritually, he did for my recovery that which none else could, in a life-time, have accomplished for it corporeally.

All his life he had been communing with the great and beautiful thinkers to whom our mysterious double nature was a beloved study. Yet no man perfected in mere book-lore was he. Without seeking apologies wherewith to excuse himself from following in the train of the dogmatists of any age, he had thought for himself, and, in the possession of an inner world thus acquired, he was independent of other resources to an extent which was equaled only by my hasheesh kingship, and by that only in degree and not in permanency. With him the spirit of all things was as much a felt presence as their gross embodiment is to material men.

From the commencement of our acquaintance I was as much with him as the pressure of cares would allow me to be, and when my own life had become to me a vague and meaningless abstraction, by participation with his thought and sympathy I somehow gradually drew into it an injected energy which made its juiceless pulses throb again, and awoke me out of the lethargy into which I was sinking deeper with every day. For months, but for him, the allotted course of my duties had been a mechanical round; a galley-slave, a mill-horse, could not have labored with less interest or more weariness.

As the mountain of exercises and compositions grew gradually more and more level with the plane of my table, and the evening wore on toward night, I was wont to soliloquize, "One hour more, and I will go to see the Doctor." Once at his rooms, and the iron mantle of pedagogic restraint fell off; I was in the human character again; nay, more, I seemed to take off my body and sit in my soul. This very resumption of naturalness and freedom by one whose position demanded all day a peculiar self-control and reticence, will be understood by those whom fortune (or misfortune) has placed in like circumstances to be the most delicious privilege for which the tired mind can yearn. The ceasing to seem to be what he is not must always be an untold relief to any one who has not, by long training in the necessary caution of a responsible place, utterly ceased to be what he was.

Yet the benefit conferred upon me by my acquaintance with the doctor was something more than could be comprehended in this mere exchange of the technical for the natural, the life of a profession for the life of humanity. A most kind and lively interest did he bestow upon all that pertained to my past enchanted existence, and never with more gentleness and care than he did could an own brother have supported me through the horrors wherein I was painfully journeying on my way to complete disenthrallment. By condolence, by congenial converse, by suggestion of brighter things, by indication of a certain hope in the distance if I would but press on, in a thousand ways did this friend nerve me to persistent effort, and close more tightly behind me the gates of return.

It was through his labors chiefly that I began once more to take an interest in the world, not through any renewed affection for its mere hollow forms, but for the sake of that inner essence which they embodied. Henceforth forever, after abandoning hasheesh, was all endurance with the external creation to be denied me unless I could penetrate deeper than its mere outside. I had known the living spirit of nature; in its husks I no longer found any nourishment, but rather the material for a certain painful loathing to expend itself upon. In my then present condition, I beheld as little beauty in the best of external things, I granted as little admiration, as any old Athenian whose eyes last fell on the divine and spirit-breathing master-pieces of Phidias, revivified to pass judgment upon some elaborately-carven gate-post.

Through the aid of the doctor I began slowly to perceive the possibility of penetrating deeper than the shard of things without the help, so dearly bought, of hasheesh. Taking up, for instance, the

subject of a spirit which works throughout all creation, by which the most microscopic plant-filament, no less than the grandest mountain, is inwrought and informed, we often talked together in parables, which, however, were never obscure to us, since we possessed that best dictionary of meanings, the bond of a close, congenial sympathy.

Let no one accuse us rashly of Pantheism, since it is not affirmed that we ascribed to that spirit of things divine, or in any way self-conscious attributes. Thus, as we were one day standing side by side before a window exquisitely arabesqued with trees by the noiseless graver of the frost, did the doctor discourse upon its process and its reasons:

"That the thing which men call dead matter has not wrought out this beauty is evident. The matter is here, but a more subtle force has moulded it according to hidden laws. The very necessary and primordial condition of matter is inertia, and without the touch of human hands inertia has here been overcome. Look at that palm-tree. We might shut out from our eyes its artificial frame, and all the other surroundings which connect it with man's workmanship, and, as we gazed upon its articulate trunk, and the plumy shoots spreading from the expanded bud which forms the capital of the shaft, believe ourselves upon an oasis of Araby.

"Wherein differs this palm-tree from its brothers of the desert, the tropical garden, and the bank of Nile? In this only. The spirit of a palm has been viewlessly wandering from zone to zone in search of a body. It reaches a warm land, and there, from ammoniacal soils, from wateratoms, from numberless elements, it slowly builds about itself, in conformance to its inner laws, roots, trunk, and branches, until some way-worn Howadji throws himself down under its shadow, saying, 'Blessed be Allah! another palm-tree.'

"A second palm-spirit, in its ethereal journeyings, comes not to the earth, but hither to this window-pane. Here it finds no soils, but only the water-drops, which all day long have been collecting from the atmosphere. Its visit is by night, and when we draw near the window in the morning, lo! the spirit has erected for itself a body of purest crystal, shaping it faultlessly, by its own unerring law, into the palm-tree which we see here.

"To-morrow the spirit of the Alga may float hither for its incarnation, and on the day after the spirit of the Fern."

Had I possessed any part in the origination of this idea, I should not venture to characterize it as I now do, singularly beautiful; yet I believe that I shall not speak without hope of sympathy in saying that such it did certainly seem to me. It chanced that in the long and severe winter which we passed together at W—, my friend and I had many opportunities of beholding the verification of his prophecy, for to our windows did come frequently both Fern and Alga, with many another spirit from the universal Flora, whose filaments and petals bitter blasts only breathed into more finished perfectness, and whose fragrance was a better, more enduring one than that of odor, since it was exhaled to the soul without mediation of corruptible organs.

As we looked upon the frost-glorified panes, our minds meanwhile tinged with this poetic theory, it was impossible to refrain from carrying up the analogy into a field which is vaster, and orbed by higher destinies than those of the unconscious creation. To a certain body of the palm alone is the breath of winter fatal. In the higher zones an incarnation reared of soils and earthy juices perishes and droops away; yet the spirit of the palm is not dead. Wafted away, it collects for itself other materials to dwell in, and crystallizes around itself a form which shall only be beautified and confirmed by that very power which destroys its other embodiment.

There is another wind in Araby, called Sarsar, the icy wind of death, which blows not upon the tree, but on the man. At its chill the bodily drops off, but the soul has never felt it. Set free by the same breath which was lethal to its shell, it voyages into another region, it crystallizes around itself "a more glorious body." Who shall say that, to this new creation which it has informed, those very influences which worked the dismemberment of its ancient covering—labor, pain, attrition, and all the thousand forces of decay, shall not the more through all the ages act to ennoble the soul, to make it a grander, better, and more harmonious being? Shall he who so clothes the grass of the field, and much rather clothes us, though of little faith, grant good uses of ill destiny to unconscious and not to conscious being?

As a legitimate and by no means unexpected consequences of our living somewhat in seclusion, and holding both opinions and converse which were not absolutely universal, there were not wanting those who dubbed us visionary, the severest epithet of reproach which can be hurled by A., whose horizon of interests is bounded by beef and clothes, at B., who inquires within a wider scope. I do not remember that we ever writhed very convulsively under this fearful thunderbolt, but bore it as became not altogether annihilated, good-humored martyrs.

As we talked of this subject upon a certain evening, thus spake the doctor in parable:

"Once upon a time there abode in a bar of iron two particles of electricity. Now one of these particles, being of an investigating temperament, to the great discredit of his family, and the shame and confusion of face of all who held high seats in the electric synagogue, set out upon a wild voyage of discovery. For a long time he was absent, and, as no tidings came from him, it was supposed he had perished ignominiously at the negative pole. In the mean while, the other particle of electricity, who staid at home and minded his own business, by gradual accretions had secured to himself size and dynamic consideration in the community. After the lapse of several seconds (which must be known is a long period to individualities which travel as rapidly as the electric) the erratic particle returned, and visiting his friends, the particle who had attained a position of high respectability, happened to let fall in conversation this remark: 'I have discovered in my journeyings that we are not the only beings extant, but that, in fact, we live in and are surrounded by a body called iron, which, from our difference of state, it possessing a far greater density than we, we do not perceive.'

"Thereat the other particle waxed wroth, and muttered something like 'humbug!' But the traveler, pressing the claim of his new fact, did so excite his respectable friend that he broke forth thus: 'Do you pretend to belie the evidence of my senses? All my life I have been going up and down about my business, and have never yet seen, heard, smelt, tasted, or felt such a thing as iron in the whole time. Why don't I run my head against it? Since that day, it is credibly stated that whenever the practical particle stands on 'Change talking with other practical particles, and the inquiring particle comes along, the former shakes his head, and says to his friends, 'Unreliable—talks nonsense about a crotchet which he calls iron— visionary, very visionary.'"

XXII.

Grand Divertissement.

As the months went on, the fervor of my longing toward the former hasheesh life in some measure passed away, and in general the fascination to return did not present itself so much in the form of pining for an affirmative as loathing of a negative state. It was not the ecstasy of the drug which so much attracted me, as its power of disenthrallment from an apathy which no human aid could utterly take away. Yet even now there were seasons of absolute struggle in which I fought as against a giant, or more truly to the nature of things should I say, in which I resisted as against a demon houri, for my tempter was more passing lovely than any thing on earth.

As in the earlier period of my warfare, I now and then caught glimpses of ravishing delight, which, through some rift in the thick cloud elsewhere completely enveloping my daily life, broke in upon me for a moment, yet lasted long enough to prove that I could not yet write myself secure, that my integrity was not yet beyond corruption.

Some of my readers will doubtless be amused, others pained, and a few disgusted at the childlike expedients to which I found it necessary to resort for the purpose of appeasing this renewed appetite for visions without a return to hasheesh. There were three different sets of circumstances which almost infallibly brought on the longing. It was never suggested by dark and stormy weather, since this was too much in consonance with my habitual mood to demand more than a passing notice. The man who has lost an intimate friend does not pay much attention to murk and mist; it is sunshine which seems to mock his melancholy. So in my own case did it happen. The season of most intense longing was a day of clear sky and brilliant light. That beauty which filled the heart of every other living thing with

gladness, only spoke of other suns more wondrous rolling through other heavens of a more matchless dye. I looked into the sky, and missed its former unutterable rose and sapphire; no longer did the whole dome of the firmament sound with grand unwritten music.

It was a pain to look into that desert wilderness of blue which of old my sorcery had peopled for me with innumerable celestial riders, with cities of pearl and symphony-haunted streams of silver. I shut my eyes, and in a moment saw all that I had lost.

A night of brilliant moonlight brought me other repentings after my enchanted life, whose tone was not so high as those of the sunshine, but deeper and more enduring. Wrapped in a melancholy which could not be imparted, I wandered by the hour through the beaming streets, and looked sadly around me to see the meanest object by the wayside

"Change
Into something rich and strange."

The stones beneath my feet gleamed like unhewn crystals. The frosty fretwork on the panels of doors which I passed, at the touch of the divine Moon-Alchemist became exquisite filigrees of silver. The elm-trees and the locust, shedding sparkles of radiance from their ice-incased twigs, might well have been those trees of gleamy ore which Allah buried when man was cast out of Paradise.

Yet mournfully I thought of the old days, when I would have walked down these shining ways as through an ever-lengthening vista of glories, when the moonlight would have fallen on me mysteriously empurpled, when over all the wondrous domain I had felt myself unquestioned sovereign, and out of the beauteous recesses of earth and sky sprite voices had musically hailed me to my kingdom.

As I thought upon these things, now forever irretrievably abandoned to the past, I have wept—yes, though it be unmanly, I have wept to find myself a discrowned king, a sorcerer ravished of his wand, a god shorn of his glories. I am not ashamed to remember that I did this; for if there be any ecstasy possible which we do not now feel imparted to us, if any excellency in things which does not now make itself tangible, it is no more ignominious to lament over it perished than to sigh after it tarrying.

There was another, a bodily condition, which I always found it necessary to avoid if I would not be smitten with repinings after the hasheesh life. It was the nervous sensitiveness induced by deprivation of tobacco.

In smoking, if in nothing else, could I boast regularity of habit. To be sure, for this regularity neither an unusually developed organ of order nor the possibility of any thing like a systematic arrangement in my multiplicity of labors was to be pre-eminently thanked. To defer for an hour the nicotine indulgence was to bring on a longing for the cannabine which was actual pain. When circumstances have occurred which made it impossible to smoke before entering my daily round of duties, until they closed I have hardly dared to shut my eyes, lest I should be borne incontinently out of the actual life into which necessity called me to a land of colossal visions. If for a moment I yielded to the impulse, I was straightway in the midst of sky and landscape whose splendors were only less vivid than the perfect hallucinations of the fantasia.

But I have not yet spoken of those expedients to which I resorted for relief and to avoid the necessity of resuming the use of hasheesh. Certainly, in them ingenuity, so far as I possessed any, was tortured to its utmost endurance.

Sometimes I spent the few moments of leisure which during the day could be snatched from business in—mention it not confidentially in Garth, breathe it not to the friend of thy bosom in Askelon—blowing soap-bubbles. Not that there is aught deserving of contempt in the enjoyment of that which has been made a philosophic toy by one of the greatest of Anglo-Saxon sages—not that the pleasure of rare beauties from humble elements is of necessity an aesthetic heresy, but because the hasheesh-eater is well aware of the existence of critics, to whom all that is childlike is also childish, who quarrel with men for being perversely happy on moderate means, and with their Creator because he has not made all the little hills as high as Cotopaxi.

Yes, throwing down the wand of professional majesty, degrading myself to the level of the most callow neophyte of an infant class, did I take up the pipe, and, going into the presence of the nearest sunbeam (a course which, by the way, might well be followed by those who for their light go farther and fare worse), did I create sphere after sphere, not, as the grotesquely but unintentionally blasphemous old poet hath it, snapping them off my fingers into space, but with careful hand taking rest over the back of a chair to counteract the tremulousness of over-anxiety not to tremble, did I inflate them to the maximum, and then sit wrapped up in gazing at their luxuriant sheen until they broke.

There I found some faint actualization of my remembered hasheesh-sky, and where the actual failed there did the ideal, thus stimulated, come in to complete the vision. Had time allowed me, I could have consumed hours in watching the sliding, the rich intermingling, the changes by origination, and the changes by reaction of those matchless hues, or hues at least so matchless in the real world that to find their parallel we must leave the glories of a waking life, and go floating through the firmament of some iridescent dream. Verily, he who would be meet for the participation in any joys must robe himself in humility and become as a little child.

There was one other way in which I measurably reproduced the past for my innocent satisfaction. Had I permitted, at certain seasons, any foreign eye to invade the sanctity of my room, it would have fallen, possibly with some surprise, upon a singular arrangement of the books upon my table into a form somewhat resembling those houses which children build at their play. Yet the stranger would have very little suspected a clew to the mystery in the fact that I had thus been embodying to myself my ideal of the ancient cavern or the resplendent temple in which many a day ago I had exulted through a whole evening, while the rocks echoed with strange music, or oracular voices spoke to me out of the inner shrine. Had he asked me the secret, he had probably not been much the wiser for my answer.

There is still another method, and by far the most efficient of all, by which I gratified the visionary propensity without returning to the old indulgence. I had been advised by the counselor to whose article I originally owed my emancipation, whenever the fascination

of the drug came upon me with peculiar power, to evade it by re-enacting some former vision upon paper. A truly wise and well-considered counsel did I find this, and one which, whenever the possibility existed from any gap in my daily occupation, I followed scrupulously. As would have resulted from once more superinducing the hasheesh delirium, my visions, marshaled out of memory, marched past beneath varying banners; some of them banded under hell-black flags, and others carrying the colors of a rainbow of the seventh heaven.

From this reproduction of the past in the order in which it had occurred, I gained a double benefit, the pleasure of appeasing the fascination without increasing it, and the salutary review of abominable horrors without any more than the echo of a pang. In this way some portion of the present narrative was sketched at first, but of necessity a very small one, since the pressure of business made my abode, even in the most innoxious dream-land, that only of a wayfaring man who turneth aside but for a night.

XXIII.
The Hell of Waters and the Hell of Treachery.

IT is not to be supposed, however, that, with all these expedients, I was now leading a life of quite tolerable calm; on the whole, rather enviable for its ideal diversions, and free from most of those sufferings which, at its abandonment, if not before, Nature sets as her unmistakable seal of disapprobation upon the use of any unnatural stimulus. If, from a human distaste of dwelling too long upon the horrible, I have been led to speak so lightly of the facts of this part of my experience that any man may think the returning way of ascent an easy one, and dare the downward road of ingress, I would repair the fault with whatever of painfully-elaborated prophecy of wretchedness may be in my power, for through all this time I was indeed a greater sufferer than any bodily pain could possibly make me.

For many a month my nights, or whatever portion of them was given to sleep, were tormented with terrific visitations. After a time Niagara began again especially to haunt me. In every variety of dangerous posture, helpless, friendless, frequently deserted utterly of every living being, I hung suspended, over the bellowing chasm, or slid down crumbling cliffs toward the treacherous pavement of ever-shifting emerald. But one consolation ever broke in upon my distress; it was that stony face, which mutely shared with me, beneath its everlasting veil, the terror of the waters. Could I but crouch beside it in my dream, one element was not wanting to my utter isolation.

Yet it was not invariably for myself alone that I feared. Sometimes a tremendous ship came floating up the river without a sign of life upon its decks of man or beast. Against the current it made headway without wheels or sails, but on coming to a certain place always stood still. I soon learned to foretell what was next coming, so that I groaned in the consciousness of an infallible prophecy of evil. A shudder shook the river, as if some dire convulsion was breaking up from its measureless abysses, and then slowly did the giant vessel begin to sink, bow foremost. Slowly she settled till her fore-chains were out of sight; then came a tumultuous surging outcry of despair; the decks, the shrouds, the stays were populous with human beings, unseen until that moment of ruin, and still clinging with iron clutch to those vain supports for the life which could not last. I saw them, one by one, lapped in as the green water mounted, and with the last bubble of their dying breath the main truck disappeared, and a moment more saw the river sliding onward as before.

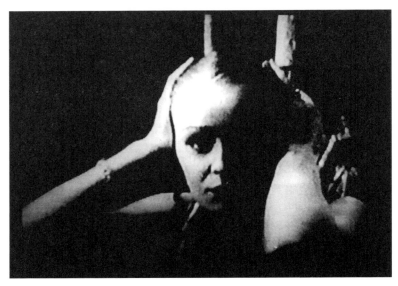

I have no idea how many times sleep rang changes of horror upon that dreadful dream, but often enough, indeed, to make me shudder with a speechless pang whenever water flowed or a ship drifted into the vast area of my nightly vision.

Gradually it grew the habitual tendency of my dreaming state to bring all its scenes, whether of pleasure or of pain, to a crisis through some catastrophe by water. Earlier in the state which ensued upon my abandonment of hasheesh I had been affrighted particularly by seeing men tumble down the shafts of mines, or, as I have before detailed, either dreading or suffering some fall into abysses on my own part; yet now, upon whatever journey I set out, to cross the Atlantic or to travel inland, sooner or later I inevitably came to an end by drowning, or the imminent peril of it. It seemed singular to me, in the waking state, that I never made use of past experience, during terrific dreams, to assure myself that a certain danger was only imaginary. Before abandoning hasheesh, in natural dreams I had frequently employed the power of logical deduction—which, in the case of many persons, remains tolerably active during sleep—saying to myself, "You were frightened by this same danger before, and it turned out to be only ideal after all"; upon which I immediately awoke, or beheld the danger pass away.

Aware of this fact, I often determined, in the daytime, to rouse myself from the distresses of the night by the same expedient, but when they came it was never once thought of. That law of hasheesh operation by which all existence is merged in the present, and there is no memory of having ever lived in a previous state, was most consistently obeyed by the sleeping horrors of abandonment. There was no way so much as conjectured by which the spell of reality might be broken, and the determination of the day being thoroughly ignored, the only remedy was to endure unto the end.

Yet there was one most agonizing vision, whose close proved an exception to the ordinary watery catastrophe, and which stamped itself upon my mind with a vividness lingering, even while I was awake, for many days. It also, like so many of the rest, was connected with Niagara.

On a cliff below the Fall, elevated to a height above the water such as only hasheesh can give, I found myself seated upon a broad flat stone.

Beside me, and resting her hand upon my own, sat a person whom I well knew, when awake, as a queenly woman of the world, who caressed society and was caressed by it in return. So far as man has a right to weigh his neighbor in the scales of private judgment, she was utterly hollow, selfish, and politic almost for policy's sake. Indeed, I felt this, when awake, acting so powerfully as a repulsion, that had I, in actual life, found her so near me, I should have arisen and walked away for fear of showing her my true dislike. Now, however, I did not stir, for a singular fascination held me.

Presently she spoke, and called my attention to some object which was going down the river. I turned to look, but almost immediately heard a grinding sound beneath me, and felt the stone on which I sat slowly sliding toward the edge of the cliff. Facing about in an instant, I saw the woman gazing earnestly in another direction. Soon again she called me to look at some appearance in the river. Strangely reckless, I obeyed her. The stone slipped forward once more. This time I turned quick enough to detect her hand just moving away from the side. I sprang up; I caught her by the arm; I glared into her beautiful icy eyes; I cried out, "Woman! accursed woman! is this your faith?" Now, casting off all disguise, she gave a hollow laugh, and spoke: "Faith! do you look for faith in hell? I would have cast you to the fishes." My eyes were opened. She said truly. We were indeed in hell, and I had not known it until now. Wearing the same features, with the demoniac instead of the human soul speaking through them—wandering about the same earth, yet aware of no presence

but demons like ourselves—lit by the same sky, but hope spoke down from it no more.

I left the she-fiend by the river-brink, and met another as well known to me in the former life. Blandly she wound to my side as if she would entrap me, thinking that I was a new-comer into hell. Knowing her treachery, as if to embrace her I caught her in my arms, and, knitting them about her, strove to crush her out of being. With a look of awful malignity, she loosed one hand, and, tearing open her bosom, disclosed her heart, hissing hot, and pressed it upon my own. "The seal of the love I bear thee, my chosen fiend!" she cried. Beneath that flaming signet my heart caught fire; I dashed her away, and then, thank God, awoke.

XXIV.

The Visionary; to which Chapter there is no Admittance upon Business.

THERE are those philosophers who, in running the boundary-line between the healthful and depraved propensities of our nature, have left the longing for stimulus upon the condemned side. Notwithstanding all that I have suffered from the most powerful stimulant that the world possesses, I can not bring myself to agree with them. Not because the propensity is defensible on the ground of being universal. True, the Syrian has his hasheesh, the Chinaman his opium; he must be a poverty-stricken Siberian who lacks his ball of narcotic fungus, an impossible American who goes without tobacco, and over all the world liquor travels and domesticates itself, being of all stimulants the most thoroughly cosmopolitan. Yet, if we make this fact our basis, we are equally committed to the defense of the quite as catholic propensities toward lying, swearing, and hating one's rival.

But there is one ground upon which the righteousness of the tendency toward stimulants may be upheld without the fear of any dangerous side-issues, namely, the fact that it proves, almost as powerfully as any thing lower than direct revelation, man's fitness by constitution and destiny by choice, for a higher set of circumstances than the present. Let it, however, be understood what, in this instance, is meant by the tendency to stimulus.

We do not mean that mere bodily craving which, shared equally in common by the most bestial and the most spiritual of men not disembodied, urges them alike to some expedient which will send their blood throbbing with a livelier thrill of physical well-being, blind them to the consideration of disagreeable truths, and eclipse all thought by the dense shadow of the Animal.

That of which we speak is something far higher—the perception of the soul's capacity for a broader being, deeper insight, grander views of Beauty, Truth, and Good than she now gains through the chinks of her cell. It is true that there are not many stimuli which possess the power in any degree to satisfy such yearnings. The whole catalogue, so far as research has written it, will probably embrace only opium, hasheesh, and, acting upon some rarely-found combinations of temperament, liquors.

Ether, chloroform, and the exhilarant gases may be left out of the consideration, since but very few people are enthusiastic or reckless enough in the pursuit of remarkable emotions to tamper with agents so evanescent in their immediate, so fatal in their prolonged effects.

But, wherever the yearning of the mind is toward gratifications of this nature—where it is calling earnestly for a nobler excellence in all its objects, nay, even wearied, discontented with those it now has, shall we pronounce this state a right or a wrong one?

Let us see what verdict we would give upon certain other yearnings. When the poor man fences in for himself a little spot of waste land, he first erects a dark and low cabin, that his household gods may not be shelterless. Pleased for a while by the hovel life, greatly better as it is than camping out upon the roofless moor, he feels all his aim satisfied, and insphered within the attainment of Nature's response to sheer physical necessities.

By-and-by, after the pleasures of not being cold, wet, exposed to suspicious eyesight, nor hungry (since he has a little potato-patch behind the cabin), have become somewhat old to him, he happens to think, "How would a few flowers look before my door? There is something inside of me which seems to approve of flowers; I think they would do me good." So the poor man wanders out into the wood, and there, in that most ancient and incense-breathing temple of our God, he kneels down on the turfy hassock, which Spring, that ever-young opener of the cathedral doors, has laid for him, and gently, without unearthing a fibre of their roots, lifts a clump of violets.

When a day or two afterward, we come along past the rude cabin, and as we lean over the fence to ask the tenant how he fares, what do we do when our eyes fail upon a little dot here and there of something more than ground, or grass, or vegetables—azure faces looking brotherly up at the same-colored heaven? Do we shake our heads, draw down our brows, purse our mouths, and say, "Ah! dissatisfied with your circumstances, I see. Restless where Providence has placed you; grasping after visionary happiness; morbidly craving for what you have not; depraved taste!" and all that sort of thing?

I had really flattered myself that I was going to make a pretty cogent combination out of this, of the *à fortiori* and *reductio ad absurdum* arguments, but I am afraid I have failed. I fear that there are some people who *would* say exactly this.

Yet I will restrict the "we" to you and to myself, my reader, since I know that you have not the ability nor I the will to be guilty of so gross a speech. *We*, then, certainly shall not say it.

Let us finish the analogy. A man who, during his childish (not his childlike) years, was growing up into all that compacts, rounds out, and confirms the animal, has in that time attended solely to those claims of nature which have a reference to assimilation and secretion. With meat, drink, and raiment he was satisfied. Practical men cherished him as a sort of typical fact of that other broader fact, the respectable community.

Just at the moment that hopes of his "making something of himself" are at their widest (I will not say "highest," since there is no height to hopes of this kind, as ordinarily understood), he discovers that he has some other need hitherto unsuspected, and not coming under any caption in the catalogue of bodily well-being. His soul wants beauty; its yearning will not be repressed. For a while he is content with the discovery of that which springs up between his feet in this really very beautiful world. Absorbed in other aims, he had never noticed it before, and now it breaks upon him as from a new heaven and a new earth.

By-and-by he thinks that, since all this loveliness is transitory, liable to be obscured by clouds and bedraggled by storms, uprooted utterly or made distasteful by the presence of a bad association which will not be exiled, his soul, as immortal and expansive, may find grander views in another region.

This other is the region of stimulus. What shall we say to this man? "You are morbid; you are depraved; your yearnings are unnatural and sinful; you must contract your wishes, or, at least, extend your arms sideways farther into the dark, not upward higher into the light?"

No; a thousand times no! Let us rather say thus: "Man, in this your longing, you have the noblest testimony to the endless capacity for growth of that germ, your soul. You can not believe more of her than she is, for you can not believe more of her than God believes, and He was assured that He had made her in His own image. You do not, therefore, flatter yourself with the privilege of looking into things too high for you; there is nothing which you can conceive of as possible to your view which shall not be actual. Your wish is approved by Heaven, for from Heaven came the constitution which made you capable of such a wish. Your Creator does not condemn you, neither do we condemn you."

If that man therefore departs, and becomes addicted to the indulgence in opium, hasheesh, or whatever other spell may in his case possess the power of prying open for him the gates to more wondrous glories, shall not the blood of the man and the tears of ruined or bitterly sympathizing friends be upon our skirts?

Nay, most just and noble-hearted reader, for that which we have said to him should be only the exordium to another, a longer address. It is not the author's will more than his province to be dictative, yet be indulgent if he shortly sketches it here.

"You sin not in your yearnings. Yet may you sin grievously, even against the grand aim of those yearnings, by a certain suicidal gratification of them. Were hasheesh, or opium, or aught else of kindred nature between the poles the only alternative to your former gross life in mere meat and drink, the only alternative even to remaining within the limits of your first acquired beauty, it were better indeed to use them than to dishonor your soul by following mere material aims, or by crippling her energies of expansion.

"Yet this is not the alternative. In Nature there is yet undiscovered glory, a spirit which gradually will interpenetrate you as you commune with her. She is not a mockery, a sham, for a truthful essence indwells, informs her. Be this communing one stimulus to you!

"In Art there is also a spirit which you have not yet read. As the spirit of Nature is the ideal of God, so is the spirit of Art the ideal of man, the mind which God has made. With this also commune. In your actions upon it, in its reactions upon you, you will rejoice in perceptions of a meaning in life which you never felt; you will have one more stimulus.

"Around you are the starving to be fed, the naked to be clothed, the captive to be set free, the persecuted to be overshadowed by your wing, the benighted to be enlightened, the vile to be cleansed. Do good as you have opportunity, and find one more stimulus in that.

"The Infinite One is communing with this illimitable soul of yours to lift it higher. At a hundred doors he comes in to you continually. There are breathings within you which are not of yourself. Do you find yourself lower than you would be? Straightway the standard of true height is shown to you, held in a hand which can help you up to it. Are you obscured by the shadow of a misused past? To you, when you muse in the twilight, come angels, like the two who came even to Sodom at evening. There is hope of a better growth, a grander life; the light of a resurrection which shoots in from the time to come through the chinks of that sepulchre, your body. Wait patiently—ah! for how few moments, and that sepulchre shall be a cenotaph. Let that hope of an advancing future, with all its unveiling of mysteries, its impulse along the path of an ever more and more glorious career, its exhaustless Beauty, and Truth, and Good, be your last, your noblest, your unfailing stimulus, until the Ideal and the Actual become the same, and it be needed no longer.

"But of the stimulus of drugs, of potions, beware. For the sake of that very majesty with which you justly wish to aggrandize your soul, beware. Their fountains will be presently exhausted, and then you shall helplessly beat your breast, as without possibility of arising from the brink you draw in their foul, their maddening lees, and curse yourself for slaying those noble powers which it was your longing to strengthen, to nourish, and to clarify."

Let this illustration be pardoned if, in spite of other intentions, it has become a sermon. The hasheesh-eater knows full well that not only in the world, but in our own country, shamelessly vilified as it is by the ignorant of other lands with the opprobrium of an all-absorbing aim at gain, there are many of those spirits who can not steep themselves in oblivion of all but physical ends, who can not rest in the mere knowledge that they are getting so many houses, so many acres of land, so much respectable consideration, to be possessed while a wind is passing by, while a twilight is fading. There are men who pine restlessly for riches which shall satisfy higher obligations of their being, shall endure longer, shall in themselves possess a nobler and more expansive essence. They are right in this pining. Yet if there be one voice which can speak from the gateway of a dangerous avenue to its satisfaction, that can say, "Ho there! pass by; I have tried this way; it leads at last into poisonous wildernesses," in the name of Heaven let it be raised.

And thus I excuse my sermon.

There are those, no doubt, who in reading it will say, "Is it not inconsistent to advise this possible hasheesh-eater to 'feed the hungry and clothe the naked,' after inveighing so much against practical aims just before?" With a desire to anticipate this objection, I would here say that it is not against practical aims, but the making them the chief, the controlling ones. Or, rather, even more boldly, not against practical aims at all, but against pseudo-practical. Paradoxical as it may be, there is no man more thoroughly, more purely practical than he who is most truly ideal. It is needless to suggest that the word "practical" is a derivative from the Greek verb "to do," and is therefore most properly applied to the man who "does" the best for himself.

Now which of two beings thus does the best for himself, he who does it particularly for that part of him which, in a few days, he is to abandon forever, or he who does it to the part which is eternally to abide by him? O practical men, judge ye.

The most perfect spirituality of aim, moreover, is not violated by any decent and orderly attention to the claims of the body. Only let the house be not more beautified than the tenant, the servant fed and adorned above his master, and, then no one in his senses can quarrel because either the servant or the house is well sustained for the master's highest good.

It is, no doubt, the perversion of this principle which has caused the word "visionary," most righteously belonging, by its first title, to souls of the grandest insight, to be held, together with the idea which it conveys, in contempt even by serious and thoughtful men. Shallow persons, urging that claim to notoriety through extravagance, which they were aware they could not press to celebrity by greatness, have been disgusting humanity with their absurdities from the time that Diogenes coiled himself in his tub down to the era of the last apostle who blew his trumpet through Broadway. They have all glorified themselves with the name "visionary"; when the radiant mantle fell from the shoulders of the last ascending prophet who had worn it in reverence, it was snatched by the ancestor of all the unseemly clan—it cloaked the rags of his spiritual beggary during his lifetime, and at his decession it was handed down through every succeeding generation of impostors. No better proof could be adduced for its primeval authentic dignity than the fact that there has never, within the memory of man, been a pseudo-poet, pseudo-philanthropist, or a pseudo- with any other termination, who has not tenaciously clung to the epithet as his birthright, his mark of the elect, his cross of the Legion of Honor.

We can not wonder at the astonishment expressed by Rogers, that most substantial banker of a most substantial country, when, after Byron had dined with him, for the sake of the spiritual man, upon one potato and a glass of water, refusing all the English cheer set prodigally before him, the moneyed man finds that, within the next hour, his brother bard has dispatched a steak and a bottle of Port at his club-house!

Yet this assumption of the spiritual where it does not exist—this counterfeit presentment of the true visionary, certainly ought not, among thinking men at least, to discredit the real fact.

There are, doubtless, more than one who, when they have heard this fine word rung mournfully from some old watch-tower of conventional respectability, as the knell of all confidence, all position, all esteem among men, or echoing portentously from the tripod of Sir Oracle, big with evil omen to an unendorsed theory, have sighed for the ancient days when it beautified the threnody over a dead seer, or pealed from the lips of harpers as they sang the forecast of a living sage.

To its old place the "visionary" will never be restored until knaves cease to make it their claim to spurious reverence, or good men refrain from looking at every theory as unsafe which does not base its request for their attention upon some tendency to promote a bodily good or explain a bodily fact. If the former can not, is it possible that the latter may not be?

For him who shall reinstate that word there is a noble meed waiting in the future. The man who leaps into a stream and brings his drowning brother safe to shore is rewarded by the Humane Society with a medal, which he is proud to hand down to his children as their best inheritance. If we are true men, Truth is brother to us all, and the representative of a great and good idea is Truth. Help! then, help! until some one comes who shall plunge even into the waves of shame, wherein this word is sinking, and draw it aland to its old place in the reverence of just thinkers. Verily he shall not lose his reward. But he must be a man of calm nerve as well as bold stroke; as able to take full in his face the outrageous pelting of the spray, as to wear the medal when he has wiped off the drops.

Then shall the soul be held worthier than the body, not only in, but outside of the pale of speculative theology, and

> "Then comes the statelier Eden back to man;
> Then springs the crowning race of human kind.
> May these things be!"

XXV.
Cave Succedanea.

I AM not aware of the existence of any in this part of the world who are now in the habit of using hasheesh. Those persons to whom, at their request, I formerly administered it, for experiment's sake, were satisfied with the one trial, upon my assuring them that any prolonged indulgence would infallibly lead to horrors.

Yet, since it is not at all impossible that these pages may meet the eye of those who, unknown to me, are incipient hasheesh-eaters, or who, having tested to the full the powers of the drug, now find its influence a slavery, yet are ignorant of the proper means of emancipation, I will not let this opportunity pass for suggesting, through a somewhat further narrative of my own case, a counsel which may chance to be salutary.

The hasheesh-eater needs particularly to resist the temptation of retreating, in the trials of his slow disenthrallment, to some other stimulus, such as liquors or opium. Against such a retreat I was warned by the same adviser whose article in the Magazine had been my prime motor to escape.

As in an early part of this narrative it has been mentioned, strong experimental tendencies had led me, long before the first acquaintance with hasheesh, to investigate the effect of all narcotics and stimulants, not so much with a view to pleasure as to the discovery of new phases of mental life. Among these researches had been opium. This drug never affected me very powerfully, not in one instance producing any thing like hallucination, but operating principally through a quiet which no external circumstances could disturb—slightly tinged, when my eyes were shut, with pleasing images of scenery. Its mild effect was probably owing to some resistant peculiarity of constitution, since I remember having once taken a dose, which I afterward learned, upon good authority, to have been sufficient to kill three healthy men, without any remarkable phenomena ensuing. Several considerations operated with me to prevent my making opium an habitual indulgence, besides this fact of its moderate potency. This, of itself, might not have been sufficient, since the capability which I acquired in its use of sustaining the most prolonged and severe fatigue was in my case unexampled.

In the first place, I was secured from enslavement by the terrors of De Quincey's suffering. I felt assured that he had not unmasked the half of it, since his exquisite sense of the refined and the appropriate in all communion with the public, showing itself in a thousand places throughout his works, had evidently withheld him, in his confessions, from giving to the painful intaglio that deep stroke of the graver which he thought that good taste would not permit, even under sanction of truth.

Again, a consideration of more narrow prejudice withheld me— the impossibility, if I should use opium, of concealing the fact from my associates, some of whom were physicians, and hardly any of them so unobserving as not to be attracted curiously to the peculiarities of the opium eye, complexion, and manner.

At this time the reputation of being an opium-eater was one very little desirable in the community which included me, had its further abominable consequences been recklessly put aside. It was impossible for any one known to have used the drug to make any intellectual effort whatever, speech, published article, or brilliant conversation, without being hailed satirically as Coleridge *le petit*, or De Quincey in the second edition. That this was not altogether a morbid condition of public sentiment in the microcosm where I dwelt, may be inferred from a fact which, occurring a few months before, I entered it, had no doubt acted to tinge general opinion.

A certain person, in reading "The Confessions," had gathered from them (it would be hard to say how, since their author every where expresses the opium state as one whose serenity is repulsive to all action for the time being) that he should be able to excel De Quincey upon his own field if he wrote while at the height of the effect. Setting apart one evening for the English opium-eater's literary discomfiture, he drank his laudanum, and locked himself into his room alone with the awful presence of a quire of foolscap. On the following morning, his friends, knocking at the door repeatedly, received no answer, and, fearful of some accident, broke in the lock. Lo! our De Quincey *in petto* was seated in his chair, with pen in hand, and his forehead resting upon a blank mass of paper, in all the *abandon* of innocent repose!

After the final abandonment of hasheesh, however, at times when distress had reduced me to the willingness to test any relief save that of return, I once or twice tried the effect of opium. It was invariably bad, not operating, as a renewal of the hasheesh indulgence would have done, to lift me into the former plane of pleasurable activity and interest in things about me, but singularly combining with whatever of the hasheesh force might be remaining in my system to cover me once more with the pall which made the worst parts of the old life so painful. Insane faces glared at me; dire voices of prophecy spoke to me even when wide awake; I was filled with foreboding of some impending wrathful visitation, and learned to my sorrow that I was only exchanging one bitter cup from another. As the opium-influence never approximated the authority of a fascination over me, I willingly and finally abjured it as an impossible relief.

It was some time after this that my constitution, broken down by hard work, which, corporeally, to use an intensely idiomatic term, was much more "cruel on me" than hasheesh had been at its most nerve-racking stages, demanded not only rest, but something immediately tonic. The former was easily attained by closing my connection with the educational "Knight of the Rueful Countenance"—a connection which all the while had not been chemical, like that of an acid with a base, but mechanical, like that of a force with a lever. The latter (the tonic) was to be found ultimately in exercise; but, for the sake of more instantaneous relief from debility, at the advice of a physician, I had recourse to spirits. A very short trial of their effect having convinced me that their stimulus was as dangerous as opium, I abandoned this also as a mean of relief. The experiment made with it renewed, sometimes for two days together, the clarity, though not the exquisite beauty of the hasheesh visionary state, and repeated, in due succession, its ideal sufferings of night and daylight.

Thus taught that every possible stimulus of any power must invariably act as auxiliary to the partially routed forces of my foe, I called in no more treacherous helps from without, but went single-handed to the fight, armed only with patience and friendly sympathies.

Since learning this lesson, the progress into recovery has been by slow degrees, yet a progress after all. Ever and anon a return of the former suffering has made it necessary to spend half the night in walking; but the sense that every step forward was also a step, however infinitesimal, upward, is a greater relief than the possibility of once more journeying through the rosiest realms of the former hasheesh happiness. At least for the present—as a proviso to the proposition let this be added—for he who has once looked upon great glories can not but hope to behold them again, when nature is freed from all the grossness which makes them painful in the present state, and they shall come to him, not through walls which they must melt to make a passage-way, but like the sunlight, which, falling joyously and harmlessly, bathes the forehead of the little child asleep.

Conclusion

NOTES ON THE WAY UPWARD.

IT is the author of "The Golden Dagon," one of our most original and interesting American books of travel, who gives to Boodh, as the deity of eternal absorption, the most appropriate title with which he has ever, to my knowledge, been glorified. He calls him "The Stagnant Calm." As I read it, such peculiar relevancy did this title seem to hold to one part of my own experience, that, but for occasional twinges of remaining humanity, remembered as having afflicted me about that time, I should have yielded to the conviction that I had myself then been an incarnation of Boodh. Hitherto my narrative has been of spell and counter-spell; of ecstasies bought on this side of Acheron, where the market was low, and paid for on the other side, where the rate of exchange is diabolic; of the checkered days of indulgence, and the one starless night of abandonment. It was during this latter period that the Boodhist state occurred. For many a month before I had been bathed in the springs of a fiery activity. I had lived in ether. Every sense had been worked at its highest power, the sense of the body, and the unspeakably more energetic sense of the imagination.

Now the exalting agency was removed. I have said how I suffered, affirmatively, from its lack in preternatural nightmares, in disgust at what seemed to me the lifeless forms of the outer world, in countless modes of pain and weariness, whose detail would be only less disagreeable to my reader than originally grievous to me. Far be it from me to recount these things again; indeed, for the past I have sometimes feared that I owed an apology, and might be a expected to say, with him who had reduced courtliness to a science, "Pardon me, gentlemen, that I am so long in dying."

But, negatively, as the months of trial went on, I came into a state which, had it been pain, would have made me fear less for myself. Gradually, after having for a long time known what it was to say, "Now I am perfectly wretched," occurred seasons whose intervals constantly lessened when I said, "Now I am totally null." It was not happiness any more than the rolling of a ball is sustained motion; like it, I went on mechanically by the not utterly extinct momentum of a removed force.

This force, too, was an hourly retarded one. There was constantly less and less hope, less volition, less interest, and the only offset to this negation was the opposite negation of disagreeable emotions. I did not despair, because there seemed nothing to despair of.

What should I do? Often (for this state of non-entity was only occasional as yet) I was visited by stern self-reprovings, admonitions to bestir myself spiritually as well as mechanically, threatenings of a final absorption into utter listlessness unless I resorted to some immediate means for quickening the pulses of thought and action.

Good people told me to sleep; Nature was reading me a lesson upon the curative properties of quiet. Good people, I could not sleep. I should never wake up again. Moreover, I attended another church of Nature's, where the lesson for the day was, "He that will not work, neither let him eat;" and the margin was illuminated, not with cherubs like Raphael's, who have nothing to do except to rest their chins upon their palms, but with certain others, sitting in rows upon a bench, diversifying their hopeless stare at the topmost pippins of the tree of knowledge by the furtive conveyance, from pocket to pocket, of a baser variety of apple, smuggled into school for the stay and consolation of the outer man which perisheth with the using.

This being the exact state of things until I left behind me, with my fulfilled responsibilities, that portentous and uncomfortable ghost, in whom my previous relations had forced me to behold Duty most eccentrically making herself incarnate, there were strong reasons for activity, besides its necessity as an energy of existence. In dissolving my connection with the portent, the latter reason still remained, and the question was how to satisfy it.

There was no further possibility of seeking activity in a research through supernatural passages. Stimulus had been abjured; the accumulation of mental facts, to serve as food for wonder, under its influence, was finished. Reason, Right, Will, all asserted this. There remained for me but one expedient.

This was to take the facts already secured, and discover, if possible, their meaning, their relations to each other; to crystallize them around the axis of some hypothesis, and determine what they taught of the operations of their source, the mind.

It was in this way that I kept up the vital heat of thought for months, and battled against an all-benumbing lethargy. The results of this practice I now go on to give, without any pretension to group them into a system; not only lack of time, but of a sufficiently broad basis of experiment having prevented that. If I shall seem to have fixed the comparative positions of even a few outposts of a strange and rarely-visited realm, I shall think myself happy. To travel farther into the interior, even for the sake of science, would have required a heroism wearing the guise, as looked at in different directions, of the martyr or the suicide. Of the first of these titles I did not hold myself worthy, nor of the last desirous.

How far hasheesh throws light upon the most interior of the mental arcana is a question which will be dogmatically decided in two diametrically opposite ways. The man who believes in nothing which does not, in some way, become tangent to his bodily organs will instinctively withdraw himself into the fortress of what he supposes to be antique common sense, and cry "madman!" from within. He will reject all of experience under stimulus, and the facts which it has professedly evolved as truth, with the final and unanswerable verdict of insanity.

There is another class of men which has its type in him who, while acknowledging the corporeal senses as very important in the present nutriment and muniment of our being, is convinced that they give him appearances alone; not things as they are in their essence and their law, classified harmoniously with reference to their source, but only as they affect him through the different adits of the body. This man will be prone to believe that Mind, in its prerogative of the only self-conscious being in the universe, has the right and the capacity to turn inward to itself for an answer to the puzzling enigmas of the world. Mind, infinite Mind, to be sure, created them and must have known their law; as an inference, Mind, though finite, may still interrogate its own phenomena for the reasons of outer existences which, however grand, are far less majestic than itself, and may obtain a clew proportionally perfect.

Arguing thus, the man, albeit a visionary, will recognize the possibility of discovering from mind, in some of its extraordinarily awakened states, a truth, or a collection of truths, which do not become manifest in his every-day condition. From this man, a few such pages as these may hope for a candid reading, if not for total assent.

Nor am I anxious to repel the charge of insanity which may be brought against the facts evolved by a hasheesh delirium. Indeed, the exaltation, in this narrative, has been repeatedly called an insanity. I only wish to be understood as believing that into some subjects the insane man can look farther than the sane. Let not idiocy here be confounded with insanity. The former is the extinction of all faculties; the latter, the extraordinary development of one faculty or a group of faculties, while the others lie comparatively dormant.

In the same way, therefore, that the characteristics of the plant are sought, not in the microscopic filaments and tissues of the germ (although they truly exist there), but in the expanded individual of the species, we may, more legitimately and with much better hope of success, search out the law of a given mental organ in its unusually than its usually developed state.

Labyrinths and Guiding Threads.

GENTLE reader—not to make this one of my speculations more labyrinthine than nature, for I hate unnatural mysteries—I will not, after the manner of an oracle, leave my title undefined until the sequel, but will here tell thee that the "labyrinths" are our bodily senses through which the outer world wanders in to commune with the soul. For a little while let us wander in together after the manner of the world, and if the clew of my speculation bring us not to the penetralia as surely as that of Ariadne, we may at least promise ourselves a safe-conduct out again. Let us try to discover the kind of communion which the world and the soul are holding together, and the manner in which they hold it.

Long before I had known hasheesh, and walked its weird uplands in pursuit of the secrets of mind, a revelation flashed upon me which, by its powers of amazement and perplexity, made the time and place of its occurrence forever memorial within me. It was a revelation in the same way that lightning is a revelation, clear in itself, yet showing hitherto unknown hills of unbroken midnight in the distance. While yet a mere boy, I was standing one afternoon by the side of two thinkers who talked metaphysics without taking me into their counsels, for they had no thought of my busying myself with any thing but the outside of nature as I met her laughing in my rambles.

"Yes, it is beyond dispute that our senses give us only appearances and not things—certain qualities of the essence, not the essence out of which they rise."

In these words there was nothing to frighten a mind of ordinarily reflective habits; no barricade of "subjective" and "objective," or any thing else technical which I had not yet learned to scale. I was smitten with a sudden interest; I did not perfectly appreciate the meaning of the sentence, but wandered to a little distance to sit down and think it over till I had made it mine. There was a meaning there which held out the strongest fascinations to discovery.

"Our senses give us only appearances, qualities, and not things." Perhaps, thought I, this is only a sophism hurled down as a sort of challenge for argument. These metaphysicians love to argue.

Of course, I did not have to look far for a test. I was leaning against a tree, and Sense, in the support given me by its trunk, seemed to be triumphantly asserting her acquaintance with things—stanch and stout things at that.

But hold! I said to myself; what do I find out in leaning here, which makes me think that I have found a thing? Why, resistance, hardness, to be sure. And it is a fact, these are qualities only. But this is nothing but feeling; let me try the senses of smell and taste. By applying nose and tongue to the tree, I perceived a fresh woody savor—quality still! I put my ear to the tree and struck it: still nothing but quality resulted, the capability to beget sound. I began to be alarmed for the dignity of the Sense, as I saw her chance of proving herself worthy of my past consideration narrowed down to one single organ—the eye. Alas for her! Quality still—a brown tint, a faculty of transmitting certain rays of light, and absorbing others. It seems strange now, but it is true that, with my knife, I began glazing the side of the tree, with a sort of fond flattery of the Sense that, though the qualities lay in the bark, "the thing" was to be detected lurking underneath. In a moment, however, I laughed perplexedly, realizing that I could make the matter no better if I hacked the tree through.

Here ended my first lesson upon the domain of the senses. I know that this incident in itself can claim no such interest as to make it part of an experience which one man, without obtrusiveness, may press upon another's ear; but I have related it, believing that it may recall to some reader here and there the circumstances under which he made the same discovery. Still further, I mention it, since it may be a sort of common ground of sympathy between author and reader, upon which will be better understood something which I wish to say upon the philosophic sufferings of a great mind, which it is our duty to appreciate as well as (and indeed in order to) pity.

David Hume, after having been feted, buried, and reviewed, has been quietly laid upon the shelf by many serious men of the present century, in that especial niche devoted to "celebrated infidels." According to our different acceptance of the term, this verdict will be just or unjust. If just, a careful and discriminating generation ought to manifest their coincidence with it by permitting him to lie under the index of obloquy. If unjust, the sentence will, sooner or later, infallibly be reversed, and whatever light, however slight a pencil any man possesses for the illustration of the matter, is due no less to truth than to the shade of a philosopher.

Infidelity properly classifies itself under two divisions—infidelity of the heart and infidelity of the intellect. The first of these is a malignant displeasure at truth for the obligations which it imposes upon life. It begins in a powerfully-felt repulsion between righteousness and the selfish will; it sometimes goes avowedly no farther, but leaves a man unjust, licentious, and in all respects, where the prudence of selfishness does not itself curb him, totally iniquitous.

In the case, however, of those who have carried on the offensive warfare of infidelity, one step farther has been taken, an utter and public rejection, namely, of the claims of truth upon self-interest. With this step has been conferred the degree, if I may so speak, of Grand Master of the Order of Heart Infidelity. It is not necessary that the man thus advanced should be pre-eminent, even above believers, in the prodigal gratification of passion and interest; temperament, society, a multiplicity of circumstances may serve as steering oars to his course, but circumstances only will direct him. The impelling force to any imaginable excess is present with him, and the certain compass of a felt obligation is gone. According to circumstances, he will go large before the wind with the graceful curvetings of a Bolingbroke, or stagger in a drunken sea like Paine.

The infidelity of the intellect is an entirely different thing. It arises, not from a hatred, but from an incorrect apprehension of truth.

When we remember how fundamental a part of human nature it is to systematize the dicta both of the written and the unwritten revelations, to build up the fragmentary formulas which express the manifold relations of our being into something like an orderly edifice, we must wonder, not so much that error infallibly vitiates to an extent more or less fatal some part of the workmanship, as that any structure so far resists gravity as not to tumble down. Not that this imperfection is to be ascribed to the habit of systematizing, but to the fact that it is human nature which systematizes—human nature, which never in any one age sweeps all truth in a comprehensive view and realizes at once the tendencies of opinions, but of necessity looks at half truths through a distorting medium, and sees only the present result of speculations. A corner-stone laid awry, some premise whose falsity is unnoticed because it has the sanction of antique opinion, may render the whole superstructure out of line and unstable, although it be reared by the most cautious workmen with unsparing scrutiny of square and plummet. In a former century, while men were contented merely with the foundation walls of a system, it mattered little whether every block was laid with perfect accuracy; there was as yet no edifice to be affected in its permanency by the error of the ground-work. But when, in the course of time, "other men builded thereon," accepting it with perfect faith as the careful structure of a master whose name was spoken reverently among men, what wonder that they pointed afterward to the marks of considerateness and caution with which they had built up their secondary walls of inference into a philosophy, as a proof that they must necessarily be stable and faultless, however much some of their compeers doubted it, though refusing to acknowledge any fault in the foundation?

The infidels of intellect have as often resulted from arguing logically upon some falsehood, hitherto universally accepted as a truism, as from any distortion of real truths or sophistical deductions from good grounds. That, if Hume was an infidel, he became one thus, we think it easy to show. Almost as easy is it to prove that, properly speaking, he was not an infidel at all.

At a central point for the consideration of Hume's infidelity, let us take the year 1746, the year in which he stood candidate for the Edinburgh chair of Moral Philosophy, and by the vote of the authorities (no doubt with the most perfect propriety) was defeated on account of his views of religion. Against the action which excluded him from a professorship so rigorously demanding an incumbent of Spartan principles upon the subject which was to be his specialty, certainly no thinking man can have aught to say. The fact of the exclusion is mentioned merely for the sake of determining some date when his bias was generally recognized among the people, who had treated with such neglect his "Treatise on Human Nature," published nine years before. In 1746, then, he had reaped the title of infidel.

For at least half a century previous, the speculative mind of the greater part of Europe (dynamically as well as numerically greater) had been under the dominion of John Locke, whose "Essay upon the Human Understanding" had been brought to light in 1690. It is perhaps rather an insincere compliment to speak of any mind as "speculative" which expatiated merely within his prescribed area. The system which bore his name is too well known to ask a statement, especially within these limits. Its parent he could hardly be called; certainly not with any more justice than we could ascribe to the man who casually remarks that it is a cloudy day the parentage of that meteorological phenomenon. His system consists mainly in the discovery that people generally get such and such ideas about their thinking faculty; that the said people have pretty nearly hit the nail on the head, and that he is glad to tell them so; all authenticated by John Locke, his mark. The majority of mankind attend to the knowledge secured through their bodily organs more closely than to any other; they elaborate truth by thinking upon this knowledge; and thus all truth comes to us through the organs, modified to a greater or less extent by reflection. In fine sense, and reflection on its data, the sources of all knowledge, form the governing principle, the "articulum stantis aut cadentis ecclesiae" of the Lockian philosophy.

Into this philosophy Hume, like all the other contemporary minds of his nation, was born as regularly as into the monarchical form of government. It was the nursery of his childhood and the school of his youth; his mind, when it wanted exercise, must run out and play in John Locke's small back yard, or not stretch its limbs at all.

Now there came a time when David Hume arrived at the very same point of speculation which I have previously mentioned as reached, on my supposition, by most of us who think. Let us see how he reasoned. Suppose him in soliloquy:

"I find that my senses give me nothing but the phenomena of things—tell me merely how objects act upon me. My eye acquaints me with color and outline; my ear with vibrations of diverse intensities; and so on with all the rest of the organs. All give qualities of things, operations which things have a capability to perform on me, appearances of things, but never *things* themselves. How do I know that they do not? By reflection, certainly; reflection on the data afforded by sense. But why do we all believe, and act upon the belief, that we see, hear, feel, smell, and taste *things*? It must no doubt be sense that tells us so; that is the only conjoint source of knowledge with reflection. Then I have within me, and so has every one else, two exactly opposite verdicts. I *do* know *things*, and I *do not* know them. Now which is the lie?"

Hume did not decide. He did not pretend to stand arbiter between these two conflicting juries, which Locke fifty years before had impaneled to settle infallibly, and without appeal, all the questions of human science. He only hung in perfect equipoise between the reality and the nonentity of all being, himself necessarily included. He became, as a strictly logical consequence of that teaching which he had drunk with his mother's milk, and which he would have rejected as much in peril of being called an unnatural son by all his contemporaries, a Pyrrhonist, a universal doubter. And who, in the name of all candor, was the parent of his Pyrrhonism? Who but John Locke, who, while a believer himself, because he did not bowl far enough in his own direction, had nevertheless opened up an easy track to the most comprehensive system of skepticism in the universe.

There may be those who will think that we have made out no better case for Hume by proving him a skeptic than an infidel. What difference exists, they ask, between doubting and disbelieving? Every possible difference. Belief and unbelief are often wrongly taken as antipodes merely on account of their antagonistic sound, and doubting is often confounded with the latter. Unbelief is, in fact, the same mental act as belief, directed by evidence or passion to a different set of statements. Doubt recognizes an equiponderance of evidence, or a total lack of evidence on both sides. Now the impulses of hate, pride, and a thousand others may bear a man's belief one way or another, so vitiate the sincerity of a judgment which ought to found itself calmly on proof. Doubt, where it is real, can never be thus produced by impulse. To sit upon the exact centre of the beam, it must be calm. Therefore, so far as any man is a sincere skeptic, so far is he proved guiltless of the charge of hostility to either side.

I do not assert this perfect calm for Hume. In the present imperfect condition of humanity we act so universally from intricately mixed motives, that it would not be safe to assert a purely ideal sincerity for any one. Doubtless Hume was influenced in the after maintenance of his Pyrrhonist principles by many of those partisan considerations which weigh with us all. But in the first susception of his doubt, acting, as he did, upon the every-where acknowledged basis that Locke was right, no man could have been more logical, more calmly, philosophically sincere. Ratiocination, and not hostility to religion, was the original cause of his skepticism.

It is particularly unfortunate for a man when he is thrown into the society of those who, by flattering that in him which his better nature feels to be a blemish and a disadvantage, if not a crime, lull his pain at its existence, and even persuade him to believe that is his honor.

We have to observe an exemplification of such misfortune in Hume, who, but for being lauded and feted as the Coryphaeus of infidels, for whom he felt no cordial attraction, might have outlived his skepticism through draughts of a better philosophy, or, at least, have kept it to himself as his most mournful secret.

Allowing himself to be applauded as the infidel which he was not, he fortified within himself the skeptic which he was; but that he never made a wholehearted consecration of himself, as some would misrepresent him, to the cause of a malignant and offensive unbelief, is evident from many facts in his history; such, for instance, was his indignant rebuff of the pert wife of the atheist Mallet, who took the liberty of introducing herself to him at a soiree: "We free-thinkers ought to know each other, Mr. Hume." "I am no free-thinker, madam;" and, turning on his heel, he strode angrily away.

There is a letter of his, also, which I only quote from memory, in which he exhibits the man he would have been if left alone, declaring that he never sat down to a game of chess with a friend, and thus threw off his logical panoply, without feeling his doubts vanish and the reality of things return. Yet this very letter has been quoted in evidence of his insincerity, because, it is said, he was forced to reason that he might support his doubts. But what if reasoning infallibly sustained them? Was he to trust in Hume playing chess or in Hume reasoning?

By his unnatural conjunction with infidels, he subjected himself to bear the obloquy of their praise. By their praise, an antagonist spirit of denunciation was excited in the society of believers. Denounced, he must reply, for the sake of his pride and his partisans. And thus, from the sincerely perplexed doubter, he came to be considered, and in a certain, though a far less degree to be, the sneering foe of Christianity.

I have dwelt thus long upon Hume and the circumstances which have tended to give him his present reputation, and to set upon him the stamp of an odium in many respects unjust, because he is an example not less striking than painful of the evil which may be wrought for a man by some unnoticed error in his mental philosophy. How easily an error which is the germ of all things hurtful may escape the notice of men who accept without examining, can be seen from the fact that the good John Locke (for he was good) was never advised of the skeptical inference from his doctrine, but died as perfectly satisfied with it as he had lived.

Most gratefully do I remember that, at the time of my first discovery of the legitimate domain of the senses, I was not left, like many others in similar case, and Hume as the representative of them all, to retreat hopelessly into a negation of all knowledge.

It is the privilege and the glory of this day that its dominant philosophy is Transcendental. Much as this word, like its kindred visionary, is in the mouth of hawkers of theological small ware—much as it has been applied, by a perversion, to all systems of error and nonsense—much as it has been branded for a stigma upon the forehead of thinkers who would not travel in a go-cart, the idea which it represents has been the regeneration of speculative philosophy. The Transcendentalists are, indeed, climbers over, as their name signifies, yet not over sound reasoning nor the definite principles of truth, but over that ring-fence of knowledge brought in through mere physical passages, with which a tyrannous oligarchy of reasoners would circumscribe all our wanderings in search of facts and laws.

Older than its oldest historic supporting names, Transcendentalism still found champions in the more enfranchised minds of Greece, and from them we come *per saltum* to its German champions of the latter half of the last, and the elapsed half of the present century. Kant, awakened, as there is some reason to think, by the very perplexity which set boundaries to the mind of Hume, stands forth as the resurrectionist of the long-buried idea, and is followed, with more or less non-essential departure from his main track, by Fichte, Hegel, and Schelling; for, although the first of the trio may be styled a pure idealist, he follows Kant pre-eminently in the assertion of far higher grounds of knowledge than the sense. It is complained that these men, and chief of all Kant, are unintelligible; that their phraseology is cumbrous and obscure. It is not difficult however, for any mind in charity with the direction of their efforts to see abundant reason why it should be so.

In the first place, while their language (when they did not write in Latin, and when they did their German modes of thought still went with them) is the most plastic in the world to all the moulds of mind, while it admits of endless word-compounding to give roundness or definiteness to ideas, still from this very fact, it tends toward obscurity, for the reason that the compounds so lengthen a sentence as to make it very difficult to carry the meaning from beginning to end.

In the second place, it is to be remembered that the ideas which these men had to communicate were to a great extent new—new even to one who looked at them fragmentarily—new particularly in their combinations as a system. They who set them forth were the pioneers of Transcendentalism; they had nothing ready to their hand, nothing open or clear; and the first entrance into a territory is always of necessity by a rugged path; it is for those who enter into their labors who come in upon the ground which they have opened, to attend to grading the causeway. First the military road, after that the turnpike. As well may we quarrel with Captain John Smith for not laying a railway through the forests of Virginia, as with Kant for not smoothing the passage into a philosophy through which he was the first traveler. It was enough for him that he had grappled with great ideas and fixed them; let his successors attend to polishing their surface.

Third, it has been put out of sight by the prevalence of a philosophy which calls itself that of common sense, but is much worthier of being named that of commonplace, that metaphysics is as true and distinct a science as chemistry, with its own peculiar and inalienable ideas, and in virtue of that prerogative demands, both as necessity and right, symbols to express its ideas which shall be its own exclusive property. Let the phrases of distinction, "objective" and "subjective," be an example. "Objective" is every thing which, in the process of mind, is not myself, but extraneous to me; "subjective," all that is myself, and my own individual part of the operation. Now the sense philosophy could have no possible use for any such words as these, since it recognizes nothing but a paper distinction between a man and his objects for all purposes of perception, all his knowledge being gained through sense, and flowing into him as its passive receptacle. So sense philosophy sneers at such technical phraseology as pedantic. But, supposing it capable of requiring some symbols for such ideas, it would most likely adopt "outward" and "inward." For speculations, or rather assertions, so little analytic and accurate as its own, these might do well enough; but how inert, how useless, how vague would they be where any subtle mental fact was to be definitely expressed. We wish to give the idea of the mind as examined by itself. Transcendentalists call this treating the mind "objectively." Our sense men would be compelled to say, treating it "outwardly." How definite would be the idea conveyed in that!

When we complain of the sailor for speaking of his masts as spars, instead of calling them sticks, to meet the comprehension of some land-lubber who will not take the pains to learn practical navigation—when the chemist is sneered at for saying crucible instead of pot—when, in fine, public opinion shall compel all men to talk of the delicacies of their arts in street slang or boudoir twaddle, then, and not till then, will it be time to deride the science, wherein, more than all others, rigorous exactitude of expression is required, for having a peculiar, even though it be not a universally intelligible language. This talk about the pedantry of metaphysics is something which the age should be ashamed of as behind it, yet even now we occasionally light upon some reviewer who, in strains of touching pathos, laments to the public that he finds it impossible to read Hickok's Rational Psychology to his wife of an evening on account of the doctor's pedantic technicality, which makes him a sealed book even to that gifted woman.

In general, it is safe to lay down this proposition as a rule: first look cursorily over a book upon Mind, to see whether its general character for neatness and system proves that its author is neither fool nor sloven; and then, reading it through carefully and with candor, you will find that in proportion to its technicality is it the repository of new and deeper truths. This, of course, is to be understood of those books on Mind which, according to De Quincey's division in his critique on Pope, belong to the literature of knowledge, and not the literature of power. The same habit of mental indolence, which is loosening the cords of our American

literature—the loving such books as read themselves to us while we lie half asleep on a sofa; the greed for dainties which may be swallowed whole, and which tickle at a moment's warning—this habit it is which has deprived of nine tenths of his legitimate number of readers such a man, for instance, as Hickok. Almost the only real metaphysician of America, perhaps the greatest now living any where, and worthy to be classed with the strongest and deepest thinkers of any age or land, he has, in his own country, about as many intelligent and appreciative readers as Pythagoras had of esoteric disciples. There is reason to fear that men love better to investigate how muslins, hay-rakes, and, above all and inclusive of all, money may be made, than how their own minds are constructed.

One might also be content to leave them and their preference alone, on the ground that they are the best judges of the respective value of their own several commodities.

Great reason have I to be thankful, again I say, that I was suckled at the breast of Transcendentalism. I am doubtless not without sympathy in others when I say that the first moment when it flashed upon me how in the Reason might be found the laws and the essences of things, and that we were not confined for our knowledge to the mere ungrouped and unsettled appearances of the Sense, was like a revelation; it expanded and dignified the soul with a sudden access of glories such as no earthly kingship could give. At that moment spirit appeared to me for the first time something more than the hopeless bond-slave of matter. For the sake of experiencing that feeling again in its full force of grand joyousness, I would like to exchange places with Locke, at the instant of his disembodiment, when he found out that he was mistaken. In having gone astray as a philosopher, he suddenly had all the more glorious surprise as a soul.

There was one question, however, which for a long time troubled me, but to which I at length got a satisfactory, although, perhaps, most men may disagree with me in the belief that it is a true answer. This is the question, How does the outer world ever become apparent to the spirit? I could see very easily how in the Reason the law conditioning an outer world might be found, but how did the appearances themselves become known? The manner of intercourse between matter and matter, between spirit and spirit, or between any two individualities of the same kind, was plain enough, or at least such an intercourse was reasonable. But with our views of matter and spirit, two existences in their very essence utterly dissimilar, how could they ever become tangent?

Take, for instance, such a case as this: I am hit by a stone. The thrill conveyed along its appropriate nerve runs up to the brain, and here we trace its ultimate footprint on the material organism. Yet an infinitesimal instant more, and my mind has learned it, is moved to anger, and reasons for revenge or remedy. I could not see the connection by which the fact of the blow, however refined by its passage, was prolonged from matter into spirit. The books said that, on reaching the brain, the fact became a *tertium quid,* a third something, neither matter nor spirit, but so etherealized that the mind could read it. What, however, was that *tertium quid?*

In the process of time, and by the aid of that ever to be blessed Transcendentalism which had helped me out of my earliest perplexity, I came to the conclusion that the *tertium quid* was a humbug, a metaphysical Mrs. Harris, upon whom the responsibility of all things impossible to be done or conceived was laid by psychological Mistresses Gamp. The answer which satisfied me was this: that there are only two kinds or modes of existence in the universe—the one, self-conscious spirit; the other, the acts of such spirit. From these data arose such a theory of the universe as the following:

The Supreme Being, as Creator of all things, is ever in activity, according to certain eternal and universal laws of right and truth. Whatever else of self-conscious Being exists, came forth originally as an efflux from him, but is now in its will, though not for the continuance of its separate existence, independent of his direct action. As spirit, man is capable of communion with the supreme spirit. Since, however, spirit itself is in its very essence imperceptible to senses, the communion makes itself perceptible by appearances. These appearances, whose cause we call "matter," are therefore, in reality, but the effects of spirit's action upon spirit. In no sense, then, does any such thing as *dead matter* exist. It is God's thinking felt by us.

If it shall be said that there is no difference between this and Pantheism, let me be allowed to show how the two systems differ *toto caelo*. I do not assert that matter is God. I say that the actor is God, and the effects of his action upon other spirit, which we call matter, are neither God, nor in any sense self-conscious. To make it clear, let my reader suppose himself striking a blow. He here appears as the self-conscious actor; yet how great an absurdity would it appear to him to call the blow itself after his name, or to attribute self-consciousness to it. He would say, The act of striking is an abstract idea, to which the other idea of self-consciousness can not be pertinent.

To carry out the parallel for further illustration, let us suppose this blow to fall upon the cheek of a bystander. The man struck would gain, from the effect produced on him, a pretty correct idea of the state of the striker's feeling, notwithstanding he did not suppose that the blow was the striker, nor that it thought for itself.

Similarly in kind, let us suppose that the Deity is forever acting out through all the universe the principles of his infinite and righteous mind. By the effects of this action he becomes known to his spiritual creatures, and in reality manifests the state of his mind toward them. By such action, in its effect upon us known as matter, he attains the only incarnation of himself for reciprocal communion which could make him known.

I have said that this resolution of the problem of the Universe is the only one which ever satisfied me. The deductions which I made from it served to keep my own activity alive through many a day of suffering; and thus from it, in its satisfaction and its energizing, I received a double good. I will state some of the deductions.

Let me be permitted, for the sake of consonance with my theory, to speak, where accuracy is wanted, of matter, known in this light as the effect of the divine action, under the name of Force. I do not employ it in its mere mechanical sense, but as expressive of the manner of communion between two spiritual beings, to an extent metaphorically meaning something analogous to what in matter would be called the result of impingement.

1. In our bodily organism is one of the most cogent proofs of the Supreme good-will toward us. By his own act he has insphered us within a force, the body, which not only resists many other forces and preserves its own integrity, but, what is of much greater importance, modifies our reception of knowledge from without, and blunts the acuteness of our action within to such an extent that truth does not come to us with a fatal shock, but gradually and softened, until we are able to bear it. Viewed as a counteractive force, the body is thus one of the highest proofs of God's benignity, since, left in our present state of spiritual infancy without it, no lidless eyeball beneath a noonday sun might be more agonized. It is as much cause for thanksgiving as for aspiration to something clearer, that we now "see through a glass darkly." Let us not repine, for there is a reason in these half opaque and tinged panes. A sun as consuming as he is wondrously glorious is shining just outside.

2. We may here find a further illustration of that which in the previous pages has been said of the symbolization, by every existence of the world, of some spiritual fact. The incarnation is as the essence; the universe is as it is because God lives as he lives. He is making himself felt in the effects of his communion with us.

A thousand times in the year do we hear it said that every plant is an evidence of God's goodness; yet how much more amply, more nobly is this true than men generally suppose! Whatever of horror or deformity exists in the unconscious creation, is but the manifestation of Creative displeasure at our wrong; whatever of beauty (and how prodigally is it spread abroad!) is a testimony, rich with meaning, of that benevolence which mixes its displeasure with pity, and the return of wondrous good for an evil which is only less boundless. The continuance of Niagara, with its wealth of ennobling influences, is as speaking a proof to every man of God's good feeling to him as the continuance of his life. In the millennium to which men are looking forward, how easily conceivable is it that the whole face of earth and heaven may be glorified by the literal fulfillment of our grandest prophecies and hopes; that an unblemished scenery, an illimitable luxuriance of greenness in the fields, an inspiration of beauty by every visible thing, may be the exponent

of the gladness in the Great Heart above us at the restoration into perfectness of his filial race.

But our philosophy does not limit us to an analytic gaze upon the earth alone. The firmament, from our eyes onward in all directions forever, is full of stars. Some of these, perhaps all of them, there is reason to believe, are peopled; but, granting that they roll on in utter loneliness, what of that? They are there, and as they are, because God is acting grandly, wisely, and righteously, and that it is all-satisfying to know. Even now they teach us lessons nightly, speaking both of Beauty and Truth. But what if they may be, also, carrying on their far-off orbits some incarnation of an attribute of God, which, in our present state, we are not sufficiently strong to bear?

It is the characteristic of the written revelation to be comprehensive. Doubtless all of God is there in the germ; yet how many a line is drawn purposely in deep shadow! We are not ready for it yet.

The natural revelation, the universe, is in itself as comprehensive; but, since we can never see it all at once, to us it must necessarily be fragmentary. Thus we now have Earth to read from; yet when we are disembodied and purified—when the incarnation through which the Divine is to come to us may with safety be made less gross than its form in the present matter, we shall learn through the stars, which have been kept waiting for us, sublimer and still sublimer truths of spirit throughout an ascending life.

Well may the man who, while his utmost gaze now catches them only as gleaming points, yet rejoices in the assurance of their significant harmony, break forth,

"O yet uninterpreted symbols, from afar I hail you as the promise of a truth which it is for Immortality to drink in! Beautiful, strange, yet not inexplicable; even now are ye beaming links of that chain which binds me to Deity; ye shall hereafter draw me close to his presence in a grander communion. Await me brightly while I calmly long for you."

In the closest circle of earthly fellowship wherein I have known what it is for heart to be knit with heart, it has ever been the beautiful custom to write the dead, who, though absent, were still one with the living brotherhood, under this title,

"Qui fuerunt, sed nunc ad astra."

How grand a meaning may there be in this!

3. Upon the ground that all knowledge through sense may be resolved into the idea of force, there are some reasons for supposing that this force may in itself be simple, and only varied by its approach to the soul through the differently modifying organs. In fine, that sight, hearing, touch, taste, and smell may be effects, to speak after the common nomenclature, of the same object, or one grand effect divided into several by transmission.

An inspection of the analogies of science must convince us that this proposition, if not *a priori* necessarily true, is, at any rate, extremely probable. The progress of philosophical research is invariably from the complex to the simple. The myriad phenomena of chemistry are all traceable to the action and reaction in various combinations of a very limited number of elements; these elements are still farther resolvable in their composition into still fewer and more ethereal bodies. In the same way, all the mechanical operations are due to differing applications of six motors; and these, by still further analysis, arrange themselves under the head of physical force. These are but two instances out of the multitude which prove the great law of simplification by research.

In many a field of inquiry the philosopher has reduced the agents effective for a given result to two or three; the next step would bring him to the all-comprehensive unity; but no, that step can not be taken, for nature here so suddenly subtilizes the springs of her activity, that she may float just before the fact of her hierophant, and laugh invisibly at baffled microscope and hypothesis. Yet enough is known in all departments of investigation to prove that the tendency of discovery is invariably from the vast periphery of facts inward to one single central law.

Yet let us not leave the theory of the all-comprehensive oneness of sense to base its plausibility upon a general analogy. We are able to particularize. What reason, then, have we, from known facts, to suppose all the senses directly referable to force? A brief analysis will discover most of the evidence we have.

And, 1st. Touch, simply considered as the organ for determining the hardness, weight, and form of bodies. The two former will be seen to be directly resolvable into force, viz., the force of resistance, in the one case particularized as cohesion, in the other as gravitation. The distinction of form may be also comprehended as an idea of force by the following statement. I move my hand in all directions in the plane of the horizon, and, finding it every where resisted *by an equal force* from below, say, "This is a flat surface."

The resistance, in another instance, occurs in a different direction, and I express this fact by saying sphere, cone, ellipsoid, etc., as the case may be.

2d. Sight. It is, no doubt, well known to many of my readers that, in modern times, two theories have obtained upon the action of light, or, more properly, its origination. Both of them arose or were resuscitated from antiquity in the seventeenth century, but that which bears the name of Huygens is by a few years the earlier. This philosopher held that all luminous bodies are in a state of almost infinitely rapid, though infinitesimally small vibration; that this vibration propagates itself in all directions with an undulatory motion through an exceedingly subtle and elastic fluid, known as ether, which fills all space; that these undulations, impinging against any material body, bound back, or, in usual parlance, are reflected to the eye, and, striking upon the retina, give through the optic nerve, of which it is an expansion, the sensation of sight.

The second theory is that of Newton, who supposed that luminous bodies are continually giving off infinitesimal radiant particles, which, through the ethereal medium, impinge upon the eye in the same manner and with the same effect as the light-waves of Huygens' theory.

The former hypothesis (viz., Huygens) is that at this day entertained by the majority of savans, but the discovered laws of optics accord equally well with either. No further dissertation is necessary to show that in either case the conception of sight is resolvable into the idea of a perceived *force*.

3d. Hearing. Upon this sense there is certainly no need of enlarging, it being universally known that sound is the offspring of vibration, and therefore a *force*, subject in its transmission, reflection, etc., to laws precisely analogous to those of light, modified merely by the nature of the medium, viz., air or grosser bodies, through which it travels, in contradistinction to the infinitely subtle ether which propagates light. There is, however, one analogy upon which we may dwell for a short time, which would seem greatly to strengthen the general theory that all sensations are, in their essential agency, one.

The relationship between light and sound does not terminate in the fact, of itself sufficiently striking, that they both obey similar conditions of transmission and reflection. True, they each pass to the human organ, not by one unbroken leap, but by a series of waves. Literally, lightning no more *darts* upon the eye than the faintest beam of dawn; thunder comes undulating to the ear as truly as the softest sigh; and the light cast upon us from a mirror is only an echo through ether instead of air.

But there is far more intricate affiliation between them. In the very possibilities of their existence they are the same. Every ray of light can be comprehended within the range of seven radical colors and the combination of them. This law of but seven possible colors is not an accident, but a primeval and necessary accompaniment of the manner of transmission.

Every possible sound likewise lies between the two termini of a gamut whose number of root sounds is seven, and this septenary law of sound is as necessary as that of light.

The universality with which these laws are practically known by means of the prism and the octave, take off, as is the case in so many other habitual mysteries, the edge of our legitimate wonder. Yet when, for a moment, we reflect calmly upon the fact that we may analyze light of any possible kind with the most rigid scrutiny without adding a single principal color to a fixed range of seven; that we may utter any conceivable sound without escaping from the same mystic boundaries; that in both cases our only changes must be rung by reduplication or blending within those adamantine gamut walls; when we reflect, I say, on these two truths, each fit food in itself for wonder, and find that in fact they are but one truth, and

that a characteristic of sensations which we have always treated as essentially different, we shall have reason to confess, with amazement, a far more intimate union between sight and hearing than any of outer coincidence. Indeed, excepting the before-mentioned difference, which their several media of travel impress upon them, philosophy can not find a mark of distinction between sight and sound.

How strong a claim to interior oneness this law of seven bestows can be fully felt only by realizing how essential a law is. So essential is it that probably, in the whole universe, it may be impossible to find a complete range of any operations which does not, in its internal nature, submit to it. I say this perfectly aware that there are insuperable obstacles, while we enjoy no more than our present development of mind, to proving this to a logical certainty. Yet the vast probability which appears to me in the proposition rests upon one fact which I have never seen noticed in connection with these senses. Doubtless it has been noticed, however, for from time immemorial the significancy of the number seven has employed the researches of philosophers and theologians. The fact is this: In the Divine philosophy of Creation, which is, at the same time, the most reverend also for age, there is a stress laid upon the importance of this number as exponent of some law of completion, of perfectness, which, unless it be granted deeply significant, can be treated upon no middle ground between that and a puerility partaking of imposture. The *seventh* day as the one whose advent expressly witnessed the completion of the Kosmos (whatever of length we may give to the days of the creation); the impress of some secret import upon *seven*, by countless ceremonial symbols, inculcated to that people who, during the whole period of the Theocracy, held more direct communion with the Divine source of all Truth than any nation before or since; the constant recurrence, in the Word, of prophetic uses of the number, and such a phrase as this: "Wisdom hath builded her house; she hath hewn out her *seven* pillars;" all these seem to indicate, beyond the possibility, in my mind at least, of conceiving the contrary possible, that this number is a fundamental law of perfectness in the Universe.

As such, therefore, and comprehending under its rule the two senses of sight and hearing, it proves a oneness in their essential conditions which seems irrefutable. In some of the more intensely awakened hasheesh states, there was a great light thrown upon this subject, but, with many other views gained like it, through symbolization, on my return to the natural state it passed away from my mind forever.

4th. Smell. Within the last ten years an attempt has been made by some Frenchman of speculative mind, whose name I forgot, to determine for this sense a septenary gamut also, in which the only two tones that have not escaped me, to the best of my knowledge, were citron and rose. If the natural existence of such a gamut could be accurately determined, it would be a great auxiliary, certainly, to our argument; but I fear that our knowledge of the catalogue and relations of all possible odors is so very imperfect as to make the research only a fanciful recreation. From the great variety of the objects, and the lack of scientific delicacy of the sense of smell, it is a very difficult one to deal with. He who investigates it through its own instrumentality, which, of course, is the only possible method for an inductive science, is very much at the disadvantage of him who should try to dissect an animalcule with his finger nail.

Yet there is, even with such obstacles in the way, a possibility of proving odor ultimately resolvable into that *force* which we have discovered as the common idea of the preceding senses. I have held the opinion, whether original with me or not I can not say, that odor, like light and sound, may be propagated by undulations; if not as the only mode, at least as one of two modes, the other of which is immediate chemical action upon the organ. As an argument in favor of this, I would instance the grain of musk, which, without losing weight at all appreciably, will for years render the room in which it is kept intolerable to its enemies.

But, granting that the chemical action is its only one, this fact, so far from precluding the idea of *force* which we seek to make general, only illustrates it. The very chemical action is itself a force. As an example, notice the effect of some such odorous agent as makes its effect particularly marked; let us say hellebore, which, when smelled, causes odic action of the nerve, in some cases only less powerful than that appropriate to galvanism. The flower of the catalpa produces a similar effect upon myself, sufficiently severe to cause very troublesome bleeding; and I know several persons affected in like manner by the carnation pink and eglantine.

5th. Taste. The theory supported by some physicists upon the operation of this very little scientifically understood sense is something such as this. The tongue, upon a foundation of muscular fibre, carries a nervous membrane, not wholly smooth even in the most delicate species, but bristling, more or less compactly, with highly sensitive minute nervous tufts, known to physiology under the name of "papillae," literally, "little teats," from their peculiar form. Sapid substances being dissolved by the saliva, and thus resolved into their ultimate particles, in the form of these particles penetrate the papillae. By something analogous to an exquisitely-refined sense of touch, these papillae detect the peculiar form characteristic of every ultimate particle of the given sapid substance, and thus define it as a certain taste.

If this be the correct explanation of the taste-phenomena, they resolve themselves into a perceived force of form, and thus come with our law. But I imagine that the operation is still more subtle; and that in every substance possessing sapidity, there is, producing the sensation, a force by itself, possessing as true an individuality as the electric, and in each case bearing a specific characteristic which gives it its peculiar taste. Perhaps it may be akin to the galvanic fluid. This seems to be suggested by the result of an experiment very easily made, viz., placing a circle of zinc upon one side of the tongue and of copper on the other, when the curious possibility will be manifest of actually "tasting galvanism."

6th. Feeling. I have made this distinction between feeling and touch for the reason that, although their sensations may be propagated along the same sets of nerves, the strongly-marked difference in nature between the facts which they separately apprehend renders it more philosophical to treat them apart. By feeling is meant here the sense of heat and its absence, pain of all kinds, and the sensuous pleasure not included under previously analyzed senses. In the latter part of this category, for instance, are included sexual gratification, the soothing effect of manipulation, whatever it may be styled, mesmeric or otherwise, and pre-eminently the exhilaration of narcotics and other stimuli.

The only argument which I shall adduce to prove the comprehension of the feeling-phenomena within the general idea of force will be simply to call to my reader's mind the fact that all such phenomena are spasmodic. Their idea is that of an injected energy of motion, manifest not only in the nerve, but in the brain, by contraction or relaxation of both, or the alternation of the two states of either.

Having endeavored, as briefly as an analysis at all satisfactory would permit, to test the truth of my theory with respect to each division of the sense, let me, in a few words, sum up the substance of that which has been sought to be proved.

It is this. That the soul in itself is capable of receiving all the impressions of all the senses from the action of the object which produces an impression upon a single sense; that in the bodily organs only and the media of transmission, which are relevant to the organs alone, lies the necessity for a divisory action; and, finally, as a consequence of these propositions, that the soul, either wholly freed from its present gross body, or so awakened, by any cause, as to be partially independent of the intervention of the corporeal organs, may behold the manifold impression from an object which now gives it only the fractional, thus seeing, hearing, smelling, tasting, and feeling in the most exquisite degree the thing which, in the state of bodily dominance, was the source of but one of these.

An opinion similar to this was held by Coleridge; and I can not but believe that it was suggested to him by some intimation of its truth which he received while in the exaltation of opium. Certainly there is no corroboration greater than he might have thus acquired for it, if the effect of that drug ever reached with him the intensity which hasheesh reached with me. By evidence of the most startling character was I repeatedly, while using the indulgence, put beyond all doubt upon the point. Indeed, at this day it lies before me in the light of as distinct a certainty as any fact of my being. Because, from the very nature of its source, I could not transfer

that certainty, in kind, to the mind of my reader, I have made the attempt to approximate it by the preceding argument, not because I felt at all the need of strengthening myself in the faith.

As, some distance back, I have referred to my own experience upon the subject, asserting my ability at times to *feel sights, see sounds,* &c., I will not attempt to illustrate the present discussion by a narrative of additional portions of my own case. It might be replied to me, "Ah! yes, all very likely; but probably you are an exception to the general rule; nobody else might be affected so." This was said to me quite frequently when, early in the hasheesh life, I enthusiastically related the most singular phenomena of my fantasy.

But there is no such thing true of the hasheesh effects. Just as inevitably as two men taking the same direction, and equally favored by Providence, will arrive at the same place, will two persons of similar temperament come to the same territory in hasheesh, see the same mysteries of their being, and get the same hitherto unconceived facts. It is this characteristic which, beyond all gainsaying, proves the definite existence of the most wondrous of the hasheesh-disclosed states of mind. The realm of that stimulus is no vagary; it as much exists as England. We are never so absurd as to expect to see insane men by the dozen all holding to the same hallucination without having had any communication with each other.

As I said once previously, after my acquaintance with the realm of witchery had become, probably, about as universal as any body's, when I chanced to be called to take care of some one making the experiment for the first time (and I always was called), by the faintest word, often by a mere look, I could tell exactly the place that my patient had reached, and treat him accordingly. Many a time, by some expression which other by-standers thought ineffably puerile, have I recognized the landmark of a field of wonders wherein I had traveled in perfect ravishment. I understood the symbolization, which they did not.

Particularly was this the case in the hasheesh experiment of a friend of mine, made not three months ago, spontaneously on his part, and unknown to me until I was "sent for." Not only was it for ecstasy and wonderful phenomena the most remarkable I ever had the care of, but so clear a light did it shed on the investigation of the few preceding pages, that I will give it here in place of any thing additional of my own, which, as I have said, I will not give.

B—, this friend of mine, for four hours supposed that he was in heaven. Infinite leagues below him he heard the old, remembered bells of the world, and their sound, as it came floating, diminished up through the immense sky beneath him, seemed the only tie which bound him to any thing not celestial.

As I sat by the side of the sofa on which he was lying, and held his hand for a greater part of the time, I became a convert to all the most marvelous articles of the mesmeric creed. The connection which his peculiar state of sensitiveness had established between us, made us, for all purposes of sensation and perception, wholly one. I was able to follow him through all his ecstatic wanderings, to see what he saw, feel what he felt, as vividly as it is possible without myself having taken hasheesh. This, however, as you will say, was nothing wonderful. It might have happened, and no doubt, in part, did happen, from my former thorough acquaintance with all such states.

But the connection did not end here. I drank a glass of water, and B. felt it as distinctly as if he had taken it himself. He experienced the spasm of the muscles of the throat, which always accompanies drinking in the hasheesh state, so vividly that he really supposed he was drinking himself, and implored me to give him no more water.

For another person in the room he had always felt strong sympathies; they were now developed to an extent most surprising. This person had a habit, when in a brown study, of industriously rubbing his forehead after a fashion painful to look upon. Suddenly I heard B. exclaim, "Oh, Bob, stop thinking! stop thinking! you don't know how it distresses my head!" My eyes had been upon B. all the time; his own had not once been opened; how could he have known that his friend was thinking? I looked around, and lo! Bob, in medio brown-studio, polishing his forefront with the usual assiduity. Merely by the sympathy between them B. had known it all. This may be laughed at, but, if necessary, I would willingly file my affidavit that B., with his outer eyes, had seen nothing for half an hour previous. I had not taken my eyes from his face once during that time.

But I will go on to the facts which more immediately bear on my theory. While, as I have said, he had not the remotest consciousness of the place in which he really was, he still conversed freely with us on the basis of his celestial locale.

To him, we all seemed to be together "in excelsis." Naturally he was a loving and gentle spirit; this characteristic the upper atmosphere brought out more fully. In terms which it would not be modest for any of us to have repeated for ourselves, he expressed his sense of the congenialities which bound us together. But this sense, no less *ethereal* than in the ordinary state, was something far more *visible*.

"I *feel*," said he, "that we have many mutual ties of fellowship, but, more than that, I *see* them. I know you are feeling kindly to me now, for there are a thousand golden and azure cords which run between us, making a network so exquisite that it is unspeakable delight to look thereon."

"Are you not fancying it?" said somebody. "Fancying it? how can I fancy that which is immediately before my eyes? Besides that, I realize that it is true; it can not be false; it is a part of each of us delicately prolonged. I see all our characteristics blended in it—oh, it is beautiful—beautiful!"

Here was that inner sense, to which, as most intuitive, we have given by analogy the name of "feeling," shown to be reciprocal, or, rather, one with sight. But the oneness of the outer senses was also to receive corroboration.

B. looked at us, and as our countenances changed in the course of conversation, that change was embodied to him in tones. "Do you know," said he, "that all your faces, your forms, have a musical idea? I hear you distinctly, in harp-like notes; each one of you, as you look upon me, has his melody; together your appearance is a harmony. Do you yourselves hear the music which you are?"

While he lay with closed eyes we still talked to him. Now, every sound which we uttered had its being to him, not only in music, in visible form. Indeed, as he afterward assured me, when in a state to philosophize upon the subject, he read in figures, while we were speaking, every idea as distinctly as from a book. Landscapes, temples, lakes, processions of all kinds of being, passed before him, borne with our voices, and impressed, not with the artificial letter-symbols of our meaning, but with the meaning itself, as in my own case I have expressed it, like an essence made incarnate.

The only sense which was not tested in this experience was that of odor. I have deeply regretted the deficiency ever since, for I am convinced that its oneness with all the others would have been exhibited as clearly as that of the others among themselves. Taste we did try with the fullest result. After much persuasion (for it seemed a degradation of his celestial nature), we prevailed upon him to eat a small piece of an apple. I took a piece of it myself, and if I, who was in heaven, could eat, he might also. Its taste he expressed as giving him likewise the idea of a tone. It was winter, and not a flower of any fragrance was within reach; but I know from my former experience, as well as the fullness of his own in every other respect, that he would have emblematized it in music immediately.

I would that every man whose eye is met by this recital, instead of reading it from my pen, and saying as coldly as is the custom at the present day, "marvelous, but doubtful," with a shake of the head, could have sat as I did by that sofa, and have learned the truth of this strange theory by an eye-witness as delightful as it was convincing. In not one single lineament of this case have I poetized; indeed, I feel deeply my most signal failure to satisfy my own ideal of what I there saw and felt. I am not aware of any recompense which would tempt me, if I could, to blot out the memory of that most exquisite lesson which I learned at the side of B.

Yet it may be said, "Your own experience had probably been pretty well known to him already, and these perceptions of his were but re-embodiments of things he had heard from you." I assure you, my dear reader, that of my own experience upon the subject of this unity of sense I had not said a word to him, not even to any person in the place where he lived. His views, from this fact, were perfectly spontaneous, as, indeed, any one present could have seen from the manner of their natural and irrepressible outflowing in his words. The only possible explanation of such perceptions, occurring

as they have in several other cases besides his without any acquaintance with my experience, is that they apprehend real truths, common to all our humanity, and needing but some instrument of intense insight to bring them forth.

Within a few days of this literally clinical lecture upon my theory occurred another case, in some respects almost as singular. Another person, making the hasheesh experience for the first time, showed the following strange characteristic in the effect of its influence. Though as perfectly conscious as in his natural state, and capable of apprehending all outer realities without hallucination, he still perceived every word which was spoken to him in the form of some visible symbol which most exquisitely embodied it. For hours every sound had its color and its form to him as truly as scenery could have them.

The fact, never witnessed by me before, of a mind in that state being able to give its phenomena to another and philosophize about them calmly, afforded me the means of a most clear investigation. I found that his case was exactly analogous to those of B. and myself; for, like us, he recognized in distinct inner types every possible sensation, our words making a visible emblematic procession before his eyes, and every perception, of whatever sense, becoming tangible to him as form, and audible as music.

There is something more than the mere fascinating activity of speculation in knowing such things as these. The excellency of their office consists in acquainting us with the fact that in our minds we possess a far greater wealth than we have ever conceived. Such a discovery may do much for us in every way, making material ends seem less valuable to us as ultimate aims, and encouraging us to live well for the sake of a spirit which possesses fathomless capacities for happiness no less than knowledge.

There is a condition in which the soul may exist, which is possible (and when we have proved any thing possible for a soul, we have, at the same time, proved it probable), in which every object of our perception shall infuse into us all the delight of whose modifications now but one alone trickles in parsimoniously through a single sense. With a more ethereal organization, the necessity for dividing our perception into the five or six modes now known may utterly pass away, and the full harmony of all qualities capable of teaching or delighting us may flow in at once to ravish the soul.

In the cases which I have mentioned, hasheesh had nearly perfected this etherealization already. Yet hasheesh must be forborne; we have no right to succeed to the inheritance till we come of age. In our longing for that spiritual majority which is to invest us with our title, we may stay ourselves on prophecies as well as patience.

Perchance we may listen to some such prophecy as this: There is a land, oh dreamer, on which the sun rises in music, and his rays are heard sounding symphony to the greeting of Memnon. The ever-shifting tints of cloudland forever rise into brightness and anthems, and fall back again to softness and lullabies. The fingers of the harper paint exquisite green fields with the pencil of a tone, and the child that sings by his side fills the soul with Claude Lorraine sunsets. The clasp of a brother's hand returning from over sea is felt in a rosy heaven, or the light of one more star and a thrill of glad-hearted song. The meaning of the brotherhood between wine and carols is known by a strain of music from the terraces of Rhine and the vineyards of Xeres, bathing the lips of the poet in added melody. With the fall of the sun upon empurpled cloud-banks of the west, the fragrance of the flowers floats to him in a hymn of good-night, and the wind from his portals rings a curfew upon lily and rose. Land twice blessed, where all things are manifold in their melodies, harmonious in difference!

Thus did I prophesy to myself as, according to my wont, with closed eyes I sat listening to a sonata of Beethoven. Within me the prophecy was even now half fulfilled, for I was dreaming in a land of palaces builded of tones, a country whose rivers ebbed and flowed with the modulations of the outer music.

Are we persuaded of these things that we may be deceived? is our hope vain? There is nothing too beautiful to believe of the soul. If its visions seem falsified by matter, it is only because they are above matter; because in prophetic gazings it mirrors a higher, a more ethereal incarnation of the Creative Spirit than yet communes with it through the passages of the fleshly sense.

Ideal Men and their Stimulants.

Of all the infinitely plastic shapes of language, perhaps the most Protean is that word "The World." Monosyllable as it is, it bears upon its back a load of incongruous meanings immense enough to have crushed into nothingness a dozen of the statelier sesquipedalia, which do not draw the marrow of their stubborn reality from so stanch a Saxon genealogy, nor plant their feet so firmly upon the usages of our hard, everyday life. In that word we see the triumph of Saxonism, for it is astonishing how any word which means so many things has not finally come to mean nothing definite at all, a "vox et praeterea nihil." While it has held its place, many other words have been banished from the common parlance of men, or are allowed only when they can be explained by their context, or when vagueness itself is an especial desideratum.

Not to multiply instances, let the English "good" and the French "vertu" be examples. The first of these who ever thinks of using (we limit its reference to human attributes) when he wishes to express something defined of the character of another? The poets only, for they, indeed, from the picturesque necessities of their art, have preserved its original outlines clear, and give it always its noble, radical force; the good man, with them, is the man of developed heart as distinguished from his clever brother of the developed intellect. But in common conversation, to say that a man is good tells about as much of him as to ascribe to him the possession of a nose. He may be, for all we know, a sour Pharisee, held righteous in proportion to the number of things which he considers sins, an easy soul who does or does not pay his little bills, a kindly person of fluent sympathies, or

"A good-humored dance with the best of intentions."

To the word "good," a man with the bump of Causality prominent must always reply "How?" and then come a host of particularizations on the other side to round out the idea.

In like manner has "vertu" passed utterly out of the universal sparkling Gallic mouth, not only for the reason that the idea which it embodies exists in a somewhat misty (as well as musty) state in the national brain, but because, very likely as a necessary outflow from this fact, it has been dissolved under the pressure of its numerous meanings into free vapor. The person who cultivates "la vertu" may be conceived of as a man who prefers reading the Constitutionnel of an evening to his wife, in slippers, to the society of Lorettes at the Bal au Masque; or again, for aught that we know, he may this moment be looking for medallions of Claudius in green spectacles and Pompeii.

But "the world," word as truly as thing, has held its course. We do not confound "the man of the world" with Humboldt, who has traveled all over it, nor "the ways of the world" with relations to its tumbling around from day to night, and from peri- into aphelion. We understand every man in the speciality of meaning which he chooses to stamp upon the word, and pass on without further questioning.

With the Geographer it means—no matter, we know what it means, not having in early youth blasphemed to no purpose the American idea of universal enlightenment over an Atlas. With the Ethnologist it is an affiliation of human manners; with the Philologist, a brotherhood of tongues. The man of society says "the world," and straightway it paints to him, if transatlantic, a vision of Almacks and the Clubs; if cisatlantic, a prodigality of entreés on the Avenue. A circle of spinsters whisper the mystic symbol over souchong, and lo! at uncontaminating distance, a dream of deluded souls dancing into inevitable destruction to a Redowa discoursed from Dodworth's balefully-fascinating tubes. Yet, by a more catholic appreciation than we give to any other word, in each case we catch the full force of the particular idea. O world, as word alone, truly there is no "transit" to thy "gloria."

Yet, from the very ease with which it carries its multiplicity of meaning, we are apt to forget how manifold they really are. We thus lose sight of a truth, than which there is none more actual, that, though we intermarry, walk, talk, and transact business together, we are each of us, this moment, living in a different world.

Even as a mere bald question of the bodily senses, this is beyond a doubt. A is a near-sighted man, and has a very defective power of discriminating colors. Like several men whom I know, he may be utterly unable to distinguish the strawberry from its leaf, or, like certain others, to discriminate between the fly on his spectacles and the eagle in the firmament. B, on the other hand, has got the focus, and pronounces dogmatically, at a glance, between two shades of blue which do not differ from each other by a tenth. A and B live in two absolutely different sight-worlds.

Again, C perceives no difference between sounds or harmonies. He is, let us say, a celebrated divine whom I have the honor to know. Some years ago, when "Oh Susannah" was triumphantly ushering in the Ethiopian school of composition to popular favor, a roguish daughter of the gentleman happened to be playing that exquisite air upon the piano, and (much as I regret to state it) upon a Sunday morning also. Her father, struck with the novel

beauty of the music, although he had heard it fifty times before, asked what it was, and was answered, with a sense of security which based itself upon his peculiar auricular failing, that it was "Greenland's icy mountains."

In the evening all the family were assembled in the parlor, and Dr. — asked the fair rogue to play the piece that had so much pleased him in the morning. Of course, by the family, "Oh Susannah" was reckoned among secular melodies, and, to speak popularly, would not "go down." Without a moment's hesitation, Miss — awoke the instrument to "Greenland," and the doctor was as perfectly satisfied as he had been ten hours before.

Such a one we will say is C. D, on the contrary, recognizes fifteen gradations between F and G of the natural scale, and whistles every air in *Trovatore* on his way home from its first performance at the Academy. If an itinerant miller of music, "knowing the wally of peace and quietness," refuses to move under a shilling, he makes over the additional sixpence, and thinks it clear gain.

The sound-worlds of C and D are as truly twain as Mars and Jupiter.

But I will not consume the letters of the alphabet in any further analysis of a statement so apparent to the slightest thought. Just briefly, in their relations to the remaining senses, let me set the opposite types apart.

In Touch, on one side stands the artisan who, with his finger, can measure that convexity in a lens which few men could determine by the eye; on the other, the person who scarcely, by his hand, discovers any inequality in a board, provided it be placed. In connection with the former, I might mention such a case as that of Giovanni Gonelli, of Volterra, who, in the seventeenth century, gave to the world the spectacle of a man entirely blind, yet a most accurate sculptor, not alone of his own ideals, but of faces which he only knew by passing his hand over them. Among the likenesses which he left were those, both faithful and beautiful, of Cosmo di Medici, Pope Urban VIII, and the first Charles of England. Yet, though I have refrained, on account of the exceptional nature of this case, I might well adduce other instances of blind dexterity and delicacy of touch far from exceptional.

Again, in Smell, there are innumerable grades between the person in whom it is an absolute lack and the one to whom, our world being unfortunately not a universal spice-grove, it is a source of constant misery. At this moment I am writing but a few feet from a lady who, a day or two ago, assured me that if, by any operation, however painful, she could eradicate her sense of smell without danger, she would willingly submit to it, even though it cost her those rose and jasmine odors in which she delights with more intensity than practical people do in a good dinner.

In Taste we may shade off humanity between the two extremes of an Apicius, desolé on account of the one quarter grain of ambergris more than the receipt in his soup of flamingos' tongues, and the Scotchman who, outside of his herring and his bannocks, is at sea upon all delicate questions of gustative interest.

In Feeling, as defined in the preceding note, the sense, to speak in general terms, of pains and pleasures not comprehended by other organs, the grades are almost innumerable.

There is a case on record of a lady so exquisitely constituted in this respect that the recital of another's pain in any particular member immediately made her feel it acutely in her own. I might offset to this the instance of a person who avowed to me that the extraction of the largest molar gave her as little suffering as the scratch of a pin, and she dreaded no possible operation to such an extent as to care to use an anaesthetic. Since she was at all times characteristically matter of fact, and never adorned the blank reality of her ideas with fiction, I had no reason to doubt that she rigorously meant what she said.

Here, then, we see both nature and cultivation making infinite variety in individual acuteness and range of all the senses. In the words of the great Chadband, "What does this teach us?"

There is, no doubt, an objective world, a something external to our perception, and outside of our originating energy, which produces the effects by us called collectively "the world." Yet, in order to become a thing perceived, that something must undergo a modification by our organs, which, after all, makes us as truly actors in the being of the world, for all purposes of perception, as if we had helped to create it. Accordingly as the senses vary, so also will the world vary, becoming all things to all men, and literally the same thing to no two men. So, not metaphorically at all, but in the most restricted sense, every human being of us has his own world which no other man has any conception of, and this, too, with all our senses wide open, and, if you please, looking in the same direction. Only upon abstract mathematical truths, or on the forum of axioms, do we ever come exactly together, and do business with each other by the same balances. Once off of this common ground, and, though we talk about things the same in words, we mean something which we see and feel very differently. The husband does not know exactly how his voice sounds to his wife, nor the wife whether to her husband her face looks precisely as it does to herself in the glass. All that they can be tolerably sure of in their intercourse with one another is that they hit the same general and necessary facts.

But if in the mere bodily senses we find such different worlds, how much more is it the case in our spiritual organism. From the characteristic of this variation we utterly exempt that faculty of direct insight which beholds truths that are necessary and therefore universal. This, which may be called the Intuition of Truth, is not only the same in its perceptions, but pretty nearly equal in its scope among all men. None but idiots, of whatever land or tribe, could fail to see that a straight line is the shortest distance between two points, and in the field of ideas to which that belongs there is at present a small harvest of similar facts, and none but men preternaturally exalted have reaped any more from richer heights.

Leave this plane, and we are all irreconcilable again. That which is one man's darling goal in life is the loathing or hatred of his neighbor. We are astonished at each other's attachments; and while we forget the old "de gustibus" aphorism, we forget also another thing whose remembrance would be much more apt to keep us calm than any dogmatic assertion of a fact without its reasons, like that of the proverb. My dear sir, the object of your friend's attachment you do not perceive in the slightest. With the index of a word out of your common dictionary he points in a certain direction. You look, and see, something which does not please you. Do not growl for that fact; if he had your spiritual eyes, he would see something that did not please him; had you his, you would see an object as lovable as he himself sees.

The importance of a proposed measure, the value of a certain end to be secured, are utterly different with different individual judgments. The majority which wins the day must not be understood as a body of men who all think alike. Each individual mind composing, it sees the question in a light varying by inexpressible shades from that which illuminates each of his colleagues. The majority is nothing more nor less than a collection of minds who, seeing one proposition in certain connections, varying in each case, think they all understand it as the same, and consent to let go their minor views with relation to it for the sake of carrying through that which on the whole they believe to be the best, though for very different ends.

There are philosophers who seriously lament over this infinite variance of perceptions, judgments, and feelings, as if it were the grand obstacle in the track of human perfection.

Deferentially, though candidly, I acknowledge that I think this a mistake. Indeed, the problem of our humanity standing as it does thus—Given our present nature, and the necessity arising out of it that investigation should be the instrument of acquiring wisdom, what is the best possible contrivance for furthering the operation? I would reply, this very state of omnipresent variance. Supposing that suddenly, and just at the point in all science which we have now reached, the law of mind should change, and a great average being struck, we should all, not to make an extreme case by saying throughout the world, but merely over its civilized area, henceforward see every thing precisely alike, and precisely alike be affected by every thing which we saw—it seems to me that a worse calamity could not happen to mankind. The wheels of our spiritual progress now roll somewhat erratically, it is true, as the impulse of the hosts who urge on the chariot is stronger now on this side, now on that, but the resultant of all the forces is a rapid and a forward motion. The check which would ensue to that progress from the coming in of an entire uniformity would be sufficient to retard for centuries the millennium of mind. True, all would push in one direction, but the grand nisus, the energy of ambition, would be lost.

In the contests—yes, even in the quarrels of opinion, we have a guarantee for the development of truth. Fertility is not the characteristic of unbroken plains; they become the torrid desert or the icy steppe; but it bestows itself upon a grouping of entire opposites; the peaks catch the clouds, and with them water the valleys. As the collision of flint and steel gives fire, so from the crashing together of many adverse views comes out Truth, the bright, the beautiful, the eternal. Let us thank God that human thought and human feeling are not one vast stagnant lake, but a sea whose ever-struggling and colliding waves keep their mass pure, and cleanse the intellectual atmosphere.

Our great need is not a reducing to uniformity, but a purging from all acrimony in our contests, the infusion of a willingness to permit and a readiness to appreciate all those differences of form, which, in every one of our neighbors, opinion must necessarily take. We have not all to bow down at the same shrine, but to respect those of all other men while we worship at our own; to put down the iconoclastic hammer, though not pretending to burn incense before one great average god of sentiment.

This tolerance is yet to be learned, for it is not a remarkably flourishing virtue even of the nineteenth century. Our great advance at this day has been made in the direction of refining our intolerance. For the stake and the dungeon have been substituted the taunt and the sneer, an invective which burns more lingeringly than the former, and a neglect which surpasses the latter in its fatal chill. We have yet to open our ears to the Past, which, up to our present summit of enlightenment and vision, is calling forever, in sad and earnest litany, "By Smithfield and the Lollards' Tower, by the poverty of confiscation and the weariness of banishment, by the blood of Savonarola, and Galileo shut up in prison from his stars, be merciful—be tolerant!"

There is one excellent result of this grand multiplicity of worlds which we seldom value as we ought. Who that of a morning walks up Broadway, in one of the two currents of that hurrying life, does not wonder that all the thousands who are rushing on, each for the sustenance or gratification of self, do not oftener jostle through that very selfishness, that the crowds do not interpenetrate each other with more friction? As a fact, we see them tolerably calm, obliging, and self-continent. As a problem, supposing it given to a philosopher who calculated only upon the data of our well-known human selfishness, could he solve it? Something else is requisite for the solution. We are none of us aiming at precisely the same mark. With no two men do the points on the target exactly coincide. The most similar of us still aim a hair's-breadth out of each other's way, and thus, in the great match, unless intentionally we tread on each others' kibes, there is room for us all.

If we wished to make a general distinctive classification which, in one way or another, would comprehend our whole humanity, living in its different worlds, there are perhaps no two divisions which would so nearly comprehend it all as those of Ideal and Non-Ideal. Each of these forms is a Kosmos by itself, which, from its great interior diversity, might, even as thus congregated, be properly translated rather system than world; but for our uses the narrower rendering will do, since all the grander laws of each Kosmos are the same for each of its inhabitants.

By these terms, Ideal and Non-Ideal, we mean very much the same ideas that a poet would get from "Visionary" and "Practical;" but these phrases are not of sufficiently catholic interpretation, the former not justly embodying that sneer, nor the latter that praise, which the language of conversation conveys in them.

We have spoken of the intuitional perception as a common ground for all men, limiting, however, the assertion to that branch of the intuitional which has its object in universal truth, and thus meaning that every body acknowledges an equal force in axioms; and, however we may dispute on other points, all agree that the whole, for instance, is equal to all its parts. Yet there are two other fields of the intuitional, which, so far from their being equally expatiated in by all men, are to some merely known by glimpses, to others, we might also believe, entirely shut. These are Beauty and

Good, higher than Truth, and therefore neither so much needed in our lower affairs, nor so much opened to all mankind by nature or cultivation.

Both the Good and the Beautiful forming each an ideal by itself, for our present purpose we need only treat with the latter. It is in relation to the Beautiful particularly that we wish to exemplify this classification of the Ideal and Non-Ideal.

That beauty is really an ideal, something of the thought inner to us, and not coming in through the passages of the sense from without, is too little perceived in our inaccurate every-day thought, and too little granted even in our moods of calmer philosophy. For this, as for so many of our other perversions, we have to thank the sense-theories.

We may examine the matter without a very painful analysis. Treading reverently and softly, as becometh umbrae who intrude upon the privacy of great men, let us steal into Abbotsford, and stand by the chair of Walter Scott, who is looking at a sunset. By his side, upon the floor beneath us, lies that faithful companion of his strolls among the heather, Maida. Since the test we are about to institute demands fairness, we will free our comparison from all imputation of artifice by placing together with the noblest specimen of man the noblest specimen of beast.

Both the poet and the greyhound are looking westward. The same tints fall through the panes upon the faces of both; far up, toward the springs of Tweed, they see the same hills bathed in a dying light, and the clouds that shift above them. Does it surprise us to hear Sir Walter bursting forth in enrapturement; or, truer still, as a meed of the heart to beauty, see him silently gazing toward the sundown with a face which glows and changes, telling more than a thousand lips? But would we be astonished or not if Maida should suddenly give vent to a lyric bark of ecstasy, or even should she refuse to be wheedled from the glories of that view by the whistle of a keeper immemorially associated with dog-meat? Not in the least, you will say; and most people would agree with you; for a hound who appreciated sunsets would be as great a sensation, even in our most *nil admirari* world, as a cow, who, like Landor, should write feelingly upon green grass, and publish it. He would have the entrée of all literary circles; dinners would be pressed upon him; he would be presented with services of plate; not an album would be without the autograph of this veritable Prince di Canino. Eclipsed in the blinding glory of his *eclat,* the learned pig would commit suicide by surfeit, and the accomplished fleas end their mortification with their own poison.

But why? A cat may look at a king, why not a dog at a sunset? "Hath not a dog eyes? Hath not a dog paws, organs, dimensions, senses?" Yet, with quite as much astonishment as Shylock asked,

"Hath a dog money? is it possible
A cur can lend three thousand ducats?"

do we all inquire, "Can a dog see beauty in a sunset?"

Anatomically we dissect his eyes, and (especially if he be a gaze-hound) find them far better calculated than man's for length and breadth of vision. In all respects they will compare favorably with the same piece of human organism, granting the latter even at the rarest point of development.

Far deeper than any sense lies this subtle appreciation. There is a something in the outer world which does not impress itself on the retina, and of which the mere visual image is but a type. That which delights us is the peculiar essence of things, and the intangible relation of harmony which the essences, manifold in unity, bear to each other and ourselves. In lakes, and mountains, and sky there is beauty to us, because the same Creator lies behind and continues us all. Sprung from the same source, we have a fitness for each other, arising out of the very fact that in our own souls and the world also creative spirit is making itself manifest; in the tangency of the two there is a delightful communion between spirit and spirit, and for the beast this does not exist, since he is not spirit. This very capability which we possess of expressing this communion in language, shows that it is not through sense that the Beautiful flows in, for what can be conceived as more cruel, more in every way unnatural, than that the hound, with senses like our own, should still be dumbly shut up to an impossibility of expression, if, while standing by our side, he was overburdened with the same loveliness as we? The idea is indeed horrible.

Yet doubtless we may wrong the animal upon the other side. Few of us being willing to carry out the sense philosophy to its ultimate conclusions by giving the dog perception of Beauty equally with ourselves, we often go to the opposite extreme, and rather pity him as a being without gratifications beyond the present bone, hearth-rug, or exciting chase. He very likely enjoys contemplation as much, proportionally to his kind, as we do. Not the contemplation of the beautiful in nature indeed, but of some other characteristic, which has as true a fitness to his constitution as Beauty has to ours. What this is, of course, from the entire difference of our plane of being, we can only conjecture.

It may be something such as this: in the creation there is a capability of sustaining animal life through food, atmosphere, and a variety of means. To us this capability seldom appears except as a logical deduction, in the form of statistics or agricultural history. To the animal it may appear stamped upon all surrounding things; it may be for him the essential truth which they embody, and in trees, herbage, fruitage, he may feel the symbolized principle which prophesies the sustenance of his highest life as our ideals prophesy ours. The Creator, who careth even for sparrows, and will not let them feel themselves unsupported in this great lonely world, may on this lower basis commune with the beast, and by it give him a suggestion of His good-will toward him, which in his case may be the source of an enjoyment measurably keen with our own.

But through the Beautiful He talks with man only, and to him alone the fitness of the conscious and unconscious creations are expressed in this way. It is a memory of the elder time to be cherished, even though it be the memory of something heard only in dreams, that all men long ago, in ages however primeval, realized Beauty, and answered back its thrill with gladness and hymns. Such a remembrance—yes, if you will say so, even such a dream—is like some not yet extinguished echo of the Creation strophe and antistrophe, when, on the one side, "the morning stars sang together," and, on the other, "all the sons of God shouted for joy!"

Sadly enough, many of the latter band of singers have been struck dumb since that day. It might be painful to read a census, could we get such a thing, of the persons who love or even recognize Beauty, by itself and for its own unmarketable sake. The bulk of such a document would probably depend upon the style of man who went around through humanity to compile it. A poet would make sad work. His best questions would be so analytic as either to render him unintelligible or obnoxious. At some houses he would be answered, "No, I am no visionary;" and at others, "Clear out! Do you mean to insult me? Can not I see Beauty? Isn't this a beautiful day, to be sure, with the sun shining so bright that I can get in all my hay?" At all events, he would come home, without having found it necessary to purchase another valise for the conveyance of his papers.

Whatever may be the reason, it can not be doubted that there is a great difference between men in the appreciation of the subtle characteristic, and in some it seems to be entirely lacking. There is one class of men who exult in beauty, who live in it, whose extreme representatives are willing even to commit all sorts of practical extravagances for its sake. There is another, whose members look at a statute of Phidias, and then at a gatepost, and in both see only something hard, white, and tall.

Yet they both have to live in what is geographically the same world. It is of the ideal man, as representative of the former class, and of some of his relations to that world, that we have to speak. A greater breadth of these relations than might at first sight be supposed is included in the question, Why do ideal men often use narcotics? Indisputably it is ideal men. The fact is there, however great a pity it may be. Let us seek, for a while, an answer to the question.

The wants of the ideal man, while in number less than those of his opposite, in degrees are far greater. Dives, as the type of the pure worldly life, is as incapable as guiltless of those vague, unsatisfied longings which he so much censures in a neighbor and discourages in a dependent. All things out of which he can extort pleasure coin themselves for him in a perfectly tangible shape. He is fully satisfied,

his wishes need no additional fulfillment to make a complete orb, if his balance strikes accurately at the counting-room, if he can go home behind his own horses when too tired to walk, his dinner is good, his wife handsome, his house comfortable, his daughters well settled, his sons imitating their father. All these requisitions he can lay his hand on; if he could not, his longings would not be vague; he would know what he wanted, and, under ordinary circumstances, could get it in time.

Ariel, on the other hand, is contented with a catalogue of enjoyments in numerical and money value far less. It was not he who originated that sneer upon love in a cottage. He was filled with infinitely more than the mere satisfaction of their material by the woodbine which clambered around his windows, the roses leading from the door-step to the gate, the lake below him, the mountains on the other side, the fruit and the loaf upon his table, and the other cleanly and kindly answers to his domestic needs.

But the tax-gatherer came to spy out the land, the insatiate genius of mill-building looked at the brook which ran by his garden, and pronounced it a "location."

Presently the waters began to run foul with dye and sawdust, gigantic band-wheels spun and hummed where birds had sung; there was a creaking, a dust, a baleful fire night and day, which invaded his library and his dreams. Provisions rose; the simplest fare upon which he had kept together soul and body now stood just where his labors could reach it upon tiptoe.

So strongly, while it does cling, does the body pull upon the soul, that, though we may be spiritually happy without being sumptuous, we can not, at the same time, be spiritual and hungry. At least most of us can not. Into what a glory, looked at through such a fact, does the Massinger tower who, with one hand stiffly holding the wolf at arm's length, with the other can indite the Virgin Martyr. Yes, there have been some such souls after all.

But our Ariel, being of less muscular make, is not among them. His "mind to him a kingdom is," but he is expatriated from it on a foraging expedition; through the jaws of Scylla and Charybdis, starvation on the one hand, and the premature old age of overwrought energies, he is voyaging in a supply-ship. If even now he could sit still in an occasional lull, and grow better by drinking in beauty, and make other men happier by imparting it to them through words, writing, or kindly offices, he sees only money-utility stamped upon the rivers, and the whole face of nature is staked off into building-lots or manufactory-sites. The features of his goddess have become the "desirable features" for a paper-speculation town.

There are a thousand ways in which his neighbors can evaporate the essence which is all in all to him, while they at the same time give to his scenery a ponderable value which to them is worth far more.

Perhaps, like Southey, he now out and out curses the mills. But this is wrong; for Southey, though a noble poet in spite of the insolence of Byron, was still no great political economist, notwithstanding the opinion of himself. Perhaps, therefore, he only sighs, and moves his household gods to another hearth—it may be where loneliness will better secure him from disturbance, it may be where labors of his particular kind yield fuller sustenance to the crying wants of life. The pangs of such a moving are little known to any one but himself, or, if he has God's crowning gift in a deep-feeling and congenial wife, to her alone beside him. The men of the world can not hear the groans of the uprooted mandrakes.

There is the hill-top, upon which, first of all visible things, his eyes for so many years have lighted in awaking. It has grown to be to him the only summit over which it could be conceived possible for the sun to rise. There is the lake along whose shores he has led his children, calling them to watch its hues and dimples at evening; along those same shores, mayhap, his father led him. Every tree, as far as the skirt of the horizon, is known to him; he has wandered over every slope; he has dreamed or written suggestions in his note-book upon every crag. The whole scenery has been to him his school, his gymnasium, his holiday-ground. He must leave it all.

And his house—it was there that he felt upon his forehead, in blessing, the hands of the now long dead; here, many a year ago, he knew man's only peace except death, childhood—knew it for a little time, while his locks were sunny and the grave shadows yet tarried from his face—then vanished it away. Hither he led home his new-made wife; here, "into something rich and strange," blossomed that mystic, intangible relation of delights when a child was born to the bosoms which are twain, yet one; here, with his children, in the fire-light gambols he kindled the dampened torch of the younger time, and for one evening was a child again.

Here, too, is his library—that cave in the rock above the world's high tide, set farther in than the surges beat or the winds blow. The tide has reached it now. There are waves and sea-weed on the floor at flood—they do not all go out at ebb. Where can he read but at that window? Where can he write but on that desk and against that wall? How can the old familiar animus of the place be left behind, unless his own soul, which had grown its twin, stays with it? Yet how can the animus be transported? No, no it can not. It knows no luggage trains; it is not a thing of drays.

Every where the tentacles of his root must give way with a wrench; the necessity being granted, the pain is inevitable; surely the only remedy is a manly patience under the irremediable—the

"Quicquid corrigere est nefas."

Now if he were to tell Dives all this, taking him into his confidence, would he not laugh? "What is the sense," would be the reply of that satisfied person, "in fashing your beard about one place or another? If you are going to town, you will probably take a far better house than this trumpery cottage—four stories high, free-stone fruit, all the modern improvements, and eligible situation. Why, my dear sir, you must be mad! Think what an exchange—gas instead of spermaceti; bathing apparatus, with warm, cold, and shower cocks, instead of this portable concern you have here, or perhaps instead of a mere swim in your twopenny lake; the market within ten minutes' staging; shopping conveniences for your wife; a daily laid, still wet, on your door-step—every thing imaginable, in place of this uncultivated, mountainous, windy, woody situation, out of call of express-wagons and solid respectability. Or, if you are going still farther into the woods (which I own, is very foolish, since you might stay here and put up a saw-mill on your own part of the brook, which would make you one of our first manufacturers), there is still no such cause as you seem to think for sorrow at moving. Probably, where you will settle, vegetables and all provisions are far cheaper—you can get your wood for almost nothing—and certainly those are advantages that a man need not pull a long face over. Be a man. Satisfy yourself with the world, as I do."

Ah! unction not in Ariel's pharmacopoeia! He is hurt where such salves will not heal him.

In many a way may the sources of his enjoyment be dried up or imbittered which the world knows not of. The ideal nature is indeed a harp of many wondrous strings, but the airs that play upon it in this life are seldom of the gentlest. The one-stringed Hawaiian guitar of the non-ideal man is easily thrummed, and never lacks tone save when its proper backbone of material well-being is temporarily lax.

If any of us, even the most tender and spiritually appreciative, could understand the various intensity with which this law works out its office in other men of the same nature, we would be much kinder in our judgment of the man who runs to narcotics and other stimulants for relief, while we regarded the habit as no less grievous. Could we, for example, enter thoroughly into the constitution of such a one as Coleridge; could we realize his temptations to the full extent; understand his struggles, and weigh all the forces of the mind which gave him, from his very birth, a perilous tendency, how much oftener with tears than with denunciations of his indolence, his neglect of duties, would we read such memorials of him as have been published, much as the most of those seem directed to bias us the contrary way.

For it seems as if there has never been a real "Life" of Coleridge. We have had, in abundance, sketches of what he himself might have called his "phenomenal existence." We have the changes of place which he made; the towns in which he lectured; the letters from home which he did not open, and the correspondences for aid from starvation which he did open; the worth, in pounds sterling,

of the laudanum which he drank per week; the number of bottles of brandy which he emptied in the same time; the extravagances of his expenditure; his repentings, his concessions to Southey and Cottle. All these are phenomenal—yes, even the last three. We have external events—movements of which we do not see the motor. Perhaps it would be impossible to see it from any thing but an auto-biography so full, so *ab intra,* that pain and humiliation would deter him from writing it, were he living. This would be a "Life" of Coleridge; the others are mere results of that life.

Perhaps the best substitute for such a work is to be found in his brief and fragmentary prose works; for, although they have almost nothing of that narrative style which is supposed to be necessary to the legitimate memoirs, they still show us, to a degree unequaled by any thing extant, Coleridge, the Man and the Mind.

A man he was to whom the world of his imagination and his reason was far more than that wherein he reaped his honors and his daily bread. Sensitive as a child to that intangible yet infinite meaning which is expressed in frowns and smiles, in love, scorn, and neglect; by nature gifted with an insight into her excellencies which cultivation and the other circumstances of his progressive being made at times even morbidly acute; living, by the very necessity of his particular inborn law of life, at the very summit of his energies, he had worn out nerve and elasticity at an age when, according to all ordinary judgments which base themselves on insurance averages and statistics of longevity, he should have been in the prime of life, and battling his way with fortitude to a competency. He exhausted by mighty drafts all his credit at the bank of healthful life, and that is a corporation which never permits us to overdraw. Up to the very last deposit of blood and sinew, nerve and spirit, prompt payment will meet every demand; then comes the crash, and the bankrupt nature is no longer known on 'Change. If all that we know of Coleridge from without, the statement of himself and his contemporaries, did not intimate to us that such was the case with him, we might determine that it would necessarily happen so, *a priori,* from that which we know of the mental constitution of the man.

He tells us through his memorializer, Cottle, and the others who have written about him, that he first used opium as a remedy for disease—a painful disease of the legs—that he found its effects a delicious and perfect relief. Furthermore, that he abandoned it with the completion of his cure, but resumed it upon his finding, with the abandonment, the pains return. That he made several attempts to free himself with the same termination, and at last settled down into the opium-eater which he was for it is impossible to say how many years of his life.

All this we have no reason to doubt. As an alleviative to severe pain the narcotic first became known to him. Yet the secret of its excessive use, the rapidly increasing doses, beyond all the demands of the body for relief—what was that? Ah! the poet himself would confess that to his mind the indulgence spoke with a fascination far greater than to his physical nature. It was, in fact, the very thing necessary for the replenishment of his exhausted capability of enjoyment.

How is it, we must ask, that opium acts upon the whole organism of a susceptible man? Physically the books of medicine tell us how—that is, to a certain distance they mark its pathway through digestion, circulation, the sympathetic nerves, and, where it causes death, leave it in an engorgement of the brain.

Probably all these phenomena are the merely external ones; they do not at all give us the mode of its action, after all. At one time, in the course of some experiments, I thought I had reached a little deeper principle of its operation; some singular facts led me to form a theory upon the subject. I will not give it here, since there is not yet a basis of tests broad enough for it to rest upon philosophically. Of all specific actions, that of narcotics is conceded by physicists universally to be one of the most recondite. Hardly any thing is really known about it by the practitioner more than by his unscientific patient. We have mere facts ungrouped about their governing principle.

But mentally we know its working better. Opium supersedes, and, by long continuance in its indulgence, actually extirpates that vital force out of which arise hope, insight into excellencies, fortitude, volition, and volition made permanent in perseverance. It is an artificial energy destructive to all natural; men habituated to it live on when what is called the nervous life is perfectly extinct.

That Coleridge could not have continued to live at all without such energy in some form is evident from the whole constitution of the man. Without the ever-present sensitive perception of spiritual beauty for which such an energy was necessary, houses, lands, comfortable family arrangements, the remunerative place in the Quarterly which his friends procured him would have seemed mere eidola. He hungered and thirsted for the spiritual. The world of dreams which he had built up in his "Pantisocracy" had been exhaled under the pressure of daily-bread necessities when to his fortuneless bosom he took a portionless wife. It is impossible that such a nature as his, emptied of the ideal Utopia, should be long void of something else as ideal. And so through all his life we see him forgetting hunger in dreams till it bites him to the heart. Then he starts up to spasmodic exertion, to sleep again in visions when the foe is driven to a respectful distance. Call this wrong, call it undutiful to relationships which he was bound to respect, yet you can not call it indolence. He was not fitted by nature to do the work of a material life, yet higher obligations called him to change his element, and he should have obeyed, against nature. In his own world he was a diligent, a glorious worker—he was not indolent—he only wrought out life according to his tendency, his constitutional fitness, and there he sinned.

Yet, oh man of the world! you who are so ready to sneer at Coleridge, let the comparison between him and yourself be put upon fair grounds before we join you in denunciation of the sin. The way in which you state the comparison is this: "Here am I, fighting the world in its roughest forms for a livelihood; there was Coleridge, who would not brace his muscles and fight like me." In another way let us state the case. Suppose yourself and Coleridge translated to that spiritual world where there are no actualities of the precise kind which you cope with. Grant that you each retained the same natural constitution as on earth, with how much ease or willingness would you change your element and labor in his province? It would then be his right to be called the actor; you would be the dreamer, and your dreams would be of things which as little suited his every-day activity as in this world his suited your own. You would be called with stentorian voices to awake to the reality of things—to dismiss the visionary figments of commerce, manufactures, credit, and capital, and to strive boldly in the arena of thought and art, and other spiritual excellences.

Do you say, "But every man's business is with the world in which he is placed for the time being?" I acknowledge that; but it is a misfortune, an imperfection of the present state. The greatest harmony is that wherein every mind works out most fully its own office. Still, the higher obligation, the moral, called Coleridge to an uncongenial activity, and in not going he was wrong. Remember in an analogous case what you would do; think what a hard thing is the change of element, and then denounce if you can.

Interpreting the opium passage of Coleridge's life by marginal references from all the pages previous, we shall see him more justly, and therefore more gently, than by any light thrown upon it as an isolated paragraph, from severe commentaries framed according to a personal and unappreciative standard.

We shall see him first as the boy. The child, as the cut-and-dried biographies have it, of poor but highly respectable parentage, that very strict economy which is so erroneously supposed to educate families into practical habits, cultivated his ideal tendency until it became exquisite. The necessity of a careful use of means in a household is the last of all things to rear its children practically. Extreme poverty, no doubt, from stimulating the very primitive activities of existence, may make a progeny which is intellectually too active to remain in the condition into which it was born, sharp-witted, cautious, provident, business-like in every respect. This fact is frequently to be observed in poor families, where sloth and viciousness do not prevent its occurrence. But the man with moderate means, who in his household affairs must be continually regulating expenditure, has reason to believe that his children, especially the more mentally active of

them, will grow up, unless great care is taken, into very unpractical views. The reasoning is something like this:

From earliest consciousness they will be thrown upon their own resources for enjoyment. The expensive toy, the luxurious recreation, will be entirely out of their reach. Yet, as the outwelling child-life must have some outlet, they will not be without toys, without recreations of one kind or another, and they will invent them for themselves. Out of the imagination they will fashion for themselves a domain where the simplest things have some rich meaning, glorified by an ideal excellence, and where all the most extravagant wishes are realized. In their plays they will be kings and queens of a garden-spot, transact weighty diplomatic business on the backs of old letters, and make boundless purchases of territory with pebbles or shells. In this cheap kingdom they will live as all-absorbing a life as the dignitaries whom they counterfeit live in theirs; and, still more, they will contract a bias very difficult to alter as increased years make it necessary. The boy who suddenly awakes to find himself a man finds it hard to believe that his old ideal efforts and ideal pleasures can not, by an elevation of their plane, be made sufficient for the satisfaction of a life-time.

More particularly is this true when, as in the present age, the world of books offers an additional asylum to the active child, to which, unless, both in mind and money, he is very poor indeed, he may retreat for the enjoyment which an outer world does not supply. He is thus reared in an ideal atmosphere until it becomes the nutriment of his very being.

From such a state as this, and through his rough experience of human mercies at the hands of Dr. Bowyer, of Christ's Hospital, we may follow Coleridge till we find him at Cambridge. How little he was fitted by nature to cope with the stern substantialities of an English University course is to be read in his final abandonment of its honors under the pressure of pecuniary difficulties, and the despair of an impossible attachment, and his enlistment into the Dragoons as a desperate indication of a desperate state of mind. Then succeed the Pantisocracy, marriage without the means of a livelihood, editorship without patrons, and without a single natural qualification for the office except the proverbially unremunerative one of out-speaking sincerity; literary labors of all kinds, from the volume of poems to the political leader, travels upon a pension, communion with German mind in books and men, of all ideal things the most ideal.

At length, by these steps, with here and there a repetition, we reach the period when his opium life commenced. In all fairness, what sort of a training had his whole previous existence been for a calm looking at the dangers of the fascinating indulgence, for a rejection of its temptation?

I dare to affirm that there is many a man who, when jaded by the day's labor, throws himself down to be refreshed by music, who in such an indulgence is committing no greater sin of intention than Coleridge committed when, coming weary from a life-time, he abandoned himself to the enjoyment of that dangerous beauty which absolute necessities and spent vitality forbade him to look for in the external world. You and I, my reader, should we abandon ourselves to the opium indulgence, would know fully the wrong we were committing; Coleridge had not any definite idea. Bitterly did he repeat it afterward; but his sorrow arose rather out of the terrible results of his course than from any self-recrimination, even in his sensitive mind, of malice aforethought.

But whether, in the case of any opium-eater, the habit be or be not contracted with a full knowledge of its evil, there is but one view which we can take of the fruitlessness of struggles made for disenthrallment at a later period of his career. That fruitlessness is not to be treated with contempt as evidence of a cowardly lack of self-denial which prevents the man from breaking the meshes of a bondage grown delightful to him. We are called rather to look upon the agonies of one who, in a nightmare-dream of fearful precipices, has not the power of volition to draw himself from the edge; we must pity—deeply pity. The protracted use of opium, not by any metaphor, but in a sense as rigorous as that of paralysis, utterly annihilates the power of will over action.

It is no mere cloak of apology which I would throw over those unfortunates who, after ineffectual attempts at being free, have subsided again into indulgence; it is actual fact that, in the horrors and the debility resulting from the disuse of the narcotic, its sufferers are no more responsible for their acts than the insane. When every man is a Scaevola, and can hold his hand in the flames till it is consumed, then may we expect men to endure the unrelieved tortures of opium-abandonment to their end in enfranchisement. Who of us would hold himself responsible for withdrawing his hand from the fire? I fancy the best of our martyrs, willing as they were to die for their cause, would have leaped out if they had not been chained among the fagots.

So far from extenuating the wrong of narcotics and stimulants, I believe myself only proclaiming (and I would it were with a thousand tongues) the perils into which they lead, as the most striking exponent of that wrong. This very emasculation of the will itself, while it may not produce the sensation of a detail of horrible visions, is in reality the most terrible characteristic of the injury wrought by these agents. A spiritual unsexing as it is, it vitiates all relations of life which exist to its victim; by submitting to it he sows a harvest of degradation, which involves in its mildewed sheaves manly fortitude, hopefulness, faith of promises, all the list of high-toned principles which are the virile—yes, still more broadly—the human glory.

To this truth let a spirit so essentially noble as Coleridge witness, agonized by the shame of those subterfuges which were necessary sometimes to procure the indulgence that had become to him the very nutriment of his being.

It is vain for us to shut our eyes to the fact that opium-eating in all countries is an immense and growing evil. In America peculiarly it is so, from the constitution of our national mind. An intense devotion to worldly business in our representative man often coexists with a stifled craving for something higher. Beginning, for the sake of advancement, at an age when other nations are still in the playground or the schoolroom, he continues rising early and lying down late in the pursuit of his ambition to a period when they have retired to the ease of travel or a villa. Yet from the very fact that his fathers have done this before him, he inherits a constitution least of all fitted to bear these drafts upon it.

The question of his breaking down is only one of time. Sometimes it happens very early; and then not only does an exhausted vitality require to be replenished, but the long-pent-up craving for a beauty of which business activity has said, "It is not in me," rises from its bonds, and, with a sad imperativeness, asks satisfaction.

How hard is it now to unlearn that habit of hasty execution which had been the acquirement of his whole previous life! The demands of business had always met from him with rapid dispatch; this complex craving must be answered as rapidly. The self-denial of recreation, abandonment of care, well-regulated regimen, might gradually restore to him health, and, with it, the elastic capacity for receiving happiness. He can not wait; the process is too slow. And the only immediate infusion of energy must be the artificial; the devil stands at his ear, and suggests opium. From that moment beings the sad, old, inevitable tale of the opium-eater's life.

Alas! it is no rare one with us. The inhabitant of the smallest village need hardly go out of his own street to hear it, and the unknown wretched who hide their shame, first in sad family hearts, last in the unwhispering grave, are even more in number, doubtless, than the known.

The only effort which can be made by a man of good feeling to his race is to suggest some means of escape to those who feel their bondage. For the terror of beginners, enough both of precept and example has been diffused widely at the present day, if that would do any good. I would not be satisfying my convictions of right did I not add to any denunciation of the habit some index toward freedom; for I believe there are many men, perhaps some who will read these words, who would escape from the opium slavery at any expense of effort, provided that the lethal stupor of their energies could be removed. Where there is one man who, like De Quincey, can at last get free by his own unaided struggle, there are a thousand to whom help from without is an absolute necessity.

It was my happiness, very soon after breaking away from the hasheesh thraldom, to make the acquaintance of a gentleman whose experience of narcotics from eyewitness in their particular mother-countries, added to the capabilities which he possessed, as a medical man, for philosophizing upon such experience, interested me much in speaking with him. It had been his good fortune to meet with some singularly inordinate opium-eaters, who were in utter despair of recovery, and, still better, it was his blessing to effect a permanent and radical cure. In one case with which I became acquainted, the patient had reached a higher point of daily indulgence than De Quincey at his most desperate stage, and had seemingly lost all constitutional basis for restoration to work upon. Yet the restoration was effected. I owe it not less to a proper goodwill to humanity than to gratitude on the part of men to say who this physician was. Sincerely desirous of being in some way instrumental in the cure of a bondage which, if not my own, was, at least, so near akin to it that I can deeply sympathize with its oppressed, I give a name whose betrayal in these pages violates no secrecy to the public, while it may do a great good—Dr. J.W. Palmer, of Roslyn, Long Island, the author-surgeon, late of the Honorable East India Company's Service, and of "The Golden Dragon," to which I have referred (See Appendix, Note B). ❏

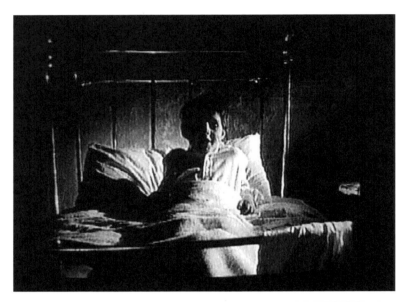

APPENDIX.

Note A, page 199

THE work referred to is a monograph upon Trance and Human Hybernation, by Dr. James Braid, of Edinburgh, and published by John Church, Princes Street, Soho, London. Besides the copy now in my hands, through the kindness of my friend Dr. Rosa, of Watertown, I have never seen any other, although it probably exists in medical libraries in this country. Aware, at any rate, that the book is inaccessible, except by considerable painstaking, to general readers, I will state the authority upon which the phenomenon of the fakeer's interment and trance is related, in order that it may rest upon a stronger basis of proof than the testimony of an exceedingly credulous and superstitious people like the natives of Lahore.

Sir Claude Wade, formerly of her majesty's service, and, at the date of Dr. Braid's writing, residing in Ryde, on the Isle of Wight, assures the doctor by letter that he was present at Lahore during the period of the fakeer's inhumation, and witnessed his disinterment. By this gentleman, Sir C.E. Trevelyan, and Captain Osborne, all that is stated of the fakeer by Dr. Braid is authenticated, and, indeed, through them did the doctor obtain the materials for his narrative.

By as strong a conjunction of testimony, therefore, as could be desired for the proof of the most startling assertion, is this recital put beyond the possibility of being an imposture.

Note B, page 254

Among a number of articles written at various times by this author upon the subject of the narcotic fascinations, is one, published some time ago over his own signature in the New York *Tribune,* relative to the employment of hasheesh in India both as a gratification and a remedy. My knowledge of his thorough acquaintance with the habits of the ultra Oriental people, among whom he so long dwelt, together with a number of astonishing cures of the opium bane which he effected when, as I have said, all hopes of restoration seemed forever gone, makes me particularly desirous to give the article of which I speak in full, as supplementary, through its specific value, to that which I have written of my own experience of hasheesh. Except as an antispasmodic in a very limited number of cases, the Cannabis is known and prized very little among our practitioners, and I am persuaded that its uses are far wider and more important than has yet been imagined.

Urged by this conviction, I have therefore transcribed the article of Dr. Palmer, and offer it here to the thoughtful attention which it deserves from all, whether professional or lay, who wish to add a most beneficial agent to their pharmacopoeia. It is entitled

HASHEESH IN HYDROPHOBIA

To the Editor of the New York Tribune:

Sir—In your journal of Friday last appeared a timely paper on hydrophobia, from Dr. Griscom, of the New York Hospital, being a report of the interesting case of Edward Bransfield, with the inevitably fatal termination. Allow me to add to the communication of Dr. Griscom another on the same subject, which may be deemed important. It is the result of medical observation in the East on the use and effects of hasheesh (*Cannabis Indica*). In thus writing for the public I shall avoid technicalities.

The Radda and Coolee bazars of the Black Town of Calcutta are the Borroboola-Ghas of heathendom—the back slums of Budhism—where the people smoke gunjah, and pray and swear by Brahma and bucksheesh—where the most abject of zealots and a very Herod among cruel heathen are presented in the same person—whither the flannel shirts and small-tooth combs of the Rev. Aminadab Sleek are sent every Friday night from Burton's Theatre, but never reach. It is there you must go to procure your hasheesh fresh from the fields, and see your living subject try experiments on himself. If you have a lively case of Rabies in your compound, and carry a copy of *Monte Cristo** in your pocket, so much the better—you are posted in the phenomena. You will find dirty, dreadful-looking shops, redolent of petroleum and the hubble-bubble,[†] and prolific in Pariah dogs, ochre-colored urchins (which, as they flounder about on their bellies, always a shade or two lighter than the rest, oddly resemble young crocodiles), and every other living thing which should make those small-tooth combs lively in the market. And, amid these essentially Oriental surroundings, you will find a fat old gentleman, with the least possible clothing, to compromise between decency and the climate, who is either galvanic like Uriah Heep, or asleep like the Fat Boy, as you happen to catch him just before or after his pipe, and who is licensed to dispense to the denizens of that quarter chorrus, gunjah, and bhang, in the name of the Lord Dalhousie, the most noble the Governor General in Council.

At the season of flowering, a resinous substance exudes and concretes on the slender stalks, leaves, and tops of the hemp plant in India, a sticky gum which causes the young stems to adhere together tenaciously in the bundles of gunjah. Men, now dressed all in leather, are sent into the fields to run to and fro, sweeping the plants with their garments, from which afterward they diligently gather the resin that has adhered. This is the chorrus, wherein is all the narcotic virtue of the herb, all the seventh heaven of hasheesh intoxication for the Hindoo and the Arab. The most potent of it comes from Nepaul. Bhang, or subjee, is the larger leaves and capsules of the Cannabis compressed in balls and sticky layers, with here and there some flowers between. Infused with water, it forms an intoxicating brew, to which, however, the Hindoos are not commonly addicted. Gunjah, mixed with tobacco and smoked in a pipe, is the shape of the drag which they popularly affect, and it is as gunjah that it is commonly sold in the shops. This comes in bundles, twenty-four or the plants entire, stalks, leaves, capsules, and tops undisturbed, and from which their resin has not been

separated, adhering tenaciously. Gunjah, indeed, is the term proper to Hindostan, hasheesh being Arabic, and used to denote the tops and tenderest parts of the plant, sun-dried and powdered.

Romantic extravagances have been written and told about the magic and the marvels of hasheesh, and Indian Coleridges and De Quinceys have been pressed into service to furnish forth characteristic stories for Oriental annuals and spectacles of the *Monte Cristo* kind. These are for the most part fictitious, though, to be sure, your kidmudgar, if he happens to be a gunjah-wallah, is apt at times to indulge in splendid fancies, to make you a grand salaam instead of a sandwich, and offer you a houri when you merely demanded a red herring. But Dr. O'Shaughnessy, the present distinguished superintendent of the Indian telegraph, who formerly administered a model system of discipline among the native hospitals, and from his Eastern look-out has added here and there a new light to the firmament of science, who was the first to pursue this subject with well-directed researches, and procure from it definite results, describes the uniform effect of this agent on the human economy as consisting in a prompt and complete alleviation of pain; a singular power of controlling inordinate muscular spasms, especially in hydrophobia and traumatic tetanus; "as a soporific or hypnotic in conciliating sleep;" inordinate augmentation of appetite; the decided promotion of aphrodisiac desire; and sudden cerebral exaltation, with perfect mental cheerfulness, in no case followed by the painful nervous "unstringing," the constipation and suppression of secretions which attend the use of opium.

Having daily under his eyes, in the streets of Calcutta, examples of this marvelous power of the gunjah, Dr. O'Shaughnessy proceeded, in a succession of judicious experiments, to apply it in several diseases attended with much muscular convulsion. Its action he discovered to be primarily on the motor nerves, promptly inducing complete loss of power in almost all the muscles; hence its timeliness in the spasms of tetanus, in the cramp of Asiatic cholera, in the sharp constriction of the muscles of deglutition in hydrophobia. In tetanus especially he met with signal success, even in his earliest experiments perfectly restoring ten cases in fourteen, and since then, to my personal knowledge, a still larger proportion. In the summer of 1852 it was administered with convincing success in cases of Asiatic cholera among the Company's troops in Burmah, even in the collapsed stage, subduing cramp and restoring warmth to the surface. Under its influence alone, that peculiar blueness and shriveling of the nails and fingers, familiarly known as "washerwoman's hands," has been rapidly dispersed, the flesh plumping out rosily again, like a decayed apple under an air-pump.

Every intelligent physician will perceive that there is nothing in the kind of virtue manifested in these cases which has not a direct bearing, and by the same modus operandi, on the phenomena of hydrophobia, since it has been ably contended, especially in India, that the three diseases are of a kindred type; that their phenomena are purely nervous and functional, and that no local inflammations are necessary to their definition.

In an occasional contribution to the British and Foreign Medical Review, and in some excellent monographs published in Calcutta, Dr. O'Shaughnessy has given the results of his experiments since 1850, by which it appears that in almost every case, with the Cannabis alone, he has succeeded in procuring perfect alleviation of pain, complete control of the spasm, and its attendant apprehension and infernal imagination—indeed, an utter routing of all the horrors of the disease; and claiming, with a saving clause, one or two cures, he makes it evident that in every instance a painless, tranquil, conscious termination is attainable. His patients have swallowed water with avidity, paddled in it and made merry with it, and been friendly with it to the end.

That it has thus overcome the horrors of Rabies and all the dreadfulness of such a death-bed, should procure for the Cannabis more consideration than it has met with at the hands of the profession in this country. The objection, hitherto valid, that its preparations are of unequal strength, and that the drug loses all its virtues by change of climate, is conclusively met and defeated at last by the admirable alcoholic extract of Mr. Robinson. The writer of this has seen a sepoy of the 40th Rifles, an hour before furiously hydrophobic, under the influence of the Cannabis not only drinking water freely, but pleasantly washing his face and hands.

In conclusion, I would invoke for the Cannabis Indica the interest of American writers and practitioners by research and experiment.

J. W. PALMER, M.D.

THE END

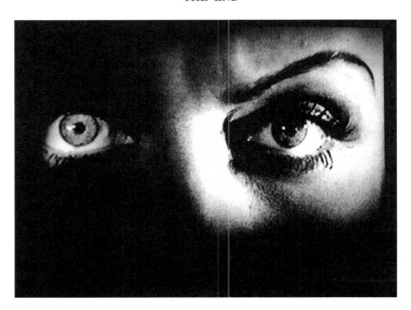

Published by Host Publications Inc., Austin, Texas
© 1999 Alfred Leslie All rights reserved
Introduction © 1995 David Lehman All rights reserved
Printed in the United States of America by Seybert Nicholas Printing Group
First edition, 1999
Library of Congress catalog number 96 - 75 - 157
ISBN - 0924047127

"Sanctity as a Social Fact" from "Saint Genet - Comedian et Martyr" by Jean Paul Sartre, translation © 1960 Lisa Bigelow. "Three Great Painters" © 1960 Pontus Hultén. "Triptych" by Gregory Corso © 1960. "Freely Espousing" by James Schuyler © 1960 with Doubleday reprint permission. "For Frank 3/31/1942" by Walter Harrison Mason, Frank Mason © 1960. "The History of Stilts" by Hannelore Hahn © 1960. "Awake in Spain" and "To the Film Industry in Crisis" by Frank O'Hara, © 1971 Maureen Granville-Smith, Administratrix of the Estate of Frank O'Hara with her reprint permission. "Four Poems" by Joel Oppenheimer © 1960 with reprint permission of Theresa Maier Administratrix of the Estate of Joel Oppenheimer. "Aether" by Allen Ginsberg © 1960. Excerpts from "a Dogtown Common blues" by Charles Olson © 1960. "Episode from The Birds by Aristophanes" by William Arrowsmith © 1960. Fragment from "The Book of Dreams (The Flying Horses of Mein-Mo)" by Jack Kerouac © 1961, 1981. "Address to the Congress for Cultural Freedom" by J. Robert Oppenheimer © 1960. "Violence in Venice" by Donald Windham © 1960. "Envy" by Alan Ansen © 1960. "Melodramas" by Kenward Elmslie © 1960. "Malcochon!" by Derek Walcott © 1960. "America" and "The Compromise" © 1960 John Ashbery.

"The world contracted to a recognizable image" by William Carlos Williams © 1962, reprint permission New Directions Publishing Corporation. "Fragments on Man and the System" by Billy Klüver © 1960. "The Need Becomes Evident" by Gael Turnbull © 1960. "On the Way to Dumbarton Oaks" by Barbara Guest © 1960. "Love is a Many Splendored" by Terry Southern © 1960. "The Promise" by Alfred J. Jensen © 1960. "Fantasy of My Mother Who's Always on Welfare" by Peter Orlovsky © 1960. "A Statement" by Alice Neel © 1960. "The Lead" by Meyer Liben © 1960. "Something Wild" by Mike Stoller, Morton Feldman and Jerry Leiber © 1960 Trio Music Company. "When the Sun Tries to Go On" by Kenneth Koch © 1960. "Condemned to Death" by Jean Genet, translated by Raymond Medeiros © 1960. All selections reprinted with the permission of the respective copyright holders.

EDITORS NOTE

I photographed nearly all of the images in this book from a video monitor using a variety of motion pictures as source material. They are images mainly of New York City in the 1940s and '50s, and they restate photographs of mine that were lost when my studio was destroyed in a 1966 fire. They were all shot between 1995 and 1999 and are what I call "Paraphrase Photos." The rest of the photos—such as Jean Harlow (p. 122) and Ernest Hemingway with his then wife writer Martha Gellhorn smoking pot in Cuba (p. 78), the World War II photos and all the ones in The Hasheesh Eaters—I call "Attachments" rather than "Paraphrases," because they do not restate my destroyed photographs. These "Attachments" are not adornments. Instead they parallel the tone of the writing they accompany, and when used in a sequence they tell a story.

CREDITS

ABOUT ALFRED LESLIE

For the past fifty years Alfred Leslie's work as a painter and filmmaker has been both extensive in its range and persuasive in its authority, influencing many artists of his and later generations. He began as one of the youngest members of that group of post World War II New York artists known as Abstract Expressionists, his path clearly marked in 1949 when he exhibited, nearly simultaneously, a work in an important group show at the then prestigious Sam Kootz Gallery in New York City, and his third film (Directions: A Walk After the War Games) at a special screening at the Museum of Modern Art. His subsequent films: Pull My Daisy, The Last Clean Shirt and Birth of a Nation 1965 are considered pioneering classics, with Pull My Daisy entering the National Film Archives.

He was awarded the Gold Medal for lifetime achievement in painting by the National Institute of Arts and Letters and has received grants from the Guggenheim Foundation and the National Endowment of the Arts. The thrust and breadth of his work has perhaps best been summed up by artist Chuck Close who, speaking in 1991 to Barbara Flynn of the extraordinary quality of Leslie's paintings and his accomplishment in creating a cohesive intellectual and political infrastructure for a resurgence of figurative art, referred to Leslie as "a hero for being the one who turned the tide." Leslie lives in New York City's East Village with his longtime companion Nancy de Antonio and is currently completing a new group of paintings and a new feature-length film, The Cedar Bar.